Adriana Trigiani grew up in Big Stone Gap, Virginia, and now lives with her husband and daughter in New York City. In addition to being the bestselling author of *Big Stone Gap*, *Big Cherry Holler*, *Milk Glass Moon* and *Lucia, Lucia*, she is an award-winning playwright, television writer, and documentary filmmaker. She has written the screenplay for the film version of *Big Stone Gap*, which she will also direct.

D1101931

Also by Adriana Trigiani

Lucia, Lucia

Big Stone Gap
————
Big Cherry Holler
————
Milk Glass Moon

Adriana Trigiani

POCKET
BOOKS

LONDON • SYDNEY • NEW YORK • TORONTO

This Adriana Trigiani omnibus edition first published
in Great Britain by Pocket Books, 2004
An imprint of Simon & Schuster UK Ltd
A Viacom Company

Big Stone Gap first published in Great Britain by Macmillan, 2001
First published in paperback by Pocket Books, 2002
An imprint of Simon & Schuster UK Ltd
A Viacom Company

Big Cherry Holler first published in Great Britain by Pocket Books, 2002
An imprint of Simon & Schuster UK Ltd
A Viacom Company

Milk Glass Moon first published in Great Britain by Pocket Books, 2003
An imprint of Simon & Schuster UK Ltd
A Viacom Company

The right of Adriana Trigiani to be identified as the author of
this work has been asserted in accordance with sections 77 and 78
of the Copyright, Designs and Patents Act, 1988.

3 5 7 9 10 8 6 4 2

Simon & Schuster UK Ltd
Africa House
64–78 Kingsway
London WC2B 6AH

www.simonsays.co.uk

Simon & Schuster Australia
Sydney

A CIP catalogue record for this book is available from the British Library

ISBN 1 4165 0203 3

Printed and bound in Great Britain by
Cox & Wyman Ltd, Reading, Berks

Big Stone Gap

For Tim

CHAPTER ONE

This will be a good weekend for reading. I picked up a dozen of Vernie Crabtree's killer chocolate chip cookies at the French Club bake sale yesterday. (I don't know what she puts in them, but they're chewy and crispy at the same time.) Those, a pot of coffee, and a good book are all I will need for the rainy weekend rolling in. It's early September in our mountains, so it's warm during the day, but tonight will bring a cool mist to remind us that fall is right around the corner.

The Wise County Bookmobile is one of the most beautiful sights in the world to me. When I see it lumbering down the mountain road like a tank, then turning wide and easing onto Shawnee Avenue, I flag it down like an old friend. I've waited on this corner every Friday since I can remember. The Bookmobile is just a government truck, but to me it's a glittering royal coach delivering stories and knowledge and life itself. I even love the smell of books. People have often told me that one of their strongest childhood memories is the scent of their grandmother's house. I never knew my grandmothers, but I could always count on the Bookmobile.

The most important thing I ever learned, I learned from books. Books have taught me how to size people up. The most useful book I ever read taught me how to read faces, an ancient Chinese art called *siang mien*, in which the size of the eyes, curve of the lip, and height of the forehead are important clues to a person's character. The placement of ears indicates intelligence. Chins that stick out reflect stubbornness. Deep-set eyes suggest a secretive nature. Eyebrows that grow together may answer the question *Could that man kill me with his bare hands?* (He could.) Even dimples have meaning. I have them, and according to face reading, something wonderful is supposed to happen to me when I turn thirty-five. (It's been four months since my birthday, and I'm still waiting.)

If you were to read my face, you would find me a comfortable person with brown eyes, good teeth, nice lips, and a nose that folks, when they are being kind, refer to as noble. It's a large nose, but at least it's straight. My eyebrows are thick, which indicates a practical nature. (I'm a pharmacist – how much more practical can you get?) I have a womanly shape, known around here as a mountain girl's body, strong legs, and a flat behind. Jackets cover it quite nicely.

This morning the idea of living in Big Stone Gap for the rest of my life gives me a nervous feeling. I stop breathing, as I do whenever I think too hard. Not breathing is very bad for you, so I inhale slowly and deeply. I taste coal dust. I don't mind; it assures me that we still have an economy. Our town was supposed to become the 'Pittsburgh of the South' and the 'Coal Mining Capital of Virginia.' That never happened, so we are forever at the whims of the big coal companies. When they tell us the coal is running out in these mountains, who are we to doubt them?

It's pretty here. Around six o'clock at night everything turns a rich Crayola midnight blue. You will never smell greenery so pungent. The Gap definitely has its romantic qualities. Even the train whistles are musical, sweet oboes in the dark. The place can fill you with longing.

The Bookmobile is at the stoplight. The librarian and driver is a good-time gal named Iva Lou Wade. She's in her forties, but she's yet to place the flag on her sexual peak. She's got being a woman down. If you painted her, she'd be sitting on a pink cloud with gold-leaf edges, showing a lot of leg. Her perfume is so loud that when I visit the Bookmobile, I wind up smelling like her for the bulk of the day. (It's a good thing I like Coty's Emeraude.) My father used to say that that's how a woman ought to be. 'A man should know when there's a woman in the room. When Iva Lou comes in, there ain't no doubt.' I'd just say nothing and roll my eyes.

Iva Lou's having a tough time parking. A mail truck has parked funny in front of the post office, taking up her usual spot, so she motions to me that she's pulling into the gas station. That's fine with the owner, Kent Vanhook. He likes Iva Lou a lot. What man doesn't? She pays real nice attention to each and every one. She examines men like eggs, perfect specimens created by God to nourish. And she hasn't met a man yet who doesn't appreciate it. Luring a man is a true talent, like playing the piano by ear. Not all of us are born prodigies, but women like Iva Lou have made it an art form.

The Bookmobile doors open with a whoosh. I can't believe what Iva Lou's wearing: Her ice-blue turtleneck is so tight it looks like she's wearing her bra on the outside. Her Mondrian-patterned pants, with squares of pale blue, yellow, and green, cling to her thighs like crisscross ribbons. Even sitting, Iva Lou has an unbelievable shape. But I wonder how much of it has to do with all the cinching. Could it be that her parts are so well-hoisted and suspended, she has transformed her real figure into a soft hourglass? Her face is childlike, with a small chin, big blue eyes, and a rosebud mouth. Her eyeteeth snaggle out over her front teeth, but on her they're demure. Her blond hair is like yellow Easter straw, arranged in an upsweep you can see through the set curls. She wears lots of Sarah Coventry jewelry, because she sells it on the side.

'I'll trade you. Shampoo for a best-seller.' I give Iva Lou a sack of shampoo samples from my pharmacy, Mulligan's Mutual.

'You got a deal.' Iva Lou grabs the sack and starts sorting through the samples. She indicates the shelf of new arrivals. 'Ave Maria, honey, you have got to read *The Captains and the Kings* that just came out. I know you don't like historicals, but this one's got sex.'

'How much more romance can you handle, Iva Lou? You've got half the men in Big Stone Gap tied up in knots.'

She snickers. 'Half? Oh well, I'm-a gonna take that as a compliment-o anyway.' I'm half Italian, so Iva Lou insists on ending her words with vowels. I taught her some key phrases in Italian in case international romance was to present itself. It wasn't very funny when Iva Lou tried them out on my mother one day. I sure got in some Big Trouble over that.

Iva Lou has a goal. She wants to make love to an Italian man, so she can decide if they are indeed the world's greatest lovers. 'Eye-talian men are my Matta-horn, honey,' she declares. Too bad there aren't any in these parts. The people around here are mainly Scotch-Irish, or Melungeon (folks who are a mix of Turkish,

French, African, Indian, and who knows what; they live up in the mountain hollers and stick to themselves). Zackie Wakin, owner of the town department store, is Lebanese. My mother and I were the only Italians; and then about five years ago we acquired one Jew, Lewis Eisenberg, a lawyer from Woodbury, New York.

'You always sit in the third snap stool. How come?' Iva Lou asks, not looking up as she flips through a new coffee-table book about travel photography.

'I like threes.'

'Sweetie-o, let me tell you something.' Iva Lou gets a faraway, mystical twinkle in her eye. Then her voice lowers to a throaty, sexy register. 'When I get to blow this coal yard, and have my big adventure, I sure as hell won't waste my time taking pictures of the Circus Maximus. I am not interested in rocks 'n' ruins. I want to experience me some flesh and blood. Some magnificent, broad-shouldered hunk of a European man. Forget the points of interest, point me toward the men. Marble don't hug back, baby.' Then she breathes deeply, 'Whoo.'

Iva Lou fixes herself a cup of Sanka and laughs. She's one of those people who are forever cracking themselves up. She always offers me a cup, and I always decline. I know that her one spare clean Styrofoam cup could be her entrée to a romantic rendezvous. Why waste it on me?

'I found you that book on wills you wanted. And here's the only one I could find on grief.' Iva Lou holds up *As Grief Exits* as though she's modeling it. The pretty cover has rococo cherubs and clouds on it. The angels' smiles are instantly comforting. 'How you been getting along?' I look at Iva Lou's face. Her innocent expression is just like the cherub's. She really wants to know how I am.

My mother died on August 2, 1978, exactly one month ago

today. It was the worst day of my life. She had breast cancer. I never thought cancer would get both of my parents, but it did. Mama was fifty-two years old, which suddenly seems awfully young to me. She was only seventeen when she came to America. My father taught her English, but she always spoke with a thick accent. One of the things I miss most about her is the sound of her voice. Sometimes when I close my eyes I can hear her.

Mama didn't want to die because she didn't want to leave me here alone. I have no brothers or sisters. The roots in the Mulligan family are strong, but at this point, the branches are mostly dead. My mother never spoke of her family over in Italy, so I assume they died in the war or something. The only relative I have left is my aunt, Alice Mulligan Lambert. She is a pill. Her husband, my Uncle Wayne, has spent his life trying not to make her angry, but he has failed. Aunt Alice has a small head and thin lips. (That's a terrible combination.)

'I'm gonna take a smoke, honey-o.' Iva Lou climbs down the steps juggling two coffees and her smokes. In under fifteen seconds, Kent Vanhook comes out from the garage, wiping his hands on a rag. Iva Lou gives Kent the Styrofoam cup, which looks tiny in his big hands. They smoke and sip. Kent Vanhook is a good-looking man of fifty, a tall, easygoing cowboy type. He looks like the great Walter Pidgeon with less hair. As he laughs with Iva Lou, twenty years seem to melt off of his face. Kent's wife is a diabetic who stays at home and complains a lot. I know this because I drop off her insulin once a month. But with Iva Lou, all Kent does is laugh.

I like to be alone on the Bookmobile. It gives me a chance to really examine the new arrivals. I make a stack and then look through the old selections. I pick up my old standby, *The Ancient Art of Chinese Face-Reading*, and think of my father, Fred

Mulligan. When he died thirteen years ago, I thought I would grieve, but to this day I haven't. We weren't close, but it wasn't from my lack of trying. From the time I can remember, he just looked through me, the way you would look through the thick glass of a jelly jar to see if there's any jelly left. Many nights when I was young I cried about him, and then one day I stopped expecting him to love me and the pain went away. I stuck by him when he got sick, though. All of a sudden, my father, who had always separated himself from people, had everything in common with the world. He was in pain and would inevitably die. The suffering gave him some humility. It's sad that my best memories of him are when he was sick. It was then that I first checked out this book on Chinese face reading.

I thought that if I read my father's face, I would be able to understand why he was so mean. It took a lot of study. Dad's face was square and full of angles: rectangular forehead, sharp jaw, pointy chin. He had small eyes (sign of a deceptive nature), a bulbous nose (sign of money in midlife, which he had from owning the Pharmacy), and no lips. Okay, he had two lips, but the set of the mouth was one tight gray lead-pencil line. That is a sign of cruelty. When you watch the news on television, look at the anchor's mouth. I will guaran-damn-tee you that none of them have upper lips. You don't get on the TV by being nice to people.

On and off for about four years straight the face-reading book was checked out in my name, and my name only. When I went up to Charlottesville on a buying trip for the Pharmacy, I tried to hunt down a copy to buy. It was out of print. Iva Lou has tried to give me the book outright many times. She said she would report it as lost. But I can't do that. I like knowing it's here, riding around with old Iva Lou.

I guess I'm staring out the windshield at them, because they're both looking at me. Iva Lou stomps out her cigarette with her pink Papagallo flat and heads back toward the Bookmobile. Kent watches her return, drinking her in like that last sip of rich, black Sanka.

'I'm sorry. Me and Kent got to talking, and well, you know.'

'No problem.'

'Face reading again? Don't you have this memorized by now? Lordy.'

Iva stamps the books with her pinky up.

'See you next week.' I wave to Kent casually, just to make him feel that there is absolutely nothing wrong with talking to single, available, willing Iva Lou and sharing a smoke. He smiles at me, a little relieved. I think most folks in Big Stone Gap know their secrets are safe with me. (God knows I don't get any pleasure in knowing that the town manager performs self-colonics.)

I have a delivery to make. I promised Mrs. Mac – MacChesney is the full surname – that I would bring her a new prescription to tame her high blood pressure. She is known around here as 'Apple Butter Nan' because nobody cans it better. Her house is way up in Cracker's Neck Holler. There are lots of twists and turns to get there, and I sort of fly around the curves like Mario Andretti (another great Eye-talian). There's an element of danger in mountain roads – there are no guardrails, so it's you and your rack-and-pinion steering. If you lose your concentration, you could go over the mountain. One foggy night the Brightwell brothers lost control of their truck and drove off the cliff. Luckily, the trees broke their fall. A state cop found the boys hanging in the branches like fresh laundry the following morning. They lost their truck, though. On impact, it fell off of them like pants. Now it rests at the bottom of Powell Valley Lake.

The Gap, or 'down in town' as the holler folks call it, is in the valley. The hollers are little communities nestled in the sides of the Blue Ridge Mountains. I couldn't give you directions to places up in the mountains, but I could take you there. There are no signs anywhere; you have to know your way. When you climb to the highest peak around here, you are standing on the borders of five states: Virginia, Kentucky, North Carolina, Tennessee, and West Virginia. You can't actually see the divider lines of course; you just know that you're standing in five states because there's a plaque that says so and because we were taught that in school. Tiny Miss Callahan, my fourth-grade teacher, would be very happy that I retained this information and shared it.

Each holler has its own name and singular history. Families found pockets that suited them in these hills and never left. Where people settle tells a lot about them. This is the only place I've ever lived, except for college. I went away to school, all the way up to South Bend, Indiana, to Saint Mary's, a small women's college. It was just big enough for me. When I got my B.S., I came home and took over management of the Pharmacy. I was needed here. My father had gotten sick and had to quit, and Mama couldn't handle it alone. It wasn't that she was a weak woman; she just couldn't handle change.

I've made it up to Cracker's Neck in record time. The MacChesney homestead sits in a clearing. It's a square stone house with four chimneys. Hearth fires smell better in stone houses, and Mrs. Mac always has one going. I park and wait for the dogs to circle. We have hundreds of wild dogs in the mountains, and they travel in packs. Most aren't rabid, and when they are, they get shot. I count six thin dogs sniffing my wheels. Buying time, I unzip my window and toss out the sign that identifies me to customers. It's a white plastic square that says: THE MEDICINE

DROPPER. (I sprung for the extra artwork, a silhouette of a nurse in a rush.)

I usually find the guts to get out of the Jeep when I see Mrs. Mac peeking out of her window. The last thing I want to appear to customers is chicken. Truth is, I appreciate her watching out for me as I open the door and swing my legs out. Ever so casually I pull myself to a rigid standing position and walk confidently through the yard to the front door, like Maureen O'Hara in every movie she ever made with John Wayne. Maureen O'Hara is short-waisted like me. She is my inspiration in wardrobe and courage. I've even taken to wearing my hair like her – simple and long in a neat braid. I pack less punch though; my hair is brown, hers lustrous red.

The porch is freshly painted gray without a speck of dirt anywhere. The firewood is stacked neatly to the side of the house in a long row, in a lattice design. I try not to have favorites, but Mrs. Mac and her orderly home definitely top my list.

'Took you long enough!' Mrs. Mac exclaims as she snaps open the screen door.

'Iva Lou and I were chatting.'

'I done figured that.' Mrs. Mac points to the fire. 'Is that a good un, or is that a good un?' The flames lick the grid in hungry yellow bursts.

'That is the best fire I have ever seen.' And I mean it.

'Come on back. I made corn bread.'

I follow Mrs. Mac to the kitchen, a sunny, spacious room with exposed oak beams on the ceiling. I hear a noise behind me. Praying that it's not another dog, I slowly turn and look, first low, then eye level. It's not a dog. It's a man. Mrs. Mac's son, Jack MacChesney, in his underwear, a faded-to-pink union suit that sticks to him like a leotard. We look at each other, and both our faces turn the color of his underwear before it faded – blood red.

'Jesus Christmas, Jack. Put some clothes on,' Mrs. Mac demands.

'Yes, ma'am,' he says to his mother, as if on automatic. 'Good morning, Ave Maria,' he says to me, and goes. I can't help it, I watch the man go. He has a fine, high rear end. I wish I did. I pull my belted CPO jacket down over my flat behind and follow Mrs. Mac into the kitchen.

Mrs. Mac and I cross the kitchen to the big table by the windows, where she pours me a cup of hot black coffee that smells like heaven. She serves me fresh cream and snow-white sugar, which I dump into the mug. 'So what's happening in town?' Mrs. Mac asks. She has a mountain-girl face – a fine nose you could draw with a compass, shiny green button eyes, Cupid bow lips, smooth cheeks. You can tell that she was a great beauty in her youth, and she still is.

'Is "Nan" short for anything?' I ask her.

'What? You mean my name?' Mrs. Mac cuts the corn bread in the iron skillet into neat triangles. 'My mamaw's name was Nan. My middle name is Bluebell because that field was covered with 'em when I got born.' She points out the window with her spatula to indicate the field in the back.

'Nan Bluebell. Pretty. What was your maiden name?'

'God-a-mighty, you got a lot of questions this here morning. Gilliam. Nan Bluebell Gilliam.'

'I like it,' I say as I sip my coffee.

Jack stands in the doorway. He lingers there for a moment, as if to assess the situation. Or maybe he doesn't want to interrupt our conversation. In town he is known as Jack Mac. He's a little over six feet but seems shorter because he's all neck and torso. His face is round and soft, with a determined chin. He has thin, straight eyebrows and hazel eyes. He has even lips – the top and bottom one match (very rare) – and a nose that suits his face – it's a strong nose, one that doesn't break where it's connected between his eyes but shoots out like a clean wedge. He has a defined jawline, which means he goes after what he wants in life and gets it. Jack Mac is dressed now, in a flannel shirt and old blue jeans. His hair is slicked down wet; in the sunlight it is gray and going. Jack Mac and I are the same age, but he looks a lot older than me. I don't think he said two words in four years of high school; he's one of those quiet types.

Mrs. Mac pours her son coffee. 'Sit down youngun,' she says to him with great affection. 'I was just asking Miss Ave here about the goings-on in town.'

'Jack Mac ought to know more than me. After all, musicians get all the dirt.'

'We do, eh?' Jack Mac says and laughs. 'You're the big director, you're in charge of the flow of information.'

Jack Mac is referring to my 'job' (volunteer, of course) as director of our musical Outdoor Drama *The Trail of the Lonesome Pine*. A mountain love story, or so the poster says. The Drama was put together sixteen summers ago. There's a lot of dramatic and musical talent in the area, so local leaders decided to capitalize on it. We figure tourism will be a good business alternative if the coal mining dries up. The Outdoor Drama draws audiences from all over the mid-South.

'Well, I don't want to say anything,' I begin ominously, 'but a certain Sweet Sue Tinsley is quite smitten with a certain picker in the pit band.'

'Mercy, Jack, are you still seeing that little slip of a thing?' Mrs. Mac arches her eyebrow, annoyed.

'Mama, I'm proud to say I am,' Jack says and winks at me.

'That girl is not built for heavy lifting.' Mrs. Mac looks at me and sizes me up; obviously, I am a girl built for heavy lifting.

'Now, Mrs. Mac, you're just a little territorial about your only son. I'm sure you'll grow to love Sweet Sue,' I say, getting off this topic. Jack Mac looks at me, relieved.

Mrs. Mac goes on a long run about some sewage problem up in the hollers that she read about in the weekly paper, the *Post*. It's hard for me to read our local paper because there are so many misspelled words in it. Spelling happens to be one of the things I'm good at, so I take notice when it isn't perfect.

As Mrs. Mac loads up the table with eggs, grits (hers are home-made pale yellow, not the store-bought kind), bacon, honey, and Lord knows what-all, Jack Mac eats. For a mountain man, he has fine manners. Delicate almost. And no matter how his mama drones on, he listens intently, like everything she says is of the utmost importance. What kind of life do the two of them have up here in Cracker's Neck? I wonder how he sneaks off to see Sweet Sue, how he maneuvers spending the night away from home, what he tells his mother. This is one of the obstacles the adult child faces while living at home with his parents. I went through it until a year ago, so I know it's hard. Maybe he goes down and stays with Sweet Sue when her kids are with their father on alternate weekends. Maybe they make love in the car on some road somewhere, like down at the Strawberry Patch, or up to Huff Rock, where the teenagers go. Or maybe they meet at a hotel over in Kingsport, Tennessee, where nobody would know them.

'Ave Maria, are we losing you?' Mrs. Mac says as she pours me coffee. I'm caught, I blush, and they both notice it.

'She's off in dreamland, Mama.'

'No, uh-uh. I was thinking about the Pharmacy. You know, Fleeta gets an attitude when I stay away too long.'

Jack Mac rises like a gentleman as I stand.

'No, sit down,' I tell Jack, a little embarrassed by his chivalry. 'Your food will get cold.'

Mrs. Mac nudges Jack. 'See her out, Jack.'

'Thanks for the coffee. And let me know how you like that new pill Doc Daugherty put you on.'

'I will, honey,' Mrs. Mac says as she waves me off with her spatula. 'Y'all scoot.'

Jack Mac is careful to let me precede him through the doorways. At the screen door it's a little awkward because I reach for it first and so does he, and he brushes my hand. 'For a coal miner, you've got mighty soft hands,' I tell him. He smiles. What possessed me to blurt *that* out?

I'm on the porch now, and he stands in the doorway, his broad shoulders filling it from frame to frame. He reaches up and plucks the coil on the screen door like it's middle C.

'Not really. Touch the tips.' Jack Mac extends his right hand and with his left takes my fingers and touches his fingertips to mine.

'You've got calluses.'

'From the guitar.'

'You've been practicing.'

'Have to. Pee Wee Poteet and I have an unspoken competition. Guitar versus fiddle.'

'I think you'll win.'

'How do you know?'

'His wife smashed his fingers in the car door last night. I had to take him some painkillers.'

'Poor old Pee Wee.'

'It wasn't an accident. His wife was in a jealous rage and went after him—' I stop myself. I am telling this man confidential things. I never tell confidential things!

'I like your perfume.'

'It's just residual from Iva Lou,' I say, turning four shades of red gingham (the curse of pale-skinned girls).

'Well, it's mighty nice, wherever it came from.' I walk down the steps into the yard. The dogs circle.

'Are any of these your actual dogs?'

Jack Mac laughs. 'No. They're all wild. This time of year, when the rain stops and the leaves turn, they get scared 'cause they can't find water. They know I'm a soft touch.' I look down at the dogs, and for a moment I sort of like them, with their soft eyes and pink tongues.

'You ain't scared of 'em, are you?'

'Me? No. Heck no. I'm not scared of much.' I guess he doesn't see that I'm invincible, like Maureen O'Hara. As I make my way back to the Jeep, Jack Mac hollers at me.

'Hey, Ave Maria, what do you think of my new truck?'

Jack Mac points to a clearing by the shed. His 1978 Ford pick-up gleams red-hot and shiny in the sun.

'It's a beauty,' I holler back.

'Fully loaded.'

'Can't beat that.' I wave good-bye and climb into my Jeep.

As I drive back to town I'm thinking about how everything at the MacChesneys' is clean.

There's a traffic jam in the middle of town. Everybody's out doing their trading. Plus, it's due date in full on the electric and gas bills. I love town when it's busy; makes me feel like something exciting might happen. Zackie Wakin, a compact Lebanese ped-dler-turned-local entrepreneur, is rolling racks of clothes out onto the sidewalk in front of his store. He is small at about five feet, his complexion café au lait, his lips full (sign of generosity). I've always loved his storefront: ZACKIE'S BARGAIN STORE: CLOTHES

& SUCH FOR THE ENTIRE FAMILY. And he's not kidding. He has everything from toasters to gold shoes. (I know because I needed a pair of gold shoes for a pharmaceutical-convention formal once, and he had them!)

'Miss Ave!' Zackie waves me over. (Zackie looks like a feriner, but his accent is pure mountain. It always sounds funny coming out of his mouth. He looks like a desert sheik from the movies, but he sounds like the rest of us.)

'Another sidewalk sale?'

'You betcha. Gotta clear out for the new fall merchandise. I got Frye boots coming in big next week. You keep that in mind, will ya?'

'I'll be over for my pair,' I promise. Zackie beams. The man was born to sell.

The lot at the Pharmacy is full, so I double-park in the alley and leave the keys in the Jeep in case I block anyone. I see that Iva Lou is still at the gas station, and Kent is now sitting inside the Bookmobile with her. (Progress.) I examine the exterior of my building as I enter. Paint is chipping off the window casings, the sign is fading, and half of the neon mortar and pestle is flashing pathetically. I let the place go when Mama was sick. Fortunately, my customers don't care about fancy trappings; I'm always busy.

Fleeta Mullins, my only employee and the thinnest woman in the Gap, chain-smokes behind the counter. I've never seen Fleeta without a cigarette in her hand, regardless of how many conversations we've had about smoking being bad for her. I hear the start of emphysema in her cough, but she refuses to give it up. She's only in her fifties, and her face is already wrinkled, a series of tiny pleats.

'Hi-dee, Ave Maria,' she barks.

'Nice do, Fleetsie,' and I meant it; she just had her hair put up.

'I copied Jeanne Pruett's upsweep.' Fleeta pats the spit curls gently. 'I wish I could sing like her, too.'

'Singing isn't the be-all. I bet she can't name all the wrestlers on the world-federation roster.'

'You got you a point there.'

'Busy morning.' I clear the register.

'I need to declare me some sort of moratorium on these damn fund-raising jars,' Fleeta complains. 'I can't hardly ring up a sale without flippin' one over.'

She's right. Our counter is overrun with homemade jars that have coin slots cut into their lids. Kids bring them by from school to raise money for all sorts of things. They glue their school pictures to the front of the jar with their names and a handwritten slogan to solicit funds. Right now the competition is heating up for Halloween prince and princess at the grade school, and I don't like to play favorites, so anybody who makes a jar can leave one. Teena Lee Ball, a cute second-grader, stands by the register. Teena Lee looks at Fleeta and thinks better of asking her for a favor, so she turns to me.

'Miss Mulligan, my mamaw said you'd put my jar on the counter 'cause we trade here.'

'Your mamaw is a smart woman, and she's got a point. It's called 'turnabout fair trade.' You put your jar on the counter. Maybe we'll raise a million dollars for your campaign!'

Teena Lee smiles and shows the space where her front teeth should be. She scoots the jar in front of the others and goes.

'You're too much of a soft touch. Let me handle them kids that come in here. If it wasn't for me, people'd run all over you all day long. I'll tell them damn kids to take their jars to the Piggly Wiggly. We ain't got the room; they do. They got three register lanes over there. We've only got the one.'

I lift a jar off the counter. 'Did that Coomer boy ever get his kidney?'

'I think it was in the paper that he did.'

I unscrew the Coomer boy's jar and pour the coins into the March of Dimes canister.

'Lew Eisenberg wants you to come see him over to his office. And I'm quitting.'

'You're kidding.'

'Ave, honey, I'm sick of people. I want to set home and watch me some TV. Portly has his Black Lung comin' through. It's time to enjoy life.'

Obviously, Fleeta hasn't let herself make the connection that in order to collect Black Lung benefits from the coal company, her husband has to be sick. This isn't exactly the time for cele-bration.

'I don't want you to go.' I sound pitiful, not like a boss at all.

'You'll get over it. I ain't met nobody yet who ain't replaceable.'

'It won't be the same.'

'It's time for a change is all,' Fleeta announces like a Greek philosopher. *Change.* Why does that word send a chill through me?

Lew Eisenberg's office is next door to the Pharmacy on Main Street. I sort of dread going in there, the place is so cluttered. Inez, Lew's wife, is also his secretary. They met when Lew came down to do some legal work for Westmoreland Coal Company. Inez had just graduated high school. They had a romance and she got pregnant. Lew did the right thing and married her. (Well, the right thing for Inez, that is).

'He's inside,' Inez says without looking up. Inez still has a pretty face, but she has gained about a hundred pounds since they married. It's been frustrating for her, since she was known for her gorgeous figure when she was a cheerleader. Now she's always on a diet. She's tried Metracal shakes, AYDS, the reducing-plan candy, and Figurine Wafers (I carry all flavors) – nothing has done the trick.

Lew sits behind his desk, smoking a cigarette. His round pumpkin head looks large atop his thin frame. He has small brown eyes behind thick glasses and a space between his front teeth (the Chinese call these lucky teeth). I haven't seen the space recently; Lew rarely smiles.

'Coffee or tea or something?' Lew asks. He always sounds agitated, but it doesn't make him unpleasant. You can see he's a sweetie underneath.

'No thanks.' Lew looks relieved that I don't want anything; the less contact with Inez, the better. He closes the door and sits in the chair next to me. He has never done that. 'We need to talk.' He is quiet for a few seconds, but it seems much longer. He stands and paces. 'I finished up your mother's paperwork. Her will. The house, the Pharmacy, the life insurance – all that goes to you. Essentially, my job is done. Except for one thing.' He stands at the window, flicking the blinds.

A floorboard creaks outside the office door, sounding like two hundred tiptoeing pounds. We look at each other. Lew turns on the radio for privacy – Inez has a reputation for snooping – and sits down next to me again. 'There's a letter.'

Lew gives me a large manila envelope. It is addressed to me in care of Lewis Eisenberg. In the upper left-hand corner it says, 'From Fiametta Vilminore Mulligan.' I'm one of those folks who opens her mail as she stands at the mailbox, so I rip into the envelope immediately and unfold the letter. I see my mother's handwriting. (The letter is written in English; I assume it's because Lew would have needed to read it, too.)

My dear Ave Maria,

    When you read this letter, I will have left you. There are things I could never tell you about myself. Many times, I tried. But then, I would think better of unburdening myself and stay quiet. The first thing I want you to know is that you are the best thing that ever happened to me.

At this point, my heart is pounding so hard it's moving the buttons on my shirt. I look over at Lew, who is now lying down on the floor, smoking and staring up at the ceiling.

'Did you read this, Lew?'

'Yup. Don't mind me, my back's out.'

    When I was seventeen, I was a very happy girl. I worked as a seamstress in my father's shop in Bergamo. My mother was beautiful, and my father a very respected man. A boy used to stop by the shop, his name was Mario Barbari. He came from a good family from Schilpario, a small town in the mountains. He was quite handsome and made me laugh. One time, my father had business in Schilpario. I begged him to let me ride along. I hoped I would see Mario, and as luck would have it, I did. Once he took care of business, Papa decided to stay in Schilpario and play cards. Mario offered to show me the town. He showed me the church, the waterwheel, the school. I felt like I had known him all of my life. I fell in love with him that day.

'May I have some water, please?' I swallow hard. Inez enters with water. Lew and I look at each other. Inez goes.

Mario came down to Bergamo to see me. My father found out about our friendship and forbade me to see him because I was too young to court. I did what no good daughter would do: I defied him and would sneak out to see Mario. I was so happy whenever I was with him. We shared such good, happy times. I knew I wanted to spend my life with him. We made a plan to run away together. He was to meet me at the Bergamo station and we would take the first train to Milan. I waited and waited but he never came. A courier arrived with a letter from him explaining that he could not meet me that day. I was going to tell Mario that I was expecting you so we could marry immediately. I am sure that he was not suspicious of my condition or he would have kept our appointment.

I knew that I must leave my home or the shame of what I had done would never be resolved. I remembered that we had a cousin in Lake Maggiore. I bought a ticket to go there, hopeful she would take me in. When I arrived in Lake Maggiore, I could not find my cousin. I had no place to go. My heart was broken But I thought of you. I had to take care of you. Then, something very lucky happened to me. I returned to the train station. Everyone rushing around, having somewhere to go, comforted me. I sat alone on a bench. I fell asleep. When I woke up, a beautiful lady was sitting next to me. I will never forget what she looked like. She was tall, slim, and wore a blue coat. The buttons were blue jewels. And on her head was a hat, exquisite blue velvet with peacock feathers and tiny blue stars. Her face was creamy pink; she smelled like garden flowers. She offered me a sweet roll. I was so hungry, I took it. She said, 'Now, my dear, what shall we do?' 'I have no place to go,' I said to her. 'But of course you do. You're coming with me. I am going to America. You will stay with me. And when we get there, we will find you a position.' I was so afraid. But this woman smiled at me and I knew we would be all right.

I am crying. Lew stands and stretches. He comes over to me, puts a limp hand on one of my shoulders, and pats me like an old dog.

I asked the beautiful lady what her name was. She said, 'Ave Maria Albricci.' I told her that she had a beautiful name and she laughed. She thought it too ornate. I told her when I had my baby I would name her Ave Maria. She laughed again. She asked me how I knew I was going to have a girl. I told her I just knew. The ride on the ship was lovely. Ave Maria had a beautiful cabin. Servants laid our clothes out. The food was plentiful, even with the war on; I felt you healthy and happy inside of me. Four weeks passed and we arrived in New York City. Ave Maria's relatives greeted us at the port. We took the train to Hoboken, New Jersey. Ave Maria bought the *Italia Oggi*, the newspaper. We read the want ads. In those days, immigrants were cheap labor and would work in exchange for room and board. 'What is Virginia?' I asked the Albriccis. They laughed. I responded to the ad: 'SEAMSTRESS WANTED: MINING TOWN: BIG STONE GAP, VIRGINIA. GOOD PAY.'

Mama had taped the actual ad to the back of the letter to verify her story.

I knew this job was a good opportunity. I wrote a letter. The gentleman that placed the ad owned a dress shop in the town. He hired me immediately based upon my letter. By chance, his friend, a merchant from Big Stone Gap, was in New York City on a buying trip. His name was Fred Mulligan, of the Mutual Pharmacy. Would I like an escort on the trip to Virginia? I was so happy. Fred Mulligan took the train to meet me. I was surprised. He was young, like me. He understood Italian, having studied it at the University of Virginia. I liked him. He told me later that for him it was love at first sight. In truth, he suspected my condition and knew it would be easier on me if I was married. I agreed to marry him. It was an arranged marriage; I arranged it.

I never heard from Ave Maria Albricci again. I sent many letters to her family in Hoboken through the years; all were returned. I prayed for her every day of my life, though, never forgetting her kindness. Whenever I spoke your name, I thought of her and how she helped me. She was an angel.

I felt you should know the truth. I hope I made the right decision in telling you this. I asked Mr. Eisenberg to be present with you. I love you, my darling girl.

Mama

I turn the envelope upside down and shake it to make sure I haven't missed anything. A small, square lace-edged black-and-white photograph falls into my lap. In gold letters it says, 'Ti Amo, Mario.' On the back, in my mother's handwriting, 'Mario da Schilpario Italia 1942.' The picture fits in my palm. The man in the picture looks to be about seventeen. He has black hair and a trim physique. He is laughing. This is my father.

Inez stands in the doorway. 'Ave, they need you up to the school. There's been an incident.' The floorboards creak as Inez ambles toward me.

'Ave, you need to get up to the school. Principal called.' Lew's voice brings me back to earth. 'They need the Rescue Squad.'

Besides being a pharmacist, I am chief of the Rescue Squad. Doc Daugherty roped me into the job a couple of years back. We're a volunteer emergency-response team – the team is the fire chief, Spec Broadwater, and me. We handle everything from car wrecks to removing buttons from kids' noses, and once we even resuscitated Faith Cox's cat.

'Spec's outside waiting fer you,' Inez says, a touch too impatiently.

Spec is wedged into the driver's seat of Rescue Squad Unit One, a white station wagon with bright orange trim. I don't know why he's called Spec; he is the opposite of a speck, he's a giant, the tallest man in the Gap, at six feet seven. I climb into the car. Fleeta runs out of the Pharmacy and hands me my emergency kit through the window. Spec steps on the gas so fast, Fleeta practically loses her hand. I hear her curse at Spec in the distance as we pull away. Spec shoves a blue siren onto the roof of the car through the driver's-side window.

'Problem up to the school.' Spec offers me a cigarette. I must look like I need one. My face is puffy from crying.

'It's bad for you, Spec.'

'Self-medication. When they come up with a healthy way for me to calm my nerves, I'll quit.'

Powell Valley High School is a stylish, brand-new red brick structure that sits back off the main road, in a wide field. It is the jewel of this town, built with monies from the War on Poverty of the late 1960s. Spec ignores all traffic laws and careens up the circular driveway in the wrong direction.

'Problem's in the West Wing,' he explains.

The principal, Dale Herron, meets us in front of the school. The kids call him Lurch. I sort of see why – he's slope-shouldered and his head juts forward. Lurch leads us inside to a rest room marked BOYS. The building is dead quiet.

'Where are the students?' I ask.

'In the auditorium,' the principal says. 'Miss Mulligan, I think you ought to wait out here.'

'I'll handle it,' Spec says, patting me like a Pekinese.

The men disappear into the rest room. A few moments pass. I hear mumbling from the lavatory. Finally, the two men emerge.

'Let's go,' Lurch says, pointing toward the assembly down the hall.

We follow the angry principal into the auditorium. Every seat is filled. The teachers line the side aisles like guards. There are some whispers but not many. Onstage is a lectern and two students squirming in chairs: the student-body president, a young man with a long Renaissance curl, and the chaplain, a pudgy girl with thick glasses. Lurch takes the stage.

'Good afternoon, students. That greeting right there is for the ninety-eight percent of you who are law-abiding kids. I'll get to the remaining two percent here in a minute. I have called this emergency assembly to alert y'all that there is a sicko among us. There is a sign outside this door which reads, UNITED WE STAND, DIVIDED WE FALL. The hijinks and shenanigans of a small percentage of us will cause the whole to suffer. To fall. Mike. Brownie. Bring up the evidence.'

Two young men rise from their front-row seats and disappear backstage. They enter sheepishly from the wings. Mike is a small platinum blond. I recognize him as the point guard on our championship basketball team. The other kid is mousy; his diminutive name suits him. They carry a large tarp between them.

'Dump it,' the principal barks.

The boys dump the contents of the tarp. White ceramic

chunks hit the stage with a clatter, making a cloud of dust. An intact toilet seat tumbles out, confirming my suspicions.

'This is what someone setting right here in this auditorium has done. Destroyed school property. Committed a crime with evil intent. How? By rigging a sophisticated round of cherry bombs to a ter-let in the boys' rest room in the West Wing.'

A few nervous giggles escape the student body.

'This is no joke, people.' Lurch searches the audience for the gigglers. Then he pauses. He pounds the podium. 'Some unfortunate young man might have been sitting on that ter-let when it blew to high heaven. I ask you, what would have happened then?'

'Jesus,' Spec says under his breath.

'Anybody actually injured?' I whisper.

Spec ignores me.

'I'm scared,' a familiar deep voice says behind me.

'You should be,' I whisper back. 'The teacher's lounge is next.'

'Dinner tonight? After the show?'

'I'd love to.'

The deep voice, and now my date for the evening, is my best friend, the band and choral director of Powell Valley High School, Theodore Tipton, formerly of Scranton, Pennsylvania. Every once in a while the mines or the school will hire someone from the outside world. Inevitably, they move in and shake things up. Theodore brought our band back to life and simultaneously goosed the libidos of all the women in town. ('He's a humdinger,' Iva Lou says with relish every time she sees him. 'The man makes a pair of Levis sing.') Theodore also stars as Preacher Red Fox in the Outdoor Drama. We became friends when he auditioned nine years ago and I cast him on the first round. I had to. His face reading told me that he was loyal and true and fiercely protective. I knew if I cast him we would spend lots of time together, and we have. His face is square-shaped, with a defined jaw. He has a firm chin with a dimple in it. He can look strong, like an Irish pirate, or intellectual, like a preoccupied poet. He is tall, with blue eyes and a red beard. Even though all the available women in town chase him (and a few married ones, too), he spends all of his spare time with me. We're 'feriners' – even though I was born here, I'm considered a feriner because my mother was one – but that's just the start of what we have in common.

The principal wraps up the assembly with a couple more threats for the student body. If the guilty party doesn't fess up, he promises to suspend the smoking areas outside. This brings a groan from the students. The chaplain places a shoe box marked ANONYMOUS on the podium. Lurch tells the kids it will be placed in the gym so anyone with tips regarding the toilet incident can leave them in there. He dismisses the assembly. The student body rises. As the kids exit in an orderly fashion, most of them acknowledge Theodore. He is popular and respected, the perfect reputation for a teacher.

Only one student stops to speak to me: Pearl Grimes, fifteen years old, a sweet mountain girl with a weight problem. She often window-shops at the Mutual. I walk down the hall with my arm around her.

'My skin's done broke out agin.' Pearl hangs her head sadly.

'I got something for that. Come by the Mutual and see me.'

'All right.' She shrugs. She doesn't believe me.

'Don't you know the more pimples you got now, the less wrinkles you'll have later?'

Finally, Pearl smiles. Her face, heart-shaped, with a high forehead, tells me that she is emotional yet fair. Her nose is small and turns up slightly. Her cheeks are full and round – the cheeks of a monarch – which means she can handle power.

Pearl blends off into the sea of students. Theodore takes my arm.

'I'll walk you to your car.'

'Sure.'

'What's new?'

'I'm a bastard.'

Theodore laughs, which gets me laughing too. 'Did you bust a shoplifter or something?'

'No. I didn't behave like a bastard. I mean the literal definition.'

'What?'

'I settled Mama's will today. She left me a letter. Fred Mulligan wasn't my father.' Theodore is surprised but remains cool for my benefit. He knows everything about Fred Mulligan and me. When I shared all those stories, Theodore always got a look like he'd kill anyone who hurt me. This new information surprises him.

Theodore leads me out the front entrance to the car. Spec sits behind the wheel.

'Get in, Ave,' Spec grumbles, lighting a cigarette. 'That was a waste of my time.'

'See you tonight,' Theodore says as he closes the door. He touches my cheek. I look up to the second-floor science lab. Pearl Grimes stands in the window, watching us. From here, in the mellow afternoon light, she has a regal countenance, like a queen looking down on her subjects. I give her a quick wave good-bye. She smiles.

CHAPTER TWO

On top of everything else, my roof leaks. It needs to be patched, and fast. The town handymen are a pair of brothers, Otto and Worley Olinger. They drive an open flatbed truck around town and pick up people's discards. Some days you'll see them with a wringer washing machine strapped to the back of the truck; another day it'll be a couple of railroad ties and a stuffed bear head. In some parts they're known as the Are Y'all Using That? Brothers because that's how they greet you when they want something from your yard.

Otto appears to be the older of the two. He is short-legged and sturdy, with gray hair and a few teeth left on the bottom. He has a distinctive nose – it has a shelf on the upper bridge, which indicates he's good with money. Worley has thick red hair and is tall and lean. His long face matches his long body. Nobody in town is exactly sure how old they are because they did not matriculate through the school system. But they seem to have been around forever.

I join them up on my roof. I manage a Thermos of coffee and a few fresh ham biscuits for the boys.

'Time for a break, gentlemen,' I say as I crawl toward them.

'Miss Ave, you afraid of heights?'

'Uh-huh.' I try not to look down as I answer.

Worley extends his hand to me. 'Don't be. We won't let you fall. Anyhow, the ground is soft. I fell off the post office when we was fixin' an exhaust fan. Landed on my head. It weren't so bad.'

'That's a lie,' Otto says. 'I caught you.'

'How bad is my roof, boys?'

'I seen worse,' Otto decides.

'I let everything around here go to hell when Mama was sick.'

'It happens.' Worley shrugs.

'I should be able to keep y'all busy through the winter.'

'We need the work. We'll do a good job for ye,' Otto promises.

There is a long silence. I've never been on my roof. I can see pretty far. Fall has definitely moved in. The treetops look like orange and red feathers to the edge of town. I wish I had brought Mama out here. She would have loved being able to see so far. I check the pocket of my overalls for her letter. I manage to carry it everywhere with me, even though I don't need to. (I've read it so many times that I've memorized it.) I wish she had left instructions. Why did she tell me this story? Did she want me to try and find Mario da Schilpario? Or did she just want me to know so I would understand Fred Mulligan? So much to think about.

'If I had a roof like this, I'd set up here all the day,' Worley announces.

'My brother don't like workin'.'

'Naw, I don't. I like sleepin' and eatin'. Workin' wears me out. Wind up all tarred and ferget how I spent the day.'

'That's how I feel after a day of counting pills.'

'Ye ought to git murried, Miss Ave. Womens ain't supposed to work like 'at.'

'Otto, I ain't husband hunting. And I like my job. Okay?' I say this flatly; inquiries regarding my marital status are an everyday thing for me. Folks always want to let me know – even though I'm not married – that I'm okay, certainly nice enough to have a husband.

'Ye oughtn't wait too long to git murried. Git set in your ways and then nobody'll want you.'

'What if they like my set ways?'

'She's done got a point there, Otto,' his brother says.

'You ever been in love, Worley?'

'No, ma'am.'

'How about you, Otto?'

Otto doesn't answer.

'Otto was sweet on a girl once. You was, brother. You was!'

'Keeping secrets from me, Otto?'

'No, ma'am.'

'Do tell, then.'

'I done had me a true love, but it was many, many years ago. Well, it was summer. I was 'bout fifteen. Mama done made me go to town fer jars. She was canning her some chow chow. Walkin' down, I passed a trailer. Lot of kids runnin' around. Their people, I could just tell, was Melungeon. They had that dark color, and that look of them. There was a girl there. She had her some black hair, shiny and straight in braids. I 'member thinkin' that the braids look like them garlands over the bank door. They was that long. And she had her some black eyes like coal. And she was small. Tiny, like a matchbox? Reminded me of that storybook about the fairy girl.'

'Thumbelina?'

'Yeah. Thumbelina.'

'What was your girl's name?'

'Destry.' Otto looks away at the mention of her name. 'Best name I ever heard,' he says quietly.

'So what happened?'

'The summer passed. And pert near every day she walked with me. I grew to like 'at and look forward to it. One day she couldn't go with me, and I missed her bad. I knew then that I loved her. Turned out her pappy moved their trailer over to Stonega. I walked over there about five miles. I done had something to give her. My mama had a little silver ring with a red stone in it. And I loved Destry so much, I stole it and give it to her.'

'How do you like 'at!' Worley said, laughing.

'You must have loved her very much to steal for her.'

'That I did, ma'am. That I did.'

'Mama done whooped the tar out of Otto when she found out. Beat him with a switch till it snapped in two.'

'Yup, and then Daddy done came home and beat me, too.' Otto reaches into his pocket. He pulls out a wad of paper crumbles, nails, and a five-dollar bill. He sifts through the stuff and pulls out the tiny silver ring. He gives it to me.

'Go ahead. Try it on.'

I put the ring on my finger.

'For a big girl, you got little fingers,' Worley observes.

'What a beautiful ring.'

'Thank you, ma'am.'

'Where is Destry now?'

'She died.' Otto sighs.

'That's the sad part of the story,' Worley says. He looks at his brother with great feeling.

'Yes, ma'am. She died. Melungeons git all sorts of things – they catch just about anything that's out there, and they're weak, so it tends to take 'em. She was sixteen when she died. I wanted to murry her, but she was too sick.'

'Why do the Melungeons die like 'at?' Worley asks.

'Well, the theory is that there's a lot of inbreeding there. Up in the mountains, folks didn't mix with the general population. And that hurt them. Because the more of a mix you get, the stronger the blood. Or so the doctors believe.'

'Where do they come from?'

'*Melungeon* comes from the French word *mélange*. It means "mixed."'

'I thought the Melungeons were them folks from the Lost Colony down in North Carolina.'

'That's another theory.'

'What's the Lost Colony?' Worley asks.

'Ye tell him, Miss Ave,' Otto says.

'I think the Lost Colony was more of a tale told in the hills rather than actual fact. But the story goes that settlers from England landed on the North Carolina coast near Virginia. The ship dropped them off with supplies, and they built a colony. There was a fort, gardens, little houses, a church – things were going well. But when the ships returned from England a year later, the colony was a ghost town. Beds were made. Books were on shelves. Clothes were hanging in the closets. But no people. The people had vanished. They looked for them but never found them. There was only one clue: the word *Croatan* was carved on a tree. Some believe that a settler carved that before he was kidnapped away by the Indians. It's just a guess, though. So, a Melungeon could be a person who descends from a mix of the settlers and Indians, who hid here in these hills and never left. Your Destry could have been a descendant of those people.'

'Well, all I know is I never loved no other.' Otto says this with such clarity, I know it is true.

The three of us sit and drink our coffee. We're all thinking about little Destry. Otto had the real thing and lost it. I hope someday my heart will open up and have a love like that.

The open-air amphitheater for *The Trail of the Lonesome Pine* Drama was built next door to the home of the only famous person to ever come from this town, the author John Fox, Jr., who wrote the book that inspired our play. Mr. Fox was a talented loner who lived with his mother and sister. His book of 1908, *The Trail of the Lonesome Pine*, was the best-selling novel in the United States prior to *Gone with the Wind*. It's the first fact you're told on the tour of the Fox home. The town turned their home into a gift shop, where you can buy key chains, postcards, and corn-husk dolls. Next to it is the theater, and next door to the theater is the original one-room schoolhouse from John Fox, Jr.'s childhood. The state funds to refurbish it haven't come through, so you can't go inside, just look through the window. The tour buses roll in to the cul-de-sac, and it sort of landlocks the audience to spend money. Visitors peruse the gift shop and eat at the Kiwanis Club sloppy-joe stand during intermission.

I love the Drama because growing up I spent most of my summers backstage. Mama designed and sewed all the costumes for the show. There was always something needing mending or replacing, so Mama and I would walk over and tend to the problem. I always loved theater people, even though I was a little scared of them with their elaborate wigs, long black eyelashes, and bright red cheeks. The cast was always nice to me, and once they even let me come onstage with them in the finale. I never forgot the excitement of those footlights, the torches that lit the back wall and the cluster of musicians in the sawdust orchestra pit down-stage. It only stood to reason that someday I would grow up and help out. Mazie Dinsmore, the grande dame director of the first season, a tugboat of a woman with the vision of Cecil B. De Mille, spotted me early on and taught me how to direct. I served as her prompter (the girl who crouches offstage and feeds lines to the actors who forget where they are or what to say). This was an important job because more than one of our lead actors was known to hit the Old Granddad before and during a performance. One night I fed a tipsy Cory Tress his line and he looked at me in the wings and said, 'What?' He got a huge laugh. But those sorts of flubs are rare. We're amateurs, but we do take the Drama seriously. There was another night when a flat of scenery painted to indicate a drawing room in a Kentucky Bluegrass mansion started to teeter and was about to fall. I slipped onto the stage and grabbed it before it crushed the actors. Mazie never forgot that. She felt I had the stomach for directing. I never panicked. She thought that was one of the most important attributes in a director.

Backstage at the Drama there is always a disorganized cacophony of kids running around, musical-instrument warm-ups, dancers doing their stretches, and actors running their lines. Tonight is closing night, the last show of our season. It's a free performance for the families and friends of the cast and crew, so it's standing room only. Nerves run high when we're putting on the show for the town; somehow, performing for strangers is easier.

The play is about a mountain girl named June Tolliver who falls in love with John Hale, a coal inspector from Kentucky. He takes this wildcat girl and sends her to the Bluegrass to be refined and educated by his aristocratic sister, Helen. When she returns to her mountains after having the Pygmalion pulled on her, she doesn't fit in. In fact, she is too cultured for John Hale, who cannot believe what a lady she has become. They get past all that, though, and admit they've loved each other all along. It's a classic story, and it gets the audience every single time. My favorite moment in the play is in the first act, when June's father, Devil Judd Tolliver, finds out that John Hale is in love with his fifteen-year-old daughter. He tries to blow the coal inspector's head off. The lines go:

DEVIL JUDD: My Juney is too young for ye.
JOHN HALE: She won't always be fifteen, sir. I'll wait.

The actual blocking has been handed down for years, so all I do is say, 'You go here; You stand there; Look surprised when the gun goes off;' and 'No chewing gum.' I just follow the instructions from Mazie's promptbook. (When she died she willed it to the John Fox, Jr., Museum.) Any of the special touches we owe to Mazie Dinsmore and her theatrical vision. She put actual gunfire into the show and added the preshow of roving bluegrass musicians and singers to entertain the audience before curtain. The preshow has set us apart from all the other outdoor dramas on the circuit. Audiences love the traditional bluegrass music, and of course, they can't wait to see our world-famous backdrop: a painting, the size of half a football field, that is an exact replica of the mountain view you see behind it. It's a dazzler at twilight, when you're sitting in the audience and you see a painting of the actual vista from your seat.

The hardest part of directing is the scheduling. Because we are not professionals, everybody has a job or two outside of the Drama. I've got musicians who are coal miners and work the hoot-owl shift (midnight to lunch), teachers who are busy all day, farmers who work weekends. It's a juggling act, but it is the most fun I've ever had. I love mountain music – the Celtic Scotch-Irish sound of regret, low wailing tunes like 'Barbara Allen' and 'Poor Wayfaring Stranger.' I always thought I loved that music because of Fred Mulligan. He was Scotch-Irish. The music was our one connection, the only mutual thing we loved. Now I must let go of that, too.

Theodore enters from stage right in full costume and beard. He crosses downstage, jumps off the lip, and comes toward me with a look of concern on his face. We have a powwow about the gizmo that leaks fake blood from his chest (he gets shot at the end of the play). Pearl Grimes is my props department, so she listens in.

My stage manager waves a clipboard in my face. 'Miss Mulligan, we're ready to open the house.' He calls off, 'Dancers! Positions, please.' The dancers take the stage. By day they are majorettes with the high school marching band, under Theodore's capable direction. Majorettes are the prettiest girls in school, even ahead of cheerleaders. Let's face it: Twirling takes skill; cheering only takes volume. By night, they're my dancers, providing storytelling through movement.

I have no twirling in the Drama, although the majorette captain, Tayloe Slagle, lobbied hard to incorporate it. I explained historical accuracy is the entire point of doing the Drama. I don't see a bunch of mountain folk from 1895 twirling batons in the middle of a hoedown.

Tayloe enters from the stage-right wings. She takes her mark at center stage, owning it like it's the only pin dot in the universe. Bo Caudill, the follow-spot operator, widens the beam of light from her perfect face to include her body – shapely, bursting in ripe perfection in a simple red dress with a scoop neck and ruffles.

Tayloe is compact but leggy, like all the great movie stars. She has a well-formed, large head with a clear, high forehead set off by smooth, small features: a prominent but straight nose (like Miriam Hopkins), blond hair (like Veronica Lake), and wet eyes (like Bette Davis). Her right eyebrow is always slightly raised in a delicate swirl, giving me the impression she is skeptical of anything she is told.

Tayloe plays June Tolliver, the ingenue lead, the coarse mountain girl who transforms into a Kentucky lady. Tayloe won the role because she has true star quality. It cannot be invented. But it sure doesn't keep every other girl in town from trying to develop That Certain Something. We have girls who practice their footwork, suffer hours of vocal coaching, and diet down to pool-cue thin, but what they don't understand is that this luminescence is inborn and unteachable, and Tayloe's got it. All any good director has to do is exploit the obvious, so we incorporated a dream ballet into the second act, featuring Tayloe in a pale pink leotard and a wee chiffon skirt. Tickets flew out of the box office.

She's our starlet, so all the girls seek her approval and imitate her. Tayloe gives them a standard, a marker by which to judge themselves. Other skills and attributes can be appreciated and duly noted, but beauty is instantly obvious to all. I have never met a girl (including myself) who did not long to be beautiful, who did not pray for her own potential to reveal itself. When a girl is beautiful, she gets to pick − she never has to wait for someone to choose her. There is so much power in doing the choosing.

Pearl Grimes touches my arm. 'I think I got a better way for the blood to spurt. I'm gonna rig a tube down Mr. Tipton's pant leg so he can step hard when he's shot.'

The summer of 1978 will forever be remembered as the summer of wily stagecraft. No matter what technique we've tried −

and we even called the folks up in New York City to find out how they do it – we have not been able to get Theodore shot on cue. Either the blood spurts too soon or too late. Either way, it destroys the authenticity of the moment.

'Did Mr. Tipton like your idea?'

'He's mighty impatient.'

'Most great artists are, you know. Michelangelo said, "Genius is eternal patience."'

'Do you think Mr. Tipton's a genius?'

'Genius or not, we gotta get him shot correctly so he can die at the end of the play. It's the last show of the season. Wouldn't it be nice to go out with the right bang?'

'Yes, ma'am.'

Poor old Pearl; what she's got, Tayloe is missing. She's got the thin brown hair, the thick ankles, and the weight problem. Pearl has beautiful hands, though. Pretty-faced girls usually have ugly hands. But then again, I don't know a lot of people who notice hands.

'Tayloe sure does look pretty,' Pearl decides as she stands there.

'Yeah.'

'That costume is mighty tight.'

I'm thinking that I would never wear that dress myself. That's the difference between me and Pearl: She still has the dream of wearing it.

'She's stuck-up, though,' Pearl zings.

I let the comment pass. It doesn't do me any good to try to convince Pearl that beauty comes from within and that age will eventually wither a pretty face. I get a pain in my left temple watching poor Pearl looking up on the stage at Tayloe like there is some answer up there. She is hoping that beauty will be truth. But that observation was surely made by a father of a very beautiful daughter, not Pearl's and surely not mine. Tayloe is conceited. But so what? Tayloe, not Pearl, is in the beam of the spotlight. Tayloe, not Pearl, is being examined and appreciated from all sides like a rare ruby. How Pearl wishes she was The One! Of course, I could lie. I could tell Pearl that being the prettiest girl in town is no great shakes, but eventually she would find out the truth. When you're fifteen, it is everything. And when you're thirty-five, it's still something. Beauty is the fat yellow line down the middle of Powell Valley Road. And it's best to figure out – and the sooner the better – which side you fall on, because if you don't do it for yourself, the world will. Why wait for the judgment?

Pearl squints at the stage and breathes the night air slowly like a drag off a cigarette. She is trying so hard to understand, trying to understand why Tayloe and not her.

'Maybe you ought to check your prop table. Curtain's almost up,' I remind her.

Pearl straightens up and goes backstage with a purpose. Having a purpose is the little secret of the nonpretties. Something to do always beats something to look at.

The cast looks terrific onstage. They've worked five shows a week all summer, yet they still have pep. They're still excited about doing the show. I'll spare you the details of the auditions and casting that take place every year from March till June. Let's just say it is highly competitive. Nothing like the theater to bring out the claws and pepper in people. Folks want the part they want and that's it. Never mind they're the wrong age, or can't sing, or can't dance. They'd leave notes on my Jeep, call me at home, give me gifts of cakes and jellies – anything to sway me. I can't imagine the competition on Broadway itself could be any more brutal than it is right here. Thank goodness there are parts that actors grow into: Li'l Bub becomes Big Bub, who can then play Dave

Tolliver, then, as he ages, Bad Rufe, all the way to the patriarch, Devil Judd. We've been doing the show so long, the cast members know each other's lines. We never have an understudy problem.

We do have an annoying stage mother: Betty Slagle. Tayloe's mom caused me so much grief with her many suggestions – of course all of them showing off her daughter to full advantage and forsaking the story – that I put her on the costume crew. She's busy pressing pants now, so she stays off my back.

I signal the Foxes to open the house. The Foxes are our women's auxiliary group named in honor of John Fox, Jr. (of course). They run the ticket sales, the concessions, and the rug-loom demonstration at the Fox Museum during intermission. They're a clique of young 'n' sexy divorcées and single girls. There's a sorority feeling to their activities. And they keep the history alive, so their form-fitting T-shirts say.

I cue the band to begin the overture. Jack Mac winks at me; I wink back. Now we have a secret – I've seen him in his underwear – and it's kind of fun. He nods to his boys, and they play. I'm always thrilled by the sound of those strings, mandolins so simple and clear. The soft melody sails over the outdoor theater and spills out into the dark. I take my place on the perch next to Bo's follow spot on the back wall. No matter how many times I've watched the show, I still get nervous before Curtain. I look down as the audience filters in. Iva Lou Wade comes in with a nice-looking man I've never seen before. (Where does she find them?) She wears a flowy mint-green pant set that makes her look like a Greek goddess. The gold armband completes the effect. She grins at me and I wave.

Our final show comes off without a hitch. The foot-stomp-blood-spurt cure that Pearl came up with worked (thank God). The show was perfect until Li'l Bub pulled a closing-night prank.

When Theodore was shot, he threw a rubber chicken onto the stage. The crowd went wild. Theodore was not amused. After three standing ovations, Bo shines a light on me and I am motioned to the stage by my cast. Two chorus boys help me up onto the stage. Tayloe whistles through her teeth in approval. How funny that looks, as she is dressed in her Kentucky-society finale gown. I embrace each of our four leads. Then I pull Pearl from backstage. I give her a big hug for her stroke of genius, and she beams. Then I give my usual 'thank you for the best season yet' speech. Sweet Sue Tinsley, president of the Foxes, walks across the stage with a bottle of champagne and presents it to me.

Sweet Sue is my age, and she was the Tayloe Slagle of our day. She is still as pretty as a teenager, small and blond, with vivid blue eyes. She's as popular now as she was in high school (accomplishment). She wasn't born with that name, though. There were three Sues in our first-grade class. The teacher got confused, so she gave each of them nicknames, which stuck. There was Tall Sue, Li'l Bit Sue, and this one, our Sweet Sue.

'A-vuh Maria, this bubbly is from the Foxes with our compliments. You're the best gosh-darned dye-rector anywhere ever on earth, and we appreciate your work so very much!' Loud applause for Sweet Sue fills the air, and enough wolf whistles cut through to conjure a Miss America pageant. For a moment I consider correcting Sweet Sue on the pronunciation of my name: It isn't A-vuh Maria like Ava Gardner, it's Ave like a prayer. Sweet Sue has been mispronouncing my name since first grade. Is she ever going to get it right? I decide to let it go when I look out over the crowd and see their warm and smiling faces. This isn't the time to be petty. I realize the pause after Sweet Sue's speech has gone on too long. Her eyes implore me to say something. And fast. She has that frozen smile and certain impatience that all pretty girls possess. *Your turn*, she seems to be saying with her eyes.

I blurt, 'Thank you kindly, Sweet Sue. And thank you, Foxes.' Sweet Sue is relieved as I accept the champagne.

'Hey, boys, how 'bout a song for Sweet Sue, the prettiest gal in town?' shouts our drummer from the pit.

'Thank you, boys,' Sweet Sue says magnanimously. Then she leans into the pit and kisses Jack Mac long and hard. The crowd cheers. Then a chorus of 'Ask her, Jack! Ask her, Jack!' The band pushes Jack Mac out of the pit, onto the stage. Wanda Brickey, who plays the mountain matriarch in the Drama, bangs the floor with her walking stick. 'Jack Mac, if you don't marry this girl, it don't make a lick of sense.'

The crowd calms down and waits for Jack's response. 'Folks, y'all know I'm a private person—'

Before he can finish, Sweet Sue pipes up, 'The answer is yes. Yes!' She kisses Jack Mac all over the face. She shouts, 'I love this man!' Her sons, still in mountain-boy costume, run up to the stage. The crowd cheers. The cold bottle of champagne I hold seems as though it's in the wrong hands all of a sudden. So I make a stage-right cross and hand it to Jack Mac.

'Congratulations!' I say happily. The crowd goes wild. Jack Mac leans into my ear and says, 'Thank you.' I look at him. 'Call your mother.'

'Yes, ma'am.' Jack Mac kisses my cheek. Sweet Sue grabs him away.

'Hey, Ava, he's mine. Find your own man!'

The crowd laughs; it's one of those long, rolling laughs. Now, when you're the town spinster, jokes of this sort aren't one bit funny. Around here, being married makes you a prize. No one has claimed me, and although it shouldn't hurt me, it does. I could cry. Instead, I bend forward and laugh louder than anyone in the house.

Theodore, as if on cue, comes up behind me and puts his hands around my waist. Then he announces, 'She has a man, Sweet Sue.' I look up at Theodore, the most beautiful man I have ever seen. I lean against him.

'Well, I didn't mean to . . .' Sweet Sue stutters. Jack Mac cues the band, gracefully saving his girlfriend's face. He shrugs at me.

Theodore takes me in his arms to dance. The music fills the theater. Somebody's singing the lyrics, but all I hear is Theodore's voice saying, 'She has a man! She has a man!' onstage, in public, and loudly for all to hear! He looks down at me and smiles. I feel wanted, claimed, and – I can't believe it – alluring. Instead of looking off as we dance, I look into his eyes, and they are as blue as the sky on the backdrop.

And then we stop. Theodore kisses me. It's not the usual friendly kiss I have become accustomed to all of these years. So at first I don't lock in. I'm confused. Then his lips, wordless and soft, persist. My spine turns from rivets of bone into a velvet ribbon spinning off its wheel and pooling onto the floor. I hold on to him like Myrna Loy did when she and Clark Gable jumped out of a two-seater plane in *Test Pilot*. My waist is on a swivel as he dips me. But the kiss doesn't end. Moments later, when it does, my body feels like it is full of goose feathers. Theodore holds my face while everyone dances around us, offering looks of approval.

'You need lipstick,' he says, squinting at me.

'You don't.' I dab the Really Red I left there off of his face. We laugh. It's one of those shared moments that can only come between two people who know each other so well that it borders on irony. Theodore pulls me close. I rest my head on his shoulder. He smells fresh, a mix of peppermint and spice. I look across the dance floor. Iva Lou gives me a thumbs-up.

'Let's get out of here,' Theodore says with an urgency I've never heard before. He takes my hand and yanks me off the stage, and I skip down the stairs behind him.

Nellie Goodloe, president of the Lonesome Pine Arts and Crafts Guild, stops us. 'Mr. Tipton, I need to speak to you about candidate John Warner's visit to the Gap.'

'We were just leaving,' Theodore says firmly. Nellie turns to me.

'Ave Maria, tell him this is important,' she says.

'It can wait,' Theodore tells her with finality.

'It can't wait. I got a call from John Warner's press person, and they want a confirmation that the town is going to go all out for his campaign stump through Southwestern Virginia.'

Nellie's mouth keeps moving, but I can't hear her. Her lips and hair are orange, and she has placed her hand on Theodore's chest. John Warner is married to Elizabeth Taylor of *National Velvet* fame, and they're coming to town and Nellie wants Theodore to put together a tribute salute in her honor. The town wants to show off its best asset: the Powell Valley High School marching band. They want a doozy of a halftime show. I can't contemplate all this right now. After tonight my life as it has been will be changed forever. I am a lover! In the scrap heaps of these hills of coal, someone found me. I am wanted! I have been waiting all of my life for this.

As folks sail by in a blur, talking and laughing, it occurs to me that they probably believe that Theodore and I, as close as we are, have a full relationship already. But since Theodore moved to town and we became friends, my mother had been ill, and I didn't feel right spending time away from her. So Theodore and I have had friendship without romance. At first I thought something might be wrong, but now I understand. He was waiting. Waiting for my heart to settle down from its grief, so it could make room for him!

Now the years seem wasted, like a lifetime, and I want to shove bossy Nellie Goodloe down on the wood chips and gag her with the polka-dot scarf she has tied around her neck chuck-wagon-style. Doesn't she understand that my body is filled with such longing that I have the strength to turn a truck over with my bare hands? That I have dreamed of wrapping myself around this man from the first day we met? Can't she see that I'm a ripe plum that will explode if touched? I interrupt them, and I am not one bit sorry.

'Excuse me. This is something you two can discuss later. Good night, Nellie.'

I grab Theodore, and we walk out of the theater onto the street. 'My house?'

'Great.' Theodore helps me into the front seat of his truck, which has now turned into a stately carriage that will take me from my dreams to a real place. He climbs in and puts his arm around me as we back out. I think to myself, Time stops when we get what we want.

I haven't made spaghetti since Mama died. I pull out her recipe book. When she found out she was sick, she wrote everything down for me. The writing starts out in good English, then loses its clarity. She tried to finish the task when she was really sick. At the end of the notebook, most of the recipes are in pure Italian.

'Cut up the garlic,' I tell Theodore. 'The basil's in the window garden. I'll start the water.'

Theodore goes about his chores. I notice we're not talking. Is this what happens to folks when things turn physical? Do kisses take the place of words? I think back on my past romances, all so long ago, and they seem insignificant, childish and silly – probably because they were. I wasn't a real woman then, a woman who knew herself. A woman alone in the world, free. Now I am a woman without strings, guilt, or parents, and I don't know what to say. How do I begin?

'How long have your parents been married?' I ask innocently.

'Forty-two years.'

'Are they happy?'

'They're perfect for each other. He drinks and she hides it. Why do you ask?'

'We've never talked about it before.'

'It seems like we have. I think you know everything about me.'

'Have you ever been in love before?'

'Have you?' he asks, quite deliberately not answering me first.

This is a loaded question for me. I don't guess that I have, although there was a nice Polish Catholic guy from Chicago – I met him at a craps table during a Mardi Gras fund-raiser at Saint Mary's. I went with him for a year and a half. He wanted to marry me, but I couldn't see it. When it was over I was sad, but I wasn't broken-hearted.

'I guess I was. Once.' I pick up the garlic and swish it into the olive oil in the pan on the stove.

'Only once?'

'Yes.'

Theodore mulls this over, and I take a seat at the kitchen table and watch him chop some basil. I wonder if I like him there at the sink chopping. Does he fit in this house? Does he fit in my life? Will we live here in this house when we're married or in his cabin out on Aviation Road? I hear my mother's voice: '*Pazienza!* Slow down! Think, Ave Maria! Think!'

I straighten the silverware on the placemat. I like two place-mats. It looks like a family lives here again. The table holds four. Children! Am I too old? Some of my classmates from high school have grandchildren. I am not too old. Thank God I have good Italian genes. No Scotch-Irish wrinkles for me. What am I think-ing? What am I saying? I catch my reflection in the steamed glass of the kitchen window. I am dewy. No! I'm soaking wet! My palms and face are sweating. I'm making myself sick and nervous. I'm a practical person, but I have always tended to daydream, and now I'm picturing myself married to this man and for some reason it's a real romance killer. I don't want to think about marriage just yet – I just want to have some sex. I need to be held! God help me!

'People are gonna talk about us,' I promise him.

'Let them.'

'Why are we cooking?' I'm asking this question to be coy and infer, Let's not eat, let's kiss.

'Aren't you hungry?' Theodore asks.

I nod. But I'm hungry for everything: food, him, and all that life has to offer. Everything seems possible to me all of a sudden. How will I tell him?

Theodore continues chopping. What beautiful hands he has! His large hand and squarish fingers are in total control of the par-ing knife. The motion reminds me of a French movie I saw in Charlottesville once. When I go on buying trips, I make it my business to see foreign movies. We don't get them down here, so they're a treat. French movies always have love scenes in the kitchen. Somebody is eating something drippy, like a ripe per-simmon, and next thing you know it's a close-up of lips and hands and off go the lights and their clothes, and pretty soon nobody's talking. I check my ceramic fruit bowl on the counter. One black banana. Please don't let this be an omen.

'I haven't . . . Well, I guess what I'm trying to . . .' Theodore keeps chopping. I persist. 'What I want to say is . . .'

'I'm thinking, Ave.'

It may have been a long time since I've been with a man, but it doesn't take a sex goddess to figure out that thinking is not a good sign. Men don't think about sex. They think about how and where and when, but they could care less about the why.

'You don't want me,' I say plainly, hoping I'm wrong. There, I've said it. The water in the pot is boiling foam. Theodore drops his knife and stirs and blows as bubbles trickle over the sides of the pot. He catches as many as he can with a spoon, but it keeps bubbling.

'Give me a hand.'

'You've got it under control.' I say this with matter-of-factness, but the truth is, my legs aren't working. I'm in a state of shock, from the ankles up. I just made a statement that scares me, and I need to stay very small, right here in this straight-backed chair, or I'm afraid of what I might do. Theodore moves the pot off the burner. The foam subsides. He pours the spaghetti into the colander in the sink. He shakes it hard. He leaves the pot in the sink and goes to the stove. He stirs the sauce.

'We call that sauce *shway shway*,' I say, making my only contribution to the dinner.

'What is that?'

'It's Italian dialect from where my mama came from. *Shway shway means* "fast." Fast sauce. Instant sauce.'

'It tastes great.'

'Fresh basil.'

Theodore pours the sauce onto the spaghetti. He pulls out plates and forks and sets the table.

'So you want to tell me why you kissed me?'

'*You* kissed *me*.' Theodore looks at me directly.

'No. *You* kissed *me*.' Oh God. I'm yelling.

'I went with the situation. You were kissing me, so I kissed back. And after what Sweet Sue said, I felt you needed to be kissed.'

'So you were doing me a favor?'

'Yeah.'

This is one of those moments when the steam between a man and a woman creates a wall. It's so thick that I can't make out Theodore's face. I do not understand him; doesn't he know how I feel? I want him. I want this. Where is the kissing Theodore? Where did he go?

'You aren't in love with me, Ave.'

'What?'

'You got stirred up, that's all.'

'I liked the kiss! It was nice! It was welcome.'

'You said you hadn't been with a man in a long time. It's understandable. A cup of water in the desert is welcome, too.'

I can't believe what I'm hearing! Theodore is comparing my aching loins to dehydration. This night is not going at all as I had expected.

'What? What?' Why is it that all I can say is *What?*

'I live alone. I like it. I grew up in a family with nine kids, and I'm still thrilled I don't have to share a bed with someone. I don't want a "thing." I like being with you. You are my best friend. I don't want a relationship.'

'Everybody wants a relationship!'

'No. You want a relationship.'

As we eat, I am sure he is right. It is me. I want to be loved. And I want to blame somebody because I'm not. So let me blame my parents. They're easy targets – one never loved me and the other leaves me scary letters after she's passed away. Let me blame life. Life keeps interfering in my plans. First Fred Mulligan was sick; then I took care of Mama, business got to booming, and I took on more and more and thought about myself less and less. Poor me. I straighten up in my chair and summon all my self-esteem in my posture. Then, very casually, I lean toward Theodore.

'I can't believe you think I kissed you.'

'You did. The whole town got a shock.'

I don't care about the whole town. I chew in slow motion because I want to digest all of this. I initiated the kiss? I kissed him? What am I really hungry for?

'You're going to find a good man, you know.'

Where? In the Blue Ridge Mountains? On the Trail of the Lonesome Pine? By the banks of the Powell River? Get serious, you transplant from Scranton, PA. Around here, men my age have been married since they were seventeen. Some of them are grandfathers already. There are no men! You are the man! Be my man!

'You'll find somebody,' he assures me.

'Somebody!' Wake up, buster! I'm not the type of woman for a Somebody. I'm picky. I take an hour to eat a tuna-salad sandwich because I pick all the sweet-pickle chunks out of it before I'll take a bite. I'm vain. I cleanse and cream my face twenty minutes before bedtime, and then I hang my head upside down over the side of my bed for an additional five to prevent jowls. I'm a snob. I want a man who reads. In thirty years I've never seen a man on the Bookmobile, except strange Earl Spivey, but he doesn't count because he's a lurker, not a reader. If this mystery man isn't smart, I don't want him. Why can't Theodore see this?

'Okay, maybe not just somebody. How about a good guy, a real winner? When you kissed me tonight, you were impulsive. Daring. People around here saw you with new eyes. You watch. Something will happen.'

'If you say so.' I say this so weakly, it's barely audible. Theodore sprinkles cheese on his spaghetti, spins a nice mound of noodles, and eats. He chews normally. Swallows. Like everything is normal! He's ready to change the subject – like it's been discussed thoroughly and there's nothing more to say. He almost seems to be saying, 'Okay, we kissed, it was nice, but it's going no further, so let's get back to our friendship.'

'Somebody needs to tell Sweet Sue Tinsley she's not the homecoming queen anymore.'

This is another reason I want Theodore. I want to be able to come home and dissect everybody and everything. Why can't I have this?

'She's afraid somebody will steal her man away.' Theodore shrugs.

Were Theodore and I even at the same event tonight? The crowd was behind Jack Mac asking Sue to marry him; they kissed passionately, and it looked all sewn up to me. Am I so deprived of physical intimacy that I did not see this? How unobservant am I? Or am I living in some other universe, one I have created out of my own strange perceptions? I look away, out the window and into my yard, and what I see there is not the Potter's oak tree that grows over the fence but a flash of Jack MacChesney in his underwear, and how strong and bear-like he was, all man, from shoulder to foot. I shake my head to erase the picture. It goes.

'I want to have sex with you tonight.' There. I just said it right out. Honestly. Clearly. Directly. Well done.

Theodore puts down his fork (another bad sign). Then he looks at me.

'You're beautiful and desirable. But it wouldn't work. We love each other; we are not in love with each other. Even if we had sex tonight, sooner or later we wouldn't be friends. I don't want to lose that. Would you?'

Around my fork I have twirled a mountain of spaghetti so large it is the size of a tennis ball.

I say to Theodore: 'I wouldn't.' But why can't I have both? The lover *and* the best friend. Isn't that the point? I know what I want. I've had many years to think about it. When I first saw Theodore at the Drama auditions years ago, my heart skipped a beat. 'Kindred spirit' doesn't begin to describe our connection.

I unravel the tennis ball of noodles. It makes a square on the plate, like the frame of an open window. In the square, I imagine a cartoon, primitive and bright. A buck-toothed gorilla is being chased by an angry mouse with a giant mallet. The mouse climbs up the gorilla and clunks him on the head repeatedly. The gorilla's eyes cross, and stars shoot out of his head. The image makes me smile, so I won't cry.

$\mathcal{F}$leeta is serious about quitting. I can tell because she has cleaned up the shelf behind the register. Her lifetime supply of Coke and peanuts is gone. Her bifocals are safe in their case. Her paperwork is stacked neatly in two piles. In one stack, her professional wrestling schedules. Fleeta and Portly go to wrestling matches in Kingsport and Knoxville every chance they get. Pictures of the great wrestling stars Haystack Calhoun, Atomic Drop, Johnny Weaver, and the frightening Pile Driver are in protective clear-plastic sleeves. The wrestlers' thick, clublike bodies are greased in oil. Their heads are smaller than their squat, muscular bodies; they look like apples on top of buildings. In the other stack, Fleeta's recipes. When business is slow, Fleeta rewrites her recipe-card file; she's had this project under way for about five years. In Fleeta's block print:

MAMAW SKEEN'S POSSUM
Skin your possum. Place in a large pot and boil till tender. Add salt and pepper to taste. Make gravy with broth and add 4

tablespoons flour and ½ cup of milk. Cook until thick. Save a foot to sop gravy!

I wonder what they do with the other three feet. I flip through the cards; many of Fleeta's specialties are included: divinity candy, a confection of whipped sugar that looks like clouds (she brings it in every Christmas), lemon squares, cheese straws, peanut butter balls, and my favorite, rhubarb pie.

'I'm putting my recipes together for my granddaughter, for when she gets murried,' Fleeta says as she stands behind me. 'You ever ate possum?'

'Not that I know of.'

'Well, you're missing out. It's the best, most tenderest meat of all.'

Fleeta grabs her smokes and motions for me to meet her in the back office for lunch. She locks the front door and flips the RING BELL sign.

Fleeta sits on a folding chair smoking. She pours a small cellophane sack of salted peanuts into her glass bottle of Coca-Cola, stops up the top with her thumb, shakes it, and when it's fizzy chugs it back. I'm going to miss our lunches.

'Fleeta, do you really have to quit on me?'

'Honey, my mama died when she was fifty-five. I'm fifty-six. The clock is ticking. I want a life before mine's over. I will miss the money, though.'

'I'll give you a raise.'

'Too late for that. Come on, Ave. You got a lot ahead of you. You're gonna get murried to that Tipton fella.'

'What?'

'His car was parked over to your house 'til all hours Saturday night, and Nellie Goodloe done spread it all over town that you and he was swapping slobbers on the dance floor over to the Drama. Now that's public. Don't hold back on me, youngun, I know you too well.'

'He doesn't want me, Fleeta. We're just friends.'

'No way. Shoot-fire, y'all do everything together. Y'all are each other's destinies.' I start to argue with Fleeta, and she stops me. 'Even when you put two rats in a box they might chew each other up at first, but give it time and they'll make baby rats.'

'Fleeta, I'm eating.'

'He's a fine-looking man. And he's clean. I like me a clean man. And he's got nice thick hair, and honey, after thirty you gotta put that in the plus column. He's got them nice Irish looks and features. The rusty hair, the blue eyes. The purty smile. Law me! What more do you want in a man?'

I don't answer her. *Nothing!* There's no one but Theodore for me. Why won't she stop this?

'Or do you even want a man?' Fleeta looks at me over her bifocals.

'Not just any man,' I say defensively, with my mouth full of food.

'I want you to git a good man like I got. You know, Portly and I still have intimate relations. Of course, it takes a lot longer than it used to to warm up my toaster. I done gone through The Change. And that's a good word for it because everything done changed on me. I have to prepare for when he gets that look. But I'll tell you one thing – Portly has him some big clubby forearms and man-hands, you know what I'm saying, he could palm my head – really, just like a basketball. And if I didn't have those gigantic arms wrapped around me of the night, I would be one cantankerous old woman. So I know what you mean.'

'How'd you and Portly meet?'

Fleeta exhales and her eyes fill with a faraway memory. She squints to make out the details of this old picture.

'Up to the school. When East Stone Gap High School was closed down, they transferred all them kids over to Powell Valley and Portly was in the bunch. First day of school, I seen him and knew he was the one. I was feeling old, though, like I'd never find nobody.'

'How old were you?'

'Sixteen. And never been kissed. My mama was so proud of 'at. But let me tell you, when I snagged Portly, I made up for lost time. I remember the very first kiss he done give me. Up behind the bleachers up to the school. Hit was around five o'clock in the afternoon, after Portly's baseball practice. He looked at me. I looked at him. Course we had to take the snuff out of our mouths first – Portly and I both love our chewing tobacky. Well, we spit it out, and then we kissed, and the rest is history.'

I'm so wrapped up in Fleeta's love life, I don't hear the persistent bang of the bell on the store counter. I come to and get up to answer it. The majorettes stand at the counter, some reading the *National Enquirer*, others thumbing through *People*. Tayloe waits at the prescription-pickup window.

'I'm here for my prescription.'

'I'll be right with you, honey.'

'It's not ready yet?' The annoyance underscores each of Tayloe's words, and she rolls her eyes. God, she's impatient. I remember that she's just a kid, and that keeps me from biting her head off.

'No, not yet,' I reply gaily.

Pearl Grimes enters the store and, upon seeing the majorettes, instantly skulks behind the hair-care rack.

'Look how fat she got!' Glenda the majorette says with authority. That's all it takes for all the majorettes to gather round *People* magazine and gloat over the picture of some formerly slim, now chunky TV actress.

'I don't know why somebody'd let themselves go like that,' says another.

"Cause she likes to eat,' Tayloe announces. It's not one bit funny, but all the girls die laughing, because in her circle, Tayloe gets to be funny as well as beautiful.

'She's not as fat as Pearl Grimes, though.' A louder laugh.

I see the top of Pearl's head disappear behind the medical-supply rack. I wonder if they saw her come in. Are they that cruel? Mrs. Spivey, Mrs. Holyfield, and Mrs. Edmonds enter the store and split up to shop. Three finer Baptist women I've never known. They're also responsible for spreading more information than the town paper.

'Miss Mulligan, could you please hurry? We've got band practice. You know . . . with Mr. Tipton?' Another round of giggles. I guess they heard about Theodore's car being outside my house till all hours. Now I wish I'd had sex with him, so the joke wouldn't be on me.

I shout out from behind the counter, 'It's gonna take a minute, girls.' More sighs and eye rolls. They continue reading the magazines.

Fleeta comes out from the back. 'Be careful with the magazines; we can't hardly sell wrinkled, used ones. Folks like their reading material virginal. And I can't blame them, as *they* are paying,' she growls.

Inspired by Fleeta's choice of words, I seize my moment. I had a microphone installed in the prescription department because the store is large, and when I get busy I can call for the customer. I blow into the microphone. All the heads look up.

'Tayloe Slagle, your birth control pills are ready at the prescription window. Tayloe. Slagle. Your. Birth. Control. Pills. Come on over.'

Tayloe lunges for the window and grabs the white sack.

'They're for cramps.'

'Really.' I ponder this possibility. The fine Baptist women look at one another and then at Tayloe with such disdain, they become a scary tableau on a stained-glass window.

'Charge it,' Tayloe barks as she sprints for the door. The girls follow her.

I hear the ladies murmuring in the dental-hygiene section – mission accomplished.

Fleeta is chuckling, and of course the chuckles turn into a hack.

'I'm done tarred of them girls coming in here and reading and never buying. You got 'em good.'

I pick up a basket of conditioner and head for the hair-care aisle. Pearl is sitting on the floor reading labels on the backs of bottles.

'Hey, Pearl.'

'I come down for the acne treatment you told me about.'

'Then what in God's name are you doing in hair care?'

Pearl shrugs. Her eyes are a mite puffy, so I know she heard the majorettes.

'You wanna help me restock the shelves?'

'Yes, ma'am.'

'Fleeta's quitting on me, so I'm looking to hire somebody part-time. You up for it?'

'I have to ask Mama.'

'Go call your mama and ask her if you can start today.'

'We ain't got no phone. And I don't know if she'd let me take a job. How would I get to and from work?'

'I could take you home after work,' I offer.

'But I live up in Insko.'

'I drive fast. How much you want an hour? For your pay.'

'I don't know.'

'Come on. Pearl. You're gonna do sales. Sell yourself.'

'Well, I git fifty cents an hour baby-sitting the Bloomer kids.'

'Not bad. They're a handful. I guess I gotta do better than Mrs. Bloomer.'

'How 'bout one dollar an hour?' Pearl looks away, embarrassed to be talking figures.

'Only a dollar? Hmm. You're a real tail twister, Pearl. How about three dollars an hour?'

Pearl's eyes widen. 'Thank you, Miss Ave! Can I start tomorrow?' Pearl straightens her spine, and I swear she grows an inch.

'You sure can.'

Fleeta watches Pearl go and lights another cigarette. 'Why in holy hell would you hire that girl?'

'I like her.'

'She don't keep herself nice.'

'You heard her. She lives up in Insko.'

'I don't care. That ain't no excuse.'

'I'm surprised at you, Fleeta. I thought you could see potential.'

'Honey, there's potential, and then there's bullshit dreaming. I think you got a case of the bullshit dreams, if you know what I mean.'

Fleeta grazes the big feather duster over the vitamins, barely tickling them.

'What I meant to say was that we could transform Pearl into a great employee if she was trained by a master.'

'I told you I don't want to work no more.' Fleeta lights up a cigarette and thinks for a moment. 'But if you're gonna throw away all I done built up here, I'd better rethink my position. All right, I'll work part-time for ye.' I am so thrilled, I hug Fleeta, who stiffens like a telephone pole. I've never hugged her before; we're both surprised.

'Three days a week and fifty cents more an hour.'

'You got a deal.'

'What? I'm no tail twister?' Fleeta says with a smile.

'You ain't no Haystack Calhoun.'

'No, I guess I ain't. But given the right circumstances, I might be able to take him.' Fleeta chuckles to herself.

Pearl shows up for work the next day in her best outfit: a smock top and eyelet-trimmed bell-bottoms. Her hair is in a low ponytail. She looks neat; but that doesn't stop Fleeta from eyeing her up and down. Pearl's work life at Mutual's begins with a shipment box haul. Fleeta and I have a system. Fleeta unloads and prices items, I break down the boxes and bring them to the Dumpster behind the store. Fleeta does product placement and displays because that feeds her creative side. She gives Pearl a dirty look when Pearl artfully places shampoo bottles in a shadow-box display. I decide it's a good idea to separate the two of them during this training period; Fleeta is an old cat with well-defined territories and the claws to protect them. Pearl joins me, already full of suggestions on how to make the box haul a more expeditious process. This kid is smart, and it's not bugging me.

'I want to thank you for the job. It's really gonna help me and my mama out.'

'I'm happy to have you. And don't worry about old Fleeta. She's mean on the outside but marshmallow on the inside.'

'Not like Tayloe and them girls up to school. They's mean to the bone.'

'Ignore them.'

'I try, but it ain't easy to hide when you're the fattest girl in school.'

'You're not the fattest girl in school.'

'I'm pretty sure I am.'

'No, you're the girl with the best after-school job.' This makes Pearl laugh as we throw empty boxes into the Dumpster. 'Besides, those type of girls talk about everybody. Even each other.'

'You know what they're saying about you?'

'Me? Why would they talk about me?'

'They say you're a bastard, that Fred Mulligan wasn't your father.'

'People say that?'

Pearl nods that they do. How naïve of me. I thought that no one talked about me in that way. I never spread stories, so I figured none were spread about me. But in a small town a good story bears repeating, even mine.

'Well, Pearl. They're right.'

'They are?'

'Yep. I guess my mama came over from Italy pregnant and Fred Mulligan married her because back in those days you had to get married if you were having a baby. Only thing, my mama didn't tell me herself; she left it in a letter. I got it after she died.'

'Aren't you mad about it?'

I guess I look off for a long time, because Pearl asks me again. I don't know how to answer her, because it's not like me to ever get angry about anything.

'If I was you, I'd be mad.'

'You would?'

'Your mama shouldn't never have lied to you about your papa.'

'Well, she did, and there's nothing to be done about it now.'

Then Pearl asks me the question that would forever change my life.

'You gonna find your real father?'

'My real one?' I ask quietly. The word *real* sounds so new.

'If he's alive, are you gonna find him?'

Who has time to think about Mario da Schilpario? I'm busy. I have the Pharmacy, deliveries, the Rescue Squad, the Drama and the Kiss.

'You gonna marry Mr. Tipton?'

'Don't tell me people are talking about that, too.'

She nods; they are.

'Well, Pearl, I don't think it's anybody's damn business who I marry, or who my father was, or what size my underwear is.'

'Good for you. Now you're mad!' Pearl says this with great pride. She's right. I'm mad. But what she doesn't know, and what I don't know, is I'm just getting started.

Ethel Bartee's Beauty Salon is tucked behind the post office in a trailer. I take the back alley from the Pharmacy and cut through the loading zone to get to Ethel. She fixed the trailer up real nice with window boxes overflowing with red geraniums. The tip end of my braid is like crispy straw; I need a haircut.

The door is propped open with a drum of pink shampoo. Ethel is putting up Iva Lou's hair.

'Can you take me for a quick trim?' I ask sweetly.

Ethel, stout with a perfect bubble hairstyle that matches her shape, looks up over her bifocals as she finishes winding Iva Lou's last curl around a plastic roller.

'I guess so,' she says, annoyed.

'I should've called.'

'Yes, you should've. But you know I ain't the type to turn nobody away.' Ethel gives me the critical once-over. 'Especially not no one who needs a clip. I got two comb-outs before I can git to you, though.' Ethel indicates her customers under the dryers.

'I can wait.'

Iva Lou rises. 'I'm gonna sit outside and let it dry in the sun, honey. It'll save you on your electric bill.' Iva Lou cocks her big head full of jumbo curlers, giving me a signal to follow her outside.

'Ethel's cranky.' Iva Lou lights up a cigarette. 'I *heard*,' she says, looking at me directly.

'Is everybody talking about it?' I ask.

'Let's put it this way. I make six stops in the Gap. It was the topic of conversation on each one.' Iva Lou points her cigarette toward the trailer door. 'And the two biddies under the dryer bubbles had themselves a field day before you dropped by.'

For a moment I am overwhelmed by it all. I figured my paternity was my business. I lean back on the steps and close my eyes.

'You know what?' Iva Lou says brightly. 'I think it's exciting news.'

'You do?'

'Follow me on this. All your life you was one thing. And now you can be something else if you want! Somebody completely different. You can actually start yourself over from scratch. Turn yourself into what you have always wanted to be!' Iva Lou continues with her Knute Rockne pep-up, and I sit up and shift so I can see the back of my pharmacy. The building looks in even worse shape from here. The mortar between the bricks is chipped, leaving spaces. They look awful. I make a mental note to get them repointed. It annoys me, though. I shouldn't have to fix them; they had a lifetime guarantee.

Closing night of the Drama signals the start of the Powell Valley High School football season. My theater life winds down and Theodore's kicks in, as he is responsible for designing and executing home-game halftime shows. The fans are as competitive about the shows as they are the football games. Every year we wonder how Theodore will top himself, and every year he does. Our downtown stores are festooned with flags in our high school colors, bright Carolina blue and ruby red. Zackie hauls out an eight-foot papier mâché Viking, spray-painted silver, letting anyone passing through town know that we are 'the Vikings, the Mighty, Mighty Vikings.'

Nellie Goodloe finally got a meeting with Theodore and impressed upon him the importance of Elizabeth Taylor and John Warner's visit coming up at the end of October. All eyes will be on us to deliver a weekend to remember. There is an excitement in the air anyway, as it is fall, our most luscious season. The mountains around us turn from dark velvet to an iridescent taffeta. The leaves of late September are bright green; by the first week of October they change to shimmering gemstones, garnet and topaz and all the purples in between. The mountains seem to be lit from the ground by theatrical footlights. Autumn is our grand opera. It even smells rich this time of year, a fresh mix of balsam and hickory and vanilla smoke. Friday nights are football-game nights, and Saturday nights find everyone in town over at the Carter Family Fold.

The Fold is famous because the originators of East Tennessee-style bluegrass music are the legendary Carter Family, led by Mother Maybelle Carter. She had a bunch of daughters, one prettier than the next, including June Carter, now married to Johnny Cash. Yes, it is their homestead and a magnet for bluegrass celebrity (like the great Stanley Brothers out of Dickenson County), and every once in a while somebody famous from the Carter Family does pass through, though that's not why we go there. We go there for the live music and dancing. You can eat there too – chili dogs and fries, the best anywhere. I usually go with Theodore; and ever since we didn't have sex, we're seeing even more of each other. The storm cloud of my lust has passed for now, so he's safe and I'm back to normal.

We enter the Fold, an old barn with flap sides, which are opened to the night air. The Fold is like a gypsy amphitheater – it has the feeling of a place that could be packed up and moved quickly overnight. And indeed, during the daytime when you drive by, you could mistake it for any old weathered barn in a field. But at night she comes alive. Folks sit in rows around the concrete dance floor on bales of hay. The bandstand is high and sets back against a permanent wall rigged with electricals for when WNVA Radio broadcasts shows live. A colorful mix of Japanese lanterns and old Christmas lights dangles over the stage. I love the crazy-quilt mess of it; it is homespun yet dramatic. I enjoy the wondrous sight until the sound of my Aunt Alice Lambert's voice ruins it. I turn to look at her and find she is busy examining Theodore from the tip of his shoe to the top of his head. Her lips are pursed so tightly, they look like two red firecrackers looking for a match.

'So, A-vuh Maria' – she too mispronounces my name – 'Hit finally come out!'

'What?' I ask, squinting up at the lights.

'The truth. You know what I'm talking about, girl.' I never imagined Aunt Alice would approach me on this subject.

She senses she caught me off guard and uses it. 'This changes everything. Don't it?' she snarls. 'My brother's estate?'

'Your brother died thirteen years ago and left everything to my mama.' I say this pleasantly, like I'm commenting on the weather.

'It ain't right. You ain't his. You never was—'

Before she can gear up, I turn and look her directly in the eye. 'I am not going to discuss my business with you. Ever. So if you'll excuse me, I'm here to be with my friends and have a good time. Good night.'

I can see her mouth – *Well!* – as I walk away. I've had time to think about what Pearl said and what Iva Lou inferred. I guess there were signs all along that I wasn't Fred Mulligan's daughter, but for me it was just something I never questioned. He seemed like my real father. Of course, I liked my mother more, loved her more, but I thought that was because I was an only child and a girl. I figured every child liked their mother more than their father. I wasn't completely unaware something was wrong, though. I do remember whispers at family functions, the fact that my first cousins never played with me, the teasing that went on at school about my first name (feriner-sounding). But I never put it all together. I hope I figure out why I didn't. I'm angry with myself for being such an idiot.

Otto and Worley spot us.

'Want to see my snake head?' Worley asks. Before I can say no, he pulls a small jar out of his back pocket and shows me a fresh snake head, floating aimlessly, with a permanent grin and thread-like tongue, which bounces against the glass.

'I got three more of 'em at home. Caught 'em up at the Roaring Branch.'

'Why did this one make the cut?'

'He had the longest tongue.' Worley throws his head back and laughs hard.

'Dance with me, Miss Ave?' Otto asks like a gentleman.

'Later, Otto. I got some business to tend to right now.'

Otto and Worley move off in time with the music. Theodore goes off for our chili dogs. Lew Eisenberg sits alone on a bale of hay licking a blueberry Sno-Kone.

'I got a bone to pick with you,' I say to him.

'You can't make me feel worse than I already do. I'm stuck in a barn with hay up my ass. What can I do for you?' Lew says pleasantly.

'Everybody in town knows about my business. I think Inez is the leak.'

Lew licks his Sno-Kone and looks off to the chili-dog stand where Inez lays hot dogs on the steamer. She is talking a mile a minute; from here we can only see her bright pink mouth moving. She looks angry, her eyebrows knit into one black V. I see my dreadful Aunt Alice with her, as well as the other ladies of the Band Boosters Club. The epicenter of the town gossip fault line rips open cellophane bags of hot-dog buns and shakes them onto the counter.

'What happened to my life?' Lew asks, and licks his Sno-Kone. 'I was so happy on Long Island. Alone. All alone. I had my little practice, my little apartment, my little problems. I like things little, Ave Maria. Little, I can hide in. Instead, I've got this.' He flails his arms around. 'I lie awake every night and wonder what went wrong.'

'I don't know what to say, Lew.' And I really don't. We don't usually talk personally like this, and it's making me slightly uncomfortable.

'One mistake.' I believe Lew is referring to Inez's unplanned pregnancy. 'One mistake and . . . this. Inez was such a nice, quiet girl. So lovely. So soft. Like a picture. Now she's impossible. When she isn't talking, she's eating, but any way around it, that mouth is going round the clock.'

'You have to think back and remember why you fell in love with Inez in the first place.'

'She had a great body.' A moment passes. 'A sleek, tight, little English race car of a body. She was the TR-6 of Big Stone Gap. She could've been in a magazine.' Lew looks at me. 'Is that terrible of me to say?' He sighs. He really misses the old Inez.

'You're just being honest.' Then we look over at Inez, completely unaware that we are talking about her. Gossips never think anybody is talking about *them*. 'Do you think she knows how you feel?'

'I cannot tell you one thing that has gone through that woman's mind in five years. I would know a stranger better.' He sighs.

'I bet she knows. Maybe that's why she eats so much.' I'm annoyed at myself for going down this road with Lew; this is not what I wanted to discuss with him. As out of touch as he thinks he is, he reads my mind.

'What was it you wanted to talk to me about?'

I don't answer him because all I see are lovers on the dance floor. Fleeta and Portly nuzzle as though they have just found each other after having been put to asleep for a hundred years. Girls I went to high school with are out on the floor, dancing close with husbands they've been married to since we were kids. They look content. (So much for the advice 'Don't marry young.') Rick Harmon, a rugged tugboat of a guy, All District Shot Put in high school, now a miner, places his hand on his wife Sherry's behind as they're dancing. She casually removes it, and they laugh privately. Otto dances with Nellie Goodloe, who waves his snake head away with a shudder. I look all around for Theodore. I want to dance. I want to be out there on the floor, gliding. Forgetting. But I can't find him in the crowd. I think he may have wandered out into the field and kept walking, never to return. He'll disappear like everything else. My heart begins to race in a way it hasn't since I pulled an all-nighter at Saint Mary's, drinking pots of black coffee and knocking back NoDoz. I put my hand on my chest and look down. My hand moves up and down against my blouse.

'You all right?' Lew asks.

'I don't feel well.'

'What are your symptoms?'

'My heart is racing.' I keep my hand on my chest, and as suddenly as it came, the rapid beating stops.

'That's an anxiety attack,' Lew says, and swats a fly away from his glasses.

'I've never had one before.'

'Welcome to the club. Once you have one, you never know when they'll strike. Part of getting older.'

'I am not old!' There she is, old maid Ave Maria again, poking through the fence like a cuckoo. Not old! Not old! Not old!

'I didn't say you were old. Older.'

My palpitations slow to a normal rhythm. I breathe deeply. I remember my medical training: Take in oxygen. As much as you can stand.

'Would you like to dance?' a voice says from behind me. At last! Theodore! He didn't leave me! I stand up. But I don't smell peppermint and apples: Instead it's a new smell, sandalwood and lime. Pleasant but unfamiliar.

'Would you like to dance?' Jack Mac repeats, extending his hand graciously.

I look all around for Theodore. But he is not there to rescue me.

'Okay, well. Sure.'

'Have fun,' Lew says, and waves bye-bye to me as though I were a child.

Jack Mac takes my hand. We shuffle into the mix and move toward the center of the dance floor. He pulls me close and rests his hand on my waist. He moves slowly, so he's easy to follow. He seems much taller to me as we dance.

'Where's Sweet Sue?'

'She took her boys over to their daddy's.'

'He's living over in Coeburn, isn't he?'

Jack Mac nods.

'I remember him from high school. Do you?'

Jack Mac nods.

'Mike Tinsley was the best in everything. His varsity jacket was decorated like a four-star general's. Remember? All-state in this and that.'

'Things have changed since high school,' Jack Mac announces, and looks off to get me to stop yapping about Mike Tinsley. Hadn't I heard about his philandering on Sue and his terrible temper and how she moved home most weekends of their married life? Besides, don't I know that no man wants to be compared with the man who came before?

Jack Mac pulls me close; his cheek rests above my left ear.

'How's your mama?' I ask. He doesn't answer for a moment. I feel him pull away to look at me. He looks me in the eye. Then he pulls me close again.

'To be honest, I wasn't thinking about my mama right then.'

For God's sake, Ave Maria! Asking a man about his mother. Who does that? You *are* an old maid! You have forgotten how to talk to a man. Say something smart.

'Could we just dance and not talk for a minute?' Jack Mac says.

I nod. Don't talk, Ave Maria. This is a man who prefers silence. You are getting on his nerves. You don't have to think of something funny to say. You don't have to entertain. Let go. Listen to the music and dance. Just dance. That's all.

The song ends. Jack Mac bows graciously and formally like a duke. 'Thank you, ma'am,' he says, and goes.

I am careful to park behind Theodore's house so as not to start any more rumors. (I don't need to be the town spinster, the town bastard, and now the town tramp all rolled into one.) And Theodore is, after all, a teacher in the Wise County public school system with a sterling reputation. He flicks the lights on. His home is simple and neat. It could be any high school teacher's house, except for the elaborate display on the dining room table. The only indication that this is a dining room is its proximity to the kitchen. Theodore has removed all of the chairs and dishes. He has turned it into a workshop, where he choreographs his halftime masterpieces.

Tonight, meticulously lined up in rows, are one hundred toy soldiers; now they represent our high school marching band. A small turntable and speakers face the table on an antique server. Albums are stacked neatly next to the turntable. He's got Sousa, classical, and Al Green, the rhythm and blues singer. The table is covered in butcher's paper. Theodore has drawn the field's yard lines onto the paper with chalk. The figurines fan out in perfect lines, in the formation of a star, leading to three small paper pyramids on the fifty-yard line. The pyramids are made of tissue paper and are scaled to size.

'You're making pyramids?'

'The shop boys are going to build them. The Vernon girl is doing the craft work. Remember her? She made the giant globe for last year's prom, "Color My World." ' How could I forget? I was Theodore's date. I couldn't believe I finally attended a prom at Powell Valley High School. I was never asked to go when I was a student. Dancing under the tinfoil stars sixteen years later was sweet retribution.

'Who's going to get them out on the field?'

'The flag girls. Two under each pyramid.'

'Flag girls? Are you kidding?'

'Papier-mâché. They'll be as light as fritters.'

'Great. Any blackouts?' There is a concert section in each half-time show in which the band faces the home stands and plays a number. This is traditional, but it can be dull. Theodore came up with a way to ignite the show; at the appropriate moment, the field lights shut off to reveal our lovely majorettes, with batons lit up like torches, spinning wheels of fire and spelling out words like *Win* or *Go*.

'The flag girls will have industrial flashlights under the pyramids. I'm using selections from the scores of Elizabeth Taylor's movies, starting with *National Velvet*. As the band plays the theme to *The Sandpipers*, we'll black out and the pyramids will light up. Then, as we segue into the love song from *Cleopatra*, Tayloe will emerge from behind the center pyramid, dressed as Cleopatra, and twirl fire.' Theodore moves the pieces around the table to show me the choreography. Then he turns out the dining room light to show me the lit-up pyramids. They do give the effect of being there, right there, in downtown Cairo.

'I think this is spectacular, Theodore,' I say, meaning it with every fiber of my being. 'It'll knock the socks off of a movie star.'

'Think so?' Theodore says as he moves the woodwinds with a ruler.

I can feel the pressure on his shoulders myself. 'Elizabeth Taylor has probably had more salutes than all the presidents combined. She's seen it all! And in a million different countries. She's going to cry or something when she sees this kind of show in little old Big Stone Gap. You'll be famous!'

Theodore lights up at the mention of fame. Who among us wouldn't? What a grand concept: to be appreciated and sought after for your God-given talent. To be revered and consulted as an expert in your field. To have the awe and respect normally reserved for movie stars.

'I don't want to be famous, Ave. I just want to be really, really good.'

'You are that! You are.' I have no problem being passionate around Theodore. I really believe in him.

Theodore moves a line of soldiers, turning the star into a triangle. I watch him masterfully make shapes and study the table as though it's an algebraic equation. Theodore loves his work. He is forever thinking about it, studying, trying things, improving. That's how my mother was. She was never satisfied with her sewing. She ripped out as many seams as she completed, probably more. There was a level of craftsmanship, a pride in her work that I have never known. She was so hard on herself. When she sewed, she would talk to herself, criticizing her work, then mumble in approval and smile when the fabric met the thread in glorious, tiny, uniform stitches that disappeared into the fabric in their delicacy. That was the hallmark of my mother's work: In order to be perfect, the seam had to disappear. The overall effect of the final garment was important. The line. The fit. The movement. Her work was never obvious, so it went unrecognized.

I am not an artisan like my mother, or a visionary like Theodore. I am a pill-counting pharmacist. I simply follow the orders of doctors; I don't even make a diagnosis. My work is not about expansion, it's about precision. Maybe this is why Theodore wants my input. Details. That's what I'm good at.

'To pull this show off, you're going to need a crew on the sidelines. I can get the folks from the Drama to help. I could put a crew together for you, and then you could boss us around.'

'You'd do that for me?'

'Of course I would. Now, all you have to do in return is sleep with me.'

Theodore and I laugh so hard at this, we shake the table and all of the soldiers fall and rattle across the table like they've just lost a war. We keep laughing until we're crying, and I'm wondering what the neighbors will say. What a boring life I'd have without Theodore. I wonder if he knows.

I gave Pearl the week off to study for her PSATs, the junior version of the college-entrance SATs. Since she's been working for me, Pearl's grades have gone from Cs to Bs. Dillard Cantrell, the high school guidance counselor, called me to express his thanks. She might make the honor roll next term. Girls like Pearl often fall between the cracks, he told me, and he would be personally thrilled to see a mountain girl exceed expectations.

Fleeta has the day off, and I'm running the store alone. June Walker, the most wrinkled woman in town, is driving me nuts with questions about face creams.

'June, you'll have to wait for Pearl to get here from school. She knows all about moisturizers.'

'Well, she better damn hurry because I got me an emergency situation.'

The Bookmobile stops outside the pharmacy. Pearl gets off. Iva Lou waves at me from her window and motions that she will be over at the gas station. (Things must be hot and heavy with Kent Vanhook because her usual spot on the street is open.)

Pearl comes into the store with a chic short haircut and a nice outfit. Could it be a cinch belt? It is! I haven't seen her in a little over a week. What a difference. She has lost weight! Enough that you can tell! I am about to fall all over Pearl when June does instead.

'Pearl Grimes, you done dropped some weight. How'd you do it?'

'I joined Weight Watchers. And I eat a lot of Jell-O.'

'Well, count me in. I'm gonna eat me a ton of Jell-O so I can drop me some weight too. Now, missie, I got me some wrinkles on my face you could hide a roll of quarters in. Which one of these here creams do you suppose I oughta slather on my mug of the night?'

'I would recommend the Queen Helene Cucumber Masque. It's thick, but it soaks in. And you get a lot for your dollar.'

Pearl leads June Walker to a little makeup table she's put together. I watch Pearl the Expert as she demonstrates all the different creams on June's hand. What salesmanship. Perhaps Mr. Cantrell is right. This girl's got a future, and it ain't in Insko.

The pleasant jingle of the tri-bells on the door signal the entrance of another customer.

'Good afternoon, Preacher.'

'Hello, Miss Mulligan.' Preacher Elmo Gaspar, our local Freewill Baptist reverend and snake handler, stands before my prescription counter and commences to go through all of his pockets.

'Preacher, you are the most disorganized man in southwest Virginia.'

'Ave Maria, I know I'm a mess. But you know, there ain't no perfection in this world, only in the next.'

'You speak the truth, Reverend!' June cries through her cream.

The preacher chuckles, reminding me of the light side to his character. When I was little, every Friday morning we had assembly in the elementary school auditorium. The speaker was always a minister from one of the local churches. Of course, as we grew older, we dreaded it. But when we were kids, we loved the fire-and-brimstone Bible stories, delivered with passion and zeal by the Protestant of the Week. The Protestants were on rotation until one week when there was a cancellation and no preacher could fill in, so the spot went by default to the only Catholic priest in the area. The schoolkids used to tease me about my religion, saying Cath-licks drank blood in our service and worshipped statues. The kids were convinced when the priest showed up that he'd have horns and green skin. They were mighty disappointed when Father Rausch, a mild man with a crew cut, brought out puppets and acted out the parable of the Prodigal Son – not exactly a barn burner. I almost wished my priest had a little of the devil in him, for theatrical purposes. I wanted the Catholics to have some pizzazz. Couldn't he have explained stigmata or weeping statues? But it was not to be. We didn't have the stuff. The Protestants did.

The Protestants knew that the hard sell was everything (there has always been a heated, if unspoken, competition among the various sects), so they came fully loaded ready to convert, with audiovisuals, pamphlets, and songs. When Preacher Gaspar came, he showed an actual filmstrip of what heaven would look like. The living room in the Palace of Heaven was made of pink and gold marble, and young, beautiful people in flowing gossamer robes were reclining on stones and staring into a bright light that came from the open ceiling. The light was God, and he was stopping by to visit the folks in one of the many rooms he had prepared for us. Then Preacher Gaspar showed us hell. It was layers of people stacked upon one another, in torment, feet crushing into faces, hands reaching out, begging for release, gnashing and wailing in horror. Preacher Gaspar left that image up a very long time and preached over, around, and in front of it, trying to scare the tarnation out of us. He succeeded because by the end of the filmstrip most of us were weeping. After we wiped away our tears and swore never to lie or steal or cheat anybody, we sang a song about the Bible.

'Preacher, remember that song you taught us at assembly when I was a girl?'

'Miss Mulligan, aren't you still a girl?' he says with a wink.

'You'll have to answer to God for lying.' I hum a bit, and then in my terrible singing voice, '*The B-I-B-L-E. Yes, that's the Book for me! I stand alone on the word of God! The B-I-B-L-E!*'

'Very good.' Preacher looks happy that I'm done serenading him and relieved that he has found his prescription order in his breast pocket.

I unfold the paper and attach it to my clipboard. It's from Doc Daugherty: a tincture for poison, for rattlesnake bites. I keep a supply on hand at all times; after all, it's hunting season and occasionally one of the men will get bitten.

'Going hunting, Preacher?'

'No, no. We got a revival down in the Frog Level. I'm preaching and handling. I promised Doc Daugherty I'd keep the medicine on hand.'

The preacher has been handling snakes at revivals since he

was very young. There's one story that he handled three rattlers at once and tamed them to sleep. Snake handling is mentioned in the Old Testament. It's a way for believers to prove their faith in God; if they truly believe, God won't let them get bitten. Preacher Gaspar's beliefs must be sincere, because in all these years he's never been bitten. He looks up at me and smiles. His expression is beatific, there is a saintly sweetness to him. He must be close to seventy now, but his face is unlined and youthful. He still has his own teeth, straight and white. His hair, once black, thick, and unruly, is gone, but his scalp is smooth and pink, an advertisement for his good health. His blue eyes shine with a knowingness and humor that can only come from a serene and intimate relationship with God. There is no pretense to him; he is the real article, kind and good.

'You be careful now, Reverend.'

'I will. I will.' He turns to go, then looks back at me. 'Miss Ave, do you remember the rest of that song I done taught you?'

'Reverend, I'm ashamed to say I don't.'

He sings, 'God's words will never fail, never fail, never fail . . .'

Pearl, June, and I join in, 'God's words will never fail. No! No! No!'

Reverend Gaspar laughs as he leaves.

'Someday you ought to come down and see him preach,' June says from the makeup table. 'He is one of the greatest, I'll goddamn guarantee you.'

Tayloe Slagle and her majorettes come in giggling and chatting. They are always loud enough to draw attention, but not so loud as to be considered obnoxious.

'What can I do for you girls?'

They swarm around the magazine rack and don't answer. If Fleeta were here, she'd swat their hands with a duster for reading the magazines and never buying them. I cut them some slack because they spend their money in other ways in my store.

Finally Tayloe asks, 'Did you get any waterproof mascara in yet?'

'I don't know. Did we, Pearl?'

Pearl continues to rub cream into June's face like she's waxing a car. 'Yes, ma'am. We got in the Great Lash.'

'See there? One-stop shopping, girls. All your needs met right here. Maybe you ought to get Pearl to show you all of our new makeup.' Pearl shoots me a look like, *Please don't mention me. If you don't talk about me, they won't notice me. I will disappear into the vat of Queen Helene Cucumber Masque.*

'Now, Miss Mulligan, let me ask you one thing.' Tayloe looks at me. Even after school, without a stitch of makeup, even under my hideous fluorescent lights, she looks luminous. She sticks out her perfect chin. 'Why would somebody who looks like me take beauty tips from somebody who looks like her?' The majorettes laugh loud and hard at this one. Tayloe takes my *People* magazine off of my rack and flips through it. Her casual cruelty makes me angry. Suddenly I don't want the likes of her touching anything in my store.

'Put down the magazine,' I warn in a voice that startles me. 'You never buy them.'

Tayloe quickly puts down the magazine. I look back at Pearl, whose eyes are not filled with tears, who is not blushing with embarrassment, who calmly works cream into June Walker's face with purpose and resolve. Pearl isn't a bundle of nerves anymore.

'I'm gonna say something to you girls. And you're gonna listen.' Two of the majorettes, one a redhead with Farrah Fawcett feathering, the other a brunette with a Jaclyn Smith center part, backtrack to the door to escape. 'You're not going anywhere, you two.' The girls stop in their tracks and turn to face me.

'I'm sick and tired of your snide comments. You're mighty proud, Tayloe. But I'd be careful if I was you. Someday you won't have your looks anymore. And all those girls, like Pearl, who weren't popular, will be the pretty ones. Why? Because they have had to work at it. So they appreciate beauty in all its forms. You only know beauty as something given, not earned. So you won't understand what's happening when your youth is gone and the pounds creep on and the wrinkles come; and you'll panic because your best days are behind you. But Pearl's best days will be ahead of her. Why? Because she had to make something out of herself from scratch. Nobody helped her. The best she got was a bunch of stuck-ups making fun of her to make themselves feel big. But trust me, that kind of power is poison. It'll turn on you. When y'all are my age, you'll be the ones envying her. Pearl will know the great power of self-acceptance and real self-love, not the shallow vanity you mistake for it. At the end of the day, Pearl Grimes will be so beautiful, she'll wipe the floor with you.'

All is silent in the store except for the creaking of the spin stool June Walker is sitting on as she leans into the mirror to examine her creamed face.

'You are so weird, Ave Maria Mulligan,' says Tayloe. Finally, somebody pronounces my name correctly. Tayloe and her twirlers go. Pearl continues with her demonstration.

I come out from behind the counter and stand in the doorway and watch them walk up the street. And I don't know how to pinpoint what I'm feeling exactly, but for some reason I see myself at sixteen walking away from myself. I know it's not me out there on the street, but it is, in the image of those girls, walking away getting smaller and smaller, and disappearing. For the first time in my life I feel the thread of who I am unravel. I am one of those people who swears she knows herself well, who in any given situation can be described and counted on to behave in a certain way. I never yell at people, nor do I make speeches. When things get tense, I usually make a joke, so everyone will feel at ease. But something, beyond defending Pearl, beyond standing up for what is right, compelled me to speak. Where did she come from? Who is this voice that isn't going to make nice anymore, but will tell the truth? It isn't Fred Mulligan's daughter. I think of Mario da Schilpario, my father, the man in the picture. Why have I tried to put him aside, thinking him dead, gone, uninterested in the likes of me? But suddenly I know – and I am as sure of it as I am sure of myself standing here – that my father is alive, and he is well, and I must find him. I put my hand on my chest, expecting another anxiety attack to come, but it does not. Practical Ave Maria must go. Me. The never-married town pharmacist who is never caught without her first-aid kit. Me. So responsible she carries two spare tires in her Jeep instead of one. Me. Who has double insurance on everything because she's afraid one of the companies will go out of business and leave me penniless after a flood. Me. The girl who built her life so carefully so she'd never have to ask anybody for anything. I have had it with me. Whoever I was! Get mad, Ave Maria! You're alone in this world. You were abandoned. Let that anger fuel the job you must do. Find him. Find your father!

I walk out of my store and into the street. I breathe deeply right down to my toes. I walk to the Bookmobile. I have a job for Iva Lou.

CHAPTER FOUR

It is quiet in my living room except for the sound of Theodore and Iva Lou turning pages as they read. I've never had Iva Lou over to my house. I don't know why. When Mama was alive, I didn't have friends over much. Mama ran her sewing business out of the house, so people were always stopping by anyhow – maybe it didn't dawn on us to formally entertain. Fred Mulligan hated having company. Mama had better have seen her last customer before he came home. Even after he died, she kept that schedule. When I came home from work, everything was put away. That must have been so hard for her. She was social. Mama loved people. She never knew a stranger. After she died, so many folks came up to me and thanked me for her kindnesses: girls, now women, who wore prom dresses that Mama had made for free. Brides who needed wedding gowns with extra fabric in front because they were a little pregnant and didn't want to show for the occasion. She'd never complain; she'd just make the adjustments.

Fred Mulligan, however, had boundaries in all things. He

could never make his customers his friends. I think he felt he couldn't make a profit from friends, so he simply never made any. Or maybe nobody wanted to be friends with him. Anyway, it feels right and glorious to have Iva Lou and Theodore sitting in my living room, eating chess pie, surrounded by stacks of books, all special orders from Clinch Valley College, a division of the University of Virginia in Wise. Iva Lou was allowed to check out these books because she knows the powers that be at the university library. (They've shared Sanka.)

She shoves a book under my nose and shows me a panoramic photograph. 'Look, here's Bergamo. It's about the size of Big Stone Gap.'

I study the panorama of Mama's hometown. There is a fountain with dancing angels in the middle of the square. Buggies led by donkeys cart people around. There are cobblestone streets. Fig trees. Small stone houses. Children. I picture my mother there as a girl. It seems to fit.

Theodore and Iva Lou leave around midnight. I clean up the dishes and walk through the first floor, turning out the lights. Then I do something I haven't done since my mother died. I go into her room.

My mother's room is simple. There is a double bed with a white cotton coverlet; over the bed hangs a small wooden crucifix. A straight-backed chair and a bureau stand against the wall opposite the window. Her sewing machine is tucked in a small alcove next to the window. The closet is small, its contents neat. I sit on the edge of her bed and look around the room as though I've never been inside of it before. I used to lie in here with her when she was dying. I took my rightful place next to her, as I was all she had. When I was little and I got sick, I would come and get her, but she never took me into her bed with my father. She would always come to my room on the second floor and lie with me there. She used to tell me that she didn't want to disturb him, but now I know she could not disturb him. He knew I wasn't his, and though he could have lovingly claimed me, he did not, and she kept me quiet. That was their understanding. And it was an understanding that lasted both of their lifetimes.

My mother was an avid reader, too. Occasionally, she bought books, but usually she just checked them off the Bookmobile as I did. She loved books about romance. Books that took place in faraway places and times. Stories with costumes. When Mama designed the costumes for the Drama, she studied the period, drew the sketches and everything. She had less theatrical tasks too. Mama has made every cheerleader uniform since anyone can remember. She made elaborate square-dancing skirts. And prom dresses, of course. When a customer wanted fancy, my mother would say in her Italian accent, 'Simple is better. Simple. Simple.' Sometimes she succeeded, but often I would hear her clucking as she sewed sequins and lace onto dresses that didn't need the fanfare. Many times when folks dropped off their clothes for altering or mending she would convince a lady to line a cloth coat in red satin or a skirt in silk. 'No one will see it, but you will know it's there and it will feel wonderful,' she'd say. My mother knew the finer things, but she didn't have a life that could celebrate them. I pick up a book off the nightstand. Glamorous Gene Tierney is on the cover. It's a book about costumes from the movies of the Golden Age in Hollywood.

Mama always took me to the movies over at the Trail Theater, right next to Zackie's. I didn't know it at the time, but Jim Roy Honeycutt, who owned the place, showed movies that, at that time, were ten, fifteen years old. I never bothered to ask my mother why the people on the screen were wearing funny hats and hairdos; I just accepted it. It wasn't until years later that I found out Mr. Honeycutt saved a lot of money renting old prints. That's how I fell in love with the leading men of the 1930s and 40s: Clark Gable, William Powell, Spencer Tracy, Robert Taylor, and especially Joel McCrea. Mama loved the actresses, costumed by the great designers Edith Head, Adrian and Travis Banton. I remember their names because Mama always pointed them out to me on the screen. We would see the same movies over and over again so Mama could study the clothes. Later she would discuss them with me in great detail. The movies were black and white, but Mama could tell when they used real gold thread on Hedy Lamarr's harem pants or real sable on Rosalind Russell's coat.

My mother was a great beauty. She had black hair so shiny it seemed lacquered; she wore it simply, combed back off of her face in a blunt bob. Her skin was golden – she died without a wrinkle or a line on it. She had deep-set brown eyes with lots of lid, like a Modigliani painting. Her neck was long and so were her fingers. She had full lips and beautiful teeth; she always was faithful about going to the dentist and taking me. Her nose was regal, aquiline. Her high forehead belied a nobility; to me she was a queen. But there was a deep sadness in my mother's eyes always, a longing to be somewhere else. I used to ask her, 'Why, Mama, why did you come *here*?' As though here were worse than a swamp, a place without air. But she loved the mountains. Mountains meant everything to her.

I begged her to go to Italy with me after my father died. We had the time, we had the means, and most important, we no longer had him. We were free, but we couldn't adjust to it. After he died, we could play Sergio Franchi as loud as we wanted, but we still kept it muted so we could hear his approaching car in the driveway. He wanted nothing Italian in this house, except food. He ate my mama's cooking with relish; in fact, that's when we could count on him to smile. My mother made everything fresh, from her own garden; olive oil she ordered out of New York. My father even drank espresso. Her cooking was his one concession to my mother's heritage. Though he had studied Italian in college, he forgot how to speak it. He preferred my mother speak English. She taught me Italian, her regional dialect; we used it as a secret language.

The summer after I graduated high school, we went to Monticello, Thomas Jefferson's home outside Charlottesville, Virginia. It bugged me when my father mispronounced Monticello – he made a soft *c*, like 'Monti-sello.' I corrected him, and he got so mad he slapped me. But that was the last time he slapped me. From that moment on I stayed out of his way. I gave up. Then Mama did too. For years she tried to make us get along, but it was not to be. When I look back, I realize that she protected me from him. We built our world around keeping him comfortable and not upsetting him. I never showed anger, frustration, or passion in front of him. I swallowed everything, and soon it became part of my character. I was there to amuse and entertain, never, ever to challenge or disrupt. When I was alone with my mother, I could have my feelings, but then I would feel guilty – why upset her?

My mother was Roman Catholic. She was allowed to go to mass and take me, but then we would have to attend the Methodist church with my father as well. The Catholic church here is run by a small missionary order of poor carpenter priests called the Glenmarys. We didn't even have a real church building until five years ago; the priests were so busy building churches in poorer areas, they kept putting ours off. Finally, we built it, and nothing made my mother happier than writing a big fat check to the Catholics after my father died. She gave them so much money, they finished building our church! When the Methodists, who have a grand big church, came for their share, my mother gave them a small token, citing their large congregation and huge donor list. They weren't happy about the slight, but being good Christians, they let it go.

Mama and I tried to be good Italians after Fred Mulligan died. We wanted to reclaim that side of ourselves that we had hidden. We decided to go to Italy. We had great fun planning our trip. We did our research, made all the arrangements, bought the tickets, and then, as the date approached, Mama panicked, complaining of a fear of motion sickness. She became so distraught, I canceled the trip. Then, after a few days, she became herself again. The incident upset her so badly, I never mentioned traveling again. I didn't try to plan another trip. She could not have gone anyway. She got cancer, and that changed our lives forever.

I look around this room and see that she had one of everything: one lamp, one bureau, one chair. She only ever had one winter coat. One pair of good shoes. One pretty hair clip. One child. One of everything, but only one, as if to keep her life quiet. She lived by her own philosophy: Be unobtrusive and maybe he'll let us stay. As though that was all she deserved! My mother deserved so much more! The best of everything! No gold, no rubies, no rare diamond would have ever been enough for my mother. She was a woman of great character. My deepest sadness comes because I know she lived a life where she wasn't treated that way.

You would think, after she died, I would have come in here and gone through her things, but I couldn't. And now I am putting too much importance on this room. I want to find clues to her. Figure out what she really wanted. What she desired. What she was secretly interested in. I pull the books off of her nightstand

and onto the bed and begin sorting. One on breast cancer. Another on regional Italian cooking. Ingrid Bergman's life story (we both love biographies). And, finally, *Lake Maggiore and Its Regions*.

I take the book, turn off the light, and leave her room. I am never afraid in this house, but tonight a chill runs through me. An urgency. I have led a life of quiet desperation (as my favorite author, Henry David Thoreau, described in *Walden*), just like my mother had, and now I want to change. As I pass through the living room to go up to bed, I pick up a small book from the large stack Iva Lou left behind. It's called *Schilpario: A Life in the Mountains*. The checkout card in the back says, 'University of Virginia Architecture Library. DO NOT REMOVE.' Iva Lou really went to some trouble to get me these books. I may have to break down and buy some Sarah Coventry jewelry from her.

Once I'm in bed, I turn on my nightlight and look through the pictures in the book about Schilpario. The Italian Alps are pointed and snowcapped. They seem three times as high as the Blue Ridge Mountains, and more dangerous, not as soft and maternal. The roads look new but narrow. There is a picture of a race car taking the dangerous curves, showing deep, jagged valley plummets to the sides of the road. No guardrails. Just like Powell Valley! I turn the page, and there is the town. This is a long-shot vista photo, probably taken from another mountain. The houses are close together and painted in muted shades of terra-cotta, gold, and soft brown. The main street leads to a waterwheel. On the next page, a picture of the waterwheel, a point of interest for tourists. In another time, before electricity, the waterwheel provided fresh water and power to the town. Now it is a museum.

I turn the next page, and there are some dignitaries from the town. They stand in a row – all men, puffed up and proud of their little village. I glance down at the names listed under the picture. As I'm reading, I look up at the row and study one man in particular who catches my eye. It's the expression on his face. I have seen it somewhere – in my own mirror. My heart begins to pound as it did the night at the Fold. I look down. My pajama buttons are moving, but this time I can hear the attack and the whoosh, beat, whoosh, beat of my blood as it chugs through my heart with force and fear. I breathe deeply, but I can't inhale very well, so I suck in the air in small gulps. I think of Lew who tells me not to worry, that it's nothing. I steady my fingers against the book. They are sweating and leave small circles on the book jacket. I rub the book on my bedspread. Then I pull the light as close as a microscope and prop the book open on my knees to steady it. I count over four names; the fourth man is the man I think I know. I scoot my finger across the faces and down to the matching name: Mario Barbari, Mayor, Schilpario, 1961-present. I flip to the front of the book and check the copyright date: 1962. That's a long time ago. I pull the small lacy picture of my father out of its envelope – I keep it with me at all times – and compare the faces. Mario Barbari is small in the picture, but I can see the shape of the face, the eyes, the eyebrows – all look similar to the young man in the picture Mama left behind for me. Is he my father?

I can hardly wait for Friday because it means Iva Lou is coming through with the Bookmobile. I wanted to call her at home, but I didn't because I wanted to tell her about Mario da Schilpario's picture in person. I can't wait for her to come to town, I'm too nervous and excited, so I drive down to her first stop in the Cadet section, just south of town, where she is parked by the side of the road. Iva Lou is sitting in the driver's seat of the Bookmobile, eating a sausage biscuit. I holler from my car window, 'Are you alone?'

'Nobody showed up yet. It's slow as Christmas.'

I park my car next to the Bookmobile and join her. 'I think I found him. Mario.'

'Lordy mercy!' she shouts, and jumps up and down. The Bookmobile rocks back and forth like a boat.

'Careful, Iva. We'll flip over.'

'Honey-o, don't worry. This old thing doesn't have to last much longer.'

'Why? Is the county springing for a new one?'

'No. But old Liz Taylor is gonna have a fried-chicken dinner over to the Coach House when she's here to raise money for our very own library. This could be it, Ave. The Big Time.'

I sit down on my snap stool. Why does this upset me? Am I that attached to this truck full of books?

'I know you love this unit, but a library! Imagine all the books we can git if we git a whole big building!'

'You're absolutely right. I am being selfish.'

'The state said they'd match whatever she came up with. Can I put you down for a couple of tickets to the dinner?'

'Sure, sure.'

'It'll be fun. We'll get Theodore for you, and I'll scrape up a date. Lyle Makin has been chasing me of late, and I just might let him catch me. He's nice and he's got a good suit. But, Lord, forget all that. Tell me about this man you think might be your daddy.'

I show Iva Lou the book; she scribbles down some notes.

'Sanka?'

This time I accept her offer. She pulls a sack out from a shelf and offers me a pink coconut snowball from the dry-bread store. I take it, tearing off one small piece at a time as I tell Iva Lou about the night I found my father in the book. She listens intently, following my every word.

Big Stone Gap has never been so atwitter. Theodore is in constant rehearsal for the halftime show; Nellie Goodloe has taken over the organization of the library fund-raiser chicken dinner; and I'm writing letters to government agencies in Italy, gathering information about Mario Barbari. It's as though the Blue Ridge Mountains around us have been peeled back and we're being discovered by a larger universe. This is equally thrilling and troubling. There is something comfortable about life the way it has been; who am I to upset the cart?

With all that's happening to me in my private life, the responsibilities of the Pharmacy still need tending to. I'm inspecting a new shipment from Dow, Fleeta is manning the cash register, and Pearl is doing inventory on our medical supplies when the familiar mine whistle blows. The coal mines are closing for the day; soon town will be filled with truckloads of men returning home for supper. I look out over my little staff as I fill prescriptions, and I feel very secure. Then the whistle blares three times in quick succession. It's not the whistle of the day being done; it's an emergency whistle. Something bad has happened up at the mine. We kick into automatic mode. Fleeta helps me out of my white jacket and into my Rescue Squad vest, and I grab my first aid kit. I hear a horn – it's Spec – and I jump into the ambulance. The whistle blares three more times. Spec cannot drive fast enough.

We speed up the mountainside to the mine. The road is not paved, it's pure gravel; we kick up dust and are pitched to and fro in the grooves carved out by coal trucks. The smoke on the entrance road is thick and gray, which confirms my suspicions that there has been an accident inside.

The first thing we do is pull up to the check-in hut, which is close to the mouth of the mine. Here each miner, before he starts his shift, leaves a silver tag bearing his name. He wears an identical tag on his belt, so his whereabouts are known to the company at all times. In an emergency we rely on these tags for a head count. There are three tags left on the board; only they remain inside the mine: A. Johnson, R. Harmon, and J. MacChesney. I take a breath. 'Come on, Ave. We ain't got all day,' Spec says as we move to join the other Rescue Squad staffs.

There are four 'holes' or entrances drilled into the side of the mountain. One entrance leads the miners to their work areas; one is for the conveyor belt, which transports the coal out; and the other two are for ventilation. There is a high level of methane gas underground, and the slightest disturbance can ignite it. There is no smoking allowed inside, but pockets of deadly gas can ignite without warning. Inspectors check the methane levels throughout the workdays and nights, but the miners travel as far as five miles into the mountain; there is always the threat of danger. As we get closer the smoke becomes deadly black, so the explosion must be deep. Rescue squads from the surrounding towns pull in around us. I see station wagons from Appalachia, Stonega, Norton, Coeburn, and Wise.

Spec and I await orders from the mining supervisor, who is on radio to survivors in the mine. The stretchers are filling up fast. Most of the injuries appear to be from smoke inhalation. Hopefully, the situation inside is not too bad. In our favor: This is a new mining site, so the construction within is modern.

Spec and I are told to join the unit from Stonega. I can't see because of the smoke, but it wouldn't do much good anyway. The supervisor shows us a map of where the explosion took place: at the third level, about five miles into the mountain.

When I trained for the Rescue Squad along with volunteers from across the county, we toured a coal mine. I remember looking forward to it, like a field trip. We dressed like the miners: one-piece coveralls; rubber knee boots; the hard hat and light; and the belt to which we attached a power pack for the hat light, an ID tag, and a mask to convert carbon monoxide to carbon dioxide in case of an explosion. Miners are required to wear safety goggles; everyone does. It is also recommended that the miners wear a protective cloth mask while they work to decrease the inhalation of deadly coal dust, but most find it difficult to communicate and work while wearing a mask, and since they are not convinced that a mask prevents Black Lung anyway, they usually skip that step.

I had romanticized the underground, thinking it would be crypt-like and eerily beautiful. Instead, it felt ominous from the moment we climbed into the transport car. The cars are shallow, tin canoes that hold about ten people. The entrance ceilings are low, so you lie down most of the trip; on a deep excursion it is nerve-racking and uncomfortable. The only person who is allowed to sit up is the driver; he operates the car on the tracks with a wooden pole connected to the electrical lines rigged on the ceiling. There is not much conversation during the ride, but there is a lot of chewing and spitting. The men chew tobacco to keep their mouths wet, as the air is very dry within the mine. The temperature remains about fifty-five degrees year-round.

I thought the interior of the mine would be black, like dirt, and well lit. Instead, the main source of light is our hats, and the walls are white. After the coal is extracted, the miners spray the walls with a white rock dust that is nonflammable, so in case of fire the mine won't turn into an oven, roasting its own coal.

Our guide explained that each car carries a work crew to a particular area. The advances in technology introduced a machine called the Continuous Miner, which actually extracts the coal from the wall. The work crew is there to load the coal onto a conveyor belt, once it has been extracted by the machine. After an area is mined, a crew places timbers on the sides and walls to create channels and shore up the walls so they don't collapse; then the roof-bolt operator and his team come in to bolt the ceiling with giant screws so the men can dig more deeply into the mine and extract more coal. The roof-bolt operator has one of the most dangerous jobs; more miners are killed by rock slides than by explosions. The guide explained that these men have superior hearing, and the slightest cracking sound is a signal to move his men out immediately. There isn't much to be done in a serious rock slide, except try to excavate the men. In an explosion, you hope they can crawl out the shafts to safety, if they can see their way through the smoke. The other threat to the miner is flooding. A man called the pumper travels through the mine during the shift and pumps out water, as there is no way of predicting underground water sources.

I remember feeling I would suffocate as the car plunged deeper into the mine, and I became more fearful as the tunnel behind us became a black river with no end. The dimensions of the mine kept changing, too. Sometimes it seemed almost large, like a cavern, and then the car would push through to a space so tiny, my arms could reach from one wall of the tunnel to the other. I never felt that I could hold my head up without getting whacked by a beam or a crossbar.

There were constant reminders of impending doom: gas meters that would sound when noxious fumes were emitted from the earth; machinery programmed for automatic use that could go off without warning and cause injury; and then, of course, the dust. You can taste it, and when you breathe it into your nose, it is a little like trying your first cigarette. At first it seems foreign and you resist it. But eventually you forget about it. Coal dust penetrates the skin and fills the lungs, causing all sorts of diseases – the least of them cancer, the worst of them Black Lung, all of them painful, protracted illnesses that cause slow death. The thing that surprised me the most was the sound inside the mine. It was deadly quiet. This was a feeling of being buried alive. I wondered how the men do it each day. I couldn't.

Coal miners in general are practical men. I get to know them long after they quit the mines and are on Black Lung benefits. That's when they need their meds, and believe me, they need a lot of them. If it isn't the lungs that go, it's repetitive injury to the joints from the picking, the loading, the hauling, and the lifting. In the same way that the mountains are depleted of coal, the men are spent by taking it from the earth.

Mining is a family tradition; usually sons follow fathers into the mines, and their sons will follow them. There are amazing stories of bravery, and I think of them as I stand and await instructions. In the 1930s, Wesley Abingdon was a local hero because he refused to give up during an accident – he took the train car, threw the men into it, pedaled out, threw the men out, and went back for more. He saved about thirty men that day, and those thirty men told their thirty families, and so on. Wesley gained saint status in these parts.

A couple of years ago there was an incident that upon repeating sounds like a folktale, but I witnessed it, so I can tell you it is absolutely true. It was late spring, and the mountains were just coming into their green. The whistle sounded, and we assembled, just as we have today, to assist in the rescue. The supervisor had determined that all the men were out but one: Basil Tate, a young miner, was still unaccounted for. The problem with explosions is that it is very hard to determine the cause until after they happen, so they are very hard to prevent. Fire and smoke are wily as well, and a good miner figures this out and works with it. The mine rescue team was deciding how to proceed, how to find Basil, when a rumbling was heard from deep in the mine. It started out softly, but it sounded like it was coming toward the exit. I will never forget what happened next. The rumble became a blast. Dirt and black smoke poured out of the entrance, and then we heard a pop. We looked up, and there was Basil Tate, flying through the air like a human cannonball. The explosion had created a vaccum, with Basil in it. Then fire propelled the fumes – and Basil – like stoking a cannon to fire. The crowd watched the spectacle in awe. Was he alive? We followed the body up over the hill and down the mountainside. Basil landed by the creek, on soft mud. We were certain he was dead. When we got to him, he was unconscious, his body contorted in an S shape. We could tell from his position that he had broken his neck and his legs. But there was still a pulse, so we wrapped him up carefully and called for a chopper from the University of Virginia to fly him out for emergency surgery. Basil was in a body cast for close to two years, and now he works the box office at the Drama. We call him the Miracle Man.

The mining supervisor, a buttoned-down city type, not from these parts, shoots me a look that says, 'What are you doing here?' Spec picks up on this and tells him, 'She's with me.' I ask an intelligent question about the explosion, and the foreman's brow relaxes like he's decided I'm okay and can stay and be of some help. He is a foreigner, too, but that's where the similarity between us ends. His demeanor and condescension are a perfect example of why locals don't like these company men. They come in with an attitude.

As explosions go, this does not appear to be a bad one. There is no fire yet; the smoke is from a power gash near the mouth of the mine. The mining foreman is trying to explain the location of Level Three to the company man when I look up and see Jack Mac crawling out of the air vent with Amos Johnson. I hear a scream as one of the wives run toward her husband. She is held back as the rescue team from Coeburn tends to him. I run toward Jack Mac as he turns to go back into the mine. The foreman shouts at me to stop him. Jack Mac turns and looks at me. I tell him, 'Rick is still inside.' Two of the company engineers try to stop him, but he throws their hands off of him and goes back into the mine. The foreman chews me out for releasing information and tells me to stay behind the line and wait for the injured.

The worst thing about these accidents is the lag time between men going in and men coming out. The waiting periods are filled with silence and some muffled weeping. For the most part, folks don't cry; accidents are an occupational hazard, and there is no sense worrying until something actually happens.

Spec is miffed at me because he's been rendered impotent by my big mouth. Spec likes to get in the middle of things, and now he is a sideliner. Twenty minutes go by. Still no Jack Mac. I feel horrible guilt about this. Why did I tell him about Rick? Couldn't I have left it up to the company men to come up with a rescue solution? Didn't I know that Jack Mac would never sit and wait for them to do something? A hand is placed on my shoulder. I turn and see Sweet Sue with a look of total terror on her face.

'Is he in there, Ava?'

'He's getting Rick out. Don't worry.' I comfort Sweet Sue as best I can, and she goes to join the rest of the women behind the line. I look over at them. Their expressions range from utter desperation and fear to pure fury. They are tired of this, and they have a right to be angry. They have sharp eyes – nothing gets past them – but there is also a weariness that comes from disappointment.

Spec shouts at me to follow him as most of the other rescue squads have already departed with injured. The foreman is still furious with me for telling Jack Mac about Rick. His job is to save as many men as he can, and now it looks as though he will lose two. Spec is starting to referee our argument when we hear a woman scream, 'Help them! Help them!'

The crowd hushes to still quiet as smoke pours out of the mine. Then, almost as if in a dream, Jack MacChesney emerges from the mine carrying a man. I hear someone yell, 'Jack Mac's got Rick! He's got Rick!' Rick Harmon's body is lifeless. We move in to resuscitate.

Spec is terrific with CPR and oxygen, so he takes charge and I assist. Jack Mac collapses and a doctor tends to him immediately. I look over at him and see that he is out cold. Rick's wife, Sherry, runs to us with her kids. They clamor to touch Rick, believing they can bring him around with familiarity and love and kisses. But the supervisor pulls them away and we continue to pump, pump, pump. Spec looks up at me. 'He's coming to.'

The doctor joins us and takes over. He tells us to move Rick away from the residual smoke, so Spec and I lift him carefully onto a stretcher and carry him a few feet to a clearing. Rick opens his eyes and says, 'My foot. Goddammit, my foot.' I smile at Rick with a look that says, *I don't think this is a good time to be cursing God*; and he looks back at me apologetically.

'Let me take a look at it.' I hadn't noticed his foot. It is mangled and bloody. I smile again and tell Rick not to worry. But I am worried; there is a deep cut across the top of his foot, and I cannot make out his toes. I fear he may lose it. 'How is it, Ave?' he asks, suspecting the worst.

'It's not too bad.' Rick looks relieved and closes his eyes. He passes out. I wrap the foot and ice it.

The Norton crew places oxygen on Rick and hoists him into the ambulance. The doors slam shut and they speed away. I turn to find Jack Mac, but he is gone. The unit from Appalachia has taken him to the hospital.

The supervisor grumbles at Spec and me as we pass. I stop and ask if everybody is for sure out of the mine. He assures me that they are. He smiles, not a smile of relief for the men who survived, but a selfish one. Saving lives for him is all about numbers; he has had a good day, and he knows his job is secure.

The women rush away from the roadside and get into their cars. They speed down the mountain to follow the ambulances to the hospital. Rick's wife comes toward me and I give her a hug. All I can think is how much she must love him, and how happy she and Rick were dancing the other night at the Fold.

Spec drops me off at the Pharmacy, and I tell the girls I'm going to make a run to the hospital to see how the men are doing. Fleeta and Pearl need no details; they got the rundown from the police radio. Fleeta stops me as I'm leaving and wipes dirt off my face with a tissue.

Saint Agnes Hospital was founded by Irish Catholic nuns who migrated here in the 1930s. The common wisdom around here is, 'When you're sick, let the sisters take care of you.' Even though the locals don't particularly care for Catholics, they make an exception when it comes to health care. The nuns built their hospital in Norton, the closest city and the location most central to the coal camps. I love the hospital because there are statues of saints and angels tucked in every corner. One time Eulala Clarkston was in for a blood clot and she swore that she saw the Virgin Mary wave at her. Sister Julia told me that, as much as they would love for the Blessed Mother to make an appearance in Norton, they were pretty sure Eulala didn't actually see her. She was on Darvon at the time and was seeing things.

Most of the miners have been released. I ask one of the nurses if there is any word on Rick Harmon, and she tells me that he is undergoing surgery at UVA Hospital in Charlottesville, and that as soon as there is word, she'll let me know. I see Spec in the hallway and compliment him on his CPR; he thanks me for helping. As I turn the corner to go, I run right into Jack MacChesney. I give him a quick hug that catches him off guard.

'Are you all right?'

'Yes, ma'am.'

Jack Mac is looking at my face funny, so I assume Fleeta didn't get all the soot off of me. I wipe my face with my sleeve. Then he says quietly, 'Thank you for telling me about Rick—'

I interrupt him. 'The supervisor really let me have it. That guy is a real jackass.' Why am I talking so loud? I'm obnoxious. Then I blurt, 'Do you need a ride home?'

Jack Mac looks like he would love one and is about to answer me when we hear a familiar voice.

'Jack!' his mother cries. 'Let me see you!'

Mrs. Mac is on the arm of Sweet Sue. Jack looks at me, confused for a moment. Then Sue runs to him and covers him in kisses. Mrs. Mac then takes her turn and keeps touching his face like he's five. All of a sudden I feel all the sad things I felt as a girl: I'm an outsider. Sweet Sue and Mrs. Mac embrace Jack, and rightly so, for he is the town hero now. He didn't save thirty men, but he did save one; in the eyes of folks around here, that is just as important.

I'm happy Mrs. Mac and Sweet Sue are fussing over him. He deserves it. To be loved like that! To have somebody to worry about you. To have your mother hold your face in her hands like delicate china! I am watching something perfect and beautiful, and I am not a part of it. They are a family. I walk back around the corner and out the door to the parking lot.

All I want is a hot bath, a glass of wine, and a long phone call with Theodore, but as I round the driveway to the back of the house, I see that I have company. Aunt Alice and Uncle Wayne's Oldsmobile Cutlass Supreme is parked near my back porch. The two of them are walking in the yard surveying the trees.

'You ought to get the forestry division over here to check that poplar. It has root rot.'

I want to say, *And how are you, Aunt Alice?* but instead, I shrug.

'We'd like to talk to ye, Ava,' my uncle says.

I invite them in and offer them iced tea, which they decline. As we pass through the dining room to get to the living room, Aunt Alice takes into account every piece of furniture, dish, and glass. It's as if her neck were on a wire, craning this way and that, to record each item and its placement in her memory.

I can't imagine why they're here. They never visit, call, or invite me to their home. After Dad died, out of respect, Mama and I would call them on holidays, but they were always so curt, we stopped trying. Aunt Alice has not aged well. She is around sixty now but looks far older. Her short hair is permed into dry, blue, tight curls. Her small face, wrinkled from a lifetime of grimaces, squints, and frowns, has an overall sour expression. She could use some Queen Helene. Her eye-glasses are too large for her face and she has false teeth now – I can hear air whistle through them when she talks. Life has settled in on her, and the results aren't pretty.

'What can I do for y'all?' I ask and sit. Aunt Alice sits, but Uncle Wayne remains standing. He looks awkward, as though he's uncomfortable around his own wife. He is tall and lean, with the face of a wizened marionette; its creases are deep, as have been his compromises.

Aunt Alice answers, 'We come down here 'cause I ain't gonna chase you all over hell to discuss business with you. So you just set there and listen to me because I got something I need to say. Now, I know your mama done came clean with you.' She used the word *clean*, implying that what came before it was dirty.

'Inez Eisenberg needs to look up *client confidentiality* in the dictionary.'

'Now, Ava, you listen here,' offers Uncle Wayne. 'We don't want no trouble.'

'What kind of trouble?' Then I look at Aunt Alice. 'And what kind of business?'

Then Aunt Alice explodes. 'You look 'ere, youngun, I have stood by all my life and watched my brother, who I loved very much, give all he had to you and your ungrateful mother, and I kept silent because he wished it so, but now, now that the truth is out, you need to know that restitution must be made to me as I am my brother's only living blood relative. Blood. You know what I mean.'

I nod.

'You are not blood. You will never be blood. It almost killed my mama when Fred came home with a wop. A pregnant one! Jesus help us! He shows up back here, on this here porch with a sullied feriner! She moved in here with her high-and-mighty attitude, looking down her nose at us, and took him for all he was worth. He done educated you, clothed you. You ate well and lived like a princess with trips here and yon and up to Monti-sello and so forth, and I done never even got as far as Roanoke. You done took all you're gonna take from me. And I mean that, missy.'

I sit quietly and look at my hands. There are three small cuts on my right index finger. I don't remember getting them, but now they pulse a little and hurt. I must have gotten them removing Rick's gear as the Norton crew lifted him into the ambulance. There is a little bit of dried blood around the first cut. I rub it off on my pant leg. Aunt Alice continues.

'After all, that business of his made you rich. That was my pappy's building, and this was the Mulligan family homestead, and I got nothing from all of this. Do you know what it does to me to think I can't live in the house I grew up in? That some stranger is living in my mama and daddy's house, instead of me? I'm treated like this, and I am his true relative?'

'His blood relative,' I say quietly.

'Damn right! And here we are! Struggling! We're on Social Security, but that ain't enough. And you're over here, rich as all get-out, and you have never lifted one finger to help us.' Aunt Alice turns to look up at Uncle Wayne. His mouth moves but no words come out, just like the mechanical Santa I put in the window at Mutual's every Christmas. She stares at him to command him to speak, but he cannot. The vein in her neck is a tight, dark blue cord. Her head snaps wildly about in anger. She looks directly at me, which she has never done. I look into her eyes. Behind the bifocals, they are light brown, googly, off center, and surrounded by whites. (In face reading, irises that float, surrounded by white, belong to folks with criminal pathologies. I'd say she's angry enough to kill right now.)

'I wish somebody had thought about me for once. Looked out for me. Nobody never done looked out for me!'

This is true. Other than those few times after Fred Mulligan died, I never looked in on them, or brought them a gift, or stopped by. But I didn't because they were the nastiest people I ever knew. Small and clannish, gossipy and mean, they didn't deserve a loving niece. Besides, they had committed the worst of sins in my mind: They were hateful to my mother. Aunt Alice never showed me any affection whatsoever. Nor could I remember a birthday gift, a card, or an Easter egg for me, ever. Really, I had no attachment to them. That is why it is so easy for me to say:

'How much do you want?'

My question catches them both completely off guard. They look at each other. Uncle Wayne is practically salivating, like I could cut them a check right now. Aunt Alice is dizzy with greed, looking around, wanting everything in this simple house, including the house itself. Uncle Wayne shifts his posture to stand up straight.

'Your aunt and I haven't actually come up with the specifics yet.'

'Well, I think you should.'

Aunt Alice looks at me. She doesn't trust me. Her eyes narrow. 'We've been talking to a lawyer down in Pennington, and he is advising us.'

'Have him call me.'

They look at me blankly. They didn't expect me to respond this way.

'I don't mean to be rude, but I just had a job with the Rescue Squad and I'm mighty tired. Maybe you heard. We had a bad explosion up at Wence. If you don't mind.' I stand and motion them to the door. Aunt Alice leaves first and doesn't look back at me. Uncle Wayne, now in a gracious mode because he can taste cash, smiles weakly at me through his thin lips.

'We just want what we got coming to us.'

'I hope you get what you've got coming to you.'

I bolt the door behind them and go directly to the bathroom. I throw up. I am scared by how much I'm vomiting, and intermittently I cry. I flush with my left hand and lean and run the cold water with my right. As soon as I can splash the cold water on my face, vomit comes up again. This happens over and over, until nothing but clear water comes up from within me. I brush my teeth. I go to put the toothbrush back in its holder and find I can barely lift it. It is as though the toothbrush is made of concrete. I begin to cry again. I want my mother. I grip the sink. I watch my tears hit the white porcelain and disappear down the drain. 'I should have killed her for what she said about you, Mama.' But deep within me, I know there is a better way to finish off Aunt Alice. I just have to find it.

CHAPTER FIVE

The old wisdom that everybody needs a good lawyer is true. I have Lew. He is thorough and competent. I just wish Inez wouldn't repeat everything she hears in his office. I don't want my personal business discussed in line at the grocery store. Fleeta almost got in a fistfight when some unflattering stories were being passed around about me on double-coupon Saturday. For the most part, though, folks are more fascinated than judgmental that I turned out to be a bastard. They can't believe the intrigue of it all, or that a regular person like me could be in the center of such a tale. The truth is, most folks around here are cautious conservatives, and the Bible is a serious guidebook for them. I'm getting looks of pity and wonderment from practically everybody I run into. I can tell which of my customers are repeating stories because they cannot look me in the eye. I surprise myself, because it seems that something like this should cause me some shame. I am more relieved than ashamed, though. The relief hasn't brought me any peace of mind yet, but I am hopeful it will.

I need to speak to Lew, and I don't want Inez to hear what I have to say, so I wait until I see him leave his office to pick up his mail at the post office. I grab my coat and follow him.

Lew juggles his keys and opens his post office box. It is stuffed with mail. As he pulls it out, he drops a periodical and I pick it up for him. I tell him about Aunt Alice and Uncle Wayne's visit. Then I tell him my plan. I was up all night, scheming and drinking coffee, so I have a crazy look about me, but my mind is clear.

'You're thinking like a lawyer. That's scary,' Lew says, as he makes a cylinder out of his mail and snaps a rubber band around it.

I wait for Lew to exit the post office. I buy a pack of stamps and wait a couple of minutes before I go. As I walk back to the Pharmacy, I see Inez grabbing a smoke on the stoop of the law office. I wave to her and smile. Any sign of warmth throws her off, so she looks at me like I'm the town kook, waves back, and smiles weakly.

I return to the Pharmacy. I fill all my prescription orders, check my inventory, and make my bank deposit. I skip lunch. I don't make any calls. I don't say much to Fleeta or Pearl. I do my work. And I wait. A few hours pass, and Pearl calls me to the front.

'Lew Eisenberg wants you to come over.'

I hug Pearl and she looks at me oddly.

'It must be good news.'

'Oh, it's not news. Not yet, anyway.'

Pearl shrugs and returns to her work. She's scraping the tips off the used lipstick samples in the display rack. Fleeta is sitting on a box of new shampoos, taking a smoke, so she doesn't notice I'm leaving. As I round the corner, I feel the first cold chill of autumn. It seems like the seasons changed in the course of this one day. The cool temperature gives me a boost.

'Is your beloved inside?' I ask Inez.

She thinks this is a little too hilarious, and laughs. 'Go on in,' she says.

Lew is sitting behind his desk. He motions for me to sit down. He turns up the radio, so Inez can't hear us. He goes over the legalities of my plan. He says one thing that concerns me: Wayne Lambert's first cousin, Buddy Lambert, is our circuit court judge at the county level, and he is known as Judge Envelope. He can be bought, and Lew believes Wayne has probably already cut a deal. There is a part of me that agrees with Aunt Alice; Fred Mulligan's money and real estate don't really belong to me. Maybe I caused all this. Maybe my ambivalence about my father, the store, the money, and the house drew all these problems to me. Maybe Aunt Alice senses my weaknesses and knows how to hurt me the most. Her brother sure did; don't these traits run in families? I don't think she'll quit until she makes me suffer.

Fred Mulligan was the most obstinate man I ever knew. His stubbornness – not his affection for my mother – is what made their marriage last. When I was in high school, he insisted that a lemon tree could grow in Big Stone Gap. No matter how much we argued with him, he could not accept that lemons need heat and sun to grow, the opposite of overcast and cool mountain weather. When the plant didn't bear fruit, he blamed the mail-order company. The lemon tree is still in the backyard. Its branches are gray and twisted, wrapped around the drainpipe by the back-porch stoop. I'll never tear it down; it reminds me not to turn bitter.

Lew sees my uncertainty. 'You're doing the right thing, Ave Maria,' he reassures me.

I have to stand up for myself. There is no one here to do that for me. For the first time in my life, I truly understand *alone*. My mother is gone. There is no brother or sister for me to turn to, no husband, just my intuition.

I don't want the Lamberts to get a dime. I think of Aunt Alice mistreating my mother, and it is all the fuel I need. Lew gives me the paperwork, which I sign. He hides it in a satchel to take to court. Then Lew shakes my hand. He places both hands on mine, to give me support and courage. I want to hug him, but I can't.

I pass Inez, who is now sitting at her desk, and turn back to Lew with one final thought.

'Lew, thank you for helping me. Aunt Alice and Uncle Wayne really deserve all they're getting. It's what Fred Mulligan would have wanted.'

Lew stands in the doorway. 'We're happy to have been of service to you.' Lew waves good-bye.

I'm out on the street, and I can hear Inez chatting on the phone already.

Insko is a tract of free land between Big Stone Gap and Appalachia that had been strip-mined. Instead of reclaiming the area, HUD put up low-income housing. When the valley floods, they move the people high up into the hills until their homes in the valley can be rebuilt. Sometimes it takes so long, folks give up and stay where they were placed.

Folks around here both rely upon and resent the government. When I was in school, we benefited from many programs. All of our vaccinations were free. Our lunch trays were filled with freebies: small bags of peanuts, a chocolate bar, or my favorite: a wedge of cheddar stamped GOVERNMENT CHEESE. They even sent entertainment from time to time. When I was in high school, a production of *Harvey* toured through, out of New York. I wasn't the only student to notice that the lead actor was drunk and actually fell asleep onstage during the second act. But we didn't care.

We were looking for any excuse to be a part of the outside world, to see what folks looked like, sounded like, and wore. For fifteen cents, you could see a show and imagine the exciting lives of those actors on the stage. We were never disappointed.

Pearl and her mother live in one of the older homes at the far end of the Insko development. I have dropped Pearl off several times, so I know where to go. I pull up in front of the two-room house. I didn't call ahead because I couldn't – they still don't have a phone, and they aren't planning on getting one, as Pearl is saving for college. The aluminum siding needs replacing, and the porch is rickety and practically separated from the house. The government is not very diligent about maintenance. The windows are thin side-by-side sliders, no insulation. I can see a light on in the house. A few kids play nearby. They stop and stare at me. I fish around my purse for some gum. I find it and give it to them. They thank me and run off.

I knock a few times. Finally, the screen door cracks opens about an inch.

'Mrs. Grimes?'

'Yes, ma'am.'

'I'm Ave Maria Mulligan, from town.'

Leah Grimes peeks out at me.

'Pearl went to fetch some leaves or something for her science project.'

'May I come in and wait for her?'

'I guess so.'

Leah Grimes opens the door to reveal a very clean but sparsely furnished room. There is an old bench, a small table, and a lamp. In the next room are two neatly made twin beds with old quilts on them. The kitchenette is neat. A pot of soup simmers on one of the two burners. Pearl comes in the door, breathless.

'Is everything all right, Miss Ave?'

'Everything is fine.'

'Mama, this is my boss, Miss Ave.'

'I know that.' Leah stands tall but looks at me funny.

'Pearl is a good worker. I don't know what I'd do without her.'

'I know. She's a good girl.'

'Has she brought you any of that miraculous Queen Helene masque yet?'

'Yes, ma'am.' Leah smiles and covers her mouth.

'I apologize if we've used you as a guinea pig for our new products, but we needed a woman with natural beauty to test it out on.'

'I used to be pretty, before I lost my teeth.'

'You know they can give you new teeth in town.'

'Someday. Right, Mama?' Pearl says, and gives her mother's hand a quick squeeze.

'Would you like some tea?' Leah asks, finally warming up.

'If you don't mind, I've got some business to discuss with Pearl.'

Pearl stands up straight and acts terribly grown-up at the mention of business.

Pearl takes me on a tour of the development. About a quarter mile down the road is one of our local natural wonders: the waterfalls of Roaring Branch. It's a magical place, natural stone steps with pure mountain water rushing over them. Folks come this way to sit and think and take in the beauty.

'You didn't know we was so poor, did you?'

'I make a lot of deliveries in these parts.'

Pearl and I sit and look at the water for a long time.

'How come you drove up here to see me? Am I fired or something?'

'No. You're doing a great job.'

'Thank you. I bug Fleeta sometimes,' Pearl apologizes. She looks at me expectantly, wondering why I've come.

'Pearl, do you have a dollar?'

'You just paid me. I got forty-six dollars.'

'I just need one.'

Pearl takes out her beaded coin purse and unfolds her money neatly. She gives me a dollar bill. 'Do you need more? Here. Take as much as you want.'

'No, thanks. One will do it. Now, let's shake on it.'

Pearl is confused, but she shakes my hand.

'Congratulations, Pearl. You just bought the Mutual Pharmacy.'

'I did? But why?'

As I walk Pearl back to her house, I explain that in order to protect the business from the scavenger Lamberts, I had to sell, and sell quickly. I had to make some big decisions in a hurry. I decided to sell my business so it couldn't be taken from me.

When we get back to the house, Pearl turns to me.

'Can I tell Mama?'

'Absolutely. Just tell her to keep it top secret until I say so.'

'Miss Ave, are you sure about this?'

'Yes, ma'am. By the way, just because you own the place, you are under no obligation to become a pharmacist. You go to college and study whatever you'd like and be whatever it is you decide you want to be. Fleeta and I can hold down the fort while you're gone. Fleeta will probably hit you up for a raise directly. I'm not so forward. But I do have a lot of experience, should you decide to keep me. I have a knack with the public.'

'But why did you pick me? Of all people?'

'Well, let's just put it this way, Pearl Grimes. You're just about the best person I ever knew.'

Pearl smiles. In the slate-blue twilight, her face is pure, unlined, and full of joy. Something good has finally happened to Pearl. At long last, somebody believes in her. Tonight in this exchange she has gained the tools with which she will build her self-esteem: she has been chosen and she has security. Maybe this is all that a person ever needs to succeed. Pearl has been picked, and that has begun to define her.

I promised Iva Lou I would meet her at the Sub Sandwich Carry-Out for a bite. This is mainly a teen hangout, but the rest of us go because the food is good. It has a nice ambiance; the plastic Tiffany chandeliers and orange Formica booths are casual and comfortable.

I tell Iva Lou about Aunt Alice and selling the business to Pearl.

'Honey-o, you ought to thank the Lord you came up with a plan like that. If your mean old aunt ever got her mangy mitts on the Mutual, nobody would trade over there. It'd close down. Ain't nobody gonna do trading with that witch.'

'Lew really knows what he's doing.'

'You know what I always say. A good lawyer is harder to find than a good husband. I'll have to swing by and thank old Lew my way.' Iva Lou winks.

'Please. I'm in enough trouble.'

'Aw, I'm just kidding with you. But what happens to you? What will you do?' Of course, I've thought about this. I've never made an impulsive decision in my life.

'I've saved a lot of money, Iva Lou.'

'Good for you.'

'I'll work for Pearl for a while, and then we'll see what happens.'

Dickie and Arlan Baker, two Mormon fellows, join us in the booth. Iva Lou makes the introductions, as she was the one who set up the meeting. The Baker brothers look to be in their twenties. They are clean; their hair is cropped short, their skin smooth and pink. (Mama always told me to cut down on the soda pop, because it's bad for the skin. As a rule, Mormons don't drink pop; their skin is an advertisement to give it up entirely.) They wear regulation black trousers and white cotton button-down shirts. For as many years as there have been Mormons, the young men have gone door-to-door wearing the same clothing combo, passing out the same literature, preaching like the good missionaries they are. The brothers have come to the Pharmacy a couple of times, but I was always too busy to talk to them.

'Boys, we need your help out of Salt Lake City. We need to climb up Ave Maria's family tree.' Iva Lou opens a spiral notebook and uncaps her pen. 'There's a man over in It-lee, and we need to find him pronto. That means "fast" in Italian.'

I laugh because this is one of the first words I taught Iva Lou.

'How can we help you?' Dickie – or is it Arlan? – asks.

'This is pretty much all the information we have on Mario Barbari presently.' Iva Lou gives them the book with the picture of Mario as the mayor of Schilpario in it. 'Don't lose it. UVA'll have my hide.' Dickie looks at Mario's picture.

'I think we can help. Most folks don't have pictures.'

Iva Lou listens as the Baker brothers explain how the Mormons came to be experts in genealogy. God bless her patience. She is such a dear friend, but I'm worried. We are so caught up in how to find Mario, I haven't had time to think about what will happen if we do. What if he rejects me? How will I handle it? I'm peeling off my old life like wet clothes. It isn't easy, but I have to do it. What will my new life be? Letting go of the Pharmacy, something

I thought I would never do, wasn't sad. It was exhilarating. I am becoming lighter. Will finding Mario da Schilpario be the one thing that brings me happiness? Will I truly be free of my Mulligan past when Alice Lambert finally gets her comeuppance?

Iva Lou rips the pages out of her spiral notebook. 'Y'all scoot. And here's my number when you get the information.'

Dickie and Arlan thank Iva Lou for dinner. They take their black valises and go.

'Iva Lou, what would I do without you?'

'Well, honey-o, somebody's got to put a fire under your butt. I see how you operate. You get all caught up in other people's dramas instead of your own. You need to be your own Rescue Squad, honey-o. Stop neglecting yourself.'

'I don't do that.'

'Sure you do. You ain't getting any, Ave, and that's a *big* problem.'

'How do you know I'm not getting any?'

'I just know.'

Iva Lou sucks the last bit of Tab through the straw. She swishes the ice around in the glass and starts chewing on it. 'It ain't healthy to go without.' I must look horrified because she holds up her index finger to punctuate the importance of what she is saying. 'You know, I've known me a lot of men. And the one thing I've learned is that they're all different. With each new experience that I rack up, I learn something new that I take with me as I move ahead in life. Sex is the most important thing there is on this earth.'

'What?' I whisper. And then Iva Lou repeats what she just said, this time with more volume. She raps the table when she's finished.

'Why?'

'Because it's the only mystery.'

I don't know if Iva Lou is profound or an idiot. Or if she has searched high and low for meaning in all her romances. Sex is a mystery? To whom? Not to her. I don't understand why she is saying this to me.

'Life is a mystery to be lived, not a problem to be solved,' she says. 'A friend of mine gave me a coffee mug with that on it a while back, and I've made it my personal philosophy. Plus, you have to find your father before you can love any man.'

'I don't believe that for a second.' I brush Iva Lou off with a wave.

'You should. It's true. Why do you think I'm helping you try to find him? I know what your problem is and how to fix it. You were told something all your life that was a lie. I happen to think you knew all along it was a lie. But that is something for you to figure out on your own after all of this is over. When people live lies, they stop connecting. When they stop connecting, trust dies. Honey-o, you can't be with a man because you can't trust one. You can't get naked, and I'm using that not literally but as a figure of speech. You follow me? To my way of thinking, if you can find your father, it will be a revelation to you. You will be able to place yourself in this world. You will finally know where you belong. You ain't one of us, Ave Maria. And not because your mama was a feriner. You separated yourself from folks around here. And I don't mean that to be cruel. You've lived here your whole life, but nobody really knows you. The first time I got a glimpse of what makes you tick was that night we read the books over at your house. You were looking at those books like old Kent Vanhook looks at my ass. There was a hunger there, a desire at long last.'

Some high school boys are playing a long song called 'Paradise by the Dashboard Light' for the third time. Iva Lou shouts at them to pick something else, like Mac Davis's 'One Hell of a Woman' (her personal favorite) or Conway Twitty's latest.

Then the bells on the entrance door jingle. They're exact replicas of the ones I have on my door at the Pharmacy. Every merchant in town has a set from Zackie's Bargain Store, and the same sweet ring happens when you go into any store in the Gap. Through the jingle, Sweet Sue comes in with Jack Mac. He sees us and walks toward us. Sweet Sue waves at us and goes to the take-out counter.

'Sue's kids with their daddy this weekend?' Iva Lou asks.

'Yes, ma'am,' Jack Mac replies.

'How's your mother?' I ask. Why do I always ask him about his mother?

'She's fine.'

'Tell her I was asking for her.' What am I? An old lady from the Methodist church sewing circle? Iva Lou shoots me a look.

'I will, ma'am.' Jack Mac looks down at the table and sees Iva Lou's open notebook.

'Y'all working on something?' he asks.

Iva Lou looks at me to answer.

'It's kind of a long story.' Jack Mac looks over to the take-out window. Sweet Sue chats with Delphine Moses, the owner of the Carry-Out, as she ladles tomato sauce onto the pizza dough.

'I got a few minutes.' Jack Mac sits down with Iva Lou, facing me.

'I'm trying to find my father.' Why am I telling him this? Couldn't I just make up something light and silly, like Iva Lou's working on a reading list for me? Why do I have to yak about my business?

'Have you heard the story going round about our Ave Maria?' Iva Lou asks as though I'm not there.

'I've heard some,' Jack Mac replies.

'We're trying to find an Eye-talian gentleman, who is our Ave's real father.'

'Yep, I'm a bastard,' I joke.

'No, you're not. That's a label adults put to babies. To my way of thinking, there isn't a soul born that wasn't supposed to be here.' Jack Mac says this as though it's the simplest concept in the world.

Iva Lou and I look at each other.

'How's the search going?' Jack Mac asks, picking up Iva Lou's notebook and scanning it.

'Iva Lou got the Mormons involved. I guess they know how to find people.'

'They sure do. Generally, they just ring your bell.' Iva Lou and I laugh. Jack Mac doesn't laugh at his own joke, and I respect that.

Sweet Sue stops by our table with her carry-out sack. 'Jack, let's go.'

Jack gets up to leave, but for a moment I don't think he wants to go. I think he wants to sit and talk with Iva Lou and me.

'Y'all take care, now,' Jack says, and follows Sweet Sue out the door. Iva Lou rises up off the seat about three inches to catch the rear view of Jack Mac as he goes. 'Nice sculpted hindquarters. Very nice. There ain't nothing like a working man.'

'What do you mean?' I ask.

'I love carpenters, plumbers, construction workers, and coal miners. The Jack Mac type.'

'He's a type?'

'Uh-huh. Had to narrow it down. When you've known as many men as me, you start making lists. The working man is a solid

man. They can fix things that are broke. They're practical. I like
that. How about you?'

'I never thought about it.' I really don't want to talk about this.

'I'll bet you haven't,' Iva Lou says, and looks at me, shaking her
head. 'Let me tell you what. Those men that sit behind a desk all
day, the office types, stay away from them. They are the weirdos of
the world. They don't get out and get air and get physical every
day, so their blood pools in their brains, and they get very strange
sexual ideas, believe you me. Kinky. I mean it.'

I try to get Iva Lou off of this subject and back to the Mormons'
notes. She is talking her favorite subject, though, and is therefore
persistent.

'I tried to have sex with him once,' Iva Lou announces.

'With whom?'

'Jack Mac.'

'Really?'

'I got nowhere. Nowhere.'

'Why? You're so pretty and fun. What happened?' Why am I
asking her this when I don't want to know? I do this. When folks
make me uncomfortable, instead of removing myself from the situation, I try to make them comfortable.

'Well, one night, before he started going with Sweet Sue, he
was up to the Fold and we had a couple of beers and a couple of
dances and I was frisky, and he was frisky, so I suggested a rendezvous up to Huff Rock. I find it inspirational up there. The
mountaintop, the sky, the big old rocks to lie on. You're getting
the picture.' I nod. 'Well, we kissed a couple of times. Good kisser. Uh-huh. Good kisser. And then it was getting time to move
things along toward some sort of something, and he stopped.'

'He stopped?'

'I asked him why he stopped, of course. I'm not bragging, but that sort of thing never happened to me before. I said, "Jack MacChesney, why on God's green earth are you stopping now? Aren't you having fun?"'

'What did he say?'

'Well, he looked at me with those eyes of his, and he said most sincerely, "Iva Lou, you are a doll. But I ain't in love with you. And I'm one of those men that has to be in love to carry on like this."'

'No!' I shriek.

'Yes. That's exactly what he said. And it was funny. My feelings weren't hurt; I wasn't embarrassed or any of that. But I'll tell you something: I couldn't believe that there was a man like that walking around in this world. I persisted a little with him, and he, very gentlemanly, kept declining my advances, so I yanked my bra straps back up and called it a night. I don't know, I guess I admired him for his principles. I didn't want to mess with it. I respected him.'

Iva Lou shrugs and picks up the last crumbs of cake with the back of her spoon. 'Does that beat all? I mean, did you ever?'

'No, that's quite a story.' What does she want me to say?

We sit quietly for a few moments. I look at Iva Lou. As she studies her notes, she looks like a little girl. I can see exactly who she was when she was little. A curious girl with a big appetite. What happened to the girl I used to be? Where did she go?

When I was seven, Mrs. White took our second-grade class to Clinch Haven Farms. It's high up the mountains; I remember being scared in the bus. It was pretty once we got there, though. There were vivid green meadows that rolled back like folds of white icing, covered in flowers, dotted with cows, just like the picture on the milk bottle. The first thing Mrs. White showed us was a creek that twisted down the rocks and flowed into a pool. Mrs.

White gathered us on the bank of the creek and explained the way water worked – how it rained and came down the mountain, making rivulets that pool and fall and then turn into rivers. We were allowed to drink of the creek. Mrs. White taught us how to kneel and, without disturbing the sediment at the bottom of the creek, cup our hands to drink the clear water off the surface. As I knelt, I examined the stones through the clear water. They were glassy brown and black stones, like the antique buttons my mama kept in a cupcake tin in her sewing closet. Then we followed the creek down to Buskers Farm and she told us how explorers always followed water. Even now, if I get lost when I'm making deliveries up in the hollers, I just remember to follow the water, and I always find my way back to town. That simple rule, for whatever reason, has stayed with me all these years and held me in good stead.

Buskers farm was gigantic. There was an open field, a barn, and a main house. There was an outhouse; we all made jokes about it, even though some of my classmates still used outhouses.

I was with Nina Kaye Coughlin, my best friend. She had straight, shiny red hair and a turned-up nose splattered with freckles. When she smiled, her front teeth turned inward to make a V shape; it didn't look bad, though. Crowded teeth are a sign of someone with lots to say. At one point I whispered to Nina Kaye that we ought to go look in the barn. So we separated from the group and went around the back of the barn to find the door. There, in a clearing, was a hog, strung up on three long poles, suspended by the head. Its gut was split from throat to groin. Two farmhands were cleaning the open gash – I guess they were removing the organs. Their hands were full of squishy blue and red entrails. They were being careful with the parts, placing them on a small, clean tarp, pulled tightly over a barrel. The hog's eyes were wide open, staring up to the sky, as if in prayer. There was a ruby red pool beneath the hog; his blood was so voluminous that it filled a small pit. We froze. Nina Kaye was holding my hand so tight, her fingernails made grooves on the side of my palm. Finally, the farmhands looked at us. For a moment they seemed annoyed, but when they saw how scared we were, they softened.

'Girls, we done drained the hog,' one of the men explained.

Nina Kaye looked as though she might faint. We both lived in town; the only farm animals we saw were on these field trips or at FFA camp in later years. We backed away from the scene and tore around the side of the barn. Nina Kaye cried and I comforted her. 'Ain't you skeered?' she said to me. 'We can't both be scared,' I told her.

'There you go again,' Iva Lou says. 'Off in space.'

'Sorry, Iva.'

'What were you thinking?'

'How I used to be so brave.'

Bullitt Park, our high school football field and town park, is full of fog. It fills up with gray mist like a soup bowl some nights, especially in early fall when Mother Nature is making her temperatures drop. It's a little dreary, and tonight it's all business. After two months of intense practice, the Powell Valley High School marching band is going to run the final rehearsal of the Elizabeth Taylor Halftime Show Salute full out, no stops. Theodore is on the fifty-yard line giving some last minute tips to the flag girls. In their gold lamé short shorts, you would never guess they were high school sophomores; they look like they could be in Cleopatra's harem.

The drum majorette blows her whistle, and the band falls into formation in the end zone, spaced across in a straight line from fence to fence. The band is magnificent in their Carolina-blue and ruby-red uniforms. From the visitor side, the pyramid crew runs out onto the field and places the pyramids. The drum majorette barks, 'Horns up!' The band begins to play.

The show is truly a wonder, but over it there is a veil of trying too hard. We are overcompensating and overprepared, but we don't know what else to do with the nervous energy that runs through us. We aren't used to famous people gracing these parts, though the great baseball player Willie Horton of the Detroit Tigers was born over in Arno. The only star that has ever passed through here was Peggie Castle from *The Lawman*, and frankly, without her makeup she didn't look like her TV self. And of course, George C. Scott (General Patton) was born in our county seat: Wise, Virginia. Until now, they were the Big Names. But we're about to top them with the biggest star of all. Everybody in Big Stone Gap has a stake in making Elizabeth Taylor's visit a success. Mr. Honeycutt has been running a 'La Liz' film festival at the Trail, and this has only fed the feverish excitement. Nellie Goodloe keeps reminding us that this an election year and the visit is really about politics. But no one seems to care about that. John Warner is a Republican, and most folks around here are Democrats, so I don't think coming through here will do his campaign much good. This is Jimmy Carter country all the way. But if anyone can sway some votes for Mr. Warner, it will be his movie star wife.

Even Tayloe Slagle is a nervous wreck. She threw up behind the bleachers before her big solo number, sending a shudder through the entire marching band. Luckily, I have a pack of Tums in my pocket – I've been carrying them around since the panic attacks started – and I run them over to her. She is embarrassed about being sick and grateful for the Tums to settle her stomach. Sitting on the ground in her mother's arms, Tayloe looks like a little girl. She is a little girl. We forget that, because kids around here marry so young. From my perspective now, at my age, she looks so small.

After he checks on Tayloe, Theodore runs onto the field, rallying the kids to focus and concentrate on the routine. You can see the fear in their faces, though. If the most perfect girl in town is a nervous wreck, it wouldn't take much for the entire band to keel over in group panic like dominoes. Thankfully, Tayloe revives quickly and returns to the field. Now she can add *vulnerable* and *indomitable* to her long list of desirable attributes.

I join Spec up in the bleachers. He just went on a Rescue Squad run to Wallens Ridge, so I'm dying to hear details.

'What happened?' I ask Spec as I sit down beside him.

'Larry Bumgarner done shot his sister.'

'No! Is she okay?'

'She's fine. He missed. Put a hole in the sleeve of her shirt is all.' Spec lights a cigarette.

'Why . . why did he shoot her?'

'She was on the phone too long. He wanted to ask a gal, you may know her, she's a majorette, Bree Clendenin?' I nod. 'Well, Larry wanted to ask Bree to Homecoming in the worst way, and his sister was tying up the line. He got fed up and went in the bedroom and got his papaw's gun and threatened her, and he says it accidentally went off.' Spec exhales.

I look off at the mountains covered in a veil of sheer gray and decide for sure and forever that I am quitting the Rescue Squad.

Spec must read my mind. 'I could have used you up there. You're good at talking sense.' Spec thinks a compliment will keep me on the job. I'll let him think so. 'You know, I had to ask him one thing. The kid. Larry. I had to know what in God's name was so special about Bree Clendenin that he had to shoot his sister off the phone. And do you know what he said to me?'

'I can't imagine.'

'He said, "Her hair." He loved her hair. Does that just beat all?' It does beat all. But what did Spec think Larry would say? That he loved Bree for her character, her mind, and her sense of humor? Isn't her thick copper hair enough to drive any boy wild? Everybody knows the old mountain wisdom: Women love with their ears and men with their eyes.

I take a good look at Spec. I spend a lot of time with him, but I've never really studied his face. His profile is outlined against the concrete wall of the bleachers like a tintype. Spec has a face of contradictions. He has the high forehead of a leader, the short, turned-up nose of a procrastinator, and no chin. According to *siang mien*, he has the big ideas but no follow-through.

'Spec? Are you happy?'

Spec exhales a puff of smoke from his cigarette. The question makes him laugh, and then he has a coughing fit. The fit lasts a few seconds. He sputters and clears his throat.

'What is so funny?'

'What kind of a question is that?'

'Are you happy? That's the question.'

'I don't think about that.'

'You don't?' I can't believe him.

'Hell no.' Spec flicks the butt of his cigarette. 'Happiness is a myth.'

'Why is it a myth?'

'I got murried when I was fifteen years old. I got me five kids. One a bigger disappointment than the next. Course, it's not their upbringing. It's the world. It's gone to hell, and ain't nothing nobody can do to stop it.'

'If you could live your life over again, would you do anything differently?'

Spec clears his throat. The definitive set of his mouth tells me that this is a question he has thought about many times.

'I'd have married Twyla Johnson instead of my wife I got now. Twyla is the One That Got Away. Everybody got one of them, you know. That's the person that you know you ought to be with, but circumstances play out a certain way and you get sidetracked and wind up settling. I think it's hard for a man once he starts having sex with a woman regular and so young, like I did with my wife. It's hard to break it off. You get into a flow and it's comfortable and you don't know nothing else, so you can't give it up. Hell, you won't give it up. I was fifteen, and let's face it, I got me a taste of the honey and I wanted the whole hive. My wife didn't know no better neither. She just wanted to get murried and have our babies. Course I had to murry her, so that might have had something to do with the decision-making process. I made a big mistake very young, and there weren't no turning back or going forward. I got myself stuck, plain and simple. I try to tell my kids, don't never settle, but they don't even have the gumption to get off the damn couch. They're born settlers like their mama. Ain't nothing I can do about it. Life gives you what you git, and you got to live with it.'

'Where's Twyla now?'

'She works at the bank down in Pennington.'

A knowing smile crosses Spec's face; for a moment he has a chin.

'Do you see her?'

'We do have lunch.'

'Just a meal?'

'Now you're getting personal.' Spec smiles at me to let me know that I haven't done anything wrong by inquiring but he's finished talking about it. Men are like that. When they've closed shop on a conversation, there's no mulling left to be done.

Spec offers me a lift home. Theodore has to put the equipment up and I'm tired, so I accept. He drops me at my house, then speeds off to the south, toward Pennington Gap. Inside, I sort through my mail – nothing exciting, only some circulars from the Piggly Wiggly and Collinsworth Antiques. I have begun to dread the mail, though I do feel a little relief when there's no word from the Mormons. I don't need any bad news. Theodore calls for my input on the halftime show. He drills me about every aspect of the rehearsal; what a perfectionist he is! There's a knock at the door. I figure it's Spec. He probably got up the road and got a radio call and did a U-turn to fetch me. I really have to talk to him about quitting. I'm sick of running around all hours of the day and night on calls. I peek out the window. No Spec. It's Jack MacChesney, carrying two jars. Still holding the phone with Theodore on the other end, I open the door.

'Mama made her first batch of apple butter for the fall, and she wanted you to have some.'

'Thank you. Would you like to come in?'

Jack Mac nods. 'You're on the phone,' he comments.

'Yeah. I'm just wrapping it up. Would you like coffee or tea or something?'

'Do you have a beer?'

I nod and go into the kitchen to fetch a can. I carry the phone into the kitchen with me.

'Who's there?' Theodore asks.

'It's Jack MacChesney.'

'What does he want?'

'His mama sent some apple butter down for me.'

'Is that all?' Theodore asks this with just enough envy to make me smile.

'No. I think he's madly in love with me and tonight we're going to make a baby.'

Theodore starts laughing, and then I do.

'Look, it's rude of me to be on the phone when company comes a-calling. I'll call you later.'

'You do that.'

Theodore hangs up. He's never been jealous before. This is interesting. I get that little jolt of adrenaline; it's probably hormonal, but it's a catlike feeling of being in charge and on the prowl.

I poke my head into the living room to tell Jack that I'll be a second. He is standing at the fireplace, looking at a small ceramic statue of the Virgin Mary on the mantel. When my mother was alive, she always put fresh flowers near it. Since she died, I've lit a candle next to it most nights. I don't know why. I've just done it.

'That's the Blessed Mother. I'm named after her.'

'You are?'

' "Ave Maria" means "Hail Mary." '

'I didn't know that.'

'I hope Budweiser is okay. All I got in the beer department is whatever Theodore brings over here.'

While I'm in the kitchen, in the reflection of the window, I see Jack Mac removing his barn jacket and folding it neatly on the rocker. He doesn't sit down. He stands and looks around the room. I pour myself a glass of water and place the fixings for his beer on a tray. I reach up into the cabinet for my mama's can of biscotti and place a few on a plate.

'The Blessed Mother is my patron saint,' I yell from the kitchen.

'Baptists don't have saints,' Jack replies. 'All we got is Jesus.'

'There's something to be said for keeping things simple,' I say as I return to the living room. Jack Mac is now seated on the couch, sort of leaning forward. He places the beer, the glass, and the napkin neatly on the coffee table. I sit in Fred Mulligan's easy chair, a few feet from him, and give him the once-over. He is spiffed up. His navy blue cords are pressed; his crisp sage-green shirt seems new. He's wearing cowboy boots. He looks like he's dressed to go somewhere.

'You're dressed up.'

'No. I just cleaned up after work.'

I curl my stockinged feet under me. I think my left sock has a big hole in it. My hooded sweatshirt from Saint Mary's is fifteen years old, and the overalls I threw on over it still have nails in the pockets from the roof patching that Otto, Worley, and I did a while back. My hair is a rat's nest of curls held up by a thousand pins. I am a mess. 'I wasn't expecting company,' I tell him, apologizing for my appearance.

'You look just fine,' he reassures me. He points to a set of white pearl rosary beads in a small crystal candy dish on the coffee table. 'Are those yours?'

I nod.

'Do you use them?'

'Not enough.'

'How do they work?'

'Well, the rosary is a devotion to the Blessed Mother.'

'Mary, who you're named after?'

'Right. And each of these beads is a Hail Mary that you say. Is this boring to you?'

'No, not at all.'

'Each of these ten beads represents a time in the life of Jesus. The joyful mysteries, the sorrowful mysteries, and so on.'

'The Cherokees have meditation beads. They sort of look like these. Mama has them. She's part Cherokee, you know. From way, way back. She had jet-black hair when she was younger.'

'I don't remember her having black hair.'

'That's because it turned when I was just a boy.'

There is a long silence. I look at the statue of Mary on the mantel. In her blue cape and crown of stars, she reminds me of the lady in my mother's letter, the Ave Maria I'm named after. I remember the Dieter's Prayer: *Lovely Lady dressed in blue, make me skinny just like you.* I bite into a biscotti. It cracks in half loudly, and a shower of crumbs goes down the front of my overalls. Luckily, most of it lands in the front utility pocket. I brush the rest away.

Jack breaks through the quiet. 'Rick Harmon quit the mines.'

'He did?'

'Well, he lost the two smallest toes on that foot of his, and the doctor told him he needed to find other work. So he got a job over at Legg's Auto World.'

'Good for him. That was a pretty bad injury. How did it happen?'

'When I went back into the mine, it took me a while to get to him. There was so much smoke, he couldn't see, so he was trying to crawl out. He caught his foot under a fallen rock. When he tried to get loose, it was bad.'

'I . . . everybody was nervous when you went back in the mine for him,' I say, speaking on behalf of the entire community.

'You . . . or everybody?' Jack says, trying not to smile.

'Everybody. Including me.' I don't think I speak this man's language. There are so many weird gaps.

We sit for a moment in silence. Finally he speaks. 'My daddy and I fixed the furnace over here once.'

'You did?'

'Remember that summer you went to FFA camp?'

How could I forget the Future Farmers of America camp? Living with a bunch of surly girls in a cabin on a farm in East Tennessee, surrounded by farm animals that *we* had to feed, brush, and milk. Fred Mulligan thought it would be good for me. I hated it. 'That was around sixth grade, right?'

'Yeah. After we fixed the furnace, your mama made us some kind of little sandwiches. My daddy was mighty impressed. I guess they were some sort of Italian specialty or something.'

'They were probably roasted-pepper sandwiches. She used to take a bunch of red peppers and broil them until the skin burned to black. Then she'd peel off the charred part, leaving the soft pepper underneath, and soak them in olive oil. Then she'd slice them up thin as paper – I still can't do it like she could – and put them on the bread with a little salt.'

'They were the best sandwiches I ever ate.'

I want to thank him for paying my mother a compliment, but I can't speak. All of a sudden, there is a knot in my throat. So I just nod and smile. I haven't cried much since Mama died, but thinking of her sandwiches, and her in the kitchen, and now she's gone forever – tears come to my eyes.

'I'm sorry,' Jack Mac says, putting down his beer, 'I didn't mean to upset you.'

'No, no. I'm not upset. I just haven't talked about her much.'

'The wound is too fresh.'

For a moment I don't understand what he means. She's only been gone a few months now, but I started to let go of her when she got really sick, which was almost four years ago. The loss doesn't seem new to me; I felt it long before she actually passed on.

'Nobody told me how much I would miss her.'

'She was a fine lady,' he says plainly and truthfully.

'The morning after she died, I went into her room. I had to go in there and pick a dress for her to be laid out in. So I went in her closet. And I found . . .' I am so embarrassed. My voice is breaking, and it never does. Why am I crying in front of this man? I remember myself and stop. 'Anyway, I found eight new blouses. They were beautiful, perfectly pressed, on hangers. Four white cottons and four patterned gingham: red, blue, yellow, and black-and-white checked. She had made them for me. She made all my clothes. But I never remember her working on them. I thought she had stopped sewing entirely when she got sick. She had pinned a note to them. It said: "Fresh blouses. Love, Mama." ' I laugh and Jack smiles.

'She even made my coats. I never had to buy anything, just blue jeans. And now that I've got the blouses, I won't need to shop for a long while.'

'A good mother is a precious thing,' he says. 'You were very lucky.'

I guess I was. But I know I never saw myself as lucky. I looked at my life as a series of small struggles and gentle, intermediate plateaus of peacefulness. But anything that I am, I owe to my mother. She taught me to revere gentleness. She brought out my good heart by example. She taught me how to read and to love books. All the places I went when I read, all the adventures I had, stayed inside the books, though. I never came into anything on my own, really. I never ventured far from my potential. I never tested myself and tried things. I wasn't afraid, I just wasn't particularly daring. It's fascinating that anyone would look at me and think I'm lucky. I don't have natural talents. I am so slow! I have to study things, ruminate, decide. I don't have grand thoughts that could change anything. I'm smart enough, and it is the *enough* that defines me. I am adequate. Hardworking. I have a sense of humor, but that's due to my prism, my point of view, and even that I cannot take credit for. Very often my odd sense of humor is lost on folks. I don't know what Jack is seeing when he looks at me. I'm not particularly special, and to me lucky is special. There's a lightness to it, an élan. I'm not that. I am fixture and hardware. Not a spritely thing.

'Would you like to go for a walk?' I ask. Jack Mac looks at me oddly – he wasn't planning on going for a walk. 'We don't have to.'

'No, no. Let's go.' He waits for me to stand up. I look around for my loafers, which I spot, shoved under the dining room table. I look down at my feet. Thankfully, the hole in my left sock is on the bottom. I scoot to the dining room and slip on my shoes.

'Let me go get my jacket,' I say.

'No. Here. Wear mine.'

'Won't you be cold?'

'No, not at all.'

Jack Mac helps me into his jacket. It is soft, and the shoulders hang down roomily over my arms. I thought I was about his size, but I'm not; I'm smaller.

'Nice lining.' It's an olive-green tufted satin. The stitches are perfect harlequin diamonds.

'Your mama put that lining in.'

'She did?'

'Last fall.' Jack Mac opens the door and lets me go outside first. It is cooler than I thought. I pull the collar up around my neck. It smells like sandalwood and lime.

We walk through my neighborhood, an area called Poplar Hill, in the oldest part of town – some would say the best part of town. I live in the smallest house on the block, a 1920s clapboard cottage-style home. It is sweet: whitewashed, with a big porch. It sits back off the road, so it looks picturesque. There's a front-porch swing, and pink squares of stained glass frame the front windows. I look back at it as I walk with Jack, thinking for the first time that it is not my father's house, it is really mine.

'How's Sweet Sue doing?'

'Well, I broke off with her.'

I stop in the middle of the road. This stuns me momentarily and I'm not sure why. Maybe it's because I saw them practically get married on the stage of the Outdoor Drama. I remember her terror when Jack Mac went into the mine, and how she claimed him when it was over. Sweet Sue is perfect for Jack Mac! Her kids. Her pep. Her community involvement – they seem to fit so nicely with the quiet dignity of the MacChesneys of Cracker's Neck Holler.

'She's a wonderful person, very caring,' he says, and kicks a stone.

'But you were getting married.'

'Not exactly, ma'am.'

Does he have to call me ma'am? He's exactly my age, for God's sake. I decide right then and there to take a box of Loving Care Chestnut Brown from the store and soak my head in it. I thought I only had two or three gray hairs, but obviously I am mistaken.

'What happened?' I ask, knowing full well it is none of my business. But I feel I have to know. I'm curious. I don't think I'm being rude or forward. Plus, reading his face, I can see that the lines from his nose to his mouth have deepened in expression. These come from guilt.

'I began to have feelings for someone else.'

'Dear God!' I shriek. I am a judgmental shrew, but usually I keep it under wraps. 'Who?' I ask, again knowing it's none of my business.

'Well, ma'am—'

'Jack Mac, please don't call me ma'am. I'm not your spinster aunt.'

'Heck, you've hardly aged since high school,' Jack Mac says, and he sounds like he means it.

'Thank you. Now, what were we talking about?'

'You.'

'No, we were talking about you. You and?'

'You.'

'Me?' What is he talking about? Me. Me as what?

'Miss Ave?'

'Jack, no "Miss" either. That's just one step above "ma'am" at the AARP.'

'Ave Maria?'

'Great pronunciation.'

Then he begins. 'We're both knee-deep in our thirties. You're all alone. You're an orphan, really. And I've got a good job. And when my mama passes, the house will be mine. And I'm in pretty good shape. I eat too much and I drink a lot of beer sometimes, but my heart's good and I'm strong. I've got some money saved. I just bought a new truck. A '78 Ford pickup. Fully loaded. And I've been thinking that I'd like a home and family. A good wife. And when it comes down to it, at our age, there aren't a lot of us left. The never-marrieds, I mean. The field sort of narrows and the pool dries up, leaving folks who have already been married, and that comes with complications. I like simplicity and I think you do, too. So, I was wondering if you'd like to get married.'

'Married?'

'Yes, ma'am. I mean yes.' He corrects himself. Good. He's quick.

'You're proposing to me?'

'Yes, I am.'

'Is there something the matter with you?'

'Excuse me?'

'Do you know anything about women?'

'I'd like to think I do.'

'In the first place, I don't know you very well. I mean, we went through school together. You have a nice mother who suffers from hypertension. You play guitar very well.' Why do I feel compelled to make a list? Why do I have to be methodical? Why do I have to make *him* feel comfortable? Can't I simply respond like a woman whose head is being blown off at this moment?

'You said I was a good dancer,' he says directly.

'Yes, I did.' I say this evenly, temperately, as if I were talking to a child who has left too many fund-raising jars on my checkout counter. I turn away from him to think for a moment. But I realize I don't need to turn away, I don't need to think; I understand everything all of a sudden, and it blazes through me like an electric shock and spins me back around.

'I don't need an answer right away,' Jack Mac says softly.

'I can give you one, Mr. MacChesney. Sir. For you to assume that I'm spent, that I'm old and without possibilities or opportunities or dreams of my own, is appalling to me. I may appear to be a pharmacist in sensible shoes, okay, maybe I have holes in my socks, but there is a river inside of me. I'm not lonely. Or desperate. Or one bit sad. I don't need to be saved!'

'You don't understand,' he says with equal force.

'I get this! I really get this! If you are sincere in this strange proposal, the answer is no. I don't love you. And I'm one of those kooks who think you ought to love the person you marry.'

'Wait a second—'

'And if you aren't sincere, I think it's mean. It isn't funny to play on a woman's station in life. As though she is somehow responsible for being married or being alone! Sometimes things happen in life, the pieces move around so that the game can't go your way. Things like cancer and mental cruelty and fear. So don't think it's funny to dangle some happy thing like that – like joy can be invented in a second. It can't! I am happy alone. I don't need you or anybody else! I take care of myself. And it might seem dull to you, or pathetic, but what you think of me does not change my life one way or another.'

'You don't understand.'

'Let me lay it out for you. I could lose everything I have, and I may. But if you think my definition of security is a mate with a job and a truck, you don't know me very well. And if I were you, I would think twice about proposing anything to anyone you don't know very well.'

I turn and walk briskly up the street. He's following me. I am sweating so hard, I get a whiff of sandalwood and lime from my neck and remember the jacket. I take it off and turn.

'Your jacket.'

He takes it.

'One more thing. In the future, if you want to win a woman, don't tell her you've got a new truck. Most women don't care about new trucks. It's not a selling point. Good night.'

About three blocks from my house, I realize that I walked a long way with Jack Mac, and this insight alone makes me more furious. Why was I walking with him, wearing his jacket, making small talk? I don't even like him. He yups and nopes and is altogether too quiet. I hate that! Those long quiet spells he lapses into, forcing me to talk, to fill the spaces with personal stories and observations that I didn't want to share in the first place. The crust of that guy! Knee-deep in our thirties! You're the one knee-deep in old age, with your bald head! I still have some glimmers of youth around my edges; yours are gone, Jack MacChesney! Don't lump me in with you and your mother in a stone house in a holler!

I break into a run so I can make it home faster, and the nails from the roof loosen in my pocket and drop out onto the street. I know that I should stop to pick them up because they could rip somebody's tires as they drive over them, but even the thought of a blowout and subsequent three-car pileup can't make me stop. I want to go home. I want to lock my door and be alone with the only person in the world I can trust: me. As I turn my corner, I see Theodore's car parked in front of my house. Theodore is sitting on my front stoop. Beautiful Theodore who understands me! I run up the walk and throw myself into his arms. He holds me tightly.

'What happened?'

'I hate him, Theodore. I hate him!'

I sound like a twelve-year-old girl. I remember myself and sit up.

'Did he do something to you?' Theodore sounds like he could kill anyone who would harm me. He slips off his jacket and wraps it around me. He looks into my eyes. In the porch light, Theodore's face has a golden glow – sepia and stone. Strength in the features! How I love this face! This Irish face. The crow's-feet. The strong nose that tilts ever so slightly down. The chiseled jaw-line, an advertisement for his determination in all things. No man could be stronger in this moment than my very own Theodore Tipton. With him I can be honest, always.

'He asked me to marry him.'

A moment passes. Theodore pulls me close. 'And what did you say?' His tone tells me he hopes I said no.

'I said no! Of course. Are you crazy? Why would I say anything but no?'

'I don't know.'

'I don't want him!'

'It's funny –'

'There is nothing funny about this!'

'About a month ago, Jack Mac stopped me at the gas station,' Theodore begins.

'What for?'

'He wanted to know if we were in love with each other.'

'Why didn't you tell me?'

'I didn't think about it. I get ribbed about you all the time, so I thought nothing of it.'

Ribbed? Am I the town joke? I am so mad I almost forget to be embarrassed.

'What a phony Jack MacChesney is! Mr. Respectful. Mr. Perfect Manners, all quiet and calm. Who's he kidding? It's all an act!'

'You mean you. He upset you.'

'Yes, I mean me!' Me. Be concerned about me. I got myself good and scared tonight. In my fury I cannot cry, so I issue orders like a commando.

'Theodore Tipton, you are sleeping over tonight.' I don't care if he wants to. I need him. I need to be held. I need reassurance, the kind you can only find in the arms of a strong man.

'I think I should.'

'You have to,' I decide, not backing down from Furious Hill for a second.

'I have to?'

'Yes. I love you. I don't love anybody else. I'm tired of this. You need me. Just like I need you. I need my friend.'

I can't see Theodore's face, so I can't read it. He just sighs deeply and we go inside.

Theodore sits in Fred Mulligan's easy chair as I straighten up the house. Headlight beams track across the walls. 'He's gone,' Theodore says, not looking up from the paper. Washing dishes, putting them up, sweeping, and straightening are my favorite things to do when I'm upset. I move around the living room and through the kitchen, back and forth like a pinball. I have a lot of nervous energy.

Theodore wants coffee, so I prepare the pot – we'll be doing a lot of talking tonight. When I look in the cabinet for the coffee, I find very little left in the canister. So I drag out the step stool to see onto a high shelf. There is a coffee tin at the back of the top shelf that looks like it came with a Christmas gift basket. I'm relieved. I need a cup of coffee right now. I pull the tin out. Theodore joins me in the kitchen and sits down at the table.

The tin is sealed around with clear tape. I grab a steak knife to unseal it and pop off the lid. There is no coffee in the tin. Just a bunch of letters. At first I don't think much of it: Mama was a pack rat. Of course she kept letters in cans. But from whom?

This thought makes me drop the tin. The letters shower all over the kitchen floor.

'What's all that?' Theodore asks.

'I don't know.' He can tell from my tone that I'm afraid, so he helps me off the step stool and into a chair. He kneels down and gathers the letters. I look down at my chest. The utility pocket is moving up and down, up and down. The palpitations are back! I breathe deeply.

Theodore sits with me and gives me one of the letters. It is addressed to my mother, at P.O. Box 233, Big Stone Gap, Virginia 24219. At the bottom of the envelope, in handwriting, 'USA.' The stamp is Italian. The letter is postmarked April 23, 1952, right around my ninth birthday.

The return address is Via Davide, Bergamo BG Italia.

'Shall I read it?' Theodore asks.

'Go ahead.'

Theodore unwraps the letter and scans it. 'Ave. Honey. It's in Italian.'

Theodore gives me the letter and I begin to read. It starts with 'My dear Sister,' and ends with 'Your loving sister, Meoli.' It's all about the goings-on in Schilpario and Bergamo. Aunt Meoli speaks of her twin, Antonietta who is healthy and happy. There are details about cousins Andrea, Federica, and Mafalda. Comments about my mother's parents! My grandparents! An uncle had died. And then she writes that she has not seen Mario. That's all it says about him.

She inquires about me. Could my mother send pictures? Don't I have a birthday soon?

'What does it say? Honey? What does it say?'

'My mother has two sisters. Twins.' I sit down on the floor. The letters are scattered all around me, filled with more shocks and surprises. I wonder how much more I can take.

CHAPTER SIX

The town paper has issued a special (lavender!) supplement with a guide to all the events involving the visit of screen legend Elizabeth Taylor. She arrives Friday afternoon, October 23, 1978, around 3:00 P.M. She is staying at the Trail Motel in their deluxe suite (boy, is she in for a surprise). At 6:00 P.M. she and her husband will be taken to Railroad Avenue, conjunct to Shawnee Avenue (Main Street), and placed in an open convertible provided by Cas Walker's grocery-store chain. At approximately 6:15 the car will follow the marching band into the ballpark. The convertible will make two 360–degree trips around the football field on the paved running track, so that Elizabeth and her husband can wave to the crowds. At 7:00 the game starts: Powell Valley vs. Rye Cove. Elizabeth will watch the game from a specially constructed platform stage, provided by the Dollar General Store, near the home stands. (This stage has been used for band-competition judges; Nellie decorated it special for this evening.) Then, the halftime show.

On Saturday morning the Republicans are having a pancake

breakfast – we'll skip that. Then, starting with hors d'oeuvres at 5:30 P.M., the library fund-raiser will commence. Iva Lou made sure that our table is right next to Elizabeth's!

The beauty of Nellie Goodloe is that she wants to do everything right. The entire weekend starring Elizabeth Taylor is in her capable hands, and she is planning it like a royal wedding. The library dinner takes the place of a reception (I'm sure Nellie's own wedding was less detailed.) She chose the theme 'Colors' for the decorations: violet in honor of Miss Taylor's eyes, and white because it is a good contrast. The Dogwood Garden Club is doing the centerpieces; the Green Thumb Garden Club is making a floral backdrop; Holding Funeral Home is supplying Astroturf runners for the entry and their funeral canopy in case of bad weather; I am donating the candles; Zackie Wakin is providing napkins printed with E.T. and the date in gold; and the Coach House Inn is making Elizabeth Taylor's favorite meal (and their specialty): fried chicken, mashed 'taters, and collard greens.

There's been a slight amount of tension between Iva Lou and Nellie regarding the dinner. Iva Lou has asserted herself in the dinner plans because she envisions herself as head librarian for the new facility. Of course, Iva Lou is no Nellie Goodloe, she couldn't care less about centerpieces, she wouldn't know a votive from a candelabra, or which side the small spoons go on in a place setting. Nellie, on the other hand, is the queen of etiquette. She went to Sweet Briar College and has a degree in home economics, so she brings a vast knowledge of elegant living to the Gap. Iva Lou wanted to do a barbecue. When she suggested this, Nellie nearly had a stroke; after all, you can't hardly ask the Queen of Hollywood to tie on a bib in Miner's Park and suck ribs. Nellie had to come up with a way to keep Iva Lou occupied, so she put her in charge of ticket sales for the dinner. Within several hours the dinner was completely sold out. Iva Lou unloaded every ticket. She knows a lot of businessmen, and evidently, they owe her favors.

Every detail of the planning for the pregame parade – in which Candidate Warner and Miss Taylor will ride through town in the convertible – must go through Theodore. He is in charge of everything from the Kiwanians who lead the parade to the drum section of the band that pulls up the rear. The cheerleaders traditionally ride on our town fire truck. Anticipating problems, Theodore makes sure that Spec has our fire truck waxed and polished and that he has secured a backup truck in case of an emergency. Spec has one truck in his arsenal. If there is a fire somewhere in town between 6:00 and 6:30, the parade is ruined. A couple of years back there was a house fire during one of our pregame parades. The cheerleaders were tossed off the truck like turnips as the unit sped off to respond to the call.

With Elizabeth Night – as it has come to be known in these parts – a few days off, I stay late at the Pharmacy to catch up on my work. Pearl is out front vacuuming and dusting. I am worried but trying not to show it. I figure I'll wait until all the big doings are over to deal with my own problems.

Pearl wraps the cord to the upright vacuum cleaner around the holder, then wipes down the front of the machine with a dust rag. 'Do you have a date for the Elizabeth Taylor dinner, Miss Ave?' she asks.

'I'm going with Mr. Tipton.'

'He'll be the center of attention after he knocks 'em dead with his halftime show; that's for sure.'

I nod and continue with my work. Pearl stands and looks at me.

'Do you need anything, Pearl?'

'Miss Ave, are you sure you want to give me the Pharmacy?'

'Yes. Absolutely. We're just waiting for the final paperwork and it will be yours. Why? Are you having second thoughts?'

'Don't you want to own this yourself? What if you get murried someday? I'm sure the place is worth something.'

I smile at Pearl. I was waiting until the paperwork was finalized before I shared the scope of our transaction. She will be shocked when she realizes that we are part of a chain of Mutual Pharmacies. She won't simply own a building and its contents, but she will have a very valuable franchise to sell or keep, if she so desires. Pearl doesn't realize she's coming into some money.

'Pearl, I'm never getting married.'

'Excuse me, ma'am, but how do you know that?'

'I just do.'

'You shouldn't never give up.'

Poor Pearl. She's a romantic. She doesn't understand what really goes on between adults. At fifteen, she could never comprehend the depth of the relationship I have with Theodore. Bells, whistles, gold bands, and a gown are not my idea of meaningful. I don't need to get married to feel whole.

'You really never tried to get murried?'

'No, ma'am, I didn't.' I'm sure she heard the rumors of Theodore's car at my house all night last weekend. She's fishing. My personal life has gone beyond gossip, and now the rumor mill wants to bump me to next level: marriage. Two grown adults cannot carry on a romance in this town without a marriage license.

'I thought everyone wanted to get murried.' Pearl shrugs.

'What makes you think I do?'

'You got rid of all the junk.'

'What are you talking about?'

'Well, you cleaned up the back. When I first worked here, it was a mess. Now it's empty. You've been fixing things up. Otto and Worley fixed your roof. Now you're paying them to repoint the bricks on this building. You're working less. You hired me to work here, even though Fleeta can handle it alone.'

'What are you saying?'

'You even gave me your business. Don't you see? Folks lighten up their lives when they're about to make a move.'

'Maybe I just got tired of having junk all over the place.'

'I don't think so. I think you're making space in your life to squeeze a man in.'

Pearl looks at me. I don't say anything, which she takes as a sign to shut up. She wheels the vacuum cleaner to the back storage closet.

'We'll be needing a new sweeper directly,' she says as she goes.

Sometimes I think Pearl Grimes is a very strange girl.

October 23 arrives gloriously without a cloud in the sky. The mountains are in the final stage of autumn, and the leaves have faded to a dull gold – the perfect backdrop for a woman who played the queen of Egypt. How I wish my mother had lived to see an actual movie star! My mother loved Elizabeth Taylor. She would go on and on about her perfect features: those eyes, that straight nose, the just-full-enough lips, that strong chin. Elizabeth Taylor is Dresden china, the finest white porcelain set off by that midnight-black hair.

Everyone is excited, and the nervousness is bringing out odd behavior in some of our townspeople, particularly the men. Ballard Littrell, our town drunk, has sobered up. He only has one ear – no one knows how he lost the other one – so he never gets his hair cut off on the left side. But he was seen at the barber, gussying up for the evening, trying to even out the sides. Otto and

Worley were seen at Zackie's store buying new shirts. They never buy anything new, so this is an important event for them. The women in town who are around Elizabeth's age, forty-five and up, took this milestone visit as a cue to upgrade their looks. Pearl noted that we have completely sold out of Black Sable hair dye and blue eye shadow.

I thought about closing the Pharmacy today, but I couldn't. I need to keep my mind busy. I am so nervous for Theodore; I want everything to be perfect for him tonight. He has worked so hard. I hope the kids don't crack under the pressure. There would be nothing worse than a fire baton going up in the air and landing on the visitors' bench instead of in the waiting hands of Tayloe Slagle. I can't imagine she'll choke, but you never know.

I decide to lock up early. Pearl is counting on it; she brought a new outfit with her to work this afternoon, and she plans to change in our powder room, then head off to the park to help Theodore set up the pyramids for the halftime show. I recruited her to work on Theodore's field crew. If there's one person who can handle a lot of pressure, it's Pearl. Just having her around is soothing.

The door bells jingle merrily. I look out the window and see a few folks milling on Main Street, staking out their spots for the parade. Two little boys stand in front of the register. They argue about whether to use their candy allowance for Good 'n Plenty or Hot Tamales. One look at their blond heads tells me they could only be Sweet Sue's boys.

'Are you the Tinsley boys?' I ask.

'I'm Jared and he's Chris,' says the older of the two.

'How much money have you got?'

'Two dimes, one nickel, and one penny.'

'You're in luck! It's two-for-one day. You get two boxes of candy for exactly twenty-six cents.' The boys jump up and down as the bells on the door ring again. I look up and see Jack MacChesney standing before me.

'What's taking you boys so long?'

'Jared couldn't pick fast,' Chris says.

'Well, go on now. Get in the truck.'

'We won't get no stickies on your seat, Uncle Jack,' Jared promises.

'Hey, how'd you get two boxes?'

'The lady give them to us.' Jared points to me.

'Did you thank her?'

'Thank you, ma'am,' they chorus, and run out. There's that word *ma'am* again. It really and truly bugs me. I must remember, these are little boys; to them, everyone is old, even their thirty-five-year-old mother.

Pearl comes out of the powder room in her new two-piece plaid suit. She looks like she's lost almost twenty pounds. She stops to check her makeup at her station but thinks better of it when she sees Jack MacChesney at my counter.

'That was mighty nice of you, Ave Maria,' Jack Mac says.

'They're cute kids.'

'Yes, ma'am, they are.'

I straighten the folds on my prescription clipboard, flattening the creases with one of the nickels Jared gave me. I can't look at Jack Mac, not because I'm embarrassed but because I don't have anything to say. What can I say to a man whose proposal I turned down? I wrack my brain, but small talk seems teeny tiny. Jack Mac just stands there, with his hands in his pockets, jiggling coins and keys. He takes the change out of his pocket and begins sorting it. I'm glad he looks down; it gives me a chance to fix my hair. I inhale. Why does he always smell so good?

'Oh no, the Hot Tamales were on the house. They couldn't

decide between Hot Tamales and Good 'n Plenty.' Jack Mac looks at me, confused.

'The kids, they only had—' Shut up, Ave Maria. The guy doesn't care what their favorite candy is; he's not their father, you idiot. He's Uncle Jack, the nice man who takes them for rides in his truck and plays catch with them. Uncle Jack, who will some-day be their step-daddy.

'You going to the dinner tomorrow night?'

'Yes.' Is he a loon or what? Asking me if I'm going to the dinner. He should hate me. I was so rude to him. And now he's standing here putting change in every single fund-raising jar on my counter. The coins drop into the jars, one clink, two clink, three clink; and it's a good thing, they fill up the silence.

'Well, I guess I better be going,' he says, and turns and walks out.

'He likes you,' Pearl announces as she rolls her lips with Bonne Bell strawberry gloss.

If only she knew. But I can't tell her.

'He looks at you like you're the most beautiful woman he ever saw. He'd dump Sweet Sue for you in a second.'

'He'd be a fool if he did that.'

'No, he wouldn't.' Pearl can be very stubborn. 'You know some-thing, Miss Ave? If I was him, and I had to pick between Sweet Sue and any other woman in town and you, I'd pick you.'

'You're very nice to say that.' I wish she would stop.

'I'd pick you because there's just something about you. You're sparkly. Yeah. That's it. Sparkly.' Pearl grabs her purse and goes to the door. 'See you on the field.'

I wear my very best coat – a red velvet swing coat – so Theodore can single me out from the announcer's booth. As I look out over the crowd in the stands, I realize that pretty much everyone in town had the same idea. We look like a hunter's convention, splashes of red and bright orange throughout the stands. Everyone wore their loudest and brightest clothing; perhaps subconsciously we are hoping Elizabeth Taylor will see us in the crowd and single us out with a smile or a wink. Fleeta flags me down from the top of the stands with a purple light wand she got at a University of Tennessee football game. She elbows Portly to wave at me; he does.

The crowd in the visitors' section is filled with overflow from our stands. Rye Cove is a small village, much smaller than Big Stone Gap. When we play them, it seems pathetic to even cheer against them since they have no manpower at all in their stands and just as little on the field. We'll beat them decisively tonight, and we should; after all, we're the side that's got the movie star.

The teams aren't on the field yet. They're lined up around the track to wave to Elizabeth Taylor. I look all around the park, and everyone is standing. There's a buzz, but it is definitely reverential. The band curves off the parking lot and onto the track, a long Carolina-blue snake, precise and pliable. And then there she is! The convertible! With her! The car harrumphs over the parking-lot median and bounces onto the track; for a moment I worry Elizabeth and her husband will be thrown off of their backseat perch. But they hang on to each other and laugh. I'm in a perfect spot to get a real good look at her.

I haven't heard this much cheering since we won the state championship in 1972. The crowd rises to their feet. The stadium fills with sound that echoes into the black mountains behind us. The chanting: 'Liz! Liz! Liz!' The occasional gut holler: 'I love you!' cuts through the din, all of us, yelling, whistling, applauding, thrilled! Notice us! Over here! See me, Elizabeth! We've sure been watching you all these many years! Watch us!

The convertible rolls around the track slowly. On the front grid of the car is a sign from the Nabisco distributor that reads, DON'T GO 'ROUND HUNGRY. HAVE YOUR NABS – short for Nabisco crackers around these parts. Cas Walker must have cut a deal with his distributors. I hope somebody explained to Elizabeth what Nabs are.

The convertible gingerly inches up to the fifty-yard line, where I am standing. Spec is behind the wheel. He sees me, and he knows I love old movies, so he practically slows to a stop so I can get a close-up look.

Elizabeth Taylor is exquisite. She is wearing a flowing emerald-green silk tunic and matching pants. The neckline is an off-center V, which is quite becoming. Her shoulder-length hair is pulled back into a low chignon, and she has a large yellow flower tucked over one ear. I am close enough to see into the car. She has kicked off a very pretty pair of matching green pumps. Her feet are bare, and her toe-nails are painted hot pink. But it is her expression, the sweet smile – not forced, genuine – that gets me. She is so happy to see us! Her eyes *are* violet! I look over at Nellie Goodloe, who seems relieved. The theme colors are a real homage now. There is something peculiar about Nellie; now I see what. She has rinsed her hair coal black. Poor old Nellie; be a leader, I want to tell her, not a follower.

Elizabeth is tiny, with delicate hands and feet, like a child's. She is a little chubby, but on her – it just softens her, so it's as though she's a little blurry, not a hard angle on her. Three of the ladies from the Methodist sewing circle stand behind me. Their comments are not as generous. Joella Reasor, who has always battled a weight problem, comments to her friends, 'All my life I wanted to look like her, and now I do.'

I see Theodore up in the announcer's booth, which angles out over the home section. He is in the window, examining the field from on high. I give him a thumbs-up, and he waves to me. Then I look back to the convertible. Candidate Warner gives me a thumbs-up; I guess he thought I was signaling to him. I feel a little guilty. I'd never vote for him, since I'm a Democrat. But you know what? It doesn't hurt anything to let him think I might. He smiles a big, beamy, vote-for-me smile, and I give him a thumbs-up too.

A team of folks helps Elizabeth and the candidate up to their seats. The football players take the field, but no one even notices the game. Luster Camp, a sweet soul of a man with a feeble mind, is our unofficial high school mascot. He takes his usual cheering spot in front of the home stands – tonight he's in direct view of Elizabeth Taylor's perch. Luster loves our team and leads very amusing cheers, but he isn't exactly the ambassador we want to flaunt in front of a visiting movie star. Luster, however, is undeterred. It's just another game night to him, and he's got a job to do. The crowd looks down at him as a mother does to a child who is about to embarrass her deeply in public. *Please don't*, they seem to be pleading with their eyes.

'Y'all. Y'all,' Luster shouts. 'It's time for a cheer!'

The kids in the stands usually cheer loudly for him, but tonight their silence sends a strong message: *Luster, sit down. Please don't humiliate us in front of Virginia Woolf.*

'Beans and corn bread got in a fight! Beans knocked the corn bread outta sight. That's what Powell Valley is gonna do tonight!'

Elizabeth Taylor laughs and applauds as though the cheer is the funniest she has ever heard.

'One more!' Luster shouts. 'Two bits, four bits, six bits, a dollah. All for the Vikings, stand up and hollah!'

Elizabeth applauds again. The crowd, taking their cue from her, stand and cheer. Luster bows deeply, then disappears into the crowd in his torn raincoat and porkpie hat. I doubt he knew Elizabeth Taylor was in the crowd.

I watch every moment of the second quarter tick off, hoping it will end and afraid for it to end. How on earth is Theodore handling this pressure? I want his show to be magnificent. We just can't make any mistakes. The band empties out onto the track silently as the final seconds of the quarter pass. The teams run off the field. The band files past the home section and across to the goal line, one by one.

The announcer in the booth, who calls the game for local radio, blows into the microphone as we all look toward him.

'Ladies and gents. We got a show fer you tonight. Now we got the prettiest gal in Hollywood here, and this here show is full of all the stuff from her movies. So sit back and relax, spit out your tobacky, and let's get happy! Here we go, folks, the Powell Valley Viking marching band!'

The crowd leaps to their feet, applauding and cheering. The pyramids are ready to roll. I see the shimmer of Tayloe's Cleopatra costume from her hiding place under the visitors' bleachers. She's right where she should be. Then something very odd happens. The drum majorette blows her whistle. Not once, not twice, but four times. And then she waits and blows it again. She isn't blowing it at the band – they are frozen in position waiting to begin. Their eyes are wide and full of horror. There on the twenty-yard line, several feet from where the band is to make its first formation, are King and Cora, the town strays, two large mutts, fed by all and adopted by no one. King has mounted Cora. Cora either senses the crowd or is through with King; either way, she does not want to be doing this right now. I can't help but think that the dogs took on all of the nervous energy in our town and now have to release it. The urgent humping is rhythmic, almost saying, *Please let this be over. Let this show be over. Let it be over now.*

Another hush falls over the crowd, and everyone looks to the queen for her response. Elizabeth Taylor is ignoring the dogs and chatting with her aide. Theodore is slumped in the announcer's booth. I look over at Pearl, who shrugs at me, wordlessly asking, *What are we supposed to do?* One of the referees can't take it another second, so he trots out onto the field to separate the dogs. Spec runs after the ref shouting loudly enough for everyone to hear, 'You can't pull 'em apart, they'll bite you, you stupid son of a bitch.' So we do the best we can in this terrible situation. We let them hump and we wait it out. This has to be the longest-lasting sex act on record. Finally, King depletes himself. He climbs off Cora and runs into the end zone with a gallop worthy of Secretariat. Cora slinks off into the shadows. The drum majorette blows her whistle. Finally. Finally. The show.

From the first pinwheel formation, the kids are perfect. They play the music so grandly, and what an arrangement! Seamlessly and beautifully, they rondelet through every major theme of every major Elizabeth Taylor movie. She stands and places her hands on the rail of the platform, leaning over the edge like she wants to be close to this majestic, loving salute. Then the flag girls pivot across the fifty-yard line, single file, and magically disappear under the pyramids. The three pyramids move into place and then BOOM! The lights in the stadium go out, the crowd cheers and whistles; and there in center field, surrounded by fire batons, is Tayloe Slagle, in full Cleopatra garb, including jet-black wig, posed Egyptian-style. Her figure is amazing; she is curvy but lean, just like Elizabeth Taylor when she was Cleopatra. Tayloe takes two batons and begins to twirl them like the pro she is. She twists and bends and tosses and catches and smiles, effortlessly, smoothly, and with such sass. The effect in this dark ball-park is dazzling. Pearl, who has run all the way from the other side of the track in the dark, comes up behind me, breathless. We stand and watch the show with awe. Even though we helped, we cannot believe how beautiful it is.

'She is so talented,' Pearl decides as she watches Tayloe.

'Yes, she is. But baton twirling is not a skill one needs later in life.' I don't know why I think I always have to teach Pearl lessons. I am not the oracle of Big Stone Gap, after all.

The lights bolt back on; everyone is cheering. The band plays off and exits the field. They pass Elizabeth's perch; she is weeping and throwing them kisses. Then the most amazing thing happens: she turns to the announcer's booth and throws Theodore a kiss. And then she bows to him! She actually bows! I will never forget this moment as long as I live.

The Coach House Inn is the only real restaurant in Big Stone Gap. We do have the Bus Terminal Café and the Sub Sandwich Carry-Out, but they are strictly casual. There is Jackson's Fish & Fry, but they only serve Sunday brunch. Punch-and-cake wedding receptions are held in the church basement fellowship rooms. So, all the rest of life's events – holidays, Lions and Kiwanis club meetings, and family buffets – are held right here at the Coach House.

The building is a simple colonial-style red brick square, with black shutters and a sloping white roof. A sign swings from the entryway: a black silhouette of a nineteenth-century coach driver whipping a team of horses with a fancy carriage behind him. The artist who painted the coach and driver is the same one who made my nurse in a rush. The eats are terrific. The food is fresh and delectable – salty, crusty, spicy, hot fried chicken (on Sundays it's called Gospel Bird), with biscuits so light and fluffy, one person could eat a dozen. Nellie made the entrance look lovely. She borrowed the large ficus plants in brass urns from the bank, so when you enter the Coach House, you are completely surrounded by lush foliage. Edna and Ledna Tackett, the town twins, now in their late sixties, are dressed alike in pale blue serge suits and hand out programs for the evening.

The programs are pretty; Nellie really has a knack. She is the doyenne of our Corn Bread Aristocracy. The program covers are made from lavender construction paper, with a tiny purple silk African violet glued on, framed by a small grosgrain ribbon. Inside, the agenda for the evening is laid out in a fancy calligraphy:

Welcome Candidate and Mrs. John Warner
Library Fund-raising Dinner
October 24, 1978 — 6.30 p.m.
The Coach House Inn

Invocation: Reverend Elmo Gaspar

Dinner: Chicken & Fixings
honoring the great career of screen legend Elizabeth Taylor
Aperitif: 'Little Women' crabbies and punch
Salad: 'Sandpiper' potato salad
Main course: 'Cleopatra' fried chicken and 'Butterfield 8' biscuits
Dessert: 'National (Red) Velvet' cake and ice cream
Coffee & Tea

Introduction: Mrs. Nellie Goodloe, Chair
Remarks: Candidate John Warner

The back cover reads: 'Compliments of the Dollar General Store'; then in musical notes, its theme-song refrain:

♪Who says a dollar won't buy much anymore?
Every day is dollar day!
At the Dollar General Store!♪
(I guess they paid for the programs.)

Theodore looks handsome in his gray slacks, navy blazer, and pale blue necktie that brings out his eyes (classic.) I'm wearing a black cocktail dress with a peacock brooch of Austrian crystals. I put my hair up in a fancy do. Through the bay windows at the front of the Coach House I can see a few hundred dressed-up folks milling around. No alcohol allowed (technically), as this is a dry county (nonenforceable), but Nellie Goodloe has made sure there's a champagne punch with lime sherbet. Nerves have calmed down considerably, but a touch of the spirits will soothe folks even more.

Liz and her husband have not arrived yet. Theodore is instantly swarmed and congratulated for his halftime spectacular. I am so very happy for him. He beams, as would any artist, having reached a mass audience. The women in the room are dressed in their finest, and it's funny, most of them wear a bright flower in their hair. Not to be outdone, I snap a white carnation off a table arrangement and tuck it behind my ear.

Iva Lou sees me and comes right over. Her dress is a masterpiece – a floor-length gown of peach quiana polyester. The skirt is full and flowing, with a short train at the back. The bodice is fitted tightly like a series of rubber bands. It looks very traditional, except for the fit. The little modern touch is an appliqué on the chest – a picture of three books standing upright on a shelf, outlined in seed pearls and dotted with sequins.

'Ave! Get this! We raised two thousand seven hundred and fifty dollars tonight! Isn't that something?'

'Congratulations!' I am thrilled for Iva Lou. Finally, all her connections have paid off.

'What do you think, girl?' Iva Lou twirls in her gown.

'You are spectacular.'

She flashes a big grin, then sticks out her chest and points to the appliqué. 'Lyle told me this dress could turn him into an avid reader. I'm gonna let him peruse my card catalog directly following this shindig. What do you think?'

'I think Lyle is the luckiest man in Wise County.'

'I think you might be right. Well, if he ain't now, we'll make sure he is tonight.' Iva Lou struts off toward a salivating Lyle, planting the seeds for later.

Lew and Inez Eisenberg are already sitting at their table. Inez looks pretty in her turquoise muumuu. She has chopsticks in her hair for that exotic touch. Their expressions are pleasant, but they aren't speaking; they're looking off in separate directions. I feel sorry for them. Spec picks the crabbies off a tray as they are passed. He gives one to his wife, who is sitting next to Inez. They don't have much to say to each other either.

I work the room and folks are pleasant; it's partly the alcohol and partly the presence of a television-camera crew from WCYB out of Kingsport, Tennessee. They've sent Johnny Wood, anchorman, reporter, and weatherman, to cover this event. He looks shorter and squatter on TV than he does in real life. He sweats in real life just like he does on TV, though. He seems cordial, but he's here to do a job so he hasn't time for small talk. Folks respect that and generally leave him alone. We've never been on the TV before, so we're on our best behavior.

'New dress?' Aunt Alice asks from behind me.

'This old thing?'

'It doesn't look old to me.'

'You look very nice tonight, Aunt Alice.' She is taken aback, and her eyes narrow suspiciously.

'Enough about that. What's going on with our business arrangement?'

'Mr. Eisenberg is handling it. You know lawyers take their sweet time.'

'I just want it done.' Before Aunt Alice can wind up and upset me further, I walk away. Theodore is surrounded by a fresh batch of admirers. I decide to place my evening bag at our dinner table. Iva Lou wasn't kidding; we are sitting right next to Elizabeth Taylor's table.

'You look very pretty,' a voice whispers. I look up and it's Jack Mac, giving me the once-over like I'm a brand-new 1978 Ford pickup truck, fully loaded.

'Thank you.' I in turn look him over, and my expression of surprise gives me away. He is crisp and classic in a navy blue suit with a barely there gray pinstripe. His shirt is pristine white, though the collar seems a little tight. The tie is scarlet red and made of fine Chinese silk.

'New duds,' he says, indicating the suit.

'They're lovely.' *Lovely?* I have never used that word in my life. It is a mamaw word, a sewing-circle word, an old-lady word. And besides, he doesn't look lovely, he looks downright handsome.

'My father's tie.'

'That's very good silk, you know.' I can't resist touching it; I love delicate silks. My mother used to smack my hands when I touched the fabric while she was sewing.

'Pap got it over in France somewhere during the Second World War.'

'Take good care of it.' Now, why do I say that? Is taking care of his wardrobe any of my business? What do I care if he wads it up and uses it for an oil rag?

'I wanted to talk to you about the other night.' For a moment I don't know what he's referring to; it's been a while since Apple Butter Night, and I haven't had time to think about any of that. He senses this and almost drops the subject, but he can't since he brought it up, so now he's stuck. I don't help matters by acting vague.

'I never meant to insult you or upset you in any way. I'm very sorry.' I don't know what to say. It's not like he shot me or anything. He proposed. His look of concern makes me uncomfortable.

'All's well that ends well. You're back with Sweet Sue, I see.' Sweet Sue is working the crowd like a canteen chanteuse. She's wearing a silvertone halter dress, her hair in a golden fountain. Her eyes are painted with a dusty lavender powder. Her teeth are so white, they gleam. She looks like she fell right out of the *Knoxville News Sentinel* style section.

'Not exactly.' Jack Mac says this with a smile and looks off to her and then back to me. This cavalier smirk really annoys me. Does he think he's juggling the affections of the town beauty and the town spinster? Does he see me as the pitiful one who needs the man, and Sweet Sue as the one who gets to pick? For a split second Jack MacChesney is the enemy. But I remember myself; I am not involved with this man. His duplicitous nonsense is not my problem. I am not the other woman. He tried to set that up but I did not play.

'You know, Jack, I'm just a pill-counting pharmacist. And I don't know much, I'll be the first to tell you. But from my seat, women ought not be trifled with. You have a beautiful girl over there. You ought to concentrate on her. Her alone.'

Jack Mac looks at me a little confused. 'You think we're togeth-er?' he asks.

'You brought her to the dinner.'

'Actually, I bought these tickets when we were together, then circumstances presented—'

'You take care of her kids.' Does he think I'm an idiot?

'I can't just drop those boys. I've been seeing her for over a year. They've come to know me and trust me. I won't just disap-pear on them.'

'Okay. Fine.' I roll my eyes and look away, hoping he'll take the hint and shove off. But he stays.

'You're here with Theodore. Explain the difference to me.'

'Wait a second. I can see whomever I please. Okay? I haven't been going around town willy-nilly, proposing to people and then jumping in bed with ex-lovers.'

'You are really something,' he growls without an ounce of kind-ness.

'Yes, I am. I have principles!' I have my hands on my hips, and my neck is three inches off its pins, thrusting my face into Jack Mac's. He does not step back. I don't either. We are eye-to-eye, nose-to-nose. His breath is sweet, and his eyes are on fire.

'You're bitter and you're lonely. You're determined to stay that way. So stay that way. I don't have to take your bull. I won't take it. Ma'am.' He turns and goes.

Theodore comes up behind me. 'What was that all about?'

'What a jackass.' Theodore and I watch as Jack Mac excuses himself through the crowd to get to his table.

'Nice suit, though.' Theodore shrugs.

Elizabeth Taylor has just pulled up. We know this immediate-ly because the headlights from the staff car are bright and aimed directly into the restaurant through the bay windows. The entire restaurant is flooded with light, and now with anticipation. It was one thing to see her in a convertible last night; she was still far away and dreamy as she is on a movie screen. But tonight she will be sitting in a room with us, having dinner! We're going to be way up close. It's thrilling.

Johnny Wood is giving directions to the TV crew, and the crowd, full of anticipation, chatters loudly. Theodore and I kneel on our chairs to watch her entrance over the crowd.

Several aides precede her through the entrance, clearing a path for her and the candidate. Elizabeth enters, wearing a floor-length royal-purple caftan, with three-quarter-length dolman sleeves and a boat neck. Her hair is down, blown straight to her shoulders. What look like large Indian beads, in agates of gold, purple, and brown, hang around her neck like royal jewels. She is absolutely breathtaking again tonight. Nellie Goodloe greets her at the entrance and gives her a quick hug. Elizabeth points to the rose tucked over Nellie's ear; Nellie blushes.

John Warner, a former undersecretary of the U.S. Navy, looks presidential in his deep navy blue suit, white shirt, and red, white and blue striped tie. He has the tall good looks of a Northern Virginia land baron. He is confident but impatient. He scoops the shock of thick gray hair away from his forehead with his hand a lot – it reminds me of President Kennedy. Folks say he's lucky to be running for the Senate at all. He came in second to Dick Obenshain in the primary last year. Then, in an unexpected tragedy, Mr. Obenshain was killed in a plane crash. The Republicans went to their runner-up, Mr. Warner, and asked him to run in Mr. Obenshain's place. He politely obliged. The papers say Mr. Warner is an old-fashioned political pot sticker; you lose a man, and he'll seal the hole. You can see he's a little put off by the attention his wife receives, but he can't exactly make her sit in the car. She brings out the voters, and that's exactly what this dark-horse Republican candidate needs to win. I wonder how he feels about always coming in second, first to Obenshain and now to his wife. Maybe he doesn't care, as long as he's in the race. He looks amazingly well-rested for a man with only ten days until the election. That's probably just good breeding. Grace under pressure is a Virginia gentleman's calling card.

Zackie Wakin strolls past the aides toward Elizabeth Taylor. He extends his hand to her. She extends hers to him, and he kisses it like a prince. The crowd woos. Zackie, the feriner peddler, charms the movie star. Zackie is small but so is she. As they stand eye-to-eye, he and Elizabeth take on that romantic Moviola glow that comes in those love scenes when the man looks down, not *at* the woman, but into her soul. Elizabeth, forever the game girl, throws her head back and laughs a few times. We can hear snippets of their conversation. She knows a lot about Lebanese culture. She accompanied Richard Burton to the Middle East when he was making a picture in the late sixties. When the aides hear her speak of a former husband, Elizabeth is hustled away, following her current husband into the kitchen to greet the staff. She turns and looks over her shoulder at Zackie, shrugs as if to say, 'Sorry we were interrupted,' and waves to him.

The kitchen doors swing open, and we hear the candidate say, 'I'm John Warner, candidate for the United States Senate. I'd like to count on y'all on November fourth.' I read in the paper that this is something John Warner likes to do. As much as he likes the muckety-mucks out front, the folks who make the meal are the ones who vote en masse.

Theodore and I are close to the galley doors that lead to the kitchen, so we scoot to the circular windows and peer in as Elizabeth and Warner take their tour. The deep aluminum serving pans are full of golden fried chicken. One pan holds only wings; they look so succulent, I want to go into the kitchen and grab a few. Elizabeth Taylor has the same thought, and as Warner blah-blahs to the chef, she bends over and samples a breast. She holds it with two hands, pinky up, and bites into the meaty part near the bones carefully, so as not to smear her perfect peach lipstick. Warner refers to Elizabeth, and she nods as she chews. He shoots her a dirty look when he sees she's sampled the chicken. She downs a large hunk quickly to finish it off and get back to the campaigning. She swallows, but something is terribly wrong. She gags. I know from Rescue Squad training that she is choking, so I burst into the kitchen. She is holding her throat and looking helpless. She cannot speak. I can see the scar on her creamy neck from an operation she had years ago. It is still pink.

'Miss Taylor. Let me get help.'

I hear the aides murmur, 'Who is she?' and the staff tells them I'm with the Rescue Squad. Theodore hollers for Spec, which triggers a buzz throughout the dining room. Spec pushes through the swinging doors like John Wayne, scans the kitchen, finds Elizabeth, and runs to her. Theodore follows.

'She swallowed a chicken bone, Spec,' I say.

'Jesus Christ. Run git the ambulance around tout suite.' Spec tosses me his key ring. Theodore and I run through the dinner crowd, out the entrance, and into the ambulance. We speed around back, open the rear chute, pull out the gurney, and wheel it into the kitchen. Warner is yelling at Spec and his aides, but mostly he seems frustrated with Elizabeth for choking.

Spec works like a pro, lifting Elizabeth onto the gurney. He carefully straps her in and checks the wheel locks. You know, folks complain that Spec runs around town in the ambulance, using it for personal reasons, but I bet they're mighty glad that he drove it here tonight. It just may save Elizabeth Taylor's life.

Spec and I load Elizabeth into the ambulance. Warner is now extremely upset, holding his wife's hand and stroking her face. Luckily, Dr. Gladys Baronagan, the Filipino physician from Lonesome Pine Hospital, came to the dinner with her husband and was recruited to help in the emergency. I hear her tell Spec that she may need to operate.

Even in tragedy, Elizabeth could not be more beautiful. She lies on the gurney like a lavender lily. She takes pain like a trouper, and believe me, I've seen all sorts of suffering and sometimes folks act pretty crazy. But she is almost beatific, like she expects that bad things will happen, and by God, you just deal with them and go through them and don't let them kill you. Her eyes say, *I won't die. Just get the damned bone out of my throat!*

Theodore and I jump into his car and follow the ambulance up to the hospital. When we get there, Miss Taylor is whisked through admissions and brought directly to the emergency room. A small crowd has gathered but no words are spoken. It's a hell of a thing. Spec paces nervously outside the ER. We pray everything will go smoothly.

Theodore and I are starving, so we eat a variety of junk from the vending machines and wash it down with instant coffee. Candidate Warner is in a special room right outside the emergency room, so we can't see him. Several aides mill about, one more worried-looking than the next.

Finally, after about an hour, a nurse comes out to talk to us. Dr. Baronagan ran a rubber pipe down Miss Taylor's throat, pushing the bone down into her stomach, where it would dissolve in digestion. No need for surgery. Miss Taylor will be fine. Johnny Wood and his crew enter and make a beeline for the nurse; he wants an exclusive for the eleven o'clock report. She holds up her hands and asks the men to leave, telling them, 'This is a hospital, not a circus.' Johnny Wood shrugs and takes his crew outside. He films his story on the sidewalk.

'What's wrong with you?' Theodore asks as he turns to me.

'I'm fine,' I tell him, holding my head in my hands.

'Let me see.' He lifts my face with his hands and examines it carefully.

'You look pale,' he decides.

'I ate too much candy. That's all.'

'Let's go.' Theodore laughs.

But I don't think it was the candy. I kept replaying the scene of Jack Mac telling me I was bitter and lonely until it upset my stomach. But I don't have to share that with Theodore. You don't have to tell your best friend everything.

CHAPTER SEVEN

We never saw Elizabeth Taylor again. After the bone was dislodged, she rested for several hours; then, in the wee hours of the morning, she was transported out of Big Stone Gap by helicopter to a large hospital in Richmond, on the other side of the state. She recuperated there for the remaining days of the campaign. John Warner won the election by a hair; many thought he got a lot of sympathy votes because his wife suffered an accident while on the stump for him. It's a shame that Big Stone Gap will be remembered not for the way we honored her but as the campaign stop where Elizabeth Taylor swallowed a chicken bone. Folks round here have a theory about it all: Maybe there's some old Scotch-Irish curse on us. After all, the coal mining boom never made us the Pittsburgh of the South; now we've choked an international movie star; maybe we're just not meant to be part of the Big World.

After all the hoopla (which gave me a chance to put my life on hold), I face myself again. I finally sit down and write my Aunt Meoli another letter. I haven't heard back from my last one to her, but I don't mind. The letter writing is cathartic. My first letter was slight and friendly, this one will be long. I figure she's in her sixties now, so I start the letter with a request for her to be with somebody before she continues reading the letter, in case she passes out or something. It is very hard for me to write about my mother's death, but knowing that this is my mother's sister, I give her every detail to the best of my recollection. Mama always expected the whole truth from me – how ironic – so I assume her sister would, too. I don't know why Mama didn't tell me about her family, especially since we had thirteen years without Fred Mulligan around. What was she still afraid of? Why didn't she see our trip as an opportunity to clear her conscience and share the truth with me? There were so many opportunities for her to tell me her story. When our passports arrived, she could have told me everything then. She could have told me on the plane to Italy. Pick any number of days, of moments inside those days, when it was just the two of us, here alone in this house, in private, without the threat of any outsider. She could have unburdened herself. What a gift the truth would have been! We could have flown to Italy together and reunited with the people I come from. She could have introduced me to her family. We could have stayed with them, learned about them, caught up on all the time that had gone by. I would have aunts and uncles and cousins who loved me. Look at all I missed in the bubble of a lie.

I'm about to dig into a nice slice of a chocolate layer cake that the Tackett sisters dropped off (the other half was delivered to Theodore). I've been getting a lot of covered dishes since I was part of the team that saved Elizabeth Taylor's life. I whip up some fresh cream. I have a nice steaming mug of coffee. I'm in my softest flannel pajamas, with my feet up, when the phone rings.

It's Spec. (Who else?) He needs me to go down to the Freewill Baptist Church with him. I beg him to make the run alone, because I'm tired (and by the way, I forgot to tell you, Spec, I'm quitting). But he begs me, so I agree to go with him. About five minutes go by before Spec honks, and I run, grabbing my kit on the way out.

As we speed across town to the church on the riverbank, Spec fills me in. Reverend Gaspar was preaching a revival to a packed house when he took two poisonous rattlesnakes out of a cage and started handling them. One bit him.

'Relax. I gave Preacher Gaspar a serum a while back. Doc Daugherty made him take the prescription.' Spec doesn't respond, he just takes a deep drag off his cigarette. This is one of those go-nowhere runs I got suckered into because Spec insisted. A snakebite is a one-man job. Wash and dress the wound, and out. I picture that moist layer cake sitting on my coffee table at home, and it makes me real cross.

The Freewill Baptist Church is a one-room building made of sandstone. The simple roof has a cross painted on it. The front door is painted bright red to keep the Devil out. Spec and I can hear wailing from the congregation, but this is typical for a revival. People come to cleanse themselves of their sins and seek redemption. That can get loud.

We enter through the rear of the church. Dicie Sturgill, a small sturdy woman with a shock of red hair, meets us at the back pew. She is very upset. She leads us up the aisle to Reverend Gaspar, who is lying on the floor of the altar with someone's coat wadded up under his head for a pillow. About twelve believers are laying their hands on him and speaking in tongues. I recognize one of the faces from a Rescue Squad run last year: a rambunctious fifteen-year-old trouble-maker named Den-Bob Snodgrass. During girls' PE one morning he came out of the boys' dressing room bouncing a basketball, buck naked. The girls saw him, start-

ed screaming, and ran out into the hallways, creating a stampede.
Den-Bob was suspended, but he never returned to finish school.
He went to work in the mines instead.

Reverend Gaspar moans softly. His wrist is wrapped in a wad
of paper towel, and the blood is seeping through. I dress his
wound while Spec quizzes him. Spec asks Reverend Gaspar if he
took the serum. The preacher cannot focus; his response tells me
he hasn't taken the serum, but I can't be sure. I ask his wife, who
is crying and praying at his feet, to take a seat. She is wailing loudly, asking Jesus to save him. I tell Spec to finish wrapping the
wound; maybe I can get through to the preacher. I ask the hand
layers to take to their seats, as the patient needs air. They oblige.
One of them puts her arms around Mrs Gaspar and leads her to
the front pew, a simple wooden bench. Spec prepares a shot to
administer to the preacher. If he already took the serum, it won't
hurt; and if he didn't, I pray this will do the trick.

'Reverend, can you hear me? It's me, Ave Maria. You got a
nasty bite.' He smiles as though he understands.

Then Den-Bob Snodgrass leaps up, pulls a pistol out of his
pants, and shoots the snakes writhing in the cage on the altar.
Blood and thin strips of brown and green snakeskin explode everywhere. The congregation screams out in horror.

'Goddamn rattlers!' Den-Bob cries. Two men grab him, take
the gun, and hustle him out of the church. Spec and I keep our
cool and continue with our business, though I feel I might throw
up. I have a fleeting thought that no one ever changes; Den-Bob
Snodgrass was a loose cannon before he chose the Lord, and he's
a loose cannon now.

'Reverend, did you take the serum?'

He does not answer me.

'We have to take you to the hospital.'

'No,' he says clearly.

'We have to. You got bit.'

'No!'

Spec looks at me like, *We're taking him anyway. Let's wrap this up and get him out of here.* Preacher Gaspar's face has begun to swell. As we lift him onto the gurney, a small vial falls out of his jacket. It's the sealed bottle of serum I sold him. I slip it into my pocket, hoping his wife didn't notice.

Spec barks for folks to clear the aisle. We get Reverend Gaspar outside and hoist him into the back of the ambulance. Spec drives, and I stay in the back with the reverend.

I hold his hand. He still has the strength to squeeze my hand, and I tell him to keep squeezing. He asks for water, and I give it to him. He has something he wants to say to me. First, he takes another sip.

'Why didn't you take the serum, Preacher?' I ask him.

'Faith,' he says. His grip on my hand loosens.

'Hurry, Spec.'

I look down at Preacher Gaspar. His expression is one of contentment. I can't understand this. He's in pain. Why isn't he crying out?

Men look so very small when they're dying. He seems like a child to me. I hold his hand and squeeze it gently, awaiting a response. I don't get one. He still has a pulse, though; he has quietly slipped into a coma.

Spec drives me home. We are silent most of the trip from the hospital. Reverend Gaspar died at 3:33 A.M.; some folks noted that Christ died at the age of thirty-three, and maybe there is some connection. Spec and I have never lost a patient, so we've never walked this territory with each other before. He drops me off and

I walk up the steps, into my old house, but I don't feel like it's home anymore. I left all the lights on; the cake and coffee are where I left them, the whipped cream now a flat sandy pool. I take the dishes to the kitchen and throw everything out. I wash the plate and the fork and the glass. I don't cry, but I can't get Reverend Gaspar's face out of my mind.

It is a glorious late-November day, perfect for apple picking or a funeral. In a simple pinewood casket Reverend Gaspar is laid out in a white gown. Field flowers are gathered with ribbons and set about the foot of the casket. The Freewill Baptist Church has never been so crowded. Almost all of the local preachers from the other denominations flank the altar, including my Catholic priest, a gentle old Irishman out of Buffalo, New York.

The Mormon brothers peruse the crowd and nod to me in recognition. I smile at them in appreciation; they sent me a family tree researched by the Mormons on my behalf. The only problem was that they were off in the spelling of Mario Barbari's name. They researched the Bonboni family instead. While the Bonbonis were talented olive oil pressers, they were not related to me. I didn't have the heart to tell the boys they made a mistake, so I sat through their spiel and acted excited about the discovery.

There is much singing and revelry. Folks stand and talk about Preacher Gaspar, how he helped them find Jesus; how he prayed with them and for them; how he was a real preacher, a genuine apostle who could tell a story and make you believe it. I couldn't help thinking about his preaching at our school when I was a girl. We were a little scared of him, and also in awe. The word *faith* keeps popping up, and I remember how he said it the night he died. It sends a chill through me.

✲

At the end of the funeral, after Pee Wee Poteet plays 'In the Sweet By and By' on his fiddle, Dicie Sturgill gets up to read a letter that the reverend wrote to his flock in the event of his death. The very mention of this letter sends the women in the church into a wailing spell. When it goes on a tad too long, Dicie gives them a look that says, *Do you want to weep, or do you want me to read this here letter after all?* The wailing trails off to nose blowing and sniffling. Then she reads:

My dear Friends in Jesus the Lord:

In my life I found Jesus, my Lord and Savior, in all things, in work and play. Jesus wasn't Somebody I turned to when I was sick or sad. I had fun with Him, too. He was with me wherever I went, whether it was to preach up at the school or fishing in Powell Valley Lake on a Saturday morning. He was always with me and I hope I knew Him well. Instead of a punch-and-cookie reception in the Fellowship Hall, I've arranged for all of you to go to Shug's Lanes and bowl the afternoon away. I want you to have some fun with Jesus. Listen to one another, laugh and see the great glory of God in each other. It is there, my friends, believe me. Sometimes we just don't have the eyes to see it. Have a set on me.

Devotedly yours, Reverend Elmo Gaspar

One thing we do very well in the Gap is follow instructions. So after we put the reverend in the ground, the funeral procession headed right down Shawnee Avenue to Shug's Bowling Lanes. Midge and Shug Hall had the lanes ready, the balls polished, the Nabs out, the pop poured, and the scorecards empty.

We pour into the bowling alley, teaming up to play a series or two. No one is impatient or competitive. We each wait and take our turn and enjoy watching others play. Even the old ladies join in the fun. There are tears here and there, but mostly there is laughter and story-telling and good eats.

Iva Lou and I excuse ourselves to go to the ladies' room. You have to walk down one of the far aisle lanes to get to the back where the bathrooms are. I remember how self-conscious I was in the first buds of puberty when I made that long walk to the bathroom. One week I was a kid with a wad of bubble gum, bouncing all around this place; within a month or two, I hit adolescence and was horrified to be on display and draw attention to myself on the way to the bathroom. Today, as Iva Lou and I make the long walk, the self-consciousness is gone. We just hope a ball doesn't pop over the aisle and hit us. Shug's is packed with lousy bowlers; balls are flying everywhere.

When we get to the back, we pause for a moment, because instead of LADIES and MEN printed on each of the rest room doors, there are two pictures to choose from: POINTERS and SETTERS. The POINTERS door has a picture of a hunting dog; the SETTERS door has a picture of a dog sitting by a hearth. 'We're setters,' Iva Lou announces as she shoves the door open.

June Walker is at the sink, washing her hands. 'Ain't this awful about Preacher Gaspar?' We nod sadly. June continues, 'You know death comes in threes, so I done guess we got two more to go.'

'I don't think you have to worry about that old superstition. There have already been three deaths.' I tell June's reflection in the mirror.

'How do you figure?' June asks.

'Well, there was Reverend Gaspar and the two snakes. That makes three.'

As we primp at the mirror, we hear the balls rolling down the lanes toward the pins. When the balls hit the back wall of the lanes to go into the return aisle, they sound like they are going to bust right through the ladies' room wall. June can't help but jump a little with each crash. Iva Lou and I laugh. The last time I was in this bathroom I was a little girl. I had forgotten how the balls smash the wall.

I don't know why I'm not sad about Reverend Gaspar's passing. I guess it's partly because he died on the heels of my mother's death and I'm still not over that, so anything on top of it seems surreal. When I get back from the funeral, Otto and Worley are putting in my storm windows on the ground floor. I tell them all about the bowling and they laugh. I'm running out of chores to assign them, and it gets me to thinking about the future. I don't know when it happened, but Otto and Worley have gone from the town junk haulers to my home-and-business repairmen. Otto left a stack of mail on the kitchen table for me. I grab it and go upstairs. I change out of my Sunday best and into my overalls. I take the mail up to the attic, through the window, and out onto the roof. I haven't been out here since we patched the roof. Where does the time go? I kept meaning to come up here and look out over town and collect my thoughts. I guess I've been busy. Or maybe I didn't need to be high up and above everything until now.

There are three requests for magazine subscription renewals. Instead of opening them and putting them in the TO PAY stack, I tear them in half. I get plenty of magazines at the store; I'll just read them there from now on. At the bottom of the stack is an onionskin envelope with swirly blue writing: The return address is Meoli Vilminore Mai! Finally!

I'm careful to open the envelope without tearing the thin paper inside. It's a three-page letter, in Italian. I must admit, I worry about losing my Italian reading and speaking ability since Mama died; each day that goes by without her, I get rustier.

In the letter Aunt Meoli tells me how sad she is to hear of my mother's passing. She had been hopeful that someday they would reunite. She tells me my mother would be happy to know that she and I found each other. She also tells me how happy she is that I am fine and asks if I could send a photograph of myself. Visions of Italian *comarei* gathered at the *groceria* with my picture, fighting over me as a potential bride for their toothless sons, gives me a shiver, so I decide not to send one just yet. Zia Meoli goes on about her life in Italy. Her twin sister, Antonietta, practically raised her two kids, since Meoli was a schoolteacher with a full-time job. Toward the end of the letter, I see the name Mario, so I skip past the newsy chitchat to the real reason for the correspondence. Zia Meoli tells me that she does not know my father well; he lives in Schilpario, up the mountain from where she lives. She does hear of him from time to time, as he is still mayor! She does not know if he's married, but she assumes he is not; when she last heard about him, he was known to be something of a ladies' man. She promises to try and find out more about him.

I lie back on the roof. It is quiet except for the sliding sounds of storm windows being tested from below. I know I should be happy that my father is alive and well. Instead, the news makes me cry. I don't know what to feel or how. So I cover my face with my sleeve so Otto and Worley won't hear me.

I have so many books to return to the Bookmobile that I half joked to Iva Lou she ought to just park it in my front yard. I gather them up in two carry-alls and head for town. Pearl and Fleeta are handling the store today – I decided I need a few days off. I don't think they miss me much. Fleeta loves to clear the register, take the money sack to the bank and put it in the night-drop slot. She says it gives her a sense of completion at the end of a hard working day.

The Bookmobile door is open, which is unusual. I hear giggling from inside; I think to knock but don't. Iva Lou is sitting on one of the snap stools next to Jack MacChesney, who is perusing one of the three national newspapers she has on board. The paper, attached to a large bamboo holder, is unwieldy, and watching Jack Mac try to balance it cracks Iva Lou up. I haven't seen Jack Mac since the Elizabeth Taylor Choke Night. He doesn't seem one bit happy to see me.

'Hey, y'all.' I empty out the two canvas sacks and turn to leave.

'Why are you in such a hurry?' Iva Lou says with a look that means *Stay*. I look back at her with a look that says: *I'm not staying*.

'I have to check on Pearl and Fleeta. Otto and Worley are over to the house.' Why do I have to justify myself to them? Can't I just drop the books and go?

'Call me sometime,' Iva Lou says with a twinge of sadness. The truth is, I was looking forward to some time on the Bookmobile with Iva Lou. It would have been fun, but He is here, so forget it. All it took was Jack Mac's scowl to change my mind; I'm disembarking pronto.

Now that I've told Iva Lou I was checking on Pearl and Fleeta, I have to stop at the store; they can see where I'm headed through the windshield, and I don't want to be a liar. So I park my Jeep in front of the post office and go into the Pharmacy. Pearl and Fleeta are back by the makeup counter. Pearl is plucking Fleeta's eyebrows. Fleeta smokes.

'I'm not checking on you two. I was forced to come in here due to circumstances.'

'Who you avoiding? Spec?'

'No.'

'He's been looking fer ye. He done got your letter that you quit the Squad. He don't want to come over by your house, so he keeps stopping by here and bothering us.'

'Did the Reverend's snakebite skeer you that bad?' Pearl asks.

'I wasn't scared. It was just the last straw. You know what I mean?'

'Well, all I know is that I don't like no damn quitters,' Fleeta remarks as she inhales her Marlboro deeply down to her diaphragm.

'I've been working on the Rescue Squad as a volunteer for years! I am not a quitter.'

'Defensive,' Fleeta decides under her breath.

I'm in no mood to argue with Fleeta. So I walk over to the post office to check my box, which turns out to be a waste. There are a few flyers for quilt shows, tours to Knoxville for the University of Tennessee football games, and several bills.

There's a truck parked next to my Jeep, so I have to squeeze in between the two vehicles to climb into my driver's seat. I hate when people park too close. There's plenty of space for everybody when you park at the correct angle. I pull my door open and I'm about to climb in when something on the passenger seat of the truck catches my eye. The word *Schilpario* pops out at me. The afternoon sun is bright, so I cover my eyes and peer into the truck through the window. It's very strange. The book I just returned to the Bookmobile, *Schilpario: A Life in the Mountains*, is sitting on the seat of the truck. Who would check that out? And why? It was a special checkout, too, so whoever borrowed it must have convinced Iva Lou to bend the rules. As I pull out, I look down the street for the Bookmobile, but it's gone. The truck is familiar. It's new. Then I remember: It belongs to Jack Mac. I don't have a good car memory, but I do remember that he pointed this one out to me long ago when I made a delivery to his mama up in the holler.

Instead of waiting to ask Jack Mac why he checked out my book, I throw the Jeep into gear and peel up to the stoplight. In the rearview I see him come out of Zackie's with a brown sack and jump into the truck. As he turns over the ignition, the light turns green. I hang a left and drive off.

Theodore and I have something special we do every once in a while. We call it our field trip. We go over to Jonesville to Cudjo's Cavern, a deep cave in the side of one of the mountains. It is full of stalagmites and stalactites, nature's majestic mineral and stone deposits – 'God's Jewelry Box,' or so the sign says.

At the entrance to the cave, there is a flat area where we wait for the guide, an old man named Ray. He senses when there are visitors; we hear his footsteps down the path. 'Oh, it's y'all. Ye ain't been up here for a while.' He chuckles. Then he leads us into the cave along a path that weaves through carved-out halls and catacombs left behind by the Indians. The rock formations that hang from the ceiling look like glittering candle-wax drips, all shapes and sizes, including some that are quite large. The ones that come up from the ground look like shimmering fingers.

Theodore and I used to keep notebooks describing the various formations. After a while, we got bored and gave it up. Still, we come back so often, the guide knows us, so he treats us to special areas of observation. Our favorite is a small crystal lake deep in the heart of the cave. Ray never takes regular folks back there because it was a sacred place of Indian prayer. It is also very dangerous; the bank of the lake is only about a foot wide, and there is one shelf of rock above it, room enough for two people to crawl up and sit.

The water in the lake itself is hundreds of feet deep. Ray is afraid a visitor could fall in. He allows us to go to the lake because he knows that we'll be careful and not touch anything.

The surface of the lake is quite small, maybe ten feet across. Ray told us to imagine a deep cylinder of stone filled with water, like a tall, slim vase. I can see why the Indians prayed here; it is so quiet, the only sound you hear is water trickling down the walls. The lake reminds me of the baptismal pool at Reverend Gaspar's church. There is just enough room to immerse a body or two at a time. (I wish I would have brought him here to show him how the Indians worshipped.) Theodore points out the far wall with the large flashlight he is holding. The water reflects off the stalactites, throwing iridescent colors all over the water-washed walls. It looks like a moving painting of blues and silvers.

Theodore, ever so sensitive, knew I needed a treat. He thinks between Elizabeth Taylor's choking and Preacher Gaspar being bitten by a deadly snake, I haven't quite been myself. He's right. I feel like the last year of my life has been one unpleasant event after another. So much for something exciting happening to me while I'm thirty-five. (Maybe I'm growing a mole or something on my face somewhere that signals disaster instead of joy.) I do have six months to go until I'm thirty-six; maybe things will change for the better – if not, I fear I will lose my faith in the ancient art of Chinese face-reading altogether. Theodore and I stay by the lake for a long time, never tiring of the color swirls nature makes.

On the way home we stop at the Dip & Cone Barn, a hamburger shack between Jonesville and Pennington Gap. Theodore orders a lot of food. We sit outside on a picnic bench even though the final day of November has a strong chill to it.

'I want to talk to you about something.'

'Sure.' I start tearing open the little ketchup packets. I like to have a substantial pool of ketchup before I start eating fries. I don't like to eat a couple and open a packet, eat a couple, open a packet. I like an orderly dinner setup.

'It's been a wild time,' Theodore offers diplomatically.

'No kidding.'

'And I don't think that I've been thinking straight.' He looks down at his hands.

'About what?'

'About us.' I look at Theodore and see a sincerity in his eyes that, I must confess, scares the hell out of me. He never said 'us' like *us* before. We were always buddies, except for that night I threw myself at him and was rejected – (a night I would like to forget).

'Remember the night of the halftime show for Elizabeth Taylor?' Remember it? Is he kidding? It was a night of nights for me.

'When those two dogs were humping in the middle of my masterpiece, I wanted to quit. But I looked down at you from the announcer's booth, and you were wearing that red velvet coat, and you smiled up at me and did this funny thing where you checked your watch, like, *How long can two dogs screw? It can't be forever*, and I actually felt the burden lift off of me. You saved my life that night. I'll never forget it.'

'You're welcome, Theodore.'

'I mean it. You're always there for me. I don't know what I'd do without you.'

The only other person in my life who ever told me that she didn't know what she would do without me was my mother, when she was dying. I make note of this, in case I have to come back to it later.

'I think we should get married.'

It's as though a shade, the kind on a roller in an old window, starts being pulled by the circle tab from the top of my head, slowly down my face, neck, torso, and limbs all the way to my feet. I want to stay behind this shade forever.

'What do you think?' he says after a moment.

'Oh, Theodore.'

'It's what you want, isn't it?'

What I want? Can't he tell that's what's wrong with me? I don't know what I want. I have spent my entire life trying to give everybody else what they want. I'm not complaining. I like to be of service. I find great purpose in it. And no one was more surprised than me when my old routines didn't work for me anymore. Somewhere along the way, I got sucked dry and started feeling like the mountain mother with sixteen kids who wakes up one morning and realizes that she's just a vessel, a way station where life passed through before it passed her by. When Reverend Gaspar was dying, and he held my hand and muttered, 'Faith,' I didn't know what he was talking about. Okay, maybe he meant the traditional Jesus story, to have faith in that, but I don't think so. I think he was talking about a deeper concept. A concept I cannot comprehend. I'd like to but I haven't yet. What did he mean? Faith in God? Faith in myself? Faith in others? Faith in the unknown? I don't know. And as for the things of this world, I am even more confused about them! I don't know what makes me happy – okay, maybe Ledna and Edna Tackett's coconut layer cake, a letter from Italy, and the lining in any of my winter coats, hand-sewn and tufted by my mother. Those things make me happy. But getting married? Is that happiness? Or is it just a container to keep happiness in? I don't know. Theodore can see that I am confused.

'I sprung this on you too quickly,' he apologizes.

'No, you didn't. I've been thinking about marrying you since the day we met.'

Theodore looks relieved that he's getting somewhere. If there's one thing I know about men, it's that they fear rejection.

'You know, I think you and Jack MacChesney asked me to marry you because you knew I'd say no.'

'This isn't about Jack.'

'No, it's not, but it sort of is. I'm the town spinster, and I've gotten two wedding proposals in the past six months. Something's up.'

I eat my french fries and sip my Tab and look at Theodore.

'I want to marry you.'

'Do you love me, Theodore?'

'Of course I do.'

'Well, thank you.'

'So, yes, you'll marry me?'

I shake my head slowly. I cannot marry Theodore Augustus Tipton. I have changed my mind. My prayer has been answered, but it was the wrong thing to have prayed for.

'Why, Ave Maria? I thought you wanted to marry me.'

'I'm going to try to explain this. I hope you'll forgive me in advance if the words are inadequate, or I am inadequate.'

Theodore motions to me that I should speak. I love when he does that; it means he's really listening.

'A while ago Iva Lou told me that I could never trust any man until I understood my relationship with my father. You can take your pick: Fred Mulligan or the mysterious Mario da Schilpario. Since that particular thing was said to me, I've made it my business to observe fathers and daughters. And I've seen some incredible things, beautiful things. Like the little girl who's not very cute – her teeth are funny, and her hair doesn't grow right, and she's got on thick glasses – but her father holds her hand and walks with her like she's a tiny angel that no one can touch. He gives her the best gift a woman can get in this world: protection. And the little girl learns to trust the man in her life. And all the things that the world expects from women – to be beautiful, to soothe the troubled spirit, heal the sick, care for the dying, send the greeting card, bake the cake – all of those things become the way we pay the father back for protecting us. It's a fair exchange. But I never got that. So I don't know how to be with you. Oh, I guess I could pretend, make it up as I go along and hope that I figure it all out later. But that wouldn't be fair to you. What if I never figured it out? You deserve a woman who can give all of herself to you. I think you should hold out for it.'

Theodore has pressed and folded the tinfoil wrapper from his hamburger into a silver square the size of a shirt button. He stares at it for a very long time.

'Let's go home,' he says. I gather up the dinner, clear off the picnic table, and toss the garbage into the can. Theodore stands by the car looking up at nothing in particular. He's going to be fine. I'm sure of it.

Pearl received the results of her PSAT's, and she's in the top tenth percentile of her class. She shows me the report, but I have to grab it out of her hand in midair, because she won't let go of it as she jumps up and down. Fleeta is excited for her, even though she has no idea what the test is; she loves when anybody she knows wins.

'Pearl, congratulations! You're a brain!' I shriek.

'I knew that the day she didn't mix the analgesics in with the laxatives.' Fleeta winks.

'Mr. Cantrell says I can get into a good school. Maybe Virginia Tech or UVA, or maybe William and Mary!'

'Go to Tech. They got a good wrestling program,' Fleeta promises.

Tayloe's mother, Betty, comes in with a prescription slip. Fleeta and Pearl fan out to the back to do their chores.

'How you doing, Betty?'

'I've been better.'

'You sick?'

Betty answers that she's not and hands me the prescription. I go behind the counter to fill it.

'Tayloe sure made a magnificent Cleopatra. We were all so proud of her.'

'Some folks thought she done looked better than Elizabeth Taylor herself.'

'I think I'd have to agree.'

I look at the prescription from Doc Daugherty. It's for prenatal vitamins.

'Congratulations, Betty! A new baby?'

'Not mine. Tayloe's. She's done found out she's pregnant.'

'Oh.' I look down at Doc's prescription. Sure enough, it's T. Slagle. I don't know what more to say. This is tragic. She's a little girl!

'Can you believe it? She was on the Pill, too. But it's too late to cry over spilt milk; it's spilt and that's all there is to it. We got to clean it up and move on here.'

'How's she feeling?'

'She's over the shock, but you know, the same darn thing happened to me when I was sixteen, and I got my beautiful baby Tayloe out of it. So we're trying to look on the bright side.'

I give Betty the prescription. She takes it and puts it in her bag.

'Kids.' Then she turns to go. 'Ave Maria?'

'Yeah, Betty?'

'She's having the baby in April. Can you keep her part in the Drama open till she's back on her feet? Playing June Tolliver means the world to her.'

'You tell Tayloe she can come back to the Drama whenever she's ready.'

Betty brightens considerably.

'Thank you kindly.'

Betty goes. She knows and I know that Tayloe's performing career is over. But Betty isn't ready to let go of all the dreams she had for her daughter. I can picture what will happen, because the outcome of this situation is always the same. Tayloe will marry, get a trailer, have her babies and be a wife. There won't be time for six performances a week.

Fleeta comes down the aisle, having overheard our conversation.

'That damn Lassiter kid. The halfback on the team. You know, with the bedroom eyes. He done knocked her up. Boys.'

Fleeta goes off to the back. I can hear Pearl, flipping the metal clip on her inventory clipboard. I join her at the makeup counter.

'Her life is ruined, isn't it?' Pearl asks.

'Of course not. It'll be hard for her, but she's a very determined girl. And her mom will help.'

'I don't ever want to get stuck in a trailer,' Pearl decides.

'Stay away from the Lassiter boys.'

Pearl nods and goes about her inventory. I check my face in the mirror. I have dark circles under my eyes. The lids droop in exhaustion. I've lost my sparkle.

The familiar jingle of the door chimes tells us we've got a customer, but there is a residual jingle, like the door was slammed after entrance. Somebody's angry and taking it out on my door. I peer down the aisle. I'm right. It's Aunt Alice.

'Where are you, you hateful bitch?'

I look at Pearl. 'Does she mean you or me?'

'I think she means you,' Pearl says fearfully.

I get out of the makeup chair slowly and take that long walk down the antiinflammatory aisle toward my aunt, who looks like she could shoot me.

'May I help you?'

She waves a letter in my face. 'You done screwed me good. You think so, don't you?'

'I didn't screw anybody.' I speak the literal and figurative truth, of course.

'Do you think I will sit back and accept this? If you do, you don't know me very well.'

'Aunt Alice, if you have any problem with my business dealings, you need to speak to Lew Eisenberg.'

'I am not talking to that feriner! I am talking to you!'

'Have your lawyer call Mr. Eisenberg.'

'If I can't have this Pharmacy, I'm gonna get my house back. You watch me!'

'You'll never get my house! Never!' The tone of my voice surprises me. Fleeta ushers Pearl to the back room. That's when Aunt Alice really lets me have it.

'You're a whore just like your mother before you. You're a sponger, a taker. And you're evil. You may think you beat me out of what's mine, but I will fight you until my last breath.'

'You need to leave. If you don't, I'll have to call the police.'

'This is mine! This is all mine! All of it! You robbed me!' She looks like a sad six-year-old girl who didn't get the doll she wanted. Her eyes fill with mist. 'I never got anything I ever wanted in my whole life!' she cries.

'You got Uncle Wayne.' This is all I can say to her? Where's my fight? Why can't I defend my mother's honor? Where's the woman who schemed to protect her assets against this cruel woman? I don't need a doctor to tell me. Something is wrong with me.

I have been exhausted lately, but I blame it on the cold weather and my schedule at the Pharmacy. I started stocking ornaments, lights, and decorations (by customer request), which attract extra business. I feel bad sticking Fleeta and Pearl with longer hours around the holidays, so I cover the extra time myself. Also, folks get the flu and colds this time of year, so I'm on the run constantly filling and delivering prescriptions. Theodore and Iva Lou check on me quite a bit, they're worried, but I keep telling them it's just the holiday rush. Maybe I'm especially exhausted because this will be my first Christmas without Mama and I'm not up to facing it just yet. If I could just get some rest, I would feel so much better. It's gotten to the point where I can't sleep through the night. I haven't told anyone. But I've been thinking about calling Doc Daugherty. I just haven't gotten around to it.

I am donating several boxes of twinkling lights to the Dogwood Garden Club for the Christmas flower exhibit at the Southwest Virginia Museum. I'm late delivering them; I had some straggling customers at the Pharmacy. I drive right up on the lawn and park by the door, too tired to walk the few extra feet from the sidewalk. I would've asked Theodore to deliver them, but he's gone to visit his family in Scranton for the holidays. He invited me to join him, but the thought of a long car trip and spending time with a large family was too tiring, so I politely refused the invitation. This Christmas, I just don't feel like celebrating.

The entrance to the museum is actually the foyer of the only mansion in Big Stone Gap. The museum was the Slemp family home for years, until they donated it to the state in the 1940s.

Now it is a sweet homespun museum with dioramas that tell the stories of the miners, quilters, Cherokees, Melungeons, and families of the area. I must be standing here a long time because two of the Garden Club members whisper to each other to fetch Nellie Goodloe. Nellie descends the grand staircase and greets me at the door. Her expression is one of concern. She looks deeply into my eyes.

'Ave Maria, honey, are you all right?'

'I brought you the lights.' I give Nellie the stack of lights, but I miss her arms and they fall to the ground with a clatter.

I wake up in my own bed, in my pajamas. Pearl, her mother, Leah, Fleeta, and Theodore stand at the foot of my bed.

'What happened?' I ask.

'You fainted.'

'I was dropping off the lights.' I move to get up, but my legs feel like they're filled with sand. The group moves toward me. 'What's wrong with me?' I am really scared. 'Theodore, aren't you supposed to be in Scranton?'

'I've been back a few days.'

'A few days.'

'It's December thirtieth, Ave,' Fleeta announces, confusing me. 'Christmas is over.'

'But I was at the museum two days before Christmas. What happened to me?'

'Doc Daugherty ain't sure,' Pearl tells me.

'What do you mean, he ain't sure?'

'You passed out up there, and since you were close to home, they brought you here. And then Nellie Goodloe came over to the Pharmacy and told me and Fleeta. We called Doc Daugherty and he came right over here. All your vitals was okay, so he said you could sleep it off. And you did. For exactly seven days.'

'Doc told me I couldn't smoke around you, so I done gave it up,' Fleeta says proudly.

'Good for you.' I'm glad Fleeta could take my medical emergency and turn it into a positive experience for herself.

'Do you remember any of this, Ave?' Theodore asks.

I don't. I feel refreshed, like I had a nap. I throw my legs over the side of the bed to stand, but I collapse right onto the mattress.

'You got bed legs, is all. Don't let it fret you. The movement'll come back when you start using them again,' Fleeta reassures me.

'Let's go fix her something to eat,' Leah announces, motioning to Fleeta and Pearl that she'll need their help in the kitchen. They go, and Theodore sits next to me on my bed.

'Am I dying or something?'

'No. Doc thinks you suffered a nervous breakdown.'

'What?'

'He says he's seen all kinds of them in his life. Some folks function through them; some have blackout episodes, and some sleep it off, like a bear hibernating in the winter. You went the cave route.' Theodore hugs me.

'Help me walk.' I try to stand, and Theodore helps steady me. We walk slowly. We get to the bathroom, where I tell him to wait outside.

My bathroom, with the black-and-white checked tile, seems huge to me. The skylight in the ceiling has snow on it. It must have been a white Christmas. The bathroom is cold; the fresh towels I hung a week ago are still there untouched. The soap is the same size it was before I went to sleep. This is so odd. I pull the light string next to the mirror. I look at myself.

My face looks like it did when I was a girl. I guess I lost some weight during my nap; my nose seems longer, and my jaw is sticking out ever so slightly. My eyelashes are crusted with sleep; they are gnarled and crisscrossed, but still thick. There isn't a line on my face, and believe me, there were plenty of them before Christmas.

I don't remember dreaming. Did a switch just go off in my mind, and I went to sleep? Why don't I remember anything? Where did my mind go?

'Are you okay in there?' Theodore asks through the door a little nervously.

'I'm fine. I'll be right out.'

I wash my face and brush my teeth. I grip the sink, then the wall, then the door. I pull it open slowly. Theodore is on the other side, there to steady me.

'Are you hungry?'

'I've never been this hungry.' He carries me down the steps to the kitchen.

*W*hoever said 'Never make any major decisions when you're tired' was a very smart person. I let January and February of 1979 pass without doing much of anything beyond the basics. Everyone in town is asking me about my Deep Sleep, as it has come to be known, but I can't tell them much. I still don't remember a thing. Doc Daugherty is checking me on a weekly basis, and he sees no lasting damage to my physical person; he is pretty certain my mind is fine, too. Pearl and Fleeta manned the store for me while I was under, and Clayton Phipps, a licensed pharmacist up in Norton, came down every Monday and Tuesday and filled prescriptions. Folks appreciated the pinch hitting.

When I do finally start back to work in March, Pearl uses my rejuvenated face as an example of the importance of sleep as a beauty must to all women. There is nothing like slumber to give the face a youthful glow. I believe this is somewhat false advertising. I believe I look so good because I didn't die. I came through something, and relief perked up my face. Either way, Pearl has been selling Queen Helene hand over fist, telling the ladies that she used it on my face twice a day, every day, during the Deep Sleep.

Pearl kept a list of all the folks who dropped by. She got the idea from Nellie, who explained that all fine families keep a guest book for visitors who pass through. I finally get a chance to look at it. Folks signed in with funny messages: Iva Lou with smiley faces; the Tackett twins with Bible verses; Doc Daugherty with Latin phrases; the book is full and it makes me laugh. It's thick, too. Nan MacChesney came twice. I look for Jack Mac's name. He never made it over.

Otto and Worley took it upon themselves to clean out the roof gutters at the Pharmacy and my house during the Deep Sleep. Pearl tells me they were so worried that I might bite the dust, Otto cried. I give them each a bonus for their initiative and loyalty.

I learned three things about myself after the Deep Sleep. I learned who my true friends are; I learned that I bury my problems until they overcome me in a full-blown crisis; and the biggest thing of all, I learned that I wasn't happy. It's a terrifying thing to admit. It puts everyone around you in a state of paralysis, because they think that they are somehow responsible for your sadness and can fix it. Of course, they cannot. I know happiness exists somewhere; and if I knew where, I would go to it and claim it. I realize I have spent my life reacting to things and not initiating them. I let myself go somewhere along the way. And I didn't miss myself. (Does that sound crazy?) Some days I wonder if something grew inside my heart during the Deep Sleep. I want a change.

March brings the most beautiful spring I have ever seen in Big Stone Gap. Purple and yellow crocuses spring up everywhere, honeysuckle blooms and fills the air, and the mountains turn green, after being gray and brittle for all of winter.

I am finally feeling like myself again. Iva Lou is shocked when I board the Bookmobile. It has been a long time, and it feels like home.

'Hey, girl!' She hugs me, so happy to see me back on the third snap stool.

'I never did thank you for all your visits when I was under.'

'Don't mention it. You had the whole town rattled.' Then Iva Lou's face fills with joy. 'I was gonna drop by and see you later. I had something I wanted to ask you. Lyle Makin done asked me to marry him, and I said yes!'

Iva Lou and I shriek like sophomores.

'We're gonna get married over to the United Methodist church. Reverend Manning said he'd be happy to do the service. And I was wondering if you would honor me by standing up for me. Would you please be my maid of honor?'

'Absolutely! I'd be honored, of course. But we can't call me a maid of honor. Call me an old maid of disrepute.'

'That's my title. Course I'll be happy to pass it on to you when I'm a fat and sassy wife!'

Iva Lou and Lyle don't want to wait long, so the date is set for March 11. I bought a new pink dress and a matching picture hat with illusion netting and a tiny bumblebee nestled in the crown. Iva Lou asked me to wear something colorful, since Lyle likes bright colors.

March 11 turns out to be a perfect day for a wedding. The weather is warm, about seventy-five degrees and sunny. I'm glad my dress has a stole that I can take off, in case it gets hot later on in the fellowship hall.

The mail comes and I'm dressed early, so I sit down and sort through it. It's a lot of junk. One of the flyers from the Dollar General Store seems thick, so I shake it out. An envelope falls out and hits the floor. I can see that it's from Italy. Zia Meoli owes me a letter from a month ago, but the handwriting on this is not familiar. There is no return address. I remove one of my hat pins and slowly rip open the envelope.

The letter begins, 'My dear daughter.' I sit down in the chair, a little stunned. I hadn't made it official to myself, but I had given up on hearing from my father. Maybe that had something to do with the Deep Sleep – I needed to give up hope to move on. But I am so happy to see this letter.

The letter is short but well written, in very simple English. He tells me that Meoli's husband came to Schilpario to visit him. My uncle told my father all about me, or at least what he knew from letters. He tells me that he has no other children and no wife. He lives with his mother in the center of town. (*His mother?* I do have a grandmother! I can't believe my good luck.) Mario has been mayor of Schilpario since 1958. He would like me to write to him and has written his address on the back of the letter. I stuff it into my purse. It's a nice, friendly letter. No revelations. Why didn't my father ever try to contact my mother after he broke off their relationship? Did she mean so little to him that he could forget her so quickly and forever?

A horn honks out front. Theodore jumps out of the car and comes around to open my door. He whistles at me. 'You look beautiful.'

'Say hello to the Strawberry Daiquiri of Big Stone Gap.'

Theodore laughs and I climb in. 'What's new?' he asks innocently.

'I got a letter from Mario da Schilpario.'

He practically stops the car.

I open my beaded clutch (my maid-of-honor gift from Iva Lou) and take out the letter. 'It's okay.' As Theodore drives us to the church, I read it to him.

There's a big crowd outside the church. Iva Lou didn't send out personal invitations, but she did run her engagement photo in the *Post*, announcing the time and date and other particulars. This is called an open-church wedding, which means everyone in town is welcome. Everyone likes Iva Lou, so she has a full house.

I haven't been in the Methodist church since Fred Mulligan's funeral. I've pretty much stuck to my Catholic church. But I know every room inside this building, including the sacristy, where brides wait before going down the aisle.

Iva Lou looks stunning in a peacock-blue gown. She decided not to wear white because it makes her look too washed-out. She, too, wears a picture hat. She is sipping vodka from a small airline-size bottle. She offers me some. I swig it – not because I'm nervous about going down the aisle but because Mario's letter has put me on edge – and I give it back to Iva Lou. She finishes it off and throws the empty bottle into her makeup case.

'You are so beautiful, Iva Lou.'

'You think?' She squints into the mirror.

'You're a little piece of blue heaven.'

'Thanks, honey-o.'

'How's Lyle holding up?'

'He got drunk last night up in Esserville. Thank God his buddies got him home so he could sleep it off.'

'Nerves.'

'Uh-huh,' Iva Lou agrees, as she applies a little more powder blush. Her hand is shaking, so she steadies herself.

'Don't be scared. You're doing the right thing.'

'I know that. I just hate crowds. And ministers give me the creeps.'

'Reverend Manning is really nice.'

'I know. I just have to focus on something besides the gravity of all this. It's too overwhelming for a girl like me.'

A girl like Iva Lou. What a girl she is. Always made up her own rules. Here she is, forty-plus, getting married for the first time, having tasted all the goodies in the county. Good for her. She understood what she needed and went after it. She drove the Bookmobile even though they said a woman couldn't handle it. She sells costume jewelry, for profit and to give women something small and sparkly that will make them feel good about themselves. She always paid her own way, and she owns her own home. She is very strong and also very feminine. Iva Lou must love Lyle very much, because of all the women I know, she has the most to lose.

Through the crack in the sacristy door I can hear the bellows of the pipe organ. Fred Mulligan bought that organ, and it sounds like it's been kept up to snuff.

'Iva Lou, I think it's time.'

'Jesus Christ Almighty on a mountain! I forgot your bouquet. It's over there in the box.'

I go to the box and remove a beautiful arrangement of tea roses in shades of pink. Iva Lou picks up her bouquet of white roses.

'Nellie. She's got the touch.' Iva Lou models her bouquet. 'Someday, when you get murried, you'll have to get her to do the flowers.'

'Let's go.'

Iva Lou and I hover in the vestibule of the church. Nellie is directing the wedding, so she'll send us down the aisle. I have to remember how these things go in the movies; we didn't rehearse. Lyle said you would only find his ass in church three times in his life: for his baptism, his wedding, and his funeral. Iva Lou dispensed with the rehearsal.

I take off with the bridal one-step, two-step down the aisle to an eight-track version of 'Say Forever You'll Be Mine' from Dolly Parton and Porter Wagoner. The pews are full, and I get lots of approving glances and winks from both sides of the aisle. Joella Reasor even cranes out of her pew to whisper 'Welcome back' to me. Now I know how holler folks feel when they finally make it down to town after the long winter.

As I reach the altar, I smile at Lyle, who looks very happy and extremely nervous. He pivots out ever so slightly to see Iva Lou start her trek down the great white (blue) way. I stop short when I see his best man: Jack MacChesney, polished up like mamaw's silver, gives me a wink.

I'm going to let Iva Lou have it later. Why didn't she tell me Jack Mac was the other half of this wedding party? Maybe she noticed that he didn't come to see me when I was sick. Maybe she thought I'd bow out if I knew he was involved. It's funny. I don't hate him when I look at him. I'm just glad I look good in this dress.

The Methodists like their ceremonies short and sweet. This one is practically over before it begins. I'm sure it was the longest eight minutes of Lyle's life; his face is the color of a cherry tomato. When Reverend Manning introduces Mr and Mrs Lyle Makin for the first time, Iva Lou weeps. Her parents are gone, too, and I know she wishes they were here to see how happy she is.

The music begins again, and though we haven't practiced the recessional, I know the proper thing to do is take Jack Mac's arm and follow the bride and groom out. I face the congregation and wait for Jack Mac to join me. He does.

'Nice hat,' he says and smiles. Then he extends his arm, I take it, and we go.

Nellie has decorated the fellowship hall in a Victorian theme. There are decorative, hand-painted fans on the walls; the ceiling is festooned with a lace canopy. The tables are covered in white linen. The cake has stacked circle tiers with a bride and groom in an antique carriage on top. Silver trays lined with crisp white doilies are filled with Nellie's homemade candy wedding bells dusted in blue and pink sugar.

Lyle is relaxed now. Iva Lou is herself again, laughing and talking and making everyone feel at home. Theodore is chatting with a couple of teachers from up at the high school. I dip my cup into the bowl of champagne punch.

'Pink is your color,' Jack MacChesney says.

'Thank you. Lyle's favorite color is peacock blue, so I'm the contrast.'

'How have you been?'

'I'm coming back strong. Thank you for asking. How are you?'

'I'm fine myself.' Jack Mac looks off. I turn to see what he's looking at. It's Sweet Sue Tinsley, escorted by her ex-husband, Mike.

'Are they back together?' I ask bluntly.

'Yes, ma'am,' Jack Mac says quietly.

'You know something, Jack? I'll buy you a new hunting rifle if you promise never to call me ma'am again.'

'I'm sorry. It's a habit from my upbringing.'

Theodore joins us at the punch bowl. 'Everybody's meeting for a potluck at Iva Lou's trailer later. Hope you can make it, Jack,' Theodore offers.

'I'll be there.'

'I'll get the car,' Theodore tells me as he places his punch cup on the out trolley.

Theodore goes. I finish my punch and nibble on a wedding bell.

'You'll be at Iva Lou's later, right?'

I nod.

'You're gonna wear the pink dress, aren't you?'

I look at Jack Mac with a half smile that says, *Yeah, right. I am going to stay in this cinched silk cummerbund and panty girdle the rest of the day.* Little does he know I can't wait to get out of here and peel it off.

'See you at Iva's.' I grab my hat off the bookshelf and go to meet Theodore.

I've never been to Iva Lou's trailer in Danberry Heights, but it's a beauty. The outside is sleek, ecru wood panels set off by crisp black shutters. Iva attached a redwood deckette at the entrance. An old-fashioned light fixture on an antique pole at the curve of the entrance that casts a pretty golden glow as you enter. I arrive alone. Theodore is coming in his own car; he has a school-board meeting in the morning and might have to cut out early.

The interior decor is beige and modern – the perfect backdrop for a cool blonde like Iva Lou. The shag carpeting is a thick salt-and-pepper mix, very cozy. Iva Lou's inner circle is packed into the trailer. She has made macaroni and cheese, salad, and slaw. There are leftover mints and lots of cake – plenty to eat. She bought wedding paper plates and napkins with a bride and groom on them. Lyle is toasting pals with a bottle of beer. He looks like the lord of the manor now; he definitely fits in. Iva Lou feeds him a biscuit, then kisses the crumbs away. I'm starving, so I dig into the hot macaroni and cheese. Mama never made this dish, but I've always loved it. The soft elbow noodles nestled in butter and cheddar cheese melt in my mouth. The crushed potato chips on top give it a delicious salty crunch. I may have seconds. Sweet Sue comes up behind me with a plate of cake.

'How's it going, A-vuh Maria?'

'Great. How are you?'

'I got back with Mike.' Mike Tinsley is laughing heartily at one of Lyle's jokes. He seems happy to be part of the Gap social scene again. 'Yeah, the kids missed him.' The space between Sweet Sue's eyebrows knit into a little square. 'I did too, of course.' I smile and chew; as long as I'm chewing, I don't have to talk. I look at Sweet Sue's face. She really is very pretty. Her eyes are a clear ocean-blue. There are little crinkles around them now, but they give her a look of knowing and experience, which she wears well. I wonder if Jack Mac ever told her he proposed to me. I don't think he did, because she doesn't seem uncomfortable with me. I am most definitely not a rival.

'Well, I'll see you later.' Sweet Sue smiles and wedges through the crowd to get to Mike.

'What happened to the pink dress?' I hear from the entrance to the den. Now I see why Sweet Sue scooted off like a possum: It's Jack Mac. He stands in the kitchen doorway with his arms folded.

'It was cutting off circulation. I couldn't take it another minute.'

'What about the hat?'

He smiles at me and moves close, and I must say, everything this guy says sounds like a come-on to me. There's something in that slow delivery and those gluttonous pauses that makes you feel buck naked. I pull my cardigan closed and button it.

'Are you cold?'

'Ever since I had the Deep Sleep, I get shivers.' I hope he buys the lie, but I don't think he does.

'Do I scare you?'

I laugh right out loud. 'No, sir, you don't.'

'I don't know. You get jumpy when I'm around.'

'I do?' I don't notice that I do, but even if I do, I don't want this man pointing out my insecurities to me.

'What did you dream about during the Deep Sleep?' he wonders out loud.

Okay, now I get it. He's drunk. He's drunk and he's making a pass at me. He probably had the Tackett sisters in the den and flirted with them and got nowhere, so he moved to the kitchenette, and it's my turn on the way to the living room, where he'll hit on Iva Lou's cousins in from Knoxville, and then he'll go right up to Mike Tinsley and punch him in the mouth and Sweet Sue will scream, and the guys will pull them apart, and Mike will be bleeding and he'll tell Jack Mac to stay the hell away from his woman, and Jack will tell Mike he was a no-good husband, and Sweet Sue will have to choose and we'll all watch and be horrified and hope nobody's got a gun.

'Did you dream during your Deep Sleep, Ave Maria?' Jack Mac asks me again.

I shrug as though I don't remember, and I keep eating the macaroni and cheese.

'Where do you go when you look off like that?' He totally caught me. Now what am I going to say? You know what? I'm going to tell him the truth.

'I imagined you flirting with every woman at this party and then working your way over to Sweet Sue and trying to reclaim her, and you and Mike Tinsley getting in a bloody brawl and turning the trailer over.' Jack throws his head back and laughs.

'Now you know never to ask me what I'm thinking.' I turn to walk away, but he grabs my arm.

'I have something in the truck for you.'

'I'll bet you do.' Sometimes the mountain girl in me comes

out. I try to gracefully remove my arm from his grasp, but he grips it more tightly.

Then he laughs again, this time even louder.

'Are you drunk, Jack?'

'I haven't had a drop since the wedding punch. And you know how cheap Nellie is with the spirits.' Okay. This is really bad. He isn't drunk. So he means everything he's saying. Now what do I do?

'Come with me.'

He gets a grip on my elbow and won't let go. He guides me through the crowd in the trailer and out to the parking field. He moves fast, and I have to skip to keep up with him. It's dark, but I'm not afraid.

Jack finds his truck and reaches into the front seat. He gives me a brown paper bag. I move to the streetlight so I can see the contents. It's a book. A shiny, new copy of *Schilpario: A Life in the Mountains*, the very book I saw on the front seat of his truck a few months ago.

'Is this for me?'

'It better be. I can't even pronounce it.' Jack Mac smiles at me as I open the book. 'I had to special-order it out of Charlottesville. It's out of print, so they had to do a search. I thought it would be of some help to you, since you were trying to find your daddy.'

I'm having a very strange sensation inside my body right now. I feel compelled to embrace him, to thank him for his kindness. But there are so many questions. When I told him about trying to find my father, he was at the Sub Sandwich Carry-Out with Sweet Sue. We didn't talk about it for very long, and why should he take such an interest in it? Why does he care? I look at his face. He cares. I have this feeling that he knows more about me than I have told him. I hug the book to my chest; the paper smells so good, and the cover is cool and shiny. And then he pulls me close and holds me. The sandalwood and lime is so familiar, and so sweet, that I breathe deeply to take it in, and also to steady my racing heart, which is in desperate need of oxygen. My heart is not palpitating; that condition seemed to correct itself during the Deep Sleep. This is a different kind of thumping, a kind I haven't felt before.

I bury my face in his chest; it seems as though there is a place carved out for me there. I can hear the Statler Brothers as they sail out of Iva Lou's trailer and into the woods; laughter and chatting underscore it; I am very comfortable right here in this moment.

A few minutes pass, and Jack Mac lifts my head with his hands. I am sleepy now; every muscle in me is relaxed.

'May I kiss you?' he asks.

I search my brain for a witty comeback, but I can't think of any. He senses I'm searching for one, and he's determined to nip it in the bud. Sometimes humor has no place in life, and this is one of those times. He traces his lips from the top of my head and down my nose until he finds my lips. Then he kisses me.

The ground under my feet is soft, and I am sinking into it. I am like a stick in a sandy creek, going deeper and farther down into the dirt, meeting no resistance but the lack of my own will.

'I think we should get back to the party.'

'Why?' He kisses me again. I stop him, remembering Iva Lou, the party, and my responsibilities.

'Thank you for the book.'

He looks at me, a little confused.

'Let's go back,' I say quietly. We walk back to the trailer in silence.

Misty Dawn Slagle Lassiter, six pounds, seven ounces, was born at 12:03 A.M. on March 17, 1979, at Saint Agnes Hospital, Norton,

Virginia. Her mama, Tayloe, is doing fine; she had an easy labor, and now she can plan her wedding. Betty came to the Pharmacy with pictures of the little one, and she looks to be a stunner just like her mother. Fleeta is concerned that Misty may develop the Lassiter underbite, but it doesn't appear to be so in the pictures.

Since I sold the Pharmacy to Pearl, I've had a different attitude about it. I don't take business problems so seriously; markups on medications don't irritate me as much; and to hell with the dusting. Fleeta and Pearl take good care of the place, but something inside me has shifted.

I am teaching Pearl the log-in procedure on medication when Nan MacChesney comes into the store. She's using a cane. Her white hair is pulled back in a tight braid. Her eyes search the store for me.

'I know you're in here somewhere, Ave Maria. I done saw your Jeep out front.'

'I'm back here, Mrs. Mac. In the pharmacy.'

'Oh.' She comes over to the pharmacy counter. She barely reaches the top of it.

'How are you?' I ask.

'I'm all right. Can you come out of there and talk to me, please?'

'Sure.' I come out from behind the counter and stand in front of her.

'Is there somewhere we could talk?' she asks me.

'There's the back room,' Fleeta offers. Does Fleeta eavesdrop on every exchange that takes place in this store? I give her a look and take Mrs. Mac to the back room. I pull out a chair, but she declines, so I sit. Otherwise, I tower over her.

'Now, I know this ain't none of my business, but I got a son to worry about. I just want you to know that he is a fine gentleman and a faithful son. They don't make 'em no better than my boy. Now, I know he likes you. He thinks you're a fine woman. And I encouraged him in that, 'cause I done think you made all the right decisions in your life. You've been loyal and you've been good, and that ought to be rewarded. I know you don't see yourself as nobody's wife or mother, 'cause you've said so from time to time to me. I'm not here to repeat hearsay and gossip, I'm only going on what I know directly from your lips to my ears. But I think you need to take some time and reflect on yourself. I'm not telling you what to do, but if you let my son slip through your fingers, you'll be the sorriest gal in the world. I know what he's made of, and it's choice. He's a man of quality. So you go ahead and do whatever it is you're gonna do, but I just wanted somebody to tell you the real story about my son. You couldn't do no better.'

She raps her cane on the floor and looks at me.

'Thank you for your thoughts. I know you mean well, and I intend no disrespect. I agree with you. You've raised a fine son. But I have other plans. I want to travel, see things. Try new things. Alone. Can you understand that?'

Mrs. Mac shrugs, unconvinced. 'I just had to speak my mind,' she says as I lead her out of the back room. She goes out the front through the jingling doors.

'What the hell did she want?' Fleeta wants to know.

'Like you don't know.'

'I don't. Tell me.'

'Fleeta. Come on. You're both in the DAR. That's the front burner of hot gossip in Big Stone Gap.'

'Well, I have heard that somebody saw you swapping slobbers with her son at Iva Lou's trailer park and it done got around.' Fleeta shrugs.

'I hate this town!'

'What do you want from me? I can't help I heard it.' Fleeta dismisses me with a wave of her feather duster and goes to work..

'Don't you think Jack MacChesney is cute?' Pearl asks from behind the counter.

'Pearl. That's enough.' God knows what she'll ask me next. It's none of her business if he's a good kisser. What is wrong with these people? Do they expect me to magically transform after one kiss? Am I supposed to drop everything for Jack Mac? What about *my* plans? What about what *I* want?

Pearl smiles and concentrates on her work. I am trying to figure out which building in the Gap is the tallest, so I can jump off of it.

Iva Lou returns from her honeymoon all refreshed. There's a wedding card from the staff of the Wise County Library on the dashboard of the Bookmobile, the only sign of change since she got married. I listen to her recount the awesome beauty of Gatlinburg and Ruby Falls (one of the three natural wonders in Tennessee), and then I ask to see *The New York Times*.

'What d'you need that for?' Iva Lou wants to know.

'The travel section.'

'Well, they only got that on Sundays. I could score you last week's edition. Is that okay?'

'Whatever you've got is fine.' I wish Iva Lou would go and get it. She never makes a fuss when I want something. Why now?

'You going somewhere?' She sounds worried.

'I don't know yet.'

'Well, don't go springing surprises on me. I'm an old married lady now, and I can't take much.'

'You'll be the first to know my plans when I make them,' I promise her. She looks relieved.

'I got it below, in the storage bin. I'll fetch it.'

What Iva Lou doesn't know is that I am leaving Big Stone Gap. I've spent my whole life here, and it is time for a change. I want to challenge myself. I want to see what people are like from other places and get to know them. I want adventure. Yes, I would even like to fall in love. I think I should start at the beginning, in the place where my people are from. I am going to Italy. Maybe I'll like it so much I will stay there forever. I am in the last minutes of my youth; I don't want to wait any longer to be young.

I take a good long look at the Bookmobile. This may be the last time I'm ever on it, and I want to remember every detail. (Now that I want to leave, tomorrow would not be soon enough.) I want to remember the shelves made of pink Formica trimmed in green; the snap elastics that hold them in place while the vehicle is in motion; the three Murphy stools that pop up against the books when they're not being used; the Styrofoam cups; the Sanka packets; the checkout stamp; the rearview mirror Iva Lou uses to apply makeup; and especially, most especially, the smell of it.

'Here you go, Ave.' Iva Lou hands me the travel section in pristine condition. She really is the best librarian there ever was. She respects library materials.

'Ave, I owe you an apology.'

'For what?'

'Well, I sort of sprung old Jack Mac on you at my wedding. I never liked nobody force-feeding me when I was a baby, and I sure as hell wouldn't like it now. I should've mentioned it to you. But I guess I got caught up in all of it and just forgot.'

'It was fine. Don't worry about it.' What is everybody getting so worked up about? I'm not going with Jack Mac. So I walked down Iva Lou's aisle with him. So what? He kissed me once. Twice. At

a party. Big deal! Women get kissed at parties all the time. I've
hardly given it a second thought since then.

I get comfortable on my stool and begin to read.

'So, where you going?' Iva Lou asks.

'Italy.'

'Italy? That far?' Iva Lou's eyes widen. 'When?'

'As soon as I can book it.'

She points out travel advertisements she thinks are effective.
One catches my eye. The caption reads: 'New Jersey's own: GALA
NUCCIO TOURS: YOU WON'T MISS THE BOAT. Join Gala, she
makes every tour a party!' There's a big photo of Gala, who looks
to be about my age. She is a very dramatic Italian woman with an
elaborate hairdo, a pile of braids that curve artfully all over her
head like snakes; she has big brown Sophia Loren eyes and an
hourglass shape. She stands in the middle of a gondola in a
Venetian canal with her arms in the air. In a flag on the gondola
the tour prices are listed. They are very reasonable. I have found
my travel agent and tour guide in one stop! Iva Lou is thrilled for
me. She wishes she could go too, but for now she must put her
dreams of Europe on hold and concentrate on her new husband.

I return home, get comfortable in Fred Mulligan's chair, and
dial Gala Nuccio. The phone rings twice, then: 'Frank, you son of
a bitch bastard, stop calling me. I am done with you! Finished! It's
over!'

'I must have dialed the wrong number,' I whisper.

'Who is this? No, no. Dammit. I thought this was my personal
line. I have two phones over here, and I get 'em confused from
time to time.'

'Are you Gala Nuccio?'

'Yes. I apologize for my outburst. I never use that kind of language. But if you had been fucked over by that goomba the way I

have, you'd pick up the phone ready to bite off somebody's head too.' Gala sighs. I can hear her take a long deep drag off of a cigarette. Her accent reminds me of all the hard-boiled New York blondes in the detective movies of the 1930s.

'Are you all right?' I ask very earnestly.

This makes her laugh loudly. 'Men. You're a woman, right?'

'Yes, ma'am.'

'Then you know what I'm talking about.'

'Say no more,' I reply pleasantly. What I really want to talk about is planning my trip. I begin to ask questions about her tour packages, but Gala needs to talk about Frank.

'I've been with Frank on and off for about four years. He's divorced, he's got three kids – they're brats of course. And I don't see him enough. He says it's work and the kids, but I don't buy that line of bull for a second. "Lipstick on His Collar" is sort of my theme song. You know the song?' She inhales again. I can hear her exhale the smoke all the way from New Jersey.

'I do. It's an oldie.'

'Yeah. Well. It still applies. What can I do for you?'

'I'd like to go to Italy. I speak Italian.' I sound like a backwoods bumpkin. What does she care if I speak Italian? Is there a test you have to pass to buy a tour ticket?

'I have several tours coming up. You wanna do the Greek Isles, too?'

'No, just Italy. Northern Italy.'

'Uh-huh. Venice, Milan, and up. I do that. And a side trip to Santa Margarita on the coast. You don't want to miss that. It's scrumptious.'

'Great. Maybe you can send me some brochures.'

'Love to.' Gala continues to puff as I give her my address and information. She is surprised that I am Italian too and live in the mountains of Virginia. She has never heard of that before. I say that I'll tell her my story on the long plane ride to Italy. She sounds genuinely interested.

'Hey, Ave Maria. This could be your lucky day.' Gala puffs.

'Why?'

'I got a seat on my Northern Italy tour in three weeks. Think you can pull it together by then and join us?'

I panic. There's so much to do. It's not like it's just a vacation, it's a reroute-the-rest-of-my-life trip. There's so much to settle up around here: the house, the business, and everything else. But maybe this is a sign to do it quick and clean. Maybe if I don't have much time to think, I won't ponder details. Maybe for once in my life I should just throw myself headlong into opportunity and see what happens.

'I can make it.'

'Great. You're booked.'

I've gone about my business quietly. I find I can get a lot done if I get up early in the morning. I've managed to pack up the house, shop for the trip, and check in on the Pharmacy without tipping anyone off. I don't want anyone else's opinion about this decision; I want it to be mine and mine alone. I wrote to Mario asking him if he would like to meet me. If so, I wanted to know a convenient time to come and visit Schilpario. I have not heard back from him. I wrote to my mother's family as well, and they are thrilled that I'll be visiting. I still haven't sent a picture. The photos that came back after Iva Lou's wedding were horrible, and I'm not showing them to anybody. The hat and the dress were a disaster, and I will never wear either one again.

I haven't told anyone that I'm leaving. I may tell Theodore in advance, but only if the time is right. My plan is to go on the trip, meet my family, and consider all my options. The only thing I am certain of is that I will never return to Big Stone Gap. This is not my world anymore. My mother is gone. The Pharmacy and now my home are in Pearl's capable hands. Spec has chosen a new captain for the Rescue Squad. Anybody can direct the Outdoor Drama. There is nothing holding me here. It's time to move on.

The front page of the *Post* has a bold headline: MOVIE STAR GIVES CHUNK O' CHANGE TO LPH. It turns out that Elizabeth Taylor was so grateful to the staff of Lonesome Pine Hospital for yanking that bone that she made a five-thousand-dollar donation to its emergency fund. I flip through the paper to the want ads. I placed one this week; I'm selling my mother's Oldsmobile Cutlass. It's amazing how much I've gotten done since I put my mind to it. I've made a list of my assets, and I plan to sell off whatever I don't need. There is only the matter of Pearl to address.

I've called a meeting with Iva Lou, Nellie, and Pearl over at Lew's office. I stop by the Sub Sandwich Carry-Out and pick up a few sandwiches and bottles of pop; we're having a working lunch. Delphine Moses throws in extra chips (she always does) and comments on how impressed she is with Elizabeth Taylor's generosity. 'You just don't expect that kind of caring from a movie star,' she says.

Inez looks slimmer. Pearl convinced her to join Weight Watchers, and the results are impressive.

'Inez, you look fantastic.'

'Thank you, Ave. You know, I haven't felt this good in years. And I love all the little pamphlets, recipes, and helpful hints they give us at Weight Watchers. Our group leader, Pam Sumpter, is from Norton, and she lost one hundred pounds herself, so she knows how hard it is. Every week she shows us her "before" picture. She had it blowed up large and sets it on an easel at the beginning of every meeting. I keep it fixed in my mind, and it helps me stay on program. Losing weight has made such a difference in me. I think he notices it too.' Inez points to her husband's inner sanctum.

'Good for you!' As I enter Lew's office, I realize that this is probably the longest conversation I've had with Inez. She does seem like a different person. And Lew is smiling. Why shouldn't he be? He's got his tight little race car back in running order.

'How are you?'

'Better.' Lew beams like a man who is getting regular attention from his wife. 'And how are you?'

'I'm just great.'

'You look it.'

Pearl comes in, having forgotten to take off her Mulligan's Mutual smock. We hear an engine blast, followed by a fan-belt hum, and then silence, signaling Iva Lou's arrival in the Bookmobile. Then the office fills with the smell of gardenia, and we know Nellie Goodloe must be in the waiting area. Lew hollers to Nellie to come on in, as I set up the lunch.

Iva Lou breezes in and kisses everyone, but I can tell she is nervous. The girls have no idea why I have gathered them here, and let's face it, it's never pleasant when you have to make a trip to a law office. I make it as friendly and casual as I can, but food can only do so much to comfort people.

'I guess you all wonder why I have gathered you here today.'

Nellie and Iva Lou nod; Pearl takes a cue from them and nods too. I find it endearing that she is acting so mature.

'Girls, I'm leaving you.'

'You aren't sick or anything, are you?' Iva Lou asks worriedly.

'No, no. I'm not dying.' They look relieved.

'You all know I believe in Chinese face reading. Well, maybe Nellie, you never heard of it.' She shakes her head slightly; she doesn't know what has gotten into me.

'Every face is a map. Mine tells the story of a woman who changes the course of her life the year she turns thirty-five. Now, you know, I've had quite a few whammies over the course of the last several months. It was fate at work. After much contemplation, I decided that it was time to take control of my destiny and figure out why I was put on this earth. I don't want to let life happen to me anymore; I want to choose my future.'

'I did the exact same thing right around thirty-five,' Iva Lou interjects. 'That's when I got my two-year degree from Mountain Empire Community College and got on the Bookmobile!'

'Good. Right. See there? Iva Lou gets what I'm talking about. Sooner or later everybody has to ask the big questions of themselves. Some of us ignore the truth, and some of us gut the interior of our lives and attempt to reinvent it. I am doing the latter.'

'Good for you,' Nellie says because she thinks she needs to say something.

'Thank you. Now, a few months back I made Pearl Grimes here my ward. I signed over Mulligan's Mutual to her.' I look at Pearl. 'To you. But what I didn't tell you at the time was that I also gave you my house in the deal.'

'You gave me your house?'

'Yes, Pearl. It's yours.' Pearl looks at Lew, who nods in confirmation and smiles at her.

'But . . . why?'

'I'm leaving town and I thought you'd like to have it.'

Pearl is overwhelmed. I know what this means to her, to live in town. To be close to the school. To have a phone. To be able to have her friends over. This is the best thing that could happen, better than owning Mutual Pharmacy. I look at Nellie and Iva Lou, who are equally stunned.

'Pearl just turned sixteen, and until the age of eighteen, she cannot fully own the properties and their assets in her own name. That's where you two come in. I would like you to be her legal overseers. Lew came up with an angle I like. You two will look over this youngun and guide her decisions regarding the business. And you will be paid for your services.'

'I've never run a business,' Iva Lou offers.

'You're a librarian. You're organized. You work within a system. Pearl needs a system. You can guide her.'

'What about me?' Nellie says. 'I'm just a housewife.'

'Nellie, I picked you because you have good taste. And Pearl needs exposure to the finer things in life. You'll show her how to make a pretty store window, teach her the proper manners for business lunches, show her how to deal with all sorts of people.'

Nellie's back straightens. She never realized that her skills were marketable. Now she knows.

'What about my mama?' Pearl asks.

'She is a great mother. She loves you and takes excellent care of you, and she always will. I've talked this over with her, and she's comfortable with Iva Lou and Nellie handling this stuff. When I met with her, all she kept saying is that she wants you to be happy.' Pearl's eyes fill with tears.

'Yes, ma'am. That's all any good mother wants,' Nellie says, backing me up.

'She's very excited about moving to town with you. You'll be closer to things that will help you develop into a self-sufficient person. She is totally in favor of my' – I look at Lew and share the credit – 'our plan.'

'You're moving away, Ave Maria?' Iva Lou asks pitifully.

'Girls, this isn't a sad thing. I've lived here all of my life, and it's been wonderful. But it's time to see what's out there, test my mettle, see what I'm made of. You understand.'

'When do we start?' Nellie asks.

'Monday.'

'Monday? Cripes, why don't you just give me a heart attack right here, Ave?' Iva Lou slumps back in her chair.

'Are you ever coming back?' Pearl asks.

'I'm sure I'll visit. I won't make like a ghost, like old Liz Taylor. I'll be back.'

I motion to the lunch set up on Lew's worktable.

'Let's eat,' Lew says as he stands. 'We can sign the papers later.'

We gather around the table. Nobody says much. We eat. Delphine can make a sub sandwich, that's for sure. Nellie unfolds a paper napkin and places it gently in her lap. She turns to Pearl, who is picking the turkey out of her sub, and gives her a napkin. Pearl unfolds the napkin and places it gently in her lap, just like Nellie.

The hardest part about packing up my house is deciding what to do with Mama's sewing supplies. The only thing I know for sure that I will keep is her button box. I used to play in it when I was little, pretending the buttons were stones when I played explorer, or crown jewels when I played princess. I've sorted out most of the plastic ones, keeping the antique and cloth buttons. Buttons are light; I can always tuck them in a corner of my suitcase, and they are very symbolic to me. When Mama made something, the last thing she did was to sew on the buttons. They were the finishing touch, the end of a creation. I just can't throw them away.

I know this should be easy. Why should any normal person be

attached to bolts of fabric: scraps, ends, and odd yardage? But I am. Each piece reminds me of something she made. There's a yard of purple satin that she used to make my shepherd robe for the kindergarten Nativity. A mint-green dotted Swiss remnant that she used to make my dress for the May Day court when I was in seventh grade. A bolt of Carolina-blue wool for cheerleading skirts and a bolt of ruby-red wool that she used in the pleats of those same skirts. Red cording and frogs that she used when she made Bobby Necessary's band uniform. Back in 1969 Bobby's mama came over all hush-hush and begged Mama to make Bobby a band uniform. He was so heavyset, they couldn't order one in his size. Mama toiled over that one. But when Bobby marched out with his clarinet during halftime, you couldn't tell that his uniform wasn't from the factory. It was a perfect match.

There are several bolts of cotton velveteen in deep shades of red, blue, and gold. Mama was a big fan of velvet; she thought it was sturdy and elegant and that it 'wore' in an interesting way. She used to crumple it and let it fall, pointing out how the light played on the folds, giving it a sheen and dimension. She made me so many things of velvet! Skirts, pants, coats, even a bedspread. I always had a poufy bed, with beautiful linens. Mama grew up with that over in Italy, and she wanted me to have it, too. In later years, when we went shopping for sheets, she would sniff them. She could tell the grade of cotton, the thread count, from the smell. She said she would rather have one set of sheets that were four hundred count than ten sets that were two hundred count. I've slept on the cheap stuff away from home; believe me, there is a difference.

Even my favorite bedtime story was about fabric! Mama told me the story of the Fortuny family in Italy who made their own fabrics and became world-famous for it. She told me how they invented double-sided velvet (her favorite to work with), and how they experimented with design, embroidering it, watermarking it, even burning it! I used to imagine the Fortuny factory and their workers. I pictured the men and women standing around cocoons as the silk was spun; the raw silk draped on the cutting table; the processes of soaking, stretching, pressing, and cutting. Mama told me that if you made fabric correctly and took care of it, it could last until the end of time. I guess she was right. Think of those medieval tapestries and even the Shroud of Turin. Good fabric, good care – eternity.

I know a couple of quilters up in the hollers, but I really want to bequeath this material to someone who is expert at quilting and would appreciate it. I settle on Nan Bluebell Gilliam MacChesney. She's one of the best quilters around. I wrap the fabric in burlap casings. Mama never used plastic because the fabric could not breathe. She would be proud that I remembered this. I load up the Jeep. There is barely room for me in the driver's seat once I fill it.

It's around suppertime. I don't know where the day went; I started this project at breakfast, and it seems just moments ago. The ride up to Cracker's Neck is smooth; everything is green. The MacChesney house looks so much larger in the twilight; it's a warm way station in the mountain, not just a simple stone house with four chimneys as it appears by day. Light pours out of every window, and all four chimneys puff smoke. It is very inviting.

I pull up and park. I don't see any stray dogs around; of course, it's spring and there's been plenty of rain, so the creeks up in the mountains are full. I balance one bolt of velvet on each shoulder. Jack Mac's truck is gone. Good. I can drop these off and scram.

I can see into the house through the screen door. The main door is propped open behind it. I hear talking and laughing. Mrs.

Mac must have company. At first I think to throw the bolts back into the Jeep and come back another time, but it is too late. The dog stands in the doorway of the kitchen, barking like mad. Mrs. Mac pokes her head out of the kitchen door.

'Who's there? Speak up or I'll shoot!' There is a wave of loud, rolling laughter from the kitchen.

'Hold your fire, ma'am. It's just me, Ave Maria.' There is dead silence. 'Uh, I can come back another time. Good night.' The weight of the bolts is starting to press me into the ground like a nail, so I turn to go down the porch steps, juggling the bolts. I almost push in the mesh of the screen door.

'Whoa. Hold up,' Jack Mac says. 'Wait a minute.'

Damn, he is here. He must have parked in the back; it's dark and I couldn't see.

'I was just dropping off some fabric for your mother. It was my mother's and I didn't want to just throw it out, so I thought I'd bring it up here because she's such a good quilter.' My voice broke. I hate that. Why am I overexplaining? I just want to go home. By now Jack Mac is on the porch steps, lifting the bolts off of my shoulders and setting them down on the porch gently.

'There's a lot more in the Jeep.'

'I can help,' a familiar voice says from inside the house. It's Theodore. What in God's name is he doing up here? I want to ask him, of course, as he is my best friend in the entire world, but I cannot, because I have chosen to project this calm, casual thing to Jack Mac, and to change course in the middle of my performance would be death.

'Hi, Theodore,' I say as though it's an everyday occurrence to find him up in Cracker's Neck Holler with the MacChesney family.

'There's a lot more in the Jeep,' Jack Mac tells Theodore. They follow me to the Jeep.

'You loaded all this yourself? Why didn't you call me?' Theodore wants to know. I think he's got a lot of crust. I should be the one asking questions. Like, *What are you doing here?*

'You guys need any help?' It's a woman's voice, but it isn't Mrs. Mac. I am not going to ask who she is, so I wait.

'I think we got it, Sarah,' Jack Mac hollers off. Who is Sarah? What is going on here?

'It got chilly,' another voice says. I look up at the porch; there, in the light, is another woman. Are they breeding slim, pretty women inside the MacChesney house? Or is this a double date? I am mortified. Theodore has a date and Jack Mac has a date, and Mrs. Mac is making them roast pork chops and potatoes, and they're all in the kitchen, laughing and talking and making plans to go on excursions together to Cudjo's Caverns or maybe to North Carolina, to Biltmore House and Gardens. Theodore is in charge of the guidebook, and Jack Mac is in charge of the parking. The girls, in their halter tops and short shorts, are in charge of nothing. They are there to enjoy. Boy, these girls are fun and ever so game! Easy to be with! Undemanding! And witty and sweet, too! And they have nice figures from my vantage point, and long hair, parted down the middle, silky and straight with no clips. These are girls who can get their hair wet and have it dry with no frizz. They're spontaneous. They don't need any time for advance planning; no, they are just ready to jump in the car, powdered and fresh, anytime, day or night, ready to just hit the open road and have some laughs. They're breezy and no-hassle and chatty and sexy and unserious, and they've probably never been depressed or suffered the humiliation of a Deep Sleep or had rattlesnake blood splattered all over them at a revival. No, these girls are the ice cream after the steak. All sweetness and light, an excellent finish to an evening.

'You got a lot here,' Jack Mac says as he hauls remnants on his third trip up to the house. I lift the last heavy bolt myself, stretching it across my shoulders horizontally, yoke-style, like the Israelite slaves in *Ben-Hur*. It is the last bolt, and I don't care if it weighs two thousand pounds; I want to get this up to the house so I can get the hell out of here. Jack Mac and Theodore have different ideas, though. They run into the yard to help me with the last one.

'Let me get this,' Jack Mac orders.

'Sure. Sure.' I hand it over to him and Theodore. It takes both of them to carry it; that's how heavy it is. I'll bet Sarah and her slim buddy can't lift a bolt of wool.

Mrs. Mac is on the porch. The tsetse-fly twins are helping her transport the fabric in small loads into the house. I wave to her from the middle yard.

'Well, thanks, everybody. Good night,' I shout gaily. I turn to get into my Jeep. I'm glad it's dark, because I think I'll start crying the second my key hits the ignition.

'No, no,' chimes the Greek chorus in hot pants. 'Stay.'

'I can't. Sorry. I have to go.'

Theodore crosses down into the yard. He says to me under his breath and firmly, 'Don't be rude.'

This is the kryptonite of nice girls: We don't ever want to be rude. And even though I am leaving town, I would like to be perceived as the good person I've been all these years, and not a rude lout who doesn't say good-bye properly. Besides, the Jeep is empty, and there's nothing more to do; how long can this humiliation last? I walk up to the house with Theodore.

He says: 'Ave Maria, I'd like you to meet Sarah.' Sarah shakes my hand. Her hand is soft and her nails are painted ballet-slipper pink. They are hands that have never lifted a four-hundred-pound man onto a gurney or patched a roof. I put my ragged nails in my coat pockets.

'Hello, Sarah.'

'And this is Gail.' Gail says hello. She's even tinier than Sarah, if that's possible. I feel very large, like I'm three heads taller than either of them, and two planks wider.

'Ave Maria is a very interesting name,' Sarah offers.

'It means "Hail Mary," ' Theodore, Jack Mac, and I say in unison.

"That's a Catholic prayer, right?' Gail asks, hoping it's an intelligent question.

'Yes, ma'am,' I reply. I hope I make her feel good and old.

'Would you like to stay for dinner?' Mrs. Mac asks.

'I couldn't possibly. Pearl Grimes has a teacher's conference tonight, and I'm subbing for her mother, who is getting some new teeth.' Nice, Ave Maria. Could you stretch the truth a little more, please? The conference, the teeth – why don't you make up a boyfriend who's waiting for you back at the house with beer and pretzels?

Theodore and Sarah look at each other confused. Oh God, no. Theodore is a teacher. He knows there is no conference.

'I'm the new English teacher at Powell Valley,' Sarah says. 'I wasn't aware of a conference tonight.'

Sarah, the new English teacher. How literary. Does she wear short shorts to class? I wonder.

'Ave probably has a private meeting with Mr. Cantrell.' Theodore comes in for the save. Just like old times.

'That's exactly right,' I concur. I look at poor Gail, who is standing there, shivering. 'What do you do, Gail?'

'I'm Sarah's sister. I came for the weekend to help her get settled into her new place.'

'That's great.' Sure, it's great. Two piranha sisters chomp their
way into town and instantly find the only two eligible bachelors
with a pulse and make a snack out of them. Couldn't their dates,
both of them standing with their hands in their pockets staring at
me like two sick fish, have waited until I left town to carry on with
these girls? What am I thinking? I turned both of these men down;
now I am very glad I did.

'I really need to be on my way.' I check the time on my wrist.
Nice. I forgot to put my watch on this morning. Maybe no one
noticed.

'Thank you for the quilt pieces, honey,' Mrs. Mac says sincerely.

'You enjoy them.' Then I turn to the girls. 'You'd better get
inside. It's gotten real chilly.' Wouldn't want you two tasty nuggets
to catch your death and die long, hideous deaths on a respirator,
would we?

Sarah and Gail smile at me and follow Mrs. Mac into the
house. Jack Mac and Theodore offer to walk me to my Jeep. I
thank them, but no, I don't need anybody walking me anywhere.
In fact, I don't need anybody. I am Maureen O'Hara in *Buffalo
Bill*; I can take anything you throw at me.

I climb into the driver's seat, shove the key in the ignition, and
turn her over. I back out of the drive and off of this mountain, and
I don't even check the rearview mirror. I don't cry. I don't even
come close. The sexy sisters are just the goose I need to leave
town. Life will go on quite nicely without me in Big Stone Gap.

$\mathcal{T}$here is something thrilling about an almost empty house.

When you crave the comfort of things, as I have for much of my life, unloading them is a very freeing experience. I was always so careful in Fred Mulligan's easy chair, not to spill on it or sit on the arms or flip the footrest up and down too much. I wanted it to last. So when it is carried out of my house, I am relieved. I won't have that to worry about anymore. Lyle Makin can bathe it in beer and onion dip forever. Enjoy it. Use it. And when you're through with it, leave it in the street for Otto and Worley. Pearl and Leah will purchase all new things for this house – their new home – when I'm gone. I figure it's a bad idea for them to move in here with my old stuff. They need a fresh start; they should never feel like renters in a home of their own.

I can see the architectural bones of this house in a way I couldn't before. The floorboards are handsome and simple. The arches in the doorways are whimsical, with funny curves along the edges. The windows are very wide and eye level. It is a romantic cottage; how funny I never thought of it that way! Shorn of heavy drapes, just the rolling shades remain; I am reminded how important it is to let light play through rooms. I will remember this rule wherever I go.

I am lying on my back in the empty living room, looking up at the ceiling, a vast expanse of pure white – it seems to be a painting. My mind clears as I stare into it. I feel a moment of deep contentment, similar to what nuns and monks must feel when they pray. Being quiet is a very nice experience.

I hear a hacking cough coming up my walk; for a moment I think it might be Fleeta with another question about accounting, but it is too deep a rattle. It must be a man. Without sitting up, I roll over, and craning my neck ever so slightly, I can see the porch steps through the mail chute in the door. It's Spec. He raps on the door.

'It's open.'

Spec takes one step into the house and stands there. He is surprised to see the interior so bare, and he is also surprised to see me lollygagging on the floor like an old cat.

'Are you all right?' Spec wonders.

'Never better.'

'I need you to come with me to the hospital.'

'Why?'

'Otto's done had himself a heart attack.'

I've ridden in the Rescue Squad wagon with Spec many times. He keeps it in prime condition. I notice that the interior has changed a bit, though. My replacement has put the clipboard in a different spot. His kit is on the hump, not under the seat, where I used to place mine. There are notes Scotch-taped to the dashboard. I never did that.

Otto asked Worley to take him to Saint Agnes Hospital instead of Lonesome Pine. The Catholic nuns appeal to his superstitious nature. When Spec and I check in, we're told Otto is in Intensive Care. The tone of her voice tells us that the situation is serious. Nurses have many excellent skills, but they are never good actresses.

Worley kneels next to his brother's bed, holding his left hand, the one without the IV, in both of his hands. It reminds me of a Buster Keaton movie, where Buster is swinging from a building, holding on to his rescuer with both hands while he flails in midair trying not to fall. Spec goes to the opposite side of the bed, close to Otto's face. I gently place my hands on Worley's shoulders. He has been crying.

'Worley, what happened?'

'My brother done ate his lunch. And then he went out back and threw up. And then he passed out. He didn't come to, so I put him in the truck and brought him here.'

'You did good.'

'Please don't let him die. Please.'

I wish I could promise Worley that Otto wasn't ever going to die. But I can't lie to him, and it's not fair to give false hope where there is none.

'Worley, let old Spec take you for a cup of coffee and a chew.'

'I don't want to leave him!' Worley looks at his brother with deep affection.

'If you leave for a couple of minutes, I can talk to the doctors and get some information for you. Just do what I say, okay?' Spec takes Worley away. Sister Ann Christina, the head of Intensive Care, comes up behind me.

'How is he, Sister?' She lowers her head, indicating that it was very bad, motioning to me not to ask any questions.

'Can I talk to him? Can he hear me?' Sister nods, so I lean in to Otto's ear.

'Otto, what in the hell are you doing in the hospital?'

He smiles at me weakly. His eyes are lively, though. He motions to the oxygen mask. He wants me to lift it off. I lift it ever so slightly, so he can catch some air to speak.

'I need you to tell Worley something.'

'Sure.'

Otto and I settle into a breathing-and-speaking routine. I push the mask up and down as he finishes a sentence. He catches his breath and continues.

'I ain't Worley's brother.' I look confused. Sometimes folks go out of their minds when their bodies shut down on them, but hallucination isn't usually part of a heart attack, nor is memory loss.

'Who are you, then?'

'I'm his daddy.'

I grip the stainless steel bed guard to steady myself. It is cold.

'Remember Destry?' I nod. 'Destry was his mama. She died when she had him. The state wanted to take him, but Mama told them Worley was hers so they couldn't.'

'He doesn't know?'

Otto shakes his head.

'You have to tell him, Otto. You have to.' I say this slowly and deliberately, emphasizing the *you*.

'I can't.'

'Yes, you can. You just told me. You can do this. You must.'

Otto takes a long breath, and his eyes fill with tears. 'I can't.'

'Why can't you?' Otto closes his eyes tightly, hoping I will change my mind once he opens them. Then he opens his eyes and looks up at the ceiling. He barely whispers, 'He will be ashamed of me.'

And there it is. The mystery I could not solve. My mother could not bear the thought of me ever being ashamed of her, so she lied to me. A lie is better than rejection by your own flesh and blood when they out that you are not perfect.

'Otto, you listen to me. Worley needs to hear this from you.' Otto has a stricken look on his face. He's just had a heart attack, he's in pain, he's facing death, and I am refusing his final request. He is so confused. I have to make him understand.

'Goddammit, Otto. I'm a bastard. Not because of the circumstances of my birth, but because I was lied to. The lie made it wrong. You had something most people only dream of: a real and true love. And you were graced with a baby! A baby that came from you and Destry. Haven't you spent your entire life thinking about it? Thinking about her? Wouldn't you have given everything to hold her again? What is wrong with that? You loved her. That is a sacred thing!'

'I was gonna marry her,' he whispers.

'Tell him that. Tell him what your plans were. Tell him what Destry wanted for him. Anything you can remember. Tell him everything. It's the best thing you will ever do for him.'

Otto breathes in short bursts. A nurse comes over and gives me the eyeball, like, *What are you doing in here upsetting people?* But Otto keeps his hand on mine, so she gets the message that he wants me to stay.

'Please go and get Worley,' I say to the nurse. She goes.

'Now, Otto. Don't you cry. You be clear with him. He has to hear this from you. Okay?'

Otto nods that he understands. Worley comes in and goes directly to Otto's side. I pat Worley on the back and give Otto a look. Otto begins his story. I pull the curtains around the bed to give them privacy. I go out into the waiting area and wait with Spec.

*

'If I threw my body down and set it on fire, would it make you stay?' Iva Lou asks me over a BYOB beer at the Coach House Inn.

'Lyle would kill me.' Lyle Makin goes all over town and tells everybody what a great wife Iva Lou is; she knows it as well as I do. She's stuck for life and she's happy about it.

'Yes, he would. He loves being murried.'

Ballard Littrell stumbles past us to take a table near the kitchen.

'Drunk again?' Iva Lou asks Ballard.

'So am I!' He smiles, and takes a seat.

'See what you're gonna miss? What his wife has gone through. At the bottom of every woman's heartache is a bottle.' Iva Lou swigs her beer.

'What happened to his ear, anyway?'

'There was a story going around that a jealous lover cut it off during a fight. But I think Ballard himself started that one around. Lyle told me that he got caught in the Continuous Miner machine up in the mines. Sliced it right off. Why do you ask?'

'It was the last open question I had about anything in Big Stone Gap.'

'You know a lot of folks that are in the Drama are dropping out because you won't be directing this year.'

'Come on. I'm hardly a director. I just follow whatever Mazie Dinsmore wrote in her promptbook. I am easily replaced.'

'I don't know about that. Theodore Tipton quit this morning.'

'No way. He's the whole show!'

'I know. Between him quitting and Tayloe Slagle having a hard time getting the baby weight off, it's gonna be a long summer. He got offered a big job.'

'Really?'

'University of Tennessee wants him to be their band director.'

'Fantastic!' I am hurt, though. I would like to have been the first person Theodore told. I used to be. He came over to my house after Sarah and Gail Night, but I didn't answer the door. Maybe that's what he came over to tell me.

'Funny thing is, they didn't hire him for his theatrical flair. They thought the musical arrangement of all the Elizabeth Taylor themes was genius. Imagine that.'

'It was.'

'Then of course, there's old Jack Mac, the best kisser in Big Stone Gap.'

'What about him?'

Iva Lou shrugs.

'What have you heard?'

'He's seeing that new schoolteacher. Fleeta saw them up to the Fold.'

'That's what he needs. A schoolteacher. Mining and teaching go great together.'

'Listen to Miss Positive, Everything Turns Out for the Best. Law me.'

'Well, it does, doesn't it?'

'You like old Jack Mac. Admit it.'

I shrug nonchalantly and finish my beer.

'No, I mean you like him, in that way that I have liked half the men in Wise County. And don't lie to me.'

'Let's say I did. Why would I admit it? What good would it do me?'

'To be loved is the only good anybody can do for anybody. And you know how I feel about sex. I must say, though, marital sex is a whole different animal. But it's still an animal, thank the Lord for that.'

'Do you ever wonder why we're made this way?'

'Who?'

'Us. Women.'

'Honey-o, I don't know. I think I understand men better than women. A man is an animal all his life. He wants to eat when he's hungry. He wants to sleep when he's tired. And every so often he wants sex when he's horny. Simple.' Iva Lou looks at me.

'It's that simple?' I wonder.

'Animals. Uh-huh. Simple creatures, men. And we got the scientific evidence right here in the Gap. Anybody who says men didn't descend from apes never went out with Mad Dog Mabe. His entire body was an homage to shag carpet. That man even had hair on his elbows.'

I sit outside Theodore's house for a long time before I decide to walk up to the door. A walk takes twice as long when you feel stupid. I suppose I'm going to have to grovel and beg his forgiveness for Sarah and Gail Night. I haven't spoken to him since; I know he's really angry with me. I've been dreading this moment. But I miss him desperately; we used to talk every day. Life is different without him, and I don't like the change.

'Who is it?'

'Ave Maria Mulligan. Town pharmacist.'

Theodore appears in the doorway. 'Former town pharmacist.'

'Not until a week from Friday.'

'Come on in.'

Theodore lets me into his house. I never entered through the front before. I always came in the back, through the kitchen. Why didn't I go to the back of the house as I have for nine years? Why did I choose this front entrance, as though I were a salesman or a missionary? Why did I do this? Why have I put a wall between me and my very best friend?

'Did you hear about my offer from UT?'

'It's wonderful. Your work will be on the TV and everything now. You deserve all of the fame and glory in the world.'

'Thank you.'

'Are you mad at me?' I say in a funny voice.

'Yes, I am,' he responds in a very adult tone.

'I figured. Don't I get to be a little mad because you made friends behind my back and went up to the MacChesneys' with a couple of hot dates and didn't tell me?' I whine.

'No.' Theodore hates whining. Why am I playing this game with the man who knows me best?

'Why not?'

'You're a very interesting person,' Theodore begins. It has been a rule in my life that whenever anybody has used the word *interesting* to describe me, it is always something bad. 'You don't want to get involved with anybody, but you don't want the anybodys you know to get involved with anybody else either. Why do you suppose that's true?'

'First of all, it isn't true. People are free to do whatever they like.'

'People? Is that what I am to you? A general person?'

'No, no, of course not.'

'Start there. What am I to you?'

I want to tell him that he's my best friend. That if the entire world collapsed and I could only save one person, it would be him. That the thought of him leaving and taking a job somewhere else in the universe where I can't talk to him every day kills me! Why is it different when I'm the one who's going? Do I expect Theodore to sit here and wait for me while I go out and have adventures, like he's some talisman I can come back and touch to remind me that nothing has really changed? Instead,

I see the wispy sisters shivering in the moonlight on Jack Mac's porch. The image makes me angry. Why am I never chosen? 'Look. You don't owe me a thing. I can take care of myself.'

'You don't need anybody.'

'That's right. I'm very strong on my own. I don't need anybody.'

'Are you sure you're not Fred Mulligan's daughter?' This comment catches me off guard, and I find it cruel. I confided in Theodore about every horrible thing Fred Mulligan ever did to me and my mama, and now he's throwing it up in my face. But I would never give him the satisfaction of knowing that he has hurt me. If you saw my face in this moment, you would think I hadn't a care in the world. This is my best area; this is where I perform at my peak. I can shut down, detach, and not feel. So, that is exactly what I do.

'You'd be the first person in the world who didn't need someone, Ave Maria. Do you think you're that person? The one girl in the world who doesn't need anybody, ever? Are you some special category of person?'

'Why are you doing this to me?'

'See, there you go. See how you operate? I'm doing something to you because I'm asking you how you feel. What you feel. It is my business. I love you.'

'Sure, sure you love me.' I roll my eyes like I'm five.

'You know, having sex with someone isn't the only way to show you care.'

'Well, it would have been nice!' Why am I shouting at this man? Isn't he on my side? Isn't he telling me that I am as deserving of love as the next person? That it's okay to need love? That I'm allowed to be scared? But it's too late. I know Theodore is really angry because he cannot look at me.

As he paces, he says calmly, 'You have big problems, okay? Big ones that you need to think about.'

'I have big problems? What about you? You think I can't connect to people?' Now I'm shouting and I'm sure I'm scaring him. Good. My voice gets even louder. 'Stop analyzing me! Stop it! I wanted to marry you for nine years and you didn't want me. Finally, finally, you propose to me, and what was I supposed to do? Drop everything and marry you in the middle of a black depression? And then what? Be happy? Maybe I loved you in the middle of my depression, and loved you enough not to saddle you with a nut case! You should have married me nine years ago when I was young and I didn't know so much! I would have had someone to love me when I went through all the worst things of my life. I've gone through all the worst things, and I did it alone. A person can't just pretend that they didn't go through it all alone. I did. I don't want any credit for it, but understand that when it comes to love, *I don't understand!* I wouldn't know what to do with a man! Hook him? Serve him? Then pray he never leaves? How do you do it without dying? How?'

Theodore goes to the kitchen. He turns in the doorway. 'How about a cup of coffee?'

I sit on Theodore's futon while he fixes a pot of coffee. I look down at the buttons on my shirt. There is no rise and fall, no palpitations. Nothing but the steady breathing that comes with the unburdening of feelings locked up, locked down, and buried for nine years. It feels good. I curl up on Theodore's couch.

'You're my best friend, Ave Maria,' Theodore says casually from the kitchen. 'I'll never leave you.'

I want to speak, to respond, to let him know that I feel the same, but I can't. So, I cry instead. I can cry here. I'm safe.

✳

The postmaster from town calls; he has a certified letter for me. I let him open it. They're my tickets from Gala Nuccio. I am very excited about my trip, and very nervous. I have called Gala nearly every day to practice speaking Italian and to discuss the trip. She is very excited to have me with the group, since I speak Italian. Also, we've become good phone friends. She has told me a lot about her life. Her boyfriend, Frank, has finally asked her to marry him, but she doesn't see herself as Maria von Trapp, a second mother who plays puppets with her stepchildren. Gala also believes Frank still has other women. She can't prove it, but he keeps strange hours and is forever calling her from phone booths (she assures me this is a sign of a cheating man, and I think she's right). I never had a girlfriend who was Italian like me, and it is so much fun. We have similar attitudes about things. Theodore and I drove all the way over to the Tri-City Mall, to see *Saturday Night Fever*. (It's been out two years but there is still a demand in Kingsport.) I never knew people were like that. Gala assures me the movie is accurate; she grew up in the same kind of neighborhood. She finds it charming that I have a Southern accent. 'You just don't expect that sound to come out of an Italian girl.' I told her all about the last year of my life, and she listened carefully. She thinks Theodore is not the man for me. She likes the idea of Jack MacChesney. I told her it's too late for all of that; Jack Mac and Sarah are hot and heavy. Gala wasn't surprised that Jack Mac turned around and got another girlfriend so fast. 'Men always have to be with somebody. It's just how the son of bitches are made.' Her words ring in my ears long after we're off the phone. I think she's right.

I wash my face, throw on some lipstick, and grab my keys to run into town. I have already had my mail rerouted to the post office, so daily chores at my house have dwindled to preparing my meals and packing.

I need a spatula to pry all of my mail out of the post office box. I quickly shuffle through. There is a postcard from Zia Meoli telling me in a line how the whole family cannot wait to meet me. I've received a card or a letter from Zia Meoli at least once a week since I wrote to her the first time. I told her I hadn't heard from Mario da Schilpario since his first and only letter, even though I have written to him three times with the dates of my trip. I've given up on him. I would like to meet him, but if it doesn't happen, if he doesn't want to see me, I am not going to barge into his home and confront him. I wonder if he told his mother about me. My grandmother. How I wish I could meet her. It's silly, I know, but the one thing I always wished I had was a grandmother to talk to. Well, the sooner we learn that we don't get everything we want in this life, the better. I am grateful to meet my twin aunts and uncle and cousins. They will be more than enough; I guess I shouldn't be greedy.

The windows in Mulligan's Mutual have never been prettier. Nellie has painted the backdrop doors a bright lime green and placed paper butterflies on the product displays, making the windows look like a happy terrarium. The mortar-and-pestle neon sign that had burned out on the building has been replaced with a giant **R**; and it's a real attention-getter. Otto and Worley did a beautiful job on the bricks. So the place finally is up to snuff, and that makes me very happy.

Fleeta is handling the store part of the Pharmacy during the day until Pearl gets off school, and that nice man from Norton agreed to take Mondays and Tuesdays for prescription filling until a permanent pharmacist can be found. We interviewed a man from Coeburn, and he may be able to start by early summer. Nellie and Iva Lou are keeping an eye on Pearl already, though Pearl has complained that Nellie is a little bossy. I told Pearl to tell Nellie that; I'm sure she doesn't realize that she's being bossy.

Fleeta is behind the counter. I hear her explaining the difference between the chicken-wing overcross and the sleeper hold to a boy, obviously another professional-wrestling fan. Fleeta begged me to start carrying World Wrestling Federation magazines, so we did. It does bring in that young male element; they also buy a lot of candy. Fleeta is downright religious about wrestling. She has started smoking again; she said it was too hard to quit because everybody smokes in the arenas where the wrestling matches are held. Plus, her nerves get frayed during the shows when the man she is rooting for falls behind. She needs her cigarettes to calm down.

'What are you doing here?' she asks me.

'Just dropped by. To say hi.'

'Shouldn't you be home, girl?' Fleeta looks around nervously.

'I was home but I already had my mail rerouted, so I came to fetch it.'

'Oh.'

'Is something wrong?' I ask.

'No, nothing.' Fleeta puffs on her Marlboro like she's blowing up a balloon in spurts.

'You seem upset about something.'

'I told you everything was fine.'

Now, I know Fleeta as well as I know anyone. Something is not right. It could be something small, like she made a bet on Haystack Calhoun or the Pile Driver and somebody's into her for twenty bucks; or it could be something big like Portly's ill. The one thing about Fleeta: She reacts exactly the same to any challenge; there are no degrees with her.

'Don't look at me like that. Don't you think you ought to be getting yourself home?'

'Fleeta. What is going on?'

'Jesus. Would you lay off?'

Fleeta has never spoken to me like this.

'You know what, Fleeta? I don't appreciate your tone.'

'I'm sorry about that, Ave Maria. I really am. But I need you to just trust me on this one. You need to get yourself home.'

'Is something wrong with Otto?'

'God, no. That shunt in his heart is working like a garden hose.'

Fleeta clamps her little lips shut and goes about her dusting. I wait for a moment, but she isn't volunteering any further information.

Something is up.

When I get home, Otto and Worley are repairing the fence in my front yard. They laugh, share tools, and consult each other about the best way to replace an old hinge. I ask them if everything is okay, and when I tell them about Fleeta, they just shrug. I ask Otto about his shunt. He opens his shirt and shows me the red staccato scar down his breastbone. (I didn't need to see that.) The doctor is pleased with the results, and Otto is feeling like his old self again. The doctor considers Otto's recovery a miracle. I think that the truth healed his heart. Once Otto unloaded the terrible burden he had been carrying all these years, the weight on his chest lifted, and he could breathe again. He doesn't huff and puff when he climbs ladders or lifts things anymore, and he gave up chewing tobacco. It's the start of a whole new era for Otto. I think he'll find a girlfriend next. He has his eye on a woman down in Lee County.

I finally found out how old the boys are. Otto is sixty-nine and Worley is fifty-five. Everybody in town is shocked by this; we thought they were much younger and closer in age. Worley has a hard time calling Otto Daddy, so he still calls him just plain Otto. The transition from close brothers to father and son has not been that much of a challenge for them. Otto always took the lead anyway; so the revelation hasn't really affected their day-to-day life. Worley seems very happy and takes every opportunity to ask folks up the mountain if they remember little Destry, the beautiful Melungeon girl. Some do, and that has brought him great comfort.

I tell them I'm going upstairs to finish packing. The house looks so cheery; Otto and Worley painted all the rooms in sheer eggshell beige, and they are pristine. All of my clothes are laid out on the bed. Italy in April is on the cool side, so I'm packing basics in navy and off-white: simple suspender pants my mother made for me, a few pressed blouses, a skirt for church, and my red velvet swing coat. Pearl saved me all sorts of travel-size toiletries and put them in a pretty makeup bag on which she embroidered my initials as a going-away present.

I go into the bathroom. It is completely bare, except for my clean, white towels. I run a bath. I have the day free. I'm going to have a nice soak, put on my makeup, test-run my casual navy travel suit, and surprise Theodore and take him to the movies in Kingsport.

As I sink into the hot water, I look up at the skylight, which for years has been my favorite thing in this house. I could always see a patch of sky through it. I never minded if there were clouds or if it was raining; all kinds of weather had a particular beauty in that square of lead glass. I could see birds go by and watch the clouds change from billowy white to gray and then, in winter, see a sky full of snow. It was my own private clock. I'm about to turn thirty-six years old. Thirty-six! I cannot believe it. I feel nineteen some days and eighty-five on others.

I am blissfully content. I'm sure there are things I could get riled up about, like Mario Barbari dropping me as a pen pal. But I see the big picture now in a way I couldn't before. I have lowered my expectations, and that's a good thing. I can't look outside of myself for happiness, or let things like letters coming or not coming ruin my life. I am ready for a change. I just know that this trip to Italy will change my life. And I'm not going to fight it.

Since Mama died, I have prayed to her. I haven't had any sense that she's around me, but I do believe she's up in heaven. Iva Lou told me for six months after her mother died that, whenever she'd turn a light on, the bulb would blow, even if it was new. Iva Lou believes that souls are full of energy. And they channel into our energy sources to talk to us. A lamp is a perfect object for them to communicate through because it runs on electricity, and that is similar to the frequency in the afterlife. All I know is that I haven't changed a bulb in this house since Mama died.

I do say my prayers every day. Mama told me to pray even if it was just mindless repetition. 'You may not need your prayers today, but trust me, eventually everyone needs to pray.' I remember Reverend Gaspar's face as he was dying. 'Faith,' he said. I hope I find it someday.

I put my hair up in a towel and put my makeup on. I go with the full Kabuki: moisturizer, spot concealer, and base applied with a sponge. Pearl taught me how to do it, and I must say, my skin looks like alabaster. She taught me how to line my lips and fill them in with lipstick on a brush, not straight from the tube. I'm not big on eye makeup, so I don't do the shadow thing, just mascara. Pearl told me that long lashes are my best asset. Maybe she's right.

The sun pours through the skylight, giving my hair a sheen when I take it out of the towel. I dry it and it doesn't frizz. It's too early in the year for humidity. I have a three-week window in the seasonal calendar when my hair behaves. This is the first week. I'm going to miss the rest of the good-hair weeks, but I don't care – my hair can do whatever it wants on a gondola in Venice.

Mama had a bottle of Chanel No. 5 in her dresser; I dab it on sparingly. I know I can always buy another, but this was hers, so every drop is precious. I don't want to use it up. I guess I feel that when it's gone, she is really gone. I screw the cap on tightly.

When I go downstairs, Otto and Worley are in the kitchen eating their lunch. They whistle at me. I give them a look, and we all laugh.

'We just ain't never seen you all gussied up like that, Miss Ave,' Otto says.

And they're right. They haven't.

'Pearl says she wants to drop some of her and her mama's stuff by later,' Worley offers.

'That's fine.'

'Where you off to?' Otto asks.

'I thought I'd go and see a movie in Kingsport. I'm getting jumpy waiting for Friday to get here. I need something to do.'

Otto and Worley look at each other and smile.

'Did I say something funny?'

'Nah,' Otto says. 'It's just that you've always been so busy, running here, running there, that's it's funny to think you don't got nothing to do.'

'Are you all packed?' Worley asks.

I nod.

The doorbell rings. It's probably Pearl. She has keys, though. So why would she be ringing the bell?

I open the door. For a moment, I feel as though I have entered a dream. Through the screen, I see a familiar face. It's the same face that appears in an ad in *The New York Times* travel section every Sunday. The hair is different and the arms aren't extended over her head in welcome, but the same face, the same big eyes, the same big smile greet me with the same largesse and joy that's in the picture. Except she's not in the paper; she is here on my porch. It is Gala Nuccio.

'Are you Ave Maria?'

'I am.'

'Oh, my God! It's me! Gala!' She pushes me into the house and embraces me. We hug like sisters, and it's so funny – she could be my sister. She's shaped like me but smaller, and she has hair that could frizz. She's much more down-to-earth and less dramatic in real life.

'What are you doing here?' I ask without letting her go.

'Before I tell you, believe me, I wanted to call and explain, but they wouldn't let me.' I'm thinking, who are 'they,' and why would Gala come over a thousand miles to see me when she would have seen me two days from now at the C Luggage area at Newark Airport in New Jersey? My nerve endings feel as though they are pushing tiny needles from the inside of my body through to the outside. I am overcome with a deep fear. Gala, my sister, can tell.

'Don't be afraid,' she says, sounding like Moses if he had been raised in New Jersey. She puts her arm around me. Otto and Worley stand in the doorway of the kitchen and watch silently. Gala leans out the door and motions for someone to enter.

There in my doorway is the man in the picture: my father, Mario da Schilpario. I put one hand on my heart and the other over my mouth, as if to make sure I am still in my body and standing here. He smiles at me. Just like he did in the picture. He is about my height, and his black hair is full and curly, peppered with streaks of white. His eyes are large and brown and turn up in the corners, like mine. He has the same slight overbite I do, but he has a dimpled chin, which I don't. He is dressed impeccably, with a long-sleeved beige cashmere sweater tied around his shoulders like Jean-Paul Belmondo in all those French movies. I am stunned that my father could be so dapper. Then he says, in very rehearsed English, 'I am Mario Barbari. I am happy to meet you.' He takes both of my hands and kisses them. Then he embraces me. It is not a phony embrace either, and not a pitiful 'I'm sorry I was never there for you all these many years' embrace; it is one of genuine joy. He *is* happy to meet me.

Finally, I am in the arms of my real father. Why, then, do I see the face of Fred Mulligan? Fred, who taught me how to peel an apple, play gin rummy, and open a checking account? Fred Mulligan, who I thought never loved me because I asked 'why' too much. Fred Mulligan, who died and left my mother everything he had, knowing that someday I would benefit from that. Fred Mulligan, who didn't know how not to hurt me, because he, too, was asked to live a lie.

When I cry, Gala weeps. My father cries too, but they aren't shameful tears; they are empathetic, like he knows how important this moment is to me.

Mario looks at me with the same wonder I feel looking at him. He is much more imposing in life than he is in his picture. I take a moment to examine the details of his face in person as I have in the photograph all these months. He has a firm jaw (decisive), thick eyebrows (a healthy libido; surprise, surprise) that frame each eye from one corner to the other (a woman would kill for such perfect arches!), and a straight nose, but it is his smile, with full lips revealing perfect teeth, that draws you in. In face reading, his is the face of a king. He isn't very tall for a man, but his posture and carriage are so regal, you don't notice.

Gala touches my shoulder, and I look at her as though I am looking into the face of an angel. I am very grateful, but I cannot thank her. How do you begin to thank someone for something so incredible? Then she says, 'Would you like to meet your grandmother?'

Through the door steps my grandmother. She looks me up and down and over like she's buying an eggplant. She is tiny but broad-shouldered. She wears a simple blue serge suit. Her hair is in a white braided bun. She has a long nose and clear blue eyes. She shoves her son out of the way and says, 'Ave Maria!' And then she hugs me hard, right from the gut; I think my tailbone will snap in two. 'Nonna?' I say to her. She grins at me. 'You speak Italian?' I nod. She is so overjoyed she slaps my arm hard. Nonna, or 'Grandma,' speaks in a hard-to-follow mountain dialect. She understands my Italian, though. I speak too fast when I am excited too. It is a wonder to me that she exists. I have dreamt of this all my life, and now it is real. Nonna does not stop talking. She tells me that I am her only granddaughter and she prayed all of her life to have a grandchild. She is sorry she never held me as a baby. Do Italians tell you everything they feel without censor? I think so. Then, she says, 'Dove è cucina?' I point to the kitchen and she trundles off. Then the most magical thing happens.

Zia Meoli and Zia Antonietta walk in together. They are identical twins, and they look exactly like my mother! The same high forehead, the same golden skin, the same smile! They were ten years older than she, but their hair is still black; they wear it in the same long braid. I embrace them both at once, and I feel like I am in the arms of my own mother again. They smell like Chanel

No. 5, just like Mama. They are followed by a tall, distinguished man, my Uncle Pietro, Meoli's husband. She introduces him, speaking in Italian, referring to her descriptions of him in her letters. I look off and see my father trying to communicate with Otto and Worley, using some sort of sign language. It is so funny that I start laughing; soon we are all laughing. The laughter clears my head, and I can think. I turn to Gala. 'How did they get here?' She tells me she put the tour together. She reads my mind: I'm thinking, Who paid for this? Gala tells me someone sent the family the tickets. Who? She shrugs and looks out on the porch.

Theodore, Fleeta, Pearl, Iva Lou, and Lyle are waiting for me. They are crying, all except for Lyle, who keeps biting his lip. I go to embrace them, but none of them can wait, so we glob into one group and hug and cry. Pearl, like the great make-up artist she is, dabs the runny mascara off my face with a Kleenex.

'Thank you for this. Thank you so much.' My dear friends must have pooled all their money to bring my family to me. How will I ever repay them for this priceless gift?

'Don't thank us,' Iva Lou says simply.

'What do you mean?'

'Thank him.' Iva Lou points to the end of my front walkway. A man stands there with his hands in his pockets, his back to us. He turns slightly and kicks a rock with his foot. It is Jack MacChesney.

'He did this for me?' My friends nod at me solemnly and look at one another.

'But why?'

'I guess you'll have to ask him that yourself, honey-o,' Iva Lou says tenderly.

I turn to go down the steps that lead to the walkway that will lead me to him. I take a deep breath, but I don't move. I see him there; he does not see me yet. The mountains rise behind him in green folds that peel back, back, back, until they reach the end of the sky. How small he looks at the foot of those hills. How singular. How lonely. I know I must go to him. I look at my friends on the porch, and they agree. What can I possibly say to him? I'll think of something. I hope.

Jack Mac is deep in thought when I reach him. I touch his arm, and he looks at me.

'You did this for me?'

He nods.

'Thank you.' I step toward him to embrace him. I am so full of gratitude; I want him to know that no one in the world ever did anything like this for me before.

He takes a step back and looks off into the middle distance. I am stunned that he rebuffs me. But I don't press it; he is not the sort of man you back into a corner.

'Why did you do this for me?' I ask him softly.

He looks at me, bewildered that I could ask such a question.

'This is something I planned a few months back . . .' A few months back? The night he came over with the apple butter? All shiny and dressed up like a boy attending his first Sunday-school class? The night he asked me to marry him out of the blue? Is this what he means?

'Obviously things have changed. I still wish you all the best. I'm glad this all worked out for you.' Worked out for me? He didn't fix my stove or paint my fence, for God's sake. He brought me my family. Why is he so cold, and what is he talking about?

'Take care of yourself.' He pats my hand and turns. He walks up the street toward town. I have an impulse to shout after him, but he is walking fast. What would I say to him, anyway? This is so strange. Where is he going? Why is he acting like this? Can't he see how grateful I am? How happy this has made me? Why won't he stay?

'Ave Maria! *Andiamo!*' Nonna calls out to me from the porch. She waves a hanky at me to come back to the house. Theodore waits for me by the gate.

'What was that all about?' I ask him.

'You are so dense.'

'Can you please explain? I don't understand.'

'Ave. The man sold his new truck to bring your family here. He is in love with you.'

'He is not!'

'Who does something like this for somebody he's not in love with?'

'Theodore, you don't know about Jack Mac.'

'What's to know? He's generous? He's a good man?'

'I'm sick of hearing about what a saint he is. Believe me, he's not perfect.'

'Oh, well, if it's perfect you want . . .' Theodore throws his hands up.

'Stop! If he was ever in love with me, he isn't anymore. I was the second course between Sweet Sue Tinsley and Sarah Dunleavy. But that's okay. He was very polite about it. Now I'll be the one with good manners. I'll reciprocate. He did a beautiful thing for me and I will pay him back. I will.'

'Okay, okay,' Theodore says, looking toward the house.

'Come on,' I growl. 'I've got company. Be entertaining!'

I will not ruin this day for my family with my own problems. Obviously, Jack Mac has changed his mind about me. It is done.

He's found someone new. He and Sarah Dunleavy are happy now. I can settle up with him about his truck later. I have a family, I think as Theodore and I climb the porch steps. They need me. And I have so many questions.

*N*onna has made a delectable lunch of risotto and wine and bread. Iva Lou has never had risotto before; she is surprised – she thought all Italian food had red sauce. Nonna explains Northern Italian cuisine, using Gala as a translator. I ask Nonna how she smuggled her ingredients through Customs. Nonna looks at Gala, who shrugs and says, 'My Frank works in Customs.'

Iva Lou corners my father and tells him how she's always wanted to have a wild international romance with an Italian gentleman, but it was not to be because Lyle Makin changed all that. (*Ciao*, Matterhorn.) My father listens intently, nodding a lot and making Iva Lou feel important. I hear my father tell her that very few Italian men live up to their amorous reputations. He convinces Iva Lou that she hasn't missed a thing having secured monogamy with a good American mountain man.

After lunch Mario sets up a card game, which attracts the men and Zia Antonietta. It surprises me that my mother and father's families get along so well. There don't appear to be any hard feelings about what happened. No anger. There doesn't seem to be any guilt either. This helps me. So much time has been wasted, it seems silly to waste more of it in sadness and regret.

As I help my *nonna* clear the table and set up dessert, I hear Gala telling Iva Lou the saga of her boyfriend, Frank DeCaesar, in detail. Iva Lou is fascinated by the twists and turns of Gala's volatile love affair. If there's anyone on earth who can steer Gala through the jungle of love with common sense, it's Iva Lou.

Zackie Wakin knocks on the screen door. Iva Lou lets him in.

'Zackie, did you smell the risotto from town?' I yell from the kitchen.

'No ma'am.' He smiles. 'Spec and me heard about the surprise you was going to get today and thought you could use some beds, since you done give yours away. If you'd like, we could set up a little hotel for ye.'

He and Spec set everything up quickly. Zackie's served in Italy; he knows about *la siesta*. The family will stay for a few days; how wonderful that the boys can turn this old empty house into an instant hotel.

After we talk, the relatives are tired and beg for a nap. Everyone except Mario, who wants to go for a walk. I have been waiting all afternoon to be alone with him. I kept looking over at him throughout the meal. I cannot believe he is here. It is an amazing thing to get what you want in life.

Mario wants to see the neighborhood. We set out for a walk, but you can hardly call it that. No more than five steps from the house, he stops. He looks all around, carefully. He lingers at each house and studies the architecture. He asks me questions about the trees, what sorts of things we grow in our gardens, and what the weather is like from season to season. It's as though he is trying to place me in the world. How did his child get so far from home? And what is this place that she grew up in? As beautiful as our neighborhood is – and it is, all fresh and green and pink with the dogwood trees in full bloom – I know a better place to take him. I ask him if he'd like to go for a ride. He brightens up and says he'd love to. 'Are you sure you're not tired?' I ask him in Italian. He shakes his head vigorously. Italians really are very expressive. Mario has such deliberate gestures; he is so alive. I am not used to this. I see similarities between us, though. He is stubborn like me. When his mother tried to sprinkle extra cheese on his risotto he waved his hand over the dish in a chopping motion, like he was wielding an ax. I do that sort of thing, and it always surprises people around here. These are the sorts of discoveries I will make with my family, and it thrills me.

Mario climbs into the Jeep. He adjusts the front knot on his sweater, pushes his thick hair back, and nods for me to go. We drive toward Appalachia, our neighboring village and the gateway to all the roads up into the mountains. Mario notices the Powell River immediately and wants to know where it goes and whether it floods. He makes me stop on the side of the road when we get to the coal transom, a long white pipe that transports coal on a conveyor from the top of the mountain, where the mines are, to the rail yard at the foot of them. He looks at the train cars. In his thick Italian accents he sounds out Southern, the name of the railroad company, stenciled on the sides of the cars. I explain that Southern is what we are. When we drive down the main drag in Appalachia, Mario wants to stop for something to drink. So I pull up to Bessie's Diner, the best burger joint in southwest Virginia. Bessie's is always packed.

When we enter, the dull roar of conversation trails off to a quiet din of whispers. Can they sense I just brought a stranger into town? What are they looking at? Then I see, it's not the men; they look up and see us and go back to their eating. It's the women.

They can't take their eyes off Mario. One woman yanks up her bra straps by her thumbs; another wipes the crumbs from the side of her mouth with her pinky and smiles; another, at the counter, straightens her posture and gives him a sideways glance. I look at Mario. He, in turn, is surveying the women in the room as though they are each individually delectable, like pieces in a box of expensive chocolates. No woman can resist. Even a baby girl in a high chair bangs her spoon for his attention. I remember what Zia Meoli told me about Mario's reputation. I order a couple of Cokes to go, and Mario asks me more questions about geography. How far are we from Big Stone Gap? Are we going up the mountain? Do I come to Appalachia often?

Once we're back in the Jeep, I am feeling more comfortable with Mario, so I begin to ask him questions.

'Are you married?' He tells me that he is not, then he looks out the window offering no further information.

'Do you have a girlfriend?' This question makes him laugh for some reason.

He shrugs and lights a cigarette.

'Why aren't you married?' I ask him.

'Why aren't you?' he asks me.

I'm sure he didn't mean that to be as snippy as it sounds. Hasn't anybody told him I'm the town spinster?

'You are beautiful,' he says simply. 'I don't understand.'

I think it is very sweet that he compliments me, even though it is somewhat to his credit, as I resemble him. I am happy, though, that he doesn't think his only daughter is a troll. How am I going to explain why I'm not married? I don't think there's a simple answer to that question.

'I don't know,' I tell him. 'It just never happened for me.'

He throws back his head and laughs.

'What is so funny?' I'm getting annoyed.

'A woman can always, always, always get married,' he says. 'She must want it.'

I don't know how to say 'Give me a break' in Italian, so I begin a long-winded speech about all the reasons I'm not married. Right man, wrong timing. Love living alone. Ambivalent about children. Job all-consuming. Other interests. Taking care of sick parents. I go on and on until he stops me.

'Ridiculous,' he says, and waves his hand with a grand gesture of dismissal.

The man is my father, and I cannot leave him on the side of the road. But I have just bared my soul to him, and he has waved it off like a summer fly.

'When a woman wants to marry, she lets the man know she is interested. That is all I am saying.'

Now I feel foolish for being so loud and defensive and yapping on and on. He senses this too and redirects the conversation to himself.

'I am the mayor of Schilpario.'

I nod.

'When you come to Schilpario, you will see that we have mountains, too. The Italian Alps. They are much higher and the peaks are sharp. The snow stays on the peaks year-round. We ski in the winter. We rest in the summer. Wild berries grow all over the mountainside – delicious, sweet blackberries. All we do is squeeze a little lemon on them and eat them. No sugar. They are sweet enough. Delicious.' He smiles.

We drive up the mountain in silence. Mario looks all around and seems to enjoy the quiet and the view. He looks over the side of the mountain where there are no guardrails, but he isn't scared; dangerous heights remind him of home. We drive past Insko and up to a clearing. I want to show him the waterfalls of Roaring Branch.

I park the Jeep. We walk into the woods and up the path. I watch the expression on his face as he sees the falls for the first time. He smiles and stands still and looks at it. He opens his hands, palms up, and stands there just like my mother's statue of Saint Francis of Assisi in the backyard.

'It is beautiful!' he says. 'Wonderful!'

I take him on the path that leads up the side of the falls and show him the way the water cascades over the rocks, leaving caverns of dry space in the overhang.

Then Mario kneels down next to the stream just like the time when I was little and Mrs. White took our second-grade class up to Huff Rock and taught us how to drink of the stream. My father cups his hands the very same way, and without disturbing the sediment he skims the surface of the clear water and then takes a drink. He motions for me to do the same. I kneel next to him and drink from the stream.

There is a place above the waterfalls where folks sit and have picnics. You can see the creeks connecting that feed into one small river that spills over and creates the Roaring Branch. We sit on the rocks and are quiet for a long time. In my mind I rehearse several ways to bring up the subject of my mother, but as I try them out, they don't seem right to me, so I don't say anything. Again, he senses something and solves my problem.

'Tell me about your mother,' he says.

I really don't know where to begin. And I don't want to get emotional. It's too late for all of that now because it can't change anything. I want to know his side of things, but the lump in my throat won't let me make words.

'Perhaps I should tell you what I remember,' he says kindly.

'Please.'

'Fiametta Vilminore was a very beautiful girl from a very good family in Bergamo. She was a hard worker. I fell in love with her when I saw her at her father's shop in town.' He shrugs as though this is the most natural thing in the world, to meet a beautiful girl and to fall in love. He pulls a pack of cigarettes from his shirt; he offers me one, which I decline, then he lights his own.

'She was strong-willed. Once, when I drove her up the mountain, she gave me orders about how to handle the horses. I just laughed at her. I think she liked that.'

'Why did you end your romance with her?'

Mario's face changes from a slight smile to no expression whatsoever. He thinks about his answer.

'I had to,' he offers. 'I had a wife already.' He looks at the water. His eyes follow it as it seeps over the rocks and down to the falls.

'I thought you said you weren't married.'

'I'm not married now. I was then.'

'Did my mother know?'

'Yes. I told her in a letter.'

This explains why Mama panicked when we were ready to go to Italy. She was afraid she would see him again, and he would reject her again. And what if he rejected me? She wouldn't have put me through that. She wanted more for me. She didn't want me to be the child of a brief affair by a woman he hardly remembered. What mother would? Of course she couldn't go back there.

'What happened to your wife?'

'She went home to her parents. I wasn't a good husband.'

No kidding. Somebody should tell this guy you're not supposed to date after you marry. But what good would it do now? One look at this man, and you can see that he would never change for anyone. Mario does not pretend to be a man of great virtue; I don't even get the sense he cares about that. He seems a little vain, but what great-looking man isn't? He is comfortable with himself and accepts himself, including whatever this thing is he does with women. If he weren't my father, I'd be fascinated by him. He knows himself, and he's not about to let anyone, any woman that is, possess him.

As we walk back down the mountain to the clearing, we don't say much. I wish I could hold Mario responsible for everything that has happened, but I can't. He was a seventeen-year-old boy. My mother was just a girl. I think of her; she spent her whole life pining for her first love. She was so loyal to Mario Barbari. I remember when she had a few minutes to herself, she would stack several records on the stereo, sit in her chair, close her eyes, and listen. She did not nap; she was dreaming of someone. I am sure that it was Mario. He is too compelling for her to have ever forgotten him or replaced him in her heart. For the first time in my life I am not sad for my mother. She had a beautiful dream. A dream of a faraway land and a dashing man who made love to her and gave her a baby. Maybe she knew he could never live up to what she imagined him to be. Or maybe when she realized that he was never going to come and rescue her, she did what all strong women do: she found a way to save herself. Very practical. So very much my mother's way.

I wish my mother could have told me this story herself. I find myself angry with her, not him – even though he is here and I could express my anger to him. I don't know him well enough yet to do that. My mother and I were so close, practically inseparable. It hurts me that she could not tell me the truth. Even shameful mistakes can be rectified, healed, and forgiven once they are dealt with. How sad for us that Mama could not let go of her shame.

As we drive back to the Gap, I picture the three of us: Mama,

Mario, and me. What if we had been able to reunite as a family after Fred Mulligan died? What if she had told me the truth? What if we went to Italy, found him, and knocked on his door? Would we have fit in his life? Mama knew there was no place for us there. She knew she must stay in his memory where she was young and beautiful and the thing men love best: undemanding. She would be the best lover in his mind's eye: the uncomplicated great love of his youth. How did she know that those memories are what warms old age? When my father speaks of my mother, a look of contentment settles into his face. He has had many, many women since. I wonder if he really cared about her.

'Did you love her?'

He does not answer me.

'It's okay, Mario. I can handle it.' I pat his shoulder.

'I never forgot Etta,' he says.

No one ever called my mother Etta; I am so happy he had a special name for her.

I cannot ask him any more questions right now, because I understand, just from the few short hours I have known him, that he does not have much of an attention span. He asks a lot of questions, but he doesn't stay on any one topic for very long. I can see that he is tired of this one. I change the subject as we drive through town. This pleases him.

Theodore is being a real doll and arranging all sorts of side trips for the relatives. He borrowed the school van to take my family around. Nonna loved Cudjo's Caverns. Her favorite local cuisine is soup beans and corn bread; she has eaten it every day. Mario and I are becoming good friends; everywhere we go, people tell me I look like him. We convinced Gala to stay for the four-day visit. Even though she is American, Big Stone Gap is like a foreign land to her. Worley has a crush on her, but he doesn't know it. He just follows her around like he's never seen a woman before.

Theodore and I plan a doozy of a final night for the family. We're going to take them to the Carter Family Fold. I hope we haven't built it up too much. My aunts can't wait to try clog dancing and eat their first chili dogs.

When we arrive at the Fold, the parking field is packed with cars, as usual. As we pile out of the van, my Italian relatives move slowly, like they are disembarking a spaceship. They look all around at the cars, the people, and the old barn, twinkling in the field against the blue mountains.

Iva Lou and Lyle are dancing when we get there. I take sweaters and purses and stake out a row of hay bales. Theodore takes Gala and my aunts in one direction. Fleeta takes Mario, Nonna, and my uncle to the food stand.

Sitting on the bale of hay, I realize that this is the first time since they've arrived that I've been alone and had a chance to think. It has all been so crazy – their arrival, our talks late into the night every night, the touring. I'm glad I live in a place I can show off easily in four days. The Fold is pretty much the grand finale of tourist sights around Big Stone Gap.

Nonna asked me to spend the summer with them in Schilpario. I think I will. I'm happy my new family has had the chance to visit Big Stone Gap before I move away entirely. They were able to stay in my mother's house. Even without furniture, my mother's spirit is very much alive there. Pearl and Leah will take good care of it. The fall will be a perfect time for me to relocate and find a job. Doesn't everyone start new projects in the fall?

Iva Lou and Lyle come off the dance floor. She gives him a

quick kiss, and he's off to get something to eat. She waves to me and climbs up to our row of hay.

'What did you do with the Eye-talians?'

'They're having their first chili dogs.'

'Good for them. Hope they like 'em.'

'They've liked everything they've eaten. I can't believe it. My father likes fried chicken, and my aunts love collard greens. Imagine that.'

The folks on the dance floor shift in a large circle, revealing Jack MacChesney and Sarah the schoolteacher waltzing gracefully. Iva Lou catches me looking at them.

'I hate that woman,' she decides.

'Who?'

'The bony schoolteacher.'

'Why?'

'She's workin' Jack Mac over. I don't like it one bit when a woman takes advantage of a vulnerable man. Unless it's me, of course.'

'He likes her,' I say matter-of-factly.

'It's more than that. She's going after him big-time. She was over at the beauty parlor today chatting me up about all the things they do together. They've even gone camping. It makes me sick.'

'Why?' I have to admit the camping part makes me a little sick too. You can take one look at Sarah and know she is not the outdoors type. Old Jack Mac better get a lot of camping trips in before he marries her because that'll be the last time he sees her frying steaks in the great wild. She's a bait-and-trap type. Once the trap shuts, no more bait.

'You know why.'

'No, I really don't. She's not in your business. You've got Lyle. So why do you care?'

'Don't do this,' Iva says, annoyed.

'Do what?'

'I think it's terrible how you've treated Jack Mac. He sold his truck to bring your family over here, and you haven't even thanked him properly. What is wrong with you?'

'Iva, I've got a house full of company. I was planning on going over to his house tomorrow night. Okay?'

'You should have chased him up the street when he left your house that day!'

'He stormed off.'

'You didn't even holler after him to stop him. He'd have come back.'

'You don't know what he said to me.'

'It couldn't have been bad. The man is crazy about you.'

Poor Iva Lou. She believes in love. I want to shake her and say, *Wake up! It's me you're talking about. No man is crazy about me. How much proof do you need? I'm alone.* Instead, I turn defensive. 'You don't know the whole story, so don't assume this is all on me because it's not.'

'Fill me in, girl.'

I whisper, 'A few months back, he felt sorry for me and came over and proposed. He was supposedly broken up with Sweet Sue, but after I said no, hardly the weekend passed and he was out with her again. So it wasn't love or apple butter that drove him over to my house, it was pity. Okay?'

'Pity? Who in their right mind would ever pity you?'

'You don't know what he's like. He's very confused.'

'He doesn't strike me that way, but all right, if you say so.'

'I tried to thank him. I went to hug him. I couldn't believe what he had done. But he pulled away, he actually stepped back and didn't want me to touch him.'

'It didn't look like that from the porch.'

'I'm not lying to you, Iva.'

Jack Mac follows Sarah outside to the food stand. He guides her with his hand on her lower back. She reaches back with her right hand and pats his leg. Iva Lou sees this, too, and she makes a disgusted clucking noise. 'Somebody needs to tell her that flats are a no-no for girls with thick ankles.'

'Let's just say he did love me once. He sure as hell doesn't anymore. Let it go.'

Iva Lou can't let it go. 'How do you feel about him?'

I shake my head. I don't want to get into all of this. How *do* I feel about him? All I know is that when I kind of liked him, he didn't like me. And then when he liked me, I didn't want him. I do think of the kiss sometimes – well, let's be honest, it's the last thing I think about when I'm in that weakened state right before sleep. I go right back to the trailer park, to the book, to the pools of light coming out of the windows, to the way he smelled, to the way my face fit into his chest like a puzzle piece, to his eyes that looked at me with such tenderness and with just a little humor, too. I re-create the whole picture, and then he kisses me. It's my good-night kiss, I guess, and the last thing I remember before breakfast. But this is my little ritual, and I'm certainly not going to share it with Iva Lou.

'Are you afraid of him?'

'God, no.'

'I don't mean of him per se.' Iva Lou struggles to find the words for the right way to invade my privacy.

'Are you afraid of having sex with him?'

'Iva Lou.' My tone says, *Stop this, please.*

'Look, I'm just your friend. And you know all about me. But I'll be damned, I don't know how *you* feel about certain things. You never talk about how you feel about men. As a woman. The most fun in life for a woman is to talk about men. Look at me. It's my favorite topic in and out of the bedroom.'

'I don't like to talk about it.'

'Well, try. I'm a girl. You're a girl. We got our own little club; and men have no idea what we talk about. Your secrets are safe with me.' From the doorway Lyle holds up a chili dog toward Iva Lou. She shakes her head and waves him off. He goes back to talking with his buddies.

'Come on. Tell me what makes you tick. Before you leave town and I never see you again.' Iva Lou looks so pitiful, I almost want to explain myself to her.

'I think he's attractive. I do.' I hope this will be enough to get her off the subject of Jack Mac forever.

'That's a start. Now, don't leave me hanging. Go on.' I don't think I've ever seen Iva Lou this excited.

'When I saw him at the end of my walk the day my family arrived, I thought he was the most beautiful person I had ever seen.'

'And you didn't throw yourself into his arms, right there and then?'

'Because he . . .'

'Follow your impulses for once! Girl, you're how old? Thirty-six? When do you think you're gonna have sex? When you're sixty? Ninety? Honey-o, get in there and have you some while you're still limber. What are you waiting for? How could you let somebody like Jack Mac slip through your fingers? I bet the sex with him is primo. I can just tell.'

I wish Iva Lou would stop talking, but she can't. She is trying very hard to make me understand. I have never seen her on such a tear.

She continues, 'Do you deprive yourself of a ripe strawberry or a spritz of nice perfume or a good book because you don't think you deserve them? Hell, no. Sex is no different. It is a delightful gift from God that makes life pleasant. Now, what could be wrong with that? You'll find out a helluva lot more about yourself in bed with a good man than you will traipsing off to some foreign country with a camera and a guidebook. You need to get honest with yourself. You're afraid. But you want sex. You ought to have you some sex.'

On the dance floor Otto and Worley are teaching my grandmother how to clog. A supportive crowd has gathered to cheer her on. Iva Lou and I join in. Nonna's body is a small barrel, her legs thin but well-shaped. Her eyes gleam as she dances. She segues from an Appalachian two-step into a folk dance we don't do in these parts – must be Alpine Italian. Otto and Worley follow her lead, and soon everyone is spinning and smiling.

Iva Lou and I run out of breath first and sit down to watch. I look off in the grass, a bit beyond the door, and see my father talking to Jack MacChesney. My father's hands are expressive as usual. Jack Mac leans into my father's ear and says something. They laugh and shake hands. Sarah joins them – does she ever leave him alone for five minutes? Jack Mac introduces her to my father. Jack Mac and Sarah leave. My father looks around for us and cuts across the dance floor to join me.

'What were you talking about?' I ask Mario, indicating the conversation he just had with Jack Mac.

'His Italian is pretty good,' my father says.

'He doesn't speak Italian.'

'He just did.' Mario shrugs. How do you like that? Maybe Sarah Dunleavy taught Jack a few key phrases she picked up from the *Godfather* movies. How continental of her.

'Jack Mac is a very kind man. Don't you think?' Mario looks off. Sure, Jack is a very kind man, and I'm very grateful. But he won't accept my gratitude, which makes a jackass out of me. I would love to tell my father all about Jack MacChesney and Sweet Sue and the proposal and Sarah Dunleavy and everything, but I think better of it. He would just smile and say something breezy in colloquial Italian about the salt in the cupboard or the eyes of a fish or some other image that doesn't make any sense or apply. Doesn't anybody see how hard all of this is for me?

Gala coralls us all into a group – she is first and foremost a travel director – and we head off for the van. On the drive home, everyone laughs as Nonna recounts how Otto and Worley tried to teach her how to clog. I don't feel much like laughing. I am filling up with sadness and regret. My family just got here, and already they're leaving. I don't want them to go! I wish this black road would never end and we could stay inside this van forever talking and laughing with Theodore behind the wheel and my father at my side.

When we get back to the house, Nonna gives Gala the dry soup beans and seasonings she bought at the Piggly Wiggly to take back to Italy.

'I'm gonna break it off for good with Frank tomorrow night. After I get Nonna's soup beans through Customs. Hey, he used me, now I use him.'

Nonna kisses me good night and goes off to bed.

I watch Gala stuff soup beans in socks. She looks at me.

'Are you okay?' I nod. 'You look sad. You're going to miss them.'

'It's gone by so fast. But I don't want to complain, I sound so ungrateful.'

'Believe me. It was a project getting these folks over here. What a logistical nightmare. Could they live any farther up in the Alps? They're a pack of goats, your family.'

'Gala, who contacted you about getting my family over here?' . 'Iva Lou.'

'Iva Lou?'

'She called first. But it was just an inquiry. You know, to find out how this sort of tour would work. So I gave her a breakdown and took notes. Of course, I wasn't sure how it would work, but then I thought of it as a reverse tour and I was fine. Iva Lou didn't talk money or anything, though. That was entirely Jack MacChesney's department. He's a cute one, don't you think?'

'When did he call you to make the arrangements?'

She shrugs. 'A couple of months ago. I could look it up.'

'Was my trip planned before or after theirs?' I wave my hand to indicate my houseguests.

'After.' Gala looks guilty for a moment and then continues. 'I was expecting your call. Iva Lou tipped me off. I'm sorry. I lied to you, I trumped up a fake trip to make you think it was happening. But we had already planned the relatives coming over, so I saw no harm in it. Frank arranged the fake airline tickets I sent you. I'm sorry.'

How could I be angry with Gala? My family is in my house, and we have had the best time.

'Don't apologize,' I say to Gala. 'I owe you so much more than you will ever owe me.' I really mean this.

That sneaky Iva Lou. That day on the Bookmobile, long ago, when Jack Mac was there with a newspaper, that's when they found Gala. So, when I needed an international travel agent, Iva Lou conveniently had the page with Gala's advertisement poised in the storage bin to give to me. Jack Mac said he started planning this back when he proposed. And those Mormons; Iva Lou set that up to buy more time for Jack Mac's plan. Is the whole town in on my business?

Everyone has gone to bed. We set three alarms so we would not oversleep. The Piedmont plane out of Tri-Cities for John F. Kennedy Airport in New York leaves at 7:00 A.M., and there isn't another connection, so they must make it. (I remember that 'Piedmont' means 'foot of the mountains.' What a poor name for an airline!) I can't sleep, so I'm wandering around the house trying not to make noise. I tiptoe outside and sit on the porch. I'm anticipating how sad I will be tomorrow after everyone leaves. Yes, I am going to Italy to visit them in a few weeks; Gala took care of everything without penalty, and she invited me to stay with her in New Jersey for a week and see New York before I go overseas! But after that, what? Where will I go? Maybe I'll like Schilpario and stay there. I ponder that for a moment. How I wish Mama were here. Imagine how happy she would have been to see me with her family, knowing that I would never be alone in the world again. Even that I could not give her. Why did my mother's life have to be so hard? I breathe deeply. I will never answer that question.

Zia Meoli stands at the screen door.

'I can't sleep,' she says. This makes me laugh. She sounds just like my mother. And even though you would never say my mother was a comical person, sometimes she could say one sentence in such a way that it made you laugh. Zia Meoli comes outside.

'I wanted to talk to you alone.' She pulls up a chair next to me. 'Please.'

'How do you like him?' She indicates the window behind which my father sleeps.

'I like him.' She shrugs. 'Don't you?'

Zia Meoli thinks for a moment. 'He's a politician,' she decides.

I figure in Italy that's not a compliment. 'Zia . . .' I begin, but from the look on her face, I can see that she knows what I am going to ask her. 'Do you remember when Mama left Bergamo?'

She nods as though it was yesterday. 'Your mother left us in the middle of the night. She did not tell us where she was going. She left a letter for me, telling me that I should not worry about her, that she would write to me.'

I can tell from Zia's expression that she has replayed these events over in her mind many times. She is still bothered by them.

'Did you want to go after her to find her?' I ask.

'Yes! Of course, yes! I thought of every place she might go. Cousins. Other towns. But no one had seen her. And she left no clue as to where she went or why. I was suspicious, because she spoke of Mario Barbari often, but I said nothing because I wasn't sure. My mother, your grandmother, was destroyed. After Fiametta left, she could never be consoled.'

'What about your father?'

'I think he knew what happened. See, he knew Mario Barbari. He knew his family, not well, but in business. When Papa figured out that Fiametta liked Mario, he felt she was too young to court. So he forbade her to see him. She was devastated. But our father was very strict. If anything improper had occurred, he would have made Fiametta leave our home. My sister knew this. Though it broke my heart that she did what she did, I understood. She had no choice. I would have done the same thing.'

'But she was only seventeen. Just a girl.'

'At that time, many Italians were leaving the country. Some to Canada, some to South America, some to Australia. All over. Many, of course, went to New York. America. I knew that if she could, she would leave Italy altogether, so as not to bring shame upon us. I also knew that when she made a decision, she would never turn back.'

'Did you know she was pregnant with me?'

Zia Meoli shakes her head; she did not know of her sister's condition.

'If you knew about Mario Barbari, why didn't you go to him?'

She nods vehemently. 'I went to him. I did.'

'Did you know he was married?'

'I knew a family up the mountain, in a town about fifteen kilometers from Schilpario. They knew of him, where I could find him. They told me he was married. I was sure he had married my sister. But it wasn't Fiametta, it was another girl. I was told it was a match, and it did not work. The girl went back with her parents after a short time.'

'How do they make a match?'

'The families come together and decide who their children will marry. Pietro and I were a match. He was one of five children, four of them sons. His father came to my father, and they discussed which daughter would be suitable for his sons. Antonietta loved a boy in Sestri Levante, near Genoa, and Fiametta was gone, so that left me. I met Pietro, I liked him very well. We courted for one year, and then we got married.' She folds her arms indicating that making matches is the most natural way to make a marriage in the whole world.

'So, what happened when you went to find Mario Barbari?'

'Oh, yes!' She remembers as she goes back to her story. I notice that Italians do digress – I am guilty of it too. In the middle of a story, one element of it grabs their attention, and then they're off the subject entirely, never to return. I am reminded of how alike we are, even though I was not influenced by them when I was growing up. These similarities, though, are deep and in our bones.

'Mario da Schilpario was very suave. The black, black hair. The black eyes. Very striking man. I figured out a way to get up the mountain without my father finding out the real reason for my trip. I was hoping that Fiametta would be there with him, and I could talk sense to her and have her come home. When I got to Schilpario, I found Mario working in the church. His family are glass and metal workers. They make stained-glass windows.' Another fact about my father I didn't know!

'I knew it was him right away, because I remembered him from town; he drove a carriage down for supplies sometimes, and all the girls in Bergamo took note of him. I asked to speak with him alone. He was very pleasant, but he knew nothing of my sister's whereabouts. He had not heard from her. He asked me to understand his position; he had a wife, and they were trying to make their marriage work, even though they did not live under one roof. He thought my sister was beautiful and sweet, but theirs was a romance that could never be. Would I tell her that when I found her? I told him that was something he needed to discuss with Fiametta himself. I remember that, at the mention of her name, his eyes had great pain in them. I believe he loved her.'

Zia Meoli has obviously given this a great deal of thought. But she is a woman, too, and she knows what happens to unsuspecting girls who fall for the town Lothario. At first, they accept that they are one of many, but they hope they can tame him, win his heart, and make him faithful and true. At seventeen, my mother didn't know that she would never win this battle. But she was so in love, she gave him her heart anyway. It is so ironic that I am Mario's only child. All those women, all that romance, and I am the only child that grew from it.

'So, I went back down the mountain, with no more information than when I left. I gathered my mother and my sister in a room, away from my father, and told them what I had learned. My mother was devastated; she was certain I would find Fiametta and bring her home. My mother's health turned at that time. She cried all the time, she took to her bed. The Italians would say that her blood turned. Her sadness had made her ill.'

'What about your father?'

'My mother never discussed it with my father. She knew where he stood on the matter. If Fiametta had done wrong, she had to live with the consequences. One time he and I had an argument about it. He told me he knew that my sister was alive and well. He knew how strong-willed she was. Papa thought that she could protect herself. I thought he was cold and indifferent, and I was very angry with him for not setting out to find her. But he and Fiametta had always had a sense about each other; I never had that with him.'

'A sense?'

'Papa knew what she was thinking. He always did. He could tell before she did something what she was going to do. It was mystical.'

'When did Mama write her first letter to you?'

'It was almost a year after she left. How happy Mama was when that letter came from America.'

'I didn't find any letters from your mother to my mother.'

Zia Meoli shakes her finger back and forth. 'Never. My mother would never go against my father! Never!'

'Did your mother know about me?'

'She was so happy. But you were only a year or so old when she died. But my mother knew your name and all of the details Fiametta sent to me.'

'Did you ever tell your father?'

My aunt shakes her head sadly. 'If he knew, we never talked about it. Don't judge him for it, Ave Maria. It was a different time.

A girl could not leave the family home without being married, nor could she—'

'Dishonor the family name.'

Zia Meoli shakes her head again. 'I knew there was no dishonor. She was young. She was in love.' Zia sits back in the chair, rocking a bit.

Mama in love. I wish I could have seen it.

Theodore and I see everyone off at the airport, but it is in no way a sad parting. We promise to call and write one another, and we're all looking forward to the long summer in Schilpario.

My father tries to give me a wad of money, which I stuff right back into his pocket.

'Papa, I don't need it.'

'Please take it.'

'Papa, you keep it. Take care of Nonna.' He smiles and we hug for a long time. We will see each other very soon, and we're happy about that.

Theodore and I watch the plane take off. After it disappears beyond the mountains, we go to Shoney's for a leisurely lunch and relive every moment of the Eye-talian visit.

I load up the Jeep to return all the pans to the ladies in town who dropped off food while my family was visiting. One of my favorite things about Big Stone Gap is the stream of covered dishes that flows from house to house in times of joy or sadness. The ladies make it easy to get their pans back: On the bottom of each, in indelible ink on heavy tape, they print their names: N. Goodloe, E. and L. Tackett, I. Makin, J. Hendrick, and N. MacChesney. It will take me the better part of the day to shuttle these back to their owners.

I drive up to Cracker's Neck first, starting at the top of the mountain with the first pan return. Then I'll work my way back down to town. Tufts of white smoke puff out of the kitchen chimney at the MacChesneys'. I knock at the door. No answer. I knock again. Still no answer. In a split second there is loud barking behind me, and I practically jump out of my skin. It's the family dog. He keeps barking and circles back around the house. I follow him.

Mrs. Mac is hanging out the laundry. The white sheets are whiter than the clouds overhead, and even outdoors the air is filled with the clean smell of fresh laundry. She looks up and sees me and smiles.

'Thank you for the chess pie. My family loved it.'

'Who wouldn't? It's good pie.'

'Do you need some help?' I ask.

'I'm all done. Come inside. I got coffee.'

I follow Mrs. Mac into the house through the back porch. I have never seen this porch or entered the house this way. In fact, I didn't even know she had a room like this on the back of the house. You can't see it from the kitchen; it is off at a different angle and easily hidden.

The sunporch is lovely. There is rattan furniture with soft cushions, quilted in elaborate designs; I recognize the traditional 'drunkard's path' motif on a matching chair. There are hanging plants everywhere, spilling over with blooms of pink, purple, and yellow. I have never seen an indoor garden quite so beautiful; it looks like it belongs in another house, not in this clean, spare stone house in Cracker's Neck.

'Yep, this is my favorite spot in the house. Plants need a lot of care, though.'

I imagine Mrs. Mac making the sunporch her own special room, full of her feminine touches. But it is more than that; it has a spiritual feeling, like a sanctuary. I follow her through a small pantry back into the kitchen that I know so well.

'Everybody get off all right?' she asks as she fetches me a cup of coffee.

'They had the best time.'

'How about you?'

'It was a dream.'

'Good.'

'Mrs. Mac, you probably know that Jack sold his truck to pay for all of it, and I—'

She holds up her hand to stop me. 'That is his affair.'

'I know. But I want you to know that I appreciate it.'

'Honey, it ain't none of my business.'

'But—'

'It ain't.'

We sit in an uncomfortable silence for a few minutes.

'You raised a very fine person.'

'Thank you kindly.'

'Mrs. Mac, are you upset with me about something?'

'I wouldn't call it upset.'

'What would you call it?'

'There is a word for it; let me think.' She thinks a moment, gets up, goes to the cake saver, pulls off the lid, cuts a couple of pieces of pound cake, puts them on a plate, fetches two forks and two plates and two napkins, and comes back to the table and sits down with me. 'I'm mystified.'

'Excuse me?'

'Do you want my son or not?'

I can't answer her. Not only am I embarrassed, I realize that I am in that horrible position of having dragged somebody's mama into my confusion, a bad place for her and me.

'Do you mind if I don't answer that?'

'Suit yourself.'

We eat our cake and drink our coffee. Mrs. Mac stares off at the field. She looks old to me this morning. Or maybe I'm afraid that I will miss her when I leave.

'I got a lot of pans in the car, so I better shove off.'

'Ave Maria?' Mrs. Mac looks at me directly and does not blink.

'My sister Cecelia is coming to git me this afternoon to take me down to her place for a visit. I'm gonna be gone about a week. My son gets off of his shift at six sharp; he comes home here through the door no later than seven. He don't know I'm going to see his aunt, so he's gonna come home here directly, expecting dinner as usual. If I was you, and if you have one tenth the brain in your head that I think you do, you'll be sitting there on the porch waiting for him. Now, is that clear enough, youngun?'

I nod.

I give Mrs. Mac a quick hug. When I let go of her, she gives me an extra-quick hug that instructs me, *Do what I'm telling you, or I can't be responsible for what happens next.*

There are some low patches of fog as I drive down the mountain. I think of the kiss in the trailer park. It's the first time I have ever thought about it during the day. As I make the turn onto Valley Road, a cat runs out in front of my Jeep. I slam on the brakes and jump out. The cat is disappearing into the ditch but I'm afraid it might be injured. I cross the road and climb down the bank just as it slips into the dark opening of a culvert. I crawl closer and brush away the leaves in the mouth of the tunnel. There are three kittens, not even old enough to open their eyes. I back away and sit at the edge of the ditch for a moment, waiting for the mother peek out at me. Eventually she does. She licks her kittens and she seems to be okay. I start to cry. I realize what a phony I am. I told Otto in no uncertain terms that he had to be honest with Worley about his shame. And yet I cannot be honest about my own. I have chosen *not* to fall in love because I thought it would heal my mother's shame if I was a perfect daughter, always upstanding and independent. I have spent my life trying not to need anyone. But I listen to Mrs. Mac again in my mind and I realize I don't want to live like that anymore.

A car horn blasts behind me. It's Nellie Goodloe.

'Ave Maria, are you all right down there in that ditch?'

'I'm fine, Nellie,' I call back to her.

She shrugs and drives off. I stand up and brush the leaves from my pants. By the time I reach the Jeep, I know what I'm going to do.

I drop by the Pharmacy with Fleeta's pan. Fleeta is restocking the candy.

'They done picked the new Drama director,' Fleeta announces.

'Oh yeah? Who?'

'Sarah Dunleavy, that new English teacher up to the high school.'

'No!' This really makes me mad. I didn't think I was territorial about the job, but her? She doesn't have any pizzazz at all.

'*Sarah*' – Fleeta pronounces it like it's a brand name for industrial sludge – 'has done been greasin' the board of dye-rectors up one side and down the other. She done joined the Dogwood Garden Club, hell, she hosted their Early Bird Breakfast, she got herself into the sewing circle at the Methodist church, and she got Don Wax Realty to sponsor her tenth-grade English class on a field trip over to the Barter Theater to see a play. This gal is takin' things over. Trust me on that one. Are you chapped?'

'Yes. I'm chapped.' I don't know exactly why, but I am.

'I would be, too. After all you done for the folks around here. Driving yourself cuckoo, volunteering for this and that. And this is the thanks you git. Your scent ain't even evaporated in the area, and they done filled your spot. For whatever it's worth, Portly thinks it's terrible too.'

'Have we got any Coty's Emeraude cologne?'

'It's in the locked case.' Fleeta points to it, pulling a key ring with ten thousand keys on it out of her back pocket and flipping through it.

'How do you know which key?'

'It's like Braille to me. I feel the grooves.'

The first key Fleeta chooses fits the case.

'It's your lucky day. One bottle left.'

'Put it on my tab.'

Fleeta laughs and it turns into a rattle. She coughs. 'That's pretty funny, bein' it's your place.' I wish I could join in the hilarity, but I'm not feeling very funny right now. Sarah Dunleavy has taken my place in Big Stone Gap, seamlessly, effortlessly; it's as though I never existed. And I haven't even left town yet! I guess I'm just going to have to be a little more careful about marking my territory. I'll start with the Emeraude.

I spend most of the afternoon getting ready for the evening. I want to make sure that I am on the MacChesneys' porch by six o'clock, sitting there waiting. I'm afraid that if I'm late, and I drive up and see Jack Mac's truck, I'll throw the old Jeep in reverse and back down the mountain. I am very nervous about all of this; my last conversation with Jack wasn't a friendly one. I don't know if he'll turn mountain man on me and order me off his property or what. So I need to get there first and plant myself. That will give me courage.

I choose something very simple to wear: one of my new Mama blouses and a pair of jeans. A skirt would look like I'm trying to impress him, since I rarely wear them. This is a business meeting for me; I need to project a certain seriousness, and I have that in pants.

As I make the drive up through Cracker's Neck, I review carefully in my mind all the twists and turns of my friendship, or whatever you want to call it, with Jack MacChesney. Back in school, he was a shy, shadowy sort of figure. He didn't join a lot of clubs. I remember that he might have played baseball, but that would be all. My real memories of him started that morning when I caught him in his long johns and stayed for breakfast. That's the first time I really took note of him – sparkling, out of the shower. And I think I fell for him for real when he winked at me at the Drama rehearsal.

But I am not the kind of woman to steal another woman's man. First of all, I wouldn't do that to any woman because I sure as hell wouldn't want it done to me. And second, situations based on one-upmanship never, ever last. Those romances are not built on solid foundations; at the first sign of trouble, they collapse. Maybe that's part of the thrill, but to me no man was ever worth the heartbreak of a woman.

I am not naïve, though. I know there are the Sarah Dunleavys out there, who make a project out of finding the best men in every group and working their way in to their hearts by being quiet, orderly, and not much fuss. But there isn't one among us who can playact for a lifetime. Men don't understand that, though. They think they know what they're marrying because it would never dawn on men to change their behavior for anybody. 'Accept me as I am,' they seem to say as they plant their feet, 'or move on, girl.' But women? We adapt. Adapting gets results. It worked for Mama, but that life is not for me. Perhaps that is the real reason I never married. I just couldn't adapt.

Why am I driving to Cracker's Neck? What do I think I'll find here? Maybe the subconscious lull of Jack MacChesney's kiss remembered each night before I go to sleep has imprinted itself on my heart and sent a message to my brain to face myself. I don't know. It unlocked something in me, though. This old Jeep cannot plow through Cracker's Neck fast enough to deliver me safely to the MacChesneys' porch.

My fear leaves me as I sit on the porch. I am amazed at the view, and I wish the sun would stay up longer so I could really study the landscape. Finally, after what seems like years, I can see truck lights down the mountain as they make the big turn onto the property.

The truck bounces over the pits and holes in the dirt road, kicking up a little dust. The headlights shine on me as Jack drives the truck to the side of the house. I shield my eyes from the glare but stand to greet him. The truck has the price $3,100 USED written on the windshield in white shoe polish. I guess Rick Harmon loaned it to Jack from the used-car dealership. I don't know how he can see through the big white writing well enough to drive. For a moment I panic. What if Sarah Dunleavy is in the truck with him? I wish I would have brought a cake pan; at least I could look like I had an excuse to be here, and then I could cut out, with my face intact. Too late to jump in the Jeep and get out of here, so I wait. Jack parks the truck; the setting sun shines into the passenger window, and I can see he is alone. I breathe deeply.

It takes him a moment to get out of his truck, gathering his lunch pail and boots. He comes around the back of the truck and up the walk. He looks at me funny.

'Is something wrong with Mama?'

'No, no. She . . . she went to visit your Aunt Cecelia.'

'Why didn't she tell me?' Jack Mac walks up the steps, past me, and up to the door with the keys.

'I guess it came up all of a sudden or something.'

'Could be,' he says, and opens the door. Jack leans in and turns on the lights. Mrs. Mac has left a note on the front-hall table verifying what I just told him. He reads it and puts it back on the table.

It's as if I'm not even here. He isn't happy to see me, but he's not annoyed either. It's just a cordial indifference. How awful. Or is this a ploy to make me suffer? I've hurt him, so now he has to hurt me? Oh, God, he's going to make me work for this. I'm going to have to get down on my knees and beg this man to forgive me. I grab the rail on the front-porch stoop and hold it.

'Would you like to come in?' His voice is so monotone that there is no way to read whether he actually wants me to or is just being polite.

'Yes, I would.'

I stand in the doorway awaiting further instruction. But he doesn't say a word. He just goes in and out of rooms, turning on lights, dropping off the lunch pail, putting the boots away, and moving the mail from the mantel to the hallway table. It is as though I'm invisible. I wish I were.

'Do you think Mama left any supper?' he asks me, finally. It's the first friendly thing he's said, but I don't trust him.

'I don't know.'

'Let's check.' Jack Mac goes into the kitchen. I could not feel more stupid than I do, standing here. He pokes his head out of the kitchen.

'Well, come on,' he says, and goes back into the kitchen.

I follow him. Sure enough, Mrs. Mac has prepared a meal. The table is set for two, and there is a patio candle, a dark blue one, in white mesh in the middle of the table. The setup makes me feel awkward; it is almost as bad as parents fawning all over their pimply kids on prom night.

'Why don't you heat up supper and I'll start the fire?' He looks at me like I'm a moron, who can't figure out that if I came all the way up here and it's suppertime, we might as well eat. I go to the refrigerator and pull out a casserole that has the indelible ink and tape strip that says 'mac 'n cheese.' I preheat the oven.

What am I doing here? This is the worst idea I've ever had. I have to make a move to get out of here, and fast. I would rather die than tell him about the kiss-before-sleeping thing, or how I love the way he smells, or how I'd just as soon rip out Sarah Dunleavy's eyes as lose him to her. Why did I come up this mountain tonight? I should have just bought him a new truck and had it delivered and moved away and forgotten all about him. I am too old to be feeling this out of control. Why is he so calm? He is doing this to me on purpose. I bet he thinks this is funny. Mr. Never Without a Girlfriend. Go ahead, make fun of the Terrified Old Maid.

'I'm going to take a shower. You make the salad.' He goes.

Where is the phone? I'll call Theodore and tell him to come and get me. I don't think I can drive in the state I'm in. This man has me completely and totally unglued. My hands feel numb, as though I could snap them off like rubber gloves. Jack Mac sticks his head back into the kitchen. I jump.

'Don't put any radishes in it. I hate them.' He goes again.

Jesus, he popped his head in here and scared me like a lurker in a horror movie. He must have seen me jump, because it's the first time I saw him smile tonight. This is torture. Should I just leave? Why don't I? I can't. My feet won't move. Deep inside, I feel my core and it centers me. I breathe deeply and evenly, regulating my nerves and settling my heart. I check my makeup in the toaster. I look good. I can do this. I make the salad. I make the dressing. I find a bowl and put it on the table. Then I choose a seat at the table and sit down. And I wait.

Finally, he comes back into the kitchen. He is freshly scrubbed and looks neat. He is dressed nicely, in a denim shirt and old jeans, but it doesn't look like he's trying too hard. He goes to the oven, pulls out the casserole, and puts it on the table. He takes a bottle of wine out of the refrigerator. Without asking me, he uncorks it.

'Wine?' he offers.

I put my face in my hands. 'I'd rather have an aspirin.' Now, why he finds this so amusing, I do not know. But he laughs like he thinks it is the funniest thing he's ever heard. He laughs long enough that I take offense.

'What is so funny?'

'You are.'

'I'm mighty glad I'm so entertaining.'

'You're more than that.' Jack Mac sits down. What is he talking about? What does he mean? I feel like he's speaking a different language. There's a good starting point.

'My father told me you spoke Italian with him.'

'I know a little.'

'How?'

'From a book. I got the Berlitz book-and-tape series from the county library.'

'Why?'

'I wanted to learn it.'

'Because of me?'

'You aren't the only Italian in the world, you know.'

'I didn't mean it to sound that way. I just assumed—'

'Well, don't.'

I have had enough, and I haven't even been inside this old, ugly, hateful stone house for an hour. But I am not going to bite his head off. I am going to be dignified about this whole thing.

'Why are you being cruel to me?'

He thinks about this for minute. 'Maybe it's self-protection.'

Okay, now I get it. I hurt him, so he has to decimate me to level the playing field. How childish. How childish for a man with more gray hair than brown.

'I am not going to hurt you.' I don't know why I say this, but it seems to me that this is the issue and I should address it.

'Too late for that.'

He is really mad at me. I don't know how I'm going to get through to him. Or should I even keep trying? Maybe he wants me to leave, and his genteel Southern manners won't let him throw me out.

'Do you want me to go?' I ask very nicely.

'Do you want to go?'

I hate when people answer questions with questions. 'No, I don't,' I say to him pointedly. I don't know where that came from; I would have given my right leg to get out of here a minute ago, but somehow, hearing that I have hurt him makes me stay.

'Are you in love with Sarah Dunleavy?'

'Why are you asking?'

'Because if you are, I will take up your offer and leave.'

'And if I'm not?'

'If you're not, I think we could work this thing out and you could get very lucky tonight, as your mother is out of town.'

Where did that come from? Thank God he's laughing, or I might have to ask where they keep the gun they use to shoot rabid dogs and just turn it on myself.

'Had I known it was that easy, I wouldn't have sold my truck.' He gets up and pours himself a glass of water.

'Why did you sell your truck?' Now I'm standing. I think the two bites of macaroni helped me get my strength back. I'm ready for him now. So I keep going. 'It was fully loaded. It was your dream truck. You loved that truck.'

'Yeah, but I've loved you since the sixth grade.'

He turns to me. I can't move. He doesn't either. He just stands there looking at me. Finally, he points to the floor in front of his feet, indicating that I should walk to him – he is not going to come to me. So I take those twelve steps and fall into his arms. I didn't think this moment would mean so much to me, but once I am in his arms, leaning against this place on his chest that I have dreamed of, there is nothing that could tear me away from him ever again. He kisses me, just like he has in my dreams every night since Iva Lou's wedding. I am so mad at myself for having wasted so much time.

It is early in the evening, and we still have a lot to talk about. We finish dinner (he is hungry, I am not). Then Jack wants to show me the house. He starts with the sunporch, which looks even cozier at night. He shows me his mother's bedroom from the doorway, a simple pale blue room. The parlor. The sitting room. And then he takes me upstairs to show me the attic, a room the size of the whole house. Mrs Mac's quilting supplies are organized on simple wooden shelves, and there is a long farm table in the middle of the room, with chairs around it. Jack Mac explains that this is where Aunt Cecelia and various friends come and quilt. He leads me to the window, which overlooks the magnificent Powell Valley. I can see for miles; though it is dark, the faraway streetlights give the small pockets of the mountains a twinkling glow.

While we're in the attic room, he shows me some photographs in the family album. There are pictures of his mother when she was a girl. I think she looked like Loretta Young in *Call of the Wild*; Jack tells me his father always thought so, too. He tells me his parents had a real love affair, and how sad she was for so long after he died.

Jack shares a little about his romantic past with me, enough to help me understand but certainly not anything to make me feel uncomfortable or envious. He confides that he was worried I'd marry Theodore and he would miss his chance with me. He has a lot of questions for me, too. He wants to know where I was going when I gave everything to Pearl. I tell him I wasn't sure. I was planning to take a long trip to Italy and then decide where to settle. He asks me if I still want to live in Big Stone Gap. I'm still not completely sure, but I am starting to see that the place didn't make me unhappy; I made me unhappy. I started to view everyday things as a burden, so they became a burden. But I tell him that it had a lot to do with my mother's death.

Jack asks me about Fred Mulligan, with whom I now feel at peace. Jack remembers him as a decent man but very stern. I agree with him. I guess I was lucky; I learned a lot from the bad stuff, too. Who would have thought meeting Mario da Schilpario would help me let go of Fred Mulligan?

I ask Jack about his father. He smiles. 'The best thing a father can do for his son is love his mother. And he did that.'

I think of Iva Lou telling me that Jack Mac didn't throw himself around town with the ladies indiscriminately. Maybe he's just like his father. He leads me out to the sunporch, taking the patio candle with us. We lie on the couch. He holds me. Then he tells me what's in his heart. 'I'd been trying to get your attention at the Drama for years. I was always offering to stay and help with the stage crew, or I offered to bring you home a lot. Do you remember?' Now I do remember. But I never thought he was interested in me *that* way. I wasn't that kind of girl. I was always so busy. 'You always seemed perfectly nice, but you never really paid me any mind.' I didn't. I was friendly to everybody, but I never chose favorites. A little of that was Mazie Dinsmore's directing style that I imitated, and part of it was my own brand of shyness with men. I never looked for a man in any crowd; I felt completely fulfilled by my friendship with Theodore.

Jack continues, 'And then there was that night, when Sweet Sue gave you the champagne and then the cast started teasing us and begging me to propose. That was just about the worst night of my life. Because I wanted to turn to you and say, "You're the one I want." Sue knew it too. That's when I decided to just be direct with you. That's when I came over and asked you to marry me.'

'You thought I'd say yes and that would be it?'

'I thought you'd think about it. I didn't think you'd say no and get mad at me. But I didn't know what I was doing. I didn't understand you then. I do now. Things have to be your idea or they don't get done.'

'But why then? Why did you ask me to marry you then?'

'Well, I thought I saw something different in your eyes up at the hospital after the explosion in the mine.'

'I wanted to drive you home!' I offer.

'Right.'

'But Sweet Sue and your mama . . .'

'I couldn't turn them away. And you looked at me as though you understood.'

'I did,' I say, meaning it.

'When I got home, I sat down and had a long, hard night of thinking. I realized that my life was half over. Sounds simple, but it isn't. Kept me up all night. See, I went in to help Rick, and when I got to him, I realized that at my age I might not have the strength to pull him out of there. I've been in the mines since I was eighteen. That's almost twenty years. I'm not what I was.'

'But you were strong! You did save him!'

'Barely.' Jack says.

'What does this have to do with me?'

Jack Mac takes a moment. 'I didn't want to grow old without you.'

I can't speak. As the town spinster, I had no picture of my old age. Being alone gave me a certain timelessness. I don't have the deep worry lines on my face that come from motherhood, or the soft body that comes from holding a lover or a child. I have perfect posture because I never stoop or look down. I froze myself in time hoping it would not catch me. I was so afraid to love someone for fear I would fail.

'Are you crying?' he asks me.

'I have a feeling I'm just getting started,' I tell him. He laughs. 'Now, tell me how you decided to bring my family over from Italy.'

'See, Iva Lou kept me informed about your search for your father. When you got in touch with him, I thought I'd take you over there to meet him. So I found Gala in the paper and called to arrange a first-class trip for the two of us. Then I came over to your house and proposed.'

'Apple Butter Night.'

'What?'

'Nothing,' I say quietly.

'You said no, so I was stuck with no pride and a deluxe trip for two to Italy. Iva Lou still insisted you were in love with me. So she thought, let's send the tickets over there to bring your father and grandmother over here. But you almost messed that up when you planned your own trip. We told Gala the whole story and persuaded her to invent a phony trip. You wouldn't have gotten anywhere with the tickets she sent you. They were fake.'

'I know. Gala told me. But what about Zia Meoli and Zia Antonietta and Uncle Pietro?'

'Well, you saw how things work with Gala. And Iva Lou, for that matter. They snowball. But if I was going to do this thing, I was going to do it right. I couldn't bring your father over and ignore all your mother's people now, could I? So—'

'So,' I interrupt. 'You sold your truck.'

'I sold my truck. The mystery is solved,' Jack says simply.

Sort of.

'Why would you still go through with it after I . . .' I don't want to use the word *rejected*, so I don't.

'Look. I thought about giving up. It was too late; the plans were made. And I'm stubborn. I wasn't ready to give up. Iva Lou kept telling me you were in love with me but you just didn't know it yet. But faith can only go so far. Sometimes you need a little proof.'

I never gave Jack a single sign. No wonder he walked away that day when my family came. He probably couldn't believe my reaction. I was grateful when I should have been loving. No man had ever bought me such a gift. A priceless gift, really. He looked deep inside me and then set off to fulfill my heart's desire. And I acted as though he had dropped off a jar of apple butter. So he looked elsewhere for affection.

'And then Sarah Dunleavy swooped in.'

'You don't know Sarah. She can't swoop. It'd mess up her hair.'

'What were all of you doing up here having dinner the night I brought the fabric?'

'My mother knew her mother years ago and invited the girls to dinner. Theodore is on the Faculty Welcoming Committee. We were going to take them to the Coach House, but Mama wanted to cook. You know how she is.'

'But you kept seeing her?'

'Not really. She was new in town. She called me to take her places, but I didn't call her. I liked it when you were jealous, though. It was the first sign of life I saw in you regarding me.'

'What do you think took me so long?' I ask. 'What took me so long to figure out I wanted you too?'

'I wish I knew.' We laugh.

It takes a long time to get to Jack Mac's bedroom. (What a gentleman.) We stop and kiss every other step; sometimes we talk a bit, but mostly we just connect and connect and connect. I have dreamt of these kisses for so long that they still aren't quite real to me. I thought I had a pretty good imagination, but I am not so sure anymore. The real thing is so much better, so much more full of surprises than the stories I created in my mind's eye.

Jack's room is simple, with an old four-poster bed heaped with lush quilts, a straight-backed chair in one corner, and three windows that look out onto the long rolling field that drops off down into the mountain. I won't let him draw the curtain; the view is so beautiful.

For some reason, I think of Iva Lou, and I laugh.

'What is so funny?'

'Iva Lou would give everything she had twice to know where I am right now.'

'You don't want to call her, do you?' Jack Mac jokes.

'Where's the phone?' We laugh. I hope that, whatever happens, we will always laugh like this.

I am standing by his bed; he is near the windows. He comes to me and lifts me up and places me gently on his bed. He covers me in small, tender kisses – can I remember each and every one of these forever? I breathe deeply, feeling the rise and fall of my breath matching his.

When I was little and playing in the yard, I found a tiny blue egg in the grass. I looked up in the tree; there, out of my reach, was a nest in the branches. I ran for my mother. She carefully placed the egg in my hands and lifted me high off the ground and up into the tree, so that I was eye level with the nest. There were two more tiny blue eggs in the nest. Very gently, I placed the fallen egg at home with the others. This is how I feel in my lover's bed tonight. I feel that I am safe and I am home.

$\mathcal{I}$ always thought that if I ever unleashed The Woman in me and gave in to my passionate nature, everybody in Big Stone Gap would know it and come running. So I am not totally surprised when I get up the next morning and no sooner do I fix the coffee than Spec is banging on the door. Iva Lou probably called my house and couldn't find me, so she called Spec, who lives in Cracker's Neck, and he's come up here looking for me. Jack is still asleep. I'm dressed, so I answer the door.

'Hey, Spec.'

'What are you doing here?'

'Making coffee. What are you doing here?'

'I'm here to fetch Jack Mac. They took his mother to the hospital down in Pennington. He needs to get to her right away. It's real bad, Ave. We need to hurry.'

'Stay here.'

I go into Jack's room, where he is sleeping soundly, like a little boy. I kiss him tenderly to wake him, and he pulls me close.

'Jack, Spec's here. Your Aunt Cecelia took your mama to the

hospital. We need to go right away.' He jumps out of the bed. I help him dress, handing him a T-shirt, boxers, socks one at a time, a pair of pants. We jump into the ambulance with Spec.

Spec doesn't turn on the siren; it's Saturday morning, about seven, and most folks are on a weekend schedule. He goes about ninety, though. I sit in the back; Jack is up front with Spec. I lean forward on the seat to keep my right hand on Jack's shoulder to let him know that I am here for him. Every once in a while he reaches up and squeezes my hand. Spec looks at me in the rearview; he raises one eyebrow and lets me know he understands.

Jack doesn't say a word the entire ride. I know he has dreaded this ride all of his life. The idea of his mother in pain or sick is too much for him to bear, but he doesn't collapse. I completely fell apart when it was my mama. Jack MacChesney is not the fall-apart type.

Spec pulls into the emergency exit at the hospital in Pennington Gap. He knows it well, so he takes us through a long corridor, a back entrance to Intensive Care. Jack goes through the door first, before Spec. He sees his mother in the corner of the unit, Cecelia at her side. He breaks into a run to reach her. When Mrs Mac sees Jack, she smiles and raises her head slightly off of the pillow.

'Took you long enough,' she says.

'I came as fast as I could, Mama.' Jack is close to her face, holding both of her hands.

'I done took a fall,' she says as she closes her eyes.

'She passed out,' Aunt Cecelia says, crying. 'I couldn't get her up. It was just the two of us there, and I had to call the hospital. I got so scared.' Jack is holding his mother tightly. I can't bear the sight of Cecelia's tears, so I put my arms around her gently. She looks at me, and though she doesn't know who I am, she accepts my embrace.

'She's the girl I done told you about,' Mrs. Mac says to Cecelia.

'They're gonna fix you right up, Mrs. Mac,' I promise.

'Do you think so?' she says with a twinkle.

I can tell that Jack wants to be alone with her, so Cecelia and I give them their privacy. Cecelia is a beauty, too, probably older than Mrs. Mac. She is taller and heavier.

'We was having such a grand time. We talked and laughed and ate. She was feeling funny last night, but we didn't think nothing of it; I thought she was just tired. But she had a bad night, she told me, like indigestion, and then this morning I went in to wake her and she was on the floor, just blacked out.'

'You did everything you could. I'm sure they can help her.' I try to reassure Cecelia, but Mrs. Mac doesn't look too good. Jack Mac calls for me, and a nurse takes over with Cecelia.

'Mama wants to tell you something,' Jack tells me, his voice breaking. I have never heard this tone in his voice before. My heart is breaking for him. He is so sad. He knows. He knows she is going, and he is powerless to do anything about it. I know that feeling, and it is devastating.

I lean over the side of the bed.

Mrs. Mac takes a good breath. 'Did you ever wonder why your mama did my mending when I was a good seamstress myself?' I shake my head; I never thought about it. 'My son wanted an excuse to go to your house.' She smiles. 'Take care of him. Because he took good care of me.'

I try to say I will, but I can't speak; I just nod and promise. I kiss her good-bye. I straighten up next to her bed; for a moment I am dizzy. This cannot be happening.

Jack leans over her bed and takes his mother in his arms. She looks like a beautiful porcelain doll, her skin a silky white, like her hair. Jack holds his mother and cries. I hear him say, 'Don't go, Mama. Don't go.' The nurse crosses over to help, but my expression tells her that Mrs MacChesney has died. She died in her son's arms. And that is what she wanted.

The passing of Nan Bluebell Gilliam MacChesney took everyone in the Gap by surprise. Except Jack. He knew she would never have endured a long illness, she wanted to go quickly. And she did. My mama knew I wasn't ready to let her go, so she stayed until her passing would be a blessing, her suffering over. The terrible things that happen to us in this life never make any sense when we're in the middle of them, floundering, no end in sight. There is no rope to hang on to, it seems. Mothers can soothe children during those times, through their reassurance. No one worries about you like your mother, and when she is gone, the world seems unsafe, things that happen unwieldy. You cannot turn to her anymore, and it changes your life forever. There is no one on earth who knew you from the day you were born; who knew why you cried, or when you'd had enough food; who knew exactly what to say when you were hurting; and who encouraged you to grow a good heart. When that layer goes, whatever is left of your childhood goes with her. Memories are very different and cannot soothe you the same way her touch did. If any sense can be made of my mother's death, it would be that I was of some help to Jack when he lost his mother. I hope I have been.

Jack was so strong through the wake and the funeral. He cried a bit at the service. But I was so proud of him; he took a moment with every person who came, to let each one know how much they had meant to his mother. I fell more deeply in love with him as I watched.

I load up the Jeep to return all the covered cake pans (again!). Then I'm taking Theodore out to lunch to thank him for being such a help through Mrs. Mac's funeral.

Bessie's Diner is standing room only, as usual. I hear Theodore call my name; over the crowd I see him wave to me from a booth way in the back. I work through the crowd to get to him.

'Did you buy old Bessie a diamond ring to get this table?' I kiss Theodore on the cheek.

'Almost.'

We haven't had a chance to talk much over the past week, and there is so much to tell him.

'How's it going with Jack Mac?' he asks.

'Well, he's sad. But he isn't depressed. He keeps saying he is thankful she didn't suffer a long time. He got to say good-bye to her. He's gonna be all right.'

'No, I mean how's it going with you and Jack?'

'I . . . love him.' I've never said that out loud. Theodore smiles.

'You do?'

'I do.'

'Why?' Theodore asks kindly.

'I don't know if I can say it.'

'Try.' Theodore sits back and makes a pyramid out of the tiny half-and-half containers.

'I love Jack MacChesney because . . . he loves me.'

'Is that all?'

I don't think Theodore understands how big that statement is, how loaded it is to me. Nobody ever loved me; yes, Mama did and some friends, but nobody Loved me. I was *chosen*. And for once, I wasn't afraid, I just let It in. How silly my fears seem now. Why did I wait so long to let go? Even Mrs. Mac knew how scared I was. She kept trying to assure me that I would be safe with her son.

'Isn't that enough?' I fire back. Theodore nods.

'Ave, I'm going to take the job at UT.'

'You are?' I'm instantly disappointed, and just as quickly I am thrilled for him. 'Congratulations!'

'I think it's time to move on. I need a new challenge. I need to look at myself, where I'm going, you know?'

Theodore! Don't go! I want my life to be perfect. I want to be in love with Jack MacChesney and have you, my best friend, in my life forever. I don't want anything to change! Instead, I say, 'You may go. But I'm not going to let you off the hook. We'll be long-distance best friends. Okay?'

'That's what I was thinking. Knoxville isn't so far. You'll come down.'

'We can talk on the phone,' I say, so upbeat.

'Every day. Just like now.' Theodore looks at me. 'Tell me I'm doing the right thing,' he implores.

'You are doing the right thing. The only thing. Sometimes you have to strip away everything to find what you were in the first place.'

'I guess that's what you did too, isn't it? Who would have thought our lives were going to change like this?'

'Chinese face reading.'

'Really? Can face reading predict what I have planned after lunch?'

'I have to bring Edna and Ledna Tackett their pie dish.'

'They can wait. We're going to Cudjo's Caverns.'

As we drive to the Caverns, I think of my friendship with Theodore, what comfort it brought me all these years, how it grew as we grew. I just know he will always be a big part of my life. How could he not? He's the only person I know who likes caves.

Ray takes us up the dark path with his flashlight.

'Can we go to the lake?' I ask him.

'I got something better to show you,' he promises. Theodore and I look at each another and follow him.

For ten years Theodore and I have come into this cave to explore, and every so often Roy has something new to show us. How is this possible? Does he keep things from us? Or does he make discoveries all the time and share them with us when he's ready? Is this old mountain so full of riches that they cannot be discovered in one lifetime or even two? The path narrows; I keep my hand on the wall as we climb into a new place. As we move in, I can feel the cool stream of mountain water that flows down the rocks to form the stalagmites. It takes the water generations to change the rocks. And yet it is so gentle on the stones, barely a gray mist.

'There it is,' Ray says. 'Y'all, look.'

There is a small alcove, a grotto, the back wall jagged rock that forms a canopy overhead. Moss grows up the sides where the water trickles. The guide shines his flashlight on the ground. It is covered in lavender sand, fine-grained like spun sugar. The light beam plays over the sand, making it shimmer.

'How did this happen?' Theodore wants to know. We cannot believe the beauty of the sand.

'I ain't so sure,' Ray begins. 'This was an ugly black pool of gunk for the longest time. I didn't go near it, because I didn't know what was in it. You never do know inside the mountain. But over the winter, it started to drain out, so I kept an eye on it. And when all the water done drained off, this is what was at the bottom. It wasn't something ugly. It was this.' Ray steadies the beam on the lavender sand; the light makes a bright circle that burns hot in the center and fades out to the edges until it falls away in a soft gloomy blue.

Ray, Theodore, and I stay for a very long time.

'I've worked in here all my life. Sometimes you just can't explain things.'

Jack Mac gets home from work at six o'clock sharp. I'm making spaghetti when he comes in. Bessie's hamburger wore off hours ago, and I'm hungry. He calls to me from the front hall and walks back to the kitchen. He puts his lunch pail down on the table and his boots on the floor. Then he looks at me.

'I called the priest.'

'You turning Catholic?' I tease.

'No.'

'What, then?'

'I told him I wanted him to marry us.'

'I don't want to marry the priest, too. Can't it just be the two of us?'

Jack Mac laughs. 'Is that a yes?'

I nod. 'Isn't this too quick, though?' Old Ave Maria is back, questioning everything.

Jack Mac stops and gives me a you've-got-to-be-kidding look that stops me from blabbering on further and ruining a very precious moment.

'I learned that it's best not to let you think about things too much,' he says, and he goes to wash up.

Never put Iva Lou Wade Makin in charge of a simple wedding. In two seconds she's convinced me to wear a dress that's too tight, a hat that's too broad, and too much makeup. We argue about the blush (I don't need it; humiliation gives me the only rose hue I need), lipstick versus lip gloss (my lips are so shiny I may slide off the groom), and powder finish (I think I look chalky).

As I look at my vivid face in the mirror, it reminds me of the glamorous women of the Ice Capades, who need a lot of makeup to be seen from six hundred feet in an arena. I don't need this kind of definition in a chapel that holds twenty people tops, so I slip into the bathroom to wash my face and start over. The corals, blues, and browns of my clown face disappear in the bubbles as I scrub. It's my wedding day. Better a few hurt feelings than Jack Mac taking one look at me and sprinting from the church in horror.

While I'm in the bathroom, I realize this fiasco is all my fault. I should have planned this better. I should have had some idea of what I wanted. I never dreamt of my wedding day. Not once. Not a single fantasy. I never imagined my bridesmaids in sherbet colors lined up at the altar, my very own ladies-in-waiting. I never saw the church festooned with flowers, heard the organ music, or thought about what color sugar Nellie Goodloe's mints should be dipped in. I never thought I'd get married. But believe me, there are plenty of women who have six, seven, eight scenarios mapped out in their minds, every detail of the nuptials planned, and they're all too happy to take over your big day and turn it into a monster of lace, ribbons, and flouncy details. Iva Lou Makin is the consummate romantic.

Once I arrive at the church, I forget all the prenuptial distress. For Jack and me, this is a simple ceremony, where we will have the great honor of promising, in front of our loved ones, to be true. This thought calms me. We are having a private mass with Jack's Aunt Cecelia and our closest friends. There will be no hoo-hah down the aisle or any other grand touches. Jack and I will enter together. The witnesses are Theodore, Iva Lou and Lyle, Aunt Cecelia, Pearl, Leah, Fleeta and Portly, Otto and Worley, Lew and Inez Eisenberg, Zackie, and Spec.

Jack Mac pulls up in his truck and jumps out. He runs up the walkway and meets me in the vestibule.

'You're beautiful,' he tells me. You wouldn't think so if you'd seen me an hour ago with four pounds of Max Factor heaped on my face. I smile at my groom.

It's the strangest thing – no one cries. There is just joy, simple and unadorned, in this little chapel with the quiet priest. Tomorrow, April 29, 1979, is my thirty-sixth birthday. How did I get to this place? Who knew?

After church, we've planned a dinner for everyone in town at the Coach House (yes, we're having the same fried chicken, taters, and slaw combo that was served on Elizabeth Taylor Night).

When we cut our cake – thank you, Edna and Ledna Tackett, for the coconut confection – Zackie emerges from the circle around us.

'Miss Ave Maria . . . I mean, Mizriz MacChesney . . .' The crowd cheers. I look at the faces of Rick and Sherry Harmon, Nellie Goodloe, June Walker, and Mrs. Gaspar. They couldn't be happier for me. How lucky I am.

'We wanted to do something special for you and Jack Mac,' Zackie says. 'So we put together a little fund-raiser.'

Iva Lou and Lyle emerge from the kitchen carrying a four-foot pickle jar stuffed with coins and bills. The crowd cheers again. There is a sign inside the jar: HONEYMOON OR BUST.

'We want to send y'all to It-lee. We hope this will help.'

Iva Lou and Lyle place the giant pickle jar at our feet. Pearl and Leah present us with a giant congratulations card signed by everyone at the reception. I look around the room. Most folks are crying. I am, too.

❉

Jack and I spend our first night as a married couple in his stone house on the hill. I open all the windows; it is warm and the breeze is full of honeysuckle and jasmine. My husband comes to bed.

'There's something I never told you,' he begins. My heart starts to race; a thousand possibilities float through my mind, all of them horrible, like he has three months to live, or he has a second family tucked away up in Insko, or that he's been in debtor's prison.

What has happened to me? I get so afraid now. I never used to. Why am I more vulnerable now than I was when I was alone, in charge of everything? I lived by myself in the middle of town, for God's sake. I checked my own oil, lit my own furnace, caught mice. I had a routine: running a home, a business, the Rescue Squad, the Drama. I was never scared then. So much for strength in numbers, I think as I look at my husband, now that we are a family.

'The fall before your mother got really sick, I went down to your house to pick up some mending. And she was sitting in the living room. She invited me to sit down, and I did. She told me some things about herself, general things, like where she was from in Italy, how she taught herself English, that sort of thing. As I was about to leave, she walked me to the door. She told me that she was dying, and if I wouldn't mind, could I look in on you once in a while to make sure you were all right. I promised her I would.'

What can I say to him? Surely he knows what this means to me. My mama picked him first, way before I was ready, back when I was afraid to. I wonder if she knows how happy I am in this moment. Though I have no proof, something tells me she does.

We cuddle down into the covers, me on my side, my husband lying next to me, on his side, holding me. He places his arm around my waist like the bar on a roller-coaster car. I am locked in for the night. We have had a long day and a lot of cake, and we are very tired. My husband tells me he loves me, and I tell him that I love him. He kisses the back of my neck and goes to sleep.

As he sleeps, I think about Reverend Gaspar and I hear him say that word, *faith*. I haven't been able to figure out what he meant that night in the ambulance until now. I don't think he was talking about faith in God. I think he was telling me that he had faith in me, that he believed I could help him. Maybe he even thought I could save him. That's why his eyes were so clear and his voice was so strong as he lay dying. He had a revelation. He knew that the great mysteries in life can only be solved person to person. We can pull each other through. He figured it out at the end of his life; I am so glad he shared it with me in the middle of mine. Maybe I can be of some use now. Maybe I can be of some good to one person. I hope that person is Jack MacChesney.

The trip to Italy that was to change the course of my life has become a honeymoon. I made Jack take a leave of absence from the mines so we could spend the entire summer in Italy. My husband is a very good traveler. He's not too persnickety about seeing everything; he's loose about missing trains; he doesn't get upset when a museum is closed or a church on our itinerary is locked. He speaks Italian with a mountain twang; sometimes I have to walk away because it is so funny. He ignores me and persists. The Italians love him because he tries so hard.

We landed in Rome and have been touring the countryside north by train. There is no way for me to scientifically explain the light here, as I am ignorant of such matters. But I swear to you, the sun is hung differently. There is a peachy golden haze over Italy that makes green fields more vivid, gives brown earth a depth and people a romantic glow. I point it out to Jack, and he tells me that I'm drunk in love with the place and it is coloring my perceptions. I don't think so. I think there is something different about the light. When the sun goes down, the sky turns a vivid blue-black, the stars seem closer, and the edges don't fade out toward the horizon. The same saturated blue hems the skyline that nestles the moon. It is no wonder the Fortuny family makes fabric here. They have a different canopy of velvet overhead to choose from each night. All they have to do is look up and copy.

Of course, we cannot wait to get to Bergamo, my mother's family home, for a two-day visit, and then on to Schilpario, where Mario and Nonna live. Mario is scheduled to come down the mountain and pick us up to take us to his home. I cannot explain the deep joy I feel. My husband is sleeping next to me on the train, and I am sailing through the place I come from. There may not be a greater feeling on earth.

The train pulls into Bergamo. I wake Jack and begin yanking suitcases down from the bars overhead. We brought so much American crap for the relatives. They had time to get home and decide which items they missed, so I am loaded down with cigarettes, Bic pens, staples and staple guns, moon pies, goo-goo clusters, and giant plastic paper clips. I didn't question their choices; I just went out and bought in bulk and loaded a trunk.

Two of my cousins, Mafalda and Andrea, are there to meet us at the station. Their happy faces walk alongside the train until it makes a full stop. I hang out the window; they see me and run to our exit steps to wait for us. I don't think anybody has ever been so happy to see us. They negotiate the cumbersome bags, leaving me to carry nothing but my new leather-bound journal, which my husband bought me in Florence.

The train station is on the outskirts of town, on a side street nestled in some trees. Andrea and Mafalda load our luggage into their small car, we squeeze in, and we're off. Andrea drives very fast, and Mafalda chides him to slow down. We take a sharp right turn that leads us to a C-shaped street that connects to the town circle. Mafalda points out the newspaper office, the government building, the church. Bergamo looks just like the picture in the book Iva Lou found at the university library. Nothing has changed. The fountain of angels, the cobblestone streets, the upright shoe-box-shaped houses painted subtle pastels, the little park, the outdoor cafés – they are all the same! There is only one change that I can see: The car has replaced the horse and carriage.

The Vilminore family lives in a four-story house in the middle of a block on Via Davide. Zia Antonietta, Zia Meoli, Zio Pietro, and my cousin Federica are waiting for us in front of the house. My aunts cry when they see us. They can't seem to let go of Jack, who doesn't seem to mind their heartfelt, sturdy embraces. The family home is neat and spare. Everything is white but the floor, which is made of glossy dark brown planks. Mafalda takes us up the stairs to our room, a good-sized simple room with a sleigh bed and a matching settee. The bed is piled high with white coverlets, just the way Mama liked. Mafalda tells us to rest, they will see us for a light supper later. Before she goes, she tells me that this used to be my mother's bedroom.

While Jack unpacks, I lie down on the bed and look up at the ceiling, smooth and white. The window and door frames are painted an almond color. It's the same white and the same almond trim in my mother's bedroom in Big Stone Gap. My mother may not have talked much about Italy, but she surrounded herself with details that reminded her of her home.

We lie down for a nap and wake at about seven o'clock. The

sun has set; we are surprised that we slept so long. The kitchen table is set for the two of us. Zia Antonietta serves us a delicious thick soup with greens in it, and soft bread with a hard, chewy crust. There is lots of creamy butter, and good, rich red wine. Italians eat their biggest meal at noon; this supper is perfectly sized, just enough for us to feel full but not stuffed.

When we are done eating, Zia Antonietta tells us to get our sweaters and we go for a walk, or 'la passeggiata,' as they say here. We walk a short distance to the main piazza in Bergamo Bassa, where folks stand in small groups chatting. Others sip coffee in the cafés on either side of the fountain. There is laughter, and the children run and play. The people here are so animated; they raise their voices to make a point, they use their bodies for emphasis; they are so full of life and comical! It is no surprise that the commedia dell'arte theatrical tradition started here in the fourteenth century. Everyone seems to have a divine sense of humor. Zia Antonietta tells us that this goes on every night. 'It is soothing to laugh before sleep,' she explains in Italian. Jack thinks it's the best idea he has ever heard. Zia Antonietta points to a rim of light above the city; in the twilight it looks like there are pillars and some buildings. 'Alta Città. That was the ancient city Bergamo Alta. Now it is very desirable real estate. Our university is there. Mafalda will take you tomorrow if you like.'

'Why did the city move down here?' Jack wants to know.

'War. Rock slides,' she explains. She sees me frown. 'But that was many centuries ago. Don't worry, Ave Maria. Don't worry.'

We join Zia Meoli and Zio Pietro. My uncle takes Jack off to show him something; Zia Meoli and I go for a walk, just the two of us. Zia Antonietta leaves the group and returns home up the side street.

'Where is Zia Antonietta going?'

'Home.' Zia Meoli shrugs.

'Isn't she going to stay and have some fun?'

'She likes to do her chores.'

'Now?'

'Yes. She prepares the table for breakfast tomorrow, and then she goes to sleep.'

'Why does she prepare the breakfast?'

'That is how we do it. Antonietta never married, so she runs the family home.'

That was me, I think to myself as we walk along. I took care of everything. I was so busy, I didn't think about what I was doing or where the years were going. I just did what was expected of me. I wonder if Zia Antonietta is the town spinster. Zia Meoli must read my mind.

'My sister likes to take care of us.'

'She seems happy.'

'She was to marry, many years ago. The third son of seven of a family in Sestri Levante, on the seacoast. Then the war came and he died. She did not want to marry anyone else. She had many suitors. But her heart was broken, and that was the end of all that for her.'

I feel better that Zia Antonietta had a great love, even though he died. But I can't help but wonder what it is about these Vilminore women; do they only ever love one man their whole lives, even if they marry another like my mother, or never marry like my aunt? Are they so clear-sighted about their great loves that there is no room for any other, ever? It seems that once their hearts were unlocked, they should have remained open to the possibilities of new love. Maybe the Vilminore girls are just one-man women.

*

Jack is waiting for me when we return to the house. I kiss my relatives good night, and Jack and I go to our room.

We sink into the layers and layers of feather-filled mattresses. We sink so deeply we can't find each other. My mother tried to re-create this effect in America, but she couldn't. Jack, used to sleeping on hard American mattresses, is afraid his back will go out in all this softness. I pound the top mattress flat to find my husband's face.

'Thank you for marrying me,' I tell him. He looks confused, like *Here she goes again, my strange wife.* 'No. Really. Thank you.'

'You're welcome . . . I guess.'

'I like being married to you.'

'Good. Because you promised to stay with me forever.'

'I know. But now it seems like time is flying by; I'm not going to have enough time with you. I just know it.'

'Why do you worry about stuff like that?'

I don't think he wants my answer. Because I worry about everything! I worry about Zia Antonietta, whose lover died before she could marry him. I worry that her entire life is doing dishes and sweeping without love to break the tedium! I worry that happiness can't stay; I know it is just like the Deep Sleep, it is just a phase, a time, and then you come out of it and start all over again. I worry that the joy in my heart will become so ordinary to me that I will forget how sad I was without him and I will take him for granted and start nagging him and turn him away. I worry that I'm too old to have children. I worry that coal dust is sifting like black sand in the bellows of his lungs and he'll get emphysema and die an untimely death. I worry that when we die, he'll go first and I'll be left all alone again. I worry that when I die and go to find him in heaven, he won't be there. He will have changed and I won't recognize him and then I'll be traipsing through all eternity reliving the first thirty-five years of my life when I could not love anyone.

'Stop it.'

'What?'

'Stop thinking. You've got that crease between your eyes. The one that comes out when you worry.'

That did it. Never tell a thirty-six-year-old that there is a crease anywhere on her. It is not something I want to hear, ever. I rub the crease away.

'That's my third eye.' Jack laughs so loud, I pull the sheet over his head.

'Shh.'

'What is a third eye?'

'In face reading. It's the all-knowing eye of your mind. It's where you create the pictures that become the reality of your life.'

'Put a pretty picture in there then,' Jack says simply.

Oh, if it were that I easy; I look at him pitifully. When it is all said and done, he is still a man, and men just don't understand.

Mario Barbari stands outside the Vilminore homestead on Via Davide like he owns the entire block. He is dapper in navy slacks, a navy, cashmere V-neck sweater, tucked in without a wrinkle (of course), and his signature ecru top sweater, tied in a knot and draped over his shoulders. He is having a smoke – so European. I don't stand on ceremony. I race down the sidewalk and throw myself on him. 'Papa!' He hugs me and we kiss. He is so happy to see me. I'm so glad I like my father. I really do. He's a character, all right, and his cologne could ignite downtown Bergamo, but he is truly an original. I love to be around him.

'So you get married and you don't even wait for your own papa to give you away.'

'You didn't miss much. I had on too much makeup, and I couldn't breathe in the dress.'

'I'm sure you were lovely,' he says, flicking his cigarette. Is this guy a movie star or what? My father embraces my husband as men do, with a quick hug and big slaps on their backs and arms, and then the two of them load the car. My family gathers on the steps of their home and wave us off into the distance, past the end of the block; Papa drives like a maniac. We're like a silver pinball whipping around the curves of the town circle surrounding the Fountain of Angels, past the park, and then to the road that leads out of town. SCHILPARIO NORD 7 KM, the green-and-white sign says. We're on our way to Grandmother's house.

Jack and my father talk about the difference between the beds in Italy and the beds in America. Jack tells Papa that he is shocked that his back is fine after sleeping on all those feathers. Papa explains that the body heat is evenly distributed when you sleep on feathers, or straw for that matter, so the muscles in the body stay the same warm temperature, and the result is you wake up without kinks and spasms.

'Look at me. I am old. And I am well rested. Yes?' Jack nods; Papa looks good for his age. Papa winks at me in the rearview mirror. He is fifty-four, but not fifty-four in Big Stone Gap years. His hair is long and thick and layers back in soft waves – the only aspect that belies his age is the white streaks throughout. His carriage is upright and youthful. And his skin is still magnificent. He looks about forty. I hope I have his genes.

About halfway up the mountain, Papa peels off into a ravine. I think we're going to land in a forest, but the road clears, revealing a chalet jutting out from the mountain. Papa looks at us.

'We rest.' He parks. We get out of the car and go into the chalet.

The chalet is a restaurant. It is midafternoon and too early for dinner. Papa nods to the owner, who is restocking the bar. He brings us each a glass of bitters, which my father throws back in one gulp. Jack shrugs and throws his back. I follow. Bitters, I know from the Pharmacy, are herbs steeped in a fizz, a tonic. They are usually medicinal; I have never heard of them being used for social purposes.

'Cleans the blood,' my father offers.

The owner brings out a tray with three small silver bowls and three tiny silver spoons. He places the summer blackberries before us. Papa squeezes fresh lemon over them.

'Go ahead. Eat.' Jack and I eat, and we can't believe how sweet they berries are. Papa is pleased.

'Now we go,' he says, and we are done. He nods to the owner. He leaves no money. I thank the man behind the bar, and he waves us off with a smile.

The road to Schilpario is really twisty, and my ears are popping as we ascend. I ask my father how high up we are, but he isn't sure. Then, with a flick of his wrist, he careens us off of the road to a scenic overlook. The protective railing is old and crumbling, and my heart beats faster when Papa parks too close.

'Come,' he says, and gets out of the car. 'Look.' Jack and I join him at the edge of the mountain. I look down the precipice; layers and layers of jagged rock, gutted by time, create a deep gulch for miles to the bottom, which from here looks to be about the size of a quarter. I get dizzy and have to step back.

'Too far down, eh?' my father says. I nod.

'Let me tell you a story,' Papa begins. I ask Papa and Jack to step back. I can imagine a strong wind kicking up and blowing them both over the side, never to be seen again.

'This is a story told to me by my father, Gianluca Barbari. His father, my grandfather, owned a carriage and two horses. He used to take people up and down the mountain to town. They paid him very well, so he kept a very elegant carriage. One morning the town widow called to arrange a ride the following day down to Bergamo. She wanted to leave before the sun rose, and my grandfather agreed to take her. He woke that morning in the dark, fed the horses, hooked them up to the buggy, and went to pick up the woman at her house. She came to the door in a beautiful gown of pale green satin. Her shawl was embroidered with tiny yellow and gold leaves. She wore a beautiful hat with a green plume. My grandfather remembered a beautiful necklace with a diamond the size of a stone. It shimmered in the lamplight. Grandpapa helped her into the carriage. He remembered that she smelled like roses and that she smiled very happily. They began their trip down the mountain. This is the place where my grandfather used to stop and rest the horses. The woman wanted to stretch a bit, so my grandfather helped her out of the carriage. He was right over there watering the horses when he heard a sound like the sound when you shake out wet laundry before hanging it on the line. So he turned to look. The old lady had jumped off the mountain. Her skirts made the terrible sound as she fell. My grandfather ran to the edge, but she was gone. He shook terribly, and he had a moment where he thought that he too would jump. But he had eight children to feed, and he could not do it. So he went back up the mountain and directly to the police station. Grandfather knew the policeman and hoped he would believe his story. The policeman said it would be difficult to prove Grandfather's innocence because the widow had no relatives in town; she was alone, so who could corroborate his story, or at least offer information as to the woman's mental state? No one. My grandfather now worried he would be thrown in prison, unjustly accused of pushing the old widow over the mountain. But then the policeman had an idea. "Let us go to her house and see if there are any clues that would help us ascertain if she was crazy, or in a weak state of mind." When they reached the widow's house, the policeman was going to break the lock, but he did not have to. The front door was unlocked. The policeman went in, asking my grandfather to stay outside. He said the minutes while the policeman was inside the house turned his hair from black to white. The policeman came out holding a letter. The letter said that the authorities were not to blame Gianluca Barbari for her suicide. She said it was her choice entirely. She was ill and had no one in the world and wanted to die. Please give whatever was in her house to the church. Then the policeman handed my grandfather the fare for the trip, explaining that the widow wanted to pay him. My grandfather returned home and told his family the story. He was so grateful that the widow had left behind a letter clearing his name that he commissioned a stained-glass window to be made for the chapel. My grandfather's brothers had a small glassworks business. They made the stained-glass window and installed it in the choir loft. The window is still there.' My father promises to show it to us.

We are high up in the Alps, and though it is summer, the breeze is very cool and sends a chill through me. Jack and Papa lead me back to the car. We drive the rest of the way in silence.

There is no grand entrance into the town of Schilpario. You happen upon it, almost by accident. It has not changed either; it looks like the pictures in Iva Lou's books. It is just much smaller than I expected. I am not disappointed, just surprised. The main drag is a narrow street, lined on one side by shoe-box houses. These homes have different details from the ones down in Bergamo, though. There are Alpine touches: dark wood trim in gingerbread curves, small porches, and colorful shutters of soft beige, and pink. The stucco on the outside is painted more vividly than down in the town. Perhaps the people of Schilpario paint the houses light colors so they are not lost altogether in the mountains and can be found by travelers as they pass through.

The town is nestled into the side of the mountain; houses are dotted over us on the hillside; narrow streets make veins that lead to the main street. Papa drives us through the town and up to the waterwheel, which spins clear, icy mountain water over its flaps. Everyone who sees us waves and smiles. I get the feeling my father is well-respected here. Papa does a U-turn and returns down the main street, pulling over to park in front of a bright green shoe-box house. Nonna appears in the doorway. She is surrounded by people – I assume I am related to all of them. As they gather around the car, Nonna shoves them aside and hugs me and then Jack. She grabs my hand to inspect my gold wedding band.

'Sposa bella!' she says to me, and hugs me so hard I hear my clavicle crack. She leads us inside. Nonna has prepared a feast of risotto, salad, and roast duck, which Jack flips for. Jack and I and Papa sit at the table. It seems there are four people serving to each one sitting at the table. We are waited on like royalty. I notice my father is treated reverentially; and I also notice that he expects it. He is the only son in this household, and he is the mayor of this town, so he is held in very high esteem. I look at him and admire his self-confidence. He wears it so naturally.

The women won't let me help clean up, and they look at Jack as though he is from Mars when he rises to help with the dishes. Nonna wallops his back with her hand so hard, he sits down and doesn't try to help anymore. Nonna brings out biscotti, berries, and espresso at the end of the meal. We eat everything. She is pleased.

Two of Papa's old pals, actually first cousins, drop by to check out the Americans. Papa and Jack invite the men to play cards. Jack asks me if I'd like to play, but I decline, not because I don't want to play cards but because I know it's a men-only thing. My cousins look me up and down like a new appliance. I return the favor by examining them just as closely; it breaks their concentration, and they stop staring at me. They aren't aware of how well I speak Italian, so one of them whispers 'nice ass' to the other as I leave the room, figuring I don't understand. I can't resist, so I lean in between them and say, 'You have nice asses too.' At first they are taken aback, and then they laugh heartily.

Nonna serves our breakfast, hard rolls, left over from the previous night's dinner, soft butter and berry jam, and a large mug of steaming milk with espresso in it. We can't figure out why, but this combination is satisfying. Jack and I decide to eat this very thing every morning when we return home. How do the Italians know how to live? We don't understand it. Everything tastes better, even hard rolls and butter! And the pace is so easy. Work a little. Take a nap. Work a little more, eat a little something, take a little nap. And so on, day in and day out. Lots of play time: cards and socializing and long walks. It is a heavenly existence in the Alps.

Papa wants to take us to the chapel with the windows his grandfather created. We walk up the narrow street and turn onto a small side street where the chapel sits, like any house, except the details are simpler and the door is painted bright red – just like the Freewill Baptist Church in the Gap. Maybe they have to keep the Devil out in Italy too. We enter the tiny chapel. A priest is tinkering up at the altar.

'Ave Maria, this is Don Andrea, our priest,' Papa says.

'Ave Maria,' he says. 'I never met an Ave Maria before.'

'Don't you say your rosary?' I ask him. At first he doesn't get the joke, and then he smiles.

'This is my husband, Jack.' Don Andrea shakes his hand.

'They just got married, Don Andrea. This is my daughter; I told you all about her.'

'Oh, yes, yes.' The old priest understands everything now.

'We're going to take a look around,' Papa tells him. Jack studies the architecture. I ask Papa to show me the Blessed Mother window. He leads me up to the choir loft and points to it. It is very small, about the size of a book. As I lean in to examine it, a shiver goes through me. The lady in the glass wears a long blue gown and a hat with gold stars and peacock feathers, just like Ave Maria Albricci, the woman who helped my mother on the boat to America. She has a serene countenance. She stands on what looks like the waves of the ocean.

'Are you all right?' Papa asks me.

How can I tell him about Ave Maria Albricci? Even Jack was confused when I told him about her. He shrugged it off, like angels appear to people every day and save them. But this is too strange. In this sea of coincidences, I am beginning to understand that we don't control our destinies; they are mapped out for us as surely as we are born.

'Papa, I want to get married again,' I announce to my father. Sometimes he looks at me like I am a little nuts, and this is one of those times.

'Who will tell Jack?' my father asks with a wry smile.

'Not to a different man. To Jack. Again. Here. I want you to give me away.'

My father shrugs, like it isn't the worst idea he's ever heard.

So on Sunday, June 3, Jack MacChesney and I are blessed all

over again, by Don Andrea, at La Capella Di Santa Chiara in Schilpario, Italy.

My father is nervous as he walks me down the aisle, but very happy too. He serves as Jack's best man, and I ask Nonna to stand up for me. She is very embarrassed, though; she thinks she is too old. But I make her do it, strong-arming her the way she commands everyone else.

Men don't like church weddings the first time around, so you can imagine the begging I have to do to get Jack to repeat the vows. But I realize something important about him in all of this, something that I never knew before. No matter what I ask of him, no matter how corny or difficult or plain old fashioned undoable it is, if I ask, he will do it for me. He loves me so completely that he cannot deny me anything. I pray that I will never abuse this gift. But knowing me, there will be times I come close. I just hope he understands.

The best summer of our lives comes to an end. We say our goodbyes, but they aren't really binding, as Papa plans to visit us the next spring. Jack and I promise to spend part of every summer for the rest of our lives here in Schilpario, my father's home. Goodbyes are not sad to me at all anymore. I have learned to enjoy what leads up to them too much to worry about finalities.

I am anxious to get home. I have missed the Blue Ridge Mountains. Jack laughs about this.

'Mountains are mountains wherever you go,' he says.

'No. Our mountains are home,' I tell him. I can't explain it to him, but Big Stone Gap has gone from the place I was running from to the place I most want to be. I have seen where I come from, but now I know where I belong. Home is with Jack MacChesney in that stone house on the hill.

*

The plane ride home is bumpy. I am sick most of the way, as is Jack. But I think he gets sick when he sees me get sick. What is the old expression about true lovers: When one gets cut, the other bleeds? When we land at Tri-Cities Airport, I am not sad. I am looking forward to returning to Cracker's Neck and waiting for the seasons to change and bring us our first autumn together.

Well, it wasn't airsickness back in August. Almost a year to the day after our American wedding, April 28, 1980, Fiametta Bluebell MacChesney was born to two very happy parents. This is all so new to me, and I have no words to describe it.

I do know, and I will explain to my daughter, that she is a very lucky girl. She need look no further than her own family to inspire her to cut her own path in life. We're calling the baby Etta, the name my mother's true love called her. I hope that she has my mother's heart; it is evident to all, in the two days she's been on earth, that she has already inherited her stubbornness. Most of the time, when I hold her, I think of Mama. I feel her around me now, guiding me. Finally, my mother's choices make sense to me. Now I understand how she found the courage to leave her family and start a new life with me. A baby gives you the strength to do just about anything.

Etta has Nan MacChesney's eyes. They say all babies have blue eyes, but I see the green there already, and they have a knowingness and a humor that can only have come from her no-nonsense grandmother. How sad I am Etta will never know her grandmothers! Why am I making a list of all the things our daughter won't have? The only thing I know for sure is that I will worry about this little one until the day I die. Jack agrees with that; he says I've been practicing worry for thirty-seven years, so I'm mighty good at it.

And what about Jack MacChesney, my husband and the father of our daughter? Will he teach her to play the guitar and whistle?

The moon is just a sliver the first night home with our baby. I'm tired, so Jack relieves me and I doze off to sleep for twenty minutes or so. When I wake up, the house is quiet. I can't find Jack and Etta inside, so I go to the backyard and circle around to the front of the house. There they are. Father and daughter. Sitting on the porch, looking at the moon. I stand there for a very long time. I don't know why. She starts to fuss and I know she is hungry. But I can't move. I want to watch the two of them forever – a daughter learning to trust, and a father doing the thing he does best: protecting her.

Big Cherry Holler

For my mother,
Ida Bonicelli Trigiani

The rain is coming down on this old stone house so hard, it seems there are a hundred tap dancers on the roof. When Etta left for school this morning, it was drizzling, and now, at two o'clock, it's a storm. I can barely see Powell Mountain out my kitchen window; just yesterday it was a shimmering gold pyramid of autumn leaves at their peak. I hope the downpour won't beat the color off the trees too soon. We have all winter for Cracker's Neck Holler to wear gray. How I love these mountains in October: the leaves are turning—layers of burgundy and yellow crinolines that change color in the light—the apples are in, the air smells like sweet smoke, and I get to build big fires in Mrs. Mac's deep hearths. As I kneel and slip a log into the stove, I think of my mother-in-law, who had fires going after the first chill in the air. "I love me a farr," she'd say.

There's a note on the blackboard over the sink in Jack Mac's handwriting: *Red pepper sandwiches?* The message is at least three months old; no one should have to wait that long for their favorite sandwich, least of all my husband. Why does it take me so long to fulfill a simple request? There was a time when he came first, when I would drop everything and invent ways to make my husband happy. I wonder if he notices that life has put him in second place. If he doesn't, my magazine subscriptions sure do. *Redbook* came with a cover exploding in hot pink letters: PUT THE SIZZLE BACK IN YOUR MARRIAGE! WE SHOW YOU HOW! Step #4 is Make His Favorite Food. (Don't ask about the other nine steps.) So, with equal measures of guilt and determination to do better, I'm roasting peppers in the oven, turning them while they char as dark as the sky.

I baked the bread for the sandwiches this morning. I pull the cookie sheet off the deep windowsill, brush the squares of puffy dough with olive oil, and put them aside. Then I take the tray out of the oven and commence peeling the peppers. (This is a sit-down job.) My mother used to lift off the charred part in one piece; I've yet to master her technique. The vivid red pepper underneath is smooth as the velvet lining of an old jewelry box. I lay the thin red strips on the soft bread. The mix of olive oil and sweet hot bread smells fresh and buttery. I sprinkle coarse salt on the open sandwiches; the faceted crystals glisten on the red peppers. I'm glad I made a huge batch. There will be lots of us in the van tonight.

There's big news around here. Etta is going to be on television. She and two of her classmates are going on *Kiddie Kollege*, the WCYB quiz show for third-graders. Etta, who loves to read, has been chosen for her general knowledge. Her fellow teammates are Jane Herd and Billy Skeens. Jane, a math whiz who has the round cheeks of a monarch, has been selected for her keen ability to divide in her head. Billy, a small but mighty Melungeon boy, was chosen for his bravery. He recently helped evacuate the Big Stone Gap Elementary School cafeteria when one of the steam tables caught fire. No one could come up with a prize big enough to honor him (an assembly and a medal seemed silly), so the school decided to put him on the show. I guess the teachers feel that fame is its own reward.

Jack Mac borrowed the van from Sacred Heart Church because we're transporting the team and I've promised rides to our friends.

The television studio is about an hour and a half from the Gap, right past Kingsport over in Bristol, Tennessee. The show is live at six P.M. sharp, so we'll leave right after school. Etta planned her outfit carefully: a navy blue skirt and pink sweater (her grandfather Mario sent it to her from Italy, so Etta thinks it's the best sweater she owns, if not the luckiest). She is wearing her black patent-leather Mary Janes, though I pointed out that you rarely see anyone's shoes on TV.

I make one final pass through the downstairs, locking up as I go. With its simple, square rooms and lots of floor space, this old house is perfect for raising kids. Of course, when Mrs. Mac was alive, I never dreamed I'd live here. For a few years, this was just another delivery stop for me in the Medicine Dropper. I remember how I loved to drive up the bumpy dirt road and see this stone house sitting in a clearing against the mountain like a painting. If I had known that Mrs. Mac would one day be my mother-in-law, I might have tried to impress her. But I didn't. I'd drop off her pills, have a cup of coffee, and go. I never thought I would fall in love with her only son. And I never thought I would be looking at my face in these mottled antique mirrors, or building fires for heat, or raising her granddaughter in these rooms. If you had told me that I would make my home in this holler on this mountain, I would have laughed. I grew up down in town; no one ever moves out of Big Stone Gap and up into the hills. How strange life is.

I check myself in the mirror. Etta is forever begging me to wear more makeup. She wants me to be a young mom, like her friends have; in these parts, the women my age are grandmothers! So I stop in the hallway for a moment and dig for the lipstick in the bottom of my purse. My youthful appeal will have to come from a tube. You would think that someone who has worked in a pharmacy all her life would have one of those snazzy makeup bags. We have a whole spin rack of them at the Mutual's. Maybe Etta's right, I should pay more attention to the way I look. (Covering up my undereye circles is just not a priority.) Folks tell me that I haven't changed since I was a girl. Is that a good thing? I lean into the tea-stained glass and take a closer look. Eight years with Jack MacChesney have come and gone. It seems once I fell in love with him, time began flying.

Someone is banging on the front door. The thunder is so loud, I didn't hear a car come up the road. With one hand, Doris Bentrup from the flower shop juggles an umbrella in the wind and with the other, a stack of white boxes festooned with lavender ribbons. Two pairs of reading glasses dangle from her neck. Beads of rain cover the clear plastic cap she wears on her head.

"Come on in!"

"Can't. Got a wagon full of flowers. Got a funeral over in Pound. I'm gonna kill myself if this rain done ruined my hair."

"It looks good." I'm about a foot taller than Doris, so I look down on her tiny curls, each one a perfect rosette of blue icing under a saran-wrap tent.

"It'd better. I suffered for this look. I sat under that dryer over to Ethel's for two hours on Saturdee 'cause of the humidity. She sprayed my head so bad these curls is like tee-niney rocks. Feel."

"They're perfect," I tell Doris without touching her head.

"Etta all ready for the big show?"

"Yes ma'am."

"We hope they win this year, on account of no one from Big Stone ever wins."

"Didn't the Dogwood Garden Club win on *Club Quiz*?"

"Yes'm. But that was a good ten year' ago. And they was grown-ups, so I don't think you can count 'at. Wait till you see who these is from. I nearly done dropped my teeth, and you know that ain't easy, 'cause I glue 'em in good."

I pull the tiny white card bordered in crisp pink daisies out of the envelope. It reads: *Knock 'em dead, Etta. And remember, the cardinal is the state bird of Virginia. Love, Uncle Theodore.*

"That there Tipton is a class act. He ain't never gonna be replaced in these parts," Doris announces as she tips her head back to let the rain drain off her cap. "Sometimes we git a ferriner in here that makes us set up and take notice. How's he doin' at U.T.?"

"He says he's got the best marching band in the nation."

"Now if they'd only start winning them some ball games."

As Doris makes a break for her station wagon, I open a box. There, crisp and perfect, is a wrist corsage of white carnations. Nestled in the cold petals are three small gold-foil letters: WIN. I inhale the fresh, cold flowers. The letters tickle my nose and remind me of the homecoming mums that Theodore bought me every year during football season. For nearly ten years, Theodore was band director and Junior Class Sponsor at Powell Valley High School. He chaperoned every dance, and I was always his date. (Parents appreciated that an experienced member of the Rescue Squad chaperoned school dances.) Theodore always made a big deal of slipping the corsage onto my wrist before the game. Win or lose, the dance was a celebration because Theodore's halftime shows were always spectacular. Besides his unforgettable salute to Elizabeth Taylor prior to her choking on the chicken bone, my favorite was his salute to the Great American Musical, honoring the creations of Rodgers and Hammerstein. Each of the majorettes was dressed as a different lead character, including Maria from *The Sound of Music* and Julie Jordan from *Carousel*. Romalinda Miranda, daughter of the Filipino Doctor Who Was on the Team That Saved Liz Taylor, was the ingenue from *Flower Drum Song*. Theodore pulled her from the Flag Girls; there was a bit of a drama around that, as folks didn't think that a majorette should be drafted out of thin air for one show just because she looked like she was from the original cast. Once the controversy died down, the Miranda family basked in the glory of the celebration of their Asian heritage. (Extra points for my fellow ferriners.)

I gently place the boxes on top of my tote bag full of things we might need for the television appearance. Extra kneesocks. Chap Stick. Comb. Ribbons. My life is all about collecting things for my family and then putting them back. Lists. Hauling. And I'd better never forget anything. Even Jack relies on me for tissues when he sneezes and quarters for the paper. Sometimes I wonder if all these small details add up to anything.

Big Stone Gap Elementary is a regal collection of four beautifully appointed beige sandstone buildings, built in 1908. In mining towns, the first place the boom money goes is to the schools; Big Stone Gap was no different. There is at least an extra acre of field for the kids to play in, a glorious old auditorium (with footlights), and a newly refurbished cafeteria (since Billy the Hero). I wait at the entry fence as my own mother did for so many years.

As the bell sounds and the green double doors swing open, the kids pour out onto the wet playground like beads from a sack. Etta stands at the top of the stairs, surveying the fence line. When she sees me, she hops down the steps two at a time and runs toward me. She has a hard time holding on to her red plaid umbrella in the fierce wind. Her rain slicker flaps about. I give her a quick kiss as she jumps into the Jeep.

"Did you remember my socks?"

"Are you nervous?"

Etta peels off her mud-splattered white kneesocks and pulls on the fresh ones. "Very."

"Uncle Theodore sent you a present."

Etta rips into the box. Her light brown hair hangs limp and straight. (I'm glad Fleeta can put it up in a braid tonight.) Her little hands are just like mine, made for work. Her face is her father's, the straight nose, the lips that match top and bottom, and the hazel eyes, bright and round. Etta has freckles—we don't know where those came from. Jack told Etta a bedtime story about freckles when she was very little, which she believed for the longest time: God has a bucketful of freckles, and when he's done making babies in heaven, he lines them up right before they're born and sprinkles freckles on them for good luck. The more freckles, the better your luck. Let's hope the freckles do their job tonight. Etta holds up the corsage. "I shouldn't wear it if Jane doesn't have one."

"Not to worry. He sent one for Jane and a boutonniere for Billy."

"Just like a wedding," Etta says. "But I ain't never gonna marry Billy Skeens. No way. He's too short."

"He's probably gonna grow," I tell my daughter, sounding like someone else's annoying mother. "And we don't say 'ain't never.' Do we?"

A horn blasts next to us. "Daddy!" Etta shouts, off the hook for her bad grammar. The van from Sacred Heart Church careens into a parking spot. My husband smiles and waves to us. Etta climbs out of the Jeep and runs to the van, where Jack has thrown open the door. She shows him her corsage, which he admires. I watch the two of them through the window as they laugh. They look like an old photograph, black and white and silver where the emulsion has turned.

Jack must feel me staring through the rain and motions for me to join them. He shoves the van door open, and I jump in and climb into the seat behind him.

"How was your day?" I ask.

"Fine."

"Daddy, kiss Mama." Jack kisses me on the cheek. "Why do they misspell 'college' in *Kiddie Kollege*?"

"I don't know." Jack defers to me.

"Maybe because it matches the 'K' in 'Kiddie,' " I tell her.

"That's a dumb reason. If you're smart enough to go on a show called *Kiddie Kollege*, you're smart enough to know that college starts with a 'C.' "

Jack looks at me in the rearview mirror. The corners of his hazel eyes crinkle up as he smiles. He finds Etta's know-it-all tone funny; I think her loud opinions are just nerves before competition. Or maybe it's confidence. I'm not sure.

My family cheers when I announce I've brought along red pepper sandwiches. As I cross to the Jeep to get the cooler, Jack gets out to help me. He looks beautiful to me, fresh-scrubbed from the mine. He's gotten better-looking as he's aged. (Men are so lucky that way, and in others—don't get me started.) His hair, which receded in his late thirties and looked like it might fall out, stayed in. It's all gray now, but with his hazel eyes, it looks elegant. He lost some weight, determined not to be Fat and Forty. I smooth down my hair, which has frizzed in the rain.

"I've got it," Jack says as he lifts the cooler over my head.

"What's wrong?" I ask him.

"Nothing."

"Something is wrong. I can tell."

"Ave. Nothing's wrong."

"Are you sure?"

"I can't talk about it right now. I'll tell you later."

"Tell me now."

"No. Later." Jack looks at me and then through the window at Etta. She looks out at us. "I don't want to get Etta all riled up."

"Okay," I say impatiently. "But you can tell me." Why won't he tell me what's wrong? What is he protecting me from?

"The mines closed."

"No!"

"Yeah," he says under his breath angrily.

"I'm sorry." That's all I can say? I don't throw my arms around him? I don't comfort him? I just stand here in the rain.

"I am too." Jack turns toward the van.

"Let's not ruin Etta's night," I say to his back. Jack turns around and looks at me as though I'm a stranger; it sends a chill through me. He straightens his shoulders and says, "Let's not."

The day we have dreaded has come. My husband is out of work. But it's worse than that; Jack's identity and heritage is tied to the coal in these hills in a deeply personal way. The MacChesneys have been coal miners for as far back as anyone can remember. My husband is a proud miner: a union man who worked his way up from a pumper to chief roof bolter. Some say it's the most dangerous job in the mine. Now what will he do? What kind of work can my husband find at his age? He has no degree. How are we going to make it? I only work three days a week at the Pharmacy. We count on his benefits. Sure, we own the house, but it doesn't run on air. I wish we didn't have this show tonight, or all these people coming. Why do I always have to make an event out of everything? I had to arrange the van, fill it with friends, make sandwiches. I couldn't let it be just the three of us.

Iva Lou Wade Makin pulls up and parks across the street. Her glorious blond bouffant is protected by a white polka-dot rain cap with a peak so pointy, it makes her seem medieval. Actually, Iva Lou looks more like the state bird as she puddle-hops across Shawnee Avenue. Her lips, her shoes, and her raincoat are ruby red. She hoists herself into the van (hips first) with a Jean Harlow grin. Her gold bangle bracelets jingle as she lifts the rain cap off her head.

"Whoo. That storm is a bitch." Iva Lou turns to Etta. "Now, don't use that word 'bitch,' hon. It's a grown-up word."

"Thanks for the clarification." I give Iva Lou a look.

"Nellie Goodloe ain't coming. She's gonna watch the show with the Methodist Sewing Circle at the Carry-Out."

"Is Aunt Fleeta coming?" Etta asks.

"I saw her at the Pharmacy. I got the last rain bonnet. She'll be along presently."

Etta's teacher (and mine way back when), Grace White, a petite lady of almost seventy, holds an umbrella over Jane and Billy, dressed for television in their Sunday finest. Jack gets out and helps them into the van.

"Jane, we got corsages!" Etta squeals. "Billy, you got a carnation."

"Okay," Billy says, less than enthused.

Fleeta Mullins's old gray Cadillac with one bashed fin pulls up next to the Jeep. She barrels out of it quickly, tossing off the butt of a cigarette. Fleeta is small, and she's shrinking; smoking has ruined her bones. I try to get her to take calcium; I'm sure she has osteoporosis.

She's still a nimble thing, though. Fleeta leaps up into the van after Iva Lou pulls open the door for her, then wedges into the middle seat next to Mrs. White, bringing a waft of tobacco and Windsong cologne with her. "I had me a line at the register, and folks was surly. Pearl Grimes needs to hire more help over to the Pharmacy," she announces over her foggy reading glasses. I shrug. I am not the boss, haven't been for almost ten years. But old habits die hard with Fleeta.

"No problem. We're right on schedule," Mrs. White promises.

"Pearl made peanut-butter balls." Fleeta gives me the tin. The kids beg for them, but I tell them, "After the show. Okay? We don't need your winning answers sticking to the roofs of your mouths."

As the kids chatter, Fleeta sticks her head between Jack and me. "I done heard. Westmoreland's out."

"Don't say anything, Fleets. The kids," Jack says to her quietly.

"Right. Right. I got me half a mind to get on the bus to Pittsburgh and go meet them company men myself and tell 'em to go straight to hell. After all we done for 'em. Sixty years of profit on the backs of our men, and now they're just gonna pack up and clear out." Fleeta grunts and sits back in her seat.

As we drive out of our mountains and into the hills of East Tennessee, Billy regales us with the capitals of all fifty states in alphabetical order. Jane divides fractions aloud. Etta squeezes into my seat with me and faces her father.

"Are y'all mad?"

"No," Jack and I say together, looking straight ahead.

"Then what's wrong?"

"Nothing," Jack tells her as she shuffles through her homemade flash cards.

"Daddy, the coal of Southwest Virginia is . . ."

"Bituminous."

"That's right!" Etta smiles. "I hope they don't make me spell it."

"If they do, you just stay calm and sound it out," I tell her.

"And if you can't, we love you anyway, darlin'," her father tells her.

"I want to win." Etta's eyes narrow.

"Etta, do you know how much coal there is in our mountains?"

"How much, Daddy?"

"Enough to mine for the next seven hundred years."

"That much?"

"That much."

"If they ask me that, I'll know," Etta says proudly.

"I don't think they'll ask you that," Jack tells her.

"You never know." Etta hugs his neck and returns to her seat.

I look over at Jack, who keeps his eyes on the road. I wish I could fill up the silence between us with something, anything, a joke maybe. I used to know what to say to my husband; I used to be able to comfort him or cut to the center of a problem and dissect it. I could always make him feel better. But something is wrong. Something has shifted, and the change was so subtle and so quiet, we hardly noticed it. We pull against each other now.

"Jack?"

"Yeah?"

"Is there really seven hundred years of coal in our mountains?"

"At least," he tells me without taking his eyes off the road.

The WCYB television station is a small, square, brown-brick building nestled in the hillside outside of Bristol, just off the highway.

"Is that it?" Etta asks as she wedges between us and looks through the windshield.

"That's it?" Jane echoes.

The building does look lonesome sitting there on the side of the road. It's hard to believe that it's the center of communications for the Appalachian Mountains. The kids were expecting WCYB to be a comic-book skyscraper with mirrored windows and an oscillating satellite dish shooting menacing green waves into the sky.

"Now, see, that's not so scary," Jack Mac says to the team.

"That ain't scary at all. It looks like a garage," Billy adds, disappointed.

"It ain't how big it is. It's if they got cameras. All you need is a camera and some wires and some electricity. That's what makes TV," little Jane says definitively. (I hope Jane doesn't get any questions about modern appliances. If she does, we're in big trouble.) Mrs. White leads the kids into the studio.

Fleeta needs a smoke. Iva Lou is so tense from the trip, she bums a cigarette. The rain has stopped in Bristol, but it's still damp, and the fresh smell of the surrounding woods makes the place feel like home.

"I don't know how you people with kids do it." Iva Lou lights up, folds an arm across her waist, and perches her other arm with the cigarette in midair. I've always liked how she leans in to smoke, sort of like the cigarette might be safe to smoke if it's off in the distance a bit.

"It weren't easy, let me tell ye. That's how I started with these." Fleeta holds up her cigarette like a number one. "My nerves was so bad from the day-in-day-out with my younguns, I turned to tobacky and it's been my friend ever since. Thank you Jesus and keep the crop pure."

"Our kids are well prepared for the show. Sounded like," Iva Lou says hopefully.

"I want 'em to whoop the asses off Kingsport," Fleeta says as she stomps her cigarette butt. "I been watching every week, scopin' out the competition. I had Ten to Two Metcalf run some stats for me." Fleeta exhales. (Ten to Two is a bookie out of Jonesville. He got his name because he has a permanent tilt to his head, forcing his neck to crick over his shoulder at the ten-till mark.) "I got twenty bucks ridin' on our team. And I don't like to lose."

If the exterior of WCYB is a big fat disappointment, the interior doesn't do much to impress the kids either. The check-in desk is an old wooden table with a backless stool on wheels. A fancy plastic

NBC peacock sign spreads over the back wall. A wide electrical cord dangles down from it like a hanging noose (it must light up). I peek in the small rectangular window of a door marked STUDIO. The familiar *Kiddie Kollege* set, an old-fashioned schoolroom with six desks for the contestants, is positioned in front of the camera. The portable bleachers for the audience fall into shadow. The host's desk, complete with a large spinning wheel full of tiny folded question cards, is bathed in a bright white light.

A perky young redhead with a small, flat nose meets us at the studio door. "I'm Kim Stallard. Welcome to the WCYB studio."

"We can read, lady." Billy Skeens points to the sign.

"Aren't you smart?" Kim says sincerely. "You must be from Big Stone Gap. Would you like to see the studio?"

"You better do something with them damn kids. They're squirrelly as hell, cooped up in that van for pert' near two hours," Fleeta tells Kim, popping a mint.

"Right. Okay. Follow me." Kim motions us into the dark studio. There is a small path to the set; on either side are painted flats, which serve as backdrops for the news shows.

"Isn't this interesting, kids?" Jack asks.

"It's a mess," Etta decides.

"These are sets for the shows," I tell her in a tone to remind her that we are guests in TV Land.

"We're what you call an affiliate. We are a multipurpose studio. Is it smaller than you thought?" Kim asks.

"Much," Jane Herd tells her as she cranes her neck to look up at the rafters rigged with lights.

"Well, TV isn't all glamorous." Kim smiles.

"Look, a bike." Etta points to an off-camera bike.

"That's mine," says the familiar deep voice of Dan DeBoard, the debonair fiftyish game-show host/weatherman/anchor of the six o'clock news (he shares these responsibilities with Johnny "Snow

Day" Wood). He doesn't seem one bit nervous as he reviews his notes. He is tall and slim; his black hair is parted neatly and slicked back. The *Bristol Herald Courier* once proclaimed him "East Tennessee's Burt Reynolds." The resemblance is definitely there, and so are the *Smokey and the Bandit* sideburns.

"You look thinner in real life," Fleeta says as she sizes him up.

"So do you," Mr. DeBoard replies. (I guess he hears that plenty.)

"It's a pleasure to meet you." Iva Lou extends her hand and right hip in one smooth move.

"And you must be a former Miss Virginia?" Dan's eyes travel over Iva Lou as though he's starving and perusing the fresh pie rack at Stringer's Cafeteria.

"No, just plain old Miss Iva Lou." She tightens her grip as her eyes travel all over Dan DeBoard.

"She's murried," Fleeta growls.

"Aren't we all?" Dan winks.

Our kids swarm the stage. "It's good to let the children get comfortable on the set. It makes for a better show," Kim tells us as she checks a list on a clipboard. They catch sight of themselves on the television monitor on the floor in front of them. "Look-ee! We're on the TV!" Jane shrieks. Etta and Billy squeeze into the seat with Jane and wave to their images on the monitor.

Then the enemy arrives. Kingsport Elementary is represented by three stern boys with identical crew cuts and creases in their little navy slacks. Their matching green plaid jackets are so stiff, they look like they were pressed while the boys were wearing them.

"Lordy mercy," Jack Mac whispers.

"They look like triplets," Fleeta announces.

Mrs. White surveys the competition, then gathers our team in a huddle. The group breaks. Jane slips into her seat and folds her hands neatly on the desk. Etta smooths her hair and adjusts her nameplate so it is square on camera. Billy sits down at his desk and removes his boutonniere. The girls follow suit with their corsages. The mountain kids get it. This is for real. If they want to win, no flowers, no shenanigans.

As the theme music plays (a swing version of the alphabet song), Dan DeBoard takes a sip of coffee and spins gently on a high stool. He nibbles on the rim of the Styrofoam cup as his eyes search the bleachers for Iva Lou. When he finds her, he smiles and double-blinks (very flirty). Then he stands and casually hooks the heel of his shiny tasseled oxblood loafer on the chrome rung of the stool. He is so calm, he might as well be playing charades at home in his living room. I grip Jack's hand so tightly, I could crush a Coke can.

"Let's welcome the challengers from Big Stone Gap, Virginia." Fleeta, Iva Lou, and I applaud, and Fleeta whistles long and low, like she's calling a cow. He continues: "This is the team captain, Etta MacChesney. Etta, tell me about your family."

"My daddy's a coal miner, and my mama sells pills."

"What kind of pills?"

"It depends. What's wrong with you?"

The host stifles a laugh. "I understand you're an avid reader."

"Yes sir."

"What are you reading now?"

"*The Ancient Art of Chinese Face-Reading.* My Aunt Iva Lou gave it to me. She works at the li-barry." Etta points to Iva Lou, who straightens her spine and beams as though she's on camera.

"How interesting. What is the Art of Chinese Face-Reading, exactly?"

"Well. It's all about how your face can tell you what kind of person you are and what the future holds for you."

"A little hocus-pocus, eh?" Dan looks into the camera, raising one eyebrow.

"Not really. Like you. Your top lip is thin, and your bottom lip is thick."

"Does that mean something?" Dan rubs his chin.

"You're cheap."

"Somebody's been talking to my wife," Dan deadpans.

"I'm sorry," Etta says, realizing that she may have said something unkind.

"I'd like to crawl in a hole and die," I whisper to Iva Lou.

"I'd like to crawl into a hole with Dan DeBoard," she whispers back.

Dan tells our team that, as the challengers, they go first. He asks Etta for a number.

"Five for my cat, Shoo, who is five," Etta says.

"If you have two baskets of peaches and in one basket there are three hundred fifty-six peaches and in the other there are two hundred ninety-eight, how many peaches do you have?"

Etta squeezes her eyes shut and tries to add in her head. Jane Herd's little blue eyeballs roll back in her head and click up and down like the digits on an adding machine. Jane starts to shake; she has the answer. Etta's expression of pure panic and desperation tells me she does not.

"Five hundred fifty-four?" Etta says weakly.

"Sorry. It's six hundred fifty-four. Let's go to the Kingsport team."

Etta's cheeks puff as though she may cry. Jane is so disappointed, her head hits the top of the desk like a bowl of cold mashed potatoes. The champions look over to see what clunked. Etta pulls Jane's head off her desk by the scruff of the neck; there's no blood, thank God, so Dan throws the next question to the opposition.

The Kingsport boys take the next three questions, answering each of them correctly, including one about the state capital of Vermont. "Look at the Skeens boy. He ain't right," Fleeta whispers. "He ain't blinking." Something *is* wrong with Billy. He is frozen, staring into the distance, his eyes round and vacant like pitted black olives. Our team has totally lost focus. Jane is obsessed with the monitor. She makes circles with her head, studying her face from all angles. She is sweating so profusely in the hot lights that the barrette is slipping from her side part. Etta obsessively twists the third button on her cardigan like a radio knob; it looks to snap off any second.

By halftime, we have managed to scrape up zero points, while the Kingsport boys have fifteen. "Turr-ible. Turr-ible," Fleeta mumbles, and she goes outside to smoke. She paces in the hallway, alternately puffing and scratching her head with a pencil she found lodged in her upsweep. Mrs. White spends the break trying to thaw Billy.

As round two begins, we hope for a miracle.

"When water flows out a drain, does it drain clockwise or counterclockwise?" Dan asks Billy. Billy's forehead folds into one deep wrinkle.

"Oh, for cripe's sake," Fleeta says loud enough that everyone in the studio turns and looks at her. Dan drops his chin and rolls his head, encouraging Billy to answer. Finally, Billy opens his mouth and says, "Uhhhh," without forming words. His mouth hangs open like an unbuttoned pocket. Then his "uhhh" turns into a strange hum. "What the hell is wrong with that boy?" Fleeta whispers.

Dan looks at the cameraman, who shrugs. Jane turns to her teammate. "Dang it, Billy. Say somethin'!" He says nothing, so she turns to him and shakes him. "Guess! Take a guess, Bill-eeee!" Billy slips out of his seat like a wet noodle. Jane lunges to yank him back into the seat, but instead he latches on to her and pulls her out of her seat. Jane's desk turns over on top of Billy's. The clanging and banging sound like a four-car pileup. As Jane tries to free Billy, her foot gets caught in the metal bottom of her desk and she flips it over again. The Kingsport boys are standing now, confused by the melee. Dan runs across the set and lifts Jane off the scrap heap, and her skirt flips up like an inside-out umbrella. He yanks her skirt down, then unpins Billy and helps him back into his seat. Etta sits with a clenched smile so creepy, her upper and lower teeth form one wall of fear (I have not seen the likes of it since we watched *Mr. Sardonicus* on the Million-Dollar Movie). I look down at Mrs. White, who is dabbing her forehead with a hanky. How thrilled we are when the buzzer goes off and the game is over.

As team captain, Etta must collect the consolation prize: a case of Pepsi for their next school party and a check for ten dollars.

"Etta, what is your class going to do with the check?"

"Well, if we won the twenty-five dollars, we were going to buy a set of Nancy Drews. Since we only got the ten, we'll probably just get a *Weekly Reader* magazine or something. The Pepsi's nice, though."

"Well, good luck with all that," Dan says, and winks at the camera. The theme music plays through. "Let's do the Good-bye Wave from *Kiddie Kollege*! See ya next week!" our host says in the same professional tone he uses when he's signing off the six o'clock news or starring on a commercial for Morgan Legg's Autoworld. He places a giant yellow cardboard dunce cap on Etta's head, as she is captain of the losers, a tradition that began when the first *Kiddie Kollege* aired. The giant dunce cap is so big it covers Etta's eyes. Billy, pressure off, has revived. He jumps in front of Dan and the kids and puts his face in the camera, barking out greetings to his kin—every Skeens and Sizemore in the Cumberland Gap gets a personalized greeting. He and Jane flail their arms so hard, it looks like they're washing a car. The three automatons from Kingsport stand in front of the question wheel (which I believe should be set on fire and destroyed) and wave like movie stars. We are all relieved when the cameraman makes a slashing motion across his throat to stop this nightmare (at least he knows how we feel).

"You guys did great!" I tell them peppily.

"We lost real bad," Jane says, looking at the ground.

"I can't add in my head," Etta says sadly.

"Mrs. Mac, do you have them peanut-butter balls?" Billy asks. Finally, a child that can shake off catatonia and defeat with his sweet tooth. We know our way out of the studio, and it's a good thing. Perky Kim has disappeared. Even a television producer out of Bristol, Tennessee, knows when to remove herself from the stink of failure.

Even though we lost, the tension is gone, so the ride home is more fun than the ride over. The blue hills of Tennessee give way to our familiar black mountains as we curl through the darkness in our big green van with the Sacred Heart of Jesus painted on the side. A lot of good the religious shield did us. And what about the Saint Anthony medal that Father Schmidt gave to Etta for good luck? Did he forget to bless it? Where was Saint Anthony, the patron saint of lost things, when my daughter forgot how to add?

The kids are gathered around Fleeta in the back of the van while she tells them a ghost story. Etta has already forgotten all about *Kiddie Kollege*, and that makes me happy. Preparing for that stupid show was an ordeal, anyway. No more cramming for questions tacked on that godforsaken wheel. No more flash cards. No more watching the show every week and taking notes. Etta's moment in the sun came and went in the same night. The kids eat pepper sandwiches, chewing slowly; Fleeta cackles like a witch. Occasional passing headlights cast weird shadows on her and make her even more scary. Mrs. White has tucked her raincoat into a neat square pillow and sleeps against the window. Iva Lou hums to a Janie Fricke song playing softly on the radio. I lean across and rub my husband's neck as he drives.

"That's okay," he says.

"No. I want to," I tell him.

"Really. It's okay."

I remove my hand from my husband's neck and place it on my lap. I look out the window. I'm afraid I might cry. He puts his hand on mine. This time, I pull away.

"I'm sorry," he says softly.

"It's not my fault," I tell him without looking at him. But I don't believe it. I think everything is my fault, including the demise of the coal industry in Southwest Virginia. I am the woman in this family; I'm supposed to make everything work. What I can't seem to say aloud is that I'm failing.

"We'll be all right," Jack says, which upsets me even more. I hate when he downplays important things, the *most* important things! I'm furious with him, yet I'm also angry at myself. I saw this coming. I tried to talk to him about this many times, and he wouldn't discuss it. Why didn't I beg Jack to quit the mines when the layoffs became routine and the coal companies shrank their staffs and the train whistles carrying coal out of these hills became less and less frequent? I want to turn to him and say, "I told you this was going to happen!," but I can't. We have a van full of kids and Etta's teacher and my friends. So instead of shouting, I bury my rage. I turn to him and tell him calmly, "I can work more days at the Pharmacy."

Jack doesn't say anything. He looks at me quickly and then focuses his eyes back on the road. "Well. What do you think?" I say, realizing it sounds more like an accusation than a show of support. He does not answer me. As he drives into the dark valley, he checks the rearview a lot. But there is nothing behind us. We're the only vehicle on the road. Thank goodness the shrieks and giggles of the kids fill up the quiet.

The road to our house is so bumpy it wakes Etta, who has been sleeping since we hit the hill into town. She slept through dropping off her teammates at their houses and our guests at their cars outside the elementary school.

"We have to fix this road," I tell my husband.

"Put it on the list."

Jack lifts Etta out of the van and carries her up to the house as I clear the sandwich basket, the tote bag, and Etta's book bag. Jack takes Etta to her room, and I go to the kitchen. As I flip the light switch, I hear a thump. Shoo the Cat has jumped from his perch and is looking up at me.

"I forgot your food!" I fill the dish, pet him, and apologize over and over. There was too much to think about today. Jack comes into the kitchen and opens the refrigerator.

"There's leftover macaroni and cheese," I tell him. Jack pulls out the casserole and puts it in the oven. "We need to talk," I tell him.

"Not now. I'm tired." Jack uncaps a beer and looks out the kitchen window. I don't know what he's looking at, the field is pitch black, and tonight there's no moon.

"We need to talk about the mines." I try not to sound impatient.

"What do you want me to say?"

"Well, what's your plan?"

"My plan?"

"Yeah. What are you going to do?"

"Well, I'm going to be out of work."

"I know that. Have you thought about something else to do? Some other job?"

"No."

"Jack, maybe it's time to come up with something."

"Maybe it is." Jack shrugs. He is not listening to me.

"I know this is hard for you—"

"You have no idea."

"Yes I do."

"No you don't."

"Yes I do. I know mining is in your blood."

"Ave. Stop. Let's just forget it."

"Forget it? Why are you mad at me? What did I do?"

"You think I get up at dawn and disappear into a mountain, and ten hours later I come out and wash it off of me and come home to you. I don't tell you the half of it."

"Whose fault is that? You have to talk to me. I'm tired of pulling information out of you. I've worried every day you've left this house. Especially lately." As the bigger companies pulled out, safety became less important. I would panic every time I heard a wildcat company was coming in to reopen old mines for quick access to more coal. I knew they weren't following codes; it was common knowledge around here. I look at my husband, who is studying the label on his beer. I hear myself raising my voice; he looks at me. At least I have his attention now. "I worried myself sick. Of course, you have no idea what I'm thinking because you never ask me."

"Maybe that's because I know what you're thinking." He takes a swig.

"Look, I've had a very—" I begin to say "tough day" but stop myself. I look at my husband, and he is wounded down to his bones.

"Ave, you don't come from coal." Jack says this matter-of-factly. He's right. I'm not a descendant of these folks, even though I was born and raised here. I am a ferriner. I do have a different point of view. I don't accept the power of a big company over a community. I don't believe in waiting until the last drop of coal is pulled from these mountains before having a plan. I don't rely on anybody for anything. If I can't work for it myself, I won't have it.

"That's not fair." This is all I can come up with?

"When my grandpap took me down in the mine the very first time, he wanted me to hate it. But I got into the transport car with him, and from the first second daylight was gone and we were inside the mountain, I loved it. I loved the smell of the earth, the white dust on the walls where the coal was taken from, and the men all together in there, figuring out how to beat the mountain. How to outfox it. How to get that coal out without anybody getting hurt."

"Jack," I start to say, but he's turned away to pull the casserole out of the oven and doesn't hear me.

"When they talk to us like we're idiots, it takes a piece out of me. I saw simple men in there solve complex problems and prevail. And that's what I wanted my work life to be." Jack sits down. I sit down too and reach for him across the table.

"You can still have that. You can go back to school and become an engineer. Whatever you want."

Jack throws back his head and laughs.

"Do you have any idea who you're married to?" He tilts the kitchen chair, balancing on the back legs, and looks at me, challenging me to answer. Why do men do this? Why do they pretend to be strong when they're hurting? And why am I angry when he's hurting? I resist the urge to push him off the chair.

"I guess I don't."

"See there? We agree on something." Jack picks up his fork and eats.

I give up. I leave the kitchen and stop when I get halfway up the stairs. I didn't want to walk out of the room, I wanted to stay and work things through. Why did I leave? Why do I always leave the moment things get really hard? I sit down in the dark to think.

The storm is back, and the rain hits the house in gusts as thunder breaks over us in loud crashes. Lightning pierces the darkness, sending jagged shadows across me like sharp fingers. I pull myself up by a dowel of the old banister and take one step down to go back into the kitchen. I am determined to fix this tonight. I am going to tell him that I trust him to take care of us. But something stops me. I go up the stairs, choosing to go to my daughter instead of comforting my husband. I have the feeling it's a decision I will regret, but I do it anyway.

"Hey. You're supposed to be asleep," I tell Etta. She's looking out the window and watching the storm.

"The thunder woke me up." Etta crawls into her bed.

"It sure is loud," I tell my daughter as I tuck the blanket in; I hope it was loud enough to drown out the fight between her father and me.

"I'm glad Mr. DeBoard didn't ask me if I had any brothers and sisters. He does that sometimes, you know."

"Yeah, he does." I sit down on the bed. "Joe would've been very proud of you tonight."

"No, he wouldn't. We lost."

"Okay. Right. He probably would have teased you and called you a big loser all the way home."

Etta smiles as she turns over and looks at me. "He would have loved it when the desks flipped over." She lies back on her pillow. "Joe's been gone so long, sometimes I forget about him."

In Etta's life, three years is a long time. For me, it's a heartbeat. Joe was only four years old when he died. He and Etta were so close in age, folks often thought they were twins, even though they could not have been more different. I got pregnant with him three months after I had Etta. You should've heard the jokes in town. "Honey, must've been nice to get wet after that drought o' yorn!" one of Jack's coal mining buddies said to me at a football game. Oh yeah. They had a good old time talking about the Former Spinster turned Baby-Making Machine. I guess they thought I got myself a little taste of the honey and had to have the whole hive.

When Joe was born, Jack took one look at him and said, "The Eye-talian genes have landed!" And it was true. Joe had curly black hair and chocolate-chip eyes. He had my father's regal nose and slight overbite. His chin was square and prominent, but it curved at the bottom as though a cleft should form there. He had a deep dimple near his eye when he smiled (we don't know where that came from). He was so different from Etta. Joe was loud, funny, and exasperating. Once he even pulled down the Christmas tree. He drove me crazy. And I would give everything I own to have him back, driving me crazy.

"Don't worry. You'll never forget your brother."

"Are you sure?"

"I promise. I know."

"How do you know?"

"Because you loved your brother. And love never dies." I say this to my daughter as plainly as I might tell her to carry her umbrella when it's raining. Now if only I believed it. I turn off her bedside lamp and switch on the nightlight.

"Ma, stay till I'm asleep."

I lie down with my daughter and wrap my arms around her. She is warm and safe. I hope that, wherever my son is, someone is holding him. I have prayed to my mother to find him and take care of him. I have to trust that my prayers have been answered, but every night, even as I say them, I am not so sure.

The headline on the front page of the Big Stone Gap *Post* says WESTMORELAND PULLS OUT, which causes a round of jokes in town that do not bear repeating. In the week since the announcement, *The Post* has been printing helpful articles for the miners about their benefits, insurance, and black-lung programs.

On the Almost Fame and No Fortune front: AREA KIDS TAKE SECOND PLACE ON *KIDDIE KOLLEGE* is the delicately worded headline on page two. Perhaps the editor, Bill Hendrick, placed it under PRAYERS REQUESTED FOR MAXIE BELCHER AND PEBBLE FIG so that folks could get a little perspective. We hate to lose, even at the elementary school level. The picture of our team is sweet; thank God they took it before the show, in happier times. It's taken a full week to shake defeat. Etta had almost forgotten about the loss, until she heard an old man point at her in a Buckles Supermarket, "Right 'ere's one of 'em kids that lost for us on the *Kiddie Kollege* show!" I fold the newspaper neatly into a basket filled with canned goods, fresh eggs, and milk.

It's my turn to leave staples for the Tuckett twins. Edna and Ledna are somewhere in their eighties and don't get out much. I leave the basket inside their screen door. When I get back to my Jeep, I hear the creak of their front door, letting me know that they got the basket. All these years, the sisters made pies and cakes for all the families in town: from birth to death and in between, you could count on the Tuckett twins and their cobblers. Now they find it hard to take what they consider "charity." But it isn't charity; as far as the folks in town are concerned, it's payback time.

Town is busier than usual. The first thing that happens when bad news comes out of the mines is that folks come into town to talk to the businesses where they have credit. Everyone from Zackie Wakin to Gilley's Jewelers renegotiates their terms in a time of crisis. Barney Gilley often tells his customers that without coal, there would be no diamonds; and without the coal miners, he'd be out of business, so he's happy to refinance.

My boss, Pearl Grimes, is sweeping the front walk when I pull into the parking lot of the Mutual Pharmacy. Pearl is a very mature twenty-four years old; if you just met her, you'd swear she was older. She looks polished and slim in a simple taupe A-line skirt and white blouse. Her smock is pressed and tied at the sides in small bows. Fleeta and I also wear the smocks, which Pearl designed, white with an embroidered pine tree on front (a salute to John Fox, Jr.'s *The Trail of the Lonesome Pine*). Pearl has permed her brown hair into a curly 'do, and she uses lots of spray on it. She has grown into her face, once round and girlish, now more chiseled, and she has mastered the art of well-placed rouge, which gives her cheekbones. Her soft brown eyes still have a sadness, but there is also a determination now, which is very attractive.

As Pearl has transformed, so has the Pharmacy. With Pearl's cum laude degree in business administration from the University of Virginia at Wise, she has transformed Mulligan's Mutual from a pharmacy that sold beauty aids to a full-service personal-needs department store. She began by talking to our customers and asking them how she could improve business. Then she goosed the staff (Fleeta permanent, and me part-time since Etta went to school) and set out to make the place more professional. We wear smocks (even though Fleeta rebels by keeping hers untied so it flaps like a vest on a construction worker). No more smoking behind the counter or eating lunch on packing boxes. No more Fleeta chugging back peanuts and Coke while sizing up a customer. No more putting the WE'LL BE RIGHT BACK sign on the door to hit a yard sale.

Pearl considered every aspect of the business before she made her changes, including ambience. She removed the garish fluorescent tubes installed by Fred Mulligan (the original owner and the father who raised me). "Soft light and music draw business," Pearl promised. And she was right. Some days we can't get rid of the browsers. Pearl even thought to stock Estée Lauder cosmetics, which attracted new clients who used to have to drive all the way over to Kingsport for that sort of high-end specialty item.

Pearl outdid herself with the window dressing this month. In her homage to autumn, she built a papier-mâché tree festooned with leaves spray-painted gold. A mannequin dressed like a farmer (he'll be Santa Claus come Christmas) holds a rake next to the tree. It's a simple concept, but Pearl put it over the top by burying a fan in a fake mound of dirt to blow the autumn leaves around. What a scene. It looks so real that Reverend Edmonds, in awe of the artistry, rearended Nellie Goodloe as he drove past one morning.

"I got an idea," Pearl says as she sweeps leaves into a dustpan.

"Fleeta and I are not doing a floor show to attract more business."

"I'm not entirely sure that would attract business."

"Thanks."

"I have a better idea. Did you know that there used to be a soda fountain back in the storage room?

"When I was little, Fred Mulligan closed it. Said it was too much work."

"The pipes are still in the wall. And they work. It wouldn't take much to put in some appliances and reopen the kitchen. We could serve breakfast and lunch. Keep the menu small at first. The only place to gather in town is Hardy's. How many sausage biscuits can you eat?" I don't want to disappoint Pearl, but the answer to that question is: a lot. Brownie Polly holds the record—fourteen sausage biscuits in one Sunday morning.

Pearl continues, "It would be fun for the town. It would be profitable for us. I think we should do it." She rattles off the list of positives with such enthusiasm, I can tell she has already made her decision.

"It sounds like you did your research."

Fleeta sticks her head out the door. And what a head it is this morning. Her hair is piled high on her head in waxy brownette curls. A tightly woven braid encircles the curls like a licorice tiara. A cigarette dangles from her mouth. In the daylight, Fleeta's rouge is so bright, it sits atop her cheeks like little orange bottle caps.

"Mornin', Cleopatra." I pat my cheeks, which makes Fleeta pat hers. She feels the two pink "X's" of tape holding down her spit curls and rips them off. The curls lie against her cheeks like commas.

"Somebody want to tell me what the hell is going on?" Fleeta pulls her smock over her head, neglecting to tie the side ribbons, as usual.

"Pearl's reopening the soda fountain."

"I ain't workin' no damn food-service job. Do you know what it is to wait on hungry people? They's beasts."

Pearl takes Fleeta's opinions seriously because Fleeta works the most hours. Ever since her husband, Portly, died from the black lung two years ago, she's been able to work more. Fleeta's kids are grown too: her son Kyle moved to North Carolina because he couldn't find a job here; her son Pavis moved to Florida because he passed bad checks in North Carolina, where he was working with Kyle. Fleeta's daughter, Dorinda, had a baby, but Fleeta told her that she wasn't raising another "damn kid." "You had the fun, now you have the baby, she's yorn, you take care of her and visit me on Mother's Day," Fleeta told her; so went the story around town. She didn't mean it, though. She takes care of little Jeanine every chance she gets. Dorinda gave her a necklace that says WORLD'S BEST GRANDMA on a little gold plate in cursive letters. Fleeta never takes it off.

"Fleeta. I think it's a great idea." I look at Pearl.

"You would," Fleeta growls. "How much more change we gonna have 'round here? Purty soon we're gonna be the Fort Henry Mall. If I wanted to work at a mall, I'd git me a job at the mall."

"With the mines closing, we need to look at ways to expand. If the fountain takes off, Pearl will be able to hire people. More jobs. Here. In town."

Otto and Worley emerge from behind the building, carrying their tools and balancing a long pipe on their shoulders (proof that Pearl's decision was made long before she asked me). Otto walks with a limp; he swears his bones got short in the one leg due to old age. He has a bright smile, thin white hair, and clear blue eyes. Their new truck has a sign on the door that says OTTO OLINGER & SON, lest anyone forget that they are father and son, not brothers, as all of the Gap believed for so many years. I notice that Worley looks good, well dressed with a certain stature. His red hair has lots of white in it. And he's had some work done on his front teeth.

"What'd Miss Ave say about reopening the soda fountain?" Otto wants to know.

"I love the idea."

"Do either of y'all two give a rat's ass about what I think?" Fleeta pats her smock, trying to locate her cigarettes.

"Not really." Otto smiles at Worley.

"You can kiss it, Otto," Fleeta barks.

"Okay, guys. That's enough," Pearl says with a smile.

"I remember old Fred Mulligan's soda fountain," Otto says wistfully. "There was a mirror on the back wall and them green leather stools that used to spin. And the cherry floats! Lord, they was good, them cherry floats."

"I 'member it too. But if I want a cherry float, I go to Bessie's in Appalachia. Let's get on it, Daddy-O," Worley tells him. (Back when

Otto confessed to Worley that he was his father, Worley stopped calling him plain Otto and invented Daddy Otto.)

I take my place behind my counter and tack up the prescription orders for the day. Pearl has left her peanut-butter ball recipe on my desk. Etta pleads for them so much, I figure they're good leverage when I want her to do something.

COUSIN DEE'S PEANUT-BUTTER BALLS
Blend: one box of confectioners' sugar
18-oz. jar of crunchy peanut butter
2 cups of graham-cracker crumbs
2 sticks of melted butter
Roll into bite-size balls.
Melt: 12-oz. package of semi-sweet chocolate chips
¼ box of paraffin wax
Dip balls into melted chocolate and wax and place on wax paper.

"Is this it?" I wave the recipe at Pearl.

"It's easy."

Fleeta grabs the recipe and reads it. "I don't use the graham-cracker crumbs in mine, makes 'em mealy. I use crushed pea-nits. Gives 'em weight plus crunch."

"I'll keep that in mind."

"Try the crackers, then be the judge." Fleeta shrugs. " 'Course, nobody round here cares what I think."

"Pearl, can I talk to ye?" Worley asks.

"Sure."

Worley's tone is serious, so Fleeta and I look at each other. I tug on her smock and move toward the office to give them privacy.

"You can stay, Miss Ave. In fact, I'd like ye to," Worley says. Worley doesn't say anything to Fleeta, who takes this as permission to stay. She turns her back to us behind the counter, lightly dusting the outgoing prescription envelopes. Her head is cocked with her good ear toward us, so I know she's eavesdropping.

"Is something the matter?" I ask Worley.

"No ma'am. I got me a full heart is all."

"Sad-full or happy-full?" From Worley's somber expression and the deep crease between his eyes, I can't tell.

"Oh, very happy, ma'am."

"Does this have something to do with my mama?" Pearl asks.

"Yes, it do. I'd like to murry Miss Leah if it's all right with you." Worley looks at Pearl and then, struck with shyness, looks at the floor. Fleeta and I look at each other. We're stunned.

"Did you ask her yet?" Pearl asks Worley.

"We have talked."

"Did she say yes?"

"She said if you said it was all right, then she'd murry me."

"Well, it's absolutely all right with me."

Worley smiles. "I always wanted me a nice Melungeon girl like my mama was. And now I got me one." He goes back to the storage room.

"Your mama and Worley have been dating?" I ask Pearl.

"I wouldn't call it dating. You know how things are at the house — it's old, and pipes go, or something goes wrong with the wiring, and Otto and Worley know where everything is, so they come over and fix it. And then it's rude not to ask them to stay for dinner or lunch or whatever."

"Put milk out and you ain't never rid of a cat," Fleeta says under her breath.

Fleeta's got a point. Before I got married, I had so many repairs on the house, Otto and Worley practically lived there. They'd take in my mail, close the windows when it rained, and sometimes even start dinner before I got home.

"I guess Mama and Worley evolved sort of naturally." Pearl sighs.

"Why on God's green would your mama want to murry him? What does he got that's worth having?" Fleeta demands.

"Companionship," Pearl says over her shoulder as she walks back to the storage room.

"Leah will see how she likes companionship when she has him hangin' 'round all the time. She'll get tarred of that directly. A man can crowd a woman worse than a bunch of kids." Fleeta cracks a roll of quarters into the register like an egg.

"Do you think you'll ever fall in love again?" I ask.

"I had me Portly. I don't need to be goin' down that road agin. I'm old. Or haven't you noticed?"

"Love doesn't have an age."

"Yes, it do. If you heard the way my bones creak of the night, you wouldn't be tryin' to get some old man to come into my bed and creak around with me." Fleeta grabs her cigarettes and goes outside.

Falling in love with Jack Mac was almost an accident, so fleeting a moment I almost missed it. I was thirty-five and figured I'd be alone for the rest of my life. But Mrs. Mac knew better. She wanted me for her son and set about to make it happen, practically ordered me to go to the house when he would be home and she wouldn't. And I did— I went up there and waited at the old stone house with four chimneys. I often think of that night when he told me he loved me for the first time. I was so scared of it, of him, of everything. What if I had gotten back in the Jeep and driven down the mountain before he got home? If he had decided not to come home that night to find me waiting there? If he hadn't seen in me what even I didn't know was there? How did he know I could love him back when I never gave him a single sign? How fragile love is. How delicate and small in its first buds, when it's just an idea, a wish filled with hope. It is so easy to turn away from it entirely and choose to live alone in your own private fear. I had one moment of courage, and it changed my life. I didn't turn to love out of loneliness. Or out of habit. I let love change me. I see why Fleeta doesn't want a new man. She doesn't want to change.

The bells on the door ring merrily.

"Saw your Jeep outside." Spec Broadwater saunters in, leans against the counter, and starts fiddling with the viewfinder key chains hanging on a wire by the register. Spec, well into his sixties, is like a tree, seeming to grow higher and higher with age. Everything about him is oversize, his big head (mostly forehead, etched with crisscross lines from the smoking), his mighty hands, even his gold aviator eyeglass frames are so big they seem like windshields on his face. "Bad news about the mines." Spec exhales like a cartoon cloud that grows a face and blows gusts of wind. "How's Jack Mac?"

"He's okay."

"The situation stinks." Spec tears a stick of gum in two and offers me half. I decline. He chews one piece and puts the other in his shirt pocket. "You know they got this new thing now."

"What's that?"

"It's a new way to get coal out. Instead of digging it, you start at the top of a mountain and mine from the outside. Kindly like peelin' an apple. You mine down the outside of the mountain and then through."

"What happens to the mountain?"

"Eventually, it's gone. It disappears."

"That's horrible."

"Yep. It is. If a bunch of ferriners come in here and mow our mountains flat, what will we be? Indiana?" Spec leans across the counter and shakes the March of Dimes coin canister. "A job's a job, though. Maybe this here new technology is the answer."

"I don't know." I smile at him, but he knows and I know that new technology isn't going to help us. The companies have decided that they can go elsewhere in the world and mine coal more cheaply. There isn't anything we can do.

"I don't neither. Maybe some of these politicians 'round here will get off their arses and get the tourism thing going."

"Maybe they will."

"We got a lot around here to offer folks. The mountains. The beauty. Huff Rock. The Valley. Keokee Lake. Big Cherry Lake. You been up 'ere lately? Oh, it's a beauty. The Dickensons put in a boat launch—no motors up there. Only manual. It's something." Spec neatens the rack of cough drops.

"Spec. Do you need something?"

He looks at me and laughs. His laugh turns into a hack. He clears his throat. "I need you to come back on the Rescue Squad."

Spec has got to be kidding. Volunteering on the Rescue Squad when I was single was a natural thing; I was the town pharmacist trained in CPR and first aid, so soon I was assisting Spec. But it's been almost ten years since I was on board. I don't have the time anymore. "You know I can't. I've got the kids—I mean, Etta."

Spec looks away at the reference to Joe. I'm not offended by that, it happens a lot. Whenever I talk about Joe (and that's rare), folks quickly change the subject. It's not that they're being rude or insensitive, they just don't know what to say. Maybe it's too painful for people to look into the eyes of a mother whose child has died, so they'd rather pretend it didn't happen. Or maybe they think if they mention Joe, it will hurt me all over again. Joe's life was so brief, just a small piece of the landscape of our long lives in these parts. Except maybe for Spec. I believe Spec remembers Joe the way I do.

Spec was Joe's godfather, even though he isn't Catholic. In fact, I found out later that Spec had never set foot in a "Cath-lick" church on account of the way he was raised. Catholics were strange and mysterious and not to be trusted. But he bucked up the day Joe was baptized, and made it to the church, even though he was shaking so bad from nerves he almost dropped the baby.

"I hate to turn you down."

"Then don't. I can't keep nobody. I had that Trudy Qualls running shotgun with me for a while, and she just didn't work out. Tried to boss me. You know how I am. I don't mind living with one bossy woman, but I ain't gonna work with one too."

I'd like to help Spec. I would. He's been there for me on some of the worst days of my life.

"Come on, Ave. For old times' sake."

There were lots of good times with Spec on squad detail: cat rescues, setting off confiscated fireworks for all the kids in town when there was no other means to destroy them, decorating the Rescue Squad wagon to ride in the parade at the state capital when Big Stone Gap's own Linwood Holton was elected governor. And when it came to Etta and Joe, there wasn't anything he wouldn't do. He used to let Joe ride around in the Rescue wagon with the siren going and the lights flashing.

When I took my son to the hospital for the first time, it was one of those bleak January days. We came off the elevator and ran smack into Spec. It was a Snow Day, and Etta was home from school, so she came along. Spec made a big fuss over them, threw them both up in the air, then sent them off to look at the newborn babies behind glass.

"What the hell you doin' here?" Spec asked with a smile.

"Joe has a bad bruise."

"Did he get in a fight?"

"No."

"Well, you know boys, they fall a lot. Who's his doctor?"

"Dr. Bakagese."

"The Indian? He's right good. I ran Myra Poff over here the other day, and he caught the first start of pneumonia in her chest."

"That's good to know."

Spec put his arm around me, which, in all the years I had known him, he had never done. I assisted him for eleven years on the Rescue Squad; in the face of sickness and accidents, I never flinched. I followed his instructions and never panicked. I think he appreciated that I could deal with things without emotion.

"Why are you gittin' yourself all upset?"

"What if it's serious?"

"Good God a-mighty, Avuh. You can't be the mother of a son and hit the panic button every time he takes a tumble. Boys are a mess. I got me two; one was a head-banger in the crib and the other one set fires. It's just how they are."

Somehow the thought of Spec's sons, one a self-flagellator and the other a pyromaniac, soothed me. I had been fighting feelings of doom for months; maybe the long winter had me in a state. Hadn't I read that folks get depressed this time of year? That the short days and overcast skies can chemically alter the brain into sadness? Hadn't I noticed that the mountains surrounded us like brown metal walls and the sky, a dismal patch of faded blue flannel, had made everything seem worse on the drive up to the hospital that day? I thought then, as Spec looked at me like I was crazy, that there was a chance I was making the whole thing up. How I wanted to believe Joe was fine. For those few seconds, I did. I gave Spec, the Mighty Oak, a big hug. He pulled away quickly, embarrassed, and said, "See ye," then off he went. That was the last time I felt hope throughout Joe's entire ordeal.

I owe Spec. He knows it and so do I. How can I say no to Spec Broadwater now?

"Okay, Spec."

"You'll come back on?"

"Yes sir. But only one week a month. I'm a mother. I can't be high-tailing it all over Wise County with you."

"I'll take you. Even one week a month. Better than nothin'. See ye." Spec goes out the door, whistling.

"You're a fool." Fleeta clucks and reloads the candy bar display.

"I know."

"You got enough on your plate."

As I load Mary Lipps's insulin into a plastic case, I am sure that Fleeta is right.

"Oughtn't you check with Jack Mac? Don't he have no say?"

"I never once heard you say you checked with Portly about anything, so lay off," I tell her pleasantly.

"I may never have said it, but I done did it," Fleeta says as she stuffs overflow Goo Goo Clusters into a basket. "I done did it."

It's dark in Cracker's Neck Holler as I drive home from work. I stopped at Buckles for milk and talked too long with Faith Cox, who is taking names for the bus trip to the revival of *Carousel* starring John Raitt next month. (Etta would love it, so I took a flyer.)

I take the curves of the roads gingerly. I'm crawling along so slowly, you'd think that I don't want to go home. Truth is, I'm tired and don't want to take a dip over the side. I don't drive as fast as I used to. (I don't do a lot of things since I became a mother.) I love my time alone going to and from work. It's my time to think and sort things out. Right now I'm reconstructing all the little day-to-day decisions I've made that led us to our present situation. It's what I always do when I have a big problem to contend with and feel stumped. I've been doing this a lot since Jack told me about the mines closing. I wonder if things would be different if I hadn't given Pearl the Pharmacy and the Mulligan house on Poplar Hill.

When I sold Pearl the business for a dollar (the technicality made it legal) years ago, it wasn't just to keep it from falling into the hands of my Aunt Alice Lambert. I did it because it was time for me to move on and start my new life. I shed the reputation of town spinster; I didn't know what I would replace it with, but it was going to be something! I had big plans. I was going to travel the world and find the place where I fit. I had lived my life taking care of my parents; at thirty-five, I felt half of my life was over, and I hadn't lived one day of it for myself. Folks were shocked when I sold Mama's car, then gave Pearl the store and the Mulligan homestead on Poplar Hill. I knew if Pearl and Leah moved into town, it would give them a new world-view, the very thing I was seeking. It seemed crazy to others, but I saw potential in Pearl and knew that, with a little encouragement, she could make something of a business that I merely maintained. I never felt like Mulligan's Mutual was mine, even though it said so in Mama's will. I never felt like anything but an employee. Once I knew that Fred Mulligan wasn't my father, I didn't have to hold on to the things he had built. And I didn't want to.

I never intended to become a pharmacist. After I went to Saint Mary's and got my degree, I came home because Fred Mulligan had gotten sick and couldn't run the place, and if he lost the business, what would happen to Mama? Then he died, and she got sick. I don't regret staying home to take care of my mother. She had peace of mind when she died, knowing I was secure financially. I wonder what she thought up in heaven when I sold the Pharmacy to Pearl.

It sure would be nice to have a little cushion now. I don't like myself for feeling this way. A little cushion is just a veil for what you really need. Don't we all need extra money? Is there ever a time we don't? The nest egg that I came into my marriage with has dwindled over the years. We needed extra cash to maintain the property. Things happened: the big pine tree that hit the back of the house two winters ago; a new truck for Jack when his old one broke down; Joe's medical expenses.

I began working at the Pharmacy again once Joe was in preschool. When I came back to work, I realized how much I had missed my work life. Maybe I initially became a pharmacist out of duty, but when I returned, it was by choice. I found out that I love what I do, the precision of it, learning about new medications, and helping folks look after their health. When I quit, I missed the delivery run and talking to folks in their own homes. I missed the way their houses smelled so distinctly from one another: the Tuckett sisters' of cinnamon, the Bledsoes' of lilies, and the Sturgills' of fresh vanilla. The job was something that was all mine, and I liked that. I missed being needed for my skills and my knowledge of medications. My job fills me up in ways I never knew until I left it behind.

The fifteen-minute commute seems more like ten seconds. As I come into the clearing, I figure I've taken a wrong turn or I'm at the wrong house. My home is lit up like a casino. Cars and pickup trucks are parked all around it. I don't remember planning a party.

As I climb the front steps, I look in the window like a visitor. I see my husband in the front room, surrounded by men. They drink beer and laugh and talk. I must stand there a long time, because the milk in the paper sack starts to feel wet on the bottom.

The laughter dies down a bit when the men see me in the entryway.

"I thought poker night was Tuesday," I say with a big smile.

"We ain't gamblin', Ave," Rick Harmon says with a wink. He has his feet on my mama's old coffee table. I push them off; the men laugh. Jack Mac takes the milk from me and leads me into the kitchen. Shoo the Cat makes a break for the kitchen and follows.

"Where's Etta?"

"Watchin' TV." Jack puts the milk in the fridge and turns to me and smiles. His face is full of news to share, his eyes full of hope again. I haven't seen him smile in days. Instead of being happy about this, I am curt.

"Did she eat?"

"I heated up the spaghetti."

"Did you make broccoli?"

"No."

"So she didn't have anything green?"

"She had that green banana for dessert."

"Not funny. I'm tired. I've been working all day, and I'm really really tired."

"I get it. You're tired."

"Where are you going?"

"I'm in the middle of a meeting."

"You're in the middle of a party." Why am I doing this? I want him to have a good time with his friends, don't I? Jack stares at me with disbelief.

"We got sidetracked."

"Sorry I interrupted the fun."

Jack looks back at me as he goes. I don't look up at him. I sit down at the kitchen table and cry. I just have a nice little self-indulgent cry. I want to feel good and sorry for myself. I came home to a mess, a child fed supper with no greens, and noise and beer and company I didn't want to see.

I check on Etta, who does not look up from a cartoon show. I kiss her and walk back through the old kitchen onto the back porch, through the creaky screen door, and out into the black field behind our house. It's cold, but I don't turn back for my coat.

The moon hangs between the mountains like a searchlight, making a path through flimsy clouds. I breathe deeply. The cool night smoke fills me with calm. The mountains, knit together seamlessly, form a black velvet fortress around me. The dark sky lightens to a shimmer of silver on the mountaintop, like a window shade that cannot reach the sash to keep out the light. The details are clean—bare branches with fluttery edges like curls, and strong black veins in the trunks and branches of the mighty pine trees. I am so small here.

There's a stump from an old weeping cherry tree in the back field that overlooks the side of Powell Mountain. When I sit on it, I'm nearly on the edge of our cliff, which gives way to a ravine and then the valley below. It's a wild, dark tangle of shrubs and branches and overgrown footpaths. When I first lived here, it scared me to come out back alone. But as time passed, I became less afraid and began to explore the MacChesney woods. I'm not afraid of falling off mountains anymore (at least when I'm on foot). And something about these old hills reassures me.

I don't know how long I've been sitting; it must be a while, because my hands are freezing. I hear the hum of motors starting in the field out in front. Jack's meeting must be over. I don't know why, but the sound fills me with dread. I feel a big argument coming on with my husband, and I don't have the energy to fight. I go inside and up to Etta's room. She finishes the second chapter of *Heidi*, reaches up to turn out her light, and dutifully lays her head on her pillow. There is a catch to her breathing—her nose is stuffed up, probably from the first cold spell of the season. I have to remember to give her something for that tomorrow. I give her a kiss and tuck her in.

Instead of going to the living room to collect beer bottles (great), I go to the sun porch and fold a load of laundry. When I'm done, I straighten up the rest of the kitchen and look in the refrigerator, making a mental note that we're low on lettuce. Enough procrastinating. The men left over half an hour ago, and the house is quiet. Time to go to bed. The light on the nightstand sends a warm glow up the walls of our room across from the kitchen. On the surface, everything seems safe, normal. I walk around the bed and see that the bathroom door is open, but I don't see Jack.

Shoo the Cat is asleep on the bench in the hallway in an empty box Etta uses for Barbie school. I look out the window. Jack's truck is there. Good. He didn't go out with the boys. I go to lock the front door, and through the small pane, I see him sitting on the porch steps, leaning back on his elbows. His legs drape down the stairs and are crossed at the ankle.

"I'm locking up."

"I'll take care of it."

"It's chilly out there."

"I like it."

I almost turn to go to bed, but something tells me to go to Jack. So I go out onto the porch and sit down next to him. He doesn't make any room for me on the stairs.

"I'm sorry about before. I'm just tired," I tell him.

"That's no excuse."

"Yes, it is. When people are tired, they get a little testy."

"You're more than testy."

"Not really."

"I'm not going to fight with you," Jack says plainly.

"I don't want to fight either." And I mean it. I hate fighting. "Jack.

Please. What's wrong?" My husband does not answer, but this is typical. I have to pull everything out of him, especially his feelings. "Just say it. Come on."

"Why haven't you talked to me about the mines closing?" Jack says quietly.

"We talked about it. Honey. We knew this was coming."

"Yeah. We did, didn't we."

"What does that mean?"

"You act like it's my fault. Like I wanted, after twenty-two years, to be out of a job, out of the only trade I've ever known."

"It's not your fault."

"Damn right it isn't."

"What good is that going to do? To be angry? It won't make West-moreland reconsider. We have to face this."

"We? You're the one who hasn't faced this."

"What do you mean?"

"You think that the solution to this problem is to take care of it yourself."

"What's wrong with that?"

"Everything. You don't believe in me. I need your support."

Oh my God, he thinks that I don't support him? That I didn't admire him every day for taking such risks in a dangerous job? That I don't respect his physical strength and leadership skills? Of course I support him.

"Don't you trust me?" Jack looks at me. He's thrown a lot of questions around, but I can see that he'd like an answer to this one.

"Of course I trust you." I blurt this out instead of saying it like I mean it. Do I mean it? Do I trust him?

"Do you think I'm going to get another job?"

"Yes. Of course."

"I'm worried about my life too. But I'm not going to sit around waiting for something to happen. I'm out there making it happen."

"I never said you wouldn't."

"You said *you'd* work extra hours. As if this were about money. Do you know how that made me feel?"

"It should make you feel like you've got a wife you can count on."

"I know that. That's not what I'm talking about. Ave, I have my pride. Okay? I thought we were partners. I thought that you understood me, that you knew that whatever comes, I would find a way for us to get through it. Instead, you make me feel like I'm expendable. You don't need me around here if you're gonna do everything yourself. Why are we married if you're gonna handle everything alone?"

"I don't want to handle everything alone!" I feel my marriage sliding off this mountain like a loose rock, with me flailing after, trying to catch it and make it secure.

"You aren't the man in the family." Jack Mac gets up to go back into the house. I grab his ankle, then pull myself up and put my arms around him.

"I'm sorry. These worries overtake me sometimes. I still think I have to do everything myself." This revelation comes from the deepest part of me, and my husband knows it. He knows how hard it is for me to let go. I know how hard it is for me, but then why do I keep making the same mistakes? Why do I push him away when I need him? I feel my husband's heartbeat slow from an angry pounding to a sweet, steady rhythm. His arms encircle me tenderly. His great shoulders protect me from the cold; I melt into him in a way that I haven't in a very long time.

"I believe in you," I tell my husband, meaning it with every cell in my body.

"I hope so, Ave."

"No. No. I do. Here. Come on. Sit. Tell me your plans." I pull Jack down onto the step and put my arms around him. My husband's face is bathed in the golden haze of the lamplight from the living room window. I see the same expression I saw in the kitchen earlier. He is excited, hopeful, full of new ideas, solutions, even.

"Rick and Mousey want to start a construction company. The three of us. We think there's going to be a lot of development in the area. There's talk of that prison being built, and that means a new highway coming through, and that'll create a need for additional housing. We thought we'd be the first to get in on it."

"Great idea. You're terrific with woodworking."

"Yeah, and Mousey knows electrics and plumbing."

"Is Rick going to quit his job at the car dealership?"

"He thinks he can do both. Until we get busy enough that he can quit."

"Okay. This is great! When do you start?"

My husband pulls me close and kisses me a hundred times, quickly and sweetly and gratefully. This is what I love the most about being married: sometimes, even after eight years, we feel new, like there's a surprise in the familiar that I wasn't counting on; the passion comes back, sneaks up on you. You gear yourself up for what might be a doozy of a fight and reach an understanding instead; instead of jabbing at each other, you kiss. And you learn to take advantage of a moment like this, because it comes and goes and may not return for a very long time.

The moonlight blankets the porch. We lean into the pale blue, and in it I see my husband's face clearly. Every detail. The strong, straight nose, the perfectly matched lips, and the hazel eyes that can show hurt and love in the same moment. We fold into each other naturally, but it isn't like any time we've made love before. We laugh as we go for each other's buttons, zippers, lips. He shushes me, tells me not to wake Etta, then kisses my laughter away. What wonderful thing is happening? How can it be so different this time? It's romantic, yes, and a little daring (we're outside, for Godsakes), but this feels like it used to, when we were first in love. Why did that go away, and why didn't I know how to get it back? We talk too much or too little and show our love so rarely. We need to show each other more. Why do I forget this simple truth when I'm tired from work or caught up with Etta? This is the center of everything, this love right here. Without it, we're nothing but an old boardinghouse in Cracker's Neck Holler with Etta, the ghosts of those who are gone, and a box of problems. We're more than our problems, aren't we? As my husband kisses me, I am reminded of why he chose me, and how we must always come back to that, even when we've disappointed each other. Especially then. He holds me tenderly, and a night breeze settles over us. I shiver.

"Let's go inside, honey," he whispers.

"I love you, you know," I tell him.

"I know." He kisses me again.

In the warmth of our bed, Jack holds me closely as he hasn't done in a long time. We're united again under these old quilts, and I like the feeling.

"Honey?"

"Yeah?"

"Spec asked me if I could come back on the Rescue Squad a few days a month. What do you think?"

"I told him I thought it was fine."

I sit up in bed. "He asked *you*?"

"Spec's old-school. He does the right thing and checks with the husband before he goes to the wife."

Before I can object, Jack begins to laugh. I take my pillow and beat him with it. Jack grabs the pillow, and then me.

"You got a problem? Take it up with Spec." My husband smiles and kisses me.

A square of homemade fudge topped with snowy mini-marshmallows and crunchy pecans is wrapped neatly in wax paper and waiting for me on my counter. I need the sugar this morning. (I forgot how much energy the love department requires; it's like starting Jazzercise after a long hiatus.)

"Hey, thanks for the surprise," I tell Fleeta as she squirts a big blob of hand cream onto her forearm from the Estée Lauder display. (Never mind that the tube is not a sample.)

"I'm just a big ole sweetheart, ain't I?" Fleeta looks at me over her glasses and rubs her wrists together. "Nobody'll miss it." She puts the tube of hand cream back on the shelf. "What are you smilin' about?" she asks suspiciously.

"Nothin'," I tell her and shrug.

Pearl walks in carrying two big bags from the hardware store.

"What's that?" Fleeta asks Pearl.

"Contact Paper for the shelves in the fountain." Pearl goes to the back of the store.

"I ain't helping ye with nothin' back 'ere," Fleeta calls after her.

"Not a problem, Fleets," Pearl hollers back.

I grab a pair of scissors and join Pearl in the Soda Fountain.

"Pearl, I need a favor."

"Sure."

"I hate to ask, and I wouldn't if I didn't have to."

"Ave, come on. What do you need?"

"I need to work more hours."

Pearl looks at me oddly at first; it is still hard for her to be my employer. "No problem."

"Are you sure? You've got the expense of this new venture back here, and I don't want to strap you."

"Are you kidding? I need you."

"Great." I turn to go back to my post.

"Ave Maria?"

"Yeah?"

"There's something I want to tell you. And it's still real new, so I can't say too much. I'm . . . I'm seeing someone."

"A man?"

Pearl nods.

"Romantically?"

Pearl nods again, and this time she smiles.

"Good for you! Who is he?"

"I don't want to say yet. In case it doesn't work out."

"Okay."

"I like him a lot."

"That's great!"

"You know I'm sort of a late bloomer. So I'm a little nervous. You know." Pearl looks at me. I spent fifteen years in this town without a boyfriend. I know all about late blooming. I was alone so long, there are still times when I forget I'm part of a couple.

"Take your time. And don't agonize."

Pearl laughs. "I'm having too much fun to agonize."

"Good girl."

"Ave Maria! Pat Bean needs her 'scription! She ain't got all damn day!" Fleeta shouts from the register. (So much for the soothing shopping atmosphere at the Mutual Pharmacy.)

"I'm on my way," I yell back to Fleeta.

"Hey, Ave. Thanks," Pearl says, and her face flushes to a soft pink.

Pearl Grimes in love? Things around here are changing fast. I wonder if I can keep up.

The Halloween Carnival at Big Stone Gap Elementary is sold out. Nellie Goodloe thought it would be fun to host an all-county carnival to raise money for the John Fox, Jr., Foundation, which funds the Outdoor Drama. "Nellie has a flair," I keep hearing over and over as I walk through the spectacular decorations. White ghosts with black button eyes line the rail of the balcony overhead; the basketball backboards are big black cauldrons; a family of black paper bats flies over the bleachers. Nellie banked the entire ceiling in a spiderweb made of thick rope. In the center, she attached a giant papier-mâché spider that dangles down like a creepy chandelier. How does she do it?

The admissions table is loaded with straw and jack-o'-lanterns of all sizes; the ladies of the June Tolliver Guild are dressed as witches. The Foxes, who hand out programs at the Outdoor Drama, are also dressed as witches, but instead of billowing black robes, they wear short skirts (to show off their fishnet stockings, I'm sure).

Nellie hauled the oil painting of Big Stone Gap's most famous resident, John Fox, Jr., the author of *The Trail of the Lonesome Pine*, over here from the museum. Fleeta thinks Nellie has a crush on him, even though he's been dead since 1940-something. "Whenever she throws a shindig, she drags his mug out," Fleeta complains. Mr. Fox's oil portrait is eerily perfect for Halloween: he sits in profile in a dark wood study; on his long, pointed nose sits a pair of granny glasses. Come to think of it, he looks like a male *Whistler's Mother*. Nellie has draped fake white cobwebs on him. He fits right in.

Local merchants and the PTA provide the booths. Nellie is raffling off six free car washes (with wax) at Gilliam's Car Wash and a month of free dry cleaning at the Magic Mart. The money raised will go toward new streetlights in town (Nellie wants the old-fashioned-lantern look). There's a cakewalk and a costume pageant. Etta is not particular about her costume. Every year she goes as a skeleton, wearing a black jumpsuit with silver bones and a skull mask. She loves games of chance; she has spent the better part of the evening shooting at ducks on a spinning wheel.

Etta runs up to me with a glossy caramel apple covered in orange sprinkles. "Mama, will you put this in your purse for later? We need to cut it."

"This is the biggest apple I've ever seen," I tell my daughter. She hands me two pretty china saucers she won in the penny toss. When I ask her where the matching teacups are, she says, "I missed."

Etta's pals—Tammy Pleasant, a tiny, wiry blonde in constant motion, and Tara Kilgore, a tall, serious brunette with heavy-lidded brown eyes—grab her.

"You got to come *now*, Etta." Tammy tugs on her.

"They got a man that bleeds actual red blood in the Spookhouse," Tara says flatly. "I wasn't skeered."

"I was!" Tammy says, her eyes widening. The girls run to get in line at the Spookhouse. I know all about the Spookhouse because I spent the better part of this morning peeling grapes for the bowl of eye-balls the kids feel on their way in. Nellie convinced Otto and Worley to play monsters: Otto lies in a casket with blue goo on his face while Worley chases the kids through the locker area with a plastic ax strapped to his head.

"Yoo-hoo, Ave!" Iva Lou hollers. She is selling used library books in a booth decorated like a study in a historical home, and is dressed in a sexy turquoise hoop skirt and a frilly peasant blouse that exposes her creamy bare shoulders. Her cleavage forms a clean line like an excla-mation point. "Is this a good idea or what?"

"The blouse or the booth?"

"The booth, silly. I'm unloading all our old stuff, making way for the new. What do you think?" Iva Lou spins like a plate on a stick.

"What a deal!" I hold up four Lee Smith paperbacks tied with string, priced at two dollars even.

"Hold off. In another hour, I'm doing a flood sale: everything must go."

Iva Lou leaves the booth to James Varner, who looks much taller in real life than he does behind the wheel of the Bookmobile. Iva Lou still turns every head in the room. (There are some women who never lose their allure.) Lyle Makin stands off with a group of his buddies. He nods and smiles at us.

"How's your husband?" I ask Iva Lou as I wave to him.

"Well, he ain't been soused this month. Of course, no full moon yet."

"What does that have to do with it?"

"He gets drunk almost exactly with the tides of the moon. It's the strangest thing. He can go dry for weeks, and then boom, he goes on a four-day bender. There's no getting around it, either. I can hide the stuff; I can try to divert his attention; I can fuss, but nothing works. When he wants to drink, he'll find a way to drink, and that's that. So I learned to live with it. He's good for weeks on a stretch; and you

know, that's more than most women git." Iva Lou unwraps a chocolate marshmallow witch and takes a bite. "How are you doing?"

"We're okay. Better than okay. Jack is fine."

"It's a big damn deal when a man is out of work."

"I know."

"They *are* their jobs. You have to be careful. He's vulnerable right
now."

"To what?"

"To getting sick. Taking to the beer. Running around. You know."

"*My* husband?" Iva Lou has got to be kidding.

"He's a man, ain't he? He's forty and change. Jack Mac's hittin' that
mortality wall."

"Aren't we all?"

"Women are different. Men ain't got markers to show them that
they're getting older. Not like us. Mother Nature takes us women by
the hand and leads us into it slowly. You got your monthly to tell you
that you went from girl to young woman; childbirth to let you know
you're in the middle; and then the Change to tell you that soon it'll all
be over. What have men got, really? Losing their hair? Losing a job?
A pot gut? What?"

"I don't know."

"You got to git a man to talk. It ain't easy to git a man to talk about
his feelings. They'd rather not have them at all. It's our job to draw
'em out."

"Ivy Loo-ee?" Lyle hollers from the Coin Toss.

"Lyle's hungry."

"You can tell what he wants from the sound of his voice?"

"I'd know that call of the wild anywheres. I don't even need him to
use words. I can tell by a grunt." Iva Lou gives me a quick hug and
goes to the Coin Toss.

Jack is shooting ducks outside the Spookhouse. As I make my way
across the crowded gym, I think about how a good woman can suss
out her husband's needs. Or how a good man can do that for his wife.

Sometimes Jack reads my mind. But do I read his? Does he know how I feel about him? Is he still attracted to me the way I'm attracted to him? My husband has a great body. Really. He has broad shoulders and strong arms. His legs are thick and muscular from years of lifting, chopping wood, mining. And though I hate guns, there is something sexy about him as he stands with a rifle cocked. He sort of reminds me of John Wayne in *Stagecoach*. (Jim Roy Honeycutt just ran the print at the Trail. Black-and-white movies are always better on the big screen.)

The crowd shifts a little, obscuring my husband. Before I can get to him, Leah Grimes stops me. I hardly recognize her. She's lost weight (must be prewedding jitters), her hair is dyed a magnificent red, and the cut is pure Dottie West, a neat chin-length bob with feathering.

"Leah, you look so pretty."

"Love done it to me."

"Congratulations on your engagement. Worley is a fine man."

"I know." Leah blushes. I look over her shoulder and see my husband putting the toy rifle down on the shelf of the duck booth. A woman I have never seen before touches him on the shoulder; he turns around and grins at her.

"Are you having a church wedding?" I ask Leah while repositioning myself to get a better look at the woman talking to my husband.

"Nope. We're gonna elope. Perty soon, too. Soon as Worley gets the pipes done at the Mutual's."

"How are things at the house?" I ask Leah. Jack is laughing with the woman.

"Good. Good. I want you to know if you ever need me to do anything fer ye, I'd like that. Baby-sit for Etta. Sew fer ye. Whatever you need."

"Thank you, Leah. But you're gonna have your hands full with a new husband directly."

Leah smiles and nods. Her friends join her, and they go off to the crafts booth. Instead of following them to check out the apple butter, or going to Jack and introducing myself to the strange woman, I go up the stairs to the balcony. I circle around the upper level so I can watch them without either of them seeing me. I feel guilty doing this (slightly). I sit down behind a family dressed as sunflowers, munching on popcorn balls. They ignore me and watch the people below. As I slide down in the seat, I can see Jack Mac and the woman perfectly.

From overhead, she looks like the Athletic Type. She is small and fit. Even though it is late October, she still has the bronzey glow of a summer tan. I thank God for the Art of Chinese Face-Reading and the bright fluorescent gym lighting, which helps me to get a good look at her. She is definitely attractive. She has deep-set brown eyes (a secretive nature, great) which flash in a way that shows a sense of humor and a certain intelligence. She has a long, angular face and a large head (means she's not hurting for money). Her short blond hair is sprayed into a casual bob, with spiky bangs. (She looks about forty, but maybe that's just the sun damage.) She is neatly dressed; even her trim, faded jeans are pressed. The collar on her pale pink blouse is turned up, as are the sleeves. The top three buttons are open, revealing a freckled chest and a high, small bust. (I quickly unfasten the second button on my denim shirt and sit up straight.)

She says something; my husband throws his head back and laughs. She holds a set of used books to her chest (good, I'll ask Iva Lou about her) and gazes all around, giving him an opportunity to take a good look at her. Isn't she a little old to be playing the coquette? It doesn't matter. My husband is enjoying this! She sways back and forth, restlessly shifting her weight from foot to foot as she chatters. She is doing most of the talking (of course she is, I'm not married to a conversationalist), then she leans in and whispers in my husband's ear. As her lips near his earlobe, I feel a stab of jealousy in my gut. Part of me wants to jump up on the balcony wall, latch on to one of the bedsheet ghosts, swing down onto the floor, and knock her over like a bowling pin. But I am his wife, so I would prefer to knock him over first and take care of her later. However, I do nothing. I sit here frozen.

Why is he still talking to her? What does he see in her? I have my answer. She laughs a final time and pats the small of his back. (That's a little low on a married man's body to pat, in my opinion.) She turns and walks away. My husband watches her as she goes. She rolls off the balls of her feet and up onto her toes to give her hips just the right swivel. Jack Mac doesn't miss one movement. I am officially sick to my stomach. Then, as if his conscience has bitten him on the ass for eyeing hers, he turns his attention innocently to the shooters at the spinning duck booth.

The popcorn-ball eaters have left. I lean forward and drape myself over the back of the seat in front of me as though I have been shot and left for dead. (I don't consider this too dramatic in light of all Iva Lou just told me!) Suddenly, as if marital radar alarms have gone off, Jack Mac feels my presence overhead and looks up at me. He smiles sheepishly. Well, maybe it's not sheepish; I don't know what it is, but whatever it is, I haven't seen that smile on his face in a long, long time. It's the kind of smile he gave me on Apple Butter Night, the night he first proposed to me. I lean back in my seat and exhale a long, deep breath toward the ceiling. (I must have been holding my breath the entire time!) The big black spider swings overhead, its crooked legs caught in the ropy web.

I'd rather die than let my husband think I saw him flirting with the Blond Mystery Woman, so I wave to him from my perch and survey the gym floor as though I'm looking for someone. He looks up at me, confused. I want to stand up and scream, in front of the entire Halloween Carnival, "Yes! Yes! Yes! I'm spying on you!" Instead I smile and give a thumbs-up to the decorations. Spec joins him. Jack points up to me. Spec motions for me as he taps the red emergency cross on his orange vest. As I run downstairs to join them on the floor, I'm hoping the kids didn't have an accident in the Spookhouse; the tile floor in there can get slick.

"We got a call up in Wampler Holler. Let's go."

"What happened?"

"Not sure. Police radioed me," Spec tells me, handing me my gear.

"Honey, look after Etta," I tell Jack, and go with Spec. I look back as we leave. God, he looks good to me all of a sudden in his white cotton shirt and his oldest jeans. (Are all men better-looking when other women want them?)

Spec takes a road up to the holler that I've never been on before.

"So what's going on?"

"We're cuttin' through Don Wax's farm, goin' to the old Mullins homestead."

Most of the Mullins family (no relation to Fleeta) has moved out of our area; some to Kingsport, others north to "O-high" (I don't know what the industry is in Ohio, but lots of our folks have gone north to whatever awaits them there). All that's left of the Mullins family is its matriarch, Naomi, who still lives in Wampler Holler. I love this holler; it cuts into the mountain in the highest point in the cliffs, and it has a great view of East Stone Gap and the dairy farms that make up this side of Powell Valley. As Spec speeds along the ridge, I figure it's a real emergency—Naomi must be close to ninety years old. She still comes to town to trade on the first of every month; her face has not a wrinkle, and her hair is still coal black—must be that Cherokee blood.

"Is Naomi all right?"

"I ain't got no details, Ave, so don't ask me. The Fraley boy from the next house over was gittin' some firewood out of her barn and saw something and called it in."

"Fine, Mr. Testy."

Spec smiles and keeps his eyes on the road. It's just like old times, with Spec's complaining and my prying. As we approach the Mullins log cabin (which has since sprouted extra rooms and been covered in aluminum siding), we are stopped by burly Tozz Ball, a deputy in the Big Stone police department. He directs us to pull into the clearing next to the neighbors, take our gear, and approach on foot. Spec and I make our way on a small footpath that leads to Naomi's front porch.

I see a group of men, most from neighboring Norton's rescue squad, looking in the windows on the side of the log-cabin portion of the house. Spec and I join them. One of the men turns to us and motions us to be quiet.

"Lordy mercy," Spec says as he looks into the window. (He's tall enough to see over all the heads.)

"What is it?"

"You ain't gonna believe it." Spec pushes me to the front of the group so I can see in the window. There in the living room is Naomi, in a long pale green flannel nightgown, standing completely still and staring into the eyes of a six-point buck. The buck seems twice as big as any horse I've ever seen, and he doesn't seem agitated, he just looks deeply into Naomi's eyes. Naomi does not move; she stares the buck down.

"It's been pert' near an hour we been waitin'. But the buck ain't flinched, and neither has Naomi," a man holding a stun gun tells me.

"What are you gonna do?" I whisper back.

"I got ten bucks on Naomi," he whispers back.

"Boys, we'd better make a move," Spec warns the group. But no one can make a move; we're in that strange place where awe and fear intersect, and it has paralyzed us.

Naomi takes a step back without breaking her stare. As she shifts, the deer cocks his head. We hold our breath outside the window. Naomi holds up her finger.

"I'm a-gonna go, Ben," she says to the buck. "Now, you go when I go. Go on. Git." Naomi disappears down a hallway and we hear a door close.

"Who the hell is Ben?" Tozz whispers.

Then the six-point buck rears up. For a second, it looks as though he, like Naomi, may back out the open front door. Instead, in a panic, he charges the bay window at the far side of the living room and jumps through the window, tearing away the wood frame with his antlers. We hear a small yelp from deep within him as he breaks through the glass, which shatters onto the wood floor like crushed ice. In what seems like a long time but is only a few seconds, Tozz leads the charge around the side of the house to the front, to see where the buck went. As we get to the front porch steps, we see his silvery-brown rump as he leaps majestically back into the dark woods.

Spec and I run into the house to Naomi. The bay window is destroyed. The simple voile sheers are torn where the buck's antlers caught; there is fresh blood on the sash, where the glass pierced his underside. This makes my stomach turn. Spec opens the door to the bedroom for me.

"Naomi, honey, are you all right?" I ask her.

She sits on the edge of her bed in a state of calm with her hands folded neatly on her lap.

"Naomi?"

"Check her breathin'," Spec barks.

"What happened?"

"Oh, Ava Marie," Naomi says and sighs. Naomi's pale skin has a pink sheen to it; there is a little dew on her forehead (from the standoff, no doubt). Her long hair, which I have never seen outside a braided bun, is loose and hanging around her shoulders in shiny ropes. Her bedroom is small, with a bed with a red and white Irish chain quilt, a small lamp, and a table. She looks like a doll in a simple cradle as she sits. "He come to me. I dreamt it, and he done come."

"Who?"

"Ben."

"Ben?"

"My husband, Ben. Ye know."

"Naomi, we always called your husband Mule. Mule Mullins."

"His Christian name was Ben."

"I didn't know that."

"Benjamin Ezra Mullins. That was his name in full. I had a dream a while back where he was a buck and I was a doe and we was talkin' to each other like we was human." I make Naomi cough three times as I listen to her heart. "I been restless, thinkin' about him here lately. And I prayed that I could talk to him dye-rectly as I was feelin' his presence here. I been thinkin' 'bout selling this farm, and I couldn't decide on nothin' on my own, so I called on Jesus and then, o' course, my Ben."

"How did the buck, I mean Ben, get into the house?"

"He just walked right in. I had left the door open for air."

"How do you know it was him?"

"The eyes." Naomi smiles.

"What did he tell you?"

"To stay."

"Well, if that was his message, he tore up the window in the living room pretty good."

Naomi chuckles. "He never did want me to put that window in. He said we got enough light with the front windows. But I wanted me some big windows, so that I could put me some purty curtains up, like I saw in the movies. I always wanted me some big windows where the breeze comes through and moves them curtains around like fancy skirts."

"Honey, it doesn't seem like there's anything wrong with you. Your heart is beating normal, your blood pressure is good . . ."

"I wasn't skeered of that old buck."

"I know. But the excitement might've caused you some trouble."

"Aww, I feel fine," Naomi tells me, and gets up.

Spec has cleaned up the glass in the living room. Two of the men are taping cardboard along the frame where the glass had been.

"I'm gonna put on some coffee, boys. Any takers?" Naomi offers.

The men grumble appreciatively. Spec leaves his number with Naomi.

"Now you call me, youngun, if you need me."

"I will."

The ride down through the veiny roads of East Stone Gap is dark except for our high beams and the occasional jack-o'-lantern on a porch. As we speed through the black night, I have a sense that time has stopped. I am somewhere in the past, when I was younger and wore the same orange vest and sat beside Spec in this very wagon that forever smells of tobacco and spearmint.

"Ave?"

"Yeah, Spec?"

"That there was a good run."

"For everybody but the deer."

"Yup." He smiles.

"It was a mystical experience."

"Don't start that stuff, Ave."

"Spec, that was a visit from the beyond."

"It was a visit from the woods. That deer saw a light through an open door and went in Naomi's house uninvited. And that there is the end of it."

"Nope. Naomi thinks it was a visit from her husband on the other side."

"You're givin' me the creeps."

"I thought you were a believer."

"I am. If it's Bible-approved, or if it makes any goddamn sense. People don't come back as animals. That's nuts."

"I wish I knew where we go when we die."

"What good would that do?"

"I don't know. Maybe I'd live differently. Maybe I wouldn't be so afraid to lose people. I get scared that I'll never see my mother again. My son."

"I shore would like to see my mama agin. And my pap, too. 'Cause if I could see 'em agin, I would ask 'em a lot of things. Things that weigh on my mind."

"Like what?"

"Like why both of 'em died on me before I could git to 'em. Both of 'em. Ma went in her sleep, and Pap died at the hospital. But I never did say good-bye to neither of 'em. I wish that were different."

"I wish I would have made my mama go to Italy. She never went home, you know. That bothers me."

"I knew your mama. You couldn't make her do nothin' that she didn't want to do. So you got to let go of that one."

"I guess so."

As Spec drives us up the holler road, I wish for a minute that the run weren't over. There are things I'd like to talk about.

"Thank ye, Ave. You done good."

"Don't flatter me, Spec. It ain't your style."

Spec smiles. I grab my gear and go into our old stone house.

Etta must be asleep, I can see the glimmer of her nightlight from the bottom of the stairs. I place my gear on the bench and head back to our bedroom. Jack is propped up in bed, reading.

"How's Naomi?"

"How'd you know?"

"They made an announcement at the carnival. A guy from the Norton fire department called down the mountain with details."

"It was something to see."

"I'll bet." Jack goes back to his reading. When I see my husband, so comfortable in our house, in our bed, I feel as though we could last forever. I want to tell him about Naomi's dream, and I wonder if he believes in that sort of thing. We never talk about things like that, so I don't know.

"Do you ever dream about Joe?" I ask him.

Jack puts down his newspaper and looks at me, surprised that I brought Joe up. "No, I don't," he says softly. "Or maybe if I do, I don't remember it." We never talk about him; it's just easier that way. I turn to go into the bathroom to wash up for bed.

"Why do you ask?"

"I wonder where he is."

"In heaven."

"God, Jack."

"Don't you believe that?"

"I tell Etta that; I guess I'm hoping it's true."

"I thought you believed."

"Oh, I believe. I just don't know in what," I say. Jack looks at me funny. "What?"

"Ave, sometimes . . . I don't know. I don't get it." He shrugs and goes back to his reading.

"Honey?"

Jack puts down his paper. "What?"

"Sometimes you don't get *me*."

I go into the bathroom and take a good, long time brushing my teeth. Jack appears in the doorway. "Is everything all right?"

I want to say, "No. I'm scared. Who was that woman at the carnival? Are you tired of me?" Instead, I look at my husband and say, "Everything is fine." He buys it and goes back to bed. And that, I am sure, is the root of our problem.

For the first time in his life, Jack MacChesney is officially his own boss. MR. J's Construction Company opened its door on November 20. MR. J stands for Mousey, Rick, and Jack. Very clever. Rick finagled a small office for them at the car dealership. Morgan Legg, the owner, was happy to oblige them, as Rick was his top salesman on the floor last year. I have never seen my husband so happy. And they're off to a good strong start. They bid on a job to renovate the Fellowship Hall at the Methodist Church, and they won. Jack is having a ball designing the new space. No money coming in yet, but it doesn't matter, my husband's smiling face is payment enough. Jack's new job frees up extra time for Etta too. When he was a miner, he left before dawn and often came home after dark. Now he controls his time, so we see more of each other. I feel our troubles lifting a bit. A real reason to celebrate come Christmas.

I'm back to working full-time, and I like it. Jack didn't like the idea at first, but I was so supportive of his new company that he let go of any misgivings he may have had about my schedule.

The grand opening of the Soda Fountain is December 1. (Otto and

Worley are practically living in the Mutual's, trying to finish the job.) We're having specials and giveaways all month. (Maybe we can unload some of that partially used Estée Lauder cream that Fleeta pinches.) Pearl has sifted through lots of employment applications, looking for two waitresses and a cook. She has decided to hire Tayloe Lassiter as head waitress, who, despite having two babies now (Misty was joined by baby Travis last year) is still a looker and can draw a crowd. Sarah Dunleavy, the high school teacher who replaced Theodore when he left for the University of Tennessee, directs the Outdoor Drama and has taken Tayloe under her wing. She gives her acting lessons, and everyone in town agrees that Tayloe has gone from amateur to semiprofessional actress beautifully. Sarah has also encouraged Tayloe to model. Occasionally, we see Tayloe in the *Kingsport Times* on the hood of a new truck or in an ad for kitchen appliances.

Pearl comes in with a large packing box. "Fleets, the tinsel is in."

Fleeta takes the box and rips into it.

Pearl comes behind the counter. "I'd like you to come over to Lew Eisenberg's with me."

"Right now?"

"Yeah. If you don't mind."

"What's the matter?"

"Nothing. Just need your help on something."

"Okay." I grab my coat and follow Pearl out.

Lew Eisenberg has gone from the best local lawyer for the coal companies to representing the townsfolk in all matters from wills to divorces. He's always busy, and he's very good. He's even happy now that his wife, Inez, has gotten back her race-car body. She is a Weight Watchers leader, having kept off fifty-eight pounds for over seven years. It's been a long time since I've heard Lew mention moving back to Long Island, New York.

Lew's hair is completely gray; other than that, you'd never guess he was flirting with sixty. "Hey kids," he says from behind his desk. "Ave, your husband was in with his buddies incorporating last week. What do you think of that?"

"If you can't keep Westmoreland Coal Company in town, we'll take it," I tell Lew.

"We're real busy over at the Pharmacy," Pearl tells Lew, cutting the chitchat in half.

"Okay, so let's get to it. This is easy. Ave Maria, Pearl wants to make you her partner at the Pharmacy."

"A partner? Why?" I turn so that I'm facing Pearl. She glances at Lew, then looks at me.

"Because I need a partner now. We've grown so much that I can't oversee everything alone."

"I can't do it."

"Sure you can."

"No I can't. I have more than I can handle." I can't tell Pearl and Lew that for the first time in three years I feel my home life is returning to normal, that the hole left by Joe's death is slowly being filled by time, routine, and change. How could they understand that?

"I'm going to hire more help for you." Pearl offers.

"No, I'm sorry, Pearl. No."

"But you need it," Pearl blurts. It's no secret that with the mines closed, anyone with a miner in the family is struggling.

"We're doing fine."

"Let's say that you *are* doing fine, I still need help. I'm looking to expand, and I want to keep the flagship going strong. I'd have to hire a manager; who better than you?" Flagship? Little Main Street Mulligan's Mutual Pharmacy a flagship? What is Pearl talking about?

I turn to Pearl. "You're expanding?"

"I'd like to open a pharmacy in Norton. I've been looking at a building."

"You're serious?"

Lew pulls out a file and shows me a picture of the old insurance building, which has been abandoned for several years, in downtown Norton.

"We're talking to the realtor right now," he tells me.

"I think my concept of a down-home variety drugstore is one that can work anywhere. And Norton needs a pharmacy. They have two hospitals but no pharmacy."

"Pearl's on to something here. You should consider this," Lew says, peering at me over his glasses.

I know I should. I'd have fewer Night Worries about the bills, college, and pensions. And the other part of all of this is just selfish. I've missed my pharmacy. I loved making the day-to-day decisions; I used to be a person who *ran* something. Being in charge gave me a sense of accomplishment that I don't get working part-time or at home scrubbing the oven. I still have to scrub the oven, and that's okay, but I love my job.

"Ave, please do this. I wouldn't have anything, I wouldn't be anything, if you hadn't helped Mama and me. It forever changed us. I owe you." Pearl looks off for a second, and then that familiar concentration crease between her eyes deepens. "And I don't like owing people. So let me at least begin to pay you back by sharing in the success of Mutual's."

"The chain," Lew pipes in.

"Let me see what you've got there."

Lew hands me papers; Pearl lets out a whoop and claps her hands. It's a simple deal. On the flagship store, I will be salaried as a manager and pharmacist and take 50 percent of the profits; the other share goes to Pearl. As I sign my name, I am thinking of my daughter and her future. She needs security. My husband will never leave Cracker's Neck Holler, and now that he's found work he enjoys, I have to contribute all I can, however I can.

As Pearl and I walk back to the Pharmacy, she chatters on about her business plans, and I think about my family. This break will help us;

I'm tired of worrying, and maybe this will help me stop. Ever since Joe died, when something wonderful happens, I have a moment of elation, then I remember my son and feel a pang of doom. What good is anything without my son to share it with? Now that I've ruined the moment for myself, I plunge further into despair. I feel a strange sense of defeat: here I go again, I'm tied down to a business I didn't choose in the first place. When I gave the Pharmacy to Pearl, it was a no-strings deal. I knew the power that guilt can have over a person because it had defined my life. How I wanted to do the choosing and be free to invent myself. I had made a plan. I was going to leave Big Stone Gap and find myself out there in the world, seek my happiness, own my destiny, have a life of adventure before it was too late. Instead of going away, though, I fell in love and stayed here. I married Jack Mac and believed that the only cage I had been in was one of my own creation. Why do I now have that old boxed-in feeling when I should feel relief?

Jack's truck is parked in front of the Mutual's when we return. "I hope Etta's all right," I tell Pearl.

When we get inside, we find Jack, Rick, and Mousey working with Otto in the Soda Fountain. Etta is wearing Fleeta's smock and painting one of the wood panels on the base of the counter.

"Hey, what's going on?" I say to the men, who look up but keep working.

"Well, we was worried that we wasn't gonna make our deadline. So I called old Jack Mac and I done tole him my troubles and he come over and here we are," Otto explains.

"I'm painting, Mama!" Etta says proudly.

"I can see that," I tell my daughter, who haphazardly streaks paint down the wood.

"Don't worry, Ave. It's just the base coat," Otto says under his breath.

"Try not to get any paint on Fleeta's smock."

"She can ruin it for all I care," Fleeta says as she stacks boxes of Christmas tree lights onto the shelf.

I watch my husband as he stands on a ladder, maneuvering a ceiling tile into place. I consider what I told Pearl about spending fifteen years in this town without a boyfriend. Suddenly, I am not in the present—I am the woman I was ten years ago, when I worked in this Pharmacy and it was my life. My husband swivels on the ladder. I don't think any man could look better in a pair of old overalls and a bandanna. We're so different; he's talented with his hands, and the last book he read was *Moby-Dick* in the eleventh grade. I can't hammer a nail, and I wait for the Bookmobile every Saturday. I must be attracted to what I don't have, but I wonder what I fill up in him. He catches me looking at him and smiles. "What are you looking at?"

"You," I tell him.

"Jack, you gots a call."

My husband and I are really looking at each other in a way we haven't in a very long time, and I don't want this moment to end.

"She says it's important," Fleeta says impatiently.

"Who is it?" I ask. My tone of voice causes every man in the room to look at me.

"Karen. Karen somebody," Fleeta barks.

"I'll be right there," Jack says, and steps off the ladder. He touches my arm as he passes; I'm going to take that as a sign of reassurance for now. I look over at Rick, who studies the trim of the counter a little too intently.

"Who's Karen?" I ask him. Without looking up, he shrugs.

Mousey interjects. "She manages the lumber store up in Coeburn. We git our lumber there."

I'm so glad I asked.

"Hel-looo?" Iva Lou calls out from the front of the Pharmacy.

"We're back here," I holler.

"Well, lookee here. This is gonna be some soda fountain." Iva Lou inspects the job. "All we need is Lana Turner on the stool and we're in business."

"Who's Lana Turner?" Etta asks.

"She was a sweater girl in the movies when I was a boy," Otto tells her.

"A sweater girl?"

"Yeah, she made me sweat." Otto laughs.

"Mr. Honeycutt shows her movies sometimes. I just haven't taken you to any of them yet," I tell my daughter.

"I got tickets over to the Barter The-A-ter in Abingdon for tomorrow's matinee," Iva Lou tells me.

"What are you seeing?"

"*Fiddler on the Roof.* Remember that Womack girl who used to understudy June in the Drama? Well, she's playin' one of the sisters. I put a group together. I was hoping I could take Etta."

"I want to go to the show!" Etta says. She puts down her paintbrush and shoves her bangs out of her eyes.

"Okay, honey."

"I'm gonna be all alone this weekend without my women," Jack Mac says from behind me.

"Really? You throwing me out?" I tease.

"Kind of." Jack kisses me on the forehead and pulls a ticket from his pocket. UNIVERSITY OF TENNESSEE VS. ALABAMA, it says in orange letters.

"What's this?"

"You're going to Knoxville to see Theodore."

"You're kidding." I'm thrilled. Utterly surprised and a little confused, but thrilled at the prospect of a weekend without chores and errands and worries. I have the most thoughtful husband in the world.

"Go on home and pack. Your bus leaves in an hour."

"Etta, you'll be all right?"

"Mama. Go," she says, and rolls her eyes.

"Okay. Great. I'm leaving." I kiss Etta and then my husband.

"I'll follow you home and give you a lift back down to town," Iva Lou says as I head for the door.

Once I'm home, I throw together a duffel bag of clothes, feed the cat, and turn up the heat so it'll be warm when Jack and Etta come home later.

"You need to git away," Iva Lou tells me as we descend the mountain into the Gap.

"I do?"

"Honey, you're worn to a nub. We've all noticed it."

"I thought I was fine."

"Not to those of us who know ye."

We travel in silence for a moment. I dismiss the fact that folks are discussing my moods behind my back.

"There was something I meant to ask you a while ago."

"Shoot."

"Do you remember a woman with blond hair buying books at the Halloween Carnival? She was small?" I was going to use the word "petite" but that sounds too pretty.

"There were so many people there."

"This one kind of had a tan?"

"Hon, I don't remember." Iva Lou looks at me. "Why do you ask?"

"I just never saw her before. I thought maybe you knew her."

"No. I could ask James. Maybe he knows her."

"No, no, that's okay. It's not important."

"Are you sure? James is a bigger gossip than any woman I know. He's carried more stories across this county than there are miles on the Bookmobile."

"Nope. It's okay."

I have always loved bus rides. When you grow up in a small town, they really are your ticket to the outside world. I've been to Washington, D.C., Cincinnati, Nashville, Memphis, and Charlottesville by bus.

Last year, I took Etta and two of her friends to Knoxville for "Holiday on Ice." Theodore showed us the town, even let the kids run on the football field at the U.T. stadium. Jack stayed home. (You couldn't pay him to go to an ice show—another one of those facts that surface after you marry someone.) I love ice shows: the cold stadium, the crowd, the smell of carmel popcorn, the pale blue ice rink, the criss-crossing beams of red and tangerine spotlights, and of course, the Stars of the Show, the skaters, lean and graceful, who shoot past in their glittering tulle skirts.

The bus is nearly empty tonight. I'm sitting behind the driver (my favorite seat), with my feet resting on the aluminum bar separating his area from the rest of the bus. As we speed along in the dark, the soft lights of the distant farms fade into the black, creating a hypnotic effect that begins to lull me to sleep. I am exhausted, so I take my duffel bag and place it on the seat next to me. As I begin to stretch out and lie down, a sudden thought causes me to bolt upright. Why did Jack rush me out of town so quickly? Does he have a date with that mysterious blond? The driver must have heard me shift quickly because he looks at me in the rearview. Honestly. Stop this, I tell myself. You're making things up. I lean over onto the duffel bag. If I sleep, we'll get to Knoxville all the faster.

"Hey. Sleepyhead. Wake up," the familiar deep voice teases me.

"Theodore!" I sit up, refreshed from my nap. "God, you look great!" And he does. He is trim; I can see the cut of his biceps through his T-shirt. "What's with the arms?"

"The beauty of working at a university is the free gym and trainers."

"Get me a job here. Immediately."

Theodore takes my bag, and I catch him up on everything as we charge through the bus station. We stop under a crosswalk light so I can show him Etta's new school picture.

"Hungry?" he asks me as he loads the bag into his car.

"Starving."

We go to a twenty-four-hour IHOP and settle into a booth, just like the old days. When Theodore lived in Big Stone Gap, we'd drive over to Kingsport after the football games and sit at Shoney's all night dissecting the halftime show and everything else going on in our lives. How simple it was! How perfect.

In the bright, warm light I can see Theodore more clearly. We talk on the phone a lot, but I haven't seen him in months. He still looks like the passionate pirate poet who moved to Big Stone Gap from Scranton, Pennsylvania, so many years ago. There is nothing boyish about him anymore, though. He is Lord of the Manor now, his strong jaw more chiseled, character and experience having given him a sort of nobility. His red hair is as full as ever, and there's some white in it at the temples; the blue eyes are a little more crinkled, but not much; overall, his face is smooth and clear. Theodore looks like a man who loves his life, and that makes me very happy.

"Tell me everything," he says.

"I've told you everything." I laugh. "Etta is great. Jack started a new business."

"Everything about *you*."

I don't know why, but that sounds like the strangest thing I have ever heard. I don't think of myself separate and apart from what I have to *do*. I think about things that need to be done. Taking care of my responsibilities. Being there for my family. When Theodore asks me about myself, I realize that I don't have anything to say.

"Come on. Talk," he says as he punches open a tiny white plastic barrel of half-and-half and dumps it in his coffee.

"Pearl asked me to partner with her at the Pharmacy. She's opening a new shop in Norton. I didn't want to say yes."

"Why?"

I shrug. "It's hers."

"Well, good for Pearl for asking you to partner. You gave her a future when you gave her your store. Let her help you now. Are you going to do it?"

"Yes. I signed the papers today. I'll be the manager and split the Big Stone profits fifty-fifty with her."

"What does Jack think?"

"He doesn't know yet."

"Oh," Theodore says casually.

"It just happened today. I haven't had a chance to talk to him." Boy that sounds lame—and it sounds lame because it *is* lame. I hold everything in, and not for any good reason I can think of!

I want to tell Theodore everything. I want to tell him that when the mines closed, I was afraid Jack wouldn't find a job; how he laughed when I suggested he take some engineering classes; how he looked at that woman at the Halloween Carnival. And how I get scared, every day, that I am going to lose him. How can I explain it to Theodore? Months after Joe died, Father Rausch came to see me. He told me that most marriages break up when a child dies. I couldn't imagine losing my son and then losing my husband. What good would that do? And Etta needed us. I still worry about her and the way losing Joe affected her. I want to tell Theodore every detail. But I can't. I want everything to be just fine. It has to be. What have I worked so long and hard for? Besides, isn't this life? Aren't things hard? Doesn't the romance come and go? Don't children take precedence over everything else? Don't all husbands stop looking at their wives instead of drinking in their beauty? Don't they learn to see past the exterior and right into our brains, where necessary facts and schedules are stored? Don't all marriages become routine? Spats? Silences? Weird open-ended arguments? Sex on the porch? Sour milk and burnt toast? Dirty laundry? Isn't money always a problem?

"What is going on with you? Your face looks like a Picasso, for Godsakes."

Looking distorted doesn't worry me. "Do I look old?" I ask him.

Theodore laughs.

"Do I?"

"No."

"Thank you."

"Why did you ask me that?"

"Because I live in Big Stone Gap, where people have seen me every day for forty-two years and don't really look at me."

"What about your husband?"

I can't answer. Instead, I start to cry.

"Jesus, what is wrong?" Theodore says as he yanks napkins out of the holder on the table and shoves them toward me.

"I'm scared."

"Of what?"

"That it's over."

"What's over?"

"Everything."

"What are you talking about? Are you sick?"

"No. I'm fine."

"What's over? Your marriage?"

"Yes."

"What's going on?"

"Jack is looking at other women."

"So?"

"Strange women with tans."

"Tans in November?" Theodore tries not to laugh.

"I know. It makes me sick." The word "sick" makes me weep harder.

"Who is she?"

"I don't know her name. She wears tight pants."

"You don't know her name but you've checked out her ass?"

"I can't help it. I had to watch them. They didn't see me. It's not like I stalked them or something. I just watched them fall all over each other at the Halloween Carnival."

"Your husband is madly in love with you. He'd be crazy to even think of another woman."

"You say that, but you didn't see her. She was working it! She was patting his back. Low. She's one of those predators. One of those women, and you can just tell, who only wants a married man. They're in it for the thrill. For the pain it causes people like me. She looks like one of those women who has all day to fix a strand of hair! And look at me. I barely have time to put on lipstick. I'm starting to look like Ma Kettle, for Godsakes."

"Have you asked Jack Mac who she is?"

"God no."

"Why not?"

"Because in every Bette Davis movie I have ever seen, when the woman asks the man that question, the man always says, 'I'm sorry, yes, you're right, you're so intuitive, yes, I love her. And I don't love you anymore. So set me free so at least one of us can be happy.' "

"Don't base your real life on bad melodrama," Theodore says, rearranging the sugar packets in their plastic holder.

"Do you have a better idea?" I ask him as I blow my nose.

The waitress comes over to take our order. She doesn't even look concerned. She just picks up my wad of tear-soaked napkins and dumps them in the trash on the way back to the kitchen. I guess a lot of people face their demons in the middle of the night at the International House of Pancakes.

"Why would your husband call me and brag about you and how hard you work and what a great wife and mother you are and how you need a weekend away because there isn't enough he could do to ever thank you, if he was leaving you?"

"I don't know."

"You have got to get a grip."

Theodore's exasperation soothes me. Maybe I am crazy. "I know I sound totally irrational—"

"Listen to me. This thing, this blackness and doom you feel, is just a tiny storm cloud of feelings passing overhead. You are at a crisis point. I don't think it's about Jack Mac and Etta. It's about Joe."

"I'm dealing with Joe."

"Joe isn't here to deal with. That's your problem," Theodore says tenderly.

"I hate myself. I was a terrible mother to him."

"You were not!"

"Do you know that I yelled at him every day? Do you know that he got spanked? And I swore to Jack I'd never spank the kids. But he turned on the water in the tub and left it and it overflowed and ruined the ceiling and I went crazy. I took him to sit in Etta's time-out chair. He laughed at it! In fact, he never sat in it. The thing had cobwebs on it!"

"So you spanked him. What else?"

"I was so busy trying to make him behave that I missed everything. I was chasing him all the time. Correcting him. Begging him to sit still. Whatever it was."

"He was a demanding kid."

"But I didn't appreciate him. I wanted him to be more like Etta. And he wasn't. He was a tornado. Even the way he got sick in the end. Etta gets a cold, and it takes her half the winter to get over it. I see bruises on Joe one morning, and six days later he's dead. Don't you see? He was this unbelievably vibrant color, this amazing shot of purple that flew in and flew out, and I was too busy trying to make him into something else. I blew it. I totally blew it. And now, three years later, I just want to apologize to him. To tell him I'm sorry for not seeing what he was." I'm stunned that I am not crying. Theodore looks at me.

"Feel better?"

"I sort of . . . do." The waitress refills my coffee and dumps some more half-and-half onto the table. "Really, yeah, I'm fine," I tell Theodore and then the waitress, who ignores me and checks her reflection in the window of our booth.

"No, you're not. You wouldn't be here. You wouldn't be asking me if you look old. Somehow Jack knew you needed a deeper conversation. One that cannot be had over the phone."

"Did he say something to you?" I rise up in the booth by my chin like a rattlesnake peeking out of a basket.

"No. He did not," Theodore says calmly. His tone of voice makes me sink right back down into the booth.

"How do you know so much about men?"

"I've been one for a long time."

"Right." I stir my coffee. I don't care if it's my second cup and it's the middle of the night. "You should thank God you're not married."

"I could never be married."

"Good thinking."

"It's not for me."

"You're smart."

"No. I'm gay."

The IHOP becomes very quiet. It's almost as though I can hear the pancake batter pouring onto the griddle through the swing doors.

"You are?"

"Yeah."

"Well, when?"

"Since I can remember."

The thoughts kick up in my head in a thousand different directions. Questions pop up: How? Why didn't you tell me sooner? Is there a special man in your life? That's why we couldn't take our friendship any further so long ago! I wasn't crazy! You just weren't available! "Couldn't you have told me thirteen years ago?"

"Why? I wasn't going to date men in Big Stone Gap."

"Good point."

"And we had each other."

"Yes, we did." Boy, did we have each other. For so many years, that was all I needed. Why does my single past seem so perfect now, so uncomplicated? Was it? "When did you know?"

"I guess I knew all my life. But I wasn't out all my life. I guess I thought I was a loner, and that I would never become attached to anyone because I didn't need it. I have a creative life, and it makes me whole. I wasn't unhappy. I was and am very fulfilled. I never saw that people in couples were very happy, so I assumed it wasn't for me. And when I met you, we had such a mind meld."

"Yes, we did."

"You never made me feel bad about being a loner. You were one too."

"I know. It explains a lot, though."

"Sure. Everything. It was that missing piece of information that made all the facts fall into place. I was fighting my instinct to be who I was—that's always a bad idea."

"Do you have someone special in your life now?"

"I did. A biochemist who was at UT on a grant, studying some kind of cells to cure some kind of something. He was terrific, but he lives in Boston, and I'm not moving, so it didn't work out."

"I would have loved to have met him." And I mean that. We sit quietly for a few minutes, but I'm never troubled by long silences when I'm with Theodore. That's just our rhythm.

"By the way, you didn't turn me gay."

"I like to blame myself for everything from laundry mistakes to the failure of world peace, but I won't take on that I turned you gay." I pat his hand.

"Good."

"It's a good thing you figured it out while you're still young."

"Yep. I figured it out in the nick of time."

"Maybe that's what I'm scared of. I feel like my life is ice in my hands. It's going by so fast, and I'm not any smarter. I don't have that peace that I read about in magazines. I'm old enough to be wise, and I'm not. I don't want to get old, though. I feel like I've never been young. Maybe I thought love was going to make me young."

"Before we go down this road," Theodore says, "let me say that aging is worst for two groups: women and gay men. Straight men are told they're potent all their lives, they can be ninety and have kids, and so on. I know what you mean about feeling old and stupid. I'm not a professional psychologist, so don't hold me to any of this, but I think what's going on here, apart from your communication problems with your husband and your grief for your son, is even more personal. It's about you. You woke up one day and realized that you were halfway through. You're middle-aged."

"I am not! Fifty is middle-aged."

"Okay, now we're squabbling about numbers. Here's the fact of the matter: there's a lot behind you. You've got some miles on you now. You're not a sweet young thing anymore."

"I was never a sweet young thing! And don't think I don't resent *that*!"

"Stop whining. Let me finish. Getting older is tough. It's depressing. But it happens to all of us. Look at me. I'm lifting barbells sumo wrestlers won't touch because I want pecs of steel, believing that muscles will hold up my youth like those pillars hold up the Acropolis. Well, they don't. The only thing you can do is accept it. Do the best you can. But accept it."

"Am I that shallow?"

"We're all shallow. But you're luckier than most. You don't really look forty-whatever-you-are. You can be one of those timeless beauties with the good skin. You can wear cardigan sweaters and a little lipstick, and no one will know if you're thirty or sixty. Okay?"

"I feel so stupid." I swing my legs sideways in the booth and sink down.

"Vanity will do that to you."

"I am vain, aren't I?"

"And a little paranoid. You had to take a three-and-a-half-hour bus ride to have me tell you that your husband is not having an affair. Look at yourself. You're letting one woman in tight jeans derail your entire life. You have *earned* a glorious marriage, because you and Jack have gone through the worst and come out the other side. And you still have your daughter. You are still a family, even though Joe is gone. And you love each other! Stop. Think. What are you doing? This woman who has no name has taken your self-confidence and run off with it. How can you let a stranger do that to you?"

Theodore's guest room is simple and comfortable. There is an old, rich chocolate-colored four-poster bed, a matching dresser, and a small Tiffany-style lamp. There's a luggage rack for my duffel bag and a full-length mirror behind the door. The walls, the linens, the rug—everything is white. I pull back the coverlet and climb under the cool sheets. This is the first time I have been alone in a bed since I married Jack MacChesney. I've never gone anywhere without him in all this time, nor he without me. I wonder if he is thinking the same thing at home in our bed. I stretch my arms from edge to edge in the double bed and my feet as far apart as they can go. I stay in this snow-angel position until sleep comes.

Big Orange does not begin to describe the University of Tennessee Football Experience. It should be called All Orange, All the Time. Thousands of fans descend upon Knoxville wearing the theme color, and many of them have painted all exposed skin to match; their devotion seems to begin on a cellular level. I have never seen such football mania (and I went to Saint Mary's College in South Bend, Indiana!). Painted people aside, Knoxville is a genteel Southern city famous for its Dogwood Festival and debutantes. You get a sense of times gone by when you walk the streets here.

Once I'm at the stadium, I weave my way through the tailgate parties (a man is actually roasting chicken on a spit in the back of his station wagon). Theodore let me sleep late and left without me. He meets me at the staff entrance and takes me up one of the aerial booths where the football staff films the games. This is also Theodore's perch, where he can watch the 125 brilliant musicians who make up the UT Marching Band. "Theodore, remember the county band competitions?"

"Yeah. We always beat Appalachia's Tricky Sixty," Theodore remembers.

"Enrollment took a dive since you left. Now they're called the Dirty Thirty."

Theodore laughs. I can't believe he's gone from the Wise County band competition to national television in less than ten years.

We barely watch the first half of the game as Theodore checks via headsets with the camera crews who are set to record the halftime show. He is a celebrity and honored auteur here—people stop him and ask for his autograph—because he delivers. Theodore, however, takes it all in stride; he knows his popularity rises and falls along with the success of the football team: no sense having a winning band with a losing team.

When the band takes the field at halftime, the crowd goes wild. If you could tap the energy in this stadium right now, you could win a war or move a pyramid. Theodore plays right into the razzle-dazzle. The majorettes are glorious, magazine-cover gorgeous: the whole weekend is an homage to youth, powerhouse athletics, and white-toothed sex appeal.

Theodore's shows are more technical, more complex, than they were back in Big Stone Gap. Of course, this is another level entirely. But it is a wonder to see how Theodore has grown with the challenge of college football, most of it nationally televised. He has assumed the mantle with little fuss. He has Elizabeth Taylor to thank for this opportunity, and he knows it. If it weren't for her fateful visit to Big Stone Gap, Theodore never would have been discovered.

As the band takes the field, Theodore is calm and focused. A row of small television monitors on the desk in front of us all record several angles of the performance at once. Theodore takes some notes, occasionally curses, sometimes smiles. I don't know how he keeps what he's watching straight. All I know is, when I look out of this glassy cube in the sky down onto the bright green field filled from end to end with crisp orange and white figures moving as smoothly as the intricate inner workings of a Swiss watch, I would be hard-pressed to find a mistake. I see only an astounding sculpture in motion, and the crowd agrees, thousands of them on their feet, feasting at the sight and sound of this display.

"Pretty good," Theodore says as the band marches off the field. "Let's go."

We leave the booth and head down what seems to be secret stairs into the belly of the stadium. We come out into daylight on the ground level of the field; the plastic passes hanging around our necks on chains give us immediate access everywhere. Security guards nod respectfully at Theodore; VIPs lean over the side of their boxes and yell, "Good show! You're the man!" Theodore takes my hand and leads me up a tiny set of stairs to the base of the band box. I look up, and as far as my eyes can see, this orange and white checkerboard reaches to the top of the sky. The band major and Theodore huddle, and the band members watch with interest. Then the captain blows his whistle, and they launch into "The Tennessee Waltz." The crowd goes wild. Theodore looks all around the stadium slowly, and for a moment, backlit by the orange and white musicians, with a breeze blowing through his hair, he is just a little bit Greek god, but surely all artist. He takes me in his arms and we spin to the music.

We have a lazy Sunday, and too soon it is time for me to get on the bus and head for home. I have an extra duffel bag full of UT paraphernalia and stuff Theodore bought for Etta—puzzles and games and an origami kit. Etta knows about international crafts because of Theodore. He is far from an absentee honorary uncle.

"I want you to remain calm," Theodore tells me as he hugs me good-bye.

"Promise you'll come for Christmas," I tell him, not letting go until he promises.

"I will be there. I'll bring the eggnog."

"I love you."

"I love you too."

I climb onto the bus and sit in my usual seat, right behind the driver. Theodore circles around and taps on the window. I use both hands to slide my window back.

"You're not old. You're beautiful."

"Thank you," I tell him, meaning it, restored after a great weekend. I'm not crazy, I'm okay. I'm just human. I get scared, and I can be comforted. That's the miracle of Theodore Tipton. He makes it all better.

As the bus pulls away, I'm not sad. Christmas is just a few weeks away. I want to go home. I miss Etta terribly. And being away from Jack, even with all of our problems, made me long for him. I haven't kissed him like I meant it in a long time. I will, though, as soon as I see him. I can't wait.

As the bus makes its descent into Big Stone Gap through the Wildcat, I am filled with anticipation. The apricot sun fades behind the blue mountains in twilight. The trunks of the trees, knotty and twisting toward the sky, wet with rain, look like they're embroidered in shiny black pearls. They make a fence down either side of the road; I feel protected, but I can see the mountains beyond spilling away in layers down the sides like cake batter. There is an awesome beauty to the Appalachian Trail, where the Blue Ridge meets Tennessee. Soon I will be inside the mountain again, inside the Gap, home.

Jack is waiting for me at the bus station. I am sitting on the edge of my seat like a kid, full of stories to tell. I want to tell Jack everything. I want to tell him how I went away so afraid and how I've come home full of hope again. I wave to him from the window, and he waves back. Etta isn't with him; how romantic! I stand with my bag before the bus can make a full stop. The driver's flinty brown eyes narrow in annoyance, and I lurch forward when he brakes. I thank him as I charge down the steps toward my husband. I throw myself into his arms and cover his sweet face in kisses. He accepts the kisses but doesn't kiss me back.

"What's wrong?" I ask him.

"Did you have a nice weekend?" he asks me without emotion.

"It was great. Is something wrong with Etta?" Now I'm worried. Why is he acting so strange?

"Etta is fine. She had a good time at the play," he tells me, taking my bag.

"Musical."

"Musical. Play. What's the goddamned difference?"

"Why are you yelling at me?" I'm yelling at him.

"It's all over town that Pearl made you her partner."

"What?" For a moment, I forget time and place. I was so happy to come home, I forgot all about last Friday, all about the deal and the papers.

"Why didn't you tell me?"

"Wait a second. I was going to tell you Friday night, but you had my trip planned. There wasn't time."

"You could've told me before you left. There is no excuse for this. None."

"Jack. This is ridiculous."

"You know, the things you think are ridiculous, I think are important. That, right there, is the problem with us." Jack throws my duffel bag in the back of the truck. If I weren't so angry, I'd be laughing. The word "problem"—that's my word, he never used that before. Men don't use that word about their relationships, they use it for cars that won't start or appliances that break down.

"Don't throw my things!" I holler, sounding about five years old.

"Get in the truck."

"Don't tell me what to do!"

"I'd like to find the person who tells you what to do and you do it. I'd like to meet him and shake his hand."

"What's the matter with you? I can't do anything right. I only agreed to partner with Pearl so you could be free to go off and be a construction worker, own your own business. I thought if I could take some of the burden off of you financially, you would be free to pursue your dream."

"You kill me."

"What?"

"Since when do you care about my dreams?"

I don't say a word. I get in the truck. He jumps into his seat and faces me. "You don't think I can take care of us. You don't believe I can make a go of the business, so you go behind my back and cut a deal so you'd feel secure."

"That is not true! I am not thinking about me. I'm thinking of Etta. Okay? If that makes me a bad person, then I'm a bad person!"

"You don't trust me. If you trusted me, you would have come home and discussed it with me. And we would have made a decision together. One that was best for our family. Instead, I hear about it all over town. Folks think it's pretty funny that I need a woman to take care of me, so I can have a hobby as a fix-it man." Jack leans back in the seat, defeated. I can't bear to see him own this like it's true.

"I never said you were a fix-it man. Who cares what people think anyway?"

Jack doesn't answer me; he just starts the truck and drives fast, back up into the holler. He pulls up next to the house. I jump out of the truck and pull my duffel bag out of the bed. I don't look back. I climb the steps, and Etta meets me at the door. She is happy and shows me the program from *Fiddler on the Roof*. I hear the gravel spit out under the tires as the truck bounces back down the mountain.

"Where's Daddy going?"

"I don't know."

"Is he mad?"

"I think so."

"Did I do something?" Etta's brow wrinkles with worry.

"No, you didn't. Daddy is under a lot of pressure. That's all."

I divert her attention with all the goodies from Uncle Theodore. Etta pulls apart the origami kit. We sit on the floor and make shapes with the delicate rice paper. I have to use both of my hands to hold the directions, I am shaking so. The rice paper is so thin, so delicate, I'm afraid I'll tear it. "Here, Mommy, let me." Etta takes the paper and lays them out on the floor in front of us.

I give Etta a snack and tuck her into bed. I check the clock; it's almost nine, and Jack is still not home. I made up an excuse for Etta, but the kid is smart. She knows. I switch on the nightlight in the hallway and turn to go downstairs, but instead, I go into Joe's old bedroom. We converted it into a playroom for Etta a couple of years ago. I turned his twin bed into a daybed, with a red corduroy cover; now it looks more like a couch. Etta has set up a blackboard and chairs. I go over to the daybed and lie down.

For the first few months after Joe died, I would go to bed with my husband, wait until he was asleep, and then get up. I'd wander through the house, then eventually I'd come up here to Joe's room and lie on his bed. It was the only place in the house where I could find rest. I tried the sun porch and the living room couch, but I never slept. Once I knew that I could fall asleep in Joe's room, I came here every night.

I never told Jack why I came up here. Any discussions of Joe's death were just too painful. And I couldn't tell him about The Dream, the real reason I came up here each night. I could hardly wait for night to come so I could have The Dream, the same dream, night after comforting night. Joe and I would run through the house. And we would laugh and laugh. The laughter was so real. It sounded like him, and it sounded like me. And then, as we were getting pains in our stomachs from laughing so hard, the roof tore cleanly away from the house, leaving no jagged edges, as though it were the lid of a pot being lifted off. Then the sky above our house filled with fantastic colors, usually shades of rose and deep blue that striated and glistened and moved like iridescent folds of oil in water. And then Joe opened his arms . . . it was always the same . . . he'd look at me and smile and say, "I love to fly!" And he would lift off the petit-point rug in the living room and ascend up and out of the house and into the swirl of fantastic color overhead. And he would fly around in it. I would try really hard to fly so I could join him, but I couldn't get off the ground. It was like my limbs had turned to stone. I would call to Joe but he had flown away. Sometimes in the distance, I heard his voice. And then the sky became a blueprint, the colors fading away like pencil lines, and it turned a flat blue like construction paper, with no movement and no depth, just a flat color, and I'd keep trying to fly, but no matter what I did, I couldn't get off the ground. I even climbed the walls of the house, but I kept sliding back down onto the floor. And I kept climbing and then I'd slide. And I'd wake up exhausted, but I didn't care. I was happy, because all night I had been with Joe, and it felt real. And it was, for the most part, a happy dream; he never cried or took a needle or slept. He was all mine, and we were together, mother and son, even though the background was skewed and strange; we were together.

"Ave?" The sound of Jack's voice startles me.

"Hi."

"Hi." He sits down on the toy chest. He folds his hands and looks at them.

I know my husband. He'll just sit there and look at me until I say something. Why is it always the woman's job to pull the information from the man? Why can't he tell me what he's feeling? That's just the way it is, and I'm certainly not going to try to change this worldwide dynamic tonight. So I take a deep breath and look at him. "Where'd you go?"

"I went up to Big Cherry Holler and walked around the lake."

Before we got married, we spent a lot of time up on Big Cherry Lake. We'd lie on the bank, or Jack would row me around in a canoe. That's the place where we really talked, shared everything we'd been through with each other. It was a magical place for us, totally private, just clean blue water as far as the eye could see, surrounded by a clean wall of regal pine trees.

"We haven't been up there together in a long time, Jack."

"Years."

"Maybe we should go sometime."

"Maybe."

Jack's one-word answers are typical. But typical isn't going to work tonight. We're in bad shape, and we have to talk about it.

"You know, I don't mean to hurt you. Somehow I always end up doing the wrong thing. I just want you to know that I don't set out to do that."

"I know," he says quietly, leaning against the window.

"I just don't know how to talk to you. Maybe I never did." Why am I using words like "never"?

"No. We got along good in the beginning."

A wave of panic goes through me. This sounds like the windup on one of those "I'm leaving you" speeches. "In the beginning" usually leads to "We're at the end of our road."

"Why do you stay?" I might as well ask him, since we're finally speaking seriously to each other.

"I love you, Ave Maria."

"You do?"

"Of course I love you."

My eyes meet his and I know that I still love him too. But loving him isn't really helping us make a marriage. Loving Joe didn't keep him alive; loving my mother didn't prevent her from getting cancer and dying; and loving Jack MacChesney isn't going to help us stay together. What will?

"Jack?" He looks at me, and I must say, I love that look. He gives of himself completely when he listens. (I don't think I do that.) "I guess I thought when we got married, since I had gone for so long without love in my life, that everything would be perfect. That because I had waited, time had made this perfect bubble, and you and I would climb in and float till we were old and died in each other's arms."

"Come on." Jack smiles and shakes his head.

"No, really. I did. I thought since I had been sad for so long, let's say for the first half of my life, that once I opened my heart, it would be beautiful and wonderful and . . . easy. So maybe what we have here is my unmet expectations biting us on the ass."

"What made you think it was going to be easy?"

"I believed the hard part was finding love."

"You didn't find me; you decided you deserved it."

"Do you think?" I sit up.

"Yeah."

"What about you?"

"I knew what we were in for."

"Am I that bad?"

"No, you're not bad. Not at all. You just don't think of me first."

I want to disagree with him, but I know he's right.

"You're not happy, Ave."

"I am. Sometimes."

"When was the last time you were truly happy? Be honest."

"January fifteenth, 1983. You made chili. It was snowing. Remember? You and me and Etta and Joe baked a chocolate cake. We drew a snowman in the icing. And we played Go Fish. And we laughed all night."

Jack sits quietly for a while; I can see he remembers Chili Night, and for a moment I cannot imagine that we won't work out our problems and be happy again. I am about to tell him this when he interrupts my thoughts. "He's gone, honey. But you and me and Etta. We're still here."

"I know."

"We matter."

Jack says this simply, and I know it's true. But it just makes me feel like a bigger failure. My mother was surely the center of my life and our family life, and here in my little family, I have let everybody down. I have a husband who feels rejected and a daughter who can't really be happy because she can't be herself and her brother too. She cannot fill that void. But she tries. Maybe that's what we've become, the three of us. We're trying to fill the space left by Joe and none of us are successful, and the harder we try, the bigger the void becomes.

"Ave?"

"Yeah?"

"You're not going to sleep in this room again, are you?"

For a second, I want to tell Jack about The Dream, but I can't. Instead, I tell him, "No. I want to be with you." I take his hand and lead him down the stairs. Sometimes, even when I'm failing, I do the right thing.

CHAPTER FOUR

$\mathcal{I}$va Lou and I sit on the old stone bench outside the Slemp Library,
eating lunch. We're bundled up; it's an overcast late November
day, but we need the fresh air. Besides, we have the entire winter to
cram into Iva Lou's tiny office for our weekly get-togethers. The
bench is a low, wide half-moon of blue slate resting on ornate concrete pedestals. It faces an old fountain, a series of jagged fieldstone
steps stacked delicately up a low hill. At the top, brass cardinals hold
a pitcher from which water cascades down rocks covered in green velvet moss. When it reaches the bottom, the water flows into a small tri-
angular pool filled with pennies. It's a romantic place, hidden by
poplar trees. At night it's a make-out spot for teenagers. Young lovers
have thrown their pennies in the pool (lots of them), hoping their
luck will last.

Delphine Moses made us meatball heroes. Iva Lou peels the tin
foil down the sides of the long bun like a banana.

"Aren't you gonna eat?" Iva Lou asks me as she takes a bite.

"I'm not hungry."

"What's the matter?"

"Jack and me."

"What happened?"

"He's mad at me because I took on managing the Pharmacy without asking him."

"Why didn't you ask him?" Iva Lou takes a swig of Coke.

Iva Lou asks me this so matter-of-factly, you'd think I'd have an equally easy, off-the-cuff answer. But I don't.

"You know, men got to feel in charge. Even if they're not. You got to let them think they are."

"Iva Lou, I'm too old for those games."

"Well, I hate to tell you, but the games go on until you're in the grave. I never met a man who didn't think he was the center of the universe."

"Do you think Jack Mac is tired of me?"

"Nope. It sounds like he's mad at you."

"Good."

"No. That's actually worse. When men get mad, they don't sit with it, they do something. They act out. You know. They go out looking for . . . I don't know. Diversions."

"Other women?"

Iva Lou nods. "And I know that for sure because once upon a time, I was the best diversion in Wise County. Now I'm just another old married woman who's kept her shape." She sits up and breathes deeply, pinching in her small waist.

"Do I need to be worried about other women?" I lean back on the bench casually, yet my spine is so rigid, it's as though there is a steel pipe in place of the bone.

"If you're a woman, you always need to be worried about that. You got a good-looking husband. And there are women out there who look for, well, they're looking for company."

"I'm not going to follow him around."

"You shouldn't! No, you have to act like nothing's wrong and gently move things back in a positive direction. You have to *act* like you have a good marriage, and then, as time goes on, if you act like it's good, it becomes good."

"How do you do that?" I want to know.

Iva Lou continues, "In little ways. Make him comfortable. Kiss him when you pass him while he's watching TV. Even if he don't kiss you back, mind you."

"Okay. I can do that."

"How's the sex?"

"God, Iva Lou."

"Are you having sex?"

"Sometimes."

"Regular?"

"Not as regular as it used to be."

"Well, girl, get on it. Make it *your* idea. That'll keep you two connected until he comes around."

"You're serious?"

"Hell, yes. A man would rather saw off his arm as live without sex. We women, well, we're camels. We can go months and months without, though I don't recommend it. We like to think about sex, and sometimes thinkin' about it's enough. Why do you think women get married to men in prison and not vice versa? We're fine just having a man sayin' he loves us, even if he's locked up with a life sentence. We don't need him home in the flesh tellin' us. A man is different; he needs a woman to be there, present, takin' care of him." Iva Lou looks at me, her left eyebrow rising up to make her point. "And I mean takin' *care* of him."

"Does everything come down to sex?"

"Yes." Iva Lou sets her hero down on the bench. "A man looks at sex like a health issue. If *it's* workin', then *he's* workin'. You got it?" I nod. "Drop by the church. They're still fixin' the Fellowship Hall kitchen, right? Surprise ole Jack Mac. Bring him a slice of pie or a thermos of coffee. And look good doin' it. Be sweet. Understand?" I nod again, but part of me resents hearing this. Why do I have to do all the work?

A squirrel, his brown coat the color of the bare ground below, shimmies down the thick trunk of the poplar tree behind Iva Lou. He stops and chatters, snapping his neck, looking all around. Then the branches rustle from above, and down the trunk, like a gumball swirling down a chute, comes another squirrel. The first squirrel waits for the second to join him. When she gets within an inch of his tail, he runs away. This reminds me of something Otto told me so many years ago. He said, "Ave, you gots to decide three things in life: what you're running from and what you're running to, and why." What Otto didn't tell me and should have: no fair running in place.

Fleeta leans against the new fountain at Mutual's. "Here I stand at the gates of hell."

"How many times do I have to tell you, you don't have to work in here."

"We'll see. This is just like when I was told I wouldn't have to handle stock reorders. Now I'm the only one who handles stock reorders."

"It came out nice, didn't it?" I ask Fleeta as I spin on one of the fountain stools. Pearl found antique etched mirrors, which she framed in white and hung behind the fountain. She copied the marbleized green linoleum countertops from the original pictures. Gaslight wall sconces with brass accents throw a soft golden light on the pale green booths with white Formica tabletops.

"Yeah, it come out good. But I don't know how it did, with Pearl's attention everywhere else in Wise County but here."

"Do you have a problem with expansion?"

"I ain't talkin' about that. Pearl's in loo-ve." Fleeta rolls her eyes when she says "love." "You know 'im too. The Indian doctor up at Saint Agnes. Bakagese. Good-lookin' sucker. He's as dark as mahogany, honey. Black."

"He was Joe's doctor."

Fleeta thinks for a moment. "Right. Right. I bet they met up your place. He's dark. But tain't nothin' wrong with it. Pearl's Melungeon herself, so she's mixed. So in a way, they match. Though lots of Melungeons don't like me saying they're mixed."

"I thought you were Melungeon."

"Part."

"There's nothing wrong with you," I point out.

"No, there ain't."

"His color doesn't matter."

"You say 'at, 'course you're Eye-talian. And Eye-talians are the great mixers of the world. Ain't no country that ain't been in yorn. And everybody knows It-lee is nothin' more than a rowboat away from Africa."

"You know your geography. Maybe they ought to put you on *Club Quiz* next time we send a team out." I hand Fleeta a note regarding a prescription. "I can't read your writing."

"It was a call-in prescription. For a delivery. To . . . Alice Lambert."

"Oh."

"I know." Fleeta clucks. "She oughtn't buy her pills from here, after all the trouble she caused you." Fleeta's right. Alice Lambert is Fred Mulligan's sister. When I found out that he wasn't really my father, she claimed I was a bastard and therefore not entitled to his estate; she even tried to take me to court. That was nearly ten years ago, and I haven't seen her since.

"When you're sick, you probably don't care where the pills come from."

"What kind of pills does she need?"

"They're for nerves."

"Uh-huh. I'd say she has nerve tryin' to trade in here."

Otto comes in with his tool chest. "Hey, Otto. Can you make a delivery over to Alice Lambert's?"

"I don't see why not. But I need to hook up the stove back 'ere. Do you think Jack Mac could help me?"

"I'll ask him." Good. Just what I needed: an excuse to pop in on my husband. Iva Lou would definitely approve.

The parking spots outside the Methodist Church are filled, so I double-park behind Jack's truck, filled with plywood sheets. I check my lipstick, which I've eaten off, and reapply it. I run a comb through my hair and fluff it. I look pretty good today, I think as I climb out of the Jeep.

The tension has eased between Jack and me, and I see this truce time as an opportunity to bring us together again. There have been small signs that he's trying too. He took my hand helping me up the attic stairs to get the Christmas ornaments. He hugged and kissed me when I made ravioli from scratch. And he rubbed my neck when I was working on the bills after Etta went to sleep last night.

The door to the church basement is propped open with a barrel trash can full of shards of old Sheetrock. I should've brought Jack something to eat, I'm thinking as I go down the familiar steps; Iva Lou would give me a demerit for not planning ahead. I hear laughter and note that the new yellow paint they chose for the stairwell really brightens up the place.

"Hello?"

"In here," my husband's familiar voice says.

I walk carefully into the hall; the floor has been removed, and new Sheetrock is being applied to the walls. Jack is measuring a large flat of wood on two horses as Mousey hammers a corner of Sheetrock to the wall.

"Hi!" I say brightly, with a big smile.

"Hi, honey," Jack answers warmly.

"I love the yellow. It's pretty. This room is really coming along," I tell them, surveying the changes. And then, as if in a dream, I see a woman emerge from the hallway that leads up the back stairs to the sacristy. It's that woman. That tanned woman from the Halloween Carnival!

"Honey, this is Karen Bell from Coeburn. This is my wife, Ave Maria," Jack says to her matter-of-factly.

"What a pretty name."

"Thank you."

"She's Italian," my husband tells her. I guess he's explaining my name.

"Yeah, I'm just plain old Karen. There's a million of them out there," she says, and shrugs.

My mind races: the name Karen. I've heard that before. The Pharmacy? A Karen called Jack at the Pharmacy, before I went to Knoxville! Why do I feel as though I've caught my husband doing something wrong?

Karen Bell wears a blue-and-tan-plaid pleated skirt and a sweater set in soft blue, a shell with a cardigan over it. She is carrying a clipboard and has a pencil tucked behind her ear (all business). She is much smaller than she appeared to be at the carnival. She's one of those women a man could carry around like a doll. And the way she moves, she comes at you one piece at a time, reminding me of the goatherd girl marionette my father sent Etta from Italy. Every movement is deliberate.

"Karen's our supplier."

"Supplier?" I guess I say this in a funny way because she laughs.

"I supply the aggravation," she says.

"That must be expensive."

"Depends." She looks at me for the first time. Or maybe she just sees me for the first time. She slides one hip onto one of the horses and perches there. Then she rubs a pencil between her palms; it clacks against her rings. (But not one of them is a wedding band.)

"Karen is a salesperson for Luck's Lumber," Jack tells me.

"Yeah, that's how we met," she says.

How we met? What an odd phrase for a salesperson to use. "Did Jack ever tell you how *we* met?" I say, wrapping my arms around him.

"No, he didn't."

"In kindergarten."

"That's so cute. Childhood sweethearts," Karen says, not meaning it.

"Not really," I tell her.

"Let's say we got together later in life," Jack adds.

"Not too late, though." I pick up a hammer and hit my open palm with it. I do this a few times before Jack takes it away from me.

"Jack, do you want to take one last look at these blueprints?" Karen is asking him the question, but she's looking at me politely, like "Could you get out of the way? We've got business here."

"Sorry. I interrupted. You guys go ahead. Do your business thing," I say nicely, and go off to the far wall to examine my husband's Sheetrock technique. I lean against the radiator to get a closer look, placing my hand on it—it's actually very hot, and I think I now have third-degree burns on my palm. But I don't scream, I just shove my hot hand into my pocket.

Karen unrolls the blueprints, which, out of the corner of my eye, look like complicated geometry to me. How hard is it to take down walls and put them back up again to reconfigure a kitchen? From the size of the blue paper and the series of complicated intersecting chalk lines: very. I watch as Karen, capable and professional, shows Jack and Mousey how things are to be done. What they need. How they can save on insulation. What size wood they need to lengthen the counter space in the kitchen. My husband listens carefully to what she is saying. She makes sense when he challenges her with a good question. Respect washes across his face when she comes up with a solution to a problem he couldn't solve until she stepped in. She taps her foot and continues to roll a pencil between her hands. She has given this project a lot of thought. This is a woman with follow-through. She always has a plan.

"Well, I guess I'd better get back to the office." Karen rolls up the blueprints. She looks over at me as if to say, "Okay, he's all yours. You can talk about what he wants for dinner, what time the PTA meeting starts, and does he need new underwear." The boring stuff that wives do, not the fascinating stuff of blueprints, raw materials, architecture, and construction—the stuff of Karen Bell.

She tucks the prints under her arm like a baton and walks across the room to her coat, dangling on a nail. Mousey watches her as she goes. She's got one of those walks where her rear end makes a complete circle as she moves. Smart and Sexy, just like *Redbook* magazine says, I think as she walks. Just what I should be, I tell myself. Jack keeps his eyes on the wall.

"Y'all let me know if you need anything else. You know where to find me," she says as she goes upstairs.

"Nice to meet you!" I call after her.

"You too" is the muffled reply.

"I've got a problem, guys." Jack and Mousey look at me. I guess my tone of voice sounds oddly curt. "Otto and Worley need help installing the oven." Boy, does that sound like the lamest excuse ever invented by a wife who suddenly had to come up with a cover story when she caught her husband with a mysterious blonde.

"We could take a look at it. Later, though, okay?"

"That would be great. There's some problem wiring, and the BTUs of the oven. That sort of thing. We may have to open a wall." What am I saying? I don't know anything about opening up walls. I'm just repeating a fragment of a conversation I heard Otto having with Worley. Who am I trying to impress? My husband? "Anyway, I don't know details, guys. All I know is we have a deadline."

"We'll stop over later," Jack promises, and kisses me on the forehead like I'm Shoo the Cat.

As I climb the stairs out to the street, Karen Bell's perfume lingers in the air. It's that Charlie cologne that makes Fleeta sneeze. It's too sweet, even in afterthought. It feels good to get out in the fresh air again.

Christmas in the Gap is a month-long affair. Of course, the kick-off was the opening of the new Mutual Pharmacy Soda Fountain. (Thank you, MR. J's Construction, for your electrical assistance in the wee hours of November 30.) Pearl wisely featured prices from the original Soda Fountain days for the first week: Cokes for a nickel, sundaes for a dime, and so forth. It has become a real hangout. Even folks just passing through the Gap stop in for a cup of coffee and pie. One man on his way to Bristol from Middlesboro, Kentucky, stopped in for Tayloe's autograph. He saw her on local TV selling storm windows and was thrilled to meet the Real Thing and leave her a big tip.

Inez Eisenberg heads the committee for Decoration Downtown; she's asked every business on Main Street to hang a wreath with tiny white lights on our entrances. Everyone complied except Zackie Wakin, who hung his wreath with blue lights (he sells them, so he used them). The Methodist Sewing Circle sponsors a door-decoration contest on private homes. Louise Camblos even decorated her doghouse door, that's how competitive folks get.

The local garden clubs boost Christmas spirit with their holiday flower shows. The Dogwood Garden Club decorates the Southwest Virginia Museum; the Intermont Club takes over the John Fox, Jr., house; and the Green Thumb ladies dress up June Tolliver's House down by the Outdoor Drama Theatre. They ship judges in from eastern Virginia to judge horticulture (you should see Betty Cline's Christmas cactus), arrangements (Arline Sharpe's centerpiece of stacked Rome apples on the dining room table at the museum is a wonder), and special creations like a ceramic Madonna and Child placed amid gold gourds.

Iva Lou, Fleeta, and I are spending most of Sunday touring the exhibitions. We're about to enter the Rooms of Historical Distinction when Joella Reasor stops us in the narrow hallway.

"Hey y'all," she says in a tone that tells us there's gossip. She wipes the corners of her mouth, where the orange lipstick bled, with her thumb and forefinger.

"Spill, Joella. We ain't got all damn day," Fleeta says impatiently.

"Pearl Grimes is in the Victorian Room with her doctor friend."

"From here on in, we'll have to call it the Indian Room." Fleeta chuckles as she searches the room for Pearl and her man.

A ten-foot blue spruce is decorated with tiny handmade lace fans. The boughs of the tree are filled with hundreds of midnight-blue satin ribbons tied into neat bows. Ropes of miniature pale lavender pearls drizzle down the branches. Moravian stars punched out of old tin nestle near the trunk, throwing oddly shaped beams of light around the room. "That's a stunner," Iva Lou says. "I wonder if they'll sell it to me."

"There they is!" Fleeta clucks. Pearl and her doctor kiss under the mistletoe hung on the pocket doors between the Victorian and antebellum eras.

"Doctor B. It's so good to see you again." I give him a big hug. We ferriners should stick together. Besides, if this romance works out with Pearl, he'll be family.

"Joe's doctor." Iva Lou whispers this as though she doesn't realize she's said it aloud.

I cover for her. "Iva Lou, you remember Dr. Bakagese."

"Of course. How are you?"

"Fine. Thank you."

Fleeta looks at me sadly; she can be sensitive once every hundred years or so, and this is one of those times.

Dr. Bakagese smiles at me. I feel instantly guilty. So many times over the past few years, I meant to call him and thank him for all he did for our family and for Joe. But I have not called him to come to dinner, as I meant to do, nor did I go to see him. I kept meaning to, but I couldn't. When I look into his eyes, he seems to understand. I flash back to the day I met him; of course, that was the day that would change our family forever.

"Mama! Joe fell!" Etta hollered from upstairs.

That kid is driving me nuts, I thought. I went up the stairs.

"I'm fine," Joe said, rubbing his hip.

"Where did you land?"

"On my butt."

"Good."

"Why? It wouldn't hurt him if he landed on his head."

"That's not funny!" Joe pushed Etta. Before they could fuss full-out, I pulled them apart.

"Stop it. Both of you. I can't take it anymore!" The tone of my voice scared them (a little), so Etta went off to her room in a huff.

"Come on. Let's get you dressed."

Joe took off his pajamas and waited for me to hand him his clothes. As he climbed into the red pants, I noticed a bruise near his knee.

"What's that from?" I asked him.

"What?"

"That bruise."

"I dunno."

"You've got to be more careful."

"It doesn't hurt."

The room was dark because of the gray day outside, so I pulled open the shades to let more light in. The sun peeked out of a curtain of charcoal clouds, enough to help me see. I turned to help Joe into his shirt. There was another bruise on his back, right under his shoulder blade.

"Jesus, Joe. You're all banged up."

His skin looked a little transparent, and there seemed to be deep pools of shadow right under the skin, almost like bruises that turn from blue to yellow as they heal.

"I don't like the way this looks," I told him, and then my son wriggled away from me. I loaded the kids into the Jeep and took them up to Saint Agnes Hospital. Looking back, that seems extreme; after all, it was just a couple of bruises. Somehow, I just knew something was terribly wrong.

Joe sat in the front seat, holding on with his hands as we bounced down the holler road. I remember looking down at him and thinking how much I loved his little face. His profile was perfect; his chin stuck out like an emperor's. Etta rested her head on my shoulder as she stood between the seats. I didn't yell at her to get into her seat belt. She had her hand on her brother's neck, the way she did when we took him into his first crowd at a high school football game. For the first time in a long while, my kids were quiet. Neither of them said a word. There was only the sound of the windshield wipers, of the wheels hitting the wet road and our breathing.

Sister Ann Christine met us at the reception desk. She's five feet tall (at most) and was dressed in a white shirtwaist habit, white shoes, and a white wimple. She was around sixty then, but you couldn't tell by her skin. It was smooth and pink, not a wrinkle in it. Her small nose dipped down in a straight line; her blue eyes stood out like patches of sky against clean white clouds. As she leaned over to embrace my children, I imagined my mother holding them and almost cried.

Dr. Bakagese entered the examination room with a big smile. "What's happening, little buddy?" He spoke American slang with an Indian accent. He was tall and slim. He had beautiful hands with long, tapered fingers. His hair was jet black and cut short. His skin was a beautiful shade of café au lait. He had a small nose, full lips, and wide brown eyes. I've always had a hard time surrendering my children to doctors, but this time, I wasn't afraid. I trusted this man.

"Ave. Yoo-hoo." Iva Lou pokes me back into the present.

"I'm sorry." I look at Pearl, whose face wears an expression that I've never seen before. It's motherly. She knows what I'm thinking. Pearl always knows. "You know, I would love to have you both to Christmas dinner." I turn to Iva Lou and Fleeta. "And you too. Lyle. Dorinda. Baby Jeanine. Everybody." I turn back to Pearl. "Your mom. Otto and Worley."

"Hell. Let me check my calendar." Fleeta searches her pockets for her cigarettes. "Yup. We can make it."

"Are you sure?" Pearl asks. She knows that I haven't celebrated Christmas in a big way since Joe died. I put up a tree for Etta, but we haven't had a party or a big dinner.

"Yeah. I think it's time. Lots of things to celebrate this year. Jack's new job. The Soda Fountain. Lots of good stuff." I look at my friends, reassuring them that this is something I really want to do. They all agree to come; we'll talk about what they can bring later. Even if you throw a dinner in the Gap, it's potluck. We live to get out our pans and fill them with our best dishes. Pearl and Dr. B. move on to the Roaring Twenties room.

Iva Lou watches them go. "They're so sweet. Like a romantic postcard."

"From somewheres in the Middle East."

"Jesus, Fleeta." Iva Lou turns to her.

"What?"

"India is not in the Middle East. Git yer facts straight."

"It don't matter. The man knows he's black."

"Indian," Iva Lou corrects her.

"Black. Indian. Brown. They's all ferriners. What's the damn difference?" Fleeta, having had enough of the Victorian era, heads into the antebellum room. Etta runs in from the hallway.

"Mommy, I barely touched Mrs. Arnold's gingerbread house and the roof caved in!"

"I told you if you touched anything, we were going home."

"I just ate a little piece of the top."

"You ate the roof? Etta, you have to go apologize immediately."

"Let it go," Iva Lou says, as Etta is heading off to make amends. "It's not a big deal. Patsy Arnold needs to get a grip. You'd think her gingerbread house was the Sistine Chapel."

I work through the crowds and down to the main floor, where the gingerbread houses are on display. I see Patsy in the corner, repairing the hole in the roof of Santa's workshop with an icing bag.

"Patsy, I'm so sorry."

"It's okay. Corey Stidham tore off the door and ate it before Etta had at the roof."

"Are you sure?"

"Hon, it's a compliment. The thing is supposed to look good enough to eat."

I head through the house looking for Etta. I go to climb up the back stairs and see her sitting outside on the porch, which serves as a loading dock for the Tolliver House.

"I told Mrs. Arnold I was sorry."

"I'm sorry I yelled. But there are judges coming around, and people work hard on their crafts."

"I want to go home."

"But we haven't seen all the rooms yet."

"I don't care."

"Why?"

"I hate Christmas."

"Come on, Etta." I take my daughter's hand. "I want to show you something."

In the study, there is a display of handmade quilts by local artists. The quilts are donated by families to the John Fox, Jr. Museum. Two of Etta's Grandmother MacChesney's creations are on display. There is a colorful drunkard's-path pattern; a king-size quilt with bright cotton paisleys; red, blue, and pink ginghams; and florals in soft pastels. A red, white, and green checkerboard with a white background covers the largest wall in the room. There is a card next to her quilts:

NAN GILLIAM MACCHESNEY, 1907–1978. I point out the card to my daughter.

"Okay," Etta says, bored. To her, this room is a bunch of colorful old blankets that smell like cedar hanging on sticks.

"See the stitch work? How tiny? And how there are layers and layers of it? It took her close to a year to make one of these. And she was fast."

"How come you don't quilt?"

"I don't know. I can sew a little."

"Your mama sewed too."

"Yes, she did."

Etta walks off to look at the diorama of the Outdoor Drama. I think about what I've tried to teach my daughter about life and love and family. The one thing I wanted to give Etta that my mother couldn't give me was the example of a happy marriage. I remember Jack told me many years ago that the most important thing a father could do for his son was to love his mother. Maybe the most important thing a mother can do for her daughter is to love her father.

The trick to the Kiwanis Club Annual Christmas Tree Sale is to find out when the truck is delivering the trees to town; if your husband is a Kiwanis member, you have an in. Then you must position yourself for the unloading, and there is a pecking order. Hospitals and churches first, then regular people. The Kiwanis Club owns the market; no one else in town sells trees. You would think that because we live in these lush mountains, Christmas trees wouldn't have to be imported. Any reasonable person would assume that we'd just take an ax, go out into the woods, pick a tree, and cut it down. I don't know why, but that is just not how it's done. We don't chop down trees in Big Stone Gap. We wait for the Kiwanians to bring them from Canada.

Otto and Worley dig holes in the ground where the trees stand until they are purchased. The empty corner lot across from the First Baptist Church became the outdoor showroom by process of elimination. The Club used to sell them up the street in front of Buckles Supermarket, but when the market needed additional parking space, they blacktopped the lot, and so went the Kiwanians. Otto swears that the trees stay fresher when they're in the ground; the men water and groom them like fine racehorses. I always laugh when the trees are gone the day after Christmas. The lot is pitted with holes where the trees were, and it looks as though a team of killer groundhogs had a battle. It stays that way until Christmas comes around again.

My husband is a new member of the Kiwanis Club, because after years of working in the mines, he can finally attend their monthly lunches at Stringer's. (Evidently, this is the backbone of membership in the Kiwanis Club—you have to be available for lunch.) Jack substitutes in the pit band at the Outdoor Drama, and when the crowds are big, he spends intermission selling popcorn and chili dogs in the Kiwanis Club concession stand (the proceeds go to the show fund), so many of the Kiwanians thought Jack was already a member. They were a little surprised to find his name on their new members list. He was elected treasurer immediately.

As we drive down Poplar Hill, cars are already parked all around the Christmas-tree lot. I pull in at the Baptist Church.

"Let's pick our tree."

"You go. I'm cold."

"Come on. It'll be fun." I put on my lipstick in the rearview mirror. "Etta, don't make me beg. I don't need a sourball in my house ruining our Christmas spirit." Etta laughs. "I'm not kidding. Come on. They have hot chocolate."

Reluctantly, she gets out of the Jeep, then sees Jack. "Daddy!" Etta says, and runs to him.

"I sold three blue spruce and one Douglas fir," Jack says, kissing me on the cheek.

"I'm impressed."

"Who knew it took selling Christmas trees?" He smiles at me.

Since Iva Lou alerted me to the fact that I must put the romance back in my marriage, I listen carefully to everything my husband says. And now I notice Little Diggers. Like that one. He said it as a joke, but there's a deeper meaning. He doesn't think I admire him, so it's my job, in this period of trying to win his heart again, to resist a funny retort and instead gently correct his misconception.

"I'm always impressed with you and everything you do." I give him a hug. He looks at me like I'm crazy. (I guess my new technique needs some refining.) "Did you pick out a tree for us yet?"

"I waited for you."

"What do you think?" I follow him into a row of fragrant Douglas firs. I stop and inhale deeply. The cold air and the clean sap make a fragrant mix of evergreen and sweet pine that sends me spinning.

"You look pretty," my husband says to me. Instead of blurting, "What? Get your eyes checked," as old, insecure Ave Maria might joke, new improved Ave Maria says, "Thank you." What I really want to do is grab him and throw him up against a tree and say, "Are you cheating on me?," but I don't. Of course not. I have a plan. And the plan is: keep my emotions in check and win him back. I am going to be so adorable that there is no way he'll want any other woman. Iva Lou swears that's the only way to keep a man in love with you, and since I have no strategies of my own, I'm going with hers.

"Ma, look. Little trees!" Etta waves from the end of the row.

"Etta honey, we've got a whole attic full of ornaments. That tree is too small."

"I want a big one too. For our house."

"Two trees?"

"This one is for Joe." Etta twirls the little tree around. "I want to take it to Glencoe."

Jack and I glance at each other. We're both surprised that Etta would want to take a tree up to the cemetery.

"I can decorate it myself. But maybe you can help me." Etta looks up at me. "I know you're busy, Daddy." Thatta girl, Etta. You tell him.

He hasn't been home for dinner in weeks, he's probably grabbing sandwiches with Karen Bell—and he should be home with us.

Jack kneels down next to Etta. "I'm sorry I'm working so much. I just started the business, and it takes up a lot of my time."

"Okay, Daddy." Etta pulls a locket of mistletoe out of her pocket and holds it over Jack's head. "Mommy?" She grins.

"Excuse me," I say to Etta. Then I throw Jack on the ground, straddle him, and kiss him. I really kiss him. Not a peck. Not a swipe on the lips. No, it's one of those French Soul Kisses you heard about in high school study hall the Monday morning after the popular kids had a wild party at Huff Rock.

"Good God a-mighty! Call Spec. Jack needs oxygen, pronto!" Zackie says loudly. "Careful, Av-uh! The Baptists will throw us off the lot!" Jack's fellow Kiwanians whistle and applaud.

"Hey." I stand up and brush the leaves off my coat. "Sometimes you just have to kiss your husband."

"Just as long as that's all you're doing," Nellie Goodloe says from the hot chocolate stand. I look down at my husband, who stares at me as though he doesn't have a clue as to who I am. Good. He wants a new woman? He's got one.

In the winter, the Powell River curls along Beamontown Road like a rusty pipe; red clay and gray rock and black ice make a path where the water will go come spring. I always thought this hillside by the river was a perfect place for a cemetery, but that was long before I knew anyone inside its gates.

An ornate wrought-iron arch stretches across two regal brick pillars in the entrance way. The cursive letters spelling GLENCOE CEMETERY are surrounded by black iron filigree flowers. A beautiful fountain sits just beyond the gate; in warm weather, water gushes over the marble shells and into a deep pool.

I used to bring the kids here on holidays. We came on Memorial Day, my mother's birthday, and every Christmas. When we visited the cemetery, I would tell the kids stories about their grandmothers. Jack always thought it was a little creepy, that I liked the cemetery and found comfort here. I tried to explain that this was part of my Catholic faith and my Italian heritage; our gravesites are as important to us as our living rooms. In Jack's Scotch-Irish tradition, a cemetery is a place you visit on the day of burial, and, hopefully, not often after that. So when I came here, I came with the kids or alone, sometimes just to sit and talk to my mother.

Four years ago this Christmas, I brought the kids here, and we placed green holly wreaths with red velvet ribbons and small glitter charms on Nan MacChesney's grave and on my mother's. Joe ran in and out among the stones, laughing and playing, hollering for Etta, then hiding and hooting like an owl or howling like a ghost. She pretended to be scared, and I, of course, teasingly reprimanded him for his lack of respect for the dead.

Now Jack's truck bounces over the gravel road on the way to the MacChesney plot. The little tree Etta chose for Joe's gravesite is safe under a tarp in the flatbed. She has a bag of bells she made out of birdseed to use as ornaments, and red ribbons to tie on the branches. She wrapped two bricks in tinfoil like gifts to anchor the trunk at the base.

Etta and I chat all the way in. Jack becomes somber the moment we drive through the gates. He pulls the truck up under the old tree that showers the ground with shiny black buckeyes (which we collect for good luck) every autumn. Our son's headstone, simple black marble with white swirls, rests near the gnarly roots of that tree.

I help Etta out of the truck. Jack lifts the tree from the back of the truck and positions it over Joe's headstone. Etta helps anchor it with the bricks. Then she carefully lays her ornaments out on the ground and begins to decorate the tree while Jack holds the tree.

I walk across the plot and over to my mother's grave, marked with the same simple marble. I pull some weeds from around the stone. I look over at Fred Mulligan's and pull some weeds from his too. My parents are buried just a few feet from the MacChesney plot (one of life's ironic little twists). I've been standing at Mrs. Mac's grave for a while when I feel my husband's arms around me.

"How's Etta doing with those ribbons?" I ask him.

"Just fine."

Together, we watch our daughter as she decorates the tree. The picture of her, reaching up inside the tiny branches to place pine cones coated in birdseed, reminds me of a Hümmel statuette my mother kept on her nightstand.

"You know what I think about sometimes?" my husband says as he pulls me closer.

"What?"

"How it all seems like a bad dream."

"I know."

"Remember the day we had all of Joe's school friends over?" Jack asks me. We had taken Joe out of the hospital so he could be home with us, with Shoo the Cat, in his own bed. Joe felt pretty good one morning and decided that he wanted to see all his buddies from school. So I called all of their mothers and threw a party.

"The boys were running and playing inside, and next thing you know, they took off in a pack and went outside into the snow. Joe took off after them. And he got as far as the middle of the field in front of the house, but he couldn't keep up. So he knelt down alone in that field. And he didn't call for us. He just knelt there. And waited. God, that broke my heart. When he couldn't run anymore."

"I hope we never forget him." I turn and face my husband.

"How could we?"

"I don't know. People do." I hold my husband so tight, it's as though he's in pieces and the only thing that can hold him together is me. I close my eyes and remember how close we have been. What is worth saving in this life? What is worth holding on to? Does anyone know until they lose it?

I look over at our daughter. Etta holds a red ribbon in her hand as she watches the two of us. She is smiling.

This Christmas is our best yet. Maybe it's because Etta feels it's a real celebration again; or because Theodore made good on his promise to spend the holidays with us; or that Jack and I seem to have come to a good place in our marriage (maybe it's temporary, or maybe it's the holiday spirit, I don't care, it's nice!). We're sitting on a Lily Pad of Calm amid a year full of setbacks and arguments. When I tell Jack we're on a pretty lily pad, he takes his fist to his head and mockingly pounds it. But the more I think of this image, the more apt I think it is. Lilies bloom on the surface of dark and murky water. There is a lot under the surface of this marriage, and I don't forget that for a second.

"Can I help?" Theodore stands behind me as I maneuver the turkey into the oven.

"Get the potatoes. Please."

"Sweetie, where's the wine?" Jack wants to know as he passes through to gather Etta and our guests.

"On the porch in the cooler. I needed the space in the fridge for Fleeta's Jell-O mold."

"Which no one eats," Theodore whispers.

"It makes a nice centerpiece."

"Until it melts lime-green goo all over the table."

"It's Christmas. Green is good," I tell him. "Thank you for coming. And being here. Especially this year. Thank you."

"You owe me. I stayed up until four-thirty putting that Barbie thing together for Etta."

"I know."

"I know you know," Theodore tells me, and kisses me on the forehead.

The phone rings, at least four times; just as I'm about to yell for someone, anyone, to pick it up, I hear Etta in the hallway.

"Ciao, Nonno!" she says, giggling. Jack takes over carving the turkey and motions for me to take the phone.

"Merry Christmas, Papa."

"How's my daughter?"

"I'm great. Just wish you were here."

"How is Christmas?"

"Hectic. Nuts. How about you?"

"Mama took a little fall, so we—"

"How? Is she all right?"

"Nothing broke. Thank God. She's bossing everyone from her chair."

"May I speak with her?" My father gives my grandmother the phone; she sounds hearty and robust and not broken at all. She tells me all the news of Schilpario in a run-on sentence, ending with the news that my father is seeing a woman seriously. Her name is Giacomina, and she's only forty-four years old! "Put Papa on the phone," I tell her. I know she must be important to him; my father has always had lots of girlfriends, so to bring home someone special must be a big deal, and for my grandmother to mention it, it's got to be serious.

"Yes, yes, it's true. I love this woman," Papa says to me, and laughs.

"Are you getting married?" I ask him.

"Thinking about it. Yes. I would prefer to only think of it and never do it."

"Don't you do a thing until I can be there!" I yell into the phone.

"When are you coming?"

"I don't know. But don't do anything until we can be there. Promise?"

"I promise."

Jack takes the phone and talks to my father. I go into the dining room and catch Theodore up on all the goings-on in Italy as he places serving pieces on the table.

The dining room table, a rustic farm table with thick legs, is dressed with my mother's china, a pattern I have always loved, which is called "English Ivy." I have placed crystal plates filled with celery, carrots, and black olives at either end of the table. Sterling silver open-weave baskets are filled with fresh rolls, and pats of butter in the shape of Christmas bells and fluffy buttermilk rolls (thank you, Hope Meade) are placed on each guest's bread plate. I dim the lights (my mother's simple crystal chandelier from our Poplar Hill house) and light the twisty red taper candles in their Santa holders (a special from the Mutual's).

Etta runs in and offers to ring the dinner bell. She grabs it and runs through the house, clanging it in every room as if she's a goatherd. Jack says good-bye to my father and goes into the kitchen for the turkey. The company drifts in, though they aren't company at all, really, but family. Iva Lou and Lyle take their places opposite Jack; Etta sits next to Iva Lou; Pearl and Dr. B. sit to one side of me, Theodore to the other; Fleeta, Dorinda, and baby Jeanine sit in the center; Otto and Worley and Leah fill in the rest. In the beauty of the moment, surrounded by my favorite people, I want to cry.

"Don't, Ma," Etta whispers.

"No, no. I'm happy. I was just thinking how lucky we are. To have each other. That's all."

My friends murmur in reply, no one 'fessing up to their holiday emotions, and maybe not wanting to deal with them, either. I miss my mother terribly; my father is a big ocean away; Mrs. Mac is gone. My son, who loved Christmas, is not here. I wonder if they're looking down on us, sorry they can't be with us. I stare into the candle for a second, hoping that the bright white of the flame will center me and help me from having a sobfest right here in the sweet-potato casserole with delicate marshmallow crust. Dr. Bakagese winks at me. Maybe he knows where my thoughts have taken me.

"Honey, why don't you lead the prayer?"

"Catholic or Baptist?" Etta offers us a choice.

"If we're goin' by the numbers, go with Baptist. We got you Cathlicks beat by about six." Fleeta moves her head around the table, counting Protestants. " 'Course, Doc, I don't know what religion you is but I'm perty sure it's one of them that meditates."

"Fleeta, with all due respect, my daughter is Catholic," Jack offers, avoiding the Cracker's Neck version of the Great Schism.

"Well, I don't much care. Jesus is Jesus." Fleeta takes a stand.

"Well, I'm half Baptist," Etta says, looking at her daddy. " 'Cause you're a full Baptist. So I will say a prayer in half and half. Bow your heads. God, the Baptists thank you for the turkey. The Catholics thank you for the cake . . ."

"And I'd like to thank the ABC store for the whiskey. Amen," Lyle says, finishing Etta's prayer. Etta makes the sign of the cross with me and shrugs. The phone rings. Etta excuses herself to go and answer it.

"Tell whoever it is we're eating dinner, Etta," I yell as I pass the gravy to Pearl.

"Probably one of 'em phone-solicitation deals," Fleeta grumbles.

"On Christmas?" Dorinda wonders.

"That's the best time. They know yer home." Fleeta takes the last drag off her cigarette, then dips the butt into her ice water. It is so quiet, I hear the sizzle. Then she places the soggy butt on her bread plate.

Etta runs back into the room. "It's for you, Mama."

"Who is it?"

"It's Captain Spec."

"I bet that Edens boy shoved another button up his nose. That boy is forever cloggin' up the holes of his head with somethin' or another."

I excuse myself and go to the phone in the hallway. I barely hang up the phone before running in to tell our guests, "I have to go. I'm sorry. There's a fire at the Trail Theatre." Chairs push away from the table, and our group moves into action, putting out candles, grabbing their coats and purses, gloves and hats. "Hell, we'll all come," Fleeta says. "It could spread to the Pharmacy." Instead of arguing with Fleeta, I turn to Iva Lou. "Watch Etta for me, honey, will you?"

"I'm going too, Ma!"

"Don't worry. She'll stay with me," Iva Lou promises.

"I'll drive you," Jack says, helping me gather my gear.

By the time we reach town, four fire trucks have parked in front of the theater. Black smoke billows out of the second story; flames pour out of the lobby below. Jim Roy Honeycutt, his white hair askew, is pacing behind the fire trucks, distraught.

"What happened?"

"My prints! All my movies is in there! From the beginning!"

I leave Jim Roy with his wife and duck under the hoses, which are being pulled off their giant spools and up to the building. A fireman from Appalachia taps the hydrant in front of Gilley's Jewelers. Barney and his son work furiously, emptying the window display into a sack. The sight of them tipping the velvet necks modeling pearls and chains reminds me of Cary Grant in *To Catch a Thief*. The chug and grind of the ladders as they extend to the roof drowns out Spec, calling to me. Jack, who is helping a volunteer fireman with an unwieldy hose, motions to me to go to Spec.

A crazy series of loud pops, followed by billows of black smoke, comes from the building. Cinders from the ornate wooden molding cascade from the building in small sprays of orange.

"Must've hit the storage room. The oil and popcorn has gone up," Spec tells me. How strange to smell the popcorn burning outside. Jim Roy's popcorn was so good, folks would stop in and buy a sack even if they weren't staying to see the movie.

"There's a man inside," a fireman shouts to us. Spec and I move in with our oxygen and gurney.

The streets are filled with onlookers, including all the merchants. Zackie gathers them together, and the postmaster from across the street manages the crowd, pushing them back and onto the Post Office steps.

Then, in a cloud of gray smoke, the captain of our Fire Department emerges from the side door to the ticket booth, carrying a man over his shoulder. Spec and I help him place the man on the gurney. He is not breathing; we administer oxygen. Doc Daugherty joins us and takes over.

"Who is he?" I ask Spec. I've never seen this man before. Spec shrugs.

Across the street in front of the Pharmacy, our Christmas dinner guests stand in a huddle watching. Pearl grabs Fleeta's hand as she watches Dr. Bakagese help a fireman who has taken in too much smoke. The crowd points and sighs as red sparks blow off the roof and out into smoke, disappearing into the cold blue air.

Spec searches the man's pockets for identification, finds his wallet, and opens it. "His name is Albert Grimes. He's from Dunbar." Dunbar is a coal camp over by Appalachia. What was he doing in the closed theater on Christmas Day?

"I wonder if he's kin to Pearl," Spec says, waving her over.

"I don't know."

"Let me see," Pearl says, running up behind me. She leans over the stretcher. "He's my father." Spec looks at her—"What?"—and then looks at me; I had no idea Pearl's father was alive or lived around here. I glance at Pearl, who gazes down at the man on the gurney. She isn't afraid for him; there is detached concern in her eyes, but certainly not worry. Spec and I lift him into the Rescue Squad wagon. I look at Pearl again and hold back a thousand questions—this is not the time.

"The building's empty!" the Fire Chief yells to his crew. "Let her have it, boys!" In earnest, they begin hosing the building through the windows; the gold flames disappear, replaced with thick black smoke.

Doc Daugherty rides with Albert Grimes in the back of the wagon. Spec and I speed up to Lonesome Pine Hospital's emergency room, which is not more than a five-minute drive through town and out through the southern section. The fireman whom Dr. B. treated did not require oxygen, but he is behind us in Appalachia's rescue squad wagon for a thorough check at the hospital.

Albert wakes up and moans; his blue eyes are fuzzy, and he cannot focus. As we wheel him into the emergency room, Tozz Ball wants to ask him a few questions, but Spec tells Tozz to beat it. Pearl and Leah sweep through the automatic doors and search the room for Albert. Pearl sees him through the window in ICU and goes to him. Leah joins Spec and me.

"Is he all right?" Leah asks.

"We think so. He took in a lot of smoke."

"He didn't mean no harm."

"I'm sure he didn't." I put my arm around Leah.

"He's basically good. He just had a bad run of it."

"Of what?"

"Of everything. Things didn't work out between us. He lost his job with the railroad on account of the disability and it all went downhill after 'at. He just lost his way, you know." Leah goes through the doors and into the ICU. She puts her arm around Pearl, who rests her head on her mother's shoulder.

I can't believe that Leah is making excuses for the man who left her and a baby. She doesn't love him anymore; she's going to marry Worley. Maybe she just feels sorry for him. Pity is a dangerous thing in a woman: it gives the man the power to treat you any way he wants; he can stay and be cruel, or he can abandon you. As I watch Pearl lean on her mother, I think of my own mother, who I could always count on when I was hurting. My mother pitied my stepfather, Fred Mulligan, felt compassion for a man who could not feel, and it left me in the middle, feeling sorry for a man who could not love me.

"I think we ought to run down and check on Jim Roy. This thing could give him a nervous breakdown," Spec tells me, and I follow him back to the squad wagon.

We pull up in front of the Pharmacy. Fleeta has opened it, turned on all the lights, and it looks as though the whole town is stuffed inside, where it's warm. The mechanical choir in the window nods and waves as though nothing has happened. There is one truck left on standby across the street outside the theater. Jack Mac and Etta stand on the sidewalk outside the Pharmacy, watching the firemen as they secure the building.

"Mama, look!" Etta points to the marquee, which has burned off the facade of the theater.

Before the fire, the bright white marquee used to have a green plastic pine tree anchoring it in the center, and THE TRAIL in plastic cursive on either side. Underneath THE TRAIL was always the title of the movie, or at least as close as Jim Roy could spell it. As the years went on, letters got lost or broken, and Jim Roy didn't replace them. So you'd see titles like GO WIND for *Gone With the Wind* or SUM 42 for *The Summer of '42*. Now the modern plastic is gone, and under it, in bold letters carved into the wood, is AMAZU.

"What's Am-a-zoo?" I ask my husband.

"Amaze You."

"What's 'Amaze You'?"

"That was the first movie house in Big Stone Gap. Way before Jim Roy bought the place and modernized it. My mama used to tell me about it. They saw silent movies there. Lillian Gish. Buster Keaton. Charlie Chaplin. And there was an organ and a stage. And before every show, old Possum Hodgins, who owned the theater, would get up and tell the audience, 'Today we're-a-gonna Amaze You!' "

I look up at the old marquee, and it sends a chill through me. How strange to see the past exposed under layers of the present.

"Honey, it's cold. Go inside," I tell my daughter.

"Fleeta opened up the Soda Fountain. She's pushin' pie and cake and coffee," Jack Mac tells me. I'm not surprised. As much as Fleeta complains, if she's not in the center of everything, she ain't living.

Spec is over at the Trail with the firemen. Jim Roy is standing out front, talking to them. I take Jack's hand, and we cross the street to join them.

"It's gone. It's all gone," Jim Roy says sadly. "All my movies. My prints done burned. All my years of collecting. Gone."

"We were able to save some, sir." A fireman joins us, just a kid of maybe twenty, and he shows Jim Roy a stack of black tin canisters which he salvaged and placed in the doorway of Gilley's Jewelers. Jim Roy sees the canisters, and his eyes light up with joy.

"Here, I got a flashlight," Spec tells Jim Roy, who rushes over to the canisters and runs his hands over the wheels of tin as though he were patting a baby.

"Let's see what we got, buddy," Spec says to Jim Roy. Then he reads the tape on the sides as I hold the flashlight: "*The Thin Man, Dancing Lady, My Man Godfrey, Stagecoach, The Heiress, Midnight* with Don Ameche and Claudette Colbert. That would've been a tragedy right there if they burned up." Spec shuffles through the reels: "There's *Bachelor Mother*, yeah, Ginger Rogers was sexy in that one; *The Barretts of Wimpole Street, Topaz, Pride and Prejudice, Jezebel, It Happened One Night . . .*"

"Clark Gable!" I shriek. Spec gives me a look.

"Let's see, there's *The Ghost and Mrs. Muir, Song of Bernadette, Test Pilot, Wuthering Heights, Dinner at Eight; Goodbye, Mr. Chips, The Women, Sullivan's Travels*; there's Claudette agin with *The Palm Beach Story*, the Duke in *The Quiet Man, How Green Was My Valley*, thank you Jesus, it looks like we saved most of Maureen O'Hara. And lookee. Henry Fonda in *The Trail of the Lonesome Pine*. It's here, Jim Roy!"

"How 'bout Kay Francis? I had all of Kay Francis," Jim Roy says nervously.

"They're here." Spec shows Jim Roy a neat stack of her movies, safe on the ground. He places a double reel on top of the stack. "*National Velvet* . . . that's Etta's favorite, isn't it?" I nod.

Jim Roy breathes deeply. Most of his treasure has been saved, and saved by a kid who probably wouldn't know Spencer Tracy from Joel McCrea. Seats and screens and popcorn machines can be replaced, but the prints that Jim Roy has collected all these years cannot.

"Come on, Jim Roy, let's take you and Mrs. Ball over to the Mutual's. Fleeta's made coffee." Jack puts his arm around Jim Roy. But Jim Roy doesn't move. He stands there looking at his theater.

"I can't believe it. And on Christmas." He sighs sadly.

As we enter the Mutual's, folks gather around Jim Roy and his wife. Soon we break into small groups in the booths or sit around the Fountain, reminiscing about our favorite movies or the first movie we ever saw at the Trail. Theodore, put to work as a waiter for Fleeta, serves pie off of a tray. Fleeta peels the cellophane and red Christmas ribbon off a Whitman's sampler box and passes the chocolates around.

Quietly, through the kitchen, Leah and Pearl come in; Worley rushes to Leah's side, and she explains all about Albert. Folks buzz around Pearl, who says that Albert will be all right. Folks around here don't even know the man but are concerned.

"He didn't set no farr," Otto tells me.

"How do you know?"

"Chief tole me. Said it was wiring in the sound system. I ought to tell Pearl that, oughtn't I?" Otto goes off to give Pearl the news.

Nellie Goodloe, dressed in her red velvet Christmas suit studded with a jeweled Christmas-tree brooch and glittering smaller trees on her ears, gets up and calls the gathering to order.

"I want to tell you something, Jim Roy. I want you to know that I had my first kiss in the Trail Theatre in 1942." Wolf whistles fill the soda fountain. "Yes sir, I did. Robert Taylor leaned over and kissed Vivien Leigh on the silver screen, and up in the balcony, Spec Broadwater leaned over and kissed me. I never forgot it."

The crowd cheers, and Spec turns so red, he matches his flannel shirt. Spec's wife, Leola, in a running suit with snowmen painted on it, shoots Spec a dirty look. Then she thinks better of her petty jealousy and chuckles. Fleeta stands up on a step stool behind the counter. "Nellie, I want to know one thang. Did old Spec know what he was doin'?"

The crowd turns to Nellie. "Honey, I hope to tell ye, he surely did."

Fleeta spins her dishrag in the air like a truce flag. Etta is laughing along with the crowd, and she looks so grown-up to me all of a sudden.

"I think Etta just got her first sex-ed lesson," I whisper to Jack.

"Could be worse," he whispers back.

Fire or no fire, once I'm home, I have to clean up the dishes. I'm one of those people who must have every dish washed and put away before they can sleep. Luckily, Theodore is one of those people too. My husband, however, is not. He went to bed after putting Etta down.

"How about I take Etta to Cudjo's Caverns tomorrow," Theodore says, stuffing the refrigerator with more leftovers.

"She'd love it."

"What are you going to do on your day off with your husband?"

"I don't know." And I really don't. I never have a day off with Jack.

"Maybe you can think of something fun to do together. And I don't mean clean the oven. I'll keep Etta away until suppertime. You can have a lot of wild sex while we're gone."

"Thanks."

"You don't even blush. What has happened to you?"

I look at him, and he laughs. He goes into the dining room to collect the last of the dessert plates while I scrub the sink and think about wild sex. I don't think of actual wild sex, I'm wondering where mine went. Ours. I expected, before I got married, that I would be the last person to trade passion for comfort and then for routine and now for, I don't know, privacy. I thought the need to communicate, to physically communicate, in marriage would grow. No one told me, and perhaps no one can, what the truth of it all is. Sex becomes another way of speaking to each other, and when you stop touching, it's just as bad as if you're not speaking. When you stop everything except those perfunctory hello and good-bye pecks on the cheek and the hugs, more a way to brace yourself than to express feelings, you're in Big Trouble. But there is no one day or one thing that sets the Big Trouble alarms off. At first you stop kissing because you're annoyed at him, and it's a way to communicate that. And when the message gets through that you're not kissing for a reason, his behavior seems to adjust to the new rule: you upset me, you hurt me, you disappointed me, no kissing. And when those tender kisses become further and further apart, so goes the sex. It's impossible to make love when you can't kiss your lover. Someone once said that sex is the thermometer in a marriage; only when something is wrong is sex an issue. And that is true. But what no one tells you is that once you stop connecting, it is very hard to bring it back. There are times when I see my husband doing mundane things like unloading the truck or stacking the firewood, or today, when he was carving the turkey, and my instinct is to run to him and tell him how much he means to me and how I want to make love to him, and let's drop everything. But I don't. Maybe I'm afraid he'll reject me or maybe it's just life—there is always something in the way. Time. Work. Etta. Company. Or something else that has to be done. And then you forget. And sex is always the first thing to go, because it's the one thing that can wait. Who knew the most natural thing in the world could become the most elusive?

Jack is snoring when I crawl into bed; I give him a gentle nudge, and he turns over. I am looking forward to sleeping long and late since Theodore is taking Etta spelunking. I sink down into the soft flannel sheets like a spoon in gravy. Jack turns over and opens his eyes.

"I thought you were asleep."

"I have an idea," Jack says, and lies back on the pillow.

"Yeah?"

"I think we should take Etta to Italy next summer to see your dad."

"Really?"

"Don't you think she's old enough?"

"I do!"

"They accepted our bid for the rec-center job in Appalachia. I think we'll be in pretty good shape financially. If we buy tickets now, we could get a good deal."

"Okay. I'll get on it."

"Does that make you happy?" he asks me.

"Oh my God, yes!" I kiss him good night.

Jack rolls over onto his side and yawns. Soon he'll be snoring again. I've never seen anyone fall asleep more quickly than my husband. Italy. Next summer. It seems so far away. And I'm happy that he got the job in Appalachia. But it's odd, he hasn't mentioned my partnership with Pearl since our argument about it. I thought it was best to leave it alone. No matter how well I think I know Jack MacChesney, he can still surprise me. His reactions to things. The things that hurt his feelings. Things I haven't counted on. There seems to be this gap between us sometimes; he doesn't know what I'm thinking, and I don't always know what he's feeling. I never would have thought that the family finances would be a problem for us. Both of us were so eager to share everything equally in the beginning. And when I had the babies, it seemed natural to work part-time; after all, we own this house, and his paycheck was enough. Maybe he felt empowered in an old-fashioned way when he was the chief breadwinner. Maybe he liked being the only one taking care of us in that way. Is Iva Lou right? Is this all about the male ego? Or are our fights about money really about something else—something both of us are afraid of, so we use the finances as an excuse? Sometimes there's a stranger in this bed, and I think it's me.

My post-Christmas present to myself is a call to Gala Nuccio, our travel agent. Gala became a big part of our lives after Jack found her in the New York paper years ago and she planned the trip that brought my dad and nonna to me for the first time.

Gala's tours are now the gold standard of Italian-American bus tours; she recently shot her first TV commercial (which airs in New York, Connecticut, New Jersey, and Pennsylvania). She sent us a videotape: there she was, an Italian goddess with golden skin, a beautiful teased bubble of black curls with red highlights, full, shiny maroon lips, arched black eyebrows, and a killer pale blue Chanel suit with gold chains on the pockets. Her perfectly manicured nails with French tips pointed out vistas of Mighty Italia in the background: Rome, Florence, Capri, and Milan whizzed by, a supersonic slide show of adventure. Then, at the end, Gala sat on a suitcase and pointed down to her 800 number, which pulsed in red, white, and green.

"Gala Tours," the receptionist says when she answers the phone.

"Is Gala in?"

"Who shall I say is calling for Mizz Nuccio?"

"Tell her it's Mario da Schilpario's daughter."

"Hold, please." I am on hold for barely ten seconds, then Gala bursts through the wires.

"Holy Mother, is that you, sister?" Gala barks into the phone.

"It's me. You dropped Nuccio? Now you're a one-name star like Cher or Liberace?"

"Or God." Gala cracks herself up.

"How are you?"

"I am fan-tab-you-luss." Then Gala lowers her voice and growls, "Yesss ma'am."

"Who is he?"

"His name is Toot Ruggerio. He lives in Manhattan. Little Italy. He's busy. And he's thrifty. He lives in the same apartment he grew up in. Rent control, you know. He's very close to the senator up there. Senator Pothole, they call him."

"Oh, Toot's in government."

"Nope. Construction. Honey, they call it politics, but honest to God, it's all construction."

I tell Gala all about Jack's new business.

"I cannot bee-leave that your Jack and my Toot are in the same line of work. We are linked by some giant bubble of karma, you and me. I tell you, we knew each other in another life. My psychic tells me I was a gemologist in Calabria. I have to remember to ask her what you were next time. She reads pictures too. She gets vibes off of them. I'll bring pictures of Etta from Christmas." Gala tells me all about her business, how it's growing by leaps and bounds; when she goes to the

Short Hills Mall, she gets mobbed because people know her from television. "Don't worry, hon. I keep it all in perspective. Success hasn't changed La Nooch. That's what Toot calls me: La Nooch. Okay, maybe now I have money and influence and I'm on TV. But believe me, at my center, at my core, fame has not gone to my head."

"Gala. I have a job for you."

"Let me get a pencil. Give me the dates."

As I give Gala the dates, I picture Jack and me in Santa Margherita, on the cliffs of the Mediterranean Sea, in the port by the sea with bright blue water where white sailboats bob like prizes and the nets are filled with shiny pink fish and the moon makes the cobblestones look like they're brushed in silver glitter. My husband will fall in love with me again in that light. I just know it.

I drive up Valley Road on my way to Norton. Pearl wants me to see the new building; the deal went through the week after Christmas. It's easy to find where Mutual Pharmacy II will be, as there are building permits posted in the window. Pearl is waiting for me inside.

"I wanted to hire MR. J's, but they're booked up."

"That's okay. How's your dad?"

"He's going to be just fine."

"There's all sorts of stories in town."

"I know." Pearl frowns.

"What was he doing in the theater?" I ask her gently.

"He was sleeping there."

"But they say he lives in Dunbar."

"Not really. After he left Mama and me, he went and lived with a woman in Dunbar, and then she threw him out after a couple of years."

"When was the last time you saw him?"

"About a month ago. He comes to me twice a year. For money." Pearl looks down when she says this. "And I give him a little, and he always promises to pay it back, and then he disappears."

"How did he find you?"

"He saw my picture in the paper when I graduated from UVA Wise."

"Did your mom know?"

"Yeah, and she didn't discourage me from seeing him. I feel bad. Mr. Honeycutt didn't know he was staying there. He snuck in through an old air shaft behind the screen."

"Don't worry. Old Jim Roy is just happy his collection got saved."

Pearl shows me the plans for the pharmacy—no soda fountain here, it will be strictly med counter and health and beauty aisles. She also tells me that the Soda Fountain is such a success, she should be able to pay off the bank loan within a year.

"I'd better get back to town. We have the sale running." I turn to go. "Pearl, where's your dad now?"

"I got him an apartment in Appalachia. I don't know if he'll stay, though."

"It's so complicated, isn't it?"

"I'll never figure it all out, will I?" Pearl asks me by way of answer.

"Did you ever ask him why he left you?"

"I did."

"And what did he say?"

"He told me it hurt too much to stay." Pearl shrugs. "I don't understand it. But that's the way it is."

The after-Christmas sale at Mutual Pharmacy is a circus. All holiday decorations, wrapping paper, ribbons, and gift sets are marked half off. Jean Hendrick has loaded her trunk with stuff twice. Mrs. Spivey and Liz Ann Noel nearly got in a hair-pulling fight over our last mechanical angel, marked down 75 percent (even though the angel was missing a wing). Peggy Slemp bought the remaining three boxes of Whitman's chocolates (we polished off the rest on the Fire Night) for half off (she freezes them!). "She gives 'em year-round. She is so cheap. Tighter than a truss," Fleeta sniffed, but she rang them up anyway.

The crowds have made the Soda Fountain lunches standing room only. Tayloe Lassiter was promoted to hostess during the post-holiday rush. We have two high school kids from Mr. Curry's Future Business Leaders Club waitressing in her place. Otto and Worley volunteered to be cooks on their days off. They're not bad, either.

By closing time, we are exhausted. Fleeta locks the door behind Reida Rankin, who bought the last few boxes of Christmas lights. "She'd stay all the night if I let her," Fleeta says, lighting up a cigarette.

"What a day!" Pearl says as she emerges from the office.

"Who's hungry?" Fleeta wants to know.

"I'm gonna head out," I tell Fleeta.

"No, not yet," she tells me firmly.

There is a knock at the front door. "Tell 'em to drop dead," Fleeta hollers, walking back to the Soda Fountain. But it's Iva Lou, so I let her in.

"Did you save me the cards with the Delacroix snow village on them?"

"I put the last three boxes behind the register."

"Good girl."

"Are you hungry?"

"Twist my arm."

If the sales staff (Fleeta and me) is half dead, the Soda Fountain staff is worse. Otto pours himself a Coke. Worley, who ended up waiting on customers because the Future Business Leader girls got flustered, sits in a booth with his feet up.

"I'm telling ye, people was so hungry, they'd have eaten a dead rat," Otto tells us.

"The sale made them hungry," Pearl says.

"What are ye talkin' about?" Fleeta asks, biting into a stale doughnut.

"When there's a sale, folks literally salivate, their mouths water at the possibility of a bargain. They have a physical reaction. It's exciting to get a deal, and the human body knows it."

"That's just fer women," Worley says.

"No, it's all people. Watch the men when Legg's Auto gets the new trucks in. You'll see," Pearl promises.

"I thought we was gonna have a full-out fistfight 'tween the Baptists and the Methodists over them religious cards you had out two for the price of one," Otto comments.

"The Baptists took 'em. Everybody knows the Baptists got more bite." Fleeta puts out plates. "Well, come on, y'all. It's buffet-style." Fleeta has displayed all the food that is left in the Soda Fountain. There are four wedges of pie, coconut or cherry ("Yer choice," Fleeta grunts), a plate of oatmeal cookies, two croissants with cheese, and several individual servings of Jell-O with a small star of whipped cream dead center on the squares. "The coffee's fresh," Fleeta says, apologizing for the hit-and-miss eats.

"You kept me hanging around for this?"

"Not exactly. This meetin' is hereby called to order. Now, who's gonna tell Ave what we heard up in Coeburn?" Fleeta announces. Iva Lou looks at her like she wants to throttle her.

"What did you hear?"

"Now, Ave, don't git pissed at the messenger is all I'm a-gonna say."

"I won't, Fleeta."

"All right. Here's what we know and when we knowed it. Pearl sent me up to Norton to check on a couple of things fer her at the new store." Fleeta looks at Pearl, who nods. "And when I was up 'ere, I done heard something. But as my mama used to say, you can put what I heard and what you heard together and hear nothin'." I nod at Fleeta. What she says makes absolutely no sense, but it seems like she rehearsed it, so I don't interrupt. "I got me a cousin up 'ere. I think you've met her. Veda Barker. Small woman. Vurry Christian woman. Well, she was over to the Coeburn town meeting, where they was talkin' about renovations and such of the town hall up 'ere, and they announced that MR. J's won the bid."

"I know they won the bid on a job in Coeburn."

"Yeah, but what you don't know is that Kurr-en Bell got up and spoke on behalf of MR. J's."

"She vouched for Jack's company. So what? She manages Luck's Lumber; they supply MR. J's with their materials."

"Kurr-en Bell is after your husband. And you need to wake up."

"Fleeta. Your tone," Pearl says to her gently.

"What do I need to wake up about?" I ask innocently. Suddenly, I realize how wives have done this for centuries. We buy time, pretending not to know what folks are talking about when they're talking about our husbands and how they spend their time and with whom. This pretend act will get me out of here so I can breathe and think.

"Karen Bell is going around telling folks she's in love with your husband. Maybe it's nothing. Maybe it's just gossip." Pearl puts her arm around me.

"Like hell. This is one story circulatin' through Wise County that has some meat on its bones. Now, get serious. You can't just turn yer husband loose up in Coeburn and expect him to find his way back home. That's too far from Cracker's Neck. He's lost. You got to make him come home. Or I'll tell you what, he'll be gone." Fleeta sits down. I've never seen her upset in this way.

I sit down. I have to. "Okay. I'm listening."

"I've followed the woman," Otto announces. "I ain't proud of it. But I done did it. I know where she lives. And I know what company she keeps up 'ere."

"You saw . . ." I look at Otto, and he looks away sadly. "Well."

I study my hands as though they're brand new and I'm seeing them on the ends of my arms for the very first time. I don't know what to say to my friends. Do I tell them that I've seen signs too, that I've been suspicious? That I had a feeling the first time I saw Karen Bell? I want to open up and tell them everything, but I can't. My loyalty to my husband, who has probably been disloyal to me, stops me.

"I need some air," I tell my friends. I stand up. So do they, and the sound of stools scraping linoleum is deafening.

Iva Lou follows me out to the Jeep and jumps into the passenger side. Mentally, I know I need to turn the key to start the engine, but I can't.

"Look. It ain't a done deal."

"Do you think it's true?"

"I been trying to tell ye. I heard bits and pieces of things. You know how stories travel."

"What do I do?"

"Nothing."

"Nothing? How can I do nothing?"

"We do not know the extent of it. Now, I know your husband. I don't think he loves her. I don't think he could. I don't think he loves any woman but you. Really. So that's good fer you. But you got a bigger problem."

"What?" What is Iva Lou talking about? What could be worse?

"Karen Bell is your problem. She wants him. And she wants him baaaaad. That's a fact. I heard that straight out of the mouth of her best friend, Benita Hensley up to the county library. She works up 'ere, and she told me herself."

Who are all these people, these strangers, who know my name and my business? What do they want? Why do they care about me and my situation? The noise in my head gets louder as Iva Lou goes on.

" 'Cause Karen Bell, you can't control. She's a wing nut and a wild card, 'cept she's a genius, 'cause she acts like a sure and steady professional woman. She's had a series of men too. Not that there's anything to judge about that." Of course there isn't. This is Iva Lou, the Siren Goddess of Big Stone Gap talking.

"I don't want to hear another thing."

"Listen to me. I have some experience as the Other Woman. I don't think there's a single scenario out there that I ain't in some way, at some point, been in. So you have what might be called a secret weapon in me, as your friend. I know what Karen Bell is up to. She can't pull anything I ain't seen before or done myself." Iva Lou fishes in her purse for a cigarette. "You need to listen to me, because I know what I'm talking about. There's Other Women who just want to play, have dinner, a movie, and some exciting sex; and then there's the Other Women who are husband hunting. And they are relentless. They don't rest till they got of yorn's what they think they want for themselves, and then it's too late for all concerned. Karen Bell is thirty-four years old—"

"She's forty if she's a day."

"Honey. She's thirty-four. Spec checked with the DMV."

"Spec!" I hit the steering wheel. Does everybody in Wise County know my business?

"He has a connection at the DMV. We had to tell him. Honey-o, here's the deal. She wants to git murried, and she wants kids, and she thinks Jack Mac would pass on a fine set of genes. She told Benita Hensley that Jack MacChesney is one of the smartest men she's ever known, that he's a man with a lot of Unrealized Potential. How do you like that? Karen Bell can spot potential. I almost threw up."

"I feel sick myself."

"I know. I know. I am so glad I'm murried and not foolin' around no more, 'cause I feel dirty just thinkin' about the pain I inflicted as the Other Woman. I hate myself for that, well not entirely, but certainly for your sake."

"What am I going to do?" I turn to Iva Lou. I almost want to grab that cigarette out of her mouth and smoke it myself.

"You can't let on to Jack that you know anything."

"Why? If I stop it . . ." And then I stop talking. Stop what? Their first kiss? Their first time together? Their falling in love? His packing up and leaving me? Their outdoor wedding at the lake in Big Cherry Holler with my Etta as the flower girl?

"Here's what you need to do. Are you listening to me?"

"Okay. Okay. I'm listening."

"She is counting on the fact that you are gonna blow this. She already knows, 'cause she's hooked your husband, that he ain't happy. So all she has to do is be sweet as pie. Uncomplicated. And that'll keep him coming back for more. If you go crazy and start following him and making him miserable and accusing him of things, it'll give her an advantage. You'll look like the hag wife, and she can be the sweet young thang." Iva Lou looks at me. "Bless your heart."

"How did this happen?"

"This happened 'cause there's a man involved. And they's vulnerable on account of the fact that they surrender their will to their ego. Don't forget that: their Will to their Ego. 'Cause their ego is what keeps them male. You got it?"

"I don't want this trash in my life! This sordid stuff. I don't want it!"

"Ave, there's that point in an affair where nothing's happened yet— nothing physical, that is. The man and the woman have established contact. They're friends. They work together. They probably talk about things. Personal things. She probably confides in him; maybe even, once in a while, pulls a little something where she has a problem at home and doesn't have a husband or any man around and something needs fixin' like a pipe or a wire and he says he'll stop by her house to fix it, and next thing you know, he's in the web."

"What web?"

"Her web. The little scene she puts together with her and him in it. Picture this. He fixes whatever she needs fixed. She has to thank him, so she makes a strong cup of coffee and a good sandwich for him. He sits down. And they get to chattin' about this and that, and next thing he knows, he doesn't know where the time went. So he gets up and says, I gotta get home to my wife, my kid, whatever. And she

looks sad, but she understands. That's the important part. She understands."

"Understands what?"

"What his life is like. What he deals with. What he needs. What his
problems are. She is His Friend. Get it?"

"Men don't talk to other men about their relationships, so they
need a woman to talk to?" I ask. Iva Lou nods. Now I'm getting it. Jack
Mac talks to Karen Bell about me. Etta. Work. Just like I talk to Iva
Lou. (If this weren't my life, I'd be thrilled at the notion of this break-
through in male-female relationships.)

"Now you see what I'm sayin'." Iva Lou leans back.

"Oh, I see it." Iva Lou doesn't know how clearly I see it.

"Jack Mac don't want to be in the web, but he's trapped, and he got
there by being nice. Men don't understand how something innocent
becomes routine, and then routine can become a relationship. You
got no idea how many men I've known who told me that they're surprised when they find themselves having an affair. They didn't see it
coming or plan it. But somehow, just by being nice, they got themselves yupped into bed. The Other Woman makes these innocent requests of their time, and they say, 'Yup, I'll help you out,' and pretty
soon she says, 'Kiss me,' and he says, 'Yup,' and the kiss leads to the
next yup."

"I don't want him to yup himself away from me."

"He won't. If you use your head. Ave Maria, that's where you've got
to be smarter than her. He doesn't want this. He knows it's wrong. But
you can't accuse him of something you're not sure he's done yet, or
for sure that will drive him right to her because he's gonna need
someone to talk to about that too." Iva Lou takes a deep breath. "I
would rather be you in this situation than her."

"Why?"

"Because he's a good man. And he's gonna try to do the right thing.
Now, I ain't sayin' he's a saint. But he's gonna wrassle right good with
it before he gives in."

"You think so?"

"I know it."

I know I should thank Iva Lou for helping me see what I should already know. But I'm not feeling much gratitude at this moment. I feel the gloom and despair of all women who have found themselves in my position, the terrible place of not knowing yet knowing all. The tricky thing is staying in the middle. I wonder if I can pull this off. I'm not going to hand over my husband like a covered dish at a church supper. If she's going to take Jack, it will be only because I let her. I guess I will find out what sort of a fighter I am. I twist my wedding band around on my finger; it feels loose. "The world's tiniest handcuff," Lyle Makin called it once. I think he was right.

*O*ne thing is for sure in a small town: if you're the toast of the town today, tomorrow you're bread crumbs. And if there are rumors that your husband is having an affair, if you wait long enough, somebody will top it with a bigger story. I'd like to thank Tozz Ball for having a second wife and family down in Middlesboro, Kentucky, and coming clean to his first family here in the Gap during a Sunday Revival at the Methodist Church. Tozz is now the headliner; I am happy to be bird feed.

Jack Mac and I talked about the rumors, in our way. I never directly named anyone (Karen), and he never admitted to anything (Karen). He told me that kind of talk comes with the territory; he works with women now, and people will talk. I told him that I understood, but I didn't want him to give anyone reason to talk, either.

I don't know if I'm getting better at following Iva Lou's instructions or if it's plain old fear that's helped me stick with my plan to be the perfect wife. I have been a joy to live with all spring: Upbeat, Warm and Tender, Uncomplicated, and Loving. I am no trouble at all. You could press me in dough and make sugar cookies out of me, I've been so sweet. I'm sure Etta wonders where my temper and occasional blue moods went this spring, but if she thinks about it much, she doesn't mention it.

It's the last week of April, which means that my wedding anniversary is coming up. April 29 will mark eight years of married life. On our first anniversary, Jack asked me what I wanted; of course, I wanted our baby to be healthy, and she was. But he wanted to buy me something. So I asked him for a book; not a book with a particular story, but one of those empty books with blank pages. He went over the mall and got me a pretty blue velvet journal and wrapped it up. When I opened it, I thanked him and then I gave it back to him. He looked confused and I told him that there was a second part to the gift. I wanted him to write me a letter every year on our anniversary, and I would write one to him, so that someday we could look back and see what we were. Now, Jack is not a writer, and neither am I, but I felt even a man of few words could come up with a page of something once a year. And he has. There are times during the year when I forget about the book, and right around our anniversary, Jack and I do this funny teasing dance with each other about writing in it; we pretend squabble and he acts like I'm asking him to yank a tooth, but we've written to each other every year, without fail.

The book has come in handy lately because I've needed reassurance. I wanted proof somehow that I didn't dream all of this, my great fortune at falling in love with a good person and having two beautiful children with him. I am trying to hang on, so I need to know why I should. I'm a woman of instinct, and my instinct keeps telling me that there's trouble ahead. I play out the scenarios in my mind: all the horrible ones, like the day he packs his clothes to go, the morning I get the divorce papers, and the day he remarries and I'm alone again. I know it's crazy, but these are crazy times around here.

The last few years have been so hard, we've written very short letters to each other. The year Joe died, Jack wrote: "I love you honey. I'm sorry." And I wrote the story of Joe's passing. But that year was the worst for us, and instead of dwelling on that, I pull the book out of my dresser and read Jack's first letter.

April 29, 1980

Dear Ave,

I know that the world is filled with lucky men. And I know that because I have met a few. And all the lucky men have one thing in common. They have a good woman who loves them. I know you worried all your life if you were pretty enough, and I hope to tell you that pretty doesn't begin to describe you. I see more in you when you're sleeping than you could ever imagine. They say your soul comes out when you sleep and, for you, this is true. When your eyes are closed, your eyelashes lie against your cheeks and you purse your lips in a way that makes you look like you're smiling. You're a peaceful girl, my Ave. And that's what I found in you. Peace. I am the luckiest man in the world. I love you. J.

I take the book and put it on Jack's nightstand with a pen. Maybe if he looks at what he's written to me, it will remind him that there is a lot here worth fighting for.

June, the month of Our Big Trip home to Italy could not come fast enough. Now that it's here, I am filled with hope again. I want to be with my husband in a romantic place where we can be together, talk, and laugh, where no one knows us. All winter the mountains felt as if they were closing in on us. Jack has spent most of the spring working overtime. There's been very little rain, so he and Mousey and Rick have been working long hours. Construction is all about the weather.

I remember the clothes Jack took to Italy on our honeymoon, and I try to copy the contents this go-round. I've asked him a few questions here and there about what he wants me to bring for him, and he just says, "You decide." So I pack for him.

The night before we're set to fly out of Tri-Cities, en route to

Kennedy Airport in New York and then to Milan, I check on Etta. She had been too excited to sleep, so I allowed her to keep the night-stand light on and read. It worked. As I pull Beverly Cleary's *Fifteen* out of her grasp and shove the bookmark into place, she turns over and hugs her pillow without opening her eyes. I give her a quick kiss on the forehead. Her bags are packed neatly and waiting in a row by the door. I can't wait to see her face when she sees Schilpario for the first time.

I hear Jack park the truck in the side yard. I am looking forward to the long airplane ride. Etta can sleep, and Jack and I will finally get a chance to talk, to catch up. Our happiest memories together are of our honeymoon, and now we'll get to relive all of that.

I meet Jack in the hallway as he shuffles through the mail. I wrap my arms around him from behind.

"How was your day?" I ask him.

"Rough."

"I bought you new socks."

"Why?"

"Your old ones were too shabby for Italy."

Jack starts to move, so I let go of him. He puts his arm around me and moves toward the kitchen.

"And by the way, these aren't the socks that come in a pack. They're the good kind that hang on the rack on the little plastic hangers at Dave's Department Store. Nothing but the best for my husband."

"I want to talk to you." He sits down at the kitchen table. I sit across from him.

"What's up?" I say cheerily. I can be cheery. Tomorrow we'll be in Italy.

"I'm not going."

"Why?" I ask. He doesn't answer me. "Is it work? Are you behind on a job?"

"No. We're okay."

"Then what is it?"

"I think we need time apart." Jack leans back in his chair and looks at me intently. His gaze makes me uncomfortable, and I look away.

"Why?"

"I think you know why."

The rumors around town? The long silences in our own bedroom? The way we bury ourselves in work, emerging only to take care of Etta?

"I don't know what you mean." Let him explain this. I am tired of filling in blanks.

"I don't think you want to be married to me anymore."

"That's not true! Not at all."

Jack gets up and turns on the tap. He pours himself a glass of water and drinks it. "Ave, you don't want to face this."

"Face what?"

"You do your chores: taking care of Etta, the house, me. And you're even sweet about it. You've been great all spring. But you're not really here in this marriage, it's an act."

"I resent that. I am doing things, living this way, out of love. I'm not pretending."

"Maybe 'pretending' is the wrong word. You're going through the motions. It's rote. You do what you think you're supposed to do. You do it well. And it's all very pleasant. Aboveboard. Nice."

"I've been doing this for you. It's not an act!"

"That's not what I want," Jack says simply. He moves and stands near the windows, yet he keeps his eyes on me the whole time.

"I'm sorry I'm such a disappointment to you."

"No. I'm sorry I'm such a disappointment to you," he says, then comes over to sit next to me.

"I'm really afraid right now. These things that you're saying sound so final to me." I take his hands into mine. I love his hands, and I don't want to let go. "Don't you love me anymore?"

"That's never been the problem. I love you so much that I'm willing to live an unhappy life for you."

"I don't understand."

"I didn't think you would," he says quietly.

"Jack, you have to explain to me what you're feeling. Because I don't get it. Please help me understand."

"When I married you, I wanted to make you happy."

"You did."

"I took it on because I wanted to."

"Took what on?"

"You. Your ways."

"Nobody is simple, Jack. We're all complicated. That's how people are. And anyone out there who you think is easy, believe me, they're not." I want to come out and say, "If you think Karen Bell is a cakewalk, you're crazy." But I can't. I will not say her name in this house.

"I knew it was going to be hard. I know a good marriage is more work than not. But I thought at the time that you would dig in and work with me. I thought that no matter what happened, we would share it."

"Haven't we shared everything?"

"No."

"I thought we had." I'm lying. We haven't shared everything, and I know it. "You're talking about Joe."

"My heart broke too when he died."

"I know." Jack takes my hand.

"And it's still broken. I've felt ready to talk about it, but you seem distant so I give up. The only time you dealt with it, with me, was at the cemetery last Christmas. And I had so much hope that it was the beginning of a new time for us. I felt like maybe you were going to share with me. Grieve with me. But that one day came and went, and that was it." Jack lets go of my hand.

"You shouldn't attack me for the way I handled our son's death. That's not fair."

"I'm not attacking you," he says quietly.

"There isn't a manual out there that tells you how to handle your child's death. Even other parents who went through this, the ones I talked to, couldn't help me. Us. I didn't handle it well. But how do you handle something like that well? Is it even possible?"

Jack Mac looks at me. He closes his eyes to think for a moment, then he opens them and looks at me. "I know he came through your body, and that's something I could never understand, but you pushed me away."

"I didn't mean to."

"Let's be clear. You did mean to. You think that there's only one person in the world who can do things right, and that's you. You've never really trusted me." I start to object, and he interrupts me. "You don't think I'm capable of taking care of our family, of you. In some way, you think that I'm not up to the task. Now, maybe you'd be that way with any man, but I only know how you are with me. And you can flit around here and smile and pretend that everything is fine, but you and I know the truth. Underneath this perfectly nice surface is a lie. I really believed in us, and you never did. It's unrequited love. I love a woman, you, who doesn't love me in the same way. A thinking man would end it all right here. A thinking man would just say, 'It's over.' But I have always let my heart rule my head. I think you need to take the summer to think about what you want to do. And I need the time to think about what I want to do. And I say we talk after you come back from Italy and we decide how we're going to proceed."

"You want a . . ." I can't, won't, say the word "divorce."

"I didn't say that. I want you to think about what you want. You may decide that you don't want to be married to me anymore."

"And you're willing to take that chance?"

He shrugs. "I can't live like this."

I look at Jack MacChesney, and he is in pain. He doesn't want to say these things. He doesn't want to believe them, yet he knows that they are true. I am not really here. When we got married, I thought happiness would come naturally. I thought he could fill me up in the way that love fills people in storybooks. I thought passion would rule us, that love would overcome any problem we had, that love itself was communication. But it's not. I haven't worked on this. I'm afraid to tell him that I don't know how. And where would I learn it at this late date? He is unhappy. I am not the woman he thought I was. I have turned out to be a disappointment to him. Remote. Private. Unwilling to share. I know myself well. I've always been able to take care of people and call it work. But the real work is being honest. The real work is admitting that what I came from had a deeper effect on me than I knew. That when our son died, it was worse for me. Maybe it wasn't, but that was what I felt. Maybe I believe that mothers are more important than fathers, and Jack sensed that. Sensed it? He downright laid it out plain for me. He has given this a lot of thought. He thinks about this all the time. How much time in a given day do I think about him in this way, if ever? I usually think about him in terms of myself. I do things for him, sure. But I do them because I'm supposed to, out of duty. The same way my mother did things. If the home was orderly and the meals were prepared, she'd provided stability. But my husband doesn't want stability. He wants a real partner. Someone who is going to dig down deep and work things through with him. I have failed him. I need to own up to it.

"Jack MacChesney." I whistle low and long.

He looks at me and smiles.

"Lordy mercy. I hear what you're saying." I collapse on the chair.

"Don't kid around."

"I'm not kidding around. And it doesn't matter if I agree with everything you've said, which, by the way, I don't. It's how you feel. And I honor that."

"Thank you."

"I'm not going to cut you loose."

"Ave?"

"What?" I sound annoyed when I say this, but come on, how much more am I supposed to take?

"Don't stay in this marriage for me. Do what is right for you."

"Okay. But I want to tell you something. And it's not to dump guilt on you in any way. But I was looking forward to being together in Italy, like we were on our honeymoon. I was hoping that this trip would be a new start for us. I just want you to know that I know you're not happy. And I wanted to change that."

Jack comes to me and puts his arms around me. "We can't go back to a magic place and hope it fixes us. It don't work that way, baby," he says simply, then he kisses my neck.

"As long as there's one spark here, just one, maybe we can make it work," he says to me. I smile at him, then I bury my head in his shoulder. One spark. My marriage rests on the notion of one spark. What a delicate, tiny, insignificant little thing. A spark. One glint of light. Is that enough to see with?

Etta walks between Jack and me, holding our hands as we walk through Tri-Cities Airport. When we get to the gate, Jack hugs Etta for a long time.

"Etta, wait for me by the door," I tell her.

"Okay, Dad, that's enough," Etta says as she gives her father a final hug. She adjusts her backpack and goes to wait for me.

"Jack. Look at me." My husband looks at me. His eyes are full of pain. I can see that he is torn, that he would like to go with us. But he too has a plan, and he is sticking with it.

"Not here," he says softly.

"No, I have to say something to you. You told me last night that you want me to decide if I want to be married to you. And I promised you that I would think about it while I was in Italy, so I will. But I want you to understand something. I may always be, I don't know . . . awkward. Maybe I didn't leave that spinster behind when we got married. I don't know. Maybe I don't express the love I feel the way I should. And maybe I don't know how to love you like you need to be loved. But I believe that even with all my shortcomings, and there are many, I am still the right woman for you. Please wait for me. I think I deserve another chance." And with that, I kiss my husband on the cheek. I hoist my duffel bag on my back and join Etta by the gate. I hand the tickets to the nice man by the door, and we follow the other passengers to the puddle-jumper plane, then climb the steps. When we get to the top step, Etta turns around and waves to her daddy.

"Mommy, wave."

"You wave for me, honey." I can't look back. I won't.

My daughter's sadness at Jack's absence gives way to the excitement of international travel in a matter of minutes. Our flight from Tri-Cities connects into Charlotte, North Carolina, we make a quick change, and head on to John F. Kennedy Airport in New York. Etta is shocked at how many people race through JFK from one terminal to another. "Mama, they look like ants!" she says, pointing to the crowd of travelers, which surges at a central point where the international terminal merges into one big space. "Stay with me," I tell my daughter cheerfully. She latches her finger on to my belt loop lightly as we walk through the throng. I'm excited by the hub of activity too. I love the way the airport smells: of soap and leather and perfume from the duty-free shop. This is just what we needed, I think as I look down at Etta.

Everything about the transatlantic plane ride enthralls her: the pretty flight attendants with their long, shiny taupe nails and perfect haircuts; the Coke in small glass bottles on her seat-back tray; the kit of amenities, including navy blue cotton booties with Italian flags embossed on them. Etta sheds her small-town, Blue Ridge Mountain reserve and sits high in her seat. She is not missing one detail of this flight. How thrilled she is when they bring her dinner in courses.

"Mama, why is it so black out there?"

"That's the ocean underneath us."

"But shouldn't there be ships with lights on them?"

"I don't think ships come out this far."

"If we crash, would anyone know?"

"Let's not think about crashes."

"We better not crash. What would Daddy do?"

"We won't crash."

"Daddy told me to be careful."

"He did?"

"He told me that you and me were his life. And that I was to watch out for you and make sure that you had a good time."

"You and Daddy talk about me?"

"There's only the three of us," Etta says, looking off down the aisle as though I am the biggest idiot in the world. Maybe I am.

Milan is a city of crisp vertical stripes, navy blue, gray, and black. Everything here is angular, from the architecture to the bone structure on the serious faces that brush past us. Even the Milanese bodies are simple and spare and thin; no Sophia Lorens here. No curves. Just straight, lean, no-nonsense shapes. Etta and I, in our cotton and denim, stick out like American tourists. (Forget that we actually *are* American tourists, we just don't want to look like it.) So before we board the train for Bergamo (there is one every hour), I take Etta into a small women's clothing shop. Lightweight wool trousers, navy blue with a flat placket and straight legs, a white cotton blouse with a gold hook and catch at the collar, and a beige cardigan are exactly what I'm looking for. I am not getting on that train with this Italian face in these American clothes. I need a uniform. And here it is. Etta thinks I'm nuts. My daughter likes her American jeans just fine and has no need to be anything but a MacChesney from Virginia, U.S.A.

As the train clicks north through the Italian countryside, low mossy hills of a deep green so rich it's almost midnight blue give way to a deep and endless pink skyline, and I am amazed at how quickly we leave modern Milan behind. Soon the world chugging past turns ancient, untouched. The sun hangs low and golden, resting on peach clouds just like it does in Tiepolo's painting on our guidebook.

I look down at Etta, who gazes out the window with an expression of wonder. I've seen that expression before, on her father's face. God, she looks just like him. Even if I wanted to leave Jack Mac behind in the mountains of Virginia, I can't. As long as she is with me, her father is here too. She is so much like Jack, even though my friends say she is just like me. She is so steady and true. Even if you hurt her feelings, she forgives you and doesn't seem to store up grudges. That's not to say she doesn't suffer; she does. She feels things deeply. But like her father, she doesn't like to linger too long on things that hurt her. There is no victim in my daughter. She is wide open and yet very private. I fold my arms across my chest and lean back, placing my legs on the seat across from us. I look down at my long legs; I could work a farm here.

A man passes by our glass-enclosed car and peeks in. He drinks me in from the tip of my toes to the top of my head and then looks into my eyes. His brown hair and mustache make him seem young, but he is around fifty. He winks at me. I smile politely, quickly look away, and sit up. I grip my knees with my hands, wedding-ring-side up. He couldn't care less about the ring; I shoot him a look that he should move on. He does.

As our train chugs into Bergamo, Etta stands in awe. I have told her the story of my honeymoon many times, and how I felt when I first saw this place, my mother's hometown in all its detail: the carved wooden bench at the train station, the fountain of angels, and my first ride on cobblestone streets. How the air smells like clean straw and lemongrass.

Etta presses her face against the window, knowing that in seconds she will be with Nonno; at last she will meet her great-grandmother (to whom she has written letters since she could write); all her cousins; and of course my mother's people, the divine Vilminores of Bergamo. I have shown her pictures of them many times, and she starts rattling off things she remembers. Some of the first words she learned were their names from the "flash cards" we made of our honeymoon pictures. Etta wants to visit the magical Alta Città and see the priests in their wide-brimmed black hats and cassocks, and the post where my grandfather used to hook his donkey named Cipi and his old wooden wagon before he made deliveries up into the Alps. I want to stand and jump up and down like she is, but suddenly, I see Joe's face as he lay dying, and I cannot be happy. Quickly, I erase the picture. I'm a terrible mother. I don't focus. Focus on Etta. She's alive and well and thrilled to see Italy. Don't think about all the things you didn't do for Joe. Don't think about how he would love this train. Don't think about how you made him frozen waffles in the toaster instead of fresh pancakes on the stove. He's gone. Etta is here. Focus on Etta.

Carefully, I pull our luggage off of the wooden rack above our seats as Etta smoothes her hair. Even the luggage racks in the Italian train cars are works of art. The lush cherry wood is curved and polished smooth. Etta runs for the steps to the platform and stops short of hopping off, turning around to wait for me. My father greets us at the foot of the stairs. He pulls Etta off the steps like he's gathered a bunch of flowers and swings her around the platform. How youthful and strong he is, though his hair has more white in it now. His eyes, a clear, dark brown, dazzle against his golden skin. I feel instantly safe around him. He wears black pants (the cuffs hit his gray suede loafers in a perfect crease) and a gray cashmere pullover sweater. Papa puts Etta down and embraces me.

"How was your trip?"

"Glorious."

"You're tired."

"A little."

"I want you to meet Giacomina." My father turns to find the woman in his life. She is a few steps behind him, smiling, with her hands clasped in anticipation. Trim and small with clear gray eyes, she has a simple beauty and thick, straight brown hair that she wears in a ponytail. Her lips are full and even, her teeth white and perfectly shaped. She has a small, delicate nose with a narrow bridge. She is dressed like the Milan version of me, except she's in beige from head to foot. In English, her name is Jacqueline—it suits her.

"Ave Maria, we are so happy you're here."

"I've heard wonderful things about you."

"Thank you. I feel as though I know you. Your father talks about you all the time." Giacomina loads my bags onto her shoulders and arms without wrinkling her silk blouse.

"Where is Jack?" Papa wants to know.

"He had too much work."

"He needs a rest, though."

"Yes, he does. But you can't tell my husband anything." I say this all so gaily that my father looks at me curiously.

"The Vilminores are expecting us at Via Davide."

Etta shrieks at the mention of Via Davide, Mama's family homestead on the side street. She has heard all about the poofy beds and the hard biscuits and coffee with sweet, hot milk for breakfast. She wants to see the tiny handmade chocolates on a silver plate that Zia Antonietta left on our pillows each night.

"Giacomina and I will stay in her apartment nearby. You and Etta will stay with Meoli. Sound good?"

"Sounds great."

"When I told her you were coming, Meoli didn't want to wait until after you stayed in Schilpario. She wanted you first. Very bossy." Papa clucks. "But I don't argue."

"Schilpario will be there tomorrow," Giacomina says, and smiles.

Via Davide has not changed. The houses are close together and painted soft corals and blues. Long shutters flap against the houses in the breeze. Small, shiny cars are parked on the street.

"It's just like the postcards," Etta exclaims.

When we get to Zia Meoli's house, I jump out of the car and race for the front door. Zia Meoli, in a simple navy blue pocodotte shirt-waist dress, greets us. Her beautiful black hair is streaked with white, and she wears shiny gold hoop earrings. Her daughter, Federica, joins her at the door, wearing jeans and a T-shirt, her red hair a mop of curls and her brown eyes crinkled at the corners. Zio Pietro walks around from the side yard, having heard our noisy reunion. He brushes his thick white hair from his forehead, takes a final drag off his cigarette and tosses it into a rosebush. When I introduce Etta to them, they fuss over her like a new toy. They feel as though they know her from my letters; I am so glad that I write to my family here regularly. It's as though they live an hour, not an ocean, away. We have a bond that connects us at the soul; we don't have to be neighbors. Zia Meoli touches Etta's hair and her face and holds her hands, examining them, all the while shooting questions in all manner of Italian—fast, slow, dialect—and broken English.

"She looks like her papa," Zio Pietro decides.

"I think so too," Zia Meoli agrees.

"Where is Zia Antonietta hiding?" I ask my aunt.

"Oh, Ave Maria. I'm sorry." Zia Meoli looks down. Her face assumes the expression of grief that I know so well. "She passed away last month."

"No!" I take Zia Meoli's hand.

"She knew you were coming, and she tried so hard to stay. But she was very sick for a long, long time."

"I'm sorry." I had a deep connection with Zia Antonietta, Meoli's twin. She never married, so the chores of housekeeping and managing the family home fell to her. That is the way it goes in Italy. The one without the husband takes care of the group. Meoli's children were Antonietta's life, and she spent it taking care of them. She wasn't sad or bitter about it, though. It was as if she was only happy to have a role, an important role, in her family and in serving them. Zia

Antonietta had been in love once, and her true love died. So she accepted fate and, instead of having her own family, invested herself in her sister's. Zia Antonietta was the most unselfish person I know.

"Come. Let's eat," Zia Meoli says. I explain that Jack could not come because of work. Zio Pietro, in particular, is sad about that. He has a woodworking shop and wanted to show Jack a sideboard he made himself. (I have to remember to tell Jack this.)

The parlor is just as it was when I came here on my honeymoon. The walls are eggshell white; the rug on the floor is a simple tapestry of gold and sage green, and it looks like there's a needlepoint tree woven in the center of it. The furniture is sleek and low and dark wood, Italian from the 1930s. A rocker, painted black with gold swirls, sits in the alcove between the windows. The fireplace is full of wood, waiting for winter. The kindling next to the mantel is tied in a bundle with a white velvet bow. The windows have no shades, only long panels of ecru lace. (The shutters close out light and noise when need be.) The mantel is crowded with framed photographs, some as old as the turn of the century, others new. The faces of my mother's family give me a sense of belonging, a point of origin. Right here. In this room. In the old black-and-white photographs, the expressions are stern; as the years pass and the pictures turn to color, the mood lifts.

If only my mother could have been a part of these new days, not the old times, when a daughter would shame her family by choosing a man they didn't approve of. I would have had my parents together. My mother never would have fled and come to America, pregnant with me. And she wouldn't have had to marry Fred Mulligan. How different our lives would have been! There are several framed pictures of Etta and Joe. This moves me. I feel that we are a part of their daily lives, even though we rarely visit.

On the screened-in porch off the kitchen, where there is a cool breeze, Zia Meoli has set the table with white linen and white dishes. In the center of the table, a cluster of delicate gardenias float in a crystal bowl. Zia directs my father to the head of the table, her husband to the other. We fill in around the men.

"Madame Vilminore?" a voice says from the doorway.

"Ciao, Stefano. Come. Sit. Eat with us," she says to him. Stefano comes out onto the porch. He's around fourteen, with brown eyes, small half-moons that disappear when he smiles. His hair is thick and unruly but beautiful: gold curls that spiral into tight corkscrew ringlets. He has a broad nose, the tip of which lifts up ever so slightly. It's a big nose, but it suits his face. He walks with his hands in his pockets, more self-effacing than shy.

"I'm Ave Maria. And this is my daughter, Etta," I tell him. He smiles at us. I hear Etta gasp. Her eyes widen ever so slightly. (Oh, no. Here we go—puberty.)

Stefano takes a seat next to Etta, who is thrilled to have A Boy sitting next to her at her very first sit-down meal in the country of Italy. And I can't blame her. He is really cute.

"I speak English," Stefano says proudly.

"Where did you learn it?" I ask him.

"School. I must learn English so I can come to America and make a lot of money," he announces.

My father laughs. "Did they tell you the streets were paved with gold?"

"Yes. Paved with gold, and you ride on them in gold Cadillacs. But I like a Ford truck better."

"Then you would like my husband. He has a Ford pickup truck," I say.

"What color?"

"Bright red," Etta pipes up, happy to have something to add.

"I like red." Stefano breaks off the end of the hard-crusted bread Zia has placed by his plate.

"Stefano is a good worker. He helps me in the shop," Zio tells us.

Zia Meoli explains that Stefano is an orphan who lives up the street in a boys' school. Evidently, orphanages aren't sad in Italy. Stefano paints a picture of a happy place, with good friends and nice rooms. I have to remember to ask Meoli later if this is true. Stefano sips the Chianti my uncle has poured.

"You drink wine?" Etta asks him, unnerved at the idea.

"Every day. What do you drink in America?"

"Milk. Pop."

"What's pop?"

"Soda pop."

"Coca-Cola?" Stefano guesses.

"Yes!" Etta says, thrilled to break through the language barrier.

"Maybe someday I try to come to America and drink your soda pop."

"Anytime, Stefano," I tell him. Etta nods in agreement.

Zia Meoli leans in. "He was Antonietta's favorite. Since she died, he's come here every day."

"You were good friends with my aunt?" I ask Stefano.

"Sí. Yes. Yes."

"What did you like about her?"

"She yelled at me all the time."

"Good preparation for marriage." Zio winks.

"Zia Antonietta didn't yell," I tell Stefano.

"Only at me. She wanted me to cut my hair." Stefano shrugs.

"That's a woman for you. Always trying to change the man," Zio says.

Zia Meoli shoots him a look. But I think about Jack, and how I'm constantly trying to change him. Did I insult him when I suggested he go to college and study engineering? I said it only because I think Jack is smart and could be a great engineer. I remember something Nellie Goodloe said to me when she found out I was to marry Jack Mac. She told me that Jack and I were very different: I ran a business and my husband was a miner—how could that work? But I laughed it off at the time. I thought I knew what I was getting into; I thought I could handle our differences. Aren't all marriages a battle of wills and a compromise of different backgrounds?

"*E vero?*" Zio looks at me.

"Yes, you're right. It's true. It's true," I tell my uncle.

We feast on delicate ravioli filled with leeks and tossed in creamy butter and shallots. The bread and butter and wine is a meal in itself, but the ravioli are so tender, they're irresistible. The breeze, filled with sweet gardenia, makes everything taste delicious.

Federica shows us to our room after lunch. It's my mother's room, the very room that Jack and I stayed in on our honeymoon. Federica has pulled out the trundle for Etta. Etta pokes at the bed piled high with fresh linens and blankets and pillows full of soft goose down.

"Mama, the coverlet is full of marshmallows!"

"Wait till you sleep on it."

"Sleep now," Federica tells us. We're ready for a nap, ready to follow any orders given us on Via Davide. She closes the door softly behind her as she goes.

I help Etta into the trundle. "Can we get me one of these back home?" she asks.

"We'll see." I climb up onto the bed.

Etta sighs. "I love Italy."

I lean over the side of the bed so I can see Etta. "You do?"

"It's not like anywhere I've ever been."

"Honey, you've only been to Tennessee and Florida."

"I know. But I didn't think it would be like this."

"That's how I felt when I first came here."

"Mama?"

"Yeah?"

"Someday I'm going to marry Stefano."

I'm glad I'm in the big bed up high, where my daughter can't see me, because my jaw is on my chest. Instead of laughing, I take a deep breath.

"You are?"

"Yes."

"How do you know that?"

"I just do."

I wait for Etta to tell me more, but she doesn't. She falls asleep, no doubt to dream of the cute Italian boy with the crazy hair. Part of me wants to wake her up and tell her to stay a little girl forever. I have to remember to tell her that love is not enough. Don't be like your mother and your grandmother whose name you share. Do better.

After a day of touring Bergamo, meeting neighbors, and going out to dinner, Etta sees *la passeggiata* for the first time. Folks leave their homes to walk around the fountain in the middle of town until the sun sets. Not much happens. Just conversation. A few laughs. Card games. Chess. Checkers. Or they simply stroll and catch up. Etta is invited to play pick-up sticks with some kids from across Via Davide. Papa and Giacomina know lots of people in town, so they walk about and greet their friends.

Zia Meoli finds a place for us on a bench under the fountain, so I can keep an eye on Etta.

"What do you think of her?" Zia Meoli points across the piazza to Giacomina and Papa, who are talking in a small group.

"Giacomina is very nice," I tell her.

"Too young for him," she says.

"At least he's settling down."

"We shall see." She shrugs.

I am happy for my father. He seems content with Giacomina. She fits into his life perfectly. She owns a shop in Schilpario that sells ski equipment. My father likes the fact that she can turn a key in the front door and close the place in a flash. He likes to pick up and do things.

"We're sorry Jack could not come," Zia Meoli says.

"I am too. I wish he could see Etta's face. She loves it here already."

"She's a beautiful girl," she says sincerely.

"Thank you."

"I am sorry we never met Joe."

"I know. I always intended to bring him here."

"What was his funeral like?" my aunt asks me.

In most countries, this would be a strange question, but in Italy, a funeral is an art form. It is the last public gathering to honor a life, and therefore, it must tell the story of that life. So there are prayers and music and speeches. They even take pictures of the deceased in the casket and make copies for all to have after the funeral. It sounds macabre, and maybe it is, but it is also tradition. When Zia Meoli asks me about Joe's funeral, she isn't trying to upset me, she just wants to know.

"It was very simple. No wake. Just a Mass and burial. His friends from school came. You know that Papa came too."

Zia Meoli sits quietly as I play the morning of Joe's funeral over in my mind. And then I remember something I haven't thought about, not during the funeral and not since.

"Remember the story of Aunt Alice Lambert?"

Zia Meoli nods and makes a gesture that indicates Alice was not a nice person. I had written to her about how Alice Mulligan Lambert tried to take the Pharmacy and house away from me.

"I just remembered something. Alice Lambert came to Joe's funeral. She was sitting in the back row on the aisle, and at the end, when we were processing out of the church, I looked down at her, and I guess I looked surprised. She was the last person I expected to see at my son's funeral. But she looked me square in the eye and said she was sorry. And that was it."

"How strange that she came at all," Zia Meoli muses.

"I know. And how funny that I didn't remember it until now."

This happened to me the last time I was in Italy. I remembered details, moments, that for some reason never crossed my mind in Big Stone Gap. When I came here the first time, I was able to see my life from a different perspective. It's as though I left myself at home in the mountains of Virginia and invented this new person to have Italian adventures abroad. I can't do that now. This time I'm on assignment, and the job is to write the plan for the second half of my life. I'm not going to be able to invent it as I go along, because Jack won't let me. He wants to know where I stand. I'm not here on vacation, and every now and then, a pain shoots through my gut to remind me of that fact. I have to make a decision. Sometimes, when I think of my husband, I get butterflies; a surge of emotion goes through me, and I long for him. Other times, I'm glad he's home, where I don't have to deal with the sadness and the stress of us. This makes me feel selfish, and I hate to admit that I haven't lived my life generously. I've sold myself on the idea that I am a magnanimous person, but it was false advertising. I always do what's good for me—what makes me comfortable—and then I dictate to my family how things will go down. Usually, they play right along. I keep telling my relatives that I wish my husband were here too. But Papa could see that I was lying when I said Jack was too busy to get away. So maybe there's another element to my summer in Italy. This is the summer I tell the truth. I will begin with Zia Meoli.

"Jack wanted me to come alone with Etta."

"Why?"

"We're having problems." There. I said it. That's not so hard.

"I am sorry."

"You don't have marital problems here in Italy, do you? The love center of the universe." I wave my hand in front of me—every age of love is in the piazza: teenage lovers speed by on their motorbikes; a young wife splashes her husband as he passes the fountain; an older gentleman buys his wife gelato. Tonight, it seems, everyone is in love in Bergamo.

Zia Meoli throws back her head and laughs. "Yes, we have problems. Lots of problems."

"Well, you're spoiling my romantic notions, but I guess that actually makes me feel better."

"Problems can be good. You solve them, and they bring you back together again."

"That would be nice."

"You've had a lot to cope with. Sometimes you take things out on each other. No?"

"I guess."

"I have a friend who got a divorce. Here in Italy, that is rare. But she was unhappy, so she divorced him. She married a new man, a very nice man. And she told me that she thought she left the problems from the first marriage in the past. But it turned out that she packed them up and took them with her into the second marriage. Sometimes it's not them. Sometimes it's you."

"Oh," I say, "I know it's me."

"Don't worry."

"All I do is worry."

"You are just like your mother."

"I am?"

"She thought love was enough."

She's right. I did think love was enough. Until my husband told me it wasn't. I am like my mother in so many ways. She invested herself in me, all of her time, all of her care. I'm sure Fred Mulligan knew that. Mama kept a beautiful home and made good meals, but she didn't love her husband. Her marriage was a safe place to raise me. I wanted so much more for Etta. But how do I change? It seems I always slide back on my bad habits, my repression, my cold core, so I don't get hurt. But I am hurting everyone around me. Just like my mother did. Fred Mulligan didn't feel her love, she saved it all for me. But it hurt me to see her hurting Fred, even though I didn't like him and he surely didn't like me. But whose fault was that? I didn't have a chance with Fred because I was the obstacle to his happiness. And Mama put me there. A marriage based upon financial security and social acceptability is not what I want for my family, yet isn't that what I have? Am I my mother?

Meoli pats me on the hand, and we get up to stroll in the piazza. The night air is chilly, and I shiver. The sound of the water spilling over the marble seashells in the fountain makes soft music as we walk. The lights above us in Alta Città are dim lavender sparks behind the black trees. I am glad the sun is sinking low behind the hills of Bergamo—I don't want Zia Meoli to see me cry.

*W*ith Papa at the wheel, we take the curve up the mountain road, out of Bergamo, north to Schilpario. Once again I am in the mountains; whether it's the Italian Alps or the Appalachians, it seems I can't escape them. As we speed up into the peaks, I am not afraid, as I was on my first visit. I look at Etta, who doesn't flinch as we climb higher and higher or even when trucks whip past us and force us over to the gravel edge of the road, our wheels inches away from the perilous edge above gaps several miles deep. I guess my kid is an old pro, having flown around the curves of Cracker's Neck Holler all of her life.

"Aren't these mountains different from ours back home?" I ask Etta, and point to the Alps.

"They're taller. And they have snow on them in the summer," she says, sounding impressed.

"Yep, they're so high up there, it stays cold and never melts."

Giacomina, strapped in by her seat belt, turns as best she can from the front seat. "We're going to take you to lots of places."

"Do you have goats?" Etta asks Giacomina.

"Many goats."

"I went to Mary Ann Davis's farm in East Stone Gap, and she had miniature goats. Do you have those?"

"We do. And they all wear bells. So when they get lost, the goatherd can find them."

"Just like Peter in *Heidi*! I love *Heidi*!"

"Etta, I will make you wear a bell!" Papa says, winking at her in the rearview mirror.

As we drive into Schilpario, for the first time in a hundred miles, Papa slows down. He has been the mayor of this village for nearly forty years. The houses with their dark beams set off by white stucco, others painted shades of pale blue and taupe and soft green, look like candy tiles glued into the rocky mountainside. Window boxes spill over with small purple blossoms and spikes of green plants I have never seen before. "Herbs," Giacomina tells me.

Etta is thrilled by the waterwheel chugging slowly around in a circle, scooping the crystal water from the stream and sending it flowing over the slats of the old wood, polished smooth from wear. I point to the stream that rushes down the mountain over clean gray stones, then widens and makes a pond next to the cabin by the waterwheel. I show her how everything is connected; I think she understands.

Nonna is waiting on a swing in the patch of grass between the street and the front door of her house when we pull up. (Nonna and Papa's home is dead center on Main Street, the perfect spot for the mayor.) She pulls herself up with a cane and opens one arm to Etta, who runs to meet her great-grandmother. Nonna's body, thick through the middle with short muscular legs, is as hearty as it was when I first met her. She is instantly in love with Etta, whom she spins around like a top, checking her out from every angle. My grandmother is as sharp as she was the day she entered my house on Poplar Hill in the Gap. I have to remember to ask Papa how old she is, because she hasn't changed a bit. What's her secret?

Mafalda, my father's first cousin, is around fifty, petite with a sweet, round face, clear, pink skin, small lips, and the trademark Barbari nose. She is bustling around the kitchen, setting the table for supper. She takes orders from my grandmother without complaint. That's just the way things are in Italy; I never hear anyone arguing with their elders. (I hope Etta makes a note of this!) Nonna runs this homestead like a general, and for her size, she packs more punch than the Italian army. Etta can't believe how loud she is, how she barks orders and seems to get angry, which then passes over like a storm cloud dissipating into mist before it can explode. My grandmother grabs Etta, hugs her, and rubs her cheeks at every opportunity. She promises to teach Etta everything about life in Schilpario—the cooking, the manners, and the family history. I have a feeling Etta will be a good student. Nonna wouldn't have it any other way.

Giacomina wasn't kidding when she told us that she has lots of plans. She brings out a calendar, and the days are full of trips and activities. She tells me when Etta leaves the room that these trips are especially for Etta, not for me. Papa wants me to rest. Only my father can see what I truly need (isn't that true of all parents?).

Nonna treats my father like a king. He is the boss, his every whim indulged. Mafalda tells me Papa has lots of company, "town business," men from Bergamo who come north with ideas for local trade. Something is always going on with Papa. He may disappear at a moment's notice, without explanation. When he returns hours later, he'll simply tell you he got caught up in a conversation. Mafalda tells me she has learned never to set the table until she sees his hat on the hook.

Papa takes us upstairs and shows Etta her own bedroom, a small, charming room with a balcony on the front and a sloped ceiling. A hand-painted yellow daybed piled high with goose-feather pillows (those poofs!) fits neatly under the eave. There is a long pillow shaped like a sausage and tied at the ends with ribbon like a hard candy. Etta holds it up and shows it to me. She's never seen one like it before. There is a trunk, an old rocker with another blanket on it, and a vase full of edelweiss that climbs out of a small silver flute. Etta loves the walls, painted beige, with the dark brown beams on the ceiling.

"Mama, don't the beams on the ceiling look like Little Debbie Snack Cakes?" She points overhead.

"They do." I laugh.

"Everything in this house looks like something to eat. Like Hansel and Gretel's house."

"You know something? You're right."

"Why?"

"Well, we're so far north in Italy, it's almost Switzerland. So you have that Tyrolean look to everything."

"What's that?"

"It's like a cuckoo clock. Gingerbread roof. Windows with shutters. Low ceilings to keep it warm and cozy in the cold. And round-topped doorways. Do you like it here?"

"I love it. I just wish Daddy was here."

I unpack Etta's things as she dresses for bed. She says her prayers and climbs under the covers. A cold breeze flaps the shutter open. I go to the window and look down on the narrow main street of Schilpario, lit only by the light that pours out of the houses in soft pools. An old man carrying a box shuffles up the street and disappears into a doorway. I can smell the tobacco from his pipe as he goes past.

On the horizon I see a rim of clouds, but I realize that they are actually the mountains' snow-covered tips, lit by the moon. The sugary caps are so close, I could lean out this little window and touch them. My face is cool from the breeze; it feels good, but I don't want Etta to catch cold, so I unfold the shutter and hook it against the frame.

I go downstairs; Mafalda is preparing the table for breakfast, Nonna has gone to bed, and Papa is watching television. I go into my father's office and pick up the phone. It's the wee hours of the morning in Big Stone Gap. As I dial our home phone number, I cannot wait for Jack to pick up. I want to tell him about our trip. The phone rings a few times, but Jack Mac is a deep sleeper. I let it ring again. And again. I count the rings. It rings thirteen times. I hang up the phone. Maybe . . . *he's not there?* Of course he's there. Where else would he be? I am not going to make too much out of this. I'm an ocean away, and there's nothing I can do. I'll try again tomorrow.

Etta is off to Sestri Levante, an old fishing village on the coast of the glorious Mediterranean. Papa's first cousins live there and want to meet Etta. The Bonicellis have a candy shop and a house on the beach. Nonna's sister has a ten-year-old granddaughter, Chiara. The girls introduced themselves to each other on the phone. Papa and Giacomina are taking her; they'll stay the weekend and get some sun. *"Bronzata,"* Papa calls it.

Mafalda lets me sleep late every morning. The only job I have is to write long letters to Theodore and Iva Lou, describing everything. I collect local postcards to send to Iva Lou. I know she'll tape them to the dashboard of the Bookmobile. I'm sending Theodore a bell for his front door—it's a small hand-painted brass bell on an embroidered rope. (Maybe next summer Theodore can come with me and see Italy for himself.) I can't believe we've been here almost a week. I'm finally feeling rested. The food makes me feel sturdy. The fragrant risottos made with saffron and sweet butter; the fresh berries drizzled in honey and served cold in sterling silver cups; and the bread, spongy and light inside, with chewy, hard crust (it's so delicious, I don't even put butter on it).

I've decided that my body could use some attention; I've neglected myself for too long. So during siesta, instead of sleeping, I climb the steep hills behind Schilpario alone. The mountain paths, worn from time, creep up through the green in all directions. I vow that by the end of the month, I will have followed most of them. Whenever I climb, I think of my mother, who loved these mountains with their emerald green fields, dangerous cliffs, and cold streams.

Today the mountain breeze is especially cool, so I borrow one of my father's soft leather car coats and wrap a red bandanna around my neck. Maybe it's just looking up at the snowcaps that makes me shiver. The sun is warm, but the ground is always cold to the touch. (I don't think the Italian Alps have ever had a good thaw.) I opt not to wear Papa's hat, one of those Robin Hood numbers: dark green felt with a feather in it. Besides, I don't want to mess up my new hair.

Yesterday Mafalda took me to the next village, Piccolo Lago, where I got a haircut. The sign in the window said MODERNA. I think "Modern" is a nutty name for anything in these parts. Everything should be called "Antica." I hadn't had a real haircut in years; I still wore it in a braid up and off of my face. Jack always liked my hair long, so I never changed it, and pulling it back is so easy. But I've needed a change for a long time. Don't I always notice women who get stuck in beauty ruts? So when Violetta, a tall blond Italian with a heavy dose of German no-nonsense in her accent, sat me down and told me to throw my head forward, I obeyed. I watched as glops of my old brown curls hit the black-and-white-checked linoleum like lengths of ribbon. When Violetta was done, she told me to sit up straight (you do whatever she tells you and fast), and the girls in the shop gathered around my chair. "Gina Lollobrigida," Violetta said and smiled, taking full credit for transforming the mouse into a va-va-voom. The other girls agreed as Violetta spun me around like a Cadillac at a car show.

The new hairdo accentuates my face. The long, boring braid is gone; this is full and thick and much shorter, with loose waves that soften my cheeks and nose, and long, delicate spiraling down my neck. One of the shop girls, a birdlike brunette with perfect lips, took a tube of lipstick out of her apron pocket. At first I was clumsy with it, so she had to unscrew the Italian top for me (different from our lipsticks, there's a latch on it). I put on the lipstick, filling out my full lips top and bottom, and my first thought was that it was too much. Too dramatic. Too purple! I felt like I was sporting a duck bill. But Violetta handed me a tissue, and after I blotted, the magenta with the little gold sparkles in it actually looked alluring. *"Bellisima!"* a customer under the dryer said, banging her head as she strained to get a look at me. I smiled and gave all the girls big tips. If I had a million dollars, I would have given it to Violetta. I needed this.

Nonna flipped for the haircut; she said, "Ornella Muti!" when I came into the house. Ornella, a Roman actress, is featured on the cover of this month's *Hello!* magazine, which has claimed a permanent spot on Nonna's coffee table. She grabbed it and pointed to the exotic green-eyed beauty, who, yes, has my haircut. Or more to the point, I have her haircut. I made Nonna take a Polaroid of me and my new hair to send to Theodore.

So it is with more than a little renewed self-confidence, a bright lipstick (God bless the kid; she gave me the tube), a new purpose, and a dazzling haircut, that I climb the Alpine trail like the Eye-talian native I would have been if my mother had not run off to America pregnant with me and without my father, Mario da Schilpario, and married Fred Mulligan instead. I look down at my thighs as I use them to power my short, quick steps up the trail. I shouldn't have such muscles in them; I've been climbing around here only a week. But they're there. I never got muscles like these hiking up Powell Mountain. The leather in Papa's coat smells like him, clean and woodsy. I feel great. Maybe it's the altitude.

I decide to take a new path today, the one that's a little more finished-looking than the rest. There are actual stones that anchor either side of the path like a garden walk. At the very top of that trail, there is a plateau that piques my curiosity.

Once I reach the top of the ridge, I have to hoist myself up and over a small shelf of ground to reach the plateau. There, high above Schilpario, in a place where only goats go, is a field of bluebells so thick, they look like a carpet stretching across the expanse. So blue, it could be a lake, or the Mediterranean Sea. Bees buzz above the sweet blossoms, so many of them that they knock into one another in midair before they dive below to drink from the flowers. Beyond the blue carpet is a green field that leads to a ledge of rock dripping with vines. I won't venture out to the edge. I know there is a drop there — probably one of those frightening gaps, so deep you cannot see the bottom. I sit down in the flowers; the only sound is the music the bees make. I think of Mrs. Mac. I must remember to bring Etta up here and tell her about the origin of the middle name that she inherited from her grandmother Nan Bluebell Gilliam MacChesney about the bluebells that bloomed in the field behind our house in Cracker's Neck the day that her grandmother "got born."

When I return from my hike, Giacomina announces that she and Papa are going to take us to a disco tonight. The whole family. (Except for Nonna, who tells me she would rather someone throw her off the mountain than make her go to a disco-tekka. Mafalda thinks Nonna is seventy-nine years old, but isn't exactly sure because Nonna won't fess up.)

Etta is back from Sestri Levante. Papa bought her a turquoise choker, which she vows she'll never take off. It lies flat and clean against her brown skin; her time on the beach brought out her freckles. Giacomina and Papa thought it would be a good idea to bring Chiara back to keep Etta company.

"Hello, Cousin Ave Maria," Chiara says to me, sounding like one of those learn-a-foreign-language-fast tapes.

"Ciao, Chiara." I give her a hug. She's a beauty, with her shiny black hair and wide brown eyes. Chiara is taller than Etta, but just as lean. She wears plastic rings on all of her fingers, a style that Etta has eagerly copied. They look like a couple of five-and-dime Cleopatras.

Then she tells my father in Italian that I am pretty and not too old. I tell my little cousin that she should have seen me before the va-va-voom haircut. Chiara looks at me like I'm crazy.

Chiara is full of mischief. In pictures, she comes off as serene and serious, but in life, her dark eyes constantly dart about, looking for excitement. She is very quick, instantly picking up English phrases from Etta. Etta is doing fine with her Italian too. Chiara is teaching her

Italian curse words, which make my daughter laugh. She is the perfect foil for Etta, who tries to do the right thing even at the expense of fun. But I instantly love my cousin; I want her to help Etta test her limits. Etta needs to loosen up. She needs to run and get dirty and play. I just want them to be careful, but I don't have to worry. Giacomina takes them under her wing like her own little summer charges, and they obey her without question.

As we drive through the mountains, Papa tells Giacomina about town business, something about tourist season come winter. Then, in a split second, he swerves off the main road and through a mass of vines and brush. We bump onto a gravel road that pitches us around like loose fruit. The girls laugh and hang on. Soon we see a clearing with tall lanterns on spikes stuck in the ground around a dance floor of portable linoleum.

I was expecting an indoor disco. When we say "disco" in America, we mean a dance club, a place where you would find John Travolta in an ice-cream suit. But here a disco can be any place there's music. The music, which sounds like Italian covers of American hits, plays out through the black night. Folks are gathered around the bar (a table set up in the field), and the kids are drinking a dark red fizzy drink, which they throw back like shots. "Bitters," Giacomina tells me. There's a crowd. A big crowd. It seems that most of the mountain villages emptied out and came here tonight. Cars are parked haphazardly along the sides of the field.

Chiara acts sophisticated and points out all the particulars to Etta. I can hardly hold on to them as they bolt from the car and head for the dance floor. Papa and Giacomina see friends from town and stop to chat. I whisper in Giacomina's ear that I am going to go exploring.

I love the way Italians look. Maybe it's because I'm relieved that there's a place in this world where I look like somebody. But I find their faces so interesting. I don't know what makes the women so beautiful—you would never see any of them on a magazine cover in

America—but they are striking. Here a strong nose is a source of pride. Most of these noses wouldn't last in America, with their length and their regal breaks in the bridge—they wouldn't be appreciated. Maybe these women are so attractive because they like themselves. They accept what they are born with; even their flaws are a source of pride, the very thing that makes them distinctive and alluring.

The men are beyond handsome. Even when they're short (I guess height is an American thing), they have a strength that makes you believe they could take one of these Alpine boulders and roll it down the hill like a basketball. They live in their skin like kings; their mothers encourage that. A son is a prized possession, more treasured than land or gold. A son means continuity. A son can become a father, and a father is the center of wisdom and policy in the home. I see it in action, in the small pockets surrounding the dance floor. Of course, the men seem to be in charge only because the women let them. Entire families are here together, enjoying the night air and the delicate paper lights and the music. (It reminds me of the Singing Convention held at Bullit Park back in Big Stone Gap. Families come with a picnic basket and stay all day listening to the music.)

"Ave Maria! *Andiamo!*" Chiara says, grabbing one of my hands while my daughter takes the other. They yank me onto the dance floor. Some Italian singer has covered an old American disco standard, and the girls want me to dance with them. At first I don't want to dance. I'm old, I want to tell them. I'm a wife and a mother and a pharmacist. There's no place for me on the dance floor; I have no business moving to the rhythm that makes the floor buckle under the impact of all these feet. But I look at my daughter's face, and she wants me to dance. She seems to be saying, "If you dance, then I can. I want a mother who is happy and free and moves without worrying about what other people think."

And for some reason, on this mountaintop, hidden inside all of these bodies as they sway and bounce, it's okay for me to let go. I feel safe in this place where I am not known. My daughter is with me, and her cousin, but really, I am alone. I'm not married in this moment, and I am not a mother. I took my wedding rings off to collect stones in the stream above Papa's house, and I forgot to put them back on. No, tonight I am Ave Maria Mulligan, the girl I left behind before I decided to give everything away to be simply a part of the Mac-Chesney family. I let the music take me to that place where I was before I knew life could be so complicated.

Chiara and Etta and I have locked arms and are spinning in a circle, laughing. People on the dance floor make room for us. I throw my head back and look at the open sky above. I am connected and at the same time completely free. I am here, in my body, in this moment, but I'm also flying overhead in the inky sky streaked white with stars.

When the song ends (and I'm so sorry it did!), Chiara and Etta giggle and run off to find my father. I breathe deeply; my heart is beating fast. I lean over and rest my palms on my knees. I am hot and winded and sweaty and I like it.

"Ciao," a man's voice says to me. I look up and into an amazing pair of blue eyes.

"Ciao," I say. He extends his hand to me. To be polite, I take it.

He looks as though he is searching for words. And he is. Italian words.

"Uh, *dove e* . . ." I do my best to follow along. In a few broken sentences, he has asked me to dance and to point him to the garage (we're in a field, there is no garage), and inquired as to what village I'm from. I'm getting a kick out of him. He has beautiful hands, which make grand gestures to help me decipher what he's trying to say in Italian.

He is also really handsome. He's tall. And what a face. He reminds me of Rock Hudson in *Pillow Talk*. Maybe it's the dark hair. Or maybe it's the look in his eyes. That's where the movie-star dazzle ends, though; he's pretty trim, but I can see he has to fight a gut. (Who doesn't? Maybe he's a little older than me, but not much.) The chest

is broad; I'll bet he's a runner. He isn't wearing glasses, but I can tell
he wears contact lenses, because he blinks a lot. He has beautiful
white teeth, with the front teeth a little longer than the rest, which is
sexy. He has thin but well-shaped lips (no cruelty there, just practi-
cality in buckets, according to face-reading). The nose is amazing:
straight, a little bulbous on the end (this is the nose of humor and
wisdom—the tip is the giveaway).

"*Non capisce,*" I say to him.

"Okay, okay," he says, more to himself than to me. Frustrated, he
looks off, giving up the Italian. "You're looking at me like I'm nuts.
Okay, maybe I am nuts." I get it: he thinks I'm a native. I feel as
though I won the Nobel Prize, I am so proud of myself! I have passed
for a Bergamosque! The pants, the cardigan, and the haircut have
worked. I appear to be a real Italian through and through! I could kiss
this guy.

"*Sí. Sí.*" I motion that he should continue in English and, with gestures, relay that I am trying to understand him. This is so much fun!

"I saw you dancing with those kids. And well, anyway, I think you're
cute. And I'd like to dance with you. I'm American. I guess you could
tell that from the English I'm speaking. You've got a great face. In fact,
everything is pretty fine on you, to tell you the truth."

"Yes?" I say.

Galvanized that I am making the attempt to communicate, he continues. "So you'll dance with me?"

"*Sí,*" I say slowly, sounding like Gina Lollobrigida in *La Bellezza di
Ippolita.*

The American takes me in his arms and pulls me close, placing his
hand on my waist, a little too low for a stranger. I reach back and put
his hand above my waist. (I'm having fun, I just don't want to have too
much fun.)

As the song ends, he seems to screw up his courage to say, "You
have beautiful eyes."

I try to smile in a way that is enigmatic yet noncommittal.

"Could I take you to dinner sometime? I'm here for another few weeks . . ."

Okay, Ave, game over. Let the nice man off the hook. "I'm married," I tell him in a pure country accent straight out of the Appalachian Mountains.

"Say that again."

"I'm married. Married. And I'm American. I can't do this to you for another second. I'm sorry."

"You're Southern!"

"Uh-huh. Virginia."

"You're just loaded with accents. Can you do Garbo from *Camille*?" I can't tell if he thinks my little game was funny or offensive. "Where in Virginia are you from?"

"Southwest. In the Blue Ridge Mountains. Where they meet the Appalachians. Near the Cumberland Gap." When you're from Big Stone Gap, you always have to overexplain the location. No one ever knows where we are.

"You aren't on the Appalachian Trail, are you?"

"We're right on it. In fact, it runs through our home-ec room at the high school. At least that's what I was told in ninth grade by my home-ec teacher, Mrs. Porier."

"I'm hiking that trail this fall!"

"You are? Well, you'll have to stop in."

I extend my hand to the tall American with the pretty eyes. "My name is Ave Maria Mulligan. I mean, MacChesney."

"You don't know your own last name?"

"I do. I just forgot it for a second. My married name, I mean." I'm so embarrassed. Why am I embarrassed? Why is he laughing in that conspiratorial way? Am I flirting with this man?

"I'm Pete Rutledge."

"Well, it was nice dancing with you." Nice, Ave. Could you sound more awkward?

"Thank you for the dance," he says. We stand and look at each other. I don't want him to go, but I don't want him to stay, either.

"Thank you for saying I was cute," I blurt.

"I meant it."

"I could tell. So thank you." I smile at him as one does when a stranger compliments your car.

He tilts his head and looks at me directly. "How married are you?" he says with a half smile. (And I thought the only wolves in Italy were Italian.)

I don't answer his question, I throw my head back and laugh. I turn to walk away and he grabs my hand.

"How long are you here?" Pete asks, then follows me off the dance floor.

"I'm leaving soon."

"You're lying."

"Yes, I am. But you make me nervous, and I lie compulsively when I'm nervous."

"That's good to know." He smiles.

"I'm here all month. Not here in this village. I'm with my father, over in Schilpario."

"What's his name?"

"Mario Barbari."

Pete leans down and pushes an unruly curl off my cheek. "Will I see you again?"

"No."

Pete laughs. "You're a Play-by-the-Rules girl?"

"You have no idea."

I hustle the girls to bed so I can be alone and think about what happened tonight. Why am I so jazzed, so giddy? I'm a grown woman. I'm acting more like Chiara and Company than the sensible woman I am! I feel guilty for replaying the excitement of Pete Rutledge in my mind, so I go into my father's study and call Jack. The phone rings three times.

"Hello?" he says, groggy with sleep.

"Hi, it's me."

"Ave?" Then he seems to wake up and listen. "Is everything okay? How's Etta?"

"She's great. We went to a disco. And she's made friends with my second cousin Chiara, who's ten. She's here with Etta now." Why am I talking so loud and so fast?

"That all sounds great."

"I missed you tonight. There was dancing."

"There usually is at a disco."

"Right. Right."

"I miss you both too," he says.

"Thanks." I don't mean to be selfish, but can't he just miss me? "Well, I guess that's all the news."

"Yep."

There is a long silence; I guess I'm waiting for him to tell me about his life, but he doesn't volunteer anything, so I don't press. "Sleep well." I hang up the phone. My body is shaking, but it's not chills. I'm happy! A fine-looking stranger thought I was pretty! And I danced with him. And he felt good, and he smelled like mint and clean woods. And he wasn't a local on the make, either, he was an American who thought I was an Italian goddess. I dial Theodore's number.

"Hello?" Theodore answers his phone sleepily. I've woken him up too.

"It's me—Ave."

"Where are you?"

"Schilpario."

"Jesus. What time is it?"

"Early. For you. Late. For me."

"This better be good."

"I danced at a disco tonight."

"Wow," he says with no enthusiasm.

"Don't be rude."

"I can be whatever I want when you wake me up at this hour."

"Sorry. Theodore, there was a man there. Pete Rutledge. He thought I was cute."

"You are cute. You're also married."

"I know. Can you print that on a postcard and send it over to me?"

"I think I'd better." I hear Theodore sit up straight in his bed. Now he's paying attention.

"He thought I was Italian."

"You are Italian."

"No, really Italian. Like from here. Born and raised. I got a haircut."

"I really have to hang up this phone."

"Bear with me, please," I beg him.

"I'm trying."

"When Violetta of the Moderna Salon cut my hair, I don't know, my face changed. And then I felt like I was walking differently. Then all of a sudden, when I was climbing in the Alps, I looked down and there were muscles in my legs, like the ones that were there when I was young and didn't have to work at it. And I got this lipstick that, I swear to you, is like magic—I put it on and I don't know, I'm sexy or something. Me. Sexy."

"Where was Jack when you were flirting with this Pete person?"

"He didn't come. He's back home."

"How convenient."

"It was his idea. It's not my fault I'm alone over here for a month—"

"You'd better be careful. A woman in her prime loose in the Italian Alps sounds like a setup for a spaghetti western with a bad ending."

"Theodore! I won't do anything! I never do anything. I'm a sensible, practical pharmacist, remember?" Doesn't Theodore know that it's the idea of an affair that excites me? I hang up the phone; my palms are sweating so much, they leave a print on the black receiver. I rub it off with the hem of my sweater.

Everyone in the house is asleep. I tiptoe up to my room on the second floor, a big, square room with a fireplace and four windows, and a high double bed with four carved wood posters that nearly reach the ceiling. It's a princess bed. And tonight, I *am* a princess who floated on a dance floor in Italy under a box of silver stars with a handsome prince.

I close the door and slip out of my loafers. I undress in the dark. When I am completely naked, I stand in front of the long mirror with the gold-leaf frame. The soft beam from the nightlight puts me in silhouette. I turn to the side and look at myself in profile. The gentle curves of my body, from having the babies, are suddenly beautiful to me. My skin is soft and warm, and I smell like the rosewater Mafalda left for me on the vanity. I shake my head, and my hair shakes loose away from my head in full, waxy curls, as curls were meant to be. Something happened to me tonight. I'm a girl again. And I like it.

CHAPTER EIGHT

*T*he rain began in the early hours of Sunday morning before I could drift off to sleep. Papa has built a fire; the smell of wood smoke, fresh rain, and Mafalda's macaroons baking in the oven woke me up. Etta and Chiara are in the basement making a mural in chalk, and I am reading all about Ornella Muti's life (she's good friends with Mussolini's granddaughter). Papa is at Giacomina's store, helping her do inventory and place orders for the ski season. Nonna went up the street to visit a friend. Papa argued with her to let her ankle heal a little longer before she went out. (Guess who won that argument?)

Jack called this morning; fully awake, he was much more animated and attentive on the phone. He had a long talk with Etta, and when she handed the phone over to me, I realized that even though she misses her daddy, she was happier than I had seen her in a long time. She is happy because she sees how happy I am. Don't I remember when I was a girl and my mother was happy? I would do anything to see my mother smile. I remember when I brought Mama to our cast party at the Drama and she sang an Italian folk song for the crowd. I couldn't believe that she had the courage to sing in front of all those people, and as I watched her, she became her best self, her most free and happy self. I'll never forget her face that night. I wished her joy could last forever. She had so much sadness, I just wanted her to forget it all and laugh. And when she did that night, I knew that it was possible for her to have a life of joy. Etta knows I'm happy here, and it brings out the best in both of us. I must not forget that I have an insight into my daughter, because I was a daughter once too.

Jack tells me about the progress he and the guys are making on the rec center in Appalachia. He catches me up on the local gossip. Leah and Worley got married by the justice of the peace; everyone thinks Tayloe Lassiter is having an affair with the jeweler from down in Pennington Gap; and Zackie Wakin, concerned that he was getting robbed, ordered a detective kit from a magazine to trap the thief. He put a special invisible powder on everything in his store and hung a sign on the door that said he was out of town ("To throw 'em off but good," he told Jack). Turns out someone was in the store at night—and when the police came and washed the powder with a special solvent and took the footprints, they belonged to Zackie. Evidently, Zackie is a sleepwalker. We have a good laugh over that one.

There is something different in my husband's voice. His tone is warm but just a touch hollow. Sort of like: you're there, I'm here, let's not talk about anything too deep. But since I danced with Pete Rutledge, all I want to do is talk about deep things. One dance made me want to dig deep and live. How dramatic, but how true.

"Ave, were you drunk last night?"

"What?"

"When you called. Had you been drinking?"

"I had bitters at the disco. But that's all."

"How much?" Jack chuckles.

"I wasn't drunk."

"You're on vacation. Live it up."

Part of me wants to tell Jack everything, as I used to do, in the beginning. We'd lie in bed for hours, and I'd share things with him I had never told anyone. It's different now. I'm not compelled to tell him everything, and I'm not sure why. When Jack hangs up, I am relieved. We ran out of things to say.

The rain is coming down so hard now, it's making a river in the street in front of the house, and it's dumping into the creek that feeds the waterwheel. The waterwheel whips around in a high-speed frenzy, throwing sheets of water everywhere. I get back to the glamorous life of Ornella Muti. Oh, the details.

Mafalda pokes her head into the study. "Ave Maria. You have a guest."

Through the door from the living room, which connects to the kitchen, I see Pete Rutledge in a yellow rain slicker, standing in the doorway. He is so tall, he has to duck his head down; his shoulders barely fit in the frame. His blue eyes stand out against the bright yellow collar of the slicker. His hair is wet, and he hasn't shaved. He reminds me of Clark Gable in *The Call of the Wild*, just a little. I wish I didn't think this man looked like all my favorite movie idols, but in certain ways, and in certain lights, he does. He's a little like my girlhood board game Mystery Date—which Etta still plays with her girlfriends—where the players spin a dial and a plastic door opens to reveal seven different specimens of young all-American manhood, one cuter than the next. I bite my lip; good, I'm wearing lipstick. (Loretta Young would never be caught without it, even in frozen tundra). Why am I worried about how I look? My heart skips, sending a flurry of butterflies through my chest, and lower. Shame on me! I take a deep breath. I am not excited he came to see me; I'm *surprised*, but I am definitely not excited. Maybe if I say this to myself enough, I'll believe it.

"Hello," I say to him as I lean in the doorway with my arms across my chest.

"Everybody in this town knows Mario Barbari." Pete smiles.

"He's been the mayor for—"

"Thirty-seven years," Mafalda finishes my sentence.

"May I borrow your Ave Maria for the afternoon?" Pete asks Mafalda.

"I cannot answer for her," she says warmly. Even Mafalda is suckered by this American male.

"There's an inn up the street. Want to get a cup of coffee?" he offers.

Mafalda instantly grabs the pot, and I stop her. "No waiting on us."

"I am happy to!" Mafalda says.

"No. If Mr. Rutledge has checked out the local coffee, then the least I can do is try it." I smile at Pete, who smiles back at me.

I grab one of my father's coats off the rack by the door. This time I wear his silly Robin Hood hat. Pete holds the door for me, and we step out into the rain. I walk ahead a few steps, and he catches up with me and opens his raincoat, pulling me inside. I resist at first, but the rain is coming down so hard that I opt to stay dry. I have to skip to keep up with him; his legs cover twice the distance mine do in the same amount of time. He looks down at me and laughs. I hope he thinks this hat is ridiculous. I do not need this man attracted to me.

Pete holds the door for me as we enter the old inn. My father has told me that in the winter, at the height of ski season, this place is packed. Today there is just me, Pete, and the proprietor, an old man with a pipe, sitting in the kitchen and reading the newspaper. The pipe smell is familiar: he's the same man who walks home late at night. I smile at him and wave, and he looks up and nods. Pete takes off his raincoat and drapes it over a chair. He helps me with my coat and hat. The proprietor comes out; Pete orders coffee in lousy Italian, and I let him. There are three stuffed deer heads over the fireplace. The room has Tyrolean touches, just like the homestead. The tables are waxed and the chairs mismatched, some with embroidered seats and some straight-backed and plain. I sit down in one of the two dilapidated easy chairs in front of the fire and stretch my legs out on the stone hearth. The chairs are so old and low to the ground, you might as well sit on the floor. Pete sinks into the other chair, scooting it to face me.

"How are you?"

"I'm fine. How are you?"

"A little wet," he says as he runs his fingers through his hair. "Why don't you wear a wedding ring?"

I look down at my hands. Why do I keep forgetting to put on my rings?

"I was helping Mafalda make macaroons."

"You weren't making macaroons last night."

"No. Last night I wasn't wearing them because I had been fishing stones out of the stream yesterday afternoon and I had taken them off."

"You wouldn't want to lose them," he says, and smiles in a way that is so sexy, I'm glad I'm sitting down: if I were standing, my knees would give out.

"No, I wouldn't," I tell him, regaining my composure, then say directly, "What are you implying?"

"Nothing."

"Good." I lean back in the chair, then shift as a spring pops up and jabs me in the center of my back.

We sit in silence for a moment. The old man brings the coffee. He looks at Pete, and then he looks at me. I can see that he appreciates the happy American couple who wandered in from the rain. You can't find a soul in this country who doesn't believe in romance. No need to further anyone's misapprehensions. I move my chair away from Pete's. I have to get this conversation on a more general, friendly plane.

"What do you do?" I ask him a bit too chirpily.

"I'm a marble guy."

"Game marbles?"

"No." He laughs. He has a good laugh—it's right up there with his smile. "Marble for houses. Mantels. Walkways. Tabletops."

"Interesting. Is there a lot of call for marble in New Jersey?"

"Are you kidding? It's the goomba capital of the world."

"Hey. I'm a goomba," I tell him.

"Me too. Half."

Half Italian. Okay. That explains the dark hair and the good nose and the hitting on married women.

"My mother was Italian," he explains. "Her people were from Calabria. They're very passionate."

"I've heard."

"You don't like small talk, do you?" he says.

We sit quietly for a moment, and I consider this stranger as he gazes into the fire and sips his coffee. Who is this guy anyway? What kind of man uses words like "passionate" and persists with a woman whether she's wearing her wedding ring or not? He eases his long legs out and rests his feet against the wall. I feel dwarfed sitting here next to him, but I shouldn't—I'm far from tiny. But there is something about this man that fills up a room. The size of him makes me want to take him on and set him straight: no, I don't like small talk. In fact, I don't like anything frivolous. I would prefer it if folks just got to the point. I learned the value of time the hard way. It's a sin to squander it.

"Maybe I don't like small talk because you're not very good at it," I tell him.

I catch him off guard and he laughs. Is there anything sexier than a man who laughs at your jokes? I don't think so. I take a sip of the coffee. I've never had a cup of coffee so good.

"Have you read *Browning's Italy*?" he asks.

"By Helen Clarke? I love that book!"

"I don't know how anyone can come to Italy without reading it."

"That's my favorite love story."

"Robert Browning and Elizabeth Barrett?" he says.

"Who did you think I meant?"

"Maybe you and me." He smiles. "I'm kidding around."

"Good." Boy, this guy is bold. "It's awfully hot in here." Let me get back to the Brownings before he says something else that makes me sweat. I push my chair away from the fire.

"Why is it your favorite love story?" he asks.

"Because it was an impossible situation. Elizabeth Barrett was living a terrible life; she was sick and housebound, writing poetry. Oppressed by a cruel father. And then Robert Browning sent her his poetry, and they began to correspond and fell in love through their words."

Pete picks up the story. "And then Browning proposed, and Elizabeth was afraid to tell her father, so they eloped and moved to Rome." The man is finishing my sentences. "You know, you can rent their apartment in Florence."

"Really?"

"I've been in it."

"You have?"

"A friend of mine rented it last summer, and I went over and checked it out."

"Did you know they had a son?"

"Penn."

"Right. And she defied the doctors; they told her that the trip to Italy from England would kill her. And that she would never have a child."

"So she followed her heart, and everything worked out. That's very reassuring, isn't it?" Pete looks at me.

"Yes, it is."

"Have you read *Casa Guidi Windows?*"

"My mother had the poem in Italian."

"It's a beaut. I think it's Elizabeth Barrett Browning's best poem," he says, then looks back into the fire. I can't believe I'm talking poetry with a man. When was the last time I did that? When did I ever do that?

"So . . . what's your story, Pete?" I ask him, feeling a jolt from the caffeine.

"You want the whole thing?"

"Sure."

"I grew up in New Jersey. I went to Rutgers. Studied theater. Set design. Graduated. Worked in not-for-profit theater in New York. Got sick of that. Hooked up with an old buddy of mine; we started this marble thing. Now I live in Hoboken. And once a year, I come over here for a couple of weeks to buy marble."

"Are you married?"

"No."

I don't know why his answer makes me smile, but it does.

"What's funny?"

"I don't know."

"You're glad I'm not married?"

"No."

"It would be nice if *you* weren't," he says, tapping my leg with the toe of his shoe. I move my leg.

"Why?" I'm only asking because I'm dying to hear what he'll come up with.

"Well, for starters, if you weren't married, we wouldn't be sitting down here having coffee." Pete's eyes travel from me to the sign that says ROOMS, with an arrow pointing up the stairs.

I don't move a muscle. I can't. Between the bad springs in this chair and my nerves shutting down one synapse at a time, I can't trust my body. "Boy, this is some haircut."

"What?"

"I never got this kind of attention with my old hair."

"It's not the hair."

"Come on. You don't even know me."

"I like what I see so far."

"Pete, let me tell you about the part you don't see."

"Please do. That's the good stuff."

"I don't know how good this stuff is. I was the Big Stone Gap Town Spinster for fifteen years."

"You called yourself that?"

"Yeah."

"So what are you saying?"

"I waited a long time to fall in love. And then I married him."

"So how's it going?"

"What?"

"Your marriage?"

I take a deep breath. "Not so great."

"Why not?"

"We're very different."

"That can be a good thing."

"Sometimes."

"What did you think it was going to be like?"

"Being married?"

"No. Loving someone. When you were a spinster—your word— did you imagine what love would be like?"

I sit back. No one has ever asked me this before. Not even Theodore. That's the sort of thing we might have talked about, but we were so busy making each other feel safe in our roles that we didn't talk about the murky, deep stuff that a potential lover might unearth. And Jack Mac doesn't talk about these things at all.

"I thought that love made everything better. I thought that it was a state of happiness and security. Yeah, that's it. And serenity. I thought love made a person whole."

"How would it do that?" Pete asks.

I think about this for moment. "It can't." Saying that almost makes me cry. I rub my eyes. I hope that Pete thinks I'm tired.

"I've upset you."

"No, no. I should think about these things more." I mean that. "You must think I'm crazy."

"I think you're fascinating."

"Me? Come on." I shift in the chair. Another spring stabs me, this time near my ribs.

"So what's the problem with your husband?"

I won't answer that because I have no answer. Instead I state the facts. "My husband was supposed to come on this vacation, and at the last minute he told me he wasn't coming because he thinks I need time to think, and he told me that I need to decide if I want to stay married."

"Do you?"

I should say yes, but I don't. "He may not want *me* at the end of this vacation."

"Wouldn't it be better if you decided what you wanted?"

"That's what he says."

"He's right."

I watch Pete drink his coffee by the light of the fire. I imagine him leaning across the chair and kissing me. I shake my head. The picture goes.

"Well, this is going to be an interesting month for you, isn't it?" He smiles at me. I wish he didn't have such great teeth.

"And busy," I tweet. Where did *that* sound come from? I breathe. "There's a big calendar at the house filled with stuff to do. Giacomina, my dad's girlfriend, came up with a month of activities. And I like a plan."

"The first thing you need to do is . . ." Pete leans toward me and puts his hand on the arm of my chair. "Throw out that calendar."

Pete walks me home in the rain. Giacomina and Papa are back from the ski shop, and it's suppertime. Where did the time go? That cup of coffee lasted for hours! Mafalda invites Pete to stay, and he graciously accepts. He instantly charms my family; he is so easygoing and fun, it's as though he's been around for years. As I watch him keep the conversation going, I think about my husband, who, in the same situation, would rather listen than talk. I like to sit back and listen, but when you're married to a quiet man, you have to do the talking most of the time. I relax back into the chair and let Pete do the entertaining.

Chiara and Etta tell Pete all about the jellyfish in the ocean at Sestri Levante. He tells them about the jellyfish on the Jersey shore. As we eat a hearty lamb stew (what does Mafalda do to the meat to make it so tender?) and bread, both of the girls develop wild crushes on him. He pays close attention to every word they say, the girls, vying to impress him, transform from kids to coquettes before our eyes. Papa asks Pete about stonework for a wall behind the house; Pete gives him helpful tips. Papa has an easy rapport with Pete, much like he has with Jack Mac. This Marble Man is just a big old American charmer. He's got everyone in this house under his spell. Everyone except me. I am not falling for him. No way. There is no way a guy this smooth can be genuine. I'm going to enjoy him and, for security purposes, I will wear my wedding band at all times. This tingling I feel in Pete's presence just reminds me that I'm alive; it doesn't mean I could fall for him; he's not a threat.

By the time I put the girls to bed, Mafalda has done the dishes, straightened the kitchen, and set the table for breakfast. (That's a good time-saver. I'll remember it once I'm home.)

Papa and Giacomina sit on the couch in the living room, cuddling and reading the paper. I sit down at the kitchen table, in Pete Rutledge's chair; okay, now I'm naming chairs after him, what is that all about? He left nearly an hour ago, though the girls begged him not to.

"How about a cup of coffee?" Giacomina says, touching my shoulder in a way that reminds me of my mother.

"Mafalda prepared the pot for breakfast already."

"I will put it back the way I found it. Don't worry." Giacomina smiles and turns on the stove. The clean mountain water makes a hissing sound in the blue-and-white-enameled pot.

"So, you met Pete at the disco last night?"

"Yeah. He asked me to dance. I wish I wouldn't have."

"Why not?"

"I'm married." Saying this aloud absolutely kills the temptation. (I must remember that.)

"Dancing with a man isn't a bad thing."

I look at Giacomina. Is she kidding? The thought of falling into the arms of another man on an Alpine cliff while music plays through the trees is a terrible thing. Giacomina doesn't know me very well. I am an all-or-nothing woman. I married Jack MacChesney the first night I made love to him. Not on paper, but in my mind, the commitment began right there. Later, when we went to the priest and said our vows, it was just a validation of what I already knew. I can't have a tall American man with a killer smile and great legs pull me away from the promises I made. What am I saying? What am I thinking? In twenty-four hours, I'm imagining a romance with someone besides my husband? Italy is a dangerous place.

"It's very complicated, no?" she says.

"What?"

"Men and women."

"No, not really. It's easy. You make promises and you keep them. That's all."

"Easy to say."

"No, it's easy to do," I insist. "I can appreciate a nice-looking man who—" why am I struggling to describe Pete? "—reads poetry and tells funny stories. But that doesn't mean anything. It's just admiration of some sort or another, I guess." I never admired any man, really and truly, until Jack MacChesney. So why I am using that word now to describe Pete Rutledge from New Jersey? "Well, I don't mean admiration. I don't know him well enough, nor will I, to use such a strong word. Let's just say I get a kick out of him."

"Who?"

"Pete."

"Oh, I thought you might be talking about your husband."

"No, I meant Pete."

As Giacomina pours our coffee, the way she holds the pot with the yellow-and-white-striped pot holder, and how her simple gold wrist-watch twists down to the inside of her wrist and dangles there, face out, and how she moves the cup toward me—scooting it on the table, not lifting it, just like Mama used to do—all make me want to confide in her. I could never lie to my mother. She would ask me questions, like Giacomina just did, and lead me gently toward the truth, so I would never *have* to lie. I could admit the worst things about myself to my mother, and she would never judge me.

"Okay. All right. Okay. I'm a little attracted to him," I confess out loud.

Giacomina smiles. "We all were. You can't be a woman and not be attracted to him. Did you see the girls?" I nod. "There are men like that out there. They sparkle. Your father is one."

I look into the living room. Papa has fallen asleep, his head lying against the back of the couch like a throw pillow. For the first time, he looks older to me. But there is an ease to his aging; a natural grace. It doesn't look like the loss of something. It's like he traded in excitement for comfort. The hair, almost completely silver now, the softer jawline, and the padding around the middle have turned him into a grandfather. And he's letting it happen. Happily.

"I have this under control, Giacomina." I reassure myself, saying it aloud.

As I lie in bed, unable to sleep because I'm wired from the caffeine (I should never have a cup of strong coffee late at night, what was I thinking?), I review my actions of the past day. This is a habit I've had since I was a child. I want to nod off with a clean slate, in case I die in my sleep. I apologize to God for my shortcomings, and while I'm at it, beg him for insight into my problems. A lot happened today. I imagined kissing a man whose attraction to me has been made abundantly clear. Bad. I opened up to him about the problems in my marriage. Bad. I allowed him to stay for dinner. Bad. I agreed to see him again. Worse. Now Pete Rutledge has a fan club at 108 Via Scalina. Now they're invested in him. Now he's a part of things! Am I falling for him? God, this is sick! What was Giacomina getting at tonight? Does she want me to leave Jack Mac and move to Schilpario and marry Pete Rutledge and start a new life? Of course not. But why do I think that's what she means?

I sit up in bed.

I realize something that makes me queasy at first, then rings through my head like a proclamation. I am still repressed! That's my problem! I hold my face in my hands. I can feel the heat rising off of my face. I thought I no longer buried my feelings and made decisions about my body and my life out of fear, but in fact, I do. Pete Rutledge unglues me, and I can't handle it! I'm afraid he's going to stir me up and then I'll really have a problem. I was so smug, so shielded from temptation, in Big Stone Gap. I was proud that I didn't want any man but my husband. That I had never wanted any man but my husband: Now I can't say that. I can't even think it, because it's not true anymore. I want Pete Rutledge. Never mind I must not have him, I want him. Why can't I tell Pete to go away? Is this retaliation for Karen Bell? No, I'm not one of those tit-for-tat people. Maybe this is what Jack Mac was talking about. Maybe he thinks I didn't live enough before we married. I got married, but I didn't leave the spinster behind: I moved her from Poplar Hill to Cracker's Neck, and now I've dragged her across the Atlantic Ocean to northern Italy! But I'm still the same woman, and Jack MacChesney is right—I am not being honest about my feelings.

Pete promised the girls a trip up into the Dolomites, a mountain range that touches the Italian Alps. (I know, I know, don't get me started on how I got myself into this one; Pete came back to the house with some slate to make the girls a chalkboard, and before we knew it, we were planning a day trip.) It's a fifty-mile ride, one way, so we plan on a very early departure. He wants to show them the marble quarry. At first I think to bring Papa and Giacomina with us, but I decide against it. Etta has been spending time with everyone but me. And Pete is fun. I am doing nothing wrong (I keep reminding myself), and there's no need to avoid our new friend. He makes us all laugh. Besides, I want to see the marble quarry.

As Pete drives, the girls jockey for position next to him. We finally decide that Chiara can sit next to him on the way over and Etta on the way home. I wasn't planning on dealing with adolescent hormones for another five years, but here they are, in all their raging glory. I sit by the passenger window as they chat and giggle. Pete and I speak occasionally, to ask and answer questions about the directions and how far we have to go, but mostly I sit with my own thoughts as we speed and swerve through the mountains.

The marble quarry is an enormous pit dug in the side of Assunta Mountain, named for a woman two brothers loved and fought over. She died, and neither of them ever loved another woman again. As Pete explains this to the girls, they nod, their eyes wide with understanding. As we walk toward the marble pit, Chiara gives Etta a tiny pot of peach lip gloss; Etta dips her pinky into it and applies it carefully to her lips. Where did she learn how to do *that*?

The marble pit is so deep and wide and black, it looks like the pit of hell in the catechism book Mama bought me for my confirmation so many years ago. I take a step back.

"Are you all right?" Pete asks.

"It's just so deep."

"Don't look, then," he says, and pulls me away from the edge.

We walk away from the pit and into a clearing, where trailers are set up. These are the mining offices, and just like our coal mines in Big Stone Gap, there is a sense that this business is temporary. No need to build an actual office; a trailer will do.

Pete takes us into the largest trailer. He shows the girls little boxes of samples, small, cool squares of finished marble, shell pink with gold veins, black with white streaks, and my favorite, the rarest of the marble, lapis-lazuli blue with accents that look like black glitter.

"You like the most expensive marble," Pete tells me. He stuffs a square into the pocket of my jeans.

"It figures." My hip tingles where he touched it. I bury my hand in my pocket to stop the sensation of that, whatever that was.

Pete lets the girls take whatever small squares they want. As we load back into the truck, Pete tells us that he has a surprise. The girls giggle and chat as we descend the mountain. Pete veers off the main road; all of a sudden, we're bouncing on an unpaved gravel road, kicking up dust.

"Mama, this is like our road," Etta says.

"Yes, it is," I tell her.

"What road?" Pete wants to know.

"Cracker's Neck Holler Road. Where we live."

"Cracker's Neck?" Pete laughs.

"Hey. Don't laugh at Cracker's Neck," I tell him.

"Yeah! Don't laugh," Etta says with mountain pride.

"If you think that's funny, you ain't been to Frog Level and It-lee Bottom," I tell him.

"I've got to see this Big Stone Gap someday," Pete says. "Yeah, right," I want to tell him, "come to the Gap and meet my husband."

At the end of the gravel road is what looks like a crude parking lot, a square of muddy field that has been driven over so many times, there is no grass, just dirt.

"Here we are!" Pete announces.

"What is this?" Etta asks, unimpressed.

"Well, not here. We have to go in there."

Pete points to the woods. We follow him in, and for a second I think, really, how well do I know this guy? He could kill us and leave us here, and we'd never be found. But when he turns around and motions for the girls and me to walk in front of him, I look at his face and trust him. It's just the trees, so high they block the sky and create a dank forest, that give me the creeps.

"Take a right," he tells the girls. They turn and we pass two big rocks; one has a red arrow painted on it.

"Look. Directions!" Etta says. I nod. Chiara nods too; her English is only rudimentary, so I don't know how she knows what Etta is talking about half the time. But they have that secret language of girls, and now I have proof that it is international. We hear a loud hissing sound, and at first it's a little scary. But it isn't the hiss of a machine, and it's too loud to be a snake.

"These are the mineral baths of Assunta Mountain," Pete announces. And there, before us, is a waterfall of deep purple rocks so dark they're almost black, covered with glistening pale green moss, leading to a natural pool of clear water. Steam rises off the top and swirls delicately upward through the trees, like cigarette smoke from a glamorous Bette Davis moment.

I turn to Pete. "Hot springs?"

"Amazing, isn't it?"

The girls circle around the edge of the pool and dip their hands in.

"It's warm, Mama," Etta says, amazed. "It's like a bath."

I sit at the edge and take off my shoes and put my feet in. The warmth settles into my entire body. This is bliss. The girls' laughter seems far away. They climb the side of the hill up to the top of the waterfall.

"Be careful!" I shout. They disappear into the ravine.

"What do you think?" Pete asks.

"I've never seen anything like it," I tell him. I wish I were alone here. I would take off all my clothes and lie in the pool and let the minerals and salts soak through my skin and replenish my soul. I can smell the salt as it bubbles in the water. Quickly, I shake off the picture of myself in this pool (just in case Pete Rutledge is a mind reader).

Pete takes his shoes and socks off and rolls up his pants legs. He wades out into the pool.

"Come here," he says.

At first I don't move. I look at him out in the mist. I like the idea of him in the mist, like a mirage, something unreal that I can't touch.

"Come here," he says again.

I roll my pants legs up, then I stand up in the water and slowly wade out to him. The bottom of the pool is filled with sand, and every once in a while something sharp, like a shell, jabs at me. Pete holds his arms out to me. Just as I'm about to reach him, my foot slides into a hole where the bottom of the pool has given way. Pete reaches out and catches me, scooping me out of the water and into his arms.

"What was that?" I look down at the water.

Pete doesn't answer me. He holds me. He looks at me. With my arms around his neck, I put my head on his shoulder, just for a second. I feel his heart beating fast; and now I know how it feels to be in his arms. I would stay here forever if I could, with the mist rising off the warm water and surrounding us. Beads of water run down my calf and onto his sleeve. He looks down at my legs; I take my hand and roll my pants legs down. When I look down, he nuzzles his nose into my neck.

I hear my daughter's distant laughter, and it brings me back to the present.

"Um, maybe, put me down," I tell him. Pete doesn't listen; he carries me back to the edge of the pool and sets me down on the ledge.

"Let's go home," he says softly.

Pete Rutledge folds into our lives in Schilpario as though he was a part of the vacation plan all along. He eats meals with us; he tours Alta Città and rides the train with us to see the Villa d'Este, the great hotel on Lake Como where the movie stars go. Since the day at the Assunta Mountain, Pete has not said or done anything flirty, and I'm relieved. Maybe fifteen years of spinsterhood taught me how to shut down suitors. I hope so.

Gala sent a telegram inviting us down to Florence. She's conducting a tour of the Big Three—Rome, Florence, and Venice—and wants us to meet her for the weekend. I wire back that we'll meet her, but I don't send details. At the last minute, Pete decides to join us because he has business in Florence. The girls are thrilled (of course). The train ride is so much fun. Mafalda packed a lunch. The girls whisper and giggle the entire trip, when they're not begging Pete to play cards or explain what they see outside the window as we speed past.

"Have you ever been to Florence?" Pete asks me.

"On my honeymoon."

Pete smiles. "Ah," he says.

When we pull into Florence, I understand why artists must come here. Everywhere you turn you see art—a painting in the way the sun hits a wall of terra-cotta tile, or a sculpture in the pattern of the cobblestone, or a poem in the way an old man with white hair feeds a flock of doves.

"Mama, can we go on the bridge?" Etta points to the Ponte Vecchio, over the Arno River. The simple bridge, a sturdy U-shaped construction of ancient brick the color of ripe peaches, waits for us in the distance.

"Absolutely. But first we have to meet Gala."

We leave the train station and find our spot in the Piazza della Signoria, where we are surrounded by rows of ornate town houses, connected but painted different shades of gray, pale blue, and beige. Only the shutters in shiny black and the touches of gold in the trim offer any glitz, but it is not necessary; the architecture is artistry enough. We stand on the corner of San Marco Street and wait for Gala.

Etta points across the cobblestone square. "Look! There she is!" Etta has never met Gala but knows her from the videotape. Boy, does she know how to make an entrance. Gala Nuccio emerges from the crowd of tourists like an exotic bird from a lake. The people in the square seem to peel back to make way for the woman who lives up to her dramatic name. Gala walks toward us in a white piqué sundress with turquoise water lilies embroidered on the hem and bodice. A wide cinch belt gives way to a balloon skirt that grazes her knees. The square neckline lies flat against her brown chest, with just a hint of cleavage peeking above the trim. She wears dark sunglasses and carries an enormous straw hat, which catches in the breeze like a flag. She manages to walk in black stiletto heels on cobblestones without tripping. How does she do it?

How happy Gala is to meet Etta and see me again. How delightful when she speaks rapid, machine-gun Italian with Chiara. How intrigued she is to meet Pete and share a couple of New Jersey anecdotes.

Pete takes the girls to the Cathedral of Saint Paul; Gala takes me for a cappuccino. "Who is *he*?" She squeals the moment Pete is out of earshot.

"Pete?"

"Who else?"

"He's a new friend."

"Where is your husband?"

"He decided not to come."

"Big mistake."

"There's nothing going on with Pete and me."

"Oh really."

"Gala, I swear there isn't."

"Maybe not for you. But there is for him."

"He knows I'm married."

"Long, tall, single lattes like that don't care about wedding rings, honey."

I feel my wedding band on my finger. Thank God I remembered to wear it today. "He's been a gentleman."

"Yeah, but you're packing two kids. Lose the kids and see how fast he jumps your bones."

"You're terrible."

"You know, your scent doesn't shut down just because you're married. Trust me. Pheromones don't know from vows. That's Mother Nature's little way of causing trouble. We're animals. Plain and simple animals, no more sophisticated than dogs or cows or pigs. He took one whiff of you, and he's hooked."

"I don't think so." I can't help but laugh.

"Jack Mac is an idiot. Letting you loose in Italy. Alone! You'd have to be dead here not to be thinking about sex twenty-four–seven. Is your husband insane? Leaving you alone in a pastoral friggin' setting with lighting so flattering we all look sixteen? A woman alone in Florence? It's like throwing raw hamburger to a starving rottweiler." Gala winks at a man as he passes. He stops, smiles, and continues on. "How I love my mother country!"

As Pete promised, the churches in Florence are filled with art so astonishing that I almost cannot take it in. In the Cathedral of Saint Monica, there is a mural of the saint with her son, Saint Augustine. It's the moment when he becomes a priest, a dream she held for her rogue son all of his life. The look in her eye, of complete joy at giving her only son to God and yet deep grief at losing him, makes me cry. I look at the corals and pinks in the painting and think of my own son's skin, how it changed from pink to pale yellow bruises when the fever came just before he died.

"Are you okay?" Pete whispers.

"How do they know?"

"Who?"

"Artists. How do they know how I feel?"

"That's their job," Pete tells me. Then, as quickly as I can, I find a door and go outside. Pete follows me.

The girls ask to go for gelato around the corner. Pete and I sit on a bench.

"What happened in there?"

"I don't know." I feel the tears come to my eyes again. He puts his arm around me. "Don't," I tell him. Quickly, he pulls it away.

"I'm sorry."

"Etta's here."

Why did I say that? So he'll think that it's okay to put his arm around me when Etta isn't around? I don't want that. Or do I?

"Why did that painting make you cry?"

"I don't want to talk about it."

"Okay," he says gently.

But as soon as he backs off, I realize I *do* want to talk about it. This is precisely what I have shut down and shut off for four years. Isn't this why I came here? Didn't I come home to Italy to learn how to feel again? I look at Pete's face, full of concern. "I . . . we had a son. After Etta. His name was Joe. He died three years ago."

"How?"

"Leukemia."

"I'm sorry."

"It was the colors of the paint and the brush strokes. They looked like Joe's bruises." I look up at Pete, and I swear he understands what I saw. I don't know how or why, but he does. Married or not, it doesn't matter to me: I need the comfort of another human being, so I let Pete hold me; but I'm not in his arms, I'm somewhere else, with my son.

Etta and Chiara have not returned. I look for them in the crowd. Pete says, "The line was long at the café, the girls won't be back for a while." I sit back. Then, Pete catches my eye in a way that tells me that he's going to kiss me. I shoot up off the bench and call for Etta. Chiara comes around the corner, followed by Etta. They're laughing. I motion for them to join us.

"Mama, are you okay?" Etta looks at me, then at Pete.

"I'm okay. I was thinking about Joe."

"Oh," she says.

"Who is Joe?" Chiara wants to know.

"I'll tell you all about him," Etta tells her.

"Who needs siesta?" Pete asks and picks up my book and bag. The girls and I take our room at the hotel. Pete goes to his room and tells us he has big plans for our dinner.

Pete takes us to Cielo, a little restaurant on a side street. It is quaint—the walls filled with old pottery and the ceiling covered with tiny white lights on wires. After the most delicious dinner of my life, gnocci (tiny, light pasta ovals made of potato—"gnocci" means knees) in delicate white cream, baby lamb chops grilled with fresh sage, a glass of hearty Chianti, hot espresso, and a bite of Etta's cream puff, I feel better.

After supper, on our way to the Ponte Vecchio, Pete surprises me and takes us by Elizabeth Barrett and Robert Browning's apartment on the corner of the Piazza San Felice. He points up to the windows and I imagine Elizabeth there, recording the parade on the street below in vivid detail. "You think of everything," I tell Pete. He just smiles.

Gala is off to Venice with her busload of Americans. (She had to skip dinner with us to take her tourists to the Opera.) We're leaving in the morning, back to Schilpario. As the girls run ahead, I can hear their laughter as it echoes off the stone walls of the narrow side streets.

"When I get you home to Schilpario, I have to go down to Rome."

I feel a pang of disappointment. What did I think, that Pete was here to entertain me ad infinitum? Or at least until my vacation ended and I was ready to pack up and go home. "Business?" I ask as nonchalantly as I can manage.

"Yeah." He pauses. "I probably won't see you again."

"I understand." Of course I do. Pete saw me fall apart about my son and realized that there is more to this picture than he realized. Fine. It's best if he goes now. I shouldn't look forward to seeing him, and I don't like counting on him to take us places and show us around and make us laugh.

"I'm getting too wrapped up here," Pete tells me as we walk.

"I know," I tell him. Boy, do I know.

$\mathcal{T}$here's a puppet show in Bergamo that Giacomina wants to take the girls to, so Papa plans a day down in the city with them. Zia Meoli will have us all over for dinner. I decide to go along at the last minute. I want to shop while the girls are at the show. I haven't heard from Pete since he dropped us off after the trip to Florence. It's been about a week, and the longer he's gone, the clearer I become. It's amazing how everyday feelings can get out of control in Italy. As the date of our departure draws closer, I turn to practical matters. I really need to shop. The dollar is pretty strong, and I haven't bought gifts for Iva Lou and Fleeta. They want leather purses, and I am going to deliver northern Italy's finest to them.

The shops in Bergamo are small and exclusive, but the prices are good. I am supposed to haggle with the shopkeepers; I even practiced the technique with Papa. He tried to drill it into my brain that the shopkeepers never expect the customer to pay the price on the tag, they want you to negotiate. But I am just too much of a people pleaser, and too chicken to haggle. I just want to pick and pay. So the shopping excursion turns into a chore almost immediately. I give up and go for an espresso. There are cafés tucked in between shops and on every corner. I choose the largest one, with friendly red-and-green-striped umbrellas and small tables with curvy little chairs that face the Fountain of the Angels. The umbrellas look like a sea of wide-brimmed hats. I settle into my chair, propping my feet on the portable fence that protects the café from the street. I close my eyes and breathe.

"Hey, look who's here."

I open my eyes and look up at Pete Rutledge. My heart skips a beat, but I cover it nicely by swinging my legs off of the fence.

"How was Rome?" I ask, too abruptly.

"I bought some terrific marble from a middleman."

"Good for you."

"I have to get home and install it. We have a customer in Basking Ridge whose middle name is Rococo." I laugh. Pete sits down. "When do you leave?"

I don't answer him at first. I want to watch the white angels pour water from their pitchers into the seashells in the fountain. "The end of next week."

"Me too."

The waiter approaches. Pete orders for the two of us. We sit in silence; what is there to say? The waiter brings the espresso.

"I need your help, Pete. I have to buy a purse for Iva Lou and one for Fleeta. And I can't haggle. Will you come with me and haggle?"

"Geez," Pete says under his breath, and then he laughs. He pays for the espresso and leads me by the elbow through the umbrellas to the sidewalk. As we start down the street, I pat his back like an old dog, hoping that my platonic warmth will soothe him. "There's a good leather place down this street. Papa told me about it." Pete grabs my hand and stops me.

"This is my hotel," he says, pointing to a simple white-brick building with a black-and-white-striped awning. HOTEL D'ORSO, it says on the brass plaque in black cursive letters.

"It looks nice."

"It was."

"It's good to know: You know. Good hotels."

I continue walking down the street. Pete stops me again. "Let's go in," he says.

I look up into his eyes. The blue of them is so clear, even though he squints. He leans down. His lips are so close to mine, I can practically taste them. If I kiss him, I know we will go to his room. I know it. My hands are deep in my pockets. I try to make the left hand into a fist. Did I remember to wear my rings today? I feel the cool gold metal against the fabric. I did remember!

"I can't." I step back.

"Why?"

"Because I'm married." Now I know why there's an ancient custom of wearing wedding rings. They're there to remind you that you're married and keep you out of trouble.

"Ave Maria! Ave Maria!" I turn to see Stefano, Etta's future husband, on a bicycle. Great. Caught in the act. Perfect.

"Ciao, Stefano."

Stefano looks up at Pete.

"This is Pete."

They exchange pleasantries and I step back, relieved. Stefano's interruption has given me a few seconds to regain my composure. I realize that Stefano could have easily been Etta; I have to stop this. This is wrong, and I don't want any part of it. I almost went into that hotel, and I hate myself for it. Stefano pedals off.

"Come to my room."

"No."

"All right. Fine. But I want to know just one thing."

I dread the next question, so much so that I close my eyes.

"Do you want to?" he asks me.

"Of course I want to. And I hate myself for it. I don't even like saying it!"

"Stay with me."

"I told you, I'm not going into that hotel with you."

"No, I mean Italy. Let's not go back. Ever. Let's just stay here. Look at this."

I look down at the cobblestones, and around at the buildings with their summer awnings, and at the people, who never rush, who always seem to savor the beautiful weather and the good food. The people move through the streets in this small town just as they do in Big Stone Gap. They look at us as they pass. And I shouldn't kid myself; they know me. They may not know my name, but they see me, a married woman on the sidewalk outside a hotel, full of guilt, trying to resist the charms of a man who is not her husband.

"Pete?"

"Yeah?"

"You're crazy." I tell him this, but I know it's really me. I'm the one who's crazy; I think I have this under control, and deep within me, I don't.

I found a gorgeous burgundy crocodile shoulder bag for Iva Lou and a buttery beige leather tote for Fleeta (perfect for candy deliveries). I look at all of my Italian vacation booty on the bed and am very proud of myself. I came, I saw, I haggled. Well, not exactly. I let the purse-shop lady haggle for me. I'd ask how much something was, then, instead of haggling, I'd shrug and she'd start driving the price down.

I bought a puffy black ski jacket for Jack Mac. And a pair of boots for me. Pearl will have a handmade white lace shawl to wear on her wedding day. We won't have to do any back-to-school shopping for Etta; her grandfather has spoiled her with clothes, clogs, and even a gold chain with a dangling angel.

We haven't seen Pete Rutledge since the day he almost kissed me. He begged out of dinner at Zia Meoli's. He called once during the week to say he was checking out some marble farther into the Dolomites before he flew back to New Jersey. I don't think about him.

That's a lie. I do think about him, and to be perfectly honest, I imagine what would have happened had I decided to kiss him on the sidewalk in front of the Hotel d'Orso.

"Ave Maria! *Teléfono!*" Mafalda calls to me from the base of the stairs.

"Ciao?"

"Girl, it's me, Iva Lou."

"Hi, honey. How are you? Wait till you see the purse—"

"I don't have a lot of time. James Varner has a summer cold he can't shake, so I took over the Bookmobile run."

"Okay. What's up?"

"When are you gittin' home?"

"Next week."

"Damn. You'll be too late. Honey, this is an emergency situation."

"Is Jack all right?"

"He's fine." Iva Lou stretches out the word "fine" until it goes from a hum to a hiss.

"Are you all right?"

"Oh God, girl, everybody is fine. But you need to git home. You got to hurry."

"Why?"

"The word up in Coeburn is not good."

"What?" My legs give out on me. I sit down on the steps.

"Yes. I don't want to hurt you, but honey, the word is that Jack Mac wants to divorce you and murry that low-to-the-ground little witch Karen Bell. We all think that he's just goin' through some silly midlife crisis or somethin', and we don't think it's anything but loneliness. I think the man misses you somethin' turr-ible. You need to git home and tend to yer business, honey. The barn is burning. Understand?" I hear Iva Lou taking a drag off a cigarette; she smokes only in times of complete duress.

"How could he do this? He said he'd wait." This is all my fault. I've been spending the summer with Pete while, thousands of miles away, Jack Mac sensed that I left him emotionally, so he has left me.

"I have got to figure out a way to get that sow out of the picture."

"Iva Lou, don't do anything."

"A man never leaves a woman unless he's got someone to go to. If she wasn't around, you wouldn't have a problem."

I must have said good-bye to Iva Lou, but I don't remember it. I hold the receiver like a tasting spoon. The buzz of the telephone line must have gotten Mafalda's attention; she takes the receiver out of my hand and hangs up the phone.

"Where are the girls?"

"They went to the waterwheel."

I go up to my room and sit on the bed. I have an amazing sense of calm all of a sudden. I believe in long leashes for men; if you give them space, they'll find their way back to you. Maybe Jack Mac is testing the length of the leash, and if he is, that's his journey. It was, after all, the point of our spending the summer apart. So we could make the journeys. Decide what we want. And there is nothing I can do about it until I get home. I am not going to poison my glorious Schilpario with schemes involving Karen Bell. I am not going to call Jack, either. I am going to remain calm. For the first time in my life, I am not going to panic and I am not going to worry about what I cannot control.

I slip out of my new pale blue suede loafers (how I love Italian shoes) and into my hiking boots. I'm going to climb the mountain. That will take the edge off any anxiety that might creep in. I tell Mafalda where I'm going, and she promises to watch the girls. I walk up the street, past the houses, and through the town square. The benches are empty, and the chess tables are plain checkerboards until *la passeggiata*, when they will be filled to capacity.

As I reach the path that will lead me up to the pastures above town, I see the door to the chapel La Capella di Santa Chiara propped open with a can of paint. This is the very place where I married Jack Mac-Chesney so many years ago (we had a second ceremony here in Italy so that my father could officially give me away). Something tells me to go inside.

The smell of paint sails over musky notes of church incense. I climb up to the choir loft, and it's as though I lost something and all of a sudden remembered where to find it. I look up and around, hoping my memory serves me well. And it does. There she is, the Blessed Lady in her turn-of-the-century ankle-length coat and a hat with stars pinned to it. This is the stained-glass window my great-grandfather made—I climb up and touch the grooves of each pane of stained glass, murky blues and brilliant burgundies; the pieces fit together perfectly. But it is only when you stand back that you can see what the picture means. I remember my namesake, Ave Maria Albricci, who took care of my mother when she was pregnant with me and on her way to America. I must never forget what I was before I married Jack MacChesney. I was a work of art. My mother's work of art. All the things I thought I was—simple and plain and sometimes funny—are very small words. They do not begin to describe me. They do not begin to express what is inside of me. I have value, and I have worth. I cannot be replaced like old shoes or taken for granted like tap water. I am more than Jack MacChesney's wife, the woman he tired of and traded in for a smart and sexy lumber supplier. Come on, Jack, you can do better than that. You married *me*, remember! So you think I'm a terrible wife. Well, maybe I am. Maybe I stopped making love to my husband, but give me a break, it slipped away from me after Joe died, I was mourning. I couldn't tend to Jack's needs when I was suffering. I couldn't even take care of myself. And then it became a habit; I started to avoid intimacy. I was hurting too much. I wanted to retreat and be alone. I couldn't share myself. If I made love to Jack, it would have been like I was cheating on myself. I wanted to control the only thing I could when Joe was taken from me. And the only thing I could control was who I let in. If Jack MacChesney doesn't understand that, if he is so shallow and so selfish, then he is not the man I thought he was. Karen Bell. Honestly.

I kiss the window of the Blessed Lady. I am not thinking of sacred relics but of my mother. She would know what to do at a time like this; she could talk some sense into me. In a way, I hope that wherever she is, she doesn't know about how I've been spending my summer. (How appropriate that I should have a little dose of Catholic shame in this perfect chapel.)

As I leave the vestibule, the midafternoon sun hits my eyes, so I close them. When I open them, Pete Rutledge is at the bottom of the path, leaning against his rental truck from the quarry. At first I don't think he's real. Why am I running down the path to him and throwing myself into his arms? And why am I crying?

"What happened to you?" he says, holding me away from his body and looking me over from head to toe.

"I haggled and got a good deal on a purse for Iva Lou," I say as I quickly wipe the tears from my eyes.

"Good girl. Sorry I couldn't come and help you drive down the prices."

"You came back."

"I had to see you again."

"Why?"

"You owe me money," he says with a straight face. "Forty-seven bucks. The train tickets to Florence."

"I'm sorry. I have the money at the house."

"I don't want the money," he says with a slight smile, pulling me close and burying his hands in the back pockets of my jeans. The timing of this is too perfect. I could have him and it would be only fair. My husband is carrying on with a woman thousands of miles away. Who would ever know?

"Do you want to see the field of bluebells?" I ask him.

"Okay."

So, surefooted and strong, my legs like sculpted stone from a month of climbing around these Alps, I lead Pete Rutledge up the path to the ridge above Schilpario. I kneel and watch him as he looks at the field of bluebells for the first time. The hum of the bees drowns out the way my heart is thumping from the climbing (or, more likely, from my nerves). I catch my breath.

"God. I've never seen anything like this."

"And look. Look. Goats." I point to a far ridge, where goats mill around a pasture and a boy herds them from the edge. "Doesn't that look like something out of the Bible?"

"It does," Pete says, squinting.

I want to tell Pete about Karen Bell, but I can't. If I tell him that, he'll think Jack is terrible, and I don't want him to think that. I want him to think that I am going home to a husband who cherishes me. A husband who worked hard all summer and missed me every night and dreamed of the sex we would have upon my long-awaited return. A husband who can't look at other women because none of them measure up, not even the young ones or the beautiful ones or the ones who flirt madly. A husband who wants sex only with me, even in his fantasies. A husband who pictures my face when he's putting up a Sheetrock wall and finishes the job perfectly in my honor. A husband who, when I have fantasies about another man, dismisses it as healthy, normal, and good for our relationship. A husband so dutiful that I could treat him badly and he'd love me anyway. A husband who doesn't expect me to put up a fight when I go ahead on vacation without him, as though he's a blow dryer I accidentally forgot to pack.

A clean, cool breeze ripples through the bluebells as one perfect white cloud hangs overhead.

"I want you, Ave Maria." Pete doesn't look at me when he says this. Instead, I study him. The breeze musses his hair, and his eyes, as they narrow in the sun, are the very color of the bluebells.

"You have a way of saying things that . . ."

"That what?"

"Unglue me." I roll over and start rolling down the hill like a child. Pete tucks and rolls beside me. Finally, we stop and I crawl back toward him. We're laughing so hard, I swear the goatherd, who must be ten miles away, looks in our direction with disgust for disturbing this perfect pastoral setting.

"Pete. You don't want me."

"Why shouldn't I want you?"

"Because I can't handle anything."

"What can't you handle?"

"Haggling. Grief. Lust. My husband's midlife crisis. You name it. I can't handle anything. I just run. Find a brave girl to love. That's what you need."

"I don't think you're the best judge of what I need."

No one has pursued me or wanted or needed me in this way in ten years. How new it all sounds. When I first heard words like these from Jack, I couldn't believe it. I love the first moments of discovery with a man. When he tells you that you're beautiful, and that there is no one like you, and that you're the only person in the world he can really talk to. What a feeling of connection and purpose!

"Why did you bring me up here?" Pete wants to know.

"I wanted you to see the bluebells."

"I've seen bluebells before," Pete says in a way that makes me laugh.

"Not like these."

"No. Not like these." He looks at me. "You asked me why I came back. Now can I tell you?"

"I owe you forty-seven dollars."

"No jokes."

"Okay. No jokes."

"When you left me at the hotel in Bergamo, I had a rough night.

That's why I didn't come up to Schilpario again. I wanted to shake the idea of you and me. And I couldn't. I had to see you one more time."

"Why?"

"For the same reason you had me climb this mountain. You want this too."

I don't answer him. We lie on our backs, talking up into the sky just like the flowers. Pete rolls over onto me. I move my leg so I can grip my boot into the earth to slide out from under him, but he hooks his leg around mine and I can't move. I could say something like "get off of me," but I love the way he smells and the feeling of his breath on me and the way his leg hooks around mine. He slides his hands under my back and lifts me off the ground a little. He kisses my neck. Now there is no place for me to put my hands, so I give up. I wrap my arms around him, and I feel his back and his shoulders, and then I take his face in my hands. I know for sure that I am in Big, Big Trouble.

His lips find mine, so tenderly that I am compelled to say something. But I don't want to talk. I want to kiss this man right off this mountain. For the first time in years, I am in my body. I feel my bones, my heartbeat, and my breath. My lips burn into his mouth like hot honey. I am beyond what I am. I am so far from what I know, I don't even have a name. The air cuts through me as though I'm a vapor. I feel his body begin to move against mine. We roll into the bluebells. I want to let him in. The sun blinds me. Pete covers my eyes and kisses me again. He unbuttons my jacket and slides his arms around my waist. I must have a temperature of two hundred degrees—I am throwing heat like a furnace. I pull away from him to breathe and look up over the ridge. The goats and their herder are gone. There are no witnesses! We are alone. I can do what I feel, be what I am, have something just for me! Haven't I earned this? Isn't life supposed to be about pleasure and connection and wild kisses? What else is there? To be alive—but how? Isn't my husband, right this second, probably having sex with a woman who carries a clipboard and wears too much Charlie cologne? Kiss this man, I cheer myself on. This man understands you.

"Pete. Stop." I say it so quietly he stops.

"Why?"

"I can't. That's the wrong word. I can do this. But I won't do this."

"Ave."

"No. I won't. I want to. But I won't. People can't just do things for selfish reasons. It has to matter."

"Who are you talking about? People? Do you mean you?"

I shake my head. Somewhere I've heard this tone and these words before. Jack MacChesney made the same observation. When someone gets too close, I always talk in generalities and speak on behalf of a large group, in this instance a worldwide community of women who are tempted to have sex with men outside of their marriages. I'm talking about Those Women—I do not say "I."

"Yes, I mean me. You make me feel good. But this is wrong."

I button my jacket and tighten the laces on my boots, which loosened when I was rolling around.

"It isn't wrong. We're not wrong," he says quietly.

"No, we're not. We could be absolutely right for each other. But I have a husband."

He stands and brushes his hair back with his fingers, as he always does. He walks several steps down the path toward the ridge. I look at him, tall, gleaming in the sun, backlit like an MGM-musical moment—silent, looking at me, waiting for the music to begin.

"Pete?" I kick the bluebells squashed by our kiss-tuck-and-roll back into their standing position with the toe of my boot. "I want to, but I'm not in love with you. I'm sorry. Once there was a man who had one rule. He'd make love only when he was *in* love."

"That guy was a saint."

"No, he's no saint. He's my husband." If only I could tell Pete the truth: Jack Mac has not been acting like my husband, and he's probably been breaking his own rule all summer.

I want to savor my last night in Schilpario, so I go to bed early. After rolling around Heidi's pasture above Schilpario with the Marble Man from New Jersey, I think it's best if I take some time to be alone. When I told Pete good-bye last night, Etta and Chiara were with me. They seemed more upset than I did. Pete just seemed resigned to the whole thing. I need my solitude and my rest. I am going home to battle. And I have a hunch that I am going to lose.

I turn over onto my side and try not to remember Pete's kisses. When I lie on my back, I can feel him on top of me. It's as though he is right here in this bed. Yes, his kisses were real. And real kisses are dangerous. I could go find him and ask for more. Thank God he lives far away!

Maybe I like the idea of that; maybe I like the idea that Pete will be in New Jersey pining for me. I could have made love to him and evened the score with Jack MacChesney. But my conscience is mine. I can't control what anyone else does, including my husband. I know only my own heart. I couldn't live with myself if I made love to another man outside my marriage. I'm going to glue this wedding band on my finger from now on. I'm sure there will be days when the idea of Pete and marble fireplaces and the woods of southern New Jersey will call to me like a corner of heaven right here on earth. I just won't choose that little piece of heaven. I have my safe place, my home in Cracker's Neck Holler. But it may not be mine anymore. Karen Bell might have taken it from me. I know one thing for sure: I have never been this confused in my life. This mess I am in has made me yearn for my days as an old maid; how simple it all was. This femme-fatale business is a lot of work.

Etta is exhausted on the flight home. She sleeps so peacefully; while she didn't sleep a wink on the way over, now she's just another blasé American who uses time on airplanes to catch up on sleep. My daughter became more beautiful this summer. More self-assured.

And her personality and humor came through. How lucky I am to have this great kid. She has written "Stefano" seventy-two times on the back of her notebook. Even Etta developed new romantic muscles in Italy.

I don't think she senses how much I dread going home. Most of the time I think I'm doing a good job of shielding her from my angst. Maybe I'm fooling myself; maybe she's like the coral sponge she brought from the beach of Sestri Levante. Maybe she soaks up everything and it becomes a part of her eternal self. Maybe she'll realize this later and resent me for it. I hope not.

The airport at Tri-Cities is empty. Etta and I deboard the little prop plane and go inside for our bags. I look up to the viewing window on the second floor of the airport and expect to see Jack there, behind the glass like a mannequin in the Big & Tall Men's Shop. But there is no one there. Etta and I walk into the luggage area.

"Daddy!" Etta screams and rushes toward her father.

He scoops her up in his arms and kisses her. She hugs him and kisses him. Jack looks good; too good, with a tan and a perfect patch of pink sunburn on the bridge of his nose. He looks slim too. His jeans hug his thighs. Must be from the construction work. I don't want to think about what else he might have been doing, or with whom. I'm all Mommy right now, watching the two of them fussing over each other. I will forever be a sucker for fathers and daughters. Jack looks up at me and grins.

"Isn't Mama pretty?" Etta says loudly.

"Yes, she is," Jack says, and kisses me on the lips lightly.

I want to say, "Pretty enough to keep you faithful?" but instead I say, "Thank you."

"Etta, honey, guess who's in the truck?"

"Who, Daddy?"

"Why don't you take a look?"

Etta opens the door of the cab, and Shoo the Cat tiptoes across the front seat with his tail in a stiff loop like a Christmas ornament hanger. He jumps into her arms.

"God a-mighty, did your luggage give birth over there?" Jack laughs as he hoists our bags into the back.

"What can I tell you, I learned how to haggle," I tell him, doing my best impression of Gala Nuccio.

Etta talks nonstop on the trip home to Big Stone Gap, and I'm glad. I don't want to start a conversation with my husband, because I know it will get serious fast. It's best for all of us if I keep it light. As we roll into the Gap, from the top of the hill on the descent into town, I see the stage lights from the Outdoor Drama. Rose and white beams shoot out into the blue twilight. I have always loved this time of day best. It wasn't so many years ago that I spent every night at the theater. We drive past, and I don't mention it. As we make the curve off of Shawnee Avenue, on our way out of town through the southern section and then on to Cracker's Neck, Etta looks up at her father.

"Daddy, can we stop in Glencoe? I brought Joe something."

Jack makes the right onto Beamontown Road. When we get to the entry arch, the curlicue gates are locked with a chain. Jack starts to turn around and head for home.

"Park. We'll jump the fence," I say. Jack gives me a look. "We do it all the time." I get out of the truck and go around the arch and over the low fence into the cemetery. Etta hands Shoo to me, then I help Etta scale the fence. Jack follows her. Night is falling and settling on the stones in a haze. I climb the hill to the Mulligan plot. I don't even feel it in my legs; all those Alpine hikes made me strong. When I climb the last little bit to the plot, I am glad that there is still enough light to see Joe's headstone. I run my fingers in the gold grooves of his name and through the words "Beloved son and brother." Black marble. White streaks.

"How do you like the impatiens?" Jack says from behind me. Etta puts Shoo down on the ground, and he trots right over to the head-stone and sniffs around it. The red and white impatiens form a beau-tiful bright border.

"It's lovely."

"Mommy, it's like the marble on Assunta Mountain."

"You know what I wish?" I tell Etta. "I wish it was the blue kind with the black glitter in it."

"What are you talking about?" Jack says gently.

"We visited a marble quarry in Italy."

"Mama, take that rock off the stone," Etta says.

"No, leave it," Jack says.

"Why?"

"Lew Eisenberg left it there. Says it's something they do in the Jew-ish faith."

So we leave the rock. I dig deep into my pocket and place the lapis marble square Pete gave me next to Lew's rock. "Honey, get Shoo," I tell Etta. She picks him up. It's too dark in the cemetery to read the stones. It's time to go home.

I take a long bath and realize how much I missed my big four-legged white enamel tub and the way our water gushes out of the pipes. In Italy, you always feel like you're trying to save water. Water barely streams out of their faucets. It's the only negative thing I can say about the entire country. In fact, if they had better plumbing, it would be a perfect place.

I climb out of the tub without even holding on to the sides. I'm in such good shape, I just lift myself out of the water like Venus. I grip the stopper with my toe and yank it out. I guess my feet got stronger too. I dry off and slip into a new nightgown, white cotton with spa-ghetti straps and small red-ribbon rosettes on the neckline, a good-bye gift from Giacomina. She's more a sister to me than a future step-mother.

Jack is in bed when I get there. He's awake. I slide into my side of the bed and under the covers.

"You look good," Jack says to me. But it isn't a come-on. It sounds like a compliment you pay to a really nice dish of chipped beef.

"Thanks. I hiked a lot. I think I'm going to start running. It's nice to be in shape."

"Great."

"Jack?"

"Yeah?" He answered me really fast, so maybe that means he has something to tell me.

"How was your summer?"

"It was pretty good."

"Did you miss me?"

"It ain't the same around here without you and Etta."

"No, I know you missed Etta. But me. Did you miss me?"

Jack looks up at the ceiling. His hands are clasped behind his head.

" 'Course I missed you," he says to the ceiling.

"Just checking," I tell him as I turn over. He turns over to spoon against me, but he doesn't reach around and pull me close. He puts his hand on the side of my thigh instead.

"You really did build some muscles in the Alps," he says.

And that's the last thing I remember before I wake the next morning.

Iva Lou meets me at the Mutual's for breakfast. I have her new purse, and she has a boatload of gossip. The Tayloe Lassiter story is true; she's been sporting one-carat diamond studs in her ears. Doc Daugherty has put Zackie on antianxiety pills to help him cope with his burglar paranoia. Pearl and Dr. Taye Bakagese are getting very serious.

"Now. Let's get down to It," Iva Lou says, buttering her toast.

"Are you sure about Jack Mac and Karen Bell?"

"Well, I haven't caught him in the act. But I'm pretty certain. Let me tell you what I know. And don't think it hasn't been an effort for me. James Varner got over his cold and is itching to get back on the Bookmobile, but I won't let him, 'cause if I let him, I lose that run up to Coeburn, and then my source dries up on me."

"Who's the source?"

"Karen Bell's best friend. Benita Hensley. The librarian up in Wise."

"Great."

"How's Jack Mac treatin' you?"

"Like a sister."

"Not good."

"Maybe it's over, Iva Lou."

"Don't say that! Don't ever say that! Y'all are true lovers! Look how long you waited to get together. Come on."

"That doesn't mean anything."

"You waited so long, to lose it all like this? Over what? Sex? What's the matter with you? Don't you care?"

"Iva Lou. Something happened to me."

"A horrible thing. I know, honey. You've been betrayed. I feel turrible about it." Iva Lou glops orange marmalade onto her toast.

"I mean something else."

"What?" Iva Lou looks up. From my tone, she guesses it must be a man. "Have you fallen in love with someone new, is that what you're sayin'?".

"No. I'm not in love. But he might be in love with me."

"Who is he?"

I tell Iva Lou all about Pete Rutledge, all the stories, all the way through the kisses in the field of bluebells.

"Well, look. On one level it's so goddamn romantic I can hardly take any more details. But you say you're not in love with him. So why would you leave what you got?"

"I wouldn't. I don't know how to explain this, Iva Lou. I really don't. But the love I have for Etta and for Joe sort of replaced the romantic love I had with Jack. And the love I have for my kids is more important to me than the love I have for Jack or the lust I had for Pete. Or any man who might come along. I'm not proud to admit it. I know I'm supposed to put my husband first, and then from there, from what's supposedly the center of everything, comes your love for the kids. But I realized when Joe got sick that things had changed between Jack and me as soon as Etta was born. She replaced him as the love of my life. And then when Joe came, I was thrilled that I could give Etta a brother and Jack a son, but I also knew that there was no question: Jack was number three. For sure. Behind Etta and Joe, my new true loves."

"Oh, you're all confused." Iva Lou rifles through her purse and finds her cigarettes. "You know, I quit." She grips a cigarette between her lips and urges me to continue as she flicks the lighter.

"I don't mean to make this sound complicated."

"Honey-o, that ain't right. It's two different kinds of love. One is not more important than the other. They're different. Love for your husband is about you. Love for your kids is about them."

"I know. It goes against everything I believe. But don't you think Jack knows that he's number three? He's not stupid."

"No, he's not. That's the first true thing you've said all the mornin'."

"I'm not even mad at him. What's the matter with me?"

"That's just a defense. You're giving up because you're afraid you'll lose him altogether."

"We don't have anything to talk about anymore."

"Do you talk about Joe?"

"No."

"There's your problem. It's all you two are thinking about, and no one's saying anything about it. You're blaming him. He didn't give Joe the cancer."

"No, but he didn't save him either, did he?" I can't believe I said it. I've only ever thought it, I've never admitted it out loud.

"Ave, you listen to me. Jack couldn't save Joe. No one could."

"But—"

"But nothin'. You stop this. You're killin' your marriage with blame. And you're holding on to bad feelings that have no place in the present."

"I know." Iva Lou is right.

"What's your plan?" She looks at me. " 'Cause, honey, I guaran-damn-tee you that Karen Bell has got a plan. What's *your* plan?"

*F*leeta, who swore she'd have nothing to do with the Soda Fountain, now stays late and bakes the desserts. And they're not simple ones, either. Pearl bought those aluminum cake stands with the glass domes to show off Fleeta's red velvet cake, her pecan and cinnamon pound cake drizzled with glaze and topped with crunchy sugar-dipped walnuts, and her mile-high chocolate cake with white butter-cream frosting. ("The secret to that one is the cup of strong coffee instead of cold water in the batter," Fleeta told me.) There is a SPECIALS! sign behind the counter and a chalkboard with folks' birthdays listed (you're entitled to a free sundae on your big day). This is unbelievable. In a few months, Pearl has hit a home run. Look out, Norton.

"I'm tellin' ye. It's a lot of work, but I love it," Fleeta says as she goes behind the counter.

"I thought you didn't want a soda fountain in the Pharmacy."

"I didn't. Till it was here. Then once it was here, I got to like doin' the bakin'. And makin' the lunches. I just added soup beans and cornbread to the menu. See?"

"Fleets, you have found your passion."

"Maybe." Fleeta blushes; she doesn't think of herself as passionate.

Ed Carleton has done a good job subbing for me in the pill department. He's caught up; the new orders are only as of this morning. I feel good as I slip into my smock and take my place on my bar stool behind my counter. I missed my job. I sort through the new orders. There is one for Alice Lambert for a very potent drug usually prescribed for cancer patients to counter the nausea that comes from chemo and radiation.

"Fleets? What's happening with Alice Lambert?"

"I told Eddie to refer her orders over to the Rite Aid in Appalachia."

"No, it's okay."

"She has cancer. I guess her meanness done turned on her."

Fleeta walks away. Now, there's loyalty for you. Fleeta cannot forgive Alice for the way she behaved after my mother died. As I count out twenty-four tiny pink pills and load them onto the knife to place them in the bottle, I wonder why I feel sad. Is it because Alice Lambert is the last person left from my old life? When she's gone, will it all be ancient history?

Etta is in town, spending the night with her girlfriends. I'm sure she will tell them all about her crush on Stefano and about Pete Rutledge and peach lip gloss. She hung a picture of Tom Cruise over her bed; Pete must have triggered her new taste for brunette men with flashy smiles.

Jack is working late. Or so he says. I go to bed at my usual time; often, when I wake up, he's already up and dressed and making coffee. I try to stay awake to see if he even comes to bed at all; I know at least one night he fell asleep in the living room in the easy chair with the television on. I keep waiting for the right time to have our talk, but there doesn't seem to be a right time. Maybe he is avoiding me. I'm not sure.

I have a chance to go through the house for the first time since our return last week. I have a stack of pictures from vacation to put away. I've bored everyone I know from St. Paul to Pennington Gap with the pictures of the summer snowcaps in the Alps—enough is enough. I sent some off to Papa, and I'll put the rest in the box where they stay until I fill albums with them. I pull the box out of the hall closet. I hear a mew. Shoo the Cat peers out at me, annoyed that I've found his hiding place. I give him a quick kiss on the head.

I sort through the box. I really need to get some photo albums. The box is practically full. I study the faces in the pictures. We look so happy; we are a family. The pictures from last Christmas are as clear and bright as the ones from years before. We were back on track. Ready to celebrate again. Weren't we happy last Christmas? And yet I sensed something. I was scared, even then, that Jack Mac was slipping away from me. I wasn't just being paranoid. I know that all men look at women. But I couldn't get that stupid Halloween Carnival out of my head. I remember it in such vivid detail, right down to the way the popcorn balls smelled so sickeningly sweet as I watched my husband chitchat with Karen Bell. What is that little voice in our head that tells us to Watch Out? How do we know when to heed the warning signs instead of chalking them up to PMS, or getting older, or just having a bad day?

I put the pictures in the box. Jack's canvas work vests are hanging in the closet. He didn't wash them while I was gone (obviously); he just wore them and hung them up again. I pull them off the hangers and head for the sun porch to wash them.

I pull keys and nails and bolts and scraps of paper out of the pockets. I make a neat stack of all the junk on the dryer. As I toss the vests into the machine, I hear something crackle. So I pull the vest out of the machine and go through the pockets one more time.

There's a square of loose-leaf paper folded many times. It reminds me of a note passed in high school study hall. The edges of the paper are ripped fringe. I unfold the paper and read:

My dear Jack: This has been the best summer of my life. Remember that I ♥ you. I'll wait. Karen.

I fold the note carefully back into a small square, just as I found it. (Why am I doing this?) I'm numb. This note makes it real, right down to the heart she put in the word "love" where the "o" goes. I met Karen Bell. She was no rival! What would my husband see in her when he had me? My ego makes a valiant effort, but it's not long before it gives way to despair and self-loathing. I feel the numbness leave me and the anger set in. I am so furious I could destroy this house, burn it to the ground and not look back. It's dangerous for me to be inside. I have to get out of here.

I look around for my keys to the Jeep. I usually leave them on the front table. When I can't find them, I begin to tear the house apart. I find myself ripping the cushions off of the sofa, then turning over the straight-backed chairs, then opening the cabinets in the kitchen, shoving out their contents—glass smashes, jars of jelly and cans of spices and boxes of rice shower the floor like rain. I go into my bedroom and rip off the coverlet, the sheets, and I tear the feather pillows apart; I'm sweating, soaked to the skin, and so angry that I cry out. I lift the mattress off the bed and shove it to the floor. What am I looking for? I am losing my mind. *Where are those keys?* I hear a deafening screech inside my ears, one so loud, I would stab myself to stop the noise.

"What are you doing?" A voice cuts through the pounding in my head. Jack stands in the doorway of our bedroom.

"You, you . . . I hate you!"

"What's going on?" he says, his voice breaking. I've caught him, and he knows it.

"Why don't you tell me the truth!"

"What are you talking about?" Now he has the look of a gentle person, a look that tells me he doesn't want to hurt me with the truth or anything else.

"You . . . you." I fish around my pockets—where did I put that letter? I find it and take it out and carefully, like a judge, unfold the clue. "Look. Look right here. You love this woman!"

"Ave. Listen to me."

"Why? You're a liar. You're just going to lie to me. I want these mattresses out of here. You fucked her all summer right here in this room. In our bed. Where my children were. How could you do that? I will hate you until the day I die."

I shove past him, out of the bedroom and to the front door. Suddenly, in the first moment of clarity I've had since I found that note, I remember where my keys are. I left them in the Jeep.

"Where are you going?"

"Don't talk to me," I tell him. I run to the Jeep. I feel him behind me. I get into the driver's seat. He reaches in and tries to pull me out of the Jeep. He has me by the waist. I swing my legs out and begin kicking him, and I'm grateful for my strong legs as I fend him off. He tries to control my kicks, but he cannot.

"You made your choice. Now go to her. Go on. Go!" He steps back. I turn the key and throw the Jeep in reverse. Before he can make another move, I am down the mountain. I don't look back.

It's a long drive to Knoxville, Tennessee. Even longer when you don't have any money. I left my purse in Cracker's Neck Holler. Thank God I have an emergency gas card taped to the bottom of the driver's seat. As I pay the man for the gas, I ask him if I can charge some food on the card. He shrugs. So I go through the Quik Mart and buy pretzels and Diet Coke, two apples, a cup of coffee, and a bottle of Tylenol for my throbbing head.

The road to Knoxville is a straightaway into the hills of Tennessee. I am glad I don't have to think too much as I drive. I go about eighty miles an hour. I hope a cop stops me. Have I got a story for him.

I feel oddly relieved after my tantrum, almost exhilarated. The pain and rage gave way to endorphins that pulse through my system, soothing me. Iva Lou was right. I had my defenses up; my lack of feeling about my husband's affair was just a facade. There's a lot inside me that I haven't addressed. The worst part is the realization that my husband is not the man I thought he was. I thought he loved me so much that there wasn't room for Karen Bell or any other woman to wheedle in and take him. How pathetic he looked when I told him I knew. There is no worse face in the world, the face of a man who gave it all away. I'll never forget it.

My marriage is over. It's sad, but it isn't nearly as sad as losing Joe. I instantly compare the two, because now, and for the last three years, everything is measured against that loss. I can't help it. And I realize that everything I've done since Joe's death has been busywork. My strategy has been to keep myself occupied until I can be with my son again. I can fill up my life with work and games and trips and even have moments when seeing Joe again isn't the only thing I think about; but as surely as I am diverted, the thought comes back. The ache of my loss never stops. It is as real to me as my breathing.

I find Theodore's house quickly (I'm surprised; my sense of direction is usually terrible). It's late. Thank God there's a light on. I knock on the door. Theodore looks out the window; when he sees it's me, he comes to the door and flings it open.

"What's wrong?"

"Jack has another woman. That woman I told you about. From the Halloween Carnival. It's all true."

"Come in."

The second I enter Theodore's living room, I am better. I need to be around things that are familiar and someone I can count on. I love his home. It smells like him. The same albums that he had in his log cabin in Big Stone Gap line the bookshelves. The same couch. The same coffee table. The same easy chair. Nothing has changed. I enter a safe realm when I'm with Theodore, the one constant in my life.

"You look like a banshee."

"I don't have any money."

"What?"

"I don't have my purse."

"You just left?"

I nod.

"Does Jack Mac know where you are?"

"No."

"We should call him and tell him you're safe."

"I don't know Karen Bell's phone number." I burst into tears and throw myself on the futon.

"That's her name?" Theodore hands me the box of Kleenex. "That's a crappy name."

The way Theodore says "crappy" makes me laugh. Great. I'm laughing and crying, just like the head case this whole ordeal has turned me into. "I'm not calling him."

"But what about Etta?"

"She's spending the night with her friend Tara. It's Tara's birthday." Theodore picks up the phone.

"What are you doing?"

"I'm calling your house. Okay? Just let me call your house."

I'm too tired to put up a fight. I hear Theodore tell Jack that I am here, and then there's a long time when Theodore listens and doesn't talk. Great. Jack is telling him the whole sordid tale. Is my husband including the fact that his girlfriend coats herself in Man Tan? She is inappropriately *bronzata* in seasons that she should not be. Theodore hangs up the phone.

"Well, now I know his side."

"I left the clue in the house!" I tell him, sitting up.

"What clue?"

"The letter. She wrote him a letter, told him she loved him and was waiting for him."

"Honey, you found a letter she wrote—not one he wrote. That's her side of things. She may be in love with him, but he's not in love with her."

"How do you know?"

"He told me."

"And you believe him? Wake up. He has a girlfriend. He's had her a long time—and he spent the summer with her. How much proof do you need?"

"I know. I get it. It sounds like the plot of a bad Connie Francis movie, not that there ever was a bad one. Let's say your husband had an affair this summer, and now it's over. Now, I don't know what 'affair' means to him—maybe they just talked about it, or fooled around a little, or maybe even a lot. But that doesn't matter now. It's over. He wants you to come home."

"Just like that."

"Well, not 'just like that,' but yeah, he wants you to come home and work through this with him."

"Theodore, why are you so calm?"

"Because you're a lunatic."

"What? Excuse me, please! Could somebody be on my side? I'm the one who's been cheated on!"

"Yeah, yeah, yeah. Poor you."

"Theodore!"

"You tore up pillows—he's spent the past four hours trying to gather up goose feathers."

"Too bad."

"You love him. Why put yourselves through this?"

"Because I'm *right*. I've been true."

"Let me tell you about men." Theodore sits down next to me.

"I don't want to talk about men."

"All right, then, let's talk about the Man. The American guy over in Italy that you were dancing with. And then you spent how many day trips with him. And meals and so on. What about him?"

"That was different."

"How so?"

"I resisted!"

"Really?"

"Yes. I have morals. Principles. I could've done whatever I wanted, but I didn't—out of respect for my marriage!"

"I'm so impressed. So you're rolling around the Alps with a guy from New Jersey. And your husband is home because he disinvited himself and you didn't beg him to reconsider; and he reaches out to someone while you're gone—and you're mad at *him*?"

"How many times do I have to tell you: I didn't have sex with Pete!"

"But you wanted to."

"That's not the same as doing it!"

"Thank you for that clarification." Theodore gets up and goes to the kitchen. I follow him. "Now, we don't know if Jack had sex with Sharon. Karen Bell."

"My husband likes a lot of sex. Okay?"

"I didn't need to know that."

"And we haven't been having any. I got back from Italy and nothing. Nothing. I mean nothing."

"Let's put this in perspective, shall we?" Theodore sounds like the professor that he is. "You're tired. And you're hurt. And you're angry. And you're—"

"Betrayed."

"Betrayed. But what you aren't is honest."

"What? I am so honest!"

"You're not. You think that you're allowed to go off and have a summer romance, consummated or not, and that's your own private domain. But you expect Jack to stay home and do the chores and be loyal and wait for you to go through whatever it is you're going through, and then you come home and he gets the great privilege of being your husband again. If he didn't have a Karen Bell, you would have to leave him."

"Why?"

"You wouldn't have a man at home. You'd have a doormat. You

want to cut off his balls, and then when you do, you're mad at him because he's not man enough."

"I don't understand."

"How dare you treat him poorly for years and expect him to take it? I'm surprised he hasn't slept with half of Big Stone Gap. At least he chose a woman in Coeburn—it's hard for gossip to travel uphill. He tried not to embarrass you, and whatever he did, he ended it when you came home. So what do you want?"

"I want . . ."

"You don't know, do you?"

I don't. (But I damn sure know that if I ever rip up the house in Cracker's Neck Holler again, the last place I'm coming for comfort is here.)

"You know, that wedding ring doesn't have magical powers. It doesn't give you license to be cruel, and it can't keep you faithful. You believe you're allowed to act in whatever ugly way you choose because you have a lifetime guarantee that he's not going anywhere. You can abuse Jack, but by God, you're married for keeps. You think you're a woman of substance and commitment and high morals, but you're the worst kind of phony."

"How can you say something like that to me? You know me."

"Right. I know you, and you didn't have sex with that Pete character because you were afraid you weren't good enough. You knew he'd have sex with you and figure out that you're just like every other lay with a smart, good-looking woman—it's lots of fun in the moment but no staying power beyond the thrill. You wanted him to want you, and you led him on, with no intention of delivering the goods. You owe that guy an apology too."

I curl up into a ball of shame on the futon. Theodore is right.

"Now I'm tired. There's a nightgown in the top drawer of the bureau in your room. You left it here last time you visited. Go to bed."

Theodore goes off to his bedroom and closes the door. I hear him turn on the television. A panel of light under the door flashes and changes as the muffled voices and canned laugh track play through. I stretch out on the futon on the floor and cry. I won't sleep tonight. I don't want to.

The ride back from Knoxville goes way too fast. I stay within the speed limit. I guess I'm trying to drag out the trip. I wish it would take a week to get home. But it doesn't. It takes me exactly three hours. Since I left at dawn, I will be home long before Etta returns from her sleepover this afternoon.

Jack's truck is parked in its usual spot next to the house. I park the Jeep and sit in it for a while. I hear the creak of the screen door. Shoo the Cat has pushed the door open and comes running out onto the porch. He lifts his head and sniffs the breeze. Then he looks over at me like I'm crazy for sitting in the Jeep. He's never seen me do this. You park and get out. But he's never seen Ave Maria the Coward before. I'm not mad at Theodore for being honest with me, but maybe I didn't want to own up to what a terrible person I've been. Shame is keeping me in this Jeep.

Maybe I thought my life would settle down and take care of itself naturally. Iva Lou's words ring in my head: "What's your plan, what's your plan?" I should have known I needed a plan. I have to work for everything I get, normalcy and routine included. So I throw my legs of lead out of the Jeep and climb the stairs and go in.

The house is orderly. I can still smell the spices I spilled all over the kitchen floor; the scent of cumin and cinnamon lingers in the deep cracks of the old wood. I walk into the kitchen, which has been put back together in perfect order. I turn and look into our bedroom, which is neat. The bed is made, with the exception of pillows. There are no pillows. I'll have to buy new ones. No way to put the old ones back together again.

I go through the kitchen and out the sun porch and into the field behind our house. Jack is there in the yard, stacking firewood in that way he does, where it looks artistic, like a latticework fence. He looks up at me. He stops his work. I know I have to make a decision, and whatever I do in this moment will determine the fate of our marriage. Now that I have been honest with myself (thank you, Theodore), there is no turning back. I have to be clear. Other lives are involved here. My daughter's. My husband's. Our extended family.

I wish I had a picture in my mind of what I think marriage ought to be. The old movies never helped; those people were always happy. And my mother and Fred Mulligan's marriage was so cold, I knew long before he wasn't my real father that mine should not be like theirs. And for a girl, now a woman, who never thought she'd marry, to be in the thick of one is surreal.

I realize now that I have not chosen this. Jack MacChesney chose me; and never once, in all these years, have I chosen him. Of course, I said yes when he wanted to marry me. But I said yes because he asked, not because I really chose. How must it have been for him, all these years of trying to please me? Of hoping every day that this would be the one that Ave Maria would choose him? But I never did. I loved him, no question. And his babies came through me and into the world. But never once did I choose him. Not really.

This field that used to overwhelm me looks like a small patch of grass. The mountains shrink back into small mounds of dirt that disappear into the wet earth. And the sky, tacked up like a pale blue sheet, looks temporary. The only eternal things are what we choose. The things we would die for. What would I die for? My children, yes. But would I die for Jack MacChesney? I walk across the field to him. He looks at me. I sit on his pretty fence of firewood. I rehearsed so many ways to tell him what he means to me on the ride back from Knoxville, but now that I'm here, I don't know where to start.

"I'm sorry I trashed the house." This is my opener?

"I had a hard time getting up the rice. It took me the better part of the day to sweep it up. How was your trip?"

"Weird."

"Ave, do you want to know what happened?" Jack is speaking of Karen Bell, I assume.

"No," I tell him.

"I can tell you," he offers.

"No, honey. That's yours. That's not mine." The only strategy I have, the only one I know for sure I must stick to, is that I mustn't have real pictures of the two of them together in my mind. Those pictures would make it impossible for me to go forward. This much I know about myself.

My husband sits down next to me. We sit there a very long time.

"Jack. What should we do?"

"What do you want to do?"

"Well, I guess most of the time, I wish you could take my pain away," I tell him.

"I can't do that."

"I know."

"If you want me to go, I will. You can have everything. This house. But I want Etta half of the year. That would be the only thing I would want," he says quietly.

"You've given this some thought."

"Because I can't bear to see you like this."

"You really love me, don't you?" I take his hand.

"Yes, I do."

"That's always been amazing to me, you know."

"What do you mean?"

"That love you've always had for me. I never could quite believe it."

"Why?"

"Maybe because I never thought I deserved it. And maybe because it's easy for me not to feel. It worked so well for me all of my life. You married a real cold cookie."

"You're not cold. You've just been hurt." Jack gets up. And then he does the strangest thing. He kneels in front of me. "And I can't believe I hurt you more."

My husband puts his head in my lap and cries. And I realize a very important thing about him, and maybe it's the thing that will help us go forward: he never blames me for what I am; and he doesn't judge me. He accepts me. And that's the one thing I never gave him in return. This guy never had a chance with me; not really. He was never enough. But who could be? No man could measure up to my standards.

"Jack, look at me." He does. "I thought I had changed. I thought you changed me with your love, by giving me the kids, by sharing this life with me. I thought I let you in, but I never really did."

"I knew what you were when I fell in love with you. I knew it was going to be hard. I knew that when I signed on. Remember when you went into that Deep Sleep?"

Of course I remember. Years ago, I collapsed and slept for one week straight. At the time, Doc Daugherty called it a nervous breakdown.

"I almost decided not to go after you anymore. I thought, there's something going on inside this woman that no one will ever know or understand. But I couldn't give up. I couldn't give you up. I had the out, I had the chance, but something made me stay. I think about that a lot. Why did I stay? Is it because I love you? Or is it more than that? I know you need me, and maybe that's my purpose, to be needed. I don't know."

"That's not your purpose."

"What is, then?"

"To be chosen." Now it's my turn to cry. "And I never chose you. But I do now. Today. If you'll still have me."

My heart is breaking. This good and decent man has been dragged through my crazy life like a wagon. It wasn't all terrible, and maybe there were times when he wasn't dragged. We've had great times together. And tragedy. And routine. Great sex. No sex. But it has all been built upon sand. There is no foundation here because I never truly committed to this. I was thirty-six years old, and I thought it was time. That's why I got married. Yes, I loved him, but I also knew that this was an opportunity that would not come again. I made myself walk into my fear and seize control. I wasn't going to let anything hold me back anymore. I was going to live. I didn't think about how I was going to live, only that I had a right to live. A right to a life with a good man who loved me.

I thought I knew my issues. I thought it was my childhood, with the strange secrets hidden under the surface. I believed that once I found my real father, everything would fall into place. Mario da Schilpario would have all the answers. I was sure of it! But he was only part of the answer. When I made peace with Fred Mulligan, I felt release. When I accepted the lie my mother told to protect me, I felt galvanized. I knew all of these things, and I thought the knowledge of them, the recognition of them, had changed me. But just because I figured it out did not mean that I had fixed it. I am shocked that I know better and yet routinely fall back into my old patterns. I shut off. I shut down. I don't feel. And I hold myself above everyone else as though I am better. I think my pain elevates me above everybody else. That weak people are destroyed by the bad things that happen to them. That weak people need sex to validate their egos. That weak people can't follow the rules. I wasn't weak! I was strong, so strong nothing could penetrate me. What a glorious prize you get for not needing people. You get to be safe and alone, even in your marriage! But all those people who live and let go and let life happen to them, good or bad, wild or serene, they aren't weak—they're human. Somewhere in my past, I learned that if you separate yourself, you don't get hurt. Pain can be avoided. And if you stuff it down deep enough, you will forget it's there. Do not acknowledge it, and it will not hurt you. Theodore is right. I do owe this man an apology. But what else do I owe him?

"When will Etta be home?"

"Iva Lou is picking her up and taking her over to her house after the slumber party. She said she'd keep her overnight."

"Good." I stand up. "I don't want to go back to what we were."

"We can't."

"I want to begin again. With what I know now."

"I don't know if you can change. Or if I can."

"It's bigger than change, Jack. It's reinventing the whole thing."

"Do you know how to do that?"

"We'll figure it out."

I lead my husband into the house. We go through the sun porch and the kitchen to our bedroom and the bed with no pillows. I will begin with how I make love to my husband. I will be present in his arms, every cell of my body in tune with his, I will listen and I will pay attention and I will treat him like the rare and precious treasure that he is. For this time and every time that will come hereafter, I choose him. My beautiful husband with the big shoulders (good thing, they carried two of us all this time) and the sweet hazel eyes. I won't wait for him to kiss me; I kiss him.

"This is new," he says, and smiles.

"Work with me," I tell him, and he laughs.

I take off his clothes slowly. First his work boots. Then his socks. I take his bare feet and rub each one tenderly. He begins to pull his shirt off over his head; I won't let him. I work the shirt off of him and, for the first time, look at his neck and the way his shoulders connect to his upper arms, and the way the muscle twists from the top of his arm around the back and down the elbow. Would I know my husband's body from any other man's in the world? I will now, as I kiss each freckle on his strong brown arm, down to his wrist. His hand, the long fingers, the tiny cuts on his thumb from stacking the wood, his square pink fingernails. How strong his chest is; as I lie on top of him, I feel his breath rise and fall underneath me, as our skin touches and then fits together in the way only longtime couples know. All of this I took for granted. How did I let so much time pass? Why did I ever think that this was expendable, that I could cut this man out of my life? What was I thinking? That I could walk out of here and find someone else? Someone better? As I run my hands down his back, I know there is no one better. In the very moment that love is mundane, it can become new. Why didn't my mother tell me that? I am able to see new things simply because I'm looking for them. How sad I am that they were here all along and I gave them away as though they had no value. Simple things: my husband's love, his faith in me, and his steadfastness. All of those things I pretended did not matter. Love is so fragile. I kiss his eyes. I really want him to see me now.

Monday brings a perfectly sunny, yet cool, first day of school. I am happy for Etta, who didn't want to wear a rain slicker to her first day of fourth grade. She wanted to show off her striped Alpine sweater from her grandfather, and happily, the weather agreed. She kisses me and jumps out of the Jeep. I feel something gooey on my cheek. It's Chiara's peach lip gloss.

I'm about to turn to drive back home (I thought I'd clean out a closet), but instead I head for the Cadet section of Big Stone Gap, in the western part of town, over the bridge and down by the Powell River. It's changed a lot; I try to remember the last time I was here. Had to be over a year ago; I delivered some pills to Oneida Mitchell. As I follow the river road, I see that they've added a trailer park and a convenience market.

There's a pink house on the dead end of Morrissey Street. It's been over thirty years since I've been here. Alice Lambert lives at Number 11. The simple ranch house has a deck on the front. The yard is overgrown; nestled in the brush are white concrete statuettes of a boy and girl who appear to be Dutch.

You can hear the river rushing by; the brown water is visible through the mud trees that line the river side of the road. The mailbox is slung open and full of flyers and junk mail. I clean it out on my way to the front door.

The old silver screen door has WELCOME written in cursive in the center panel, flanked by two rusted daisies. The plastic Greek urns that anchor either side of the door are full of weeds. A couple of wild yellow blooms choke through. I knock on the door. I see the Lamberts' old Cadillac in the carport, so I assume she's home. I hear a shuffling from the back of the house. Finally, the door opens. I am shocked when I see Aunt Alice. I hardly recognize her. She might weigh one hundred pounds.

"Aunt Alice?"

"Hello," she says through the screen door.

"I wanted to stop by and say hello. I was thinking about you."

"You was?"

"Yes ma'am."

"Why is 'at?"

"I was thinking about how you came to my son's funeral so many years ago and how I never thanked you."

"It weren't nothin'," she says, looking away.

"No, no, it was very kind of you. Thank you." After I filled Alice's prescription at the Pharmacy, I felt bad every day for not calling or stopping by.

Aunt Alice stands there. She doesn't move to close the door, but she doesn't invite me in, either. This was always the way it was with my father's side of the family. They never knew what to do to make people feel at home. Or at ease. Maybe they had good intentions underneath it all, but basically, they had no manners. My mother used to say that they didn't have *creanza*, proper upbringing.

"May I come in?" I ask her.

"Sure," she says, and shrugs.

I push the door open. Her little house is neat as a pin, but it's dirty. There is a layer of dust on everything, the windows are cloudy, and the rug needs sweeping. Poor thing. She is too weak to do the chores.

"Would you like a cup of tea?"

"No, thank you."

"I ain't got much in the house."

"I don't need a thing."

We sit quietly until Alice blurts, "I got the cancer."

"I'm sorry."

"You know'd I lost Wayne."

"Yes ma'am."

"He had him the black lung. That's worse than what I git. He couldn't hardly breathe at the end; they put him on a tank. He done filled up with water and choked to death."

"I'm sorry."

"It were turr-ible. And Bobby ne'er did come home to see 'im. That were the greatest tragedy of all. I don't got a son no more."

Wayne and Alice's son, Bobby, was the light of their lives. I never liked him at all. He was several years older and a tease. I heard that he moved to Kingsport and took to drinking. He was on his fourth wife at last count.

"Sure you still have a son. Bobby just gets sidetracked, that's all."

Alice chuckles. "That there's a good word fer it: sidetracked."

"So what does Doc Daugherty say?"

" 'Bout me? Not much."

"What kind of cancer do you have?"

"It was breast. Then it done went to the bone. On account of I wouldn't let 'em take my breast. No. I come in with 'em, and I'm a-gonna go out with 'em too."

"Do you have a lot of pain?"

"I can't hardly sleep a'tall it gits so bad of the night. I can't find a good spot, you know."

"What do you eat?"

"I ain't hungry much. Once in a while I have me some Nabs. Coca-Cola."

"Aunt Alice?" My tone of voice causes Alice's spine to stiffen.

"Yes?"

"I know we've had our problems—"

"Nah, don't dredge all that there up. It's not nothin' no more."

"I wasn't very nice."

"You got a temper on ye, that's all. You're Eye-talian. They's like 'at." Her slur, instead of upsetting me, makes me smile. She's right. Italians *are* like that.

"I'd like to help you out. Can I come over once in a while?"

I go to Buckles Supermarket and shop for Aunt Alice. I pick up easy things, like eggs and bread and cheese and cold cuts. Soup. Pasta. Pancakes. I pick up magazines and puzzle books. Nellie Goodloe is at the next register checking out.

"Hello, Ave Maria. How was your summer?"

"It was good."

"I see Jack Mac's mighty busy."

"That's for sure," I say. "They have lots of work."

"Did they finish that rec center up in Coeburn, by the by?"

Then the strangest thing happens. I feel surrounded. Maybe it's because it's Monday and folks go trading, but it's also something else. I can't put my finger on it. The Methodist Sewing Circle is ready to check out: Mrs. Shoop, Mrs. Quillen, Mrs. Grubb, Mrs. Zander, and Mrs. Messer, each has a shiny cart, and they're lined up like train cars on a track. The smiles on their faces are so sweet, like they're glad to see me. But why are they all listening?

"It was a right long month with you gone. It was about a month, wasn't it?" Mrs Quillen asks.

"Yes ma'am."

"That's a long time to be gone from your husband," Mrs. Shoop chimes in.

"He thought so," I say with a smile.

"It-lee is mighty far. You know, if there was an emergency or something," Mrs. Messer says in a sweet singsong voice, half chiding me.

"I think my husband can handle anything."

"I'm sure he can," Nellie chimes in. "And I'm sure he did." She looks over her bifocals at the ladies.

"Well, it's sure good to see y'all again." I grab my groceries and get the hell out of there. As I drive back to the Cadet section, I realize why: the ladies wanted to see how A-vuh Marie survived her husband's affair. They smelled blood and they came to check out the casualty. I expect they thought I might just throw myself on the checkout and stab myself repeatedly with the outdoor barbecue tongs they had on sale.

Alice is napping when I get there. I make up a tray of macaroni and cheese and boil up some broccoli. Before long, she joins me in the kitchen.

"Smells good."

"You sit." I help her to the table. She is so tiny, I can feel her ribs as I guide her to a chair. As soon as I put the plate of food in front of her, she eats. She gulps down the macaroni and cheese and mashes up the broccoli with her fork before eating it.

"Thank ye for all this." Alice pats my hand.

"It's my pleasure." I give Alice a hug, something that I have never done. And I hold her for a good long time.

Fleeta has a lot on her plate. She won't give up cashiering, but she won't take the Soda Fountain over, either. So she's doing both, and she's worn out. She insists upon fixing Iva Lou, Pearl, and me grilled-cheese sandwiches. It's closing time, so we let her.

"Guess who I went to visit?" I say.

"Law me. You weren't up in Coeburn, were ye?"

"Fleeta. That is not nice!" Iva Lou admonishes her.

"I ain't nice."

"I think we should have a rule," Pearl says. "No mention of Coeburn ever again."

"How'd you hear about Karen Bell?" I ask Pearl.

"In Norton."

"Who cares in Norton?"

"Whoever's up there shopping from Big Stone Gap."

"Lord a-mighty." I sit back on the bar stool.

"I told you that this entire county is filled with vipers. And they's got feet. 'Cause everything that happens 'round here travels. So if you want to keep your husband's cheatin' under wraps, you got to kill him, kill her, then send them bodies north and let them Eye-talians take care of 'em." Fleeta slides the golden-brown grilled-cheese sandwiches from her double-wide spatula onto our plates on the counter.

"What? No garnish?" Pearl teases.

"I went to see Alice Lambert."

"Why would you bother with her?" Iva Lou asks.

"She's dying."

Fleeta, Iva Lou, and Pearl sit with this new information for a moment.

"Better send Reverend Bowers over there so she can repent, or she'll be frying like hot lard in the outskirts of hell," Fleeta says as she brushes potato-chip crumbs off of her smock. "I only say send him 'cause he's known to make house calls."

"Fleeta, make her some fudge. And Iva Lou, she needs some books to read."

"I don't believe my ears," Iva Lou exclaims.

"Me neither." Fleeta shakes her head.

"Find out what medicine she needs and give it to her for free," Pearl says quietly.

"I hope that when I'm sick and distended and bloated and full of the cancer, you send me some medicine for free. I work in this joint, and all I ever git is a ten percent discount." Fleeta ashes her cigarette into the sink.

"And all the Estée Lauder you can poach." Pearl winks at her.

Etta is in full swing with her schoolwork and her new social life, which includes gathering her girlfriends together to paint their nails and make crank calls to boys. It's very annoying, but I try to be patient.

I remind myself that this is just another phase of child rearing, no different from dealing with teething or mouth breathing. The entry into the Boy Years sure can get loud.

Jack comes home from work in a great mood.

"Let's go to the Fold tonight," he suggests.

"I can't. I have the Lip Gloss Girls in there for a slumber party."

"Is Fleeta around?" Jack asks.

"I hate to ask her again."

"She loves Etta." Jack picks me up and spins me around.

"Is that your hand on my ass?" I ask my husband.

"I think so. And I hate to tell you, but that situation is only gonna get worse." He kisses me.

"Okay, okay. I'll call Fleeta."

I call Fleeta. Of course, she complains a little, she wants to see a story on *20/20* about granny dumping, but I promise her we get better cable reception up here in the holler.

So she comes.

The Carter Family Fold is overflowing with folks. It's just the right time of year to gather up in the Carter family's barn and listen to music and dance. Jack wanted to come because he heard on the job that one of the Stanley Brothers was showing up. And indeed he did, so the music is glorious. I never heard such fine fiddling. We dance so much and so hard, my denim shirt is soaked.

Lew Eisenberg has turned out to be the best clogger in Southwest Virginia. He shows me a two-step that reminds him of the hora he did at his bar mitzvah many years ago. We have a good laugh over that one.

"Honey, you need to towel off," Iva Lou says to me as I collapse on the bleachers.

"I'm having a ball," I tell her.

"How's it going with your husband?"

"Very well, thank you. It's good to have him back."

"Are you kidding? It's great. It's the best of all things. It's the triumph of true love over base lust. It's a story of forgiveness and redemption, honey. You want me to go on?"

"No."

"Then I won't. I'm doin' my own brand of celebratin' tonight. Lyle stopped drinkin' again and we are flush solid, honey."

"Good for him and good for you."

"Maybe there is something to astrology. You know, maybe the planets do line up and everybody has good vibes at the same time."

"That's totally possible."

The Methodist Sewing Circle is gathered by the door, chatting furiously.

"Jesus Christmas, what has got them so agitated?" Iva Lou wonders.

"Somebody probably came up with a better apple-butter recipe."

The Sewing Circle stops chattering. Their little circle widens and fans out.

"Or not," Iva Lou says in a tone that forces me to look up. "Oh my," she says quietly.

Karen Bell stands in the doorway wearing black leather pants, a white blouse, a chain belt, and a white cowboy hat cocked on the back of her head. She rolls her pink lips together as though she's trying to bite off a bit of chapped lip. She looks worried, and the groove between her eyes is deep. Of course she's worried. I'm here, aren't I? I look around the room for my husband; he's not here, but he said he was going for a chili dog. I wonder if she's looking for him. I can see from one look at the Methodist Sewing Circle that they have the same idea. Their heads are swiveling around on their necks like geese looking to land.

"I'll be right back," I tell Iva Lou.

I ignore her call of "Where are you going?" as I walk away. The Other Woman, the Girl on the Side, the Strumpet from Coeburn, is unaware that I am walking toward her, but she is the only woman in the room unaware of me. All eyes are on the battle-ax, the wife who hung in there till her dang knuckles bled; the poor little ole thing, me. Joe Smiddy's Reedy Creek Band plays an old ballad that underscores my steps; I feel the layers of onlookers fall away as I pass. The Sewing Circle turns into a nervous Greek Chorus as they whisper what gore may ensue if Ave Maria gets mad enough. I can feel the nervous tension as it flows through the crowd and makes a path to the Other Woman. I follow that path to its bitter end.

"Karen?"

She turns to me. When she connects me, the real person, to her life, she has a moment of surreal disbelief. I am someone whose face she tried hard to remember, having met me only once. Maybe if she could find some flaw in me, it would make her plan to steal my husband all right. But all that stands before her is a sweaty Eye-talian wearing good lipstick. She can't quite make the connection, so I will do it for her.

"I'm Ave Maria. I don't know if you remember me."

She looks at me oddly, and at first her little chin juts out as though she's looking to fight. I've confused her, so the thought crease between her eyes deepens even more.

"We met at the Methodist Church," I remind her.

"Yeah. A while back." She looks away. I guess she's had enough eye contact.

"I'd like to thank you for being such a good friend to my husband this summer."

She doesn't know what to say. She's so nervous, the cowboy hat slides off the back of her head and down her back. The chin string catches on her throat. "You're welcome," she stammers.

I turn and walk back to the bleachers, past the whispers of the well-meaning Christian ladies and to my spot next to Iva Lou.

"Girl, where on God's green did you get the courage?"

"Bette Davis. There's that scene in *Jezebel* where she wears the red dress to the ball where all the nice girls are supposed to wear white. I imagined myself in the red dress, walking across that dance floor, defying all of society. Nobody ever messed with Bette Davis, and by God, nobody is ever gonna mess with me."

"Did you tell her you'd whoop her ass if she took off after your husband agin?"

"Oh yeah."

"That's my girl," Iva Lou says as she cocks her head back and takes a gulp from her beer. "In all my years and all my married men, I only had one confrontation."

"Only one?"

"Yeah. Billie Jean Scott met me up at Skeen's Ridge one night, right after I'd been with her husband. And she looked me in the eye, after she'd blocked the road and stopped my car, of course, and said, 'Iva Lou Wade, were you with my Hank?' I was caught and I knew it, so I 'fessed up. I told her, 'Yes ma'am.' And she said, 'Thank you, kindly. I've been trying to get rid of that son of a bitch for forty-one years. And you just give me the perfect excuse to give him the old heave-ho.'"

Iva Lou and I laugh so hard, the Methodist Sewing Circle looks at us as though we're crazy. And I think we just might be.

*W*hen folks say that Big Stone Gap is for the newlywed and the nearly dead, they ain't kidding. Alice Lambert is getting a send-off worthy of a statesman. The women in town have come down and taken over her little pink house by the brown river. They've scrubbed the windows, vacuumed, and waxed the kitchen floor; they wash her clothes, they bathe her; and the delectable food dropped off in shifts is not to be believed. Ethel Bartee even came over and did Alice's hair. And folks can't help but comment that "Alice Lambert is as sweet as pie." And she is.

Doc Daugherty told me that it's a matter of days for Alice. He can't say how many, and in a way, I don't want to know. I go and see her every day (as do the other ladies), and it's strange to say this, but I think these are the happiest days of her life.

I am sitting in the living room with Aunt Alice. Ethel gave her an upsweep with tendrils worthy of the great Loretta Lynn at the Grand Old Opry. She even wears a little lipstick. There's a rap on the door; it's Spec.

"My wife done made you a cobbler, Alice. How do you like rhubarb?" he asks.

"Thank 'er for me. I love it," Alice says.

"So how are we doin', girls?" Spec says as he sits down.

"Fine," I tell him.

"Alice, I done want to run somethin' by ye."

"Yeah?"

"Bobby's outside."

"My Bobby?"

"Yes ma'am. Yer son. I went over to Kingsport and fetched him. Now, number one: he's sober. Number two: he feels like a shit-heel for not gittin' over here sooner. Number three: I don't have a number three. He just wants to talk to ye. Are ye up fer it?"

Alice nods that she is.

Spec doesn't move from his seat, he simply shouts. "Bobby, git in here."

Bobby Lambert, forty-six years old, comes in the door. He is short like Alice but has his father's face, long and hangdog, with eyes that droop in the corners, a wide mouth, low ears, and a shock of thick hair that hangs down the center of his forehead in one curl. He is thin and has the purple-veined nose of a drinker. He's very nervous and shifts from one foot to the other. He is wearing his best clothes, but the cotton button-down shirt is yellowed, and the hems of his pants are frayed where they rest against the top of his shoes. His fourth wife must have left him.

"Hey, Mama," he says, holding on to either side of the doorframe.

"Git over here and hug yer mama's neck!" she says with a bass tone to her voice I've never heard before.

Then Bobby starts talking so fast it's as though he's conducting an auction. He's dazzling his mother with information, about this deal and that deal and this new car he got and how the transmission's the best and what kind of leather seats take the heat and which ones don't, and I look at Spec and he looks at me and we're thinking the same thing: this guy is a first-class huckster.

But Aunt Alice loves it. And him. This is her only son, and she loves everything about him. Her eyes travel over his face as though she has found a precious jewel that throws back her own reflection. She doesn't let go of his face, she is so madly in love with it. And she just nods as he drones on. Soon he's kneeling, and the picture of that, of a son at the feet of his mother, begging for her forgiveness without asking for it, is one of the most beautiful things I have ever seen. No matter what Bobby would ever do, she would forgive him. No matter what, he would always have a place here, and the only reason he didn't was his own shame. Now that he sees that his mother still loves him and always will, he can stay. And he will, until the very end.

In just three days, Alice Lambert goes to bed for good. Fleeta helps me get her to the bed. She thinks Alice didn't digest Annie Hunter's apple dumplings too well and that's why she's taken the turn. I tell Fleeta that it isn't anything that Alice has eaten, it's the cancer. Cancer is very strange; it grips a patient, and then it seems to go, then it can rage back like a fever and take you. This is what has happened to Alice. Bobby helps with the sheets, smoothing them under Alice as we turn her. I tell Fleeta to run and call Doc Daugherty.

Bobby sits on the corner of the bed and holds his mother's hand. I see in his face all the things I went through when my mother passed. The great sorrow of being separated from the one who brought you, the guilt at not doing enough for her (there is never enough we can do for our mothers), and the desperate hope that the pain will be minimal. He is trying not to cry, for her sake.

"Bobby, hon, I need me a minute with Ava." I decide to let it go. She has always mispronounced my name and that's that. Bobby looks at me kindly and leaves the room.

"Yes, Aunt Alice?"

"Do you know why I came to your boy's funeral?"

"No ma'am."

" 'Cause I lost a son too."

I'm confused, and I look at Alice quizzically.

"Not Bobby. Calvin. Calvin died at four months."

"I didn't know that."

"You wouldn't. He was born right around the time you was. I never got over it. Some folks think it turned me bitter. I don't know about that."

"Aunt Alice, will you do me a favor?"

She nods.

"When you get there, will you—could you—look out for my Joe?"

"Yes ma'am, I will."

I hear the screen door slam. Doc Daugherty must be here. I kiss Alice on the forehead. What happens next is all a haze; Doc comes in with Bobby; and Spec takes his place by the door. I feel myself leave my body as I watch this scene with me in it. And I see something that I could not have known before this moment; I watch Alice let go. She lets go of her life, of her problems, her pain, and her secrets. A burden lifts off of her as she lays dying. A smile crosses her face, one of peace and duly earned solitude.

In her final moments, her thoughts were of her sons, Bobby and Calvin. Isn't this the truth of any good mother? That in all of our lives, we worry only about those we brought into this world, regardless of whether they loved us back or treated us fairly or understood our shortcomings. As Alice lets go, so do I. I let go of my mistakes, the unattainable standards I have for my husband, my daughter, and myself, and my bitterness toward those who hurt me; mostly, I let go of my pride, which I thought had kept me whole but in reality almost ruined me. I was holding on so tightly to being right, to being perfect. There is only one lesson in all of this: let go. And when you think you've let go completely, let go again. Aunt Alice sailed out of here with such grace. She really did it right.

"She's gone." Bobby weeps and holds his mother. Doc Daugherty turns to me. But I already knew. I close my eyes and smile; Aunt Alice will find my son. She will make sure he's all right.

Johnny Teglas over at *The Post* asked me to write Alice Mulligan Lambert's obituary. And in so doing, I learned many things about her. She was a WAC in World War II; she took enough courses at Mountain Empire Community College to earn an associate's degree in business (who knew?); and those weren't her real teeth (I won't put that part in the paper). But I do mention baby Calvin, and Bobby, of course. I type up the story of her life and seal it in an envelope. I holler to Fleeta back in the Soda Fountain that I'm leaving and will see her tomorrow. When I get outside, I feel the first cool breeze of autumn as it blows through. Monday is Labor Day.

I put the obit in the slot of the newspaper office. I think old Johnny's in for a surprise when he reads about Alice Lambert.

When I get home, I smell fresh butter and garlic simmering; I follow the delicious aroma into the kitchen. Jack is barefoot, in his jeans and an old sweatshirt, making us dinner.

"Hi." He looks up and smiles at me.

"What are you cooking? It smells divine!"

One of the bonuses of marrying Jack is that he is attentive in the kitchen. He's a better Italian cook than I am now. I give him a big kiss.

"Linguini carbonara, with Virginia ham. Who's Pete?" he asks casually.

"Pete who?" I try not to choke on the name.

"Pete Rutledge."

"Oh, him. We met him in Italy."

"Oh, the guy Etta talks about. The marble guy."

"Really. She told you about him?" I say casually but my vocal tone gives me away: I squeak. That kid. Does she have to tell her father everything?

"Yeah."

"Why do you ask?"

"He called."

"That's nice."

"He's in town."

"What?"

"He's here."

I don't know what to say. I figured the guy had a crush, we kissed, and that was it. What is he doing here?

"Ave, honey, tell me what's going on."

"Nothing's going on. I love you." Man, if blurting "I love you" isn't a dead giveaway for guilt developed after an Alpine make-out session, I don't know what is.

"Here's his number. He's at the Trail."

Jack puts the number on the table, as though I should call Pete Rutledge right here on our phone in this house, this house where we, a newly devoted married couple, live. I do not want to make this call.

"I'll call tomorrow."

"Call him now. Invite him to dinner. I'm making plenty."

Jack stirs the garlic in the pan. My eyes bulge out of my head like rockets. Is he serious? Have him to dinner? He's the enemy, you idiot. He wanted me to stay in Italy with him for all eternity. Tear up that number if you know what's good for you.

"Go on. Call him."

I drag myself to the phone and dial. It rings a billion times. Conley Barker, the night receptionist (as well as the airport cab driver), finally answers the phone and puts me through.

"Hello?" The sound of Pete's voice makes me happy, but just for a second.

"Hi. This is Ave Maria."

"Oh, hey, thanks for calling me back."

"What are you doing here?" I say gaily.

"Hiking the Appalachian Trail. Remember? I told you I was coming through in the fall. Well, guess what? It's fall."

"Isn't that great?"

"Yeah. I'd like to see you."

"Sure. Why not?"

"Great. Where do you live?"

I decide that it's easier for me to ride down into town and pick him up rather than give him the complicated directions to get here. When I get to the Trail, Pete is waiting for me out front. He leans up against one of the entry columns, reading the town paper. He looks like he belongs here. And he looks every bit as good in southwestern Virginia twilight as he did in the dusk of northern Italy.

"Hi!" I say too loudly and too long, with about eighteen overenthusiastic syllables.

"How are you, babe?" Pete gives me a big kiss on the cheek. "What a place you live in. It's amazing. So beautiful."

"Thank you. Can't take any credit for it. These mountains were here long before I was."

I point out a few sights on the way back to Cracker's Neck. I am determined to be a tour guide, and determined that there will be no talk of Alpine kissing or dancing. Pete seems respectful, and I'm relieved. When we climb out of the Jeep, Etta is waiting for us on the porch.

"Pete!" she squeals, and runs down the field to meet us. She throws herself into his arms.

"Chiara's not here. She's in Italy. It's only me here."

And what is that on Etta's mouth? Oh dear God, it's my Gina Lollobrigida magenta lipstick from the Moderna beauty shop in Piccolo Lago. My daughter looks like a hooker.

Jack greets us at the door. I love how warm and gracious he is to Pete. Shoo the Cat runs out from under a chair, sinks his teeth into Pete's ankle, and sprints off. We check Pete's ankle, but there's barely any blood. Between the attack cat and my trampy daughter, this is going to be a long night.

Jack takes Pete (and Etta, of course, who follows) into the kitchen.

Pete and Jack will have a beer, and the way this night is going, Etta may have her first Jack Daniel's on the rocks. The phone rings; Etta rushes to answer it.

"She never used to run for the phone." Jack Mac shrugs. "Now she's either running to it or she's on it."

"It's called being a girl, honey."

"Ma, it's Uncle Theodore."

I excuse myself. I am relieved to be out of the hot kitchen. I close the bedroom door, pull the phone off the nightstand, and sit on the floor, so no one can hear me.

"Thank God it's you."

"What's wrong?"

"He's here."

"Who?"

"Pete."

Theodore laughs. "The inamorata? No way."

"It's not funny! He's hiking around here and he stopped and called and Jack invited him to dinner. I'd like to die."

"What are you going to do?"

"It's awful. I'm so embarrassed."

"Imagine how Jack Mac feels."

"He doesn't know anything."

"Right, you're hiding under the bed whispering on the phone, and he doesn't suspect a thing."

"No, he doesn't. It would be nice if you could make me feel better in this situation."

"How does he look?"

"Oh God. Even better than he looked in Italy."

"You're in trouble."

"It's like tenth grade. Why couldn't I go through this nonsense at an age-appropriate level? No, here I am now, in middle age, dealing with this stupidity."

"It wasn't that stupid up in the cockerbells."

"Bluebells."

"You'll have to tell Jack."

"I will never tell him! Never."

"Don't you think he's going to wonder why you're acting like a fool?"

"I'll tell him I'm sick or something."

"Sexual tension isn't a disease."

"You're not helping."

"Call me later." He laughs. "Good luck."

I cannot believe how weird it is to eat dinner with my husband and my summer almost-boyfriend, who with some amazing kisses could have brought down the House of MacChesney entirely. I look across the table at the two of them, doing a compare-and-contrast. They are different, and yet there is an all-boy quality to both of them. They instantly like each other (how bizarre is that!), and they seem to have lots to talk about. Etta interrupts whenever she can think of ways to get Pete's attention. My daughter is never going to be the town spinster, that's for sure. She can't wait to be a grown-up woman. She awaits her first period like it's the Preakness of Womanhood.

Headlights flash across the living room; we see the end of the beams against the wall outside the kitchen. Jack looks at me.

"Expecting anybody?"

I shake my head and take a look out the window. It's Iva Lou.

"Sorry to barge in," Iva Lou says as she throws open the door without knocking.

"Hi, honey. We have company. Pete Rutledge."

Iva Lou's eyes roll around as she tries to place the name, and when she does, it's her turn to have her eyeballs bulge out of her head like rockets. I quickly motion for her to act casual (my first mistake) as she puts a frozen smile on her face that borders on ghoulish.

"Hi-dee. Pleased to meet you, Pete."

"I spent a lot of time with Peter in Italy this summer, Iva Lou," Etta says in an accent no one has heard since Grace Kelly used it in *High Society*.

"Yeah, well, I would've too." Iva Lou winks at Pete.

"Iva, can we get you something to eat?"

"No, no. I just had a chili dog at the Mutual's. I just stopped by on my way home to tell y'all about Spec."

"Something wrong?"

"He's having an emergency triple bypass tomorrow at Holston Valley Heart Center."

"Oh my God."

"Don't worry. He's okay for now. In fact, he drove himself over there in the Rescue Squad. He said if it got rough, he could give himself his own oxygen. Well, I've got to go."

"I'll walk you out."

Iva Lou says her good nights and meets me in the hallway.

"Man alive, and I mean man alive!" she whispers. I motion for her to hush until we get outside.

"What is he *doing* here?"

"He's hiking the Appalachian Trail."

"Well, you tell him to get himself down to the trailer park and practice on Mount Iva Lou."

I push Iva Lou out the door; when she's worked up like this, there is no telling what she'll say or do.

I drive Pete back to the motel; I wanted Ella to come along, but Jack made her stay behind to do her homework. I didn't want to look suspicious, so I didn't press it. I cannot explain how strange it feels to be in my Jeep with Pete Rutledge. I am not comfortable entertaining him here at home; he is strictly a European vacation fantasy.

I pull up in front of the hotel. I can see the top of Conley Barker's crew cut behind the desk.

"Well, have a great hike."

"Thanks."

"You want to come in?" Pete asks.

"No," I tell him so loudly it's a shout.

"You don't have to."

"I can't. But thank you." I say this with a cool I didn't think I had.

"Have you thought about me at all?"

"Pete."

"Just a little?"

"Here's the only way I can explain it. I live in a holler here in these mountains, where the weather is pretty good most of the time. And once in a while, a hell of a storm comes through, and it stirs everything up. When it's over, this amazing blue sky appears, and things become so clear and clean that I actually see better; and from my field in Cracker's Neck Holler, I can see as far as Tennessee, in such detail that I can make out the veins on the leaves. Without that storm passing through, you'd never get that crystal-clear vision that follows. You came through my life like a hurricane. You stirred me up and made me look at myself. You made me look at what I wanted and what I needed to choose. And there is a part of me that wishes I had thrown you down in that field of bluebells and had the wildest sex I could imagine, just for the thrill of it. But a thrill comes and goes, and we both know that. We did the right thing. I'm happy with Jack Mac-Chesney. I really love the man. And I'm really happy that you're my friend."

"Okay, babe. I know when I'm licked." Pete opens the door of the Jeep and swings his long legs out to the ground. He swivels and looks at me. "Thanks for dinner. And Etta. And Jack. I really like Jack." Pete leans over and kisses me on the cheek. Then he gets out of the Jeep.

"Pete?" I call after him. "Good luck."

"Thanks." He smiles and waves.

I watch him walk into the lobby of the Trail Motel. He has to drop his head under the walkway awning. And he looks to me a little like the great Gary Cooper—Pete sort of rode into town, set things straight, and is gone.

When I get home, the kitchen is clean, Etta is in bed, and Jack is in our bedroom, in the overstuffed old club chair, reading *The Post*.

"He's taking off tomorrow morning. He's meeting the hikers in Asheville."

"Great." Jack puts his newspaper down. "How come you were so nervous?"

"Oh, the news about Spec really threw me."

"No, it was before that. You didn't want to call Pete at the hotel. How come?" Jack looks at me, and I'm thinking, this is what marriage is. It's like a giant washing machine. You throw everything in there, and you pour on the soap, and the water gushes in, and you think you're gonna wash it all away. But no matter what, even after it's spun around, you open that tub and right there at the top is the thing you tried to bury at the bottom. The thing you tried to deny and walk away from. The truth about Pete Rutledge was bound to come out, because I am not a good liar. And more importantly, I don't want to keep anything from my husband anymore. The truth is so much easier. (Another thing Mama taught me that has turned out to be true.)

"Honey, when I was over in Italy with Etta, I was trying to forget about you. It was just too painful. I'm not proud of that. I got so tired of the knife in my gut that I just wanted it out. And so I got a haircut."

Jack laughs. "Okay."

"It's insane, I know, but it transformed me. I heard the scissors and I saw the clumps of my hair on the floor and it changed me."

"How?" Jack leans in and listens.

"I went out that night, and that's when I met Pete. I felt so good, I forgot about our troubles and danced. Pete saw me in that moment. And he sort of fell for me. But I wouldn't get involved with him."

"Why?" Jack asks me this with a catch in his voice.

"The truth?"

"The truth."

"I'd like to say that it was something noble, like our marriage vows. But the truth is, I didn't go to bed with him because he thought I was perfect. And as someone who worked her whole life to be perfect, I didn't want to shatter the illusion. If I had the affair it would have made me a cheater. And I wanted to stay on that pedestal; otherwise I'd just be another summer lay for an American in Italy."

"Honey?" Jack gets up and sits with me on the bed.

"What?"

"I'm glad you didn't."

"Me too." I put my arms around my husband. "Do you want to know why you . . . went with Karen? Because I made you feel bad about yourself. I wasn't there for you when the mines closed, I didn't get behind your business; I didn't think that what was happening to you was serious. I treated your crisis like a glitch. And I was holding on to stuff, holding you accountable for things that you had no control over, because I had to blame somebody. Like when Joe got sick, I blamed you, because I wanted you to be the hero who comes in and fixes everything so I didn't have to worry about it. I was horrible to you. But now I understand what I did. And it won't happen again."

"If it did happen again, we'd be able to name it. For the longest time, we just couldn't name it." Jack kisses me tenderly. "So that's the story of Pete, huh? How about a cup of tea?"

"How about Jack Daniel's? Or did Etta finish the bottle?"

"I meant to ask you, what was with the lipstick?"

"Welcome to womanhood."

"Great." Jack groans. He puts his arm around me as we go into the kitchen.

Spec's triple bypass became a quintuple. When Doc Turner got inside, he "found enough goo to fill a shoe box." (That's Spec's description, not mine.) So as I tiptoe through the halls of the Holston Valley Heart Center, I am expecting the worst. The get-well balloons I bought at L. J. Horton Florists keep getting caught on the pressboard ceiling ducts overhead. I hold them down by my waist. Finally, Room 456.

"Spec, now you listen here. I ain't sharin' you with no goddamn whore. You got to choose. You choose me or her. Now that's that. I didn't give up my goddamn life since the age of goddamn fifteen to get to this point and be by my goddamn self. If you wanted out, you should've gotten out when I could still get me out there and find me another man. Who is gonna want me at sixty-four? You might as well set me on farr right here, right now in this room, and watch me burn. Now that's the goddamn truth."

The barrage keeps me in the hallway. Soon I hear the sound of soft sneakers on linoleum.

"Hi, Leola."

"Hey, A-vuh."

Leola has a yellow bouffant hairdo and big Oscar de la Renta glasses. Her face is small, so the glasses cover most of it. She has an unlit cigarette dangling from her mouth. She is tiny, and you can see the remnants of a great figure from her youth. She was always busty, but now she's low-busty. She wears tight pink stirrup pants that pick up the pink letters on her oversize sweatshirt, which reads MYRTLE BEACH MAMA.

"Are you okay?"

"I need a smoke. Nice balloons." Leola walks up the hallway.

Spec is lying in the bed attached to tubes of all kinds. He's wearing his sunglasses, which I think is weird.

"Hey, Spec. I heard it went great."

Spec holds up five fingers.

"I heard. Quintuple. Well, might as well unclog all the pipes while the doctor's in there."

Spec nods. "Doc Turner split my breastbone in two with an ax. He's a fine surgeon. The scar is vurry thin, but it's right long." Then he whispers, "Is she gone?"

"Leola?"

He nods.

"She went for a smoke."

"I got caught," he says quietly, rolling his head back into the groove of the pillow.

"What do you mean?"

"Just what I said. Twyla was over here last night. She come to see me."

"Oh no."

"And I got caught."

For years, Spec has led a double life, seeing Twyla Johnson, his off-and-on girlfriend, while married to Leola, the mother of his five children. Twyla works at the Farmers and Miners Bank down in Pennington. She's a petite brunette with a gorgeous smile and lots of time on her hands (bank hours are ten to three). She's probably sixty now, still a young thing to old Spec.

"I'm sure Leola thinks she saw more than she saw. Didn't she?"

"No, she pert near saw it all."

"Well, what did she see?"

Spec won't say.

I press him. "Did Twyla kiss you or something?"

"No."

"Was she holding your hand?"

"Not my hand."

"Oh no."

"Yeah, she was, well, you know what she was doing. It's been a vurry vurry stressful time for me. Vurry much so. And Twyla come all this way, and frankly, she wanted to make me feel good."

"Oh, Spec."

"I know. It's like your worst nightmare. It's like your mother catchin' ye, for Godsakes. It could turn you off entirely. You know what I'm sayin'."

"Yes, I do."

"I mean. Is it so wrong? Is comfort so wrong? I mean, let's say I was about to die in here, which I was, they practically spelled it out, I mean, I was a goner. Every damn avenue to my heart was clogged,

Ave. It was dirt nap, *Good Night, Irene,* and kiss-your-ass-good-bye time. And if I had my pick of ways to spend my last moments, it sure weren't gonna be with my sorry kids and my hateful wife gaping at me like a carp in a fish tank. I wanted my Twyla." Spec sounds pitiful.

"Well, what's gonna happen now?" I sit down on the bed. The movement jostles the cloudy tubes connecting in and out of him like overpasses on Appalachia Strait.

"That remains to be seen. Leola's not left the room since. Poor Twyla burst into tears and run out of here. I ain't seen her since. She ain't called, neither."

"She's probably afraid."

"It's just a mess."

"Yes, it is."

"What ought I do?"

"What do you want to do?"

"I want out of this hospital. And then I want to be happy."

"Who makes you happy?"

"The truth?"

"Yes. The truth."

"Twyla."

"Well, then you have to choose Twyla."

"But what about Leola?"

"Leola can get another man."

"You think?"

"Yes."

"But she done took care of me when I was sick."

"Give her combat pay."

"That's true. I can't believe you're sayin' this. You bein' a Cathlick and all. Y'all ain't never supposed to go for divorce."

"Well, Spec, we've known each other a long long time. And I think I know you pretty good." I don't want to say what I'm thinking, but something tells me I should. "Spec, I think you deserve more than a hand job on a gurney. I think you should be happy all the time."

Spec is a little stunned at my blunt assessment. He appreciates it, though, and twists the food IV needle stuck in his hand like a sewing needle in a pin cushion. "Well put. Well put." Spec looks away, but I can't tell what he's looking at through the sunglasses. "Thank you for that," he says, and looks toward the window.

"Spec, I read something once that helped me a lot."

"What was that?"

"Sometimes it's hard to tell the difference between true love and lust."

"Yes ma'am, it surely is."

"Do you want to know how you tell the difference?"

"I think it would shed some light," Spec says from behind his sunglasses.

"True love energizes you; lust exhausts you."

"And women will ruin you."

"That wasn't in the book, Spec."

"It ought to be."

$\mathcal{P}$earl Grimes and Dr. Taye Bakagese are to be married tonight on the stage of the Trail of the Lonesome Pine Outdoor Drama Theatre. Pearl chose the Friday night after Thanksgiving because she knew most folks had the day off and could party into the wee hours. I am rushing around, ironing Jack's shirt, hunting for Etta's tights, and trying not to nick my freshly painted toenails on anything.

"Theodore?"

"What?" he says from inside the bathroom.

"Do you see Etta's tights in there?"

Theodore hands me Etta's tights through a crack in the door. He drove up to spend Thanksgiving with us. I convinced him that he shouldn't miss Pearl's wedding. The entire cast of the outdoor drama is invited, and they all wanted to see him.

Etta grabs her tights. I finish Jack's shirt and pull the curlers out of my hair. Jack comes in from the kitchen.

"Your hair looks nice."

"Thank you."

We decide to go in Theodore's car, since it's a four-door. When we get to the theater, it looks like a sold-out show. Pearl Grimes has cast a wide net in her life already: she went to college, then she opened a second pharmacy in Norton, with a third scheduled to open in Pound. She's amazing. As we join the folks filtering in, Otto sits by the door asking each person for tickets. Of course, everyone laughs at his joke.

"Can you believe my little grandbaby is gettin' murried?"

"Isn't life something?" I give him a hug.

"I mean, she's my new grandbaby, little Pearl, since my son murried her mother. But I can claim her, can't I?"

"Of course you can."

As we gather onstage, the ceremony is simple and elegant. It's a mix of Indian and Bluegrass, two cultures that have some things in common, like love of nature and family. Leah, radiant in a long red velvet dress, takes her place with Worley, who is wearing a new suit. Albert Grimes, hair slicked down, wearing gray slacks, a navy blazer, and a tie, fidgets nervously in the row behind Leah. (I think the insurance claim that the fire at the theater was caused by faulty wiring has taken the heat off of Albert.)

Taye looks at Pearl with so much love, it makes the hardest among us tear up. Nellie Goodloe runs out for more tissue (or maybe she's jittery because the crowd is too big and she didn't order enough mints).

Pearl's simple white gown is exquisite. It has a scoop neck and long sleeves, the kind that trumpet out. The tiny seed pearls on the bodice catch the light. She wears the shawl I brought her from Italy over her shoulders. Her hair, soft in the cool air, curls down to her shoulders like a loose ribbon. She has placed tiny sprigs of baby's breath throughout. As Taye puts the ring on Pearl's hand, Otto nudges me.

"That there is my Destry's ring."

I put my arm around Otto. He has tears in his eyes as he thinks of the love of his life, the beautiful Melungeon girl who died in child-birth bringing Worley into the world. Pearl holds her hand and looks down at the ring and adjusts it with her other hand. The judge pronounces Taye Bakagese and Pearl Grimes man and wife, and the applause echoes up and into the mountains behind us.

I feel Fleeta's breath on the back of my neck. "Them babies of theirs is gonna be real brown," she whispers.

"And beautiful," I whisper back.

"Yup," she says. I turn and look at Fleeta. Could she be softening up after all these years?

The tent, lit by tiny blue lights, showcases a feast of Southwest Virginia and Indian cuisine. Who knew that buttery sautéed kale tasted so good with grilled lamb kabobs?

"Hey, Ava!" Sweet Sue Tinsley says as she pats me on the back. In Big Stone Gap, we have open-church weddings (in this case, open-theater); they are announced in the paper and everyone is welcome. Sweet Sue Tinsley evidently kept her subscription to *The Post*, so she stays in the loop and on our party circuit. I take a good look at Jack Mac's old girlfriend. She is aging just as I thought she would: very well. She's cut her hair very short. Little spikes of white-yellow hair stick out all over her head. She wears a strapless white dress with a red patent-leather belt.

"How's Kingsport?"

"The boys love it. Mike is working at the paper plant."

"Great."

"How are you?"

"Busy. But fine."

"I'm a grandmother, you know."

"I didn't know!" I look at Sweet Sue. It seems impossible that she could be a grandmother.

"Yeah, my oldest, Chris, fell in love with his high school sweetheart. And she got pregnant. Little Michael is three months old."

"Congratulations. You're the foxiest grandma I've ever seen," I tell her, and I mean it.

"Thank you, honey. I appreciate that. I do. You're lookin' good yourself!"

Sweet Sue excuses herself and runs off to say hello to lots of folks she hasn't seen in a long while. I knock back an egg roll. I may look all right, but it's depressing to think that I am actually old enough to be a grandmother.

"I'll give you a hundred bucks if you dance with me right now," Theodore says in my ear.

"I'm eating."

"Starve." He grabs me for a slow dance by the Jerome Street Ramblers.

"What is your problem?"

"Sarah Dunleavy has a jones for me like you wouldn't believe."

"She's harmless."

"She's forty."

"You're forty-four."

"Yeah, but I'm not trying to score a husband and a baby in the next six months. She's on a mission."

Then, as though we have glided into an old memory, Jack cuts in.

"I'd like to dance with my wife," Jack says, and smiles.

"I'd like you to dance with Sarah Dunleavy," Theodore tells him.

"No way!" I step into my husband's arms and out of Theodore's. Theodore heads for the dessert table as Jack sways with me under the glittery canopy (the same one used every year at the Powell Valley High School prom).

"What was that all about?"

"Nothing."

"Why'd you cut in?"

"I don't know. Sometimes you've got to dance with your wife."

"Don't you want to dance with Sarah Dunleavy?"

"She's too skinny."

"But she's quiet, and she choral-reads Shakespeare."

"I like noise, and I hate Shakespeare."

"Uh, Jack?"

"Yes, darlin'?"

"Honey, is that your—" As we sway on the dance floor, I carefully move Jack's hand from my butt to my waist.

"It better be my hand," he says.

Pearl and Taye kiss by the band; Spec presses his fork into Nellie Goodloe's cherry jubilee; Leola has a smoke with Fleeta (I'm sure Leola is catching her up on all the News); Iva Lou and Lyle stand over the steam tables surveying the choices; and Theodore takes the last seat at the table with Rick and Rita Harmon and their kids, so he doesn't have to sit at Sarah Dunleavy's, where there are two open seats on purpose. Etta waves to me from the corner of the tent, where the kids eat sugared mints and tell silly jokes. I wave to her; she smiles.

As the clock hits midnight, Pearl and her new husband take to the dance floor for one final go-round. The remaining guests, and there's just a few of us, leave the floor to the bride and groom. Otto rigged up a couple of portable heaters under the tent, so it's warm inside. The stage of the Outdoor Drama, fully lit and bathed in pink light, is empty now.

"Your shoes," my husband says to me as he hands me the strappy sandals that stayed on my feet for about ten minutes into the reception. "Why do you wear shoes that hurt?"

"Because they're pretty."

Jack shakes his head and motions for Etta to join us. Theodore waits by the flap of the tent.

"Wasn't it beautiful?" I ask Theodore as I look back at Pearl and Taye on the dance floor, shimmering beneath the canopy.

"It was fine. It would have been better if I didn't have to play Hide the Band Director with Sarah Dunleavy."

Etta climbs into the front seat with Theodore; Jack and I settle into the backseat.

"Mama, is Daddy drunk?"

"No honey, he's just very very happy for Pearl and Dr. B."

Theodore looks at me in the rearview mirror and smiles.

As we circle around the cul-de-sac and back onto Shawnee Avenue, we stop at the turnoff to Beamontown Road at the light. The black gates of Glencoe Cemetery glisten in the middle distance where the road meets the river. For a moment, I think to ask Theodore to make the turn. But I think better of it and let it go.

"Cracker's Neck?" Theodore asks.

"Yeah."

Jack puts his head on my lap as Etta tells Theodore about a small drama at the wedding between her friend Tara and some cute older boy named Chad. Soon the lights of Big Stone Gap blur behind us, and we're speeding in the dark toward home.

Milk Glass Moon

For my father,
Anthony J. Trigiani

The Wise County Fair is my daughter's favorite event of the year, and I think it's safe to say that includes Christmas. Etta has been on her best behavior for the past two weeks, so perfect down to the smallest detail (including unassigned chores like making *my* bed and weeding *my* garden) that I'm worried.

We have the window flaps of the Jeep down, and the warm August air whipping through is sweet with honeysuckle. Still, it is no match for Iva Lou's perfume, which wafts up to the front seat whenever we peel around a curve. Etta looks out the window for road signs, searching for proof that we're almost there. I've taken the quicker route, the valley road out of Big Stone Gap up to Norton. As we ascend the mountains in twilight, we pass Coeburn nestled in the valley below, where the cluster of lights twinkles like a scoop of emeralds. Etta smoothes her braids and settles back in her seat.

"Here's the plan. First we eat," Iva Lou announces as she

unfolds the special to the newspaper. "I myself am having a jumbo caramel apple with nuts, and if I have to go see Doc Guest for a bridge on Monday, then so be it. Them caramel apples are worth a molar."

"I want the blue cotton candy," Etta decides.

"I want a chili dog with onions," I reply.

"I have a lot of money," Etta says proudly as she sifts through her change purse.

"Ask Dad to spring for dinner. That will leave you more money for the games of chance."

Etta smiles and carefully counts her money without lifting it out of the purse. I see a five-dollar bill folded neatly into a small square (some lucky clay-pigeon operator is about to score a windfall).

"What if we can't find him?" she asks.

"We'll find him."

"Just go straight to the outdoor the-a-ter. He's up there with all them men checking out the rehearsal for Miss Lonesome Pine."

"He built the stage," I remind Iva Lou in a tone that says, *Don't start with that again.*

"That's as good a reason as any, then." Iva Lou meets my eye in the rearview mirror and winks.

We find a parking spot under a tree overlooking the fairgrounds and climb out of the Jeep. Iva Lou checks her hair in the driver's side mirror and then smiles at us, ready to go. She's wearing a pair of dark blue denim pedal pushers and a red bandanna-print blouse tied at the waist. Her Diamonelle hoop earrings peek out from under her platinum bob like giant waterwheels. Iva Lou is ageless; you would never know she is fifty-something. Her look, however, is best viewed from a distance, like a fine painting. You don't want to get so close that you get lost in the details.

Etta looks at the fairgrounds with a clinical eye, surveying the faded striped tents surrounded by torches like birthday candles. She smiles when she spots the Ferris wheel. "Ma, will you go on the rides with me?"

"Sure." But Etta knows that at the last second in line, when we're ready to go up the metal plank, I'll send her father with her instead.

"Do we have to go to the beauty pageant?" she asks.

"I thought you liked it."

"I like the dresses all right. The talent's always terrible." Etta shrugs. She's right. Last year, leggy blond Ellen Tierney, representing Big Stone Gap, did a dance routine to "Happy to Keep Your Dinner Warm"; her tap shoe flew off when she did a high kick, clocked a man in the first row, and knocked him out. The victim was rushed to the hospital and revived, but he may have the imprint of the metal tap on his forehead for life. "And I hate the physical-fitness part when they come out and jump around in bathing suits. Anybody can do that stuff."

"Etta, hon, it don't take a lot of talent to look good in a bathing suit. That you're born with." Iva Lou breathes deeply and straightens her shoulders. "I ought to know."

"I'm never gonna be in a beauty pageant," Etta announces.

"Me neither." I give my daughter a quick hug.

The benches in the outdoor theater are filling up fast. The aisles are covered in Astroturf runners; the stage is banked in garlands of red paper roses; the backdrop is a cutout of a giant pine tree with MISS LONESOME PINE written in gold leaf.

School starts in a few weeks. I can't believe Etta is twelve years old and going into the seventh grade. My mother would have been sixty-six this year. I feel oddly lost between them: not old yet, not young anymore. I thought motherhood was a job with security, but it's not. It's the least permanent job in the world, the only job in which your skills become obsolete overnight. It was that way from the beginning. When I finally got a handle on breast-feeding, it was time for solid food. I worried that Etta wasn't turning over in the crib on her own, but soon she was crawling, and then, before I knew it, walking. When she went to school, I thought she'd need me more, but all of a sudden she had a life apart from me and was just fine. And now, after we've established a routine as a family, in which Etta has responsibilities, she's developed a newfound independence and her own opinions. This is, of course, the point of all of it—preparing your children to leave you—yet I'm so afraid to let go. I don't know how I'll handle it when she's eighteen and leaves for college. How did my mother do it? I wish she were here to lead me through these changes.

"Dad!" Etta waves to Jack, who waves back to her from a platform at the side of the stage. He finishes helping the spot operator set the light levels, then climbs down the ladder to join us. My husband is still agile; his strong arms hook down the ladder rhythmically. His jeans are faded to dusty blue, and his white T-shirt frames his gray hair beautifully. Sometimes, when I see him in the distance, I forget he's mine and think, What a fine-looking man. He still makes my heart race— quite a feat after all these years. His straight nose and lips are surrounded not by wrinkles but by expression lines. He's damn cute, my husband. I try not to hate him for aging so well.

Otto Olinger approaches, wiping his face with a bandanna. "We barely got that stage up in time. Ain't that right, Worley?" Otto turns to his son, whose white hair makes him look around the same age as his father.

"It was rough," Worley agrees.

" 'Cause you ain't got your minds on your work. Too busy ogling the girls," Iva Lou tells them.

"We did us some looking." Worley smiles.

Otto shrugs. "Can't hardly help it, they's so purty. Of course, I ain't never seen me no ugly women, just some that's purtier than others."

Jack gives me a kiss and takes Etta's hand. "You want to watch from up there?" he asks her.

"Yeah!"

"We've got a couple of seats down front for you."

I turn to Iva Lou. "Do you want to stay?"

"What do you want to do?"

"I'd rather wander around."

"Let's wander, then." Iva Lou turns to go up the ramp.

"Okay, we'll catch up with you later." Jack Mac takes Etta to the ladder and helps her to the top. She kneels on the platform as her father explains something about the equipment. She listens and nods. I can't believe she's my kid and not afraid of heights. In fact, she's fearless about everything—picking up stray animals, speaking in public, boys. Etta cares about how things work; in that way, she is just like her father. She is all MacChesney, and that's not always easy for me to accept.

"What are we gonna do?" Iva Lou asks.

"We're going to see Sister Claire."

"Who the hell is that? A Catholic?"

"No. She's a fortune-teller."

"No voodoo for me, girlfriend."

"Come on. After she makes you drink a cocktail of eye of newt and puts a spell on you, it's all uphill."

Sister Claire has a small dark green tent by the edge of the grounds. Two folding chairs are set up outside the flap. I'm surprised there isn't a line of people waiting. Sister Claire is well known in these parts; she's from the mountains of North Carolina near Greensboro. A pharmaceutical salesman out of Raleigh who traveled through Big Stone encouraged me to see Sister if she was ever in the area. He told me that she was the genuine article, a true mystic. I'm surprised when a small, gentle woman of sixty, with a heart-shaped face and skin the color of strong tea, emerges from the tent to greet us.

"Are you here to see me?" she asks. "I'm Sister Claire."

Iva Lou turns away and grabs my arm to return to the hub of the fair, where no one knows the future, not even the judges of the Miss Lonesome Pine Contest.

"Yes ma'am. We are." Iva Lou shoots me a look, so I correct myself. "I am," I say earnestly, not knowing exactly how to address a psychic.

"Welcome."

"I think most of the people are at the beauty pageant," I tell her, apologizing for her lack of clientele.

Sister Claire turns to Iva Lou and looks her straight in the eye. "I understand if the idea of a reading makes you uncomfortable. I don't like to have my cards read."

"Really?" Iva Lou squeaks.

"Really. It's a commitment to believe. It takes blind faith. Sometimes not even I have that."

"Well, it's not that I'm scared, and I certainly believe in the comings and goings of the spirit world. It's just that I, well, I live my life a certain way, and I don't want to know where it's all going."

"I understand."

"Wait here, then. Okay?" I give Iva Lou a wink and follow Sister Claire inside. The tent is sparsely furnished with two folding chairs and a small red lacquer table between them. An electric cord attached to a small generator runs up the side of the tent to a low-wattage bulb, which dangles in a protective metal sleeve overhead. Sister Claire motions for me to sit, then pours us each a glass of water. She sits down at the table and rests one hand on a deck of large tarot cards.

"I hear you're a Native American," I say as she shuffles the cards.

"Cherokee. Descendant of the great Chief Doublehead. 'Course, all of us that's Cherokee claim that." She smiles.

"Mother and father both?"

"Yes. But I'm mixed. I also had a grandmother who was African-American and a grandfather who was Irish."

"The green eyes give you away."

"Every time."

"How did you discover your talent for this?"

"It's not so much a talent as a way of being. It tends to run in families. My mother read cards and had visions, and so do I." She stops shuffling the cards and asks me to pick one. "How can I help you?"

I was prepared with an answer—I have lots of questions about the future—but suddenly I can't speak. "I'm sorry."

"Don't be sorry. Let's look at you." Sister Claire shuffles again and places twelve cards on the table, creating a sunburst pattern.

"What is your name?"

"Ave Maria."

"That's unusual."

"Especially in these parts."

"That's the name of the Blessed Mother. You can tell a lot by a person's name."

"What does my name tell you?"

"You're named after a strong woman, some would say a goddess. You've been surrounded by strong women since the day you were born. You're very lucky. You are loved and protected, and I see many women around you, almost making a fence. Your mother passed?"

"Yes."

"She did and she didn't. She's with you always." Sister Claire sits back in the chair and closes her eyes. "She's wearing purple."

"My mother?"

"Yes."

"I buried my mother in a purple suit. She made it herself out of crepe silk she bought on one of her husband Fred Mulligan's buying trips to New York. She told me that, for the longest time, she didn't want to make anything out of the fabric because it was so beautiful she couldn't bear to cut it into pieces."

"Fred Mulligan was not your father."

"No ma'am."

"And it caused you great pain when you learned the truth."

"It did. But in a way, it was also the great blessing of my life. I found my real father in Italy, and my whole family."

Sister Claire leans back and closes her eyes. "Your mother is showing me a house with many rooms. She is hanging curtains in the windows."

"She used to make curtains."

"There's a boy in the room. He just walked in. He has brown eyes and curly brown hair. Who is he?"

"My son."

"He passed?" she asks me quietly.

"Yes ma'am."

"Very young?"

"He was four years old."

Sister Claire laughs. "He's funny. He's happy with her. She is looking out for him." She opens her eyes and looks at me.

Sister Claire goes on to tell me lots of things—about my job, about Jack, about Etta. She sees us traveling together, and she sees Etta taking a new path, which validates my feeling that my daughter is going where she wants to go, with or without my blessing.

"Sister, how does the afterlife work?"

"What do you mean?"

"Will my son always be four years old and my mother the age she was when she died? And when I die . . ."

"What do you think?"

"I thought that they were in a holding pattern, waiting for Judgment Day."

Sister Claire laughs, though I wasn't trying to be funny.

"That's a possibility, and it all depends. Your mother and son wanted you to know they're okay, so they came to me in a way you would recognize them. This doesn't happen every time."

"So they are . . . somewhere, right?"

"I like to think the *idea* of them is somewhere, but that their energy is eternal and that it's very possible they'll return to life as different people to learn new things."

"So they could be here?"

"Anywhere."

"Should I be looking for them?"

"You won't have to look for them; they'll find you." Sister Claire shuffles the cards and this time lines them up in a single row. She asks me to pick another from the deck. "Now for your future."

I take a deep breath. "I'm ready."

"You've set many goals for yourself in your lifetime. And you've met most of them. But what I see here is that you have to begin anew. You have to decide where your life is going; you must redream."

"Redream?"

"You have to reinvent your life. You have to think about what you want to accomplish in the second half of your life. Do you understand?"

I nod that I do, but I don't really, or maybe I'm not ready to think about the rest of my life. My present path is so clear—I want to raise my daughter, nurture my husband, and keep working. I don't think much beyond that, though I know it is dangerous not to. "Sister Claire? I never think about what I want anymore, or about what the future holds. I barely have time to get everything done in the present. How do I redream?"

"There are two times a day when the soul is open to new ideas. The first is when you rise, in the stillness of morning. The second is at night, when you're in that hazy place between being awake and going to sleep. At those times, ask your inner voice to guide you. Your intuition will lead to the answers you're looking for."

"My mother used to say that all the answers were inside me."

"She was right. The problem is, we don't trust our inner voice. But that voice will guide us in the right direction every time. It really is the key to happiness: just listen." Sister Claire slides the cards into a single deck once more.

I pay her and quickly review all she said to me. There's so much to think about. I am a little stunned that my mother and son could be looking for me but I might not know them. What good will that do? The smell of Iva Lou's cigarette brings me back. She's sitting on one of the folding chairs outside the tent, puffing away. "All set," I tell her.

"Well, honey-o, since we're here, maybe I'll get a reading too." Iva Lou turns to Sister Claire and points with her pinkie finger. "But I'm warnin' you, Sis, don't tell me when I'm gonna die, even if you know. Okay, I amend that. You can tell me when I'm gonna die if it's at a hundred and one with all my faculties intact and a young man up in the bed next to me who thinks I'm better than pepper jelly."

Sister Claire laughs. "You got a deal."

They go inside the tent, and I can hear the quiet muttering between them. I sit down, stretching my legs and leaning back in the chair. From this angle, I can see the spotlight at the beauty pageant make a tunnel of silver light against the black mountain. It is a smoky beam, barely visible as it competes with the Ferris wheel spinning streaks of pink glitter. The mountains funnel the sound of the applause and the wolf whistles up into the night sky; the way the sound carries in these hills, the pageant could be a thousand miles from here. How easy it is to get lost in the noise of this world, to find yourself leading a life of acceptance and resignation. When will I find the time to question my life again? Is there anything new ahead of me, or is this it? Being a wife, a mother, a pharmacist? What does Sister Claire mean when she tells me I have to invent myself all over again? To be what? And how?

After what seems like a much longer time than my reading took, Iva Lou emerges from the tent, fishing in her purse for another cigarette.

"So?"

"Oh, honey, I've never heard such good news. Sister Claire was chock-full of all kinds of information. I just hope I can remember it all so I can write it down. She said I'm an eagle."

"Is that a good thing?"

"Absolutely. I'm regal and self-possessed and all that. But of course, tell me something I didn't already know for fifteen bucks. How about you?"

"Mama and Joe came to me."

"What did they say?"

"They didn't say anything. But it's okay. They showed up; that's all I needed."

Iva Lou puts her arm around me as we head back into the lights and the noise, but I don't see them or hear it. My mind is in that house with many rooms.

*

After helping Etta scrub the last of the blue veil of cotton candy off her face, I tuck her into bed. She wants to read one more chapter of *Harriet the Spy*, but she's exhausted, so I convince her to go to sleep. Etta is fascinated with the story of Harriet, an eleven-year-old girl who doesn't play with dolls but has a notebook and goes around the elegant Upper East Side of Manhattan spying on her neighbors and recording their activities. Etta checks it out of the library so often, I wonder if anyone else in her class has read it.

"Mama, someday can we go to New York City?"

"Sure." I look down at my daughter, who is still a girl but is starting to look like a young woman in subtle ways. As I tuck the blanket around her, I know that soon this ritual will end, and that fills me with sadness.

"I think I'd like it."

"The big city? All that noise and confusion?" I kiss Etta and walk to the door.

"It would be fun and different, Ma," she says, rolling onto her side.

I turn the light out. I'm already in the hallway when I hear her voice softly call out to me. "Mama?"

"Yes?" I turn back and lean against the doorframe.

"Am I pretty?"

"Yes, you are."

"How do they decide who's pretty?"

"Who?"

"People. You know, it's like the group knows who's pretty, and then they treat that person like they're the prettiest, and that person always knows it."

"I don't know, Etta. I've never figured it out."

"I mean, sometimes I can see it. But sometimes I don't think the prettiest girl is the pretty one."

"You're pretty," I tell her plainly and sincerely.

"Okay." Etta says this in a tone that says, *You've got to be kidding*. I wait for her to say something else, but she doesn't, so I head downstairs.

Jack is in the kitchen making coffee to have with the cherry pie we bought at the fair.

"That was weird," I say.

"What?"

"Etta asked me if I thought she was pretty. Doesn't she know I think she's pretty?"

"Maybe not."

"Don't I tell her?"

"You tell her she's smart and a good reader, and capable and all that, but you don't heap a lot of compliments on her in other ways," Jack says matter-of-factly.

"God, isn't it more important to be smart?"

"Sure. But she's a girl, Ave."

"I'm well aware she's a girl."

"Well, I've been married to one for thirteen years, and been raising one about that long, and it seems to me that girls can't hear they're pretty often enough, even when they have other things going for them." Jack smiles.

"I'll compliment her more often." I can tell I sound defensive.

"I don't think you're doing anything wrong. I just think Etta's entering a new phase. She's going to be a teenager. Misty Lassiter told them all about sex tonight."

"What?"

"Yeah. She decided to drop the bomb."

"Oh God. Where did Misty get her information?"

"She's two years ahead of Etta in school, and you know, she's like *her* mother. Let's say she's slightly advanced."

Misty Lassiter is the daughter of Tayloe Slagle Lassiter, Big Stone Gap's most beautiful homegrown girl. I see Misty when I pick up Etta at school. She's the Willowy One, taller than her classmates, the leader, with blond hair in perfect yellow ropes tied with ribbons that look sophisticated, not cutesy. Back when I directed the Outdoor Drama, I cast Tayloe in the lead when she was just fifteen. She wasn't a great actress, but it didn't matter; you wanted to watch her, her delicate features, long limbs, and those eyes, so clear, blue, and heavy-lidded. She was so beautiful, you thought she knew the secret to something, some ancient truth born in her and obvious in her every movement. Tayloe has taught her daughter well. Misty is every bit as popular and perfect as she was. Quite a feat when you live in a small town, particularly if Bo Lassiter (of the low-forehead Lassiters of East Stone Gap) is your daddy.

"Etta's got so much more going for her than Misty. What did Misty say about sex?"

"Everything." Jack pours our coffee. He sits down and slices the pie with his fork.

"Well, what exactly is everything?"

Jack does his best to do an impression of Misty giving the girls the goods. " 'Now, first, there's a man. And the man has a different part from the woman.' "

"Oh no." I don't want to hear this, but I indicate to Jack that he should continue.

" 'And the man takes his part and lets the woman know he has one. Then she decides if she wants his part or not. Now, if she does, it's called sex. If she doesn't want no part of it, she's a virgin.' "

"Great." I rest my head, which feels like it weighs a hundred pounds, on my hands.

"I thought it was funny."

"Etta told you this?"

"I overheard them when they were waiting for their cotton candy. The line was long."

I wish I had been there. Why was Jack with her when she heard the facts of life the first time, and I was off in a tent getting my cards read? That is not how I planned this. "I am going to talk to Tayloe."

"What for?"

"She needs to tell her daughter not to be scaring the kids."

"Etta's not scared."

"What do you mean she's not scared? Who isn't scared of sex—" I stop myself. Jack looks at me. I open my mouth wide and yet no words come out. Jack is well aware of my so-late-I-almost-missed-it blooming. I honestly thought it didn't matter anymore, but thanks to Misty's sex talk, those old feelings of separation and alienation just went from a trickle to a roaring river within me. Once the town spinster, always the town spinster. "No wonder." I cut another piece of pie.

"No wonder what?"

"She doesn't talk to me about it. She can tell I don't want to talk about it."

"You got that right." My husband looks at me and smiles.

"She should be able to come to me about anything. I just

didn't see the signs. She's still coloring with crayons, for Godsakes. This is happening too fast."

"Well, fix it."

"What do you mean?"

"Talk to her." Jack shrugs like it's as simple as teaching her how to play checkers.

I take a long sip of the hot coffee (Jack always puts in just the right amount of cream). Then I slip off my loafers and put my feet in my husband's lap. "I wish she would stay a girl forever."

"That's not an option, honey." Jack squeezes my foot. And he's right. This is like a tire race down Stone Mountain— once you let it loose, it's gone.

We're having a sidewalk sale at the Mutual Pharmacy. It isn't a big deal, just a couple of folding tables borrowed from the First Baptist Church and loaded with stuff that hasn't sold—pale orange lipstick, strawberry hand cream, and shoe boxes filled with greeting cards neatly arranged by holiday. We start the sale with everything 50 percent off, but by Friday, we'll be giving the stuff away. Folks know this, so they wait a few days, linger after lunch in the Soda Fountain, and then hit Fleeta up for a freebie. Fleeta, in her smock and tight black leggings, is leaning against the building to light a cigarette. Once it's lit, she stands up straight and lightly touches her blue-black upsweep (she's tried the new Loving Care line that just came in) to make sure it's in place. I wave to her as I pull into my parking spot.

"Pearl's pregnant," Fleeta barks.

Before I can ask her to repeat the news, Pearl comes out to the sidewalk. "Fleeta!"

"I know it's supposed to be a secret, but you know I can't keep one. You shouldn't never have told me," Fleeta says to Pearl, taking a long drag off her cigarette. "Besides, when you upchuck three times in one morning, I ain't gonna be the only one 'round here that's suspicious."

"Is it true?" I ask Pearl, whose smile tells me it is. "How's your husband?"

"Thrilled."

I hug her. "How far along are you?"

"About two months."

"Fantastic."

"I just didn't want to say anything until I knew for sure."

I watch Pearl walk back to the Soda Fountain, and now that I know, I can see the pregnancy. I figured she had put on a couple of pounds, as we all do from time to time, but this is different. Pearl is chang ing. Her waist is beginning to fill out; she's walking more slowly, feeling the burden of the new weight on her knees. I remember the stages of pregnancy, all right. It's true that the suffering is worth it in the end, but for every moment of those nine months, I felt as though I had rented my body out to a tenant who had no respect for the property. The morning sickness, which is really daylong seasickness, the bloated breasts, swollen ankles, and for me, painful big toes from having to walk in a whole new way—I remember every one of these details as though it were yesterday.

Pearl turns around and says to me, "I'll be counting on you for advice."

"Oh, I have plenty of it."

"What about me?" Fleeta asks. "I done blowed out three

babies, and Pavis—he was a back birth—snapped my tailbone like a cracker on his way out. I got me a lot of advice to give, 'specially about the birthing itself.'"

"I'll need your advice too, Fleets." Pearl goes into the kitchen.

"Pavis really broke your tailbone?"

"Yeah, and that was a goddamn omen. That boy never give me nothin' but trouble and heartache and pain, of both the physical and the mental variety. First he stepped on my tailbone, then on my feet—you know, when he was a-crawlin'—and then when he went to prison, he done stepped on my heart."

"You ever hear from him?" Pavis has been in prison in Kentucky for as long as I can remember.

"When he gets a phone day." Fleeta pulls another box of greeting cards out from under the folding table. "This here sidewalk sale is already a bust," she tells me, sorting through the cards like they're junk.

"You have a bad attitude."

"If it was a good idea, every vendor on the street'd have one. You don't see Mike's Department Store hauling out the Aggner leather goods, or Zackie putting out the Wranglers. But we have to make a show peddling crap nobody bought all year." Usually when Fleeta gripes, you can see that she's just having a little fun, but today it sounds entirely serious.

"Is something the matter? You're not your sweet self," I tell her.

"Doc Daugherty told me I have to quit smoking."

"Did he find something?"

"He saw a spot on an X ray, said it weren't nothin' now, but if I didn't quit the smokes, it would turn to the emphysema. And I'm mighty pissed about it."

"Fleeta. It's simple. You have to stop smoking."

"I can't," she says simply and sincerely.

"You have to."

"Don't you understand how bad my mood would be without my smokes? I'd kill three people by breakfast if I couldn't light up."

"You don't know that."

"I don't? Ave, my nerves is so bad that I shake most days. I need 'em, and I told Doc that."

"What did he say?"

"He tole me he understood but he didn't want me gittin' the emphysema neither. He tole me to quit gradual. Keep cuttin' back till I'm down to one a day. One smoke a day. Can you beat that?"

"You can do it. I know you can."

"I'm not gonna be easy to be around," Fleeta promises.

Spec Broadwater, Otto, and Worley are sitting at the counter in the Soda Fountain eating the lunch special: beef stew and biscuits, with a side of fried apples. Spec's cigarette smolders on his saucer. I put out the cigarette on my way to the coffeepot.

"Hey, what'd you do that fer?" Spec bellows. He adjusts the name tag on his pressed khaki shirt. His legs, too long for the stools, are slung to the side like railroad ties. Spec has taken to putting gel in his thick white hair. The sides are so shiny and close to his head that he reminds me of the great George Jones, who is as famous for his coiffure as for his singing.

"You're not supposed to smoke. Remember your bypass?"

"Quintuple. Don't worry, Ave. I'm cutting back."

"While you're cutting back, you need to set an example for Fleeta. She needs to quit."

"Since when is Fleeta Mullins my problem?"

"Since she went to the doctor and he told her to stop smoking."

"Jesus, Ave. I got enough on my plate. Don't make me surgeon general of Wise County on top of everything else." Spec adjusts his glasses and fishes for his pack of cigarettes.

I stop him. "You're in here every day for lunch. She needs your support." I pour myself a cup of coffee and freshen Otto's while I'm at it.

"I can stand up for my own damn self," Fleeta announces from the floor. "I don't need the support of any of y'all."

"Aw, Fleeta, relax."

"Don't tell me what to do, Otto Olinger. Just 'cause you is president of the Where's My Ass Club that convenes up in here every day for lunch don't mean I got to take any bull off of ye."

"What do you mean, Where's My Ass?" Otto asks.

"Look at ye, all y'all. Not a one of ye has an ass. I don't know how your pants stay up."

"It's called a belt, Fleets," Otto says with a chuckle.

"I ain't never gotten a single complaint about my hind end," Spec tells her, sounding hurt.

"Somebody down in Lee County's bein' nice. If old Twyla Johnson was honest . . ."

The mention of Spec's woman on the side down in Lee County sends Otto and Worley into a giggling fit. (I thought Spec had given up his girlfriend, but I guess not.) Fleeta continues, "She'd tell you the truth: it's flat and square. Looks like somebody dropped a TV set down your drawers." Fleeta goes into the kitchen.

"She's on a royal tear," Worley says, shaking his head.

"Jesus, does she have to get personal like 'at?" Spec dumps cream into his coffee.

"It's only gonna get worse, boys," Fleeta bellows from the kitchen.

I make a run over to Johnson City to pick up some olive oil Jack ordered. He's become quite the chef, picky about his ingredients and accomplished in his techniques. Sometimes he dreams about opening an Italian restaurant. It never dawns on him that folks around here are not interested in sampling pesto made with fresh basil; they much prefer their own cuisine, biscuits and gravy and name-your-meat chicken-fried. Besides, the Soda Fountain at the Mutual is all the food service I can handle, and it's strictly lunch fare. Pearl and I were surprised when we saw the profit sheets last year. With our local economy struggling as the coal industry dies out mine by mine, it's a good thing Pearl is such a risk taker; the fountain did more business than the pharmacy.

As I cut through Wildcat Holler and head back into Cracker's Neck, I practice my opening to the Sex Talk between Etta and me. There is so much to say on the subject that I wrestle with whether I should begin with the physical and segue into the emotions; or if I should just start out by asking about her feelings and what she knows already; or if I should make it a family meeting and invite her father into the discussion. It bothers me that I want Jack there. This shouldn't be so hard. I want the sort of closeness with my daughter that I had with my mother. She was my protector, and I was her defender. We never talked about sex, but I felt I could surely ask her anything if I wanted to. The truth is, I never felt comfortable asking her about sex, relationships, or intimacy. I knew she was in a less than romantic marriage, and maybe I didn't want to remind her about what she didn't have. I never wanted to make my mother uncomfortable, to say or do anything to cause her pain. Maybe this is the root of my repression—the feelings I could not express. I don't blame my mother for that, though. It was my choice.

As I drive up to our house, negotiating all the pits where the stones have settled on the road, I see Otto and Worley on my roof. Jack used to tackle all home repairs, but the irony of a career in construction is that he no longer has time to fix things around here. (They say, "A shoemaker's child goes barefoot"; well, a construction worker's wife has holes in her roof.) I don't mind it, though. Having Otto and Worley around reminds me of my single days, when they would come to my house down in town and take care of whatever needed fixing without my having to ask. As I jump out of the Jeep, I see a third figure on the roof: my daughter.

"Etta, what are you doing up there?"

"Helping Otto and Worley."

"I want you to go inside."

"Why?"

"Because it's not safe."

"It's safe," Etta says defiantly.

"I got an eye on her, Miss Ave," Worley says without looking up.

"Me too," Otto says to reassure me.

"Go inside anyway, Etta."

Etta looks so small from the ground. As she gingerly crawls across the roof toward the window, it reminds me of when she first learned to crawl, and instead of being thrilled that my baby was learning a new skill, I was terrified that she was beginning to move in the world without me.

"Etta! Watch it!"

The toe of Etta's right shoe gets caught where a shingle has not been bolted. She tries to pry the shoe free, but she is on all fours and cannot. She tries to use her left foot for leverage, but it hits a slick spot and she begins to slide toward the gutter. Otto and Worley drop their tools and crawl over to her, but Etta's weight against the slope of the roof makes her slide even faster.

"Ave, git the ladder! Git the ladder!"

The ladder is propped against the far side of the roof. I'm frozen, thinking I can catch Etta if she falls. But I know this isn't possible. The drop is almost twenty feet, time is passing, and the fabric on her jacket is tearing away as she slides. I heave the ladder from the side of the house to the front gutter, where her feet are dangling dangerously over the edge. Worley has thrown his body sideways across the roof and has grabbed one of Etta's hands, which stops her from falling.

"Come up, Ave. Come up and git her," Worley says, panting. Otto attempts to crawl closer to Etta, but he is afraid to disrupt the precarious balance of their weight on the roof, so he stops. I dig the feet of the ladder into the soft earth and climb up quickly. I feel more confident when I get to Etta's feet and can get a grip on her legs. She feels so small in my arms; I remember what it was like when I could control everything to keep her safe. I carefully pull her to me. Worley lets go when I have a good hold on her. I hold Etta by her waist and slide her onto the first step of the ladder, shielding her with my body.

"Do you think you can climb down?" I ask her. Etta barely whispers a reply, and we descend the ladder one step at a time. I try not to look to the ground, it seems so far away. With each step I take, and each one Etta takes, I breathe a little easier. By the time we reach the ground, Otto and Worley have come through the house and are waiting to help us off the ladder.

"Sorry about that, Miss Ave. We thought she was safe up 'ere with us," Otto says.

"That's okay," I tell him. Then I turn to my daughter, who examines the palms of her hands, streaked with a little blood where the shingles burned them during her downward slide. I wince. I have never been able to stand it when she bleeds.

"Come on, let's wash up." I take Etta into the house and hold back until we are out of Otto and Worley's earshot.

"What in the hell were you thinking, Etta?" She has never heard me yell this loudly, so she backs up several steps. "You are not allowed on the roof. You know that. I don't care who is here doing what, you know the rules. You could've fallen and broken your neck."

"But I didn't!" She turns on me.

"What?"

"I didn't!"

"Because you're lucky. Lucky I was there to catch you!"

"Yeah, I'm lucky you were there," Etta says sarcastically.

"Are you mocking me?"

"What do you care, anyway?"

Etta has never spoken to me in anger, and I don't know how to respond. I don't know whether to admonish her for sassing me or to answer the question.

Etta looks me in the eye. "You don't care about me."

"Where do you get that idea?"

"All the time." Etta storms off and up the stairs.

I follow her. "Stop right there!"

She turns and faces me.

"That's a very cruel thing to say to me. Of course I care about you. But when you do something stupid, something you know you're not supposed to do, you can't turn around and blame me for it. You're the one who's wrong here. Not me."

"That's all that matters to you. Who's right and who's wrong."

"Watch your tone."

"You just don't want me to die like Joe. That's all." Etta slams her bedroom door shut.

For a moment, I think I might honor her privacy, but my anger gets the best of me. I throw the door open. "What is the matter with you?"

Etta is on her bed. My heart breaks, and I go to sit beside her. She pulls away.

"We need to talk about this."

"I don't want to talk to you. I want Daddy."

When I attempt to reach out to her again, she gets up off the bed, goes to the old easy chair with the broken arm, and throws herself into it and away from me. I have never seen this sort of emotion from my daughter, and I am stunned. But I am also so hurt that I don't know what to say. So I rely on my rule about being consistent in my discipline. I'm not going to let her off the hook. "Dad is not going to bail you out of this one. You need to think about what you did this afternoon. And about the way you talked to me."

I leave the room and close the door quietly behind me. I walk down the front stairs and go through the screen door to the porch. I sit down on the steps as I have done so many times at twilight. Otto and Worley pack up their truck without saying a word. They take full responsibility for Etta being on the roof, and I don't want to say anything more. They get into their truck and wave somberly as they descend the hill.

I lean back on the stairs and take a deep breath. The mountains, still green at the end of summer, seem to intersect like those in a pop-up book. This old stone house is hidden in their folds like an abandoned castle, with me its wizened housekeeper, taken for granted and obsolete. I feel myself hitting the wall common to all mothers: the day your daughter turns on you. And it happened on such an ordinary day in Cracker's Neck Holler. Nothing strange or different or particularly dramatic in the weather or the wind. The sky meets the top of the mountains in a ruffle of deep blue. The sun sets in streaks of golden pink as it slips behind Skeens Ridge. I get lost in the quiet, the color, and the breeze, and I'm back in simpler days, the brief time before Jack and I had children, when this house was a place where we made love and ate good food and tended the garden.

The cool air soothes the throbbing in my head. I am making a mess of motherhood. What do I know about children, really? I was an only child. Maybe I baby-sat here and there, but I never had a grand plan that included children. When I found out I was pregnant, I made Iva Lou order me every book on parenthood from the county library. I read each one, choosing concepts that made sense and figuring out how to implement them. When my kids came along, I thought everything would fall into place. But my daughter isn't who I expected her to be. I thought she'd be like me, like my side of the family, marooned Eye-talians in Southwest Virginia who made a good life and fit in. But she's pure MacChesney, freckled and fearless. My kid has no dark corners, no Italian temper or Mediterranean largesse. And I know that I have disappointed her too—she needs an outdoorsy, athletic mom, one who encourages her to take risks. I do the opposite; I encourage her to stop and think. My goal is to keep her safe, and she resents that. Sometimes I am filled with dread at what lies ahead. How do I stop fearing the future? No book can tell me that.

The high beams on Jack's pickup truck light up the field as he takes the turn up the holler road. He slows down to check the mailbox, and I see him throw a few envelopes on the front seat. Then he guns the engine again, spitting gravel under his wheels. Soon I hear my daughter's footsteps as she runs down the stairs. The screen door flies open and she jumps down the steps two at a time, ignoring me, and over the path to meet her father as he parks. I hear the muffled start to her version of the Roof Disaster and wish briefly that I weren't the mother but the wizened housekeeper after all, so I wouldn't have to rat her out. But I know that I have to be unwavering so that at some point when she must make hard decisions, she will remember these days, find the wisdom born of experience, and make the right choice (yeah, right). I have to be the bad guy. Jack puts his arm around Etta as they walk up the path. I stand up. Etta passes by in a businesslike huff without looking at me. She bangs the screen door behind her.

"Are you okay?" Jack gives me a kiss.

"My nerves are shot," I tell him with a nice teaspoon of self-pity.

"We're going to have to come up with a doozy of a punishment," he promises.

"Great." My carefully rehearsed Sex Talk is ruined for now, another plan gone awry.

"Kids taking chances, taking risks, it's all a part of life, Ave." Jack sighs.

As we walk up the stairs, I want to tell my husband that I'm scared. It is one thing to parent a helpless infant and then a child, but when that child develops a will, the future becomes clear—I won't be in charge anymore, and I won't be able to protect her. My husband will have to guide us through these rough patches, since parenting seems to come so naturally to him. I have to learn how to calm down and lead my family. And then I have to find a way to love my job as a mother as the requirements change, and I'm going to need Jack to help me do it.

CHAPTER TWO

*I*t's been three weeks since Etta almost fell off the roof. She survived two weeks of being grounded, which was pretty terrible for her because she missed all the end-of-summer barbecues and the picnic trip with her friends to the Natural Bridge. She moped around for days, and then at the one-week mark, things began to get a little better between us. She made French toast for us on Sunday morning and did her laundry without my asking. Since things are back to normal, Jack has taken her over to Kingsport for their annual father-daughter shopping trip for the first day of school. Etta wants a backpack she saw at Miller and Rhodes.

I go through the house with a laundry basket, loading it up with things that need to be put away. Etta's shoes, comic books, notebooks, pencils, and gear fill the basket. As I go up to her room, Shoo the Cat bounds up the stairs next to me. He charges into Etta's room, and I follow him.

Last summer we let Etta paint her room. She chose

periwinkle with white trim. Her iron bed, painted antique beige, is covered with one of her grandma MacChesney's quilts, a pattern called "Drunkard's Path." She has a poster of Black Beauty over her bed (does every preteen girl in America love purple and horses?).

Etta has a map of the world on her far wall. In red she's circled where she's been, and in pencil the places she wants to go someday. (I'm surprised to see locations in India and New Zealand circled in pencil.) I trace my finger from the United States to Italy and find my father's hometown of Schilpario, north of my mother's: the city of Bergamo, high in the Italian Alps. Etta has written the names of her relatives next to the dots that mark the mountain villages. South on the Mediterranean coast she has circled Sestri Levante and written her cousin Chiara's name enclosed in a heart. Since I took Etta to Italy, she and Chiara have been faithful pen pals, and in many ways, Chiara, who is fifteen, is like a big sister to Etta. Chiara wants to come to the States one day. Judging by the length of her letters, she will have a lot to say when she gets here.

Etta's toy chest, only a year ago filled with dolls and stuffed animals, is now filled with equipment. There's a fishing basket, Roller-blades, a basketball, and several small branches (what she uses them for, I have no idea). She should have been a boy, I think as I prick my finger on a fishhook. I gather up some loose pencils from the bottom of the trunk and return them to the cup on her desk.

The top of the desk is covered in butcher paper, on which she has drawn a map of the heavens and written STARS OVER CRACKER'S NECK HOLLER in calligraphy along the top. She has made diagrams of the constellations and labeled each one. This pencil drawing was done with a ruler; it is so precise, I'm surprised it's hers. Granted, there are many places where the paper is worn thin from erasures, but for the most part, her work is sure-handed. Etta loves astronomy— she points out the Milky Way on clear nights, or a planet when she recognizes it sparkling in the sky—but I didn't know she was so passionate about the subject that she would take time to study the night sky in such detail. Evidently, Etta has an inner life that I know very little about.

When I was a girl, I spent a lot of time thinking about why I'd been born in Big Stone Gap, of all the places in the world. I would look up at the sky and wonder where it ended. I had such longing to explore that I couldn't make the connection that my fate was somehow tied to a mountain town in the hills of Southwest Virginia. I thought a girl like me, who loved to read big adventure stories from centuries long ago, should have been from a more exciting place, a magical place. So when I found out that my mother had in fact left Italy pregnant with me and without a husband, I had my exotic point of origin at last. Etta might be very different, but she has my longing for the Big World deep in her bones. These mountains may protect us from the outside world, but they won't hold us. We can see our way through them and over them, something lots of folks around here could never imagine.

At the bottom of the butcher paper is a very detailed drawing of our stone house, square and rustic, with its four chimneys and the front door painted pale blue. Etta has drawn the windows and their filmy lace sheers rustling in the wind. She has penciled in the roof shingle by shingle (now she knows the shingles firsthand), and her bedroom window, which overlooks the roof. Sitting in the window is Etta herself, with huge eyes and caterpillar eyelashes. In her hands, she holds a small telescope through which she gazes up to the stars above. She must have been out on the roof plenty before I caught her.

The phone rings. One of Etta's punishments was the removal of her phone, so I have to run downstairs to answer it. I pick up on the third ring.

"Ave!" When I hear the voice of my closest friend of twenty years, I become the woman I used to be—young and trouble-free. The worst problem I had when I was single, a hole in the roof of my house, seems silly in comparison to my daughter falling off one.

"Theodore! How are you?"

"Moving."

"Finally, you've come to your senses and you're moving back to Big Stone Gap."

Theodore laughs. "Not likely."

"Come on. We got killer majorettes, and our horn section is the best in the county."

"Don't tempt me."

"You're not going far, are you?" I have loved having my best friend so close in Knoxville. Many weekends, I jump in the Jeep and ride down to see his theatrical halftime shows at the University of Tennessee.

"It's a dream move."

"No. You didn't get a job in—"

"Yep. New York City!"

"No!" Theodore used to talk about New York City as though it lay between heaven and Oz, a place of perfection and possibility. Now he'll see for himself.

"I've only wanted this all of my life, and now it's actually happening," Theodore says gratefully.

"What school?"

"Not a school."

"Not a school? Are you switching careers?" I can't imagine Theodore giving up the life of a band director. He's just too brilliant at it.

"No. I'm just going pro. I've been offered the job of associate artistic director at Radio City Music Hall."

"Oh my God! The Rockettes!"

"The Christmas show, the Easter show, the concerts. All of it. I'm going to be working with the great director Joe Layton. He directed *The Lost Colony*, that outdoor drama. Remember when we drove down to North Carolina to see it?"

"One of our better road trips," I remind him.

"Who would have thought playing Preacher Red Fox in your drama would have gotten me in the door?"

"That's hardly what got you the job. You're a theatrical genius, and now everyone will know it. You're going to the big city! New York City!" I hope I'm not yelling, but I'm so excited for him.

"Now all we have to do is figure out when you're coming up."

Etta and Jack get home around suppertime carrying her new backpack, a three-ring binder with Halley's comet on the

cover, a hot-pink down vest, and more. I meet them outside
to tell them Theodore's news.

"When can we go?" Etta asks excitedly.

"He'd like us to come up for Columbus Day weekend in
October."

"Dad's coming too, right?"

"I'm not slick enough for New York City, Etta." Jack winks
at me.

"You don't have to be slick. You just need to move fast and
cuss and push people out of your way," Etta tells him with
great authority.

"Etta knows all about New York. She's read *Harriet the Spy*
about seventeen times."

"You and your mama will do fine without me."

I've made Etta's favorite dinner: spaghetti in fresh tomato
sauce with meatballs, a big salad, and brownies with vanilla
ice cream for dessert. She clears the dishes without a fuss.

"You girls got mail." Jack comes in from the hallway with
the familiar blue airmail envelopes. Etta practically dives on
her father for her letter. "I forgot about them in my pocket,
they're so thin," Jack apologizes.

"It's from Chiara!" Etta shrieks. "Here, Ma. You got one
from Grandpop."

"Those two keep the Italian mail service in business." My
husband takes the newspaper and goes into the living room.

"No kidding." I rip into my father's letter. It is full of news.
Papa and his new wife, Giacomina, are getting along great,
but his mother is causing her share of agita. Nonna is having
a hard time letting Giacomina take over the household. Papa
says the negotiations continue; I guess Jack isn't the only man

in the world who plays referee to two women. Papa has been down to Bergamo quite a bit and over to see my mother's family, the Vilminores, on Via Davide. There's even an update on Stefano Grassi, an orphan my Zia Antonietta cared for as though he were her son. After she died, the rest of the Vilminore family began to look out for him. He'd come for dinner and help Zio Pietro in the wood shop, though he continued to live at the nearby orphanage. He is a few years older than Etta, and she developed a big crush on him during our last visit. Evidently, the Barbari family has as well: Papa took Stefano to the opera with Giacomina and has included a picture of the three of them on the steps of Teatro alla Scala in Milan.

"Stefano Grassi sure is cute." I give Etta the picture.

"Ma, he is Major Cute," Etta corrects me. And she's right. He's lanky with a great face, a straight prominent nose, dark eyes, and blond curls that make him look like a Renaissance poet. "Stefano is way more mature than the boys around here."

"He wants to come and work in the States next summer. He's studying building and architecture and wants to apprentice with Dad," I tell her.

"Ma, can he come? Please?" Etta lights up like a Roman candle.

"We'll have to ask your dad. But I don't see why not."

Etta sits down and studies the picture. "That's the famous opera house La Scala," I tell her.

"I like Italy better than Big Stone."

"You do?"

"Maybe not better. I love my friends and my school and

everything. But I miss our family over there. Like Grandpop. He's the only grandparent I have."

"We don't have a lot of kin around here anymore, do we?"

"Only Aunt Cecilia. And she's about four hundred years old."

"Well, your dad was an only child, and I'm an only child—"

"I know, I know, and you got married later in life, and therefore you didn't have lots of kids like people that get married when they're young."

"Who says that?"

"You do. All the time." Etta smiles. "Is it okay if I keep the picture?" I tell her it's fine, and she goes up to her room. I suddenly feel like following her and explaining every choice I've ever made, how not every one was designed to deprive her of siblings and cousins, noise and competition and long waits for the bathroom, but rather the result of chance or luck or fate that blew through my life, woke me up, and changed my single path to this married one, and then unexpectedly, delightedly, to motherhood. But I am not going to justify my choices tonight. And I certainly can't explain her brother's death and the fundamental changes it wrought. I don't know how to tell a twelve-year-old there are things that happen in this life that have no explanation. I wonder why I am always defending myself to my daughter. When I figure that one out, perhaps I'll be ready to tackle the big issues with her, including the ones Misty Lassiter has prematurely placed on the front burner of our lives.

The Tuesday lunch special at the Soda Fountain is soup beans and corn bread, so all the regular diehards pile in for the bargain. (We're doubly busy when the first of the month lands on a Tuesday because the black-lung benefit checks arrive.) I'm stuck in the pharmacy filling meds while Fleeta mans the Soda Fountain. It gets crazy.

"Ave Maria Mulligan MacChesney, I'm a-goin' to Florida, and don't try and stop me!" Spec announces from the door.

"You're going on vacation?"

"Yup. Surprised?"

"Very. You've never had one."

"No, only if you count when me and Leola take the kids to the lake. But we ain't never left the state. I figger after forty-seven years, my wife deserves a sandy beach and a mai tai. What do you think?"

"I think it's fantastic. When are you going?"

"Thanksgiving. First off, we're gonna drive down and spend six days at Disney World, then we're gonna hit Sarasota—she got her a cousin down there—and then we'll circle back up the coast of the Sunshine State and come on home."

Fleeta hollers from the Soda Fountain. "Spec, stop jackin' your jaw. I ain't holdin' this seat of yorn no longer, I got me a wait list over here." Spec never misses a lunch special, so he motions to Fleeta that he's on his way.

Iva Lou greets me from the door (I guess everybody in town has a yen for soup beans today). "I had to double-park behind your Jeep, it's so crowded," she says as she places her purse on the counter.

"No problem. I'm not going anywhere."

"Need a hand?"

"You can do labels if you want." I give Iva Lou the labels

run off the computer. She adheres them to the prescription bags as I load the sacks.

"I hired Serena Mumpower out of Appalachia to be my assistant at the library. Top of her class at Mountain Empire."

"How's that working out?"

"She's on the phone constantly. Most popular girl in the county, I believe."

"She's pretty."

"Ain't nobody *that* pretty."

"You'll have to have a talk with her."

"I guess. I don't want her to use the Slemp Library as Dial-A-Date."

"Feel like running over to Appalachia later?"

"Sure. What do you need?"

I whisper, "Etta needs a—a bra. I thought we'd go to Dave's."

"I wouldn't miss it. Etta's first bra? Nothing like a bra to define a figger and emphasize a waistline. I can't believe it. Etta is a young woman who needs support! This is my favorite feminine rite of passage. Well, maybe my favorite was hittin' the hair dye for the first time. I was fourteen when I got yeller streaks in my hair, did 'em myself with peroxide. Big chunky streaks like Tammy Wynette on her greatest-hits album. That's when I discovered that not only do blondes have more fun, they have *all* the fun."

"We're going for utilitarian here, not Wonderbra," I remind Iva Lou.

"Well, if you want plain industrial bras, why don't you just cross the street over to Zackie's and get 'em in a box? Mike's has training bras too, and they're just across the way."

"Etta doesn't want to shop in town. She's a little sensitive about the whole thing. She tried to convince me to go to Kingsport, but I don't have time."

"I'll wear my darkest sunglasses and a Lana Turner scarf so nobody recognizes us."

"Don't laugh. I think Etta would like that."

Iva Lou and I have worked out a routine to make Etta's first bra-shopping expedition casual. Iva Lou is going to buy a pair of boots; I'm going to look at a skirt set that's on sale; and buried in a list of things that Etta needs is her first bra. I called Julia Isaac, who owns the place, ahead of time. She laughed, as she's been down this road with every girl in Appalachia.

Dave's Department Store has been around for years and carries a variety of clothes, from miner's overalls to chiffon mother-of-the-bride dresses that Julia picks up on buying trips to New York. The juniors' section is more hip and, for our area, fairly cutting-edge. Etta skims past the bras on their small plastic hangers and goes to look at shoes. Iva Lou and I look at each other. "I know what to do," Iva Lou whispers.

I watch Iva Lou as she fawns all over a pair of loafers Etta likes. As Etta tries them on, Iva Lou tries on her boots, and then they place both pairs on the checkout counter. Iva Lou leads Etta over to the accessories, showing her a small purse that clips on a belt and matches the loafers. Then Iva Lou stacks several packages of panty hose by her boots. The checkout counter is filling up. Iva Lou stops and admires a lace bra on her way to the juniors' section and makes Etta look at it. It's too mature for Etta, but I don't interrupt; I'm hoping Etta will choose a more appropriate style. She does.

She takes a sporty bra off the rack and shows Iva Lou, who guesses Etta's size and hands her several in that range. Then Iva Lou takes the lacy one to try on herself; Etta goes behind one changing curtain, Iva Lou behind another. Lord love her, Iva Lou is making this fun. My friend is the most natural mother in the world and has never raised a child.

"Ma, I'm done," Etta hollers to me from the checkout desk.

"Where's Aunt Iva Lou?"

"She's still trying things on."

I look down at Etta's stack of items as Julia rings them up. Three tasteful cotton bras with a piqué trim are hiding under the T-shirts Etta wanted.

"Iva Lou?" I say through the curtain of the dressing area. She doesn't answer. "Are you in there?" She still does not respond. I look around the store. It's empty, near closing time. "Iva?" I ask again. I peek through the curtain. Iva Lou is inside, sitting on the bench with her head in her hands.

"What's wrong?" I ask her.

"I'm just draggin', honey-o." Iva Lou looks up at me. Under the fluorescent lights, I see through her makeup that she is exhausted.

"I'm sorry. Did Etta wear you out?"

"No, it's not the shopping. I'm tarred all the time."

"What do you mean, all the time?"

"Around five o'clock every day, I just need to set down and rest."

"Have you been to the doctor?"

"Doc Daugherty said it's gettin' older. That I need to slow down. The usual BS."

"Oh, please."

"What else could it be?"

"A million things." I sit down on the floor next to her. "You may have an insulin problem."

"I don't have the sugar."

"Could be you're vitamin-deficient."

"That could be, 'cause I never do take no pills."

"We can get you over to Holston Valley Hospital for them to do a complete workup on you."

Iva Lou stands. She doesn't argue, which tells me that she's hurting.

"We'll get to the bottom of this, okay?" I reassure her. She pats me on the shoulder, then breathes deeply, peels back the curtain, and walks to the checkout.

"You girls can do some shopping." Jack looks up from watching the news.

"We needed everything we bought. Right, Etta?"

"Yep." Etta takes her shopping bags and goes upstairs.

"I'll bet," Jack says, going back to his program. The phone rings. Jack doesn't make a move for it (he never does), so I pick up in the hallway.

"Ave?"

The familiar voice sends a surge through me. "Pete?"

"How are you?" he says in a tone that makes me feel like I need to sit down.

"I'm doing fine," I tell him. Pete Rutledge has gone from my Italian Summer Crush (okay, old crush, it's been five years since I romped with him in a field of bluebells above Schilpario in the Italian Alps) to family friend.

"Me too. How's Etta?"

"Growing up fast."

"Uh-oh."

"Yeah, she'll be thirteen next April."

"I'm sure you can handle the changes."

"I'm trying."

"Is Jack around?"

"Sure, let me get him."

I call Jack, who smiles and comes to the phone when he hears that it's Pete. When I first met Pete, he was in Italy looking for marble; he's an importer from New Jersey. Actually, he recently added guest professor at NYU to his résumé—there aren't many marble experts in the world. In the time since that tumultuous summer, he's become friendly with my father and Giacomina and still visits them every time he goes to Italy on buying trips. Jack often uses marble on his jobs now, so he buys it from Pete. Their business relationship eventually turned into a friendship, which gave me the creeps at first but now is completely natural. I never realized until I got married how hard it is for men to make good male friends. Most men just have a pleasant, jocular relationship with one another; they don't get emotional or seek advice, something that comes so naturally to me and my women friends. So, even though sharing Pete Rutledge with Jack Mac is strange, I'm actually happy that my husband has made a friend.

I hear Jack hang up the phone. He comes into the kitchen and puts his arms around me as I bread chicken cutlets at the stove.

"What'd Pete want?"

"We're redoing the foyer at the Black Diamond Savings

Bank up in Norton, so I need some marble. He said you should be sure to call him when you and Etta go to New York."

Jack goes and washes up for dinner, and I break into a sweat. Nothing happened with Pete, I remind myself, except that I was tempted. And, of course, I always offset my temptation with the fact that Jack was back here getting chummy with Karen Bell, a lumber-supply saleswoman from Coeburn. (Jack buys his lumber locally now. It's a little unspoken agreement we have.) These trials didn't sink us— in fact, they helped our marriage. We looked hard at our relationship and began to resolve our differences. If Karen Bell and Pete Rutledge hadn't come along, I don't think Jack and I would still be together. Don't get me wrong, I don't want to send Karen Bell a thank-you note for her trouble, but in retrospect, I see that she did me a favor.

"Ma?" Etta interrupts my thoughts.

"Yeah?"

"Thanks for the clothes." Etta sees the table isn't set, so she goes about gathering plates and silverware.

"That was fun."

"Yeah, it was fun," Etta agrees.

I turn around and look at her. "Did you try it on?"

"I have it on," Etta says, adjusting her bra strap through her T-shirt.

"What do you think?"

Etta shrugs. "A bra's a bra, Ma."

I laugh. This is so typical of Etta. I go out of my way to make things easy for her, and she doesn't need me to! She is just like her father, who tackles a problem, finds the solution, and doesn't dwell on it further. Of course, this makes me look like the great overreactor of all time, since I'm asking for a follow-up report on the shopping trip I planned like a CIA run.

"Come on, Ave. They's at Zackie's already. Shake a leg!" Fleeta calls to me from the front doors of the Pharmacy, swinging the doors back and forth to make noise with the chimes in case the hollering didn't get my attention.

"I'm on my way."

"Hell's bells! I hear the snares! Hurry it up!" Fleeta bolts out the door into the street.

A good-size crowd has gathered on Main Street for the Powell Valley High School marching band practice parade and mini-concert on the post office steps, a pre-football-season fall ritual. The kids are fresh from band camp and anxious to show us what they've learned.

Leading the parade is Big Stone Gap's state-of-the-art fire truck, driven by Captain Spec Broadwater (also captain of the Rescue Squad). The wax job on the fire truck is so shiny, it's hard to look directly at. As Spec goes through the first stoplight, he hits the switch to activate the truck's flashing red light, which is the band's cue to pivot right and create a formation on the library steps. Spec has a look of such seriousness on his face, you'd think he was heading into a meeting with General Patton about how to split Berlin. There's plenty of decoration on top of the truck, though—the cheerleaders are draped on the ladders like fan dancers in a Busby Berkley musical. They wave their Carolina-blue pom-poms, which match the afternoon sky. Spec slows the truck to a full stop, leaving the light flashing for dramatic effect. He lights a cigarette and scans the crowd. When he makes eye contact with shopkeeper Zackie Wakin, he nods solemnly instead of waving. Not far behind, the band, marching to a snare-drum cadence, continues to drain off Main Street in perfect rows that stretch from the post office all the way back to the Dollar General Store.

The band is not in uniform; they are wearing jeans and crisp white T-shirts. The majorettes are in red short shorts and tank tops; evidently there was some coordination between them and the cheerleaders, who are wearing white short shorts and red tank tops. My Etta is one of two banner carriers selected by Kate Benton, the new band director. The banner carriers are always middle-school-age; it encourages the younger kids to see their peers march with the big kids, and it certainly encourages them to try out for the marching band when they reach high school. I have never seen such a focused band. Theodore would be so proud. Of course, on weekends Miss Benton is a sergeant in the National Guard, so she knows her stuff.

Etta's posture is perfect. She nods to the other banner carrier, little Jean Williams, whose braids are laced with red ribbons and look glamorous against her rich brown skin. Jean nods back solemnly. I resist the urge to wave to them (I don't want to embarrass them in their official capacity as parade leaders).

As the band falls into formation on the post office steps, the crowd pushes in to watch. The director hands each of the girls a red cellophane hat (the bowler type they give out on New Year's Eve) while the woodwinds pipe the opening bars of "Puttin' on the Ritz." The majorettes use their batons as canes in a Charlie Chaplin dance, but the woodwinds are suddenly drowned out by the fire whistle, which rings long and loud from across town. The drum major doesn't know what to do, so he continues to direct the music.

Spec leans his head out of the fire truck. "Everybody off!" he bellows. The cheerleaders look at one another in confusion (nothing like a pack of panicking cheerleaders).

"I said *off!*" Now the crowd gets into the act, extending arms to help the girls disembark.

"Girls, get off my goddamn truck!" Spec bangs the door with his fist, scaring everyone.

"Calm down, Spec!" Fleeta hollers from the sidewalk. "You'll give yourself a heart attack!"

The girls climb down off the truck quickly, putting their feet in places they shouldn't, making sounds that are less than ladylike, yanking at the hardware, grunting as they shimmy over spikes and notches on their way to the ground. Kelly Gembach, the most agile and petite, rappels down the back using the hose as a rope. The rest of the girls hit the ground like a spray of Red Hots. Only solidly built Kerry Necessary, the captain and the base for most of their gymnastic stunts (she also placed first in the all-county girls' division shot put last year), takes her time sliding down the windshield, creating a big red eclipse for Spec and his buddy Don Wax, who rode shotgun for fun (I'll bet he's sorry). Kerry's sweaty hands leave streaks all over the spotless glass. When she finally comes to a stop, she is on her belly and eye to eye with Spec. The look on his face scares her so badly, she tucks and rolls off the engine to the curb. Her fellow cheerleaders gather around and dust off her shorts.

"Clear the urr-ree-uh!" Spec turns on the siren. The onlookers recoil at the blast, covering their ears, then push back to let Spec through, and he speeds off down the street toward Frog Level, where something is burning.

"That's a bad omen. Gonna be a shit football season, you'll see," Fleeta says under her breath. The drum major cues the band, but the woodwinds, still paralyzed from Spec's rant, barely have the breath to blow out the opening bars. I look over at Etta, who sees me and shakes her head slowly. This wasn't the grand start to her band career that we were hoping for.

With Etta back in school, Iva Lou and I are determined not to let anything interfere with our once-a-week lunches. We've devised a system where we rotate our lunches between the library (pack your own), Stringer's (serve yourself, all you can eat), and Bessie's Diner (the classic burger joint in Appalachia).

"You'd better set down." Iva Lou rises out of her seat at Bessie's to make room for me in the booth. She has ordered for me, my usual sloppy joe and Diet Coke, and has already picked at her macaroni and cheese.

"I'm sorry I'm late. What's wrong? Did your tests come back?" Iva Lou had a full-service physical at Holston Valley— blood, stress test, the works.

"Hell, they told me I was fine over there. I just have to go back for a couple more things, but so far, I'm as healthy as a horse."

"Good."

"No, honey, this is about Etta. I'd rather you hear it from a friend."

"What?"

"It's a beaut. I gotta say, at least your daughter sticks to the tried and true."

My mind races, but I can't imagine what could be wrong. Etta has been an angel since the Roof Incident. She went to the band festival in Bristol, which Jack and I chaperoned. Her first report card of the year was all A's. She doesn't talk on the phone too much and isn't boy crazy. In a week, she and I are going to New York City to see Theodore, just the two of us. I can't imagine what Iva Lou is talking about.

"It's gonna be all over town, and you need to know first."

"Know what?" I say in a measured tone.

"Etta pulled a prank."

"A prank?" This is a word a mother hates to hear.

"Well, here's what happened. Ole Kate Benton made the kids run laps after a bad band rehearsal. Evidently, the kids were really slacking off, and of course, she made everyone run the laps, from the flag girls to the banner carriers."

"So?"

"The kids thought this was unfair, and they rebelled."

"How?"

"Etta and a few other kids ordered a ton of coal to be delivered to Miss Benton's house over on Wyandotte Avenue."

"Oh, no."

"Yep, and she has gas heat."

"No." Delivering coal to someone with a gas furnace is one of the classic pranks that local kids pull, and it surfaces every ten years or so. Basically, some kid calls the coal-delivery service and asks to have a ton of coal delivered for the winter.

In these parts, everything, including coal delivery, is done on an honor system; no deposit, they bill you after they deliver. The customer sets the date (usually sometime in November), and the truck shows up and dumps a mountain of coal in the yard. The customer is responsible for shoveling it down into the basement. You can tell how much of the winter season is left as these mountains of coal diminish in backyards all over town.

"I don't believe it."

"It's true." Iva Lou laughs.

"It's not funny. It's against the law."

"Oh, loosen up. I remember when I was girl, we called the Roy A. Green Funeral Home over in Appalachia, and we told them our principal died of a heart attack and to come fetch him. So old Roy got in his black Buick and drove over to the principal's house. His wife came to the door, and Roy looked at her with them sad bug eyes and said, 'Ma'am, we've come for the body.' She fainted dead away. Now, that was a good un."

"Hilarious," I tell Iva Lou. But I'm not laughing.

I call Jack, who heard the news from the principal, who is first cousin to Jack's business partner, Rick Harmon, and is about to head up to the school. He's furious and tells me that he will handle it.

As I drive back to town, I take a turn toward Wyandotte Avenue to assess the damage for myself. I'm not sure which house the band director lives in, but then I remind myself, don't be stupid, just look for the two-story pile of coal in the backyard.

I find her house, and it's even worse than I imagined. The mountain of shiny black lumps glistens in the afternoon sun like the diamonds they would be someday if left in the earth. The ranch house actually looks smaller than the pile of coal, but that's probably due to my fury and perspective. There's a car in the driveway (it too looks miniature compared to the coal pile), so I pull up and park. I see Spec's Rescue Squad wagon parked near the coal. He makes his way around the side of the house and joins me, shaking his head. "It's a humdinger."

"Hey, Spec. What are you doing here?"

"Miss Benton didn't know who else to call, so I told her I'd come and make the arrangements."

"I can't believe my kid did this."

"She had her some help."

"Don't defend her, Spec," I tell him gently.

"Oh, I ain't. I ain't. But you know how them kids is, they git that group-think goin', and here's the result of it."

"It just makes me sick."

"I talked to Delmer Wilson over to the coal company, and he's ready to send a truck over whenever y'all figger out who's going to pay for the labor."

"I'd like to send Etta to a military academy."

"Now, Ave." Whenever Spec says this, it means fatherly advice is to follow. "You need to keep a cool head in a hot 'tater of a situation. Overreactin' is as bad as no response. Remember what I taught you about responding to emergencies? Stay in charge and remain calm. Okay?"

Spec walks me to the front sidewalk, pats me on the back, and heads back to his wagon. My legs are weak as I take the steps up to the front door; I am so full of dread, you'd think I had pulled this prank myself.

Miss Benton comes to the door. She is wearing a wind-breaker and white sweatpants and has a whistle around her neck. She has an aristocratic face—a fine nose and the high forehead of a leader. Her sharp jawline is softened by her auburn curls, pulled into a loose ponytail. She might be forty, but she is tall and lean with square broad shoulders, so she's in that ageless category.

"Hi. I'm so sorry, Miss Benton."

"It's a mess," she says quietly.

"We will punish Etta."

"I just put sod in the backyard so it could take before the winter. Now it's ruined."

"We'll replace it."

"Well."

"I'm really sorry." I don't know what else to say. She doesn't invite me in, but then why should she? My daughter has ruined her property. Suddenly she turns away.

"Miss Benton, are you all right?"

She turns to face me, her eyes full of tears. "It's just so . . . shitty." She takes a deep breath. "You know I moved here from Richmond, the big city, and I thought, well, Big Stone Gap, in the mountains, it's a small town. It'll be fun, a new adventure. All my friends warned me, it's a dead end to move to a place where there's no life outside of school. But I love what I do, and on weekends I have the National Guard, so I thought I'd give it a shot. But this is just, well, it's too much. I don't mind not being liked, but I don't want to be hated."

"They don't hate you!"

"Oh, okay. This is something that kids who like you would do," she snaps.

I am standing face-to-face with a woman whose shoes I've been in, whose frustrations I shared for most of my adult life, and I want to tell her that I understand what it means to be single in a small town, to be alone, to have to take care of a house, from leaks in the roof to kinks in the furnace to mowing the lawn, to deal with bad news from family far away and hear good news from the same and have no one to share it with. To long for connection, to want to be a part of the bigger picture and yet to love your solitude, to have time to think and silence to read with no one to answer to or tend to. To hoard privacy, the greatest luxury, knowing that though it's the very thing that keeps you separate from people, it's so meaningful and delicious that you don't care. I know about working hard all week and being so busy that weekends aren't weekends, just two extra days to be useful. I know what she is feeling, and I want her to know that.

"I understand. I was alone in this town for a long time," I tell her.

"Then you know."

"Yes ma'am, I do."

Kate puts her hand on the door, signaling that she is done opening up to me. I turn to go down the steps. She stops me.

"What's a ferriner?" she asks quietly.

"Someone who moves to these parts from the outside. A foreigner. Why do you ask?" But I have a sick feeling I know the answer.

"I was just wondering. One of the kids called me that."

"We'll get the coal cleaned up and the sod replaced," I promise her.

She closes the screen door.

I feel so bad for Kate Benton. She might feel like a ferriner, but now she knows that is exactly how she is perceived. Every time we attract talented people to this area, we end up driving them away when they dare to do things differently or take a firm stand with our children. Ferriners are outsiders, but we make them outcasts. Why should she stay here? What is here for her? At least I had Theodore to share things with, to go places, to have a life outside my work. We loved all the same things—good books, good food, and the theater. I hardly noticed time passing in the ten years that Theodore lived here, I was so happy to have a like-minded friend. We'd go and climb around caves and see movies in Kingsport and go to the mall. When one of us needed an escort to some party or event, we'd always go together. Kate Benton doesn't have a Theodore. I don't know how long she'll last around here without one.

Fleeta is locking up when I stop by the Pharmacy on my way home.

"How bad was it?" she asks as she sorts through the keys on a large brass ring.

"It's terrible."

"Yeah, Misty confessed the whole thing to her mama, who told Iva Lou at the li-berry." Fleeta pauses, waiting for me to respond. When I don't, she continues, "Yeah, it's a bad thing them kids did. But at least Etta made the group confess to the principal. That ought to make you feel better." Fleeta lights up one of the two cigarettes she's smoking per day now.

It should make me feel better, but it doesn't. "I don't want to talk about it, Fleeta."

"All youngins git into messes one time or another. You

know what I went through with Pavis." Fleeta exhales so deeply, it's as if she blows out an additional pocket of old smoke from deep within her lungs.

How could I forget Pavis? When he was in high school, I had to advance Fleeta her paycheck several times so she could bail him out of the town jail for infractions that varied from public drunkenness to selling illegal fireworks to minors.

"Poor pitiful Pavis," Fleeta says as though it's his given name. She continues, "When the police picked him up the first time, they come by my house to let me know they had him. And I don't even remember the charges, I just remember I took a fit of cryin'. I said to the cop, 'Why? Why do I have two normal youngins who act right and one Pavis who's forever in a mess? How could one child turn out so badly?' And he said, 'Ma'am, there's an old saw, and it's true: You plant corn, you git corn.' " Fleeta sighs and goes to lock up the Soda Fountain.

My hands begin to shake on the steering wheel as I make the turn up Cracker's Neck Road. I try to remember what Spec told me, try to stay calm, but my body has other ideas. When I told Jack I would meet them at home, we were both furious, but I think he was still a bit taken aback by my tone of voice. And now that I've seen the pile of coal, my mood is even worse. I park my Jeep and take a moment to sit and breathe before going inside.

"Etta. Come down here. Now."

Jack stands back from the stairs, signaling that he wants to have a private talk with me. I raise my hand to stop him. I don't even put my purse down. Etta appears at the top of the stairs and grips the banister in fear.

"I just came from Miss Benton's house."

"I'm sorry, Mom."

"Really."

"I really am."

"Have you told Miss Benton?"

"The principal called us into the office before band practice, and Miss Benton came, and we all told her that we were sorry."

"So it's all better now?"

Etta shrugs.

"Answer me."

"No."

"No, what?"

"No ma'am."

"Come downstairs."

Etta gingerly makes her way down the stairs. I go into the living room. Jack and Etta follow me. I motion for her to sit. "How did this happen?"

"Me and Misty—"

"Misty and I."

"Misty and I were in the library, and she told me that when her dad was in high school, he called Westmoreland Coal and had a ton sent to Mr. Bates, his biology teacher. And we thought it was funny."

"Oh, it's funny. Did you see what you did?"

Etta shakes her head.

"Do you know that Miss Benton just moved here and she's all alone? Can you imagine how she feels?"

Etta looks at me. Clearly, she hasn't thought about Miss Benton.

"First of all, you're going to clean up the mess. You and your pals."

"She knows that." Jack looks at her sternly.

"And you're not going to New York."

Etta looks up at me. "What?"

Jack almost says something, but I don't give him a chance. "You heard me. You're not going to New York."

"But it was a joke!"

"I hope you had a good laugh, because that's all you're getting out of it. Go to your room."

Etta gets up slowly and walks to the doorway. I can tell she wants to say something, but she thinks better of it and climbs the stairs to her room.

I collapse onto the couch. Jack sits down next to me.

"How could this happen?" I ask him.

"They're kids."

"That's no excuse. I'm really worried about her."

"Why?"

"She runs with all these older kids. That's not good."

"You mean Misty?"

"Misty, the kids in the band."

"She carries the banner."

"Still."

"She's really sorry."

"Too bad."

"No, she really means it. She cried at the principal's office."

"What is it, Jack? Do you think I'm overreacting?" Jack

doesn't answer me. "I went to see Kate Benton, and she was devastated. I bet she moves out of town over this."

"Why?"

"God, Jack, don't you get it? She's all alone over there. She moved here on a lark, thought it would be interesting to live in a small town, and look at this. She's a joke to those kids. How would you feel?"

"I'd take control of the situation. You have to when you work with kids." Jack leans back and puts his feet on the coffee table. This nonchalant movement infuriates me further. I want to shake my husband, wake him up to what this *is*, show him that it's not just about a cruel prank, it's deeper than that. It's about Us and Them, Ferriners and Natives. How do I explain that I've been a ferriner all of my life, and that I relate to Kate Benton? My daughter will never have the experience of being an outsider. With her MacChesney name and her lineage, she is one of Them. I can't get into this with my husband. He is one of Them too. He doesn't see it, doesn't think it's important. So instead, I blast him for his indifference.

"You know what? *You're* not taking control of this situation."

"She said she's sorry."

"Maybe that's my problem. I don't believe her. She's old enough to know this was a terrible thing to do. Where's her conscience? Her compassion? Don't you worry that she's not sensitive to other people's feelings?"

"Like you're sensitive to mine?" Jack asks softly.

"What?"

"When did we talk about a punishment? You just sort of

sprung the New York thing on her and me. I want to back you up, but you need to at least let me know what you're going to do."

"I don't believe it! You're turning this into something *I'm* doing wrong."

"If you want me to help, you have to let me make the decisions with you. That's all I'm saying." Jack's tone is even and calm, as though we've had this argument before. (We have.)

"I'm sorry. This incident hit a nerve."

"I see that." Jack puts his arm around me. I sink into him like a spoon in cake batter.

"All the books say to get a grip on your emotions before you discipline your child. Haven't I done that in the past? I usually have a grip, don't I?"

"Yes, you do. Most of the time."

"But this time I saw myself in it. I was like Miss Benton for a lot of years. It's like Etta did something personal to the person I used to be."

Jack holds me for a long time, and I don't say a word. No matter how many years go by, I'm never very far from who I was, the ferriner, the unmarried one, the lone Eye-talian. And no matter how many years go by, I carry her inside me. Somehow I know that I always will.

Etta has left for school early. She has the Girls' Athletic Association preschool basketball game, but I'm sure she wants to avoid me. Jack is off to work already, so the house is quiet. As I pull a mug from the kitchen cabinet, I see a letter addressed to me propped on the windowsill. With the end of a teaspoon, I open the letter and unfold it, then I pour myself a cup of coffee.

Dear Mom,

I know you hate me right now but I wanted you to hear my side of things. I did do the wrong thing. I did call the coal company and place the order on a Friday when we knew they were rushing to get out of there and wouldn't check. I don't hate Miss Benton, except for the laps she makes us run, she's been a pretty good band director. We thought it would be funny to see a pile of coal in her yard. I didn't think about how we would get it out of there. I am very sorry. I am sorry I hurt Miss Benton and sorry I can't go to New York where I've always wanted to go. I won't order a coal dump in anyone's yard anymore.

Etta

I grab some paper and a pen and write Etta a note back.

Dear Etta,

I don't hate you. I don't like what you did, there's a difference. I believe you are sorry for the coal dump and that you won't do it again. But next time you think of doing something for the sport of it, would you please consider the person's feelings? How would you like someone to do that to you?

Love, Mom

I leave the letter on Etta's bed, noting that her room has

never been so neat. She's not a bad kid, I remind myself as I pack up for work. She didn't try to weasel out of her punishment or blame anyone else for the prank. Maybe she even learned something. But it's uncanny to me, how my kid can zero in on my sensitivities. She knows I'm protective of new folks who move to town. And she knows equally well what is required for me to set myself on the path of forgiveness.

Life in Cracker's Neck Holler has been so quiet since the coal dump a month ago, you'd think this old house was a monastery. I chose not to back down on my punishment. Etta will not be going to New York City with me (this time), and Jack agreed. It is so hard to follow through with this decision, because one of my dreams for my daughter is to travel, to expose her to the outside world, to museums, plays, culture. A couple of days ago, I almost buckled, but Jack reined me in. It won't be Etta's last chance to visit New York City, he reminded me. And both Jack and I feel it's more important to stand by the punishment than to let her think we can be softened up with a few nicely made beds. I keep a picture of Pavis Mullins in my head at all times to remind myself that once children think they can get away with something, they'll continue to try.

Iva Lou volunteered to chauffeur me to the airport—I got a great fare, and I'll be in New York City by suppertime. Etta has a football game, where Jack is working the Band Boosters' refreshment stand; Conley Barker, who runs the taxi service, is unavailable because he also announces home games for the radio, so Iva Lou generously volunteered, even though she loves Powell Valley football and hates to miss a game. I apologize for putting her out.

"It is no problem. So, you gonna see that hunk from New Jersey when you're up there?" Iva Lou adjusts the rearview mirror and looks at me. The road to the Tri-Cities airport is hilly, and I get butterflies as Iva Lou sails over the bumps.

"Who?" I play dumb.

"Pete Rutledge." Iva Lou draws his name out slowly.

"I don't know." I'm lying, of course. I would like to see Pete, my what-if fantasy. What married woman doesn't have a Plan B? You know, the handsome man from the past who, if the circumstances were different, would be the Man of the Present. Pete was very romantic and very interested four summers ago in Italy, but of course, I was married. So I safely placed him on a back burner, to lift the lid on *that* pot only when I was mad at Jack or bored with my life or stressed by my daughter. Pete Rutledge is like a good old movie that I return to in my mind's eye when I need a lift. In those moments I tell myself that if anything ever happens to Jack, there is always Pete. I do feel guilty about it, but I consider it Practical Fantasizing: when I'm being taken for granted or I get bogged down by drudgery, I can return to that field of bluebells and imagine what might have been.

"I thought New York and New Jersey were as close as Coeburn and Norton."

"They are."

"So he's right *there*, and you're right there. Did you pack your high heels?"

"What for?"

"So you can walk all over him."

"Don't you think I have enough to worry about?"

"Yeah, you do, honey, I'm just messin' with you." Iva Lou laughs.

"We're talking about me, not you. I'm not a flirt."

"Hmm. So you been thinkin' about how to get away with something."

"Absolutely not. I have a good husband, and I don't need any excitement."

"Oh, honey-o, excitement is the only thing worth livin' for." Iva Lou stops at the light outside Gate City. "But I'll make sure that things are as dull as dirt in the Gap. I'll keep an eye on your husband while you're off *not* gettin' excited."

"Not necessary."

"I'll be the judge of that. We just hired him to build us come storage units at the library, should keep him busy about a week." Iva Lou winks at me.

"Isn't that funny—the exact amount of time I'll be gone."

"Uh-huh. We murried gals got to stick together and form a shield around our men," Iva Lou says with a resolve I haven't heard since she went before the county to request a new Bookmobile (she got it).

As I board the plane, I look back and wave good-bye to Iva Lou. I have no problem leaving my life in her hands, none whatsoever.

The first rule about living in New York City (according to Theodore Tipton) is that no one ever picks up a guest at the airport. Never. Apparently, La Guardia Airport is a zoo, and it's up to the guest to get in the taxicab line (I'm not taking the bus; Theodore's instructions were too confusing), tell the driver your address, and sit back and hope he doesn't take you on a hayride to Connecticut or beyond.

I went digging into my mom's trunks for my wardrobe for this trip. I found a vintage cropped jacket in a navy blue velvet and embroidered pants, the wide-legged, high-waisted style from the early 1940s. Theodore said the weather had turned cold early and to dress warmly, so I figured the velvet would be perfect. I want to dazzle Theodore's friends, so I even threw in some of Mama's jewelry. She made a brooch of jet beads, which I'll wear to a night out at the theater. My only wardrobe worry is shoes—mine are woefully not up to snuff, so I'll splurge on some new ones in Greenwich Village

(Theodore calls Eighth Street, near his apartment, Shoe Town). I'm wearing a black turtleneck and black jeans; I figure that's a standard New York look, so I won't look like I have "tourist" tattooed on my forehead.

It's surprising how self-reliant I become when I'm alone. Part of being married is getting lazy; when I'm home I leave all the logistics (directions to Biltmore House and Gardens for a school field trip) and icky weird chores (cleaning the furnace, trapping mice) to my husband. It's empowering for me to negotiate my way through one of the busiest airports in the world. I pass under the entry portal, where LA GUARDIA pulses overhead in giant red letters; how thrilling, a fellow Eye-talian and former mayor of New York City with an airport named after him!

As I wait for my luggage, it seems like thousands of people are milling about, no two of them alike. New York really is the capital of the world, and I'm as intrigued by the wide-eyed Indian woman in her turquoise sari with strips of gold lamé on the hem as I am by the tall Russian in a bad mood who yanks his oversize duffel bags off the carousel and loads them onto a cart. I reach my hands up over my head, embracing the whole scene, and have a good stretch, thrilled to be here, so happy to be a part of something so exciting and new (to me, anyway).

"Your first trip?" a voice says behind me (I guess my look of wonder and appreciation has given me away). I drop my arms and turn.

"I went through JFK once on my way to Italy." Do I sound like a defensive tourist or what?

"Hmm. You Italian?"

"I am." In New York, you're an American second and where you immigrated from first.

"Me too." The man is around sixty, with a shock of salt-and-pepper hair. He is small and trim, and has a long nose with a very fine bridge (according to the ancient art of Chinese face reading, he may well live to be a hundred years old).

"Where are your people from?" I ask.

"Napoli."

"You're southern."

"And you?"

"North. The Alps."

"They're pieces of work up there." The man laughs.

"How do you know?"

"I married one." The man doesn't take his eyes off the baggage carousel as it rotates. "Once my wife and me, we were in Atlantic City and went to a show, and they had a comedian there—you know, the warm-up guy. Anyway, he came over to our table and said, 'You two married?' and we said that we were, and he said, 'Ladies and gentlemen, these two agree about *nothing*.' And everybody laughed, and so did we, 'cause it's true. Northern Italians and southern Italians might as well be from two different planets, you know what I mean?"

I nod that I do. I can't believe how fast people talk here. That same observation would have taken someone in Big Stone Gap about three hours to relate. Of course, back home we *have* the three hours to spare. Here everyone is in a hurry.

My cabdriver is Pakistani, and he is happy to tell me all about his homeland. I am having more interesting conversations in five minutes in New York than I do in a year in Big Stone

Gap. We turn off the Grand Central Parkway and onto the road that leads to the Queens end of the Fifty-ninth Street Bridge. The driver waves his hand over the Manhattan skyline as though presenting a box of jewels. At any moment I expect Fred Astaire and Ginger Rogers to spin across the sky; I see the clouds as her marabou cape and the stars, the heels of his black patent-leather wing tips, their glittering shoes barely touching down on the emerald-cut horizon as they dance. What could top the magnificence of this picture? Theodore is so lucky, and I am so lucky that my best friend now *lives* under these lights and inside this fabulous madness. I feel a pang of guilt, though. Etta should be here.

"You okay, lady?" The driver looks at me in the rearview mirror.

"I wish my daughter were here," I tell him.

"New York City is not going anywhere. It will always be here," he says, and smiles. And, oddly enough, that makes me feel much better.

A doorman in a navy blue uniform with gold epaulets greets me in the small but ornate rococo lobby of Theodore's building on the corner of Fifth Avenue and Ninth Street in Greenwich Village. After I got out of the cab, I must have spent five minutes looking down to the arch at Washington Square Park, a four-story pale blue horseshoe that conjures the Champs-Élysées in Paris. "I just want to take one more look," I tell the doorman as he buzzes Theodore. I go back outside and look up Fifth Avenue to where the yellow stripes in the center of the street become one giant arrow that disappears into the darkness of uptown.

"Hey, the reunion's inside!" Theodore says, stepping out of the elevator. "You made it!" He looks handsome. His red hair is sandy with gray. He is in great shape, as though auditioning for the dance corps at Radio City instead of directing it. He looks younger somehow. The worry creases between his eyes are gone, and it seems like the whole of him has relaxed (no small feat for a perfectionist).

Every detail of Theodore's new home interests me: the elevator with the shiny brass buttons; the walnut panels inlaid with 1930s Chinese foil wallpaper in the hallways; the carpet, a black and gray wool harlequin pattern (very deco). Any moment I expect Carole Lombard to peek out one of the doors looking for William Powell. We reach the door to Theodore's apartment. The small name tag over the doorbell that reads TIPTON proves that this whole trip is not a dream.

"What do you think?" Theodore stands in the middle of his living room, tastefully done in simple grays and off-white, very spare and neat. There are three large windows that overlook Fifth Avenue. I walk over to take in the scene below. The traffic streams toward Washington Square like a loose string of pop beads.

"Sure beats your log cabin in Powell Valley."

"I wish I had the closets I had in Big Stone Gap. But the only people with big closets in this city own the buildings." I follow Theodore down a small hallway with track lighting. "Check out the bedrooms. This one is yours." He drops my bags in a room so small, there is only a single bed, a nightstand, and a straight-back chair. He has decorated it simply with an antique quilt made by my mother-in-law (a gift from me when he got the job at the University of

Tennessee). "And this is mine." Theodore pushes open the door to his bedroom. It looks sleek, with a platform bed and a gray slipper chair in the corner. It's almost the size of the living room, except it overlooks Washington Square Park.

"Oh my God" is all I can say.

"I know, I know. Every night before I go to bed, I think of Henry James."

"That's the actual spot where Dr. Sloper lived, isn't it?" I point to a row of brownstones that faces the park.

"Could be."

"Remember when we used to read *The Heiress* aloud?"

"Yep. Your interpretation of Catherine Sloper will never be topped. Even though I am the only person in the world who heard you read it." Theodore laughs.

"Let's just say I could relate to the story." And boy, did I. The story of an oppressed daughter of a cruel father rang true to me. "Who would have ever thought you would be living in Henry James country?"

Theodore hasn't changed so much as evolved. He is comfortable in his skin, in this apartment, in his life. There is an ease to him that was never there before. "You look better than you've ever looked. I'm not kidding."

"That's what happens when you find the place where you fit."

"Weren't you nervous to move here?"

"Oh, God no. I couldn't wait. I'm just glad I finally made it." Theodore looks at me and smiles. "You look good."

"Oh, come on."

"No, you do."

I follow Theodore into the kitchen. A bar counter separates

the kitchen from the living room, and he's set the small dining table and chairs in front of the counter with white china and a white tablecloth. Then we hear a buzzer.

"Dinner's on."

"Dinner?"

"I can't possibly top Charlie Mom's Chinese. Wait till you taste the honey spareribs. Sit here so you have the view."

Theodore answers the door. A cute Chinese kid delivers two brown bags. Imagine. Dinner delivered hot to your door. How I wish I had this sort of setup in Big Stone Gap! Theodore unloads the bags, filling the table with small white boxes. "Tell me why you didn't bring Etta."

I tell Theodore every detail of the coal prank. He listens without interruption.

"What was the punishment?"

"We made the kids shovel the coal back onto the truck and resod her yard."

"They got off easy. I would've made them shovel the coal into wheelbarrows and walk it back to Appalachia." Theodore loads my plate with all sorts of delicacies—tiny shrimp, fluffy rice, chopped vegetables. "Etta organized five other kids to pull this off?"

"Yes. I couldn't believe it. She was in charge, but she had Misty Lassiter egging her on."

"Tayloe's daughter?"

"Yeah. She's got all of Tayloe's beauty and talent plus a cunning criminal mind, which really adds to her allure."

Theodore smiles. "That bad, huh?"

"Well, I'm a little put out by the whole thing." I stab a sparerib. "I feel like I can't trust Etta now, and I hate that. If she's not climbing on our roof, she's pulling pranks. I don't want to monitor her every move. I don't want to hover. But she doesn't leave me a choice."

"You need to keep her busy."

"She's in the band; she plays basketball before school; she works with her dad on weekends. How busy can I keep her? I don't know what else to do, short of sending her to convent school."

"There's a good one right across the river in Jersey."

"Don't tempt me."

"Back when I was teaching kids, I noticed patterns—"

"What kind of patterns?" I blurt nervously. As usual, my mind leaps to the worst-case scenario.

"Relax. It's just that the smartest kids were the ones who pulled stuff. Now, I'm not talking about the suck-up brainiacs, I'm talking about the kids who, no matter how many clubs and activities you put them in, still have time to cut up. Etta sounds like she's bored. She's hanging out with older kids, she's got time on her hands during the school day. These are all the classic signs of a troublemaker. You have to help her find a way to engage her mind."

"I'd like to find a way to engage her heart," I tell Theodore plainly.

"What do you mean?"

"I'd like her to think of other people and their feelings. Don't get me wrong. I know it could be worse and I know she has a good heart, but she's more headstrong than loving."

"She sounds like Mrs. Mac." Theodore leans back and laughs, remembering my mother-in-law. "That was one tough lady. She had that cane. She didn't carry it around because she needed the support, she used it to intimidate people. She was always banging it on the floor or catching a closing door with it. I remember I was in the post office once, going out, and she was coming in. I was in a rush, so I sort of sprinted out of there. She stopped me and said, 'Mr. Tipton?' And then she whacked me on the butt and said, 'Youth! Always in a hurry!' "

"How about when she came into the Pharmacy and asked me why I didn't accept her son's proposal? I was humiliated."

"She wound up getting her way, didn't she?" Theodore laughs and refills our wineglasses.

"How *are* you and Jack doing?"

"We're in a good place."

"No distractions?"

"You mean Karen Bell?" If there are even rumors about your husband straying, it becomes the touchstone of every conversation you'll have about your marriage. But I don't mind, because this is Theodore. "Well, I haven't found any notes, and there haven't been any phone calls, and Iva Lou says that Karen found a serious boyfriend up in Honaker, and Fleeta says she hasn't heard tell of her in Norton, so I guess she's out of the picture entirely."

"Well, that's good. It's funny about affairs, though, isn't it? They're so—I don't know, *urgent* when they're happening, uncontrollable almost, and then once they're over, it's hard to remember why the passion consumed you in the first place."

This is why Theodore and I remain so close after all these years. He can look at my life and see it clearly, in ways that I cannot. He reads my heart like a passage from a play, with emotional understanding of the moment but with one eye always on the bigger picture. Wherever he is, I feel at home with him, even in New York City, a place that once lived only in my imagination.

The guest bathroom is loaded up with all sorts of bubble baths and soaps in a basket. I take full advantage of a faceted bottle marked CALM, pouring the opulent lavender milk into the hottest water I can stand. The stress of my trip and all the anxiety leading up to it float up and out the transom in the steam. I let it go and breathe deeply.

Theodore knows how to treat a guest. The candles, nestled in a series of crystal cups, are scented like sugar cookies and throw shadows of snowflakes onto the wall. There's a stack of fluffy white towels in a wrought-iron antique stand; they're monogrammed not with initials but with the word RELAX. There's even a shower radio, and I turn on some music while I soak. (It's set on a country station, which makes me laugh.) Theodore thinks of everything; maybe that's why Radio City Music Hall snapped him up — great art is in the details.

Theodore gets me up early with a large paper cup of coffee and a giant cinnamon and raisin bagel in a brown paper bag (does everything to eat in this city come in a sack?). He wants me up and dressed so we're ready to hit the day running. Theodore has to be in the office, and he has mapped out places around Radio City that I can visit while he's working. He has a whole itinerary worked out; we'll see shows, sightsee, and even watch the Columbus Day Parade down Fifth Avenue on Monday. "You'll really get your fill of Eye-talians," Theodore promises.

The offices at Radio City aren't really offices at all. They're small beige cubicles, sort of like a giant egg carton. The walls overflow with charts and calendars and swatches of fabric, braids and trims for costumes, watercolors of set designs, and shoes (you'd be surprised how many kinds of tap shoes there are). The phones never stop ringing. Everyone is young, and everyone seems rushed. They barely look up when Theodore introduces me; they aren't rude, just busy. When he walks to the center of the maze, he is besieged by everyone from the dance captain to the receptionist. Of course, this is their busiest time of year; they're in preproduction for the Christmas extravaganza. As a small group gathers around Theodore, I reach into his jacket pocket and pull out the list of places for me to check out on my own and indicate that I'll be back for lunch.

There must be a hundred makeup kiosks on the main floor of Saks Fifth Avenue. I think of Fleeta, who complains about having to load two measly spin racks at the Mutual's; I wonder what she'd do if she had to help stock this operation.

I am spritzed with four different perfumes on my way through (they asked politely and I couldn't say no) and invited to have my makeup done, French look, high-fashion look, the natural look, or any look I want—these salesgirls are wide open to the possibilities of the paints they're peddling.

There is a girl around Etta's age sitting on one of the high-backed chairs in front of a mirror at the Clinique counter. Standing next to her is her mother (obvious from the analytical expression she wears while studying her daughter). As the makeup consultant dabs a little concealer on the girl's face, the mother leans in.

"Too much."

"Mom."

"Amy, don't argue with me."

"Use a light touch and it won't even seem like she's wearing it," the consultant says, reassuring the mother.

The girl examines her face in the mirror. "It hardly looks like I have anything on."

"I don't want it to look like you have makeup on."

"I need it," Amy responds in an all-knowing tone my daughter uses on a regular basis.

"Makeup doesn't make you pretty, it's what's inside that counts," Amy's mother reminds her.

"If you're a nun," Amy says flatly.

"There's nothing wrong with nuns. They serve humanity. Plus, you'll get much further in life focusing on your brain." Now she's gone too far; she sounds like the Universal Mother whose generic wisdom can be cracked in two and read aloud like advice in a fortune cookie.

As I take the escalator up to the next floor, I look down on Amy and her mother, who become smaller and smaller as the stairs lift away. Suddenly I don't see them, I see Etta and me. That's just the sort of conversation we have, where we disagree and haggle back and forth about the most insignificant things. After we finish one of these sessions, Etta feels misunderstood and I feel like I can't say anything right. I wonder why it is so hard for mothers to remember that daughters are just learning about being women and that this time in their lives will never come again.

＊

"How was your day?" Theodore asks as I hang on to the strap in the back of a particularly speedy cab on our way to dinner.

"Busy. I went to Saint Patrick's. Rockefeller Center. Saks. Then I walked up to Central Park. As I was walking around, I saw a stray cat, but when I looked more closely, it was a rat. Once I realized it was a rat, it was too late to scream, and he went behind a rock anyway. And then I went to the carousel, and I just sat there for a long time and watched people. Women really know how to dress in New York."

The doors to Blue Pearl are painted bright blue with gold tassels drawn on them trompe l'oeil style. Theodore opens the door for me. "Ignore the decor. It's over the top," he whispers as we enter.

I like the decor. We're inside a blue cave, with booths lit by low-hanging fixtures. The tables are small squares, perfect for two, with blue rose petals sprinkled in the center. Even the mirrored walls are smoky blue, reminding me of a 1920s speakeasy. The maître d' leads us through the crowded restaurant to a corner table, handing each of us a menu.

"How did you pick this place?" I ask Theodore.

"I know the chef. He's a special friend of mine."

The way he says this makes me think that the someone special is *his* someone special. "You have a boyfriend?" I say too loudly. Theodore nods. "Why didn't you tell me?"

"Wouldn't you rather just meet him?"

I follow Theodore to the kitchen doors. He points through the porthole window. The kitchen is small but neat. There is a long silver prep table, and behind it, an open grill with two deep overhead ovens. Theodore takes my hand and we go through the doors; we wedge into a corner observing the action, but we're in the way in this tight space. There's a phone with rows of blinking lights that look like they need to be answered, and quickly. Theodore points to the phone. "Told you the place was hot."

"Torch the brûlée!" The chef, his back to us, bellows through the din, and an assistant obeys him instantly.

"That's Max." Theodore points to the baritone in the tall white hat. Max has a stocky build (mostly muscle), and big forearms and hands. His hair is black and cut close to his large head (which, in face reading, means he will always make a good living). His black eyes don't miss a trick; he scans the pots, rearranging them as the food simmers. Finally he senses invaders and looks up. He smiles and wipes his hands on a dish towel looped through his belt as he joins us.

"This must be Ave Maria." Max takes my hand.

"This is Max Berkowitz," Theodore says proudly.

"I'm so happy to meet you," I say. Max has a great smile and deep dimples (though I don't think his staff sees them very often).

"I hope you're hungry."

"I am."

"Go sit and relax, and get ready. I'm gonna dazzle you." Max winks at Theodore.

The feast brought to our table begins with a lobster bisque so light and buttery that I want a second bowl, but I'm too ashamed to ask. It's a good thing too, because what follows is so scrumptious, I would have been sorry to miss it. Max makes us baby lamb chops on a bed of sweet-potato puree, followed by a salad of spinach, pears, walnuts, and curls of fresh

Parmesan cheese—it's the dressing that kills me; it's made with raspberries and balsamic vinegar.

"I wish Jack were here. Max would have an apprentice. Jack still talks about opening a restaurant."

"You're lucky you have a man who cooks."

"So are you. How did you meet?"

"One of those introduce-the-new-guy-to-town parties."

"You met and that was it?"

"Sort of. It grew slowly. Thought he'd be a good friend. He was so interesting, I never met anyone like him. He's so expressive and passionate."

"And talented!" I add.

"Definitely. And I haven't changed much: it's still hard for me to get close to anyone. So Max has to spend a lot of time pulling my feelings out of me. And I have to say, I like it."

"You deserve someone who understands you completely."

"I think Max is The Guy."

"You *think* I'm the guy?" Max pulls up a chair next to me. "Hardly sounds like an endorsement. Table six is having risotto, I got two seconds to kill. Ready for dessert?" The waiter brings two small dishes filled with some sort of custard. "Lavender flan," Max announces. "Sounds like a weird combination, but it just works." Max smiles at Theodore and goes back to the kitchen.

"Was he talking about your relationship or the flan?" I ask Theodore.

"Both."

Theodore and I are full, so we walk the twenty blocks or so from the restaurant to his apartment. I love the twisty Greenwich Village streets lit by lamps and old sconces in the doorways. The brownstones stacked close together, walls touching, remind me of my favorite thing, a shelf of books. And they are not unlike great books, full of characters and their stories. How I wish I could live in a place like this, maybe not forever but just long enough to hear their secrets.

Theodore turns on the lights in his apartment, dropping his keys with one hand while hitting the answering machine with the other. He takes my coat and hangs it in the closet.

"Uh, Theodore Tipton? This is Pete Rutledge," the familiar voice on the machine begins. "I understand you have a houseguest. I've been tipped off by her husband. Ask Ave Maria Mulligan if she can give me a shout at my office at NYU. Two-four-three, five-four-one-zero. Thanks."

"Mulligan? I haven't heard that in fifteen years. Does he think you're still single?"

"Oh, please." I say this casually as I throw myself down on Theodore's easy chair. I would never admit that I'm secretly thrilled Pete called. Why should I tell Theodore that Pete is my escape-hatch fantasy?

"What are you thinking about?" Theodore asks suspiciously.

"Nothing." My voice goes up an octave.

"You went off somewhere. Somewhere dangerous," Theodore observes.

"I was thinking about Jack and Pete. You know."

"No, I don't."

"I'm not going to do anything with Pete on this visit, don't worry."

"Who said anything about you doing anything with Pete Rutledge?"

"That's what you meant, isn't it?"

"No, it's what *you* meant." Theodore looks at me as though I'm up to something, and I kind of like it. At my age, I like to look into the eye of danger—okay, maybe take a peek, because *that's* as much of a thrill as I can handle.

I sleep peacefully and wake up feeling so refreshed, I believe anything is possible. I had a flying dream. It's my favorite kind of dream, where I'm walking along (in this particular dream it was Schilpario in winter, high in the Italian Alps with snow coming down like powdered sugar out of a sifter), and I'm with my father on an alpine path, chatting about nothing in particular, and then the breeze abruptly kicks up, and I hold out my arms and the wind lifts me off the ground and into the sky. I rise, higher and higher toward the stars, until the world below loses all detail, and any movement looks like coffee grounds scattered across a countertop. I can't hear anything, the sky is perfectly quiet, and even the sound of the wind stops. And for what seems like hours, I am flying, dipping, and sailing, so lightly I could disappear into the clouds I float through.

Theodore has already left for work, leaving me another sack breakfast; this time a large cappuccino and an oversize cinnamon bun. I'm going to gain ten pounds on this trip, but I don't care—I'm on vacation. I feel so good, I pick up the phone and dial Pete Rutledge's number. A secretary answers the phone and asks if I am attending Pete's lecture to the graduate students in architecture that night. I ask her if visitors can attend, and she says I'm welcome, so I tell her sure, put me on the list, since I know Theodore is working late. I tell the woman that Pete doesn't have to call me back,

I'll see him after the lecture. When I hang up, I instantly regret that I agreed to attend. What if Pete acts distant or doesn't have time to see me or doesn't look good? (How shallow of me!) It will take the rosy glow off my favorite Italian daydream. Okay, if it does, I'll live with it. But I am going down in style. I'm going to look good tonight, and I will start with my feet. I set out for Eighth Street in search of the perfect shoe (it worked for Cinderella).

What am I going to say to Pete when I see him? After all, it's been a long time. We've spoken on the phone quite a bit, Christmas cards and all that, but I haven't *seen* him. Have I changed in four years? I'm sure he hasn't—men barely skip a beat between forty and fifty. He's probably as desirable as ever. He's probably met thousands of women on his travels, thousands of women with whom he hikes the Italian Alps, wades in natural hot springs, and rolls around in fields of bluebells. Do I think I'm the only one? I know I'm not. And maybe it's this knowledge that convinces me to go to this thing tonight; after all, we're Just Friends.

The Casa Italiana Zerilli-Marimo building is only a couple of blocks away from Theodore's apartment, and I'm grateful for the cold night air and the walk. I had put on Mama's pants and jacket but decided the pants made the whole thing too dressy, so I kept the jacket but changed to jeans instead. Then I put on my new black suede New York boots, which took me half the day to find and all of my shoe budget to purchase. I feel I look my best, and it's always a good idea to look your best when you're half of an unplanned reunion.

The lobby is crowded with students and assorted professional types. I follow the crowd into a large lecture hall and take an aisle seat toward the back. When the room is full, a studious-looking professor comes from the back of the room and stands in front of the lectern. Her opening remarks are dry until she mentions Pete Rutledge, and then a wave of excitement seems to peel through her body, forcing her to rise onto her tiptoes and hold the position for a second until she realizes she is punctuating her introduction with a bit too much enthusiasm. She rolls back down onto her heels and explains that Pete is a marble expert and guest professor in their architecture department. The next thing I hear is applause. Pete has emerged from a door halfway up the aisle and is making his way to the podium, carrying a bottle of water.

The women in the audience sit up in their seats. They study Pete the same way I did the first time I saw him. All the things that made my heart stop at that outdoor disco are still there: his height, the chiseled features (he looks even more like Rock Hudson now), the perfect lips and smile, and those eyes, slate blue and bright. He is wearing jeans and a brown tweed jacket, and the look is sexy. Why does he have to look so good?

Pete puts down the water bottle and scans the crowd as though he's looking for someone. I want to dive under the seats in front of me, but I don't, and I'm glad when I see the look of total surprise on his face as our eyes meet.

Pete lectures extensively about the marble mines in Italy—his favorites are located in Bari, near the Adriatic Sea—and describes the mining process in detail. After the talk is over and the enthusiastic applause has subsided, a group of students gathers around the podium. Pete listens to their questions, but he keeps looking up at me, as if to make sure I'm still there. I indicate that I'll wait for him in the lobby. After a minute or two of nervous pacing in the lobby, I am tempted to bolt, to run back to Theodore's; okay, I've seen Pete Rutledge, he's the same, still gives me butterflies and that's all I wanted to know, now I can go back and let this infatuation or whatever it is go. I decide to slip out. He won't miss me a bit; he's got a roomful of fans. Just as I'm turning toward the door, I feel a hand on my shoulder.

"Where are you going?" Pete stands in the doorway, folding his speech into a tube, which he bangs against his thigh.

"I was just going to get some air."

"No, you were leaving." Pete takes my hand and kisses me on the cheek. "You look beautiful."

"Great lecture."

"Glad you could make it."

"I'm interested in indigenous Italian marble."

"Really."

"Yeah. I was particularly enlightened by your description of the new mining techniques."

"You were."

"I was."

"Are you hungry?"

"Very," I blurt. I should have lied. I certainly didn't intend to have dinner with him. I just wanted to say hello and get back to Theodore.

"I want the whole story. What you're doing here, how long

you're staying, especially how long you're staying." He smiles *that* smile, and I think I'm going to pass out (maybe it isn't him, maybe I'm really hungry). I casually put my hand on the frame of an enormous painting by the door and lean against it. The security guy shoots me a look. I pull my hand away.

"Professor Rutledge?" A beautiful girl in her early twenties approaches us. She has gorgeous red curls that spiral out in every direction, a sprinkle of freckles on her nose, and a body that, well, I'll never see the likes of in *my* mirror.

"I'm Sharon Hall. I'm in the architecture school here."

"Congratulations."

"Thank you. I'd like to interview you for our newsletter."

"Sure."

"Where can I reach you?"

"Um, you know what? Call the office and leave me a message, and I'll get back to you."

"Great. Great. Sorry I interrupted." She smiles at me warmly. "And thank you so much." She smiles demurely at him (redheads always have great teeth).

"I didn't know architects looked like that," I say after she's walked away.

"They don't generally," Pete says, laughing.

As Pete and I walk through the Village, I tell him why I'm here and what I've been doing since I landed. Every time I try to get him to talk about what's going on in his life, he somehow eases the conversation back to me. When we reach the public library on the corner of Sixth Avenue and West Tenth Street, Pete finds a small X carved into the sidewalk cement and makes me stand on it.

"Now look up. See the owl?"

"I see a clock." In a bell tower, there is a beautiful clock with four faces, each pointing in a different direction.

"Look again." Pete stands behind me and casually puts his arms around me; as I look up a shiver runs through me.

"I see it!" The two clock faces form the eyes, and the roof the head, of the owl. "Etta would love that."

"Show her next time." Pete rattles the wrought-iron gate on Patchin Place, a series of small brownstones painted in yellow and white separated by a small cobblestone street. "This is where e. e. cummings lived."

"The Patchin Place poems!"

"That's right. Greenwich Village has been home to a lot of great writers. Bret Harte lived up the street; Eugene O'Neill down a ways. This is the biggest advantage of working at NYU. I'm in the middle of literary history. It's romantic, isn't it?"

It's bad enough that I'm thinking romance, worse that he's pointing it out to me, but that's Pete: a perfect man in a romantic setting (I wonder, does he *plan* these settings?).

"Here we go." Pete takes my hand and leads me up a small staircase into a quiet bistro filled with mahogany antiques, odd chairs with needlepoint seats, and benches along the wall. The only light is coming from a refrigerator case that holds some of the most ornate pastries I've ever seen: tortes layered with frosting, éclairs festooned with tiny pink roses on their chocolate sleeves, a strawberry napoleon with stripes of custard and jam nestled between paper-thin crust.

"They have real food too."

"This *is* real food!" I insist.

"Let's go in the back." Pete takes me to the garden room and points to a booth in the farthest corner. We sit down, and though the wood is old and mottled, it's comfortable.

"You like this place?"

"I love it." The waiter places a basket of bread and butter on the table. "And I love fresh bread!" I tear off a piece of bread.

"You're an easy woman to make happy. So, how's Etta? How's Jack?"

"She's fine. He's fine."

"I like him, you know."

"I know. But hey, he's a great guy. Why wouldn't you like him?" I rush to promote and support my husband like the good soldier I am.

"I usually don't like the competition."

I ignore his flirting and bite into the bread, so Pete redirects the conversation (thank God). "I saw your dad last time I was in Italy."

"He told me. It was so nice of you to visit."

"He's an interesting man. There he is living in a mountain village, but there's nothing about him that's small-town. He reads, and he's interested in the bigger universe. He wants the place to grow yet maintain its charm. He'd be a kick-ass urban planner if he lived in the States."

"Sometimes I wish he did."

"Do you ever want to move over there?"

"I couldn't. Jack's construction business is going really well, and I have the Pharmacy, and Etta's in school—"

"I'd like to drop everything and move there tomorrow," Pete says convincingly.

"Why don't you?"

"Complicated." He smiles when he says this, and it makes me laugh.

"How so?"

"I'm getting married."

Now, I'm a bad actress and I know it, so I smile supportively even though his news is the last thing I expected to hear. "Oh," I say instead of "Congratulations."

He doesn't wait for me to thaw, just tells me his love story in technical steps, as if he's describing how to dig a quarry. "You know, I've lived with a couple of women, and it never seemed right. And then I met Gina about a year ago. She's divorced, has a thirteen-year-old son. At first I wasn't interested at all. She's not my type. She's small and blond and analytical. But we hit it off. She's small, and she's caring. And she's into commitment. She wants a family structure for her son, and I can't blame her. It's important."

"When's the big day?" I must have said this too loudly, because a man at the next table looks over at me.

"We don't know."

"Oh."

"Well, what do you think?"

"I'm thinking what took you so long?"

Pete throws his head back and laughs. "Well, there was just one thing holding me back."

God, do I need to hear this? Do I need to hear how hard it will be for him to give up women, as various and delectable as the French pastries in the display case? "What's that?" I ask, knowing the answer.

"You." He reaches across the table and takes my hand.

"Me?" I pull my hand away, not just to defuse the tension but also to support my head before it hits the table like a slab of marble.

"Yeah. But I can't have you. So what can I do?" He picks up the menu and begins to read it.

"Pete?" The tone of my voice makes him put down the menu and look at me. "Did you ever see *The Ghost and Mrs. Muir?*"

"Gene Tierney."

"Yeah. And Rex Harrison."

"What about it?"

"Sort of like you and me. You're like the sea captain."

"Wasn't he dead?"

"He was the ghost who lived in the cottage Gene Tierney rented from his estate. And he didn't want anybody living in the house, so he haunted the tenants. But Gene Tierney fell in love with him, even though he wasn't real. He was unavailable to her just like you're unavailable to me and I am to you."

"But I'm real."

"I know. But I'm already married, and I love my husband. So, truthfully, you might as well be a ghost. You know, we get one lifetime, and we make choices. And we can't have everything we want. Gina sounds wonderful. And you care about her. And you shouldn't think about what you're going to miss out on, but what you *have.*"

"You make a lot of sense." Pete looks away for a moment.

Now, what I can't tell him is that I liked the idea that he was an eternal bachelor, an Unattached International Bon Vivant tied to no woman, no vows, and no country. I liked knowing he was out there traveling the world, collecting rock samples, and occasionally thinking of me. Ciao to my Plan B. As we eat, I make him laugh with stories of home. We talk about poetry and architecture and Italy. We have many things to cover (this was always the case), so we zigzag from subject to subject, feeding the hunger we have for each other's conversation, knowing that we may never visit alone like this again.

As Pete walks me back to Theodore's, we don't say much, which is weird because there's still plenty we haven't covered. When we arrive at the building, we stand under the awning and look at each other. It isn't normal gazing, it's as if we're studying each other, wondering what this means, what we mean to each other. I get very still inside myself, so still I can feel my breathing. I take my hands and place them on Pete's chest. Why I'm doing this, I don't know, but in the quiet, I feel his heart beating, and it reassures me.

"I've got to go." Pete looks down Fifth Avenue as though he's seen something in the distance that is calling him. He starts to say something else and stops.

"What?" I ask.

"If someone had told me that this would be the story of my romantic life, I would've laughed," he says with a smile.

"I'm sorry." For some reason, in this instant, I feel that it's all my fault.

"It's all right. It's timing." Pete puts his hands in his pockets.

"Can I tell you something?"

"Sure."

"When I'm sad, I think of you."

Pete looks at me carefully. "Why?"

"Because." I close my eyes as though the words I need are written on the front page of my mind. "Because you see the girl in me." It's true. Nobody remembers her anymore. She got lost on the road of responsibility and within the natural process of aging (ick). When Pete Rutledge tells me I'm beautiful, I believe him. And boy, do I need to hear it. I need to *know* it. When I'm with him, I'm not taken for granted, I'm not just a pharmacist or a wife or a mother, I'm me, the real me. I'm celebrated. It's something that even the best husband can't deliver; it must come from the unfamiliar, or the new, or memory itself. That's the trade-off we all make in the security of commitment: excitement for comfort.

"Good night, Ave."

"Bye, Pete."

I watch him as he walks down the street. He turns. "Ave?"

"Yeah?"

"Tell Jack I'll send the samples this week, okay?"

"Okay."

Pete turns the corner and is gone. But just like Gene Tierney, I have a funny feeling that this is not the end of this fantasy. This is not the end of Pete Rutledge.

CHAPTER FOUR

"*D*on't ask. Let me get into my pajamas," I tell Theodore, who perches on the couch like a cat waiting to be fed. "I can't believe you stayed up this late. Are you that curious about Pete Rutledge?"

"What can I say? I love a soap opera. I'll get the wine." Theodore jumps up and goes into the kitchen.

"I could've gotten into Big Trouble," I tell Theodore on my way to the bedroom. "But I didn't." As I change, Theodore hollers from the kitchen, "Boy, are you lucky. You had the 'my best friend the gay guy is waiting for me upstairs' excuse."

I take a glass of wine from Theodore and gulp it down.

"Now, give me all the details."

"Where's Max?"

"Never mind him. He's home. Exhausted. Come on. What happened?"

"Well, I went to the lecture, and then we walked around,

and then we went to the Caffe dell'Artista on Greenwich Avenue."

"The cannoli there are as good as foreplay."

"No kidding."

"Go on."

"And he told me that he was going to get married."

"No."

"To a nice woman named Gina with a son."

"He didn't hit on you at all?"

"Yes, he did. Sort of. A little. And I was very happy about it, okay?"

"Don't get mad at me. I'm only asking the questions. Does he love the Gina woman?"

"He didn't say that. He said Gina wanted a commitment, and that her son needed him, you know, it was like a Red Cross deal. He's saving them or something."

"Uh-oh."

"And then he told me that—"

"Let me guess. He loves you but he can't have you."

"Yes! That's it! That's exactly what he said!"

"This is too good."

"It's terrible."

"It's perfect."

"How is it perfect?" I pour myself another glass of wine.

"You know that there's a great guy out there who adores you, and you never have to clean up after him or feed him or wonder if he's out catting around, or any of the bad stuff. You get only the good stuff. Who said fantasy is better than reality?"

"Everybody says that."

"Because it's true. Once you fall in love, and you're *in* love, the magic gets used up. That's not to say that the day-in and day-out routine of love isn't totally reassuring, of course it is. But it's flannel sheets instead of satin."

"Jack and I are definitely flannel. But it's more complicated than that. Pete helped me get over Joe's death. And because that bond was so strong, I had to decide if I was going to stay married to Jack. In my marriage, there's the world before Joe died, and then there's the world after. And sometimes at night, when it's just Jack and me, we talk about how everything changed after Joe, which we could never do until I went away that summer with Etta and met Pete. He helped me see where I was in my life. In a way, he even helped me to see that Jack was the right man for me."

Theodore doesn't say anything. What can he say? I just admitted that Pete Rutledge was, in a very real way, responsible for my ultimate happiness because he made me look honestly at myself and decide where I belonged. I chose Jack MacChesney, and maybe I'll always wonder what might have been. But who doesn't?

I cry all the way through the Columbus Day Parade. When the float made of red paper roses carrying Miss Italy drifts by, I see youth and beauty and possibility and feel at odds with myself. When the cornet band of old Italian men with handlebar mustaches marches by playing "Oh Marie," I think of my mother and her Louis Prima records, and how she never got the man she wanted the most. I wonder if there is some old village curse on the women in my line. I hope Etta avoids it. Somehow I think she will, as she has the

MacChesney feistiness. I don't think an evil-eye curse would get my daughter down.

When I was growing up, my mother and I were the only Eye-talians in Big Stone Gap. I thought we were the only ones in the world, because we were so removed from life beyond the Blue Ridge Mountains. But I was wrong. There were lots of us out there, and today I'm surrounded by them. I feel at home among the strong features, the prominent noses, the thick hair, the posture, the pride, all the characteristics I think of when I think of my father in Schilpario, or my mother. Sometimes her face flashes before me. I see her by the sink, or in the garden, or kneeling before me as she pins up a hem. I remember her smile and how she made me feel safe. I see her in these young women, in the strength of their dark eyes.

I want to run into the middle of the parade and tell everyone, "I am one of you! I belong here!" My dream since childhood, to belong, to be part of a bigger family, a family that looked like me and felt the things I did. And here they are, thousands of them, on the sidewalks cheering and marching down the street. Finally, I fit in the world, and yet I'm still alone. I look around, and I'm the only person crying.

When the plane takes that first dip out of the clouds and into the clear, I see the Blue Ridge Mountains roll out before me in full autumn. The trees have turned bright yellow topaz; there won't be much orange or red tint to the leaves this year because of the Indian summer. I am happy to see these mountains again, to be home, where my husband and daughter wait for me. Southwest Virginia is an uncomplicated place for a complex person, and I miss it whenever I go.

I bought Etta lots of little things, not to make up for the punishment but to let her know that she was in my thoughts the whole time. I have a goal this fall: I want to get on good footing with my daughter. I want to understand her. I want her to understand me and why I parent the way I do. I hope she learned that when she does wrong, there are consequences. Now we need to work on her compassion. I know it's in there, I just have to help her find it.

"Yoo-hoo. Girl! Over here!" Iva Lou waves to me from beyond the checkpoint. I don't hide how thrilled I am that she came to pick me up. "How was it?" she asks as she gives me a big hug.

"Theodore is so happy. He's in his groove."

"I want to hear all about it." She lifts an eyebrow, and I know her next question is about Pete Rutledge. "So?" she says, dragging out the "o" until I answer.

"He's getting married."

"I knew you'd see him!"

"I saw him."

"Are you sad?"

"No."

"How did he look?"

"Better than ever," I tell her.

"Of course he does. That's how they keep us hooked. The rats."

As we wait for my luggage, I notice that Iva Lou is fidgeting nervously. And she seems to be chatting loud and fast as she gives me the Gap update since I've been away—the manic chitchat is not her style.

"Are you okay?"

"Uh-huh."

"No. Something is not right."

"Oh, Ave." Iva Lou exhales deeply and buries her hands in her jeans pockets.

Immediately I think of Iva Lou's husband. "What is it? Lyle?"

"No, no. He's okay. It's me, hon, and it's probably nothing."

"What, then?"

"You know how I've been draggin'. Not myself."

"So you went to the doctor. And you did your tests, right?"

"Yeah." Iva Lou takes a deep breath. "They found something."

"What did they find? And where?" I know in moments like these, it's best to collect the facts and not show any panic. Iva Lou needs reassuring; her eyes are filling with tears.

"On my breast. A lump. It's about the size of a pea. But it was hard, so they did a biopsy."

"Okay. What did it show?" I know all about this stuff, as I went through it with Mama.

"It was malignant."

"God."

"Malignant. Can you imagine?" Iva Lou taps her foot.

"First of all, don't panic."

"That's what my doctor said."

"They can get you better."

"He said that too. I went to that new wing at Holston Valley. They have a comprehensive breast center. They're very up-to-date over there, so if anybody can help me, they can."

"What's the next step?"

"They told me they caught it early, but I still have to move quickly."

"That's good news." By the time they found my mother's breast cancer, it was too late. It's as if Iva Lou reads my mind.

"I been thinkin' about your mama a lot."

"Yeah, but that was a long time ago, Iva Lou. And Mama didn't want to be aggressive in her treatment. She didn't want chemotherapy or any of that. She felt it best to let nature take its course, and that was a huge mistake. There was so much they could've done, and she might still be here if she had listened to the doctors."

"Well, I'm determined not to die."

"Good."

"I mean, I feel fine otherwise. I'm just so ding-dang tarred all the time. It just drains you, and maybe it's the mental part of it, but I ain't myself. I git home around seven, and I'm in bed by eight. It's crazy. I've always been a night owl, and now I'm acting like a shut-in senior citizen. That ain't like me!"

"It sure isn't." I put my arm around my old friend. "I'll be with you every step of the way."

"I know you will. Now, tell me about that Radio City. Did you get me an application to be a Rockette like I asked ya?"

I don't answer her. After all, what is a trip compared to what she's going through? We stand there a long time and finally look up and realize that all the other passengers have left. We're alone, and my luggage is circling around the carousel waiting for me to claim it.

"Let's go home," I tell Iva Lou.

☆

Iva Lou and I ride most of the way home talking gossip and funny stories. Iva Lou isn't one to dwell on her problems, so we make light of things. I give her a big hug and tell her everything is going to be fine as she lets me out in front of my house. She's anxious to get home to Lyle, and I'm happy to be back in Cracker's Neck, surrounded by these old mountains, whose every ridge I know and every path I've followed. It's so peaceful here, I think as I stand on the front steps and look out over the dark field that leads to the lower road into town. New York is magical, but I missed the sound of the wind and the low rustle it makes through the trees before the leaves fall.

"Hello, beautiful," my husband says to me as I drop my bags in the front hall.

"I'm going away more often," I tell Jack as he takes me in his arms and kisses me.

"Nope. Not without me. I wanted to fetch you, but Iva Lou insisted—"

"No problem." Iva Lou asked me to keep her problems confidential, and though I'd like to tell Jack, I'll keep my word.

"Where's Etta?"

"Upstairs. She has a slumber party tonight."

"That's right. It's Tara Kilgore's birthday."

Shoo comes down the stairs. I stoop to pet him, but he sniffs and walks away. "Not everybody around here missed me."

"She did," Jack says and points up the stairs.

"Seriously?"

"We did a lot of talking while you were gone. You may see a little difference."

The door to Etta's room is open. She is packing her overnight bag, taking the neat pile from her bed and stuffing it into the duffel.

"Hey, Etta!" I stand in the doorway. She smiles at me (good sign). I go to her, and she hugs me (even better).

"How was New York City?" she asks, then continues packing.

"It was great. I made a list of all the places I'm going to take you when we go back. And Uncle Theodore sends his love. Now, tell me, what's new?"

"Let's see. While you were gone, I got an A on my geography test. I was the only one in class that knew all of Asia Minor. And we had to take Shoo to the vet. He had a respiratory problem. He stayed out all night when it rained."

"He seems fine now."

"He is. We gave him drops. And Dad made polenta."

"How was it?"

"Hard. But you know how he is about his cooking, so I ate it anyway."

I smile. Maybe there is more compassion in Etta than I realize.

"You know, Ma, Miss Benton ain't so mad anymore." Etta corrects herself. "Isn't so mad."

"She isn't?"

"No, she was sort of laughing about it at school on Friday. We were complaining that we had an extra practice, and she said after the coal incident, she was adding in seven more practices a week. After we got the coal picked up, Dad went and put down new sod. I helped."

"Good. I'm glad she's feeling better."

"You ain't mad at me anymore, are you?" Etta asks without looking at me.

"Only when you use 'ain't.' " I sit down on the bed. "Is Tara having a big party?"

"Six of us. Her mom asked Ethel Bartee to come over and teach us how to do manicures. Mrs. Bartee is not real patient, though. She did our hair for the band photo and went so fast it hurt when she teased it. I'm sure she's gonna get over there and try to show us stuff and then just give up and give us the nail polish to do it ourselves."

Etta zips her bag and sits down next to me. She doesn't say anything, but it isn't awkward. Our conversations are funny to me. Often she answers a question in one word or a quick sentence, but I always feel that she wants to say more. Sometimes she even takes a breath like she's going to and then stops herself.

"I got you a present in New York." I give Etta a preteen makeup kit I got at Saks. There's nothing conspicuous in it: sheer lip gloss, a facial cleanser, and a perfume that smells like vanilla.

"Cool!" Etta digs through the kit. "Thank you!"

"And, most important, this." I give Etta a hardcover copy of *Harriet the Spy.*

"My own book! Now I don't have to check it out all the time."

"Give the other kids a turn to read it, right?"

"Thanks, Mom." Etta gives me another hug, and it's worth everything we've been through. As I hold her, I wish for a second that I had another lifetime just to be her friend instead of her mother.

*

When I get home from dropping off Etta at the slumber party, Jack is waiting for me on the front steps with a picnic basket.

"What's that?"

"I'm taking you out to dinner."

"You are?"

"Yeah. I found this chef. He's ornery, but he makes real good fried chicken, and his biscuits are almost too good to eat, they're so fluffy. And he recommends this Tuscan wine, a robust red, and he swears it puts his wife in the mood."

"Really. And where did you find this chef?"

"He lives around here."

"Hmm." I play along. "In an old stone house in Cracker's Neck that needs a new road, a new water heater, and a sump pump in the spring because the basement fills with rain?"

"You know what? That sounds familiar." He smiles. "So, you want to go out with me?"

"Sure."

We take Jack's truck and go down the mountain, turning onto the valley road that will take us up to Big Cherry Holler. I slide over to the middle of the seat and put my arms around my husband just like the kids do when they borrow their daddy's truck and head for the Strawberry Patch, Big Stone's number one make-out perch, for a date.

"You missed me?" I ask my husband, knowing the answer.

"Yes, I did."

"Why?"

"It's no fun around here without you."

"Come on."

"No, you don't appreciate what a constant source of

amusement you are to Etta and me." My husband pats my leg.

"Thanks." I remove his hand from my leg and put it back on the steering wheel, but I stay snuggled against him.

A full moon the color of sandpaper floats over Big Cherry Lake like the face of an old clock. Jack is loaded down with a duffel bag, a picnic basket, and a flashlight. He shines the beam down the narrow path covered with pine needles. When we get to the water's edge, he pulls a camping lantern from the basket and lights it. The glow makes a pale golden mist on the water's edge.

I laugh as he unpacks his parcels. "You're a regular Sherpa."

"That's what I was going for. As a rule, those Sherpas are pretty sexy, right?" He winks at me.

"I don't know. You're the first one I ever met."

Jack lays an old quilt on the ground. I sit down next to him. "Are you hungry?" he asks.

"Not yet." I climb into my husband's lap and take his face in my hands. I do love him, I'm thinking to myself as I study his hazel eyes and the bridge of his perfect nose. I kiss him over and over and hold him close. "You don't change," I tell my husband.

"Good thing or bad thing?"

"Good thing."

"Do you know what tonight is?"

"The night my husband surprised me with a picnic?"

"You're worse than a guy. You don't remember."

"Remember what?"

"October fourteenth. It's the night I proposed to you the first time."

"Apple Butter Night!"

"Whatever you want to call it, darlin'. I call it the Night You Turned Me Down Flat."

I can't believe he remembers the date. Jack used two jars of his mother's fresh apple butter as an excuse to visit; he blew into my house and started chatting, and pretty soon he was talking marriage out of the blue. It was the worst marriage proposal of all time. He compared me to a fully loaded pickup truck and implied that neither one of us had enough time left to be choosy. I said no, and not too politely, but I am not going to remind him of any of that. I say, "I'm glad I came around, honey."

"Me too. Are you happy now?" he asks.

"Very."

Over breakfast this morning, Theodore told me that I should use my attraction for Pete on my husband. I thought this was strange, although I realize you can love your husband and still be attracted to other men. To use Theodore's metaphor, Pete "stirred me up," but I've come home to let Jack finish "cooking the dish." I kiss Jack again, this time like I really mean it.

"You *did* miss me." Jack laughs.

"Shh." I try not to laugh as I hear our echo across the lake. In the event that some mountaineer is out here hunting grubs, I don't want him to find us. Jack reaches across the quilt and turns off the lantern. Now all the light we have is from the moon glistening off the reservoir. As Jack kisses my neck and rolls over onto me, I look up at the moon, and now I see the hands of the clock speeding around. I close my eyes. For the first time in my life, I feel time passing quickly, and I want to stop it. I feel full and whole and loved and wanted, and there isn't a place inside of me that is lonely or disconnected. Each kiss my husband gives me tells me that he is here to stay and I am the only woman for him. The ground is cold beneath me as I hold on to him. Tonight I choose him all over again, and I know that every time I do, it's the best decision I make.

The prescriptions are so backed up at the Pharmacy, you'd think I was gone a year instead of a week. As I count out Nancy Toney's sinus medication, I get a whiff of Jade East cologne, and there's only one man left in Big Stone Gap who wears it.

"What's up, Spec?"

He stands at the door, sorting change from his pocket. "I need to talk to you. In private."

"There's nobody here but me."

"I heard about Iva Lou."

"How?"

"I was dropping off Arline Sharpe over to the heart center, she's fine by the way, and ran into Beth Hagan, Lyle Makin's sister-in-law, and she told me the bad news."

"Iva Lou doesn't want anybody to know."

"I don't know why she wouldn't. Get them Methodists and Prezbees and Freewill Baptists all competing with their prayer circles, and by God, she'll be cured PDQ."

"For now she wants it kept quiet." I make a mental note to stop by and tell Beth about Iva Lou's wishes.

"It ain't right." Spec fishes for his cigarettes.

"I know, people talk too much." Of course, what did I

expect? Iva Lou should have just gone ahead and run an ad in the paper announcing her illness.

"No. No. I mean about Iva Lou and her . . . Well, she's got the best figger in Wise County, including those gals half her age. Truthfully, she could win Miss Lonesome Pine tomorrow if she wanted to."

I want to shake Spec, or yell at him, but he doesn't mean it like it sounds. "Spec, when it's your health, you really don't care about appearances. It's more about life and death."

"I know. I know. I'm just saying, as a man, I think it's a helluva thing for her, of all people, to git *that*. Iva Lou Wade Makin's assets are like the Natural Bridge, or the Roaring Branch, or Huff Rock. They're a thing of beauty, God-given, and by God, we should be God-grateful. That shape of hers is landmark status."

"There's more to Iva Lou than her great body."

"I know. I'm just saying." Spec breathes out impatiently. "I'm runnin' down to Pennington. You need anything?"

"No, thanks anyway," I tell him.

Fleeta pushes through the doors juggling two Tupperware cake domes. "Jesus, Spec, you live here?" Spec holds the door for her on his way out. "Git yourself a home or something, would ja?" She coughs, then says to me, "Ave, you heard about ole Iva?"

I shoot Fleeta a look. "Where did *you* hear it?"

"Supermarket. I ran out of eggs."

"God forbid anybody around here wants to keep things private."

"God forbid anybody'd tell me anything around here before I hear it thirdhand out in the street. What are you gittin' mad at me fer? Cripes a-mighty on a mountain, I'll stay home if I'm gonna git my head bit off." Fleeta heads back to the Soda Fountain to open up.

Pearl pulls up in front of the Pharmacy. As I watch her get out of her car, I can really see that she's pregnant now.

"How was your trip?" she asks. "How was Theodore?"

"He's having the time of his life. He sends his best to you. How are you feeling?"

"I have morning sickness all day."

"It's rough. Have you tried Sea-Bands?" When I was pregnant with Joe, I wore the elastic pressure bracelets they give you on cruises to keep down the nausea. They worked.

"I got 'em up my arms like gypsy bangles. Cleared the stock of the Norton store." Pearl smiles.

"Got the baby something on my trip," I say.

Pearl opens the package from Saks Fifth Avenue and shrieks with delight when she lifts out a tiny yellow sweater with a taxicab design. "I love it. Thank you!"

"You tell Pearl about Iva Lou?" Fleeta wants to know.

"No, I didn't."

"Iva Lou's got the breast cancer," Fleeta announces.

"No!"

"Yeah, but they think they got it in time."

"I'm surprised you're not passing around copies of the X rays," I tell Fleeta. She grunts at me and heads for the supply room. "Iva Lou wanted it kept confidential," I explain to Pearl.

"Well, this is confidential, Big Stone-style. People know everything about you in this town, including your underwear size."

"For the record, I wear a six," Fleeta calls from the supply room.

"She's going to be all right, isn't she?"

"It's very early, so yeah, we're hoping," I reassure Pearl, but I'm not so sure about anything anymore. I can't believe that two of the most important women in my life have gotten breast cancer. And I don't ever forget my aunt Alice Lambert, who let it go untreated until it went to her bones. Pearl looks worried, so I tell her what I keep telling myself, that treatments and technology have improved vastly, and there is real hope for Iva Lou.

"It's not just Iva Lou." Pearl sighs.

"Is something wrong?"

"Ave, I've been thinking about closing the store down in Lee County. We're not doing well there at all. They have a Rite Aid now, and it's more like a department store. And there isn't enough of a population to justify two pharmacies. I hate to do it, but we're losing money."

"Hasn't the prison brought in more business?" We were all so excited when the government decided to build a federal prison in Big Stone Gap. Our people were hurting from the coal-industry bust, and the new jobs created by the prison seemed like the answer.

"It helped. But we need more industry here."

As I watch Pearl go into the office, it's hard to believe that she's the same mountain girl who used to stock my shelves when she was in high school. Pearl is a rare person. She hasn't forgotten what she came from, or the folks who helped her get where she is today. I was afraid she'd be too kindhearted for business, that people would take advantage of her, but she has natural street smarts—I'm sure she could show the hard-boiled businesspeople in New York City a thing or two.

Part of my plan to cheer up Iva Lou (she acts like she doesn't need it, but of course she does) is to fuss over her, so on Saturday I take her for a girls' night over in historic Abingdon. We have a delicious dinner at the Martha Washington Inn, an old, sprawling colonial landmark that looks like something out of a storybook, with gas lanterns and a grove of pink dogwood trees, perfect for strolling. I bought tickets to the Barter Theatre show for after supper, so we're really making a night of it.

The theater is across the road from the inn, so we decide to walk. It's early November, and the breeze is changing. Folks are using their fireplaces already; we inhale the smell of smoky applewood, my favorite sign that fall is here.

"Look, Ave," Iva Lou says, pulling me behind a tree.

"What's the matter?"

"Look in the carriage." Iva Lou urgently points to the inn's horse and carriage, moving up a stately circular driveway.

The horse clops the carriage past us. Sitting in the backseat with a blanket over their knees are Fleeta and Otto, dressed in their Sunday best. We stay behind the tree so they don't see us.

"Are they on a date?" I ask, mystified.

"They ain't collecting buckeyes. Did you know about this?" Iva Lou asks me.

"I had no idea!"

"How could this happen and none of us would know about it?" Iva Lou wonders.

"Maybe it's a new development."

"They don't look like it's a new development. Otto had that 'I'm pitchin' woo on a Saturday night' face, and Fleeta seemed pretty durn happy to be on the receiving end of his attentions."

"What do we do?"

"We go to the show and act like we didn't see 'em." Iva Lou smiles. "I always thought old Otto had the fish eye for Fleets."

"You're kidding, aren't you? She's always so mean to him. One time she told him he didn't have an ass. I heard her say it."

"What'd he say to her?" Iva Lou wants to know.

"He laughed."

"See there, he likes her. She was flirting with him. I've yet to meet the person on the face of this earth who doesn't need a little sex."

"I haven't noticed that it's helped Fleeta's mood any."

"Well, there are those people, few and far between, who indulge in sexual relations, and instead of calming them down, it serves as an agitator. Fleeta might fall into that category." Iva Lou shrugs.

Iva Lou and I have been coming to the Barter for years. It's been the state theater of Virginia since the Great Depression, but it is most famous for being the oldest regional theater in the United States and the launchpad of many great actors, including Ernest Borgnine. We always enjoy the opening-night speeches by the artistic director, Robert Porterfield, and the prize drawings in which the winner gets a Virginia ham. In its early days, lots of folks couldn't afford tickets, so they bartered goods or services instead (hence the theater's name). There is a long history here, inside the pristine white walls with wedding-cake trim around the ceiling, a grand crystal chandelier, and a balcony that swoops over the orchestra seats and wraps around to the downstage area. The seats are ruby-red velvet, and Iva Lou thinks they look like roses when they're not filled.

"You want something?" Iva Lou asks as we stand in line at the refreshment counter during intermission. "I'm having myself a white wine. Stop looking around. They're not here. Fleeta doesn't like plays, only wrestling shows."

"You're right." I don't think Otto and Fleeta are theater people. "How do you like the play?"

"It's about time they put Lee Smith's words to music. 'Fair and Tender Ladies.' That about describes us, doesn't it?" Iva Lou laughs.

"On a good night."

"Well, Ave, I done made my mind up." Iva Lou gives me a glass of white wine.

"About what?"

"I saw Dr. Phillips over at the hospital."

"What did he say?"

"He laid out all of my options, and he recommended a lumpectomy—that's where they take part of the breast—and then chemotherapy and radiation. He said there was a bit of a spread to the lymph nodes, but not to worry, the radiation would zap it. Now some of them nodes is on the other breast but he said he could git them too."

"So when do they operate?"

"Soon. But I'm not going with that plan exactly."

My heart sinks. I went through this with my mother. She had her own ideas about how to deal with her cancer, and no doctor was going to tell her how to handle it. "Oh, Iva Lou, listen to the doctors, they know best. If he tells you this will work, it will work."

"You're probably right. But I'm a hundred-percent girl."

"What does that mean?"

"I want a one-hundred-percent guarantee that I am cured. I want to come out of this thing knowing that I won't git it again. I don't want to go through all this and then five, seven years down the line find out I have to go through it all over again. And with maybe even less chance of success. I want it done with."

"So what do you want to do?"

"I told him to take them."

"Take them?"

"Both. I want a double mastectomy."

"Iva Lou, why don't you think about this a while longer? This has happened so fast. There's so much research going on, and the drugs are better, and chemotherapy gets results . . ."

She cuts me off. "No, I decided. And I sat down with Lyle, and he's with me on this. My doctor said to get a second opinion. He understands how I feel, but he thinks he can help me with the other line of treatment, and I'm sure he could. But he cannot guarantee that I'm cured. Remission, yes, but not a cure. I want a cure."

"Oh God. I don't know, Iva Lou. In a strange way, I understand. You know, I learned a lot from my mother. I learned that every person handles this sort of thing in her own way. I might even do what you're doing in the same situation.

I don't know. Now, Mama, she was ready to go. She had done her job raising me, and I don't think she saw a bright future for herself. But you're different. You want to live, and live a long time."

"That's right!" Iva Lou looks so relieved. For the first time in weeks, that little crease between her eyes is gone. She is done thinking about it. "Look, this ain't easy. I love my breasts. I have loved them and celebrated them from one end of Wise County to the other for most of my life. I was always so proud of my figure. I had it all. Honey, I worked it, I knew I had something special, and I'm, well, I'm the age I am now, and I've had a nice amount of years to enjoy them. And now they gotta go, because they have ceased to serve their purpose, and now they're just gonna cause me problems. I am grateful that I had 'em. It's been tremendously fun. But now I want something more. I want a guarantee that I'm gonna wake up every morning and live."

I can't argue with Iva Lou. She is going to do this, second, third, fourth opinions notwithstanding. She has made up her mind.

"What's the matter with you?" Iva Lou gives me a poke. I must be frowning.

"I just wish you didn't have to go through this at all."

"Honey, that ain't on the list of options. There's so much I want to do with my life. I'm not gonna let this get me down. I got plans. I think of all the places in this world that I want to see, and how happy I'll be when I get there. I've never looked at my life like it would end. But now I have proof that the clock is ticking. And by God, I'm not leavin' until I've seen and done everything I've always wanted to do." Iva Lou's words tumble out of her. She's resolute and relieved, has made her decision, and is clearly at peace with it.

Iva Lou and I go back to our seats, and as beautiful as the music and words are, I don't hear them. I'm thinking about my friend the "one-hundred-percent" girl.

The doctors weren't kidding when they told Iva Lou they were going to schedule her surgery quickly. They wanted to get her in before Thanksgiving, and they have. I worked today, but it was a blur, knowing that Iva Lou would be operated on tonight. I picked up Etta after school, came home, and took a long, hot bath, and now I'm getting ready to drive over to Kingsport. Iva Lou didn't want a crowd there, just Lyle and me. I'm putting on my makeup in the bathroom. Etta comes in and sits on the edge of the tub.

"Ma, can I go to the skate rink with Tara?"

"Is Dad going?" I ask, applying lipstick.

"He said he would."

"Then you can go."

Etta stays and watches me, as she has done so many times since she was little. I remember when I used to do the very same thing with my mother. I was fascinated by the way she powdered her perfect skin and drew her lips red with precision. She used to run a little water on her hands and then smooth her hair down. I imagine Etta with a daughter someday enacting the same rituals. I put on my perfume and then give Etta a quick dab (our little addition to Mama's routine).

"Is Aunt Iva Lou gonna die?" Etta asks quietly.

"I don't think so."

"But your mama died from cancer, didn't she?"

"Yes, she did."

"Were you scared?"

I sit down on the tub ledge next to Etta. "Terrified."

"How did it feel when she died?"

Most people focus on the grief that follows a death, or the process that comes before it, but no one, until now, has ever asked me about the day she died. "I thought it was the worst day of my life. And it was, until your brother died. But I could sort of understand when my mother passed away; she was sick a long time, and toward the end I begged God to take her. She was so thin, and she was in a lot of pain. They always tell you that they can give you something for the pain, but they really can't. I don't think it's just physical pain either, it's the sadness at leaving the world and the people you love."

"Were you with her when she died?"

"No." I breathe deeply.

"Why?"

"I went to work. Mama insisted. She felt okay, and I had been home for a few days tending to her. She was never bedridden. She could always walk around and do a few things, and then she would just get weak and tired and have to sit in her chair. I didn't want to argue with her, so I went to work. I remember Nellie Goodloe brought me a sack of Red Delicious apples that day, and I knew Mama would love a baked apple, so I was looking forward to getting home and making her one." We sit quietly for a few moments. I would like to end the story here, but Etta wants to know more.

"Then what happened?"

"I got home and I went into the house, and I called to her,

and she didn't answer. It was so quiet, it scared me. I dropped the apples, and they scattered across the floor. It seemed to happen in slow motion, with no sound. I knew something was terribly wrong, but I couldn't seem to move my feet to go to her. Then I sort of came to and ran into her bedroom, and she was in her chair. She was gone."

"Do you think when I die that your mama will recognize me?" Etta wonders aloud.

"Oh, yeah."

"And Joe, will he know us?"

"I hope so."

"He was so little, maybe he wouldn't," Etta says quietly.

I don't know how to answer Etta. No matter how long you've been a mother, sometimes your children ask you things for which there are no answers. The pat descriptions of an eternal life, of pearly gates and angels on clouds and God in a white beard, seem as removed from reality as Santa Claus at the North Pole. Etta is too big for the pretty stories, because she's asking the deeper questions.

"I hope he'll know us." I sit down next to her.

"You're not sure, are you, Ma?"

"No, I'm not." Maybe I shouldn't be honest; I should reassure her. "I know it helps me a lot to think that I will see my mother and Joe again."

"Then you will." Etta smiles and gets up. "Might as well believe in something, Ma. It can't hurt."

Holston Valley Hospital sits above Kingsport, Tennessee, like a castle. As I pull into the parking lot, the sun disappears behind the brown mountain in streaks of orange and gold like a tiger's-eye agate. I'm not afraid as I walk into the hospital, I'm confident for Iva Lou. I don't know where this optimism is coming from, but it feels real.

"Now, Lyle Emmett Makin, don't talk Ave's ear off." Iva Lou is lying on a gurney in the preop hallway with an unattractive paper shower cap on her head. The nurse tucks a blanket around her. Even without makeup, Iva Lou looks luminous. She has the unlined face of a woman at peace with her decision. Judging from the look in her husband's eyes, he is thinking the same thing. Lyle kisses his wife's forehead as she is wheeled into the elevator for her surgery. I blow her a kiss, and she smiles as the doors close. "I'm gonna git a face-lift while I'm in here, y'all!" she shouts from behind the doors. I hear the nurse laugh as the elevator pulls up and away.

"How about coffee, Lyle?"

"Thank you, ma'am."

Lyle Makin has been Iva Lou's husband for thirteen years, and I can honestly say I know him as well today as the first day I met him. He never says a lot (though he's mannerly), and I haven't heard much about his past (he's from Roseville, down in Lee County) or his work (he repairs heavy mining equipment), but I never needed to—he's Iva Lou's husband, and I love him because she does.

Lyle is over six feet tall. He, like Iva Lou, has kept his shape trim over their years together. His salt-and-pepper hair has turned to white, and he's grown a beard now, so he looks like one of the old guitar pickers at the Carter Fold. He has deep-set dark blue eyes (sign of a private person; boy, is that accurate) and a tawny complexion. I wouldn't be surprised if he was part Melungeon. Melungeons, our local mountain folk, once scorned, have become popular lately, and their exotic looks have been celebrated in books and plays. Lyle has their bronze coloring, which indicates a mix of Cherokee, Turkish, French, African, and English.

"How you holding up, Lyle?"

"I'm all right. How about you?"

"I'm okay."

We walk the long hallway in silence, and when we get in the line in the cafeteria, I'm surprised to see Lyle load up a tray. He has baked cod, a side of creamed spinach, two dinner rolls, black coffee, a small container of orange juice, and a slice of coconut cream pie. "Iva told me to eat," he says, and shrugs.

"She told me you've been very supportive."

Lyle doesn't say anything for a minute, then takes a deep breath. "She's my girl."

"I know."

"I was in Vietnam. Did you know that?"

"I didn't."

"Yep. I volunteered late. I'd served in the Korean conflict, and then when Vietnam came around, I felt I needed to go. So I volunteered."

"There weren't many people who felt that way."

"The army was the best thing that ever happened to me. I dropped out of high school in 1951, and they took me, so I felt like I owed 'em something." Lyle shakes his container of orange juice before he opens it. "I was in active duty over there, and it was a sight. I lost a few of my buddies, saw several more of 'em injured bad, and one night, we was settin' around and I told 'em that if I ever got wounded and was paralyzed that I wanted one of 'em to promise he'd finish me off right there. I told 'em I didn't want to live like 'at. So one of my buddies, a guy named Bill Kelly out of Lansing, Michigan, promised me that he'd carry out my wishes should the time come. 'Bout a month later, I got hit. I told Bill, 'Scratch what I told you, buddy. I want to live.' And he looked at my leg and said, 'It's a good thing. They just got your thighbone. But I'm gonna shoot you anyway, 'cause you said I could have your watch.' We had us a good laugh, and he carried me out of there and got me to the doctor, and sure enough, it wasn't the end of my road, and they saved my leg. I tole Iva Lou this story last night, hoping it would make her feel better; like I understood, as much as a man can, what she was goin' through. And she looked at me the way she does, and she said, 'For Godsakes, Lyle, I can't walk on my boobs.' " Lyle laughs. "She missed the point." He stirs his coffee and looks at me. "You know, she's all I got." He pushes the tray away without having touched his food. "My kin is gone."

"She's gonna be fine, Lyle."

"You think so?"

"I know it. She could whup anything or anybody that comes in her path."

"That's for true."

I'm sure this is the longest conversation I will ever have with Lyle Makin, but it certainly gave me insight into why Iva Lou gave up years of Happy Swinglehood for him. Lyle loves her in that everlasting way, and Iva Lou sensed that somewhere down the line this would be exactly what she needed.

The ride home from the hospital flies by (it helps that I'm going eighty miles an hour and that there are no trucks on the road between Gate City and Big Stone Gap). The doctors met with us after Iva Lou's surgery and told us they thought they "got it all." Iva Lou was still under anesthesia when I left; the doctors hoped she would sleep until morning. The staff was nice enough to provide Lyle with a cot so he could sleep in the room with his wife.

By the time I get home, Jack and Etta have had dinner, and he's now in our room watching TV. I give him a report on Iva Lou, then go upstairs and check on Etta, whose bed is covered with open schoolbooks, notebooks, and pencils.

"Looks like you got a lot of work ahead of you."

"I do. How's Aunt Iva Lou?"

"She's okay. She's gonna be fine."

"When can I go see her?"

"Saturday," I tell her.

"Good. Dad left you some pizza in the kitchen."

Etta goes back to her homework. Instead of heading into the kitchen, I go out the front door and sit on the steps. I'm not hungry, I need air, lots of air. I roll my head in circles slowly, as Theodore taught me to do years ago, in order to relieve an oncoming headache. It works. I can hear my neck bones crack at first, and then, after a few rotations, nothing. I walk around the house to the backyard. I think about going into the woods but decide I'm too tired, so I lie down on the ground and cross my arms under my head. I feel spent. I've been worried about Iva Lou and burying it, afraid to show my feelings to her or my family, and now it's all catching up with me. I feel a cold teardrop at the corner of my eye.

The sky is a strange color tonight, gunmetal gray, and the texture of the clouds makes it look like a skein of old wool. It reminds me of storms in adventure movies where all is calm but the sky, which churns overhead in anticipation. Maybe that's why it's warm; any minute the sky, like a ceiling soaked through by a broken pipe, will come crashing down and with it the cold rains of winter.

"Here, Mama." Etta joins me and gives me my jacket. "Don't get up." She lies down on the ground next to me and looks up. "Those clouds are creepy."

"Aren't they?"

"Have you ever seen them that color before?" she asks.

"I don't think so."

"Isn't it weird that it's not cold? It's almost Thanksgiving, and it hasn't been cold yet."

"It's very weird," I agree.

We lie there for a while until Etta asks, "If you got cancer, what would you do?"

"I guess I'd find the best doctors. Then I'd listen to what they had to say. After that, I'd come home and talk to you and Daddy. Why do you ask?"

Etta does not answer. The sound of the old coil on the screen door interrupts us. Jack stands on the porch. "What are my girls doing out here?"

"Talkin'." Etta shrugs.

"No moon tonight," Jack says, and sits down next to me.

"Oh, it's there," Etta promises.

"Where?" her father wants to know.

"Northeast." Etta points.

"How do you know?" I ask her.

"Well, at the end of the week, we'll have a rising crescent moon, which is a bright moon because it's lit by the sun. Plus, it gets a dose of earthshine, which is sunlight reflected off of the earth and onto the moon."

"Where did you learn that?" I sit up and look at my daughter with newfound respect.

"In books. Plus, Mr. Zander lets me stay after school and study his maps. 'Course, he told me that I could study the constellations for the rest of my life and not even make a dent in understanding what's out there."

"You used to stand in your crib to look out the window at night. I could never figure out what you were looking at. Now I know." I nudge Etta, and she laughs.

"I like the constellations because they're fixed. Like tonight. You can't see any stars because of the clouds. And when the moon is full and there's a lot of light, it overpowers the sparkle of the stars, so you think they're gone. But they're there. In science, the only concept you can prove is that things always change. But the truth is, they also stay the same."

"Now, that's a philosophy," Jack says as he looks up at the sky.

"It means that, like the stars, we have a fixed place. A destiny. There are facts and then there is fate, which is out of our control."

The clouds shift overhead, and in the exact spot Etta pointed to, the moon emerges, a white half-smile covered by a filmy veil of clouds.

"All right, my little scientist," Jack begins. "What do you call that moon?"

Etta looks up. "A quarter-moon?"

"Nope, although that's probably the right measurement. My grandpap called it a milk glass moon, because the clouds give it a smoky haze like milk in a glass after you've drunk it. And he said that meant it would rain the next day."

"That's nice, Dad, but I don't think it's very scientific."

Jack and I laugh; this is the best moment to be a parent, when you see that your child is going to surpass you, that her curiosity will take her places and teach her things you never even thought about. As for Etta's idea that the stories of our lives have already been written, well, this is one I'll have to think about. It makes me feel better to think the things in this world that have no explanation or cause pain (like Iva Lou's cancer) are part of a bigger picture; it makes them seem manageable and less overwhelming. But it's hard for me to accept that notion and cling tightly to everything I love. When the clouds come, I'm not so sure the stars are behind them.

*

Fleeta, Pearl, and I decide to drive over to Kingsport to see Iva Lou after visiting hours at the hospital. Between the staff of the county library, Iva Lou's old Bookmobile customers, and a round of old boyfriends, she has not lacked for company. I checked in three times today by phone, and each time she told me of another floral tribute delivered to her room. "It's a shame I ain't dyin'," she told me, " 'cause these flowers would fill the sacristy at Freewill Baptist." The most stunning flowers come from Theodore Tipton, who ordered a spray of yellow roses edged in gold glitter. Iva Lou calls them her "Viva Las Vegas" bouquet.

On the drive there, Pearl sits in the back so she can put her feet up (a must for pregnant women) while Fleeta fidgets in the front seat. She keeps pressing the nicotine patch on her arm like it's a call button. "Fleeta, it's not like a morphine drip. Pressing it won't send more nicotine into your bloodstream," I inform her.

"To hell it don't. I press on this thang every few minutes, and it gives me a jolt."

"I think that's in your imagination."

"I guess the fact that I got the shakes twenty-four-seven is imaginary too."

"You're doing great," I tell her. And she is, she's down to one cigarette a day.

"Fleeta, have you been keeping a secret from us?" Pearl wants to know.

"What sort of a secret?" Fleeta hacks.

"A boyfriend secret," Pearl says softly.

"Hell noooo." Fleeta looks out the window.

"I heard you're dating Otto Olinger." I can't believe Pearl came out with it, just like that!

"Where'd you hear that?" Fleeta coughs.

"Folks have seen you around. Arby's in Kingsport. The Galley up in Norton. You know, around." Pearl shrugs nonchalantly.

"I saw you in a horse and buggy over in Abingdon," I chime in.

"When?"

"Awhile back."

"Why didn't you say hello?"

"You and Otto looked like you wanted your privacy."

"You were right about that. So let's drop it." Fleeta smoothes the creases on her new jeans.

We ride in silence for a few moments. Finally, Pearl says, "I think it's nice."

Fleeta turns to face Pearl. "Now, don't make a big deal out of it. It's a vurry vurry casual thing. I resisted as long as I could. Menfolk are nothin' but a brand of rash—they have this way of gittin' under yer skin and makin' it itch. Now, I know for a fact that April Zirkle had the hots fer Otto fer quite a spell. Her husband's been gone about three year', 'course he ain't dead, just missin', but still. And I told him that ole April would love to go with him and she's still got all her breath, she don't git winded like me goin' from here to there, she's a nonsmoker, I think. So I tole him call her up and take *her* out."

"But he likes *you!*" I interject.

"I know that. I'm not an idiot. Otto Olinger's been chasin' my tarred ass since we lowered Portly into the ground over at Glencoe Cemetery." Fleeta settles back into her seat and folds her arms across her chest like a little girl.

"That long? No way!" Pearl leans forward in her seat.

"Yes ma'am. And I done tried everything to deter him. But he likes what he sees." Fleeta inhales deeply through her nose and sticks out her chest. "But I don't need it."

"You're not attracted to him?"

"Now, Ave. Honestly."

"It's okay if you are."

"If I'm gonna make a move, I don't want me an old man. I know, you look at me and you say, Fleets, you're old yourself. I know I am. But I never liked me old men, not when I was young and not now. I don't like lookin' at stick legs and a saggy bottom in my bedroom. I'm sorry. I see a Pierce Brosnan or somebody like 'at in my mind's eye when I let my mind's eye roll in that direction. I certainly don't see some ole hilljack with a beer gut, a flat ass, and a set of fake choppers from Doc Polly."

"You've always been particular, Fleeta," I tell her.

"I'm glad you noticed." Fleeta sniffs.

"It's very sweet," Pearl says softly.

"You're so gullible. You'd believe anything a man told you, wouldn't you?"

"If I respected him, I would."

"You can respect a man and he'll still tell you a pack o' lies. Trust me on that one."

I can't hold it any longer, and I begin to laugh. Soon Pearl joins me, and we laugh so hard, we cry. Finally, Fleeta joins us, and as we pull into the lot at Holston Valley Hospital, you'd think we were going to the circus.

☆

Hospitals are lonely places at night. I'm glad the girls are with me as we make our way down the corridor.

"She's in 602," Fleeta announces, looking at a scrap of paper from her pocket.

Iva Lou is in a corner room, and as we approach, we hear her crying. We don't bother to knock, we just barge right in. Iva Lou lies in the bed, a box of Kleenex in her lap.

"Hey, girls," she says, and blows her nose.

"Are you okay?" I ask her gently. Iva Lou nods that she's all right.

"Brought you some divinity." Fleeta gives Iva Lou the tin, plopping down on the foot of the bed.

Pearl gives Iva Lou a kiss on the cheek and places her gift on the nightstand. "I know you like hand cream." I go to embrace Iva Lou, but I can't; she's wrapped in bandages and obviously in pain.

Fleeta sneezes. "Must be the lilies." She points to the wall of flowers. "So, how are ye, girl?"

"I feel odd," Iva Lou says simply. "Is this medieval or what? My coat of armor," she says, pointing to the bandages that bind her from her neck to her waist. "Now, girls, don't look at me like that. I'm not sorry 'bout my decision. Just sometimes it all hits me at once and I git sad."

"Where's Lyle?"

"My aunt Shirley Jackowski from over in Johnson City came to see me, and I made Lyle take her out for something to eat. I'll really owe him one for that—she's a handful."

"The doctor said the surgery went well," Pearl says, offering support.

"It did. I'm gonna be all right. I do a little chemo, you

know, and then I'll be good as new," Iva Lou promises. "Otto and Worley came over earlier with Spec."

"Did they bring you something nice?" I ask her.

"Two dozen Krispy Kreme doughnuts. They ate about three quarters of them, and I gave the rest to the nurses." Iva Lou winks at Fleeta. "You got something to tell me?"

"Jesus Christmas. You too?" Fleeta gives the patch on her arm a slight pressing.

"Otto Olinger is quite smitten with you, young lady," Iva Lou tells her.

"Well, that's his problem." Fleeta picks a piece of lint off the blanket.

"Fleeta's a little annoyed at us because we talked about her love affair on the way over," I say.

"It ain't a love affair!"

"What do you call ridin' in a horse carriage under an autumn moon in Abingdon?" Iva Lou asks.

"A goddamn hayride to the pumpkin patch!" Fleeta says defensively. "Look. Love ain't on my radar screen. A surf and turf at Scoby's is. I like to go out once in a while, and it's nice to have company. That's the extent of it. God a-mighty, it's dry in here." Fleeta stands and reaches over to crack the window open.

"Okay, okay, we've tortured Fleeta enough. Who wants a Coke? I'll run down to the cafeteria." I take their drink orders.

The elevator is on the far side of the floor, so I loop around the hallway. As I'm following the arrows, I bump into a woman.

"Excuse me," I tell her.

"That's all right," she says.

I look into her eyes and am about to say something else when I realize that I know this woman: eerily tanned in November—it can be only one person. "Hi," I say as my mind connects a series of facts quickly.

"Hi," she says. "You're . . ."

"Ave Maria MacChesney," I tell her. How happy am I that I put on lipstick, changed into a new pair of jeans and a sweater, and lost the ten pounds that were hanging on my thighs like fat wallets. "And you're . . ."

"Karen. Yeah. I didn't know if you'd remember me," she says as she pushes a lock of hair behind her ear.

Remember you? I think to myself. You almost stole my husband, left my kid fatherless, and made a fool out of me from the pit of the Cumberland Gap to the tip-top of Cracker's Neck Holler. Remember? I'll never forget you. I wish my husband were here to see you in this green fluorescent light, so he could see what happens to "cute" as it ages. Four years have made quite a difference in my husband's paramour.

"Karen, honey?" A man emerges from a patient's room. He's around sixty. He has the biggest head I've ever seen (including Spec Broadwater's), gray hair combed a little too neatly, a pug nose (odd on a man this size and a sign of lack of wisdom in Chinese face reading, though I need to look that up, as I'm not sure what the combo of big head and small nose means), and low ears (this man would have trouble working a simple crossword puzzle).

"This is my boyfriend, Randy Collier."

"Hi!" I say so loudly that a passing nurse turns around to look at me. "Nice to meet you. I'm Ave Maria."

"Hello." Randy smiles.

"His daddy just had surgery. They took out about six feet of his intestines. He's gonna be all right, though," Karen offers, filling up the silence. "How's your family?" She and I both know what she means; she doesn't mean my family, she means my husband.

"Oh, we're great. Just great. I'm here visiting a friend. Well, I hate to keep you."

Pearl comes around the corner. "Here you are. I came to help out."

"I just ran into Karen Bell and her boyfriend, Randy," I tell her.

Pearl's mouth falls open, and then she forces a smile. "Hello."

"Nice meetin' you," Randy says.

"I hope your dad feels better soon," I tell him.

"This hospital is something," Randy says to his girlfriend, "we're always running into folks you know." He puts his arm around her and looks at us. "Yep, she's popular, my girl."

"Oh, yes. Very," Pearl pipes up at last.

We get in the elevator and Pearl leans against the railing. "What are the chances of you running into *her*?"

"Just my luck."

"She changed!" Pearl laughs.

We fill up a tray with cups of Coke quickly. I can't wait to get back to Iva Lou's room and tell her the news. She got me through the most difficult time in my marriage by giving me solid advice about how to handle Karen Bell. I don't know what I would have done without her. Iva Lou is one of the few people who deal honestly with everyone; she never holds a grudge, and if she gets angry, there's a reason. She taught me how to handle my feelings, to stay cool and think things through. Iva Lou has as clean an emotional slate as anyone I have ever met.

"Guess who we ran into?" I announce over the tray of Cokes.

"Who?" Fleeta asks.

"Karen Bell."

"No! What is that old toy doing here? How'd she look?"

"Bad," Pearl answers.

"How bad?" Iva Lou leans in for details.

"That tanning bed has given her the skin of a crocodile purse," Pearl tells them.

"How 'bout the hair?"

"The worst. I think she uses Frost and Tip from the drugstore," I tell her.

"Perox-fried." Iva Lou shakes her head.

"Like hay." Pearl looks at me and smiles.

"Good thing you dressed up tonight." Fleeta eyes me from head to toe.

"That's exactly what I thought when I was standing there face-to-face with her."

"She'll go home and beat herself up all night over how good you look," Iva Lou promises.

"You think?"

"I know. You're so lucky. Eye-talians don't age, it's like the Greeks or the Africans. Y'all just defy time. But Karen Bell? She has a soufflé face. The kind that caves in at forty and never snaps back." Iva Lou sips her Coke.

"We met her boyfriend too," Pearl adds.

"What did he look like?"

"Well, he had a hangdog face, big teeth, and a small nose."

"The kind where you can see every nose hair in his head?"

"His name is Randy Collier," I tell her.

"That old buck? Please. I dated him. He's from Pound. Cheapest man I ever went out with. Took me to Cab's over in Norton for doughnuts. Doughnuts! And it was nighttime! We sat right there in the car and ate 'em out of a sack. Then he wanted to have sex. I told him, 'I don't know what you've heard, but it takes more than a shower and shave and a sack of Cab's fresh-fried doughnuts to get me in the bed.' He took me home immediately, and I never saw him again."

Iva Lou offers us divinity from the tin and takes a piece herself. For a moment, her mind is off her troubles; she is back in the world again.

"He's no Lyle Makin, that's for sure," I tell her.

"Don't I know it? Ladies, I thank God for the man. After the surgery, Lyle climbed up here in the bed with me and wrapped himself around me real gentle-like. He was so happy I made it. I think he thought I'd die in there. I told him that things had come a long way since the days when the doc would come over to your house and do surgery on your kitchen table. You know, his people are from Lee County, and they're self-sufficient. I think his aunt took out her own appendix back in the forties."

"That's where his strength comes from," Pearl says.

"I guess." Iva Lou shrugs. "We made love right before he brought me over to the hospital. Yeah, we decided to have a formal good-bye to my breasts, and when we were done, we just laughed, because we both realized how little a part they played in our happiness, and yet like any part of a person, they're important because they're part of the whole. You don't realize *that* till you have to. And, of course, I had to. Lyle got real quiet after a while, and he said, 'Ivy, I want to get old with you.' Now, I ask you, how're you gonna argue with that?"

"I don't think you can," I tell her.

"No ma'am. You can't."

"So, why were you crying when we got here?" Fleeta lies across the bottom of Iva Lou's bed, munching on divinity.

Iva Lou takes a moment to think, looking off to the bare wall as if the answer is there, painted in bold letters.

"Because I ain't never gonna be the same. That's a tough pill to swallow when you like yourself."

"We're so sorry, Iva Lou," I say. Fleeta and Pearl nod in agreement. And it's true. I am sorry that this had to happen to one of the best people I know.

"Well, I'm sorry you had to run into that floozy," Iva Lou says.

"No, no, it was fine. In fact, I'm kind of glad it happened."

Fleeta sits up. "You gonna tell Jack Mac you seen her?"

"Not a word!"

"That's my girl!" Iva Lou pats my hand. "You're finally getting with the Wade-Makin regimen. Men want women to be adorable and no trouble. Sweet as pie, that's what they're lookin' for. And forgiving. They don't need to be reminded of past mistakes.

Fleeta looks at me. "Quickest way to lose a man is to remind him of a weakness. 'Cause when they feel bad about themselves, they go right back to the woman that made 'em feel good."

"You make men sound like idiots." Pearl takes a sip of her Coke.

We sit in silence for a moment, until Fleeta, Pearl, and I crack up. Then Iva Lou laughs with us, and it's the sweetest sound I've ever heard.

Fleeta has planned a welcome-home party for Iva Lou at the Mutual's. Spec insisted we delay the festivities until he returned from Florida, so here we are, at the height of Christmas shopping season, throwing a big bash at the Soda Fountain for our returning soldier.

Nellie Goodloe took charge of the program. She is going to read a poem; Cindy Ashley is going to present Iva Lou with a gold heart pendant (she raised the money by passing the hat at the homecoming game); Nicky and Becky Botts are going to sing one of Iva Lou's favorite songs, "Sleeping Single in a Double Bed"; and evidently, my husband has agreed to spike the punch (there was a note at home: *Bring the Rum*).

"Don't touch that icing, Spec Broadwater!" Fleeta hollers from the kitchen. I don't know how she can see Spec hovering over the sheet cakes from back there, but she can.

"You should have let me lick the spoon," Spec yells back playfully.

Fleeta comes to the doorway. "Don't you get enough sugar down in Pennington?"

The crowd has a good laugh on that one, and thank the Lord, Spec's wife, Leola, is not here yet. She doesn't need Spec's friendship with Twyla Johnson rubbed in her face, and we certainly don't need a marital knock-down drag-out at Iva Lou's party.

"I'd say you know more about gittin' sugar than I do, Fleeta Mullins," Spec says loudly. Everyone goes quiet and looks at Fleeta.

"Now, Spec." Fleeta points a spatula at Spec. Will she admit to the crowd that she and Otto are an item? The buzz of the overhead fluorescent lights is the only sound in the place. Spec takes a drag off his cigarette and looks at Fleeta. I haven't seen this kind of Mexican stare-down since the Trail Theatre showed *A Fistful of Dollars* at the Clint Eastwood Film Festival.

"You got somethin' to say to me?" Fleeta does not flinch, and the spatula stays pointed at Spec.

"No ma'am." Spec backs down. Fleeta returns to the kitchen. The chatter resumes.

"How was your vacation?" I ask Spec. "You're so tan!"

"Well, we was never out of the sun. And we was on the water a lot. Went fishin' with Leola's cousin. We had us a good time. I took a spill down there, though."

"What happened?"

"Well, I passed out. You know, Florida sun, a six-pack, and wrangling a swordfish for three hours will deplete anybody. They took me to the emergency room, so I got to see what it was like to ride in the gurney in the back instead of driving the vehicle. I can't say I enjoyed the experience."

"What was wrong?" I should be able to accept that my friends are getting older (so am I) and sometimes get sick, but it's still hard when I consider what they once were and that we'll never see our youth again.

"I had me old-fashioned heatstroke. I was dehydrated too. So I drunk me some Gatorade for the rest of the trip. Didn't have another problem." Spec shrugs. "Gonna have one helluva crowd tonight. SRO, looks like."

Fleeta returns from the kitchen with another sheet cake and sets it down on the counter.

"How many cakes did you make?" I ask her. The parking lot is filling up, and the Italian in me is always afraid there won't be enough food to go around.

"Six. Iva Lou's favorite. Chocolate Coca-Cola Cake."

"I want that recipe," Nellie Goodloe says cheerfully.

"Then go in the kitchen and git it. It's hanging on the bulletin board. Make and eat it at your own risk. This cake is rich. One of them Delph girls got addicted to it when she was pregnant and ballooned up eighty pounds beyond recognition."

CHOCOLATE COCA-COLA CAKE

CAKE
2 cups plain flour
2 cups sugar
1 cup Coca-Cola
2 sticks butter
3 tablespoons cocoa
1½ cups miniature marshmallows
½ cup buttermilk
2 eggs, well beaten
1 teaspoon baking soda
1 teaspoon vanilla
A pinch of salt

ICING
3 tablespoons cocoa
1 stick butter
6 tablespoons Coca-Cola
1 pound powdered sugar
1 teaspoon vanilla

1. For cake: Combine flour, sugar, and salt in a saucepan, combine & heat butter, cocoa, Coca-Cola and marshmallows until it begins to boil (add marshmallows last) . . . remove from heat & stir to dissolve marshmallows. Pour over sugar & flour and blend well . . . add remaining cake ingredients and blend well. Pour into greased 9 x 13 pan and bake at 350° for 30 to 40 minutes.

2. For icing: Combine butter, cocoa & Coca-Cola in saucepan and bring to a boil . . . mix with powdered sugar till it makes a thin paste, then drizzle over the cake while it's hot from the oven.

The sound of wild cheers, wolf whistles, and applause can only mean that Iva Lou has arrived. There must be over a hundred people, including the staff of the Wise County main library, where Iva Lou restocks the Bookmobile. Lyle has his arm around Iva Lou, who looks slim and radiant in an electric-blue leather jacket and matching pants. Her earrings are two marcasite pyramids with enamel bluebirds swinging from the bottom.

"Thank ye all, thank ye for showing up to this shindig," Iva Lou announces from my microphone behind the counter. "I am happy to be here. So happy I don't have words. But I do have a story to tell ye." The crowd cheers. "Y'all know I am not a religious person. I was raised in several Protestant faiths, none of which I can remember, because my mama never decided where to park her soul and my daddy never much cared where his soul went on Sundays or any other day of the week. Now, I'm a believer in God and Jesus and all that, but I never liked going to church or any of the socials, because we couldn't dance or drink liquor or do any of the wonderful things that result as a combination of those two activities."

"You must've been a Baptist," someone hollers.

"Yep. For about a week." Iva Lou winks. "Anyhoo, when I was in the hospital, a kindly preacher from the Higher Ground Baptist Church came to see me, and I confessed all my sins to him. He promised me that God had forgiven me, and I felt a sense of peace. I slept through the night and felt like a new woman. Well, the next day around the same time, another preacher came to see me, this one from the AME church, and he asked to hear my sins, so I complied and he absolved me. I had another good night's rest and actually started to think, Well, maybe there is something to this confession stuff. It does cleanse the soul! Anyway, the next day, I got another visitor, this time a lovely minister from the Presbyterian church, and he took a listen to my sins too, and then, once more, graciously washed them away. But on that fourth day, when the friendly minister from the Seventh-Day Adventists came to see me and I confessed my sins, I began to wonder: Does every patient get this kind of spiritual attention when they come to this hospital? So I asked the Reverend Du Jour, who came a-callin' the following day. I don't remember what his affiliation was, but it did have Jesus in the title. He too inquired about my past. So I said, 'Rev, I've had every man of the cloth in East Tennessee come visit me. What gives?' And he said, 'Mrs. Makin, no patient in the history of Holston Valley Hospital has ever confessed a litany of sins as colorful as yours. In fact, you make Mary Magdalene look like a wallflower. I speak on behalf of all the preachers, we are truly grateful for the spice you put in our soul saving.' "

The crowd's laughter erupts into applause, wolf whistles, and general whooping. Pearl, Fleeta, and I put on our aprons and take our place behind the buffet table as the guests form a line. Iva Lou works the crowd, hugging and kissing her friends. If I ever doubted that she made the right decision regarding her surgery, I am positive now that she did. Iva Lou loves living, and whatever choice gave her peace of mind was the right one.

*I*t has rained for months, so when the sun finally came out, it actually made a headline in the town paper: WINTER GONE, SPRING SPRUNG. Fleeta's so tired of hearing it that she wants to put a jar on the counter at the Mutual's requiring anyone who says "Thank God winter's over" to put a quarter in. Yet there is still cause for celebration. Pearl is a new mother!

India Leah Bakagese was born April 3, 1993, at Saint Agnes Hospital, after a long labor. Our Pearl did a magnificent job, and her husband, Taye, was so proud of her he almost insisted their daughter be named Pearl. "One Pearl in the house is enough," she told him and named their daughter after his homeland. Pearl is bringing India to the Pharmacy for the first time today. I've attached balloons to the front door to welcome her.

Fleeta enters, battling balloons as she comes through the doorway. "Turrible idea. This is a place of business, not a day-care center. I guess we're gonna put an entire nursery in the office," she grouses.

"Just a crib for now," I tell her.

"Whatever happened to the days when women stayed home with their babies?"

"What's the difference if they stay home or bring them with?" I ask her.

"It's a big difference to me. I went back to work to git away from my youngins. But I don't own the joint, so I guess I have to live with it."

"She's so cute, Fleeta. You're gonna love her."

"I ain't sayin' the baby ain't cute, I'm sayin' I don't want her around." Fleeta says this in a tone that tells me she doesn't really mean it. "Is Etta coming in for her free sundae? Ain't it her birthday?"

"This Saturday. She's having a party and everything. Can you believe Etta is thirteen?"

"Jesus, I'm getting old." With her palms, Fleeta lifts the jowls on her face up a good half inch.

"But your hair looks good."

Fleeta shoots me a look that makes us both laugh.

"Introducing India!" Pearl announces, carrying her daughter through the balloons. Taye follows with a jumbo diaper bag. He is beaming with the look of a man who has everything he wants in the world. He greets us, placing the bag on the counter. "Call me if she does anything special," Taye says with a wink.

"Yeah, I'm gonna have her make out the bank deposits, Doc," Fleeta says wryly.

"That's fine, as long as she gets her naps in." Taye kisses Pearl, then India, and goes.

"Well, well," Fleeta says as she comes from behind the counter. She studies India in the soft pink blanket. "Now, that's a brown baby."

"Well, she's half Indian," Pearl says pleasantly.

"And you're Melungeon, don't ferget that. That's some black hair on her. Now, I know them ferriners got the black hair, but this here is the shiny Melungeon variety."

"Isn't she beautiful?" I nudge Fleeta, hoping to get her off the bloodline topic. She doesn't bite.

"Every once in a while, my daughter Janine comes over and spends Fri-dee night with me. And we pop us some corn and rent us a movie. We like them Ali Baba movies set in them sand dune countries, you know, where the snakes dance out of baskets and virgins get thrown into a flaming pit on holidays. And there's always a sword fight between a homely prince and a good-lookin' poor man for the hand of the Indian princess. Somehow the good-lookin' poor man is always a real prince in disguise, but then he always gets found out and marries the princess. Well, that's what your little girl reminds me of—one of them black-eyed princesses with them Bambi eyes. She's a beauty, all right."

"Thanks, Fleeta." Pearl looks at me, and we laugh.

"Well, that's what she looks like to me." Fleeta shrugs and goes back to the Soda Fountain.

"Is she still annoyed about the crib?"

"So peeved she put it together for you," I tell her.

To Jack's amusement and my horror, we are hosting the first boy-girl birthday party ever to take place in the MacChesney homestead. Jack's family tradition for birthdays was always simple: every great-aunt and -uncle and distant cousin came for Sunday supper, and at the end of the afternoon, Mrs. Mac would bring out a red velvet cake with candles and everyone would sing. Birthdays were strictly a family affair.

My childhood birthday parties were all-girl events. Mama said I could invite boys, but I preferred my girlfriends' company. We didn't dress up, we ate lots of cake, and we played cards for hours. We were big gigglers, and that always gave Fred Mulligan an excuse not to come. Noisy girls drove him crazy, so he'd work late at the Pharmacy until the party was over.

I look over Etta's guest list. There are two Trevors, two Codys, one Jarred, one Dakota, and one Homer; two Tiffanys, one Tara, a Crystal, a Kristen, and a Chris. My daughter definitely prefers the coed birthday party.

Jack comes into the kitchen. "Everything is done. The pizza's in the oven. Fleeta dropped off the coconut cake. We have lots of pop. I borrowed the softball equipment from the church." He looks at me. "What's the matter?"

"Our girl is thirteen."

"Uh-huh. Last year she was twelve."

"You're not funny."

"You can't stop time, Ave."

"I just don't want her to grow up yet."

"We don't have a choice, honey," Jack says practically.

As I set up the picnic table on the sun porch, I look at the paper plates with Barbies on them, and suddenly they seem ridiculous, so I throw them in the drawer and pull out real china instead. I don't want to embarrass Etta, and Barbies and boys simply don't mix.

"Letter from It-lee!" Etta hollers as she comes into the house. She joins us in the kitchen. "It's from Stefano Grassi!" she announces. "It's addressed to you."

Etta stands by as I read the letter from Stefano, in which he accepts our "kind invitation" for him to come and work this summer and promises to write again soon with his travel itinerary.

Etta rolls back her shoulders—I have never seen this gesture before. She flips her hair and looks at us. "Thank you both for hosting Stefano this summer. I'm sure he'll do a good job for you, Dad," Etta says, and leaves the room.

"What was that?" Jack points in the direction of his daughter.

"She's a teenager now. She's sophisticated," I tell him.

"No, the accent. Where did that come from?"

"That was her imitation of Audrey Hepburn in *Breakfast at Tiffany's*. We watched it last night."

If the empty cake plate, punch bowl, and pizza pans are any indication, Etta's birthday party was a success. Jack is out in the yard putting away the last of the softball equipment while Etta helps me with the dishes.

"Everybody seemed to have fun," I remark.

"Yeah. Until Tara and Trevor got together."

"What do you mean 'got together'?"

"After we played softball, she chased Trevor up the path when I took everyone into the woods. Trevor Gilliam, not Trevor Bailey."

"How do you keep them straight?"

"Trevor Gilliam's cuter."

"That's as good a system as any, I guess."

"Tara got him down the path and then made out with him."

"Define 'made out.' " I try not to let my voice break.

"Ma. You know."

"I know. I want you to tell me."

"They kissed three times."

"How did they find the time?" I wonder aloud. We had the revelers scheduled with games and refreshments down to the last minute. Furthermore, how did they manage a make-out session with steely-eyed chaperone Jack MacChesney on the beat? (I'll deal with him later.)

"Tara said she's gonna marry Trevor as soon as we graduate from high school."

"She's awfully young to be thinking about marriage." This is the perfect entrée into our mother-daughter sex talk, but I am completely thrown that anyone Etta's age would even think about marriage (it's an even bigger issue than sex, isn't it?).

"Dad told me Grandma Mac got married at seventeen. That's only four years older than me."

"I know, but that was in the 1920s, for Godsakes." Etta had one grandmother who was a child bride, and the other was a single teenage mother, and while I'd be thrilled for her to take after them in every way, this is the exception.

"Dad told me that even though they were young, they had true love."

"Etta, it was a different time. Now we have so many more options. You're going to college. Grandma Mac didn't have that kind of an opportunity."

"Tara's mom got married when she was seventeen too. She's thirty now." Etta climbs on the step stool and puts the cake plate away. "You weren't even married at thirty, were you?"

"Nope."

"I have the oldest parents in my class. But I don't care. Y'all don't act old."

"Thank you for that ringing endorsement," I tell her. "Did you have a good birthday?"

"My best yet." Etta takes the rubber band off her wrist and twists her hair into a ponytail with it.

"What did you like best about your birthday?"

"The letter from Italy."

"Can I lie and tell Aunt Fleeta it was her coconut cake?"

I'm hoping if I don't make an issue out of Etta's old crush on Stefano, it will dissipate on its own by summertime. Jack comes into the kitchen with a package. "Happy birthday, Etta. This is from Mom and me."

"But you gave me a party," she says as she rips into the package. She lifts the lid off the box, and her eyes widen with excitement. "My own telescope!"

"Dad will help you put it together."

"Not that you need my help. I think you know more about this stuff than I do."

Etta throws her arms around us. "Thank you! I love it! I'm going to go and set it up right now." Etta and Jack sort through the box, lifting out parts and directions. They go upstairs as I put away the last of the dishes.

I'm exhausted, so when I'm done, I sit on the rickety bench under the windows and rock on the leg that was sawed off short for a reason no one remembers. I hear Etta and Jack fussing over the directions upstairs, and it makes me smile. This house hasn't been quiet since the day Etta was born. If I ever missed my single life (and, I confess, I have from time to time), what I missed most was the quiet and glorious solitude of my own thoughts. As I listen to the taps the three good legs of the bench make on the wooden floor, I think about what it means to be the mother of a teenager and how fundamentally my relationship with Etta has changed. Are the best days behind me, when I could hold her and kiss her as much as I wanted? This morning I went to hug her, and she pulled away. She wasn't being rude, just her idea of grown-up. But I would be lying if I said it didn't hurt my feelings. Before I had my children, I would hear parents complain about the teenage years, and I'd think, Not my kids. I'll love them so much, they'll never push me away. Well, here it is, the day Etta pulled away, and I wasn't ready (though I doubt there is any way to prepare for this).

Mr. J's Construction Company has really grown since Jack and his partners, Mousey and Rick, began their venture as general contractors. Now, with the help of some adjunct courses from Mountain Empire Community College, they have expanded their skills to include plumbing, tile work, and even some design. The Southwest Virginia Museum has hired them to refurbish all the mantelpieces in the building (a considerable amount of work, since there's a fireplace in every room of the old mansion).

Etta works with Jack now, mostly after school and occasionally on weekends. As I pull the Jeep into the alley behind the museum, I see that the load of marble from Pete Rutledge has arrived. Glistening planks of sea-foam-green granite with black veins are stacked on the back of Jack's truck.

I find Etta and Jack in the front parlor of the museum, a grand sun-washed room with many windows. It's a construction site now, with tarps covering the hardwood floors and windowsills. Jack has removed the fireplace facade to reveal a chicken-wire web of plaster underneath. Etta is on the floor measuring small squares of shiny black marble, which will become the border of the mantel. "Well, look at Michelangelo and his daughter."

"It's more like Michelangela and her father," Jack says as he takes a brush and applies a wet coating to the plaster. "Your daughter figured out how to make a border within a border so the design pops three-dimensionally."

"Where did you learn that?" I ask Etta.

"In math class. I took the measurements and made a grid. It's not that hard." Etta continues placing the small squares in neat rows on butcher paper.

"Pete sent you a present." Jack stirs the plaster.

"He did?"

"It's on the table there." Jack points with the brush.

There's a small black velvet sack. I untie the drawstring and pour the contents into my hand. There are about ten deep blue lapis lazuli marbles the size of pearls. They are streaked with gold stripes that glisten in the sunlight.

"Cool," Etta says from behind me. "That's the same kind of marble he gave you when we were over in Italy. Remember, he gave you a square when we visited the quarry?"

"I don't," I lie. I don't want Etta to think that was a day I remember in particular, though it was the day Pete Rutledge took us to the waterfall in the Alps and told me how he felt about me. I remember the steam of the hot springs, the way the smooth stones felt on my feet, and how I felt in his arms when he carried me in the water.

"Ma, you put the marble on Joe's grave at the cemetery when we got home." Etta's voice brings me back to the present.

"Oh yeah. Right. Right."

"It's still there. God. Don't you remember anything?" Etta asks impatiently.

"I guess not," I lie. The truth is, I remember everything in vivid detail, but that isn't something I want Etta or my husband to know. Like every woman, I have secrets, moments really, that are just for me. It's a way for me to stay a whole and private person while being a part of my family. I may seem to my daughter like a practical woman, but I am every bit the dreamer that she is; someday I hope to share that side of myself with her. But for now I'm a leader in her life, and boundaries are crucial.

Stefano Grassi's much anticipated arrival date is finally here. My daughter is never on time, but today she corralled us to leave early for the airport. Etta has done a three-month countdown to this big day. I hope Stefano is as nice as I remember him to be. Otherwise, we're going to have one long summer in Cracker's Neck Holler.

"How will we know him?" Jack asks me as we stand near the gate at Tri-Cities Airport.

"He'll look foreign. And probably like the picture Papa sent." I fan myself with an old program from the Barter Theatre that I found in the bottom of my good purse. It's only June, and already we're hitting the nineties.

"I'll know him," Etta says impatiently, keeping her eyes on the gate. She looks stylish in her new jeans, white cotton blouse, and clear lip gloss. (I drew the line: no eye makeup till she's fifteen.) "There he is!" Etta points.

No one is more shocked than me when a very tall and handsome Stefano Grassi sees us and separates from the crowd of passengers to join us.

"Mrs. MacChesney?" Stefano says politely.

"It's good to see you again. Please call me Ave Maria."

"And I'm Jack Mac." My husband extends his hand, and Stefano shakes it heartily.

"My God. You grew up!" I blurt. And he did, he's a man now. He still has the same curly blond hair and mischievous brown eyes and prominent nose, but the small orphan boy I remember is now six feet tall and obviously shaves on a daily basis. You wouldn't call him classically handsome, but there is an appealing Henry David Thoreau quality to him; he looks like he belongs in another century, in a cabin with his sleeves rolled up, writing serious poetry about the woods.

"Do you remember my daughter?" I ask him.

"How could I forget Etta?"

Etta beams, and if she were on a runway, that smile would win her the Miss America crown. "Hi, Stefano."

"Did you put some Coca-Cola in the refrigerator for me?" She nods. "And Mountain Dew."

As we drive back to Big Stone Gap, Stefano is full of

questions and looks out the window often, drinking in the mountain vista. He and Jack have a long conversation about surveying and construction. Etta and I sit in the back of the Jeep. My daughter leans forward, listening intently to their conversation.

The sound of Stefano's accent brings Italy back to me, and suddenly I am homesick for Schilpario and Bergamo and my people. I understand what Etta means when she complains that she doesn't have any kin here. There are times when nothing can replace the extended family of aunts and uncles and cousins rounding out life and making it full. Today the sound of Stefano's voice will have to do. Etta and I promised to speak Italian with him all summer. I grew up speaking Italian with my mother as much as English, and I taught Etta when she was a little girl. We use it occasionally, most often when we're in public, like a secret language. It will be nice to hear it spoken with a genuine native accent every day. I'm sure that will shrink the distance between the Blue Ridge Mountains and the Italian Alps considerably.

"You didn't tell us Stefano was hot," Iva Lou says as she dips her spoon into one of Fleeta's sundaes. "That's one good-lookin' man. He's got every single girl in town in an uproar. The women around here are more excited than they were when Tommy Lee Jones came through to make *Coal Miner's Daughter*." Iva Lou has rebounded beautifully from her surgery last fall, and evidently so have her hormones.

"It's the accent," Fleeta says, rinsing utensils behind the Soda Fountain. "Women love an accent. Especially Eye-talian accents. Makes 'em believe whatever the man is saying is true."

"Serena Mumpower is all over him. Ole Stefano came down to the li-berry to check out some books, and she followed him around through the stacks like a hungry kitten. I didn't discourage her from helping him, though. It's the first time that girl left the desk and did any work."

"That one will go for anything in pants." Fleeta sniffs.

"Serena's got appeal, I'm here to tell you," Iva Lou says, defending her assistant. "She's got movie-star looks. She resembles the young Natalie Wood, if Natalie Wood had a bigger nose."

"Has he brought any girls 'round yer house?" Fleeta wants to know of me.

"No. If he's entertaining girls, it's elsewhere."

"Where'd you put him?"

"Downstairs in our old bedroom. Jack and I moved upstairs into Joe's old room. It's nice." I don't elaborate on the reason for this switch—I don't think it's appropriate to have a thirteen-year-old girl on a separate floor with a male guest.

"I couldn't stand a boarder. When I git home of a night, I like to peel down to my underwear and walk around. I couldn't stand having a stranger mess up my schedule." Fleeta sits down next to us.

"What do you do with Otto?" Iva Lou wonders aloud.

"He ain't a stranger." Fleeta shrugs.

"Stefano isn't either," I tell them. "He's like family. He's no trouble at all. And he talks about Italy a lot, and I like that. Jack says Stefano is a great worker and very ambitious."

"You Eye-talians are good workers in general," Fleeta comments. "Not as good as them Greeks, but close."

"Thank you." Over the years, I have grown used to Fleeta's

bizarre compliments (I'm not going to point out that she's probably never actually met a Greek person).

"So having Stefano around is like giving Etta an older brother," Iva Lou observes.

"Exactly," I tell her. I don't want to betray Etta's confidence. Besides, it sounds like every girl in Wise County has a crush on Stefano Grassi.

I get stuck at work with a pharmaceutical salesman out of Middlesboro who talks my ear off, so I wind up buying two extra cases of antihistamines (that's okay; it's been a terrible pollen season!). It's pitch-black as I head for home. From the lower holler road, I see that Jack has lit the mosquito torches around the house. When I pull up to park, I hear Etta's voice in the backyard, so instead of going inside the house, I follow the sound to her. She has set up her telescope and is showing Stefano the night sky. Jack is cooking hamburgers on the grill; the smell of onions and peppers simmering in a small cast-iron skillet makes my mouth water.

"That's Aldebaran," Etta tells our guest as he looks through the telescope. "It's the brightest star in the sky right now."

"Yes, it is. It sparkles," Stefano tells her as he continues to look.

"The best place to observe it this month is Schilpario, well, really any location in the Dolomites and the Italian Alps. The combination of perfect weather and position is rare."

"You're such an expert!" I say proudly.

"Hi, Ma." Etta looks up at me and smiles. "Come and look."

Stefano steps aside. I peer into the lens, and what I see is astonishing. The summer sky is a rich black punctuated by small silver stars that shimmer so, they seem to overlap like pavé diamonds.

"Do you see Aldebaran?" Etta asks.

One star glitters like the surface of water in sunlight. It is round and faceted, larger than the other stars, and a deep turquoise at its core. Maybe the blue is an illusion, but it gives a rich center to the dazzling white around it, burning hot around the edges. "I see it, honey."

"You almost can't describe it, right?" Etta asks me.

"It's true. It would be impossible to describe something so beautiful."

Jack comes up behind me and puts his arms around me. He looks into the telescope and is as mesmerized as I am.

"Dad, the burgers!" Etta cries.

Jack bolts back to the grill and flips the hamburgers before they burn. Stefano and Etta go into the house for the plates, utensils, salad, and drinks. I sit down at our old picnic table and put my feet up on the bench. I feel the workday, too long and too hot, settle down to my bones.

"How's work?" I ask Jack.

"Stefano is a big help." Jack nods toward the house.

"I'm glad."

"He just fits in. I don't know how else to explain it. All the guys like him. Even the lunch crowd at Bessie's loves him. He's great with Etta. It's like he's part of the family."

Etta and Stefano throw a red-and-white-checked tablecloth onto the picnic table while I set the places for dinner. Jack joins us with a platter of burgers, the skillet, and roasted corn on the cob, which he wrapped in foil and grilled. "Smells delicious," I tell him.

"Mrs. Mac, could I ask a favor?" Stefano says. "Could I borrow your Jeep Friday night?"

"Sure."

"Are you going on a date?" Etta teases him.

"A gentleman never tells," Stefano says, sounding a lot like Mario da Schilpario with that accent.

"You're going out on a date," Etta says definitively. "It's Saturday night in Big Stone Gap. What else is there to do?" She acts like she doesn't care. My girl *is* becoming a woman.

"Who's the lucky girl?" Jack joins in the fun.

"Serena Mumpower."

Jack, Etta, and I laugh.

Stefano looks worried. "Is there something wrong with her?"

"Nothing at all," I tell him. "In fact, Iva Lou said that Serena likes you a lot."

"I know. She told me herself. American girls are bold."

"Yes sir, they are," Jack agrees. "Gettin' bolder all the time."

"How do you know?" I ask my husband.

"I observe from afar, honey." He winks at me.

"Why shouldn't a girl be bold? I would ask a boy out if I was allowed to date." Etta takes a bite of her hamburger.

"You would? Really?" I ask.

"Why not? It's not like when you and Dad were young and boys did all the asking. That's crazy."

Jack and I look at each other. Etta continues, "If girls can ask boys out, then it's more equal. Then boys do more stuff that girls usually do — like cooking."

"Hey, there," Jack says, feigning defensiveness.

"Or taking care of kids, or household chores like laundry," Etta says.

"Etta. Are you a feminist?" I tease.

"I didn't know there was a word for common sense," she fires back as she pours the iced tea.

"I agree with Etta. All people should take care of themselves, regardless of sex," Stefano announces. "I worked in the laundry at the orphanage. I was very good at it. The hard part was ironing the altar linens for church."

"What was the orphanage like?" I ask him, moving the conversation away from men and women.

"It was fine."

"Fine? They're usually terrible. I think of *Oliver Twist*."

Stefano laughs. "No, though I'm sure that there are many bad places. I was lucky. We lived in a converted monastery in Bergamo. It was a small group of us, boys only, and we were cared for by the nuns. They tried to be second mothers to us."

"You seemed to have a lot of access to the town."

"The nuns encouraged that. They wanted us to feel like part of a family. I was very lucky to have the Vilminores. They took care of me on holidays. Meals on the weekends. Once a year your uncle took me to buy shoes before school started. Your aunts bought me schoolbooks and haircuts."

"Do you know what happened to your parents?" Etta asks Stefano.

"I only know they both died when I was small."

"That's terrible," Etta says softly.

"But I didn't feel alone. All the boys were just like me." Stefano smiles.

As we eat our dinner, Jack steers the conversation to

construction. Soon the three of them are laughing. I look at Stefano in a new way, thinking about the life he's had. I wonder if there is anyone in the world who isn't broken in some way, who isn't full of questions about the past, who hasn't wondered "what if" in the face of loss. Can a person who has lost his parents so young ever heal? Stefano seems to possess all the good qualities of a stable childhood, but can he be whole? Or is he complete in a different way, a way he earned on his own?

The best part about loaning my Jeep to Stefano on the weekends is that it comes back sparkling clean with extras like the engine tuned and the tires rotated. The perfect house-guest and the perfect contractor's apprentice has also turned out to be the perfect mechanic. Everybody's happy.

"Where are my girls?" Jack says from the bottom of the steps. It is the hottest night of the summer, and Etta and I are upstairs rearranging the furniture in her room (she's bored with the setup).

"Why do you want to know?" I yell back.

"Let's go sailing!"

Jack's idea of sailing is borrowing a pair of old canoes from Otto and Worley and heading up to Big Cherry Lake. As Etta and I pile into Jack's truck with the canoes in the back, Stefano pulls up in my Jeep.

"Don't you have a date?" Jack asks Stefano.

"She stood me up." Stefano shrugs.

"You're welcome to come with us," I tell him. He smiles and jumps in the back of the truck.

Big Cherry Lake is most beautiful in the summer, its dark

blue water surrounded by trees so lush, they look like draperies of deep green. "What do you think?" Etta asks Stefano as he surveys the lake.

"It should be called Big Blue Lake," Stefano replies.

"No, it's Big Cherry because of the cherry trees. See them?" Etta points across the water to a grove of cherry trees surrounded by pine trees so tall that they could touch the windows of the penthouse in Theodore's apartment building.

"It's a small lake." Why am I apologizing for our lake?

"Ave, don't put our lake down," my husband teases me.

"Stefano's from the Italian Alps. Near Lake Como and Lake Garda. He knows big lakes. Historic lakes, world-famous lakes."

"But this is just as beautiful," Stefano says.

"Thank you," Jack and Etta say in unison, looking at me.

"Mama thinks everything in Italy is better than in America."

"Except the husbands." I put my arm around Jack.

"Too late for the suck-up. You're gonna row anyhow." He hands me an oar.

Stefano rows Etta out to the middle of the lake. Jack watches as Etta dips her hands into the water. "Are you thinking what I'm thinking?" Jack asks me without turning around.

"That our daughter is a young lady now?"

"Yeah. You don't think she's getting a crush on him, do you?"

"Getting one? She's *had* one," I tell him.

"When did that happen?"

"It happened in Italy. But she's way too young for him, so I don't think there's anything to worry about."

Etta points to the reservoir in the distance. The sound of her voice, explaining how we supply most of the water used in Wise County, carries across the lake, sounding self-assured and knowledgeable, even mature. As Stefano rows Etta across the water, I feel something very strange.

Instead of seeing Etta and Stefano in that canoe, I see Jack and me when we were young, before Etta was born. Having children makes a woman mark time in a different way. Sometimes it takes a moment to remember how old I am, but I can tell you in years, months, and days how old Etta is and how old Joe would have been.

Jack turns and looks at me. "What are you so quiet about?"

"What are we going to do when she's gone?"

"I guess we'll be lovers again."

"Just like that?"

"You got a better idea?"

"Not really," I tell him.

"Then that's the plan."

I am happy to let my husband row the canoe and answer the big questions. "Whatever you say, honey."

I'm going to miss Stefano when he goes, not just because he's good around the house but because of his personality. He's genuinely interested in everyone around him. I would say his summer in the Gap has worked out beautifully. This is his last weekend here. Tonight he's going with us to the Fold.

"Yoo-hoo, Ave?" Iva Lou calls from the front porch.

"What are you doing here?"

"Takin' y'all to the Fold. I saw Stefano down in town, and he told me to tell you he got sidetracked and to go on to the

Fold without him. So shake a leg. The Reedy Creek Band is playin' promptly at eight, and I don't want to miss Dr. Smiddy."

"The father or the son?" I ask Iva Lou, grabbing my purse.

"Either one. I don't like to be late. Besides, when you're late for the Fold, the field fills up, and then you gotta park in Gate City and walk ten miles."

"Let's go, Etta!" I call up the stairs.

Iva Lou wolf-whistles. I turn to see why, and have to say, "Etta, you look beautiful." She is wearing a denim skirt, a black T-shirt, and sandals, and has on hoop earrings, just like her aunt Iva Lou.

"Those mountain boys are gonna be all over you. But don't you worry, we'll protect ye," Iva Lou says.

"Thanks," Etta says, blushing. "Where's Dad?"

"He went to the car show in Knoxville with Rick Harmon," I tell her.

"Oh. So it's just us and Stefano?"

"Stefano isn't coming either. He sent Aunt Iva Lou to take us."

"But it's his last Saturday night here," she says.

"He changed his plans, honey. Don't let that hurt your feelings."

"But he's leaving on Monday!" Etta says emotionally.

"So he's squeezing in one last rendezvous with Serena Mumpower." Iva Lou sounds impatient.

"A date?" Etta looks confused. Her posture collapses a little.

"You know he's been seeing that Serena Mumpower. 'Course, with his work schedule and her dance card forever on the full side, it's catch-as-catch-can, but Serena is a catch-can girl."

Etta's eyes fill with tears. "Excuse me," she says, and runs up the stairs.

"Did I say something wrong?" Iva Lou asks me.

"I don't think so. Give me a second." I run up the stairs after Etta. She has closed the door to her room. I throw it open and follow her up the second set of stairs. "Honey, are you all right?"

Etta doesn't answer. She is crying.

"I'll be right back," I tell her, and run back down to Iva Lou. "Iva, go without us. She's upset."

"Oh, Lordy, let me talk to her."

"No, no, it's okay. It isn't you. I just don't think we can make it tonight. I'm sorry."

"No problem. Call me later. Let me know what happened."

"Absolutely."

Lyle taps the horn, and Iva Lou hurries out the front door. I go upstairs and sit next to Etta on the bed and place my hand gently on her back.

"Oh Mama." She's still crying.

"What is it, honey?"

"I like him so much."

"Stefano is very nice, I know. But he's eighteen, honey."

"I know."

I point out the obvious. "And he lives in Italy."

"I know," she wails.

"Is he the first young man you've ever liked?" I ask her gently.

She nods. "He's cute, and he's not stupid like the boys I know."

"Those are two good reasons to like a guy."

"And he listens to me."

"That's good too."

"But I'm just a kid to him, aren't I?" She punches her pillow, then lies down on it.

Part of me wants to say I hope so, but this is Etta's first big crush, and I have to be careful. "No, I think he thinks you're a smart girl."

"He does?"

"Sure."

"Do you think he thinks I'm pretty?"

"He'd be crazy if he didn't."

Etta kicks off her sandals, which hit the floor with a thud, and it's as though the rattan sandals have magical powers — when she wore them down the stairs, she was a young lady, but now she looks like a thirteen-year-old again, with puffy eyes, thin legs, and a broken heart.

"Why would he want to see Serena Mumpower on his last Saturday night in America?" Now Etta sounds angry, and I want to encourage that. She should let all of these feelings out. "I thought he liked us."

"He does."

"Then why does he need Serena?"

I thought my husband had a preliminary sex talk with Etta, but I see that he evidently passed right over the Nature of a Man and went straight for cellular reproduction. I make a mental note to kill him when he returns from the car show. I scratch my head, hoping that the words will come. What the hell, I'm just going to wing it. "Men are funny," I say loudly. Etta looks confused. "A man doesn't necessarily go out with a girl because she's smart or beautiful or because he has similar interests. Sometimes he goes out with a girl because she's no trouble."

"I don't understand."

"Neither did I until my fortieth birthday, so bear with me."

"Okay." Etta blows her nose and looks at me with Great Expectations, as though I'm an oracle sitting on an altar with smoke coming out of my ears and soon will predict the romantic proceedings of the next century.

"Sometimes, for a man, there isn't a great romance involved. Sometimes it's just killing time. Sometimes he picks somebody to have dinner with and a conversation, so that it's light and uncomplicated, and feelings aren't so important or even involved. Sometimes he picks a girl to be, I don't know, a diversion."

"Do you think he'll marry her?"

"Oh, Etta, I don't think there's any way he'll marry her. Is that what you're worried about?"

"Yes."

"Why?"

"Because Stefano Grassi is my destiny," Etta says without a single note of irony or drama.

"How do you know that?"

"Because of the stars."

"Do you mean the horoscope in *Seventeen* magazine, or the stars in the sky?"

"The ones I see through my telescope."

"What do they tell you?"

"There are patterns to the stars and planets. And sometimes it seems like there's a big shift up there, that everything is moving, that sometimes stars get lost and disappear. But they don't disappear, they're forever fixed. They always come back to their point of origin."

"So you think that you're like a star, and Stefano is like a star, and you're somehow fated to connect?"

Etta nods, and for a moment I think she's going to throw her arms around me. Right now I *am* her friend as well as her mother, though it's a new, and probably temporary, place for both of us.

"That's beautiful. But what about stars that burn out and fall away?"

"Those weren't meant to be."

First of all, I think I just had a sex talk with my daughter by way of Copernicus, and that gives me some comfort; and second, I still can't believe that she knows so much about something I never think about—stars and constellations and universes that exist or don't—and that she believes somehow all of this plays directly into her life and affects her choices and her future. What thirteen-year-old thinks about life on such a cosmic scale? She should have a crush on Cute Trevor or Medium-Cute Trevor, not on an eighteen-year-old Italian hunk here on a work permit. But she's been hurt tonight, deflated, and I can't bring myself to tell her that this will pass and next week it won't hurt so much, that Stefano will fly home and school will start and band practice will resume and that all of a sudden boys her own age will become alternately interesting and unbearable to her, that there will be many crushes, many mini-romances, many hurts, heartbreaks, and disbeliefs on her way to True Love Town. But she won't hear that tonight even if I say it, because the object of her ardor is dancing with Serena from Appalachia to a chorus of "Hot Buttered Beans" on the floor of the Carter Family Fold. Tonight she loves Stefano Grassi, and if she's anything like her mother, it's mostly because she can't have him.

"Don't I look older than I am?" Etta says proudly as she looks at her new passport photo.

"You look fifteen because you *are* fifteen," I tell her.

"You're no fun." Etta smiles and goes upstairs to finish packing.

Isn't time flying fast enough for my daughter? Jack has been teaching her how to drive; the bottle of Mr. Bubble that has been a staple in our bathroom since she was a girl has been replaced by vanilla bath beads; and the cupcake tins that used to hold her pebbles, fishhooks, and spare change are filled with different colors of eye shadow and lip gloss. What other road signs do we need to direct us toward womanhood?

I promised Etta that we would go back to Italy by her fifteenth summer, and she has held me to it. Of course, I don't need much encouragement when it comes to Italy, and Jack needs even less. He hasn't been back since our honeymoon, and he wants to take his Italian cooking to the next level. To do that, he needs to be in its country of origin.

I've convinced Iva Lou to go with us this time (to fulfill her life-long dream of seeing It-lee and also to celebrate the fact that she's been cancer-free for two years). Lyle has begged off; the only foreign place he wants to go is Hawaii, so Iva Lou promised him a trip next year. She's already had a conversation with local tour organizer/high school guidance counselor Jack "Nobody Comes Home Without a Lei" Gibbs.

I invited Theodore to join us as well, but he and Max took a share in a house on New York's Long Island for the summer weekends. I'll have to send them lots of postcards to make them jealous.

Etta has dated the same boy for a year, a nice kid named Dakota Clasby. She's gone to school with him all of her life, and the part I like best is that she likes him, but it's as much a friendship as a romance. Jack thinks I'm nuts and says I don't see what's really going on. But Etta talks to me about him, and I listen, and I don't see any need to worry. Besides, she gets excellent grades and even had an internship with the Thompson & Litton architectural firm in Norton. As much as she loves astronomy, she has come to love building design and construction more (thanks to her father!).

The planning of our trip has brought out the true librarian in Iva Lou. She has been packing for six months. She kept a log for three weeks to figure out the exact amounts of shampoo, soap, and personal-hygiene items she uses over the course of twenty-one days, so she'll have all she needs. She read an article on how to roll clothes instead of folding them square (it also involves tissue paper—don't ask). She has an adapter for her blow-dryer, a mini tool kit for breakdowns, and a cosmetics case that looks like Doc Daugherty's satchel, filled with small vials and tubes. She has broken in three pairs of walking shoes and one pair of stilettos (for a night out in Venice).

I'm keeping it simple. One bag for my clothes and a backpack for everything else. Jack has a natural sense of how to pack lightly (all those years of camping), and has warned us that he isn't hauling bags all over northern Italy, so we'd better keep them light.

Gala Nuccio, my honorary sister and our family travel agent (who helped me track down my father and then conspired with Jack to bring him to Southwest Virginia for a visit), has had the time of her life planning this trip for us. She called upon many of her personal contacts in Italy so that we will have tickets waiting in Florence to go to the Uffizi Gallery; accommodations at a small private hotel in Venice; and a tour of a pottery factory in Deruta. During my previous visits to Italy, I have stayed mainly in Schilpario, but this time we're branching out and taking in more of the Tuscan countryside (bringing Iva Lou gives me a good excuse to act like a typical tourist). This way Schilpario and Bergamo will be the dessert of our grand tour.

"Ma! Spec is here!" Etta hollers from the front porch.

"Load the bags, please," I yell back from the bathroom, where I'm putting on my lipstick. I slathered moisturizer on this morning, knowing the plane ride would dehydrate me.

Jack pokes his head into the bathroom. "You look great. Let's go."

"I'm coming," I tell him, dropping my mascara wand in the sink.

"What are you nervous about?"

"I don't know."

"Fleeta's coming over to feed Shoo."

"I know."

"Are you worried about the plane?"

"No."

"What is it, then?"

"You know I get funny feelings sometimes." I wish I knew what's giving me the jitters. What am I afraid to find in Italy? (Ever since I went to Sister Claire years ago, I'm a little *too* in touch with my inner voice—sometimes it's downright noisy!)

I grab my purse and follow Jack outside. Etta and Jack have loaded the luggage into the Rescue Wagon; evidently, Spec's car is in the shop.

"I hope the mayor doesn't see us riding around in an official vehicle," I tell Spec.

Spec smiles. "I called him, he gave me permission."

"Good thinking."

"Come on, Ave. You ride shotgun, just like the old days."

Iva Lou is in the backseat with Jack, and Etta is in the way back with the bags but perfectly happy to be there.

"Honey-o, I have never been so excited in my life!" Iva Lou straightens the collar on her pale blue denim jacket. Her hair is a masterpiece, highlighted with gold streaks and styled in the upsweep made famous by Verna Lisi.

"You look like a blond Italian goddess," I tell her.

"That's what I was goin' fer! Well, that and a little Ivana Trump thrown in for effect," she says proudly.

"Let's go, Spec!" Etta calls out pleasantly.

"You got it, kid!" Spec floors it, kicking up dust as we peel down the old stone road. Spec speeds through the Wildcat Holler so fast, we're practically off the ground as we make the turn onto Kingsport Road.

"Look, Etta. Your buddies are at the Quik Stop!" Spec points.

"That's fine, Spec. Keep driving." Etta's tone is even and dry. She is not above being embarrassed to be in this bright orange station wagon with the white stripes.

"Let's send you off to It-lee with a bang!" Spec laughs and puts on the siren. Etta buries her head in her purse as Iva Lou and Jack laugh.

Iva Lou flirts with every Red Cap when we land at New York's JFK Airport, and when she tries to tip the man who hauls her bags to our gate, he won't take her money (that's never happened to *me*). Once we're on the plane, she sits back in her seat and looks out the window. "I'm so happy. How do you like my outfit?" Iva Lou is wearing a simple black jumpsuit with a cinch belt, her jacket, now thrown over her shoulders, and very cute black loafers. "I love it. It fits like a glove."

"Can't tell I'm wearing falsies, can you?"

"Not a bit."

"You wanna know my secret?"

"Sure."

"Different boob sizes."

"What?"

"Yep, I have a small case of them in various sizes. See, different outfits require different boobs. A turtleneck needs high and small; a peasant blouse requires larger and centered; a suit jacket, the classic Jane Russell torpedoes; and so on.

You can bet I wasn't goin' to It-lee, the land of Claudia Cardinale and Gina Lollobrigida, flat as Fleeta's tortillas. No, I want to look every inch the American beauty rose."

"Well, you do."

"Sometimes I can't believe I made it." Iva Lou leans back in her seat.

"I always knew you'd come to Italy."

"No, I mean I can't believe I made it, period. Through the cancer. That fortune-teller was right."

"She was totally off! She told you smooth sailing, no problems. We should have gotten your money back."

"No, ole Sister Claire predicted everything."

"What?"

"Yeah. I lied to you that night. I told you that the news was good because I didn't want you to worry. The truth is, Sister told me I was in for a real tough time and to just hold on, that it would pass."

"I can't believe you didn't tell me!"

"Now, what good would *that* have done? It wouldn't have changed a thing. I still would have gotten sick. Still would have had the double mas'. And I guess in the back of my mind, I wanted to prove Sister Claire wrong. But I couldn't. She knew something I didn't. So much for knowin' myself better than anyone else does. That's the last time I don't believe a mystic."

After a smooth flight (we were all too excited to sleep), we land in Milan, then jump into the rental car and head south to Florence. Jack researched restaurants and found a jewel on a side street near the Duomo. The decor is simple: comfortable upholstered chairs and square marble tables.

Once we've ordered, Jack excuses himself and goes into the kitchen to watch the food preparation. He read an article in *Food & Wine* magazine that said Italian chefs love to be observed in the kitchen, so he's taking them up on it. He wrote letters to a couple of restaurants requesting observation time and they agreed.

"Is he going to watch the chefs make every meal we eat in Italy?" I wonder aloud.

"Ma, he wants to open a restaurant. Why do you think he tries recipes out a million times?" Etta says.

"He's a perfectionist?"

"No, he's experimenting. He says he's tired of construction." Etta shrugs.

I look at Iva Lou. "Better to open a restaurant in a midlife crisis than to buy a Harley and trade in the wife for a new model," she adds.

"Who's going to keep an Italian restaurant in business in Big Stone Gap? Stringer's is a hit because it's like a Baptist potluck supper with the steam tables and the all-you-can-eat Friday-night shrimp fries. Nobody in Big Stone is going to pay for fancy pasta," I say.

"Who says he wants to open it in Big Stone Gap?" Etta says without looking directly at me.

"Well, where does he want to open this restaurant, then?" I sound pitiful, but I am out of the loop on this one.

"Kingsport, maybe. Knoxville. I don't know. Ask him."

"I didn't think he was serious about it. I thought he was kidding around. You know, like when I say I want to go back to college and study spelunking."

Etta gives me one of those looks like I'm insane, snaps a

bread stick in two, and munches on it quietly. Iva Lou looks at me and pours me a glass of wine, then pours one for herself.

"Excuse me," I tell the girls. I pretend I'm heading to the ladies' room, but instead I take a sharp left and sneak past some red-and-gold-striped curtains with enormous red tassels across the top, which separate the kitchen from the wait station. A waiter looks up at me, I smile, and he shrugs, so I enter the kitchen, hovering close to the curtains, so as not to draw attention to myself. Here is something I have never seen before: my husband is assisting the chef. The chef, a short, balding man around sixty, continues to work at a clip as he explains what he is doing. He allows Jack to take the homemade noodles off a drying rack and throw them in the boiling water; he pinches salt into the water and hands Jack a slotted spoon to stir with. When Jack stirs too hard, the chef grabs the spoon and demonstrates a gentler technique. About three minutes go by before Jack asks the chef if he can drain the noodles. The chef looks at Jack suspiciously, and Jack indicates the sink, then explains that in America, we strain the noodles in a colander and run water over them before we add the sauce. The chef feigns a heart attack and asks Jack to watch closely as he lifts some of the steaming noodles out of the water into a colander, shakes them, and puts them aside. He explains to Jack that if you rinse the noodles, you kill the flavor of the pasta and make it impossible for the noodles to absorb the sauce.

The chef then takes another pan and pours olive oil into it. In a flash he dices up some fresh garlic and throws it in. As it sizzles, he takes strands of pancetta, a salty ham sliced so thin it's see-through, and lays them in the pan (it reminds me of the hunk of pork fatback Fleeta uses when she makes collard greens). Then the chef dumps in about a cup of fresh cream, followed by some pasta. Quickly he cracks two eggs on top of the mixture and, just as fast, tosses the eggs through the pasta and the sauce below until all the noodles are coated evenly. The pasta is whispery golden, like yellow rose petals when they've faded.

You'd think I would know this from my mother's cooking, but the truth is, we rarely ate pasta. Mostly we had risotto, a creamy rice dish, in many variations. When we did make pasta, it was often baked in small pots, or layered like lasagna in a pan, or gnocci (which means "knees"), a pasta made from potatoes and flour (rolled by hand into small round puffs light as clouds and coated in a light cream sauce). Spaghetti with tomato sauce was not a typical meal in my mother's hometown of Bergamo.

Jack is still unaware that I'm watching (a testament to his passion for cooking) and asks a question. The chef motions for Jack to remain quiet, and what he does next is pure art. He takes the pan and turns to a butcher block behind him. He has only to pivot, like a ballerina; every spoon and pot, strainer and lid, hangs within overhead reach, and his pristine cutting board and knives are lined up along the counter. The chef flips a wooden cap off a wheel that is a foot and a half across and about ten inches deep; at first I don't know what it is, but then I realize it's Parmesan cheese. He takes the steaming pasta, now coated with the buttery mixture, and throws it into the wheel—which is dug out deeply in the center, from many such dishes, I imagine—and then, putting the hot pan aside, he picks up two wooden instruments (they actually look like hands) and tosses the pasta while a thin layer of cheese peels off the sides and bottom of the wheel and onto the pasta.

"Hi, honey," Jack says, looking up at me. I am startled and smile back. *"Mia sposa,"* my husband says, introducing me.

"Italiana?" the chef says, smiling in approval at me.

"I'm a better one having seen you cook," I tell him in Italian.

"Andiamo!" he tells the waiter, who takes the plates from the worktable and hurries them to our table. "Go. Go. Eat!" The chef pats Jack on the back. I practically run to the table. I can't wait to taste the masterpiece.

When it arrives at our table, Iva Lou rolls the tender pasta around the fork and takes a dainty bite. "Jesus Christmas. This is better than—"

"You can say it," Etta says as she dives into her spaghetti puttanesca.

"It's better than sex," Iva Lou declares. "And you know for me to say that, well, it's a mouthful."

I take a bite and agree. Jack chews carefully and closes his eyes, then he reaches for his wine and takes a taste.

"I think this is the best meal I have ever had," he says, opening his eyes.

"Me too, honey," I tell him, squeezing his leg under the table.

"Now, y'all, none of that. This is Mood Food and therefore dangerous," Iva Lou says as she savors another bite and nudges Etta. "We single gals have to be very careful tonight. This sauce has magical powers. We may fall under the spell of some Eye-talian man."

"But you're married," Etta reminds her.

"You sure know how to bring the groove down."

"Uncle Lyle would want your groove down." Etta laughs loudly, and Iva Lou joins her.

For a moment I wish I had the camera out; I would capture this moment forever. But I decide not to. I want to retain this night in the warmth of memory, this meal consumed in an Italian bistro where the walls are washed in an iridescent gloss the color of pumpkins, where the candlelight makes us all look like movie stars, and where, behind the striped curtains, the chef stands proudly, watching with delight as we eat.

I am so glad we rented a car instead of taking trains, I'm thinking as we drive through the hills of Umbria, the gentle green gateway to Tuscany. The four of us feel safe and at home in the familiar landscape of small towns connected by single roads.

Jack has been very cagey about plans for Tuscany. He knows that I wanted to spend more time in Florence because I love the Duomo, the art galleries, and the Ponte Vecchio, loaded with more gold treasures than Cleopatra's jewelry box. "Ladies, next stop is Loro Ciuffenna," he announces.

"She sounds pretty," Iva Lou teases.

"She is a place, Iva Lou," Jack corrects her.

"Why do you want to go there?" Etta asks as she studies her map.

"I want to meet the King of Olive Oil," Jack says.

We girls have a good laugh. "Is there such a person?" I ask him.

"According to Renzo, the chef in Florence."

"What's the king's name?"

"Giuseppe Giaquinto."

"He sounds sexy," Iva Lou decides.

"I don't know about that. I do know that some chefs will use only Tuscan olive oil when they cook or bake, but Renzo uses only Giaquinto olive oil."

"That's a pretty strong commitment."

"I thought so. Renzo gave me the address and called ahead."

I can't believe that this is *my* husband making plans with total strangers in a foreign country. He's from Big Stone Gap, a place so small no one's ever heard of it, and yet when he ventures outside its borders he becomes daring, curious, and bold. This is not the man I married, but I have to say, I like him.

Loro Ciuffenna is south of Florence and west of Siena at the foot of the mountains. We drive up a mountain pass that is worse than any in Wise County: extremely narrow, hollowed out, and pitted from wear, with no guardrails on the driver's side. On the opposite side is a menacing wall of jagged rock, which, if you drive too close, could peel the car doors off like the lid on a can of tuna fish.

"This is a tight space," Iva Lou says, shutting her eyes and sounding like she feels slightly ill.

"Wait till we go to Schilpario. The Alps are really, really high. And the roads are more narrow than shoelaces," Etta warns her.

I hadn't mentioned any of this to Iva Lou. Why scare her so far in advance? Luckily, we begin our descent to the town through a picturesque passage. The road widens, and the terrain becomes smooth. On one side is a deep green valley, and on the other, a hillside dotted with olive trees almost precisely the same distance apart.

"That ground under them trees looks mighty dry," Iva Lou observes.

"It's supposed to. That's how you grow good olives," Jack tells her.

Etta makes Jack stop so she can get a picture of a white Tuscan farmhouse with a brown tile roof, set back off the road behind a spectacular iron gate. Even the most ordinary things are artful in Italy.

"That's the two-story traditional farmhouse I've been looking for. I want examples of architecture from the eighteenth century on," Etta says as she gets back into the car. "See the front? That opening on the ground floor is where the animals stay, and the second floor is where the family lives."

"I don't know if I'd want a cow that close to me," Iva Lou says. " 'Course my mamaw had a goat that lived in her kitchen. Fresh milk on tap. So I guess it ain't so bad to keep an animal indoors."

"Everything stays warmer that way in the winter," Etta tells us.

"You could be a tour guide," Jack tells her proudly.

I turn to look at Etta, who reloads her camera and smiles.

"This looks mighty modern," Iva Lou comments as we pull up to the metal gates outside the Giaquinto olive-oil plant in Loro Ciuffenna.

"Look up," Jack says, pointing to the hill above the factory. "There's your old Italian town with the castle." He presses the speaker panel. When he mentions Renzo's name, the gates open instantly, revealing a simple stone building, a long rectangle whose only marking is an olive tree in relief over the glass doors. Iva Lou quickly powders her nose and snaps her compact shut. "I ain't meeting the King of Olive Oil with a shiny nose."

A young woman around thirty greets us on the steps of the factory. "Welcome!" she says in an accent that can only be described as American Deep South.

"Lordy mercy, honey, where you from?" Iva Lou wants to know.

"Mississippi."

"Bless your heart!" Iva Lou looks at us and nods in approval.

"My name is Elaine." She is tall and slim, with long brown hair tied back in a simple bow. Her heavy-lidded green eyes are rimmed in soft brown, but that is her only makeup; she is a natural beauty. We follow her into the hallway; several doors lead off it to small offices. She takes us to the back, to the largest office. The sign on the door reads G. GIAQUINTO.

Mr. Giaquinto motions for us to enter, though he is on the phone shouting every Italian curse word I know. We do enter the office but hover by the door, afraid to interrupt. Giuseppe motions for us to sit, in a broad sweeping gesture that tells us to follow his instructions immediately. He continues to rant to the person on the other end of the line. Iva Lou's nose is now shiny, as is the rest of her face. She's nervous, poor thing; she's never heard anyone go full-out Eye-talian before. Suddenly, without warning, Giuseppe slams the phone down. Etta jumps in her seat a bit, then quickly shifts.

"Welcome," he says, looking up at us. The King of Olive Oil stands. He's around five feet eleven, trimly built, and simply dressed in black trousers and a white button-down shirt. He is in his mid-forties and has a handsome face, not rugged but refined. His nose ends in an elfin tip that swoops up (he's optimistic), and he has a high forehead with a widow's peak.

"You study me intently," he says to me with a smile.

"Tell him," Iva Lou says under her breath.

"Tell me what?" Giuseppe looks at me.

"I'm Iva Lou Wade Makin." Iva Lou extends her hand. Giuseppe takes it and shakes it with both hands. "I'm a librarian, and my friend here studied the ancient art of Chinese face reading. And she's right good at it."

"What does my face say?" Giuseppe asks, turning to me.

"That you're a brilliant perfectionist," I tell him. Elaine laughs from the doorway.

"You think that's funny?" Giuseppe says to her with a wink. "You met my girlfriend?"

"I find it hard to believe that a robust Eye-talian such as yourself had to go all the way to Mississippi, U.S.A., to find himself a woman," Iva Lou comments.

"She found me. At a food show in San Francisco."

"And my life has never been the same," Elaine says dryly.

Jack Mac introduces himself, and then all of us, with beautiful southern manners. Giuseppe seems soothed by my husband's tone and latches on to him as we tour the factory. I don't mind being left out of their conversation as I look at the rows of dark green glass bottles. The labels are beautiful, and some have gold leaf on the edges, an elegant touch. The explanations of the contents are pure poetry.

"You really believe in your product," I tell Giuseppe.

"Olive oil is a religion to me. I worship its natural perfection."

Iva Lou learns that olive oil is the best moisturizer. Etta takes pictures as Iva Lou rubs olive oil into her hands.

"Can you use olive oil for everything?" I wonder aloud.

"Absolutely. If it's good," Giuseppe tells us. "Good olive oil, meaning it is made from the olives grown here in Tuscany. When you eat olive oil, it nourishes your body. When you apply it topically, it soothes your skin. You need never use anything on your skin but olive oil, and if you ingest anything but this natural oil in cooking, I think you are insane."

I rattle off brands sold in the States. Giuseppe grandly dismisses them with a wave of his hand. "I would not put those oils in my car."

I name an expensive brand.

"I would not wash my feet with that!"

"Why?"

"Because the olives come from all over the place and are picked whenever it's convenient, not when nature dictates. Those brands take olives from Tunisia, for example, Greece, where the standards of pressing are not good, so the product is not pure. They mash everything and anything together. Stems! Leaves! Crap! They add colors to olive oils. Either green dye to make it look extra virgin, or gold to make it look standard. This is a black mark on our industry, but it happens all the time."

"How can you tell good olive oil from bad?" Iva Lou asks.

"Once you taste my oil, you cannot ingest another. The other oils taste like gasoline. You'll see. My family has made olive oil since nineteen thirty. I've been running the company for the past twenty years. To not be educated in this, I would have to be the village idiot. Let me show you."

We pile into Giuseppe's van to tour the farm where his olives are picked. As we drive along a long, dusty road, he points to the trees, small and spindly with a sprinkling of green leaves, many anchored to the ground by string. "I use the best pickers. Some have been doing this for fifty years. It takes a trained eye to know a good olive. They can feel if the olive is good as they pick it. I never have to check their work. They are more selective than me!" He laughs.

"I find *that* hard to believe, Big G," Iva Lou tells him, giving him a nickname now that she feels at home.

As Giuseppe explains the evolution of olive oil from tree to bottle, we are mesmerized. It really is a simple process, with three steps: growing, harvesting, and mashing. Etta is amazed that the pits, as well as the meat of the olive, are crushed to make the oil.

"I work in the only pure manufacturing business in the world. Nature does the work, I collect the gold." Giuseppe raises his hands in victory. "But I must be a soldier, watching every step without taking my eyes off it for a second! If I look away, maybe an imperfect olive makes its way into the tubs, or the storage drums are the wrong temperature, or God knows what could happen. I have to watch everything!"

"Now you taste." Giuseppe gives Jack three small pieces of unsalted bread, then pours three types of oil into small cups and sniffs the first before handing it to Jack. Giuseppe taps the side of his nose. "This, this is my la-bore-a-tory."

Jack sniffs the oil, then dips the bread into the cup and tastes it. "This one is spicy."

"Aha! Good taste buds. This oil is made from olives that have just begun to ripen. Full-bodied, yes?"

Jack nods and tastes the next oil sample. "This is . . . flowery."

"You are a genius! This oil is made from olives about to peak. We snatch them at the last possible moment." Giuseppe claps his hands together. "I may have to hire your husband."

Jack tastes the third sample. "This is very mild."

"Because the olives it comes from are very ripe! Now try this one." Giuseppe gives Jack a sample from an unmarked bottle. He tastes it and makes a face.

"What is wrong?" Giuseppe asks.

"I'm sorry. This is bad."

"Of course it is! Tell your wife! It is the brand she cooks with in the States! Terrible! I would not use this to—"

"Wash my feet!" Etta, Iva Lou, and I say in unison.

"There is a huge difference. Really, you cannot compare," Jack says to us.

As we pile back into our car, Giuseppe and Elaine wave from the steps of the factory. Iva Lou snaps a few pictures of them from the car. Elaine promises to ship a case of olive oil to Big Stone Gap. "We can be in Bergamo by sunset," Jack promises.

Etta puts her hand on my shoulder, and I reach back to take her hand. She is as happy as I am to return to Bergamo and Schilpario, to our Italian Alps. I grasp her hand tightly and look back at her. Etta loosens her grip first, but I continue to hold her hand, pulling it close to my face. We're both a little embarrassed; it reminds us of when Etta was little and we were close. Then she does something she hasn't done in years—she leans forward and rests her head on my seat. I think about what I have learned from my daughter over the years. She taught me that the stars, even when they seem to disappear, always return to their origins. And here we are, back to the place we came from, only one generation after my mother left to find her destiny in America. Who knew we would return so soon?

"There. Dad. Turn there." Etta leans between us into the front seat, pointing to the turn to Via Davide.

"You know where it is?" Jack can't believe she remembers.

"Third house on the left," Etta says confidently. "Black shutters. Lemon trees. There!"

"It's adorable." Iva Lou climbs out of the car. "How long's it been since you were here?"

"Seven years," I say.

"And it hasn't changed a bit!" Etta says excitedly, running up the familiar walkway with tiny purple flowers.

My cousin Federica peeks out the window (her brilliant red hair gives her away instantly) and shouts for Zia Meoli when she sees us coming up the walk. Federica greets us at the door. She is very pregnant, and luminous. Her red curls are cropped close to her head, and a three-year-old girl hovers around her knees. "Welcome home!" Federica throws her arms around me, remembers Jack, cannot believe how much Etta has grown, and is delighted when Iva Lou presents her with a gift of Outdoor Drama baseball caps from Big Stone Gap.

"This is Giuliana." Federica picks up her daughter to introduce us at eye level.

"She looks just like you!" I tell her.

"The hair, no?" Federica laughs and runs her fingers through Giuliana's thick curls.

"Ave Maria!" Zia Meoli stands in the entryway with her hands on her hips. She is older, her hair nearly white now, but her posture is still perfect and her energy as vital as ever. I give her a good long hug.

"Etta! Etta, you are all grown up! I can't believe it! *Bellisima!*"

Etta is thrilled to see her aunt, so happy she cries. Iva Lou fishes in her purse for a tissue. "Jesus, now you're gonna make *me* cry."

"How is Zio Pietro?" Jack wants to know.

"Come see him."

Zia Meoli leads us back through the house to the sun porch, through the familiar hallways that smell like lavender, past the old photographs in simple gold frames, through the sparkling kitchen with the white metal cabinets and the black and white harlequin floor. "Everything looks beautiful, the same," I tell my aunt, and then "Zio Pietro!"

My uncle sits in a wicker rocking chair with his hands folded in his lap. He opens his eyes when I call to him. At first he is overwhelmed by the sum of us, but he sees who we are and smiles broadly. "How are you?" I kneel down and embrace him.

Jack introduces Iva Lou, and Etta makes a big fuss over Zio Pietro, reminding him of how she learned to make boxes in his woodworking shop.

"I haven't made anything in a long time," he says.

"I could help you," Etta offers.

"Too much for me now. I am old," Zio Pietro says, and smiles.

"Hello, everyone." We hear a familiar voice in the doorway.

"Stefano Grassi!" Iva Lou throws her arms around our old friend.

"How are you, Miss Iva Lou?"

"How do I look?"

"Magnificent."

"Then that's how I am!"

"It is so good to see you all again," Stefano says graciously as he shakes Jack's hand and kisses me on the cheek.

"You remember Etta?" Iva Lou pushes Etta toward Stefano. Etta doesn't lurch; in fact, she is refined in her movements and extends her hand.

"Etta has grown up!" Stefano's eyes narrow and he looks at me, then to Jack and then back to Etta.

"Little Rose here has blossomed," Iva Lou says smugly.

The term "sparks fly" takes on new meaning as we stand with Stefano and Etta. He looks at Etta as though this is the first time he has ever seen her.

Etta is tall and lean, her light brown hair falls below her shoulders in waves, and her eyes are soft, tilting upward, the color of mossy green velvet. The only Italian element I can see in her face is the set of her mouth: her lips are full and her front teeth have a slight overbite, which gives her an endearing pout. Here in Italy, her Scottish-American coloring stands out.

"How have you been, Stefano?" Etta asks him, sounding grown up.

"Very well. Thank you."

Iva Lou nudges me as she notices how Etta smiles at Stefano. I look over at my husband. He too has not missed a beat of this. He puts his arm around Etta's shoulder.

"We're all so happy to see you again. We've planned a wonderful dinner in Città Alta," Stefano says.

"That will be wonderful," I say, speaking for the American contingent. Federica asks for a rain check. She will stay home with Zio Pietro, who is too tired to join us. We do our best to convince him to come, but he is stubborn, so we promise to bring him something from the restaurant. Zia Meoli joins us, and I'm very happy about that; we have so much to catch up on.

Stefano takes our group to Bergamo Alta (also known as Città Alta), the ancient town above the modern city (known as Bergamo Bassa), to a hillside restaurant with a view of the valley. Stefano is a delightful host, ordering such local delicacies as risotto with fresh truffles (it's the hunting season for them now) and costolette, veal cutlets coated in bread crumbs and pan-fried in butter. Etta fills Stefano in on all the news in Big Stone Gap, and Iva Lou, her loyal sidekick, adds the spicy details, while Jack laughs.

"Zia, how have you been?" I ask her.

"It's hard to get old."

"You're not old!"

"Eighty-three. And Zio Pietro is eighty-eight. We are old."

"You look terrific."

"I am doing well. I have shrunk a bit, though that's what happens to old bones. But Zio has had some problems with his heart, and his memory is not so good anymore."

"Does he go to the wood shop?"

"Not in several years. He likes Stefano to come by and talk to him about architecture and building. That was always his passion." Then Zia says with admiration, "Etta is a woman now, isn't she?"

"Almost. She looks so much older than she is."

"What are her interests?"

"Zia, she is a complex girl. She's sensible but headstrong. Sometimes that serves her well, and sometimes it causes problems."

"She is very different from you, isn't she?"

"Very."

"It's difficult to know what to do. We think our daughters will be just like us, or at least appreciate who we are. It wasn't really until Federica had her daughter that she realized that I wasn't crazy or old-fashioned. It took a long time." I sit back and exhale a long, deep sigh. Zia takes my hand. "It's difficult now, but eventually, you will be happy you have a daughter."

"Oh, I am happy I have her."

"No. What I mean is, a daughter will stay by the mother all of her life. A son is different. A son will leave you. Sons are easy until they are grown. But when they're grown, they're gone." She sighs.

"There's an old expression in America. 'A son is a son till he marries a wife; a daughter's a daughter the rest of her life.' "

"Exactly," Zia says, nodding.

We're staying the night on Via Davide. Papa is due to pick us up in the morning. Federica has prepared our rooms beautifully with all the details we remember—the embroidered sheets, the down comforters, the silver cups on the dresser filled with wild roses. Iva Lou is setting her hair in the bathroom down the hall, so I know Etta is alone, and I go into the room they're sharing. She is writing in her journal, which she closes gently when I enter.

"I'm not interrupting, am I?"

"No, come on in."

"That was fun tonight, wasn't it?"

"Yeah."

"What did you think?"

"Of what?"

"Stefano Grassi."

"He's the same, Ma."

"How so?"

"Well, he's very self-absorbed."

"Really." I'm taken aback. Where's my daughter who had a mad crush on the older Italian boy?

"Yeah. He talked about his work a lot, and where he's been. He spends a lot of time in Rimini, on the coast. He went on and on about the Adriatic Sea. Iva Lou asked him if he had a girlfriend, and he said, 'Several,' which I thought was cheesy."

"That *is* cheesy."

"He's got a big ego."

"He's young. He's Italian. No surprise there," I tell her.

Etta leans back on the pillows. "I think about things too much. I analyze stuff to death. I'm too critical."

"Sounds familiar," I tell her.

Etta smiles knowingly. If I've had fifteen years to observe

her, she's had the same fifteen to mirror me.

"I've always been that way. It's the one thing I wished I could change about myself. I admire people who can be light, and move through life like small birds, you know, landing, pecking a bit, and then flying off. Not getting too involved. Not caring too much."

Etta looks at me as though she understands exactly what I am saying. "You know when Stefano was leaving Big Stone Gap? And I got so upset?"

"I remember."

"I promised myself that I would never let any boy upset me like that ever again."

"How's that worked out?"

"Pretty well. I don't let myself get too wrapped up, Ma. I keep a distance. Boys are just too fickle, whether they're American or Italian."

Part of me is thrilled that my daughter is so poised and confident, that she has A Plan when it comes to boys. But another part of me worries that she will isolate herself, much as I did for so long. I don't want Etta to be repressed, as I was; that's part of my personal legacy that I hope she rejects. But there is something within the women of my line that spends too much time worrying about being worthy, and being strong in the face of love, and rejecting it to avoid the pain if it doesn't work out. Etta is only fifteen, too young for some of these concepts. And now that she is opening up to me, I want to encourage her to continue. I don't want to say the wrong thing.

I sit down on the foot of the bed. "You know what my mother always told me?" I ask.

"What?"

"That all the answers to all your questions are already inside of you. You just have to listen."

"Is that true?" Etta asks, putting her book aside.

"I think so."

"How do you learn to listen?"

"Well, that's something that comes with experience. And trusting yourself. At night, before I go to sleep, I think about what is troubling me. And then I ask myself to work it out while I sleep."

"And you wake up knowing the answer?"

"Sometimes. But I always wake up feeling as though I'm on the right track."

"That's interesting," Etta says as she braids the tip of a lock of hair.

"What do you see yourself doing, honey? After you leave Dad and me and go off in the world. How do you see yourself?"

"Well, I see myself working. I like cities, but I hope I'll live in a small one."

"You don't see yourself in Cracker's Neck Holler?"

"Maybe when I'm older."

"Do you see yourself married?"

"Ma." Etta's tone tells me not to go down this road.

"I was just wondering."

"Did you?" She turns the question on me.

I guess I'll be honest. "No."

"But you married Dad."

"And no one was more surprised than me. I guess that's what I'm trying to get at, Etta. Stay open to the big surprises, because I swear, they'll come."

"What are you two yammering about?" Iva Lou wants to know as she comes in. Her hair is rolled on curlers the size of orange-juice cans. "Oh, it's serious." She turns to go back out the door.

"No, no. We're done." As I stand to go, I ask Iva Lou, "Are you having a good time?"

"Do you have to ask? Look at me. I'm spillin' over with joy unabandoned. My pap used to say that, and I have no idea what it means exactly, but it sort of fits how I feel about It lee."

"We're happy you're here."

"I feel like family. I can't thank y'all enough."

As I go down the hall to my room, I hear Iva Lou squeal with delight, just as I did, when she lies down on the poufy cloud bed for the first time and sinks a good foot or two into the soft goose feathers. I stand in the hallway and listen to her and Etta laughing and realize that maybe my daughter did miss out on a big family life as an only child, but what she got instead was just as valuable. How many girls have an honorary aunt like Iva Lou? Sometimes what we don't get in life makes way for something even better.

"Where are my girls?" my father yells up the stairs at Via Davide in his rich Barbari baritone. Etta and I fly down the stairs into his arms.

"Does that include me, Mario da Schilpario?" Iva Lou says from the top of the stairs.

"Of course."

Papa is in good health, robust and youthful. He is wearing faded jeans (with pressed creases, of course) rolled about a half inch at the hem, with a beige cashmere V-neck sweater. His face hasn't aged much since his last visit to Big Stone Gap. The sharp angles of his jaw and cheekbones and thick arched black eyebrows are as pronounced as ever. I'm glad I was born when he was young, because now I have him in my middle years. The thought of this makes me wince. I hope I will be around when Etta needs me later in *her* life. "Where's Giacomina?"

"She's in Schilpario, preparing for your arrival."

"Couldn't take that mountain road I've been hearing about, eh?" Iva Lou teases.

"No, she doesn't mind the road."

"Mario da Schilpario, is that road as bad as these folks say? Should I be nervous?"

"Not with me as your coachman."

Iva Lou, Etta, and I ride with Papa, who has a thousand questions for Etta about school, her internship, and even Shoo the Cat. (We put Iva Lou in the front seat in case the winding roads get to be too much for her.) Jack Mac follows us in the van with the luggage. I offered to ride with him, but I think he'd like some time alone; he has been surrounded by women since the start of the trip. It's times like these that I think of my son—he should be here for his father, who was so proud of him; no matter where we go or what we do, Joe is always missing. When I look back and see Jack following close behind, I feel sad for him.

"Should I have ridden with Dad?" Etta asks me. I think she's reading my mind.

"He looks like he's okay."

"Are you thinking about Joe?"

"Always."

"Me too."

I wonder what life would be like if my son were here. Or what life would have been like with more children. We tried, but it didn't happen. I took it as a sign not to push things, to enjoy Etta, to focus on her. I wonder what she wishes; surely she hoped to have sisters or brothers. I was an only child and used to imagine a house full of siblings and what joy that must be. Jack was an only child too, but he looked at it differently.

He liked being alone and loved having the attention of both of his parents. Jack still can't speak of his father without getting emotional. They were very close, and Jack has told me he would never change that.

"Whenever I'm really happy, I think of Joe and feel bad he's not here," Etta says to me softly.

"Me too," I tell her, knowing that I shouldn't encourage that kind of guilt. "He would want you to be happy, Etta."

"I know."

"Remember the day of the big snowstorm?"

"The one where we made ice cream?" Etta asks.

"The very one," I tell her.

"It was so cool. You and Joe and me got all bundled up and went out into the woods with a bucket and lifted clean snow off the branches. Joe and I were so little, you had to do it all. And then we went back inside, and you took sugar and cream and stirred it into the clean snow. It tasted so good."

"That was a great day, wasn't it?"

Etta doesn't answer me. She looks out the window, still remembering. Sometimes I forget she was there through the whole ordeal, and think I'm the only person who lost Joe. Maybe that's because I'm the mother and he was born of me. But it's really not true; Etta lost her brother and Jack lost his son, and there isn't one of us who will ever be the same. No matter where we go, we are always looking for him, whether it's on a curvy alpine road or in the field behind our house in Cracker's Neck Holler.

Iva Lou makes sounds I have never before heard from her as Papa takes the sharp curves, then speeds up on the straightaways, then decelerates around dark corners, only to emerge speeding higher and higher up the alpine road. "Does anyone ever go over?" Iva Lou asks Papa, gripping the handle on the dashboard like the hand of God.

"Not often."

"How often is not often?"

"Every few years or so." Papa smiles, keeping his eyes on the road. "You make your living as a driver of the Bookmobile, no?"

"Uh-huh," Iva Lou squeaks.

"You know that nothing can go wrong when you know your road."

"Whatever you say, Mario," she replies weakly.

"Papa, pull over so Iva Lou can look down," I say.

"I don't want to look down," Iva Lou insists, her eyes shut.

"It's really cool, Aunt Iva Lou," Etta tells her.

Papa pulls over at a roadside viewing spot, and Jack follows suit. Iva Lou takes deep breaths while Etta coaxes her out of the car.

"Come. Over here," Papa orders. "Is this spectacular? Lago d'Iseo!"

"Lordy, now, that's deep." After taking a peek, Iva Lou turns back for the car.

"Iva Lou, you shouldn't miss this. Look," I tell her gently.

Lago d'Iseo has all the elements of a perfectly imagined place: a thin, milky mist and pink morning light and the movement of the wind that is almost musical as it brushes over us. The air is full of the scent of sweet grapes, growing over simple arches of wood down a never-ending footpath connected by small bridges. The bridge swings out over a mighty waterfall, which pours off the mountaintop so loudly that we must shout to hear one another. The waterfall begins somewhere high in the hills in giant white waves and cascades down the mountainside like silver streamers, falling into a pristine sapphire-blue lake below. The far side of the mountain has a steep crag that is filled with rock formations protruding from the ground in a series of shivering stone fingers that reaches to the sky.

"What are those, Papa?" I ask, pointing to the rock formations.

"We call it the Forest of the Fairies. They're a mystery. A natural wonder. No one knows how they got here."

"Must've been magic. How would anything get here? This high. Or that low," Iva Lou wonders aloud.

"Worth the ride?" Papa asks her.

"Definitely."

We make the turn to enter Schilpario, and Papa takes us through the old town, down the twisting main street, through a series of connected white stucco houses with dark brown alpine beams and shuttered windows. Papa gently taps the horn, driving slowly as the pedestrians move single file to one side of the narrow cobblestone street. When we emerge out into the sun, the familiar town square comes to life, the waterwheel spins grandly, a woman waters her garden patch of snow-white edelweiss, and several girls around Etta's age come from the bakery with long loaves of twisted bread, making their way up the mountain toward home.

At Via Scalina Number 5, Giacomina meets us on the front porch. "Welcome!" she says, with her arms open wide. Giacomina wears a straight navy blue skirt and a pale blue sweater set, and her reading glasses dangle on a pearl string around her neck. She has lovely classic features.

Nonna joins Giacomina from behind, pushing her aside a bit. "Ave Maria!" my grandmother announces at a volume normally reserved for football coaches. Nonna doesn't age. Perhaps with Papa's marriage to Giacomina, she has something to fight against, and that has given her a new lease on life.

"Etta!"

We turn around to the road to see who could possibly be shouting so enthusiastically at our daughter. It's her cousin Chiara, who is jumping up and down at the sight of her pen pal.

"Chiara!" Etta shouts back.

The two girls run toward each other and embrace, but the word "girls" no longer applies to these two. Chiara is an eighteen-year-old woman. Her black hair is full and wavy, and her once gangly legs are now long and womanly. She has found her style in a long linen skirt and an embroidered white peasant blouse tucked in and accented by a wide belt. Her espadrille sandals are tied up her ankles Roman-style, and her gold hoop earrings give the whole look a touch of Spain. To say that Chiara has turned into a beauty is to underestimate the whole process—she is a knockout. After Chiara greets Jack and me, Etta introduces her to Iva Lou, who takes an instant liking to the brunette bombshell, perhaps recognizing an alpine Iva Lou in the making. Chiara's English is excellent. She attends the university in Bergamo, where she is studying journalism, with the goal of becoming an international correspondent.

Jack and I take the room that Etta and I shared. Just being in this room again fills me with a sense of belonging and security. I feel it is *my* room in my father's house, and somehow Giacomina understands how important that is to me. She has placed Etta next door in a lovely single room with a daybed and a small desk. Giacomina has papered the room in a print of small daisies; I feel as though I'm inside a candy box.

Iva Lou is given the suite, which has a fireplace and a window seat that faces the road leading off Via Scalina and up into the Alps. Giacomina even left a pair of binoculars on Iva Lou's dresser, so she can look at the stars or up to the top of the mountain peaks.

After a hearty lunch of pansoti—delicate folds of pasta filled with ricotta cheese in a sauce of olive oil and pine nuts—crusty bread, and a plummy, rich Dolcetto wine, we all part ways for various side trips. I convince Iva Lou and Jack to go on a hike with me. Iva Lou takes to the mountain paths like a goat; after all, she was raised in the Blue Ridge Mountains. She stops occasionally to drink in the wonder of what she is seeing. "Picture books just don't do this justice." She sits down on a rock and swigs water from her shoulder carrier (which matches her overalls and pale blue kerchief).

"Isn't it amazing how close together everything in Italy is?" I wonder aloud.

"Perfect place to vacation because you can take in so many different places," Jack adds. "I'm going to wander ahead. You girls take your rest."

"Don't get lost!" I shout after him.

"I'm just gonna follow the sound of the water, honey," he

shouts back, disappearing up the path.

"I know you told me about this place, and you showed me the pictures you took, but I really can't believe it." Iva Lou rolls up her pants to get some sun on her legs. "How can a place have a hot sun and cool breezes at the same time?"

"I don't know."

"Where's that field of bluebells?" Iva Lou whispers.

The famous field of bluebells where I took Pete Rutledge and almost broke my wedding vows. That day could have changed my life forever if I had let it. That field is my place of secrets, and I'm not too anxious to share it with anyone, even Iva Lou.

"It's in the other direction," I tell her. I think Iva Lou gets the point and doesn't press me.

"How does it feel to be at the ole Eye-talian homestead?"

"When I come here, I never want to leave."

"I can understand that. And how about that waiting on you hand and foot? Now I know what it feels like to be a princess. This Eye-talian hospitality is no joke. It puts the southern brand to shame."

"They care about details, you know?"

"No kidding. Giacomina even left me a fresh nightgown in the bureau. I mean, come on. That's thinking ahead! Your nonna is a pistol, though."

"Poor Giacomina. I don't know how she puts up with it."

"Well, ole Grandma was part of a package deal."

"I couldn't do it."

"Me neither. Why do you think I married a man ten years older than me? I was looking for an orphan. I did not need to be forty-plus and dealing with a mother-in-law."

"I'm sure Lyle feels the same."

"Nah, he would've loved my mama. But my daddy, now, that would have been a different story. Lyle doesn't like anyone who shirks responsibility. And my daddy was the all-time shirker. I've been thinking about ole Pap a lot lately. About how he left us. Why he left us. How that formed me. Maybe spending time with your daddy got me to thinking about it. I don't know."

"What was your dad's name?"

"Jessie Creed Wade. I said if I ever had a son, I'd name him Jessie. I guess I wanted to replace my dad all my life."

"I like that name. It's strong."

"He was Scotch-Irish and French-Indian."

"I guess that's where you got your cheekbones."

"That's what Mama used to say. That and my temper."

"What was he like?"

"I remember him being nervous. Skittish almost, around us, like family life was too much for him. You know, a lot of folks have bad nerves when it comes to raising children, and he certainly was one of them. And he'd get sad when he had to leave us. You know, when there was no work, he'd head north to Michigan to work in the factories. And then one time he left, and by God it was a good eight years 'fore we saw him again. Mama was devastated, kept trying to find him, and eventually, you know, she tracked him down. Somehow he always made his way up north. Mama would complain that he didn't love us. But I always looked at it differently. I thought he loved us so much it was painful for him. He didn't come from a happy home, and he didn't know how to make one. Skeered him to death, I think."

"You don't sound very angry."

"I never was. Mama didn't like that neither. She thought I should hold him accountable, I guess. But I understood the man, even as a youngin I just understood him. I knew what he was made of, and I didn't expect anything more from him. And then, of course, you know, I've known me some men, and it's held me in good stead never to expect too much."

"So when Lyle comes through and is there for you . . ."

"I'm surprised. And happy to be surprised, by the way. No, Lyle Makin is a shocker. I can't believe how well he handled my cancer, or how he stuck by me when I'd get that fidgety wandering feeling in my bones, my wantin' to be alone a lot. I guess I'm just like my daddy. I want to move, find the action."

"You're a mountain girl who longs for the ocean."

"I guess I am. I can't believe I'm here. Me. The Wade girl from Appalachia. I'm in the Eye-talian Alps. And how, I ask myself? How did this happen to me? Number one in her steno class, president of the Lucky Leafs Library Club. And now a goddamn world traveler. What a life."

As Iva Lou and I follow the trail after Jack, we don't say much. I'm thinking about my father, Mario, and the man who raised me, Fred Mulligan, and my mother, who loved Mario until the day she died but served Fred until the day *he* died. I thought as I grew older that my parents would become less of a focal point for me, that my child would take precedence. And I do put Etta first in all my decisions, but it is also true that I have never really resolved how I was parented or let go of my sadness that my mother revealed the secret of my real father only after her death. I often wonder if my life would have been different without the shame of that secret. Would I have been more daring? Would I have stayed in Big Stone Gap? Once a woman falls in love, her vista changes. She becomes a helpmate, an organizer, and leaves behind her solitary existence. Men seem to control their destinies. Didn't Iva Lou's father walk away when, for whatever reason, family life was too much for him? Fred Mulligan, who raised me but never really embraced me— didn't he find a way to carve out his solitude even with a family to support? And Mario da Schilpario, his whole life a testament to his choices and not his obligations? I never like to say it's a man's world, but it often seems like it is, and it will be for my daughter. And I know, as surely as I pick up these loose rocks on this path and toss them into the woods, that my own daughter will feel an obligation to take care of me in my old age. I don't know that my son, had he survived, would have done the same. He would be off pursuing his life. The daily care of his old parents would be woman's work. And I know that no matter how I would have raised him, sensitivities and all, his selfhood would have won out over any responsibility he would feel toward me.

"Girls, this way!" Jack Mac shouts from a distance. Iva Lou points toward the sound of his voice, and I follow her up the path.

"What's all the noise about?" I ask as we reach my husband's side.

"I'll be damned. Peacocks. A slew of them," Iva Lou whispers.

"Watch." Jack whistles, and the sound makes the peacocks scatter, leaving the safety of their group to create individual spaces in the field where they strut solo. Suddenly, making a big flapping sound, we see the first of the peacocks' fans unveiled. The peacock stops, poises his neck, and spreads his glorious feathers, a mix of bright turquoise and pure white plumes that open wide, revealing tips of burnished orange and horizontal stripes of polished black. Each feather has a circle in the center of its design that shimmers like the horn of a seashell.

"You know, the peacock is the symbol of eternal life," I whisper to Iva Lou.

She doesn't say anything, just watches the spectacle like a little girl, not missing one detail of the show and in awe of every movement, as though it were choreographed just for her.

"You know, this is Italy," I tell her. "There's always something around the corner that you weren't expecting."

Etta and Chiara go into the old town for *La Passeggiatta*, the traditional after-dinner stroll, while Jack, Iva Lou, Giacomina, Papa, and I sit in the front yard and eat fresh berries from the bushes behind the house.

"I must show you the pictures of Pete and Gina from when they came to visit last year." Giacomina gets up and goes inside.

"Have you met Pete's wife?" Papa asks us.

"No, we haven't. They were supposed to hike through Big Stone but postponed it," Jack tells him.

"We had a good time with them."

Giacomina returns with a pack of pictures and shows them to us.

"That's Gina." Mario points to the petite woman with a chic blond haircut. She wears sunglasses and smiles in the picture. Good teeth. Lots of them. Long. Narrow. White. Pete looks, well, Pete looks gorgeous.

"Well, that is a fine-looking man," Iva Lou says, studying a photo. "And woman too," she adds quickly, looking at me.

I'd like to stand up and say, "This is all too weird," but I don't. I just smile and look at the pictures with everyone else. I'm crazy about my husband, but the truth is, when I look at Gina in these pictures, I envy her a little. She got the guy who talks poetry and is as sensual as he is intelligent.

"We have a gift for you," my father tells Jack and me.

"Papa, you've done enough," I say.

"No, this is one that's just for the two of you." Papa hands me an envelope. "My cousin Battista helped with this one."

I open the envelope. There is a single card trimmed in gold, written in Italian, inviting Jack and me to two nights at the Villa d'Este on Lake Como.

"Battista Barbari is one of the managers of the hotel. He is your second cousin, and when he visited us last month, he wanted to meet you. So, this came in the mail. You really should not miss it." My father rarely endorses something this strongly.

"When should we go?"

"Tomorrow. You can drive. It will take you about an hour and a half. You have to go down the mountain and then north a bit until you get to Cernobbio."

"What about Iva Lou and Etta?" I turn to her.

"Honey, I have a list as long as my arm of stuff I want to do around here. You and ole Jack Mac could use a set-down in a romantic setting."

Giacomina pats Iva Lou on the back and looks at me. "Don't worry. I will take good care of Iva Lou. Your father and I will take her to Bormio to the spa for a facial and a steam, and then we'll shop in Clusone. She won't even miss you! And don't worry about Etta. Chiara will keep her busy for the entire visit."

Laughter coming from the kitchen rouses me in my royal bed on the second floor of Via Scalina. I wake up happy, as this is the day Jack and I depart for the Villa d'Este.

The aroma of rich coffee and sweet steamed milk greets me at the door of the dining room. Everyone is around the table, talking, enjoying crusty bread with soft butter and raspberry jam.

"Stefano!" I'm surprised to see him.

"He missed us, Ma." Etta laughs.

"I thought you could use a tour guide." Stefano smiles at me.

"Jack and I are off to the Villa d'Este today."

"He knows already, Ma. Dad told him all about it."

"We're making big plans while y'all are gone. Stefano here is gonna take us all up through these hills," Iva Lou assures me.

Jack rushes me to pack a small bag to take on our trip. Iva Lou follows me upstairs to help.

"Iva Lou . . ."

"Honey-o, you don't even have to say it. I will watch Etta like a hawk watches raw hamburger. Don't you worry."

"Thank you. I really appreciate it."

"Ole Stefano has that look in his eye. Well, the look might be in his eye, but his entire body is electrified with possibilities, if you know what I mean." Iva Lou takes one look at my face and knows I'm concerned. "Now, don't worry. If there ever was a chaperone who knows the wily and secretive ways of men, it is yours truly. I'll keep 'em apart, and just friends, I promise!"

The Iva Lou plan is in place, but I don't hedge my bets. I pull Papa and Giacomina aside and tell them to please watch Etta while I'm gone. I know Etta has a good head on her shoulders, but even I was tempted by romance in these Alps. This is a place made for love, and my daughter is young. Even though she *says* she's not interested in Stefano, she might become enchanted under the right circumstances. Giacomina understands more than Papa, who you'd think would have instant insight into this but does not. He knows Stefano is a good guy and doesn't believe that he would try anything. "It's not just Stefano I'm worried about," I tell Papa. This, finally, he understands.

The gates to the Villa d'Este are so impressive, I feel I should be in a glass carriage and wearing a tiara to enter. The guard, with his long, serious face, checks a clipboard for our names. When he finds them, he grins broadly and waves us in. I order Jack to drive slowly, as I don't want to miss a detail of this entrance that looks like the start of a winding road in a fairy tale, with its perfectly manicured bushes, beds of red satin begonias, trees plumed with open cups of white magnolia, and a family crest carved into the hillside in flowers. The gardens are the least of the beauty, though. There is a low walkway with a rococo handrail along Lake Como, which might very well be made of midnight-blue lapis and not water, as it glitters so brilliantly in the sun.

As in all fairy tales, the road leads to a castle, known on this lake as the Cardinal's Palace. The Queen's Pavilion, a burnt-umber-faced villa with a boat launch at its base, faces the main building, where Battista has booked us. Jack says nothing, as he has never seen anything like this either. Only the most glamorous and elegantly dressed, coiffed, and perfumed belong here. No wonder Ava Gardner and Frank Sinatra honeymooned here; Caroline of Brunswick, Princess of Wales, was kept in exile here; Clark Gable roamed these grounds; and Ginger Rogers swam in the pool that floats on the lake. This is heavenly, and stars belong here. Jack and me? We'll do our best not to gape our two days away in awe of all we see.

"I am so happy that you decided to come," Battista, my cousin who looks like an elegant duke, says as he leads us to our room. We banter in Italian, and Jack turns and looks at the architecture. The high ceilings are shades of yellow, and the marble staircases with their flecks of silver reflect light in every direction. Battista takes a large key from an envelope (even the key has a tassel on it) and opens Room 218, a suite with a view of the lake. He opens the windows and lets the lake breeze play through the draperies, which are boldly striped in shades of dusky blue. The living room has a gray velvet couch and blue-and-gray-striped chairs; there is a bowl of fresh yellow roses on the glass-topped table. The bedroom is set off by more draperies and boasts a walk-in closet, and French doors lead out to our own private balcony overlooking the lake. Battista can see that I am overwhelmed. "But you haven't eaten a meal here yet. The cuisine is what we are famous for!"

He leaves us to our unpacking. Jack and I keep looking at each other as though we have landed on another planet.

"We only have two days!" I wail. "Let's stay right here on the lake and see everything we can."

As soon as we have unpacked and made plans for the morning, like visiting the statuary and going to the floating pool, we want to start for the lake. But before we get out the door, Jack turns to me and sweeps me into his arms and kisses me like the first time he ever kissed me in Iva Lou's trailer park so long ago. He takes the camera out of my hands and the sunglasses off my face and we tumble onto the bed. As we make love, I can hear the gentle waves of the lake and smell the jasmine that coils around the balcony. I feel young again, utterly connected to Jack, not just by our vows but in this moment. My husband, I know, feels the same. He looks at me and understands what I am thinking (one of the pluses, or minuses, of being married for so long). We laugh at our urgency and our passion—where is *this* coming from? I learn something very important today: environment matters! When a country girl is in a castle, she behaves like a princess and expects as much from her man.

There is a formal dinner dance each evening on the veranda. Thank God I brought my mother's vintage dress, a simple pale blue silk off-the-shoulder sheath with a ballerina-length skirt. Jack looks handsome in his navy suit and red tie. Battista promises something special tonight, and we can't wait to see what awaits us. (Fine dining and cuisine has become a theme in our family; in New York it was Max, in Florence, Renzo, and now the Villa d'Este!)

The waiter seats us at the water's edge and tells us that Battista has ordered for us. As soon as our drinks arrive, Jack points out over the lake. "Look, Ave!" By the Queen's Pavilion, two hot-air balloons, one with the face of the moon and the other with the sun, float over us, with two trapeze artists twirling from their baskets. The dinner guests erupt into applause, and I hear a woman at the next table tell her husband that this night is called "A Midsummer Night's Party." No wonder Papa wanted us to come right away. We won't have to dream tonight—what could be more fantastic than this?

Later, as Jack and I prepare for bed, we keep looking up at each other and laughing. This tops our honeymoon, or maybe we're just old enough to appreciate a night like this, to savor it.

"You know what I love about you?" Jack wraps his arms around me as we lie in bed. I am studying the trompe l'oeil doors on the closet, depicting a scene of a picnic on Lake Como.

"What?"

"You have a sense of wonder."

"Who wouldn't have a sense of wonder in a place like this?"

"I know lots of people who wouldn't." He pulls me closer still. "You know I never loved anyone like I love you."

I don't know what to say. My husband never talks like this. Well, not until recently, anyway; maybe it was the champagne. Or the Courvoisier after dinner. I don't care. I like it. And frankly, I'm going to pump him for more. "Why's that?" I ask demurely.

"I just never have, and I don't think I ever will." Jack kisses me good night and turns over. The soft warm breeze off the lake and the smell of gardenias take me back seven years to the summer in Schilpario when I left Jack to bring Etta to Italy. I think of him alone, back home, and his friendship with Karen Bell. It seems long ago, almost as though it happened to someone else. Instead of yanking at the picks in the fabric of our past, I leave it alone. We survived our problems, I remind myself. Love or something else saved us. Maybe it was just the timing, but we made it through. I know I was meant to take care of my husband, and I've seen him grow contented with our life together. I must remember to always be tender with him, because he always has been with me. I cover my husband with the duvet, centering the embroidered crest on his backside like a label. This makes me giggle.

"What's funny?"

"Honey, you have a royal ass. You are actually stamped and certified."

Jack and I want never to leave the Villa d'Este, but we also can't wait to go back to Schilpario to tell everyone what we saw. We decide to tour the quaint village of Cernobbio on the way back and to have lunch in Bellagio, which we saw from our boat tour of Lake Como. Our captain, Sergio, would speed down the center of the lake until he saw the home of a celebrity, and then he would turn off the motor and tell us about the owner as we bobbed on the water. The homes often matched their owners. The house of Fiorucci (the madcap shoe designer) was lime green with forest-green shutters; Catherine Deneuve (the regal French film star), a tasteful three-story beige villa with brown shutters; the Versace family (fashion designers), an old Hollywood-style white castle trimmed in gold and black. At the Ratti silk outlet, I buy six yards of silk wool in a multicolor bouclé to have a coat made for Etta. I hope she likes it. My mother would swoon at the quality of this fabric. Jack picks up some wine and cheese in Saronno on our drive back. I call ahead and tell Papa that we won't make it for dinner, we'll probably roll in around midnight.

There is a single lamp on in the front window at Papa's house when we pull into the driveway. We load ourselves down with the parcels so we only have to make one trip and enter the house through the garage. I take the perishables to the kitchen.

"What's that racket?" Jack asks as he drops a bag on the table.

"What racket?"

"That." Jack points to the street. We go to the window. Four figures come down the narrow street singing. And it's a song we know. It's the theme of the Outdoor Drama, "The Trail of the Lonesome Pine."

"Jesus, it's Iva Lou. She's drunk," I tell Jack as he follows me to the door.

The volume of the singing escalates. "Etta?" Jack asks, obviously hoping it's not her.

"Daaaa-dee," she says, one arm slung over pie-eyed Iva Lou and the other over Chiara, whose mascara has smeared into two black triangles under her eyes. A man, holding Iva Lou upright, emerges from the shadows.

"Stefano? Is that you?"

"Yes ma'am."

"What is going on here?" I sound like everyone's mother now, including Iva Lou's.

"We went to the disco up there!" Iva Lou points to the hill above us and attempts to do a couple of dance moves that look slightly dangerous. Jack stops her before she topples over.

"And had bell-eeeeee-knees." Etta throws her head back and laughs. My daughter is dead drunk.

"Get in the house," I say sternly; even in her inebriated state, Etta can tell I mean business. "Now."

Jack helps Etta and Iva Lou into the house. Chiara, also tipsy, follows. "You stay here tonight, Chiara," I tell her.

"*Va bene,*" she says. Evidently, she loses her ability to speak English when she's wasted.

"Bye-bye, Stefano!" The trio of lushes waves good night to him as Jack pushes them through the door.

"Are you drunk too?" I turn and face Stefano.

"No."

"How could you let this happen?"

"I didn't think—"

"No, you didn't think. Etta is only fifteen years old."

"I know how old she is, Mrs. Mac," he says evenly.

"Then you know that she's too young to be at a club drinking."

"I understand." He turns to get into his car. "I'm sorry."

*

Iva Lou is snoring by the time I check on her. Chiara is facedown and sound asleep on the trundle in Etta's room. Etta is throwing up in the bathroom, and I decide it's better for her long-term health to let her father hold her head while she hurls, as I might kill her.

"She washed her face and got into bed," Jack reports when he comes to our room.

"Do you believe this?"

"She's a teenager."

"Jack, she was drinking!"

"We let her drink wine on this trip."

"This is different. This is going-out-partying drinking!"

"We're on vacation."

"That is no excuse."

"Iva Lou was a wreck too."

"Iva Lou can get drunk. She's over twenty . . . *fifty*-one!" I bellow.

"What happened to Stefano?"

"He went home. I yelled at him."

"Iva Lou gave me the whole story before she passed out."

"Didn't you see how he looked at Etta down in Bergamo? She's a pretty young thing, and he's Italian and he was giving her That Look. I don't like it."

"Honey, I think we'll all be better off if we don't make a big deal out of it. Okay?"

"She should be punished!"

"And ruin the vacation?" Jack says sensibly.

"Here we go again. Mr. Loose, Mr. Let Her Do What She Wants, thinks all of this is just fine, a natural part of growing up. 'Go on back to the still and git you some hooch!' Well, I don't go for it. I never came home drunk, and I don't want a daughter who is underage and drinks. Call me a fanatic, call me too strict, I don't like it!"

"Ave, I can't do this tonight. I'm beat. Can we table this till the morning?" Jack sounds genuinely weary. Besides, I don't want my yelling to wake Nonna, Papa, and Giacomina, so I let it go for now.

This is a recurring pattern, I think, as I lie down in bed with my husband: he goes right off to sleep, and I spend my time stewing. There is a pattern with Etta too. We have a coast period when we get along great and she follows the rules, and then suddenly, she does something completely out of character and ruins whatever good behavior points she has built up. I am speaking of her as a prisoner, and I know it. I'm not proud of that. But I don't know how else to mother her. When I'm lenient, she takes advantage, and when I press the discipline, she sulks. She knows she is not to drink, and she knows that wine with dinner is not the same thing as champagne cocktails while partying. No, she figured we wouldn't be back tonight, and she was going to test the rules. And what a chaperone Iva Lou turned out to be. What was she thinking?

Jack, Giacomina, Papa, and I are the only ones at breakfast. Not much is said as Papa reads the paper, and the cuckoo clock behind him ticks loudly. Jack and I drink our caffe lattes and Giacomina fills the sugar bowl. We look at one another when we hear the Less Than Holy Trinity come down the stairs.

"Keep your cool," Jack says to me quietly.

Iva Lou, in sunglasses, Chiara, looking far younger than eighteen with her disco war paint washed off, and Etta, still a bit green, sit down quietly at the table.

"Well, y'all look like a pack of river rats," Jack says as he surveys the damage of the night before.

"Don't rub it in," Iva Lou says.

I can contain myself no longer. "What happened last night?" Giacomina offers the girls bread, and in unison they slowly shake their heads. Instead of the usual large mugs of steaming milk, Giacomina serves them espresso, black, in tiny cups (good hangover cure).

"We was dancin' at the club. And we all started with OJ and ice. Right, girls?" They nod in agreement. "And then we thought we'd try the bitters, 'cause I ain't never had bitters. So we chugged them back. And then there were these broad-shouldered alpine hunks at the next table, and they bought us a round of drinks. Now, Stefano put out a warning that maybe we shouldn't take the offer, but I figgered why not. So you see, all of this is my fault." Iva Lou adjusts her sunglasses and continues, "Well, I tasted the bellini first, and it was delicious. I told Etta she could have a sip. And the rest is, well, the rest is a hangover."

"Etta?" I look at my daughter, who looks contrite, but that could be due to the fact that she's on the verge of vomiting.

"I'm sorry," she says softly.

Jack nudges me under the table.

"Apology accepted," I say in a tone that implies it's not. "Let's not ruin the rest of our trip."

☆

The remainder of our vacation goes smoothly (Iva Lou became a teetotaler after Bellini Night). We make our way through the Milan airport, hauling more bags than we brought (boy, did we shop). When we reach the gate, Etta asks if she can go and buy magazines. There's a bit of a line to check in, so I let her.

"Mrs. Mac?" I hear from behind me.

"Stefano! What are you doing here?" Jack and Iva Lou greet him.

"I wanted to apologize again for the disco," he begins.

"It's all been settled," Jack tells him politely.

Stefano looks around; he must be wondering where Etta is. "Etta went for magazines," I tell him.

"Could you give her this for me?" He gives me a small parcel.

"What is it?"

"A lens for her telescope. This one is high-definition."

"I'm sure she'll love it. Thank you."

Etta rejoins us in the line and lights up to see Stefano.

"Stefano brought you a present," Iva Lou announces.

Etta rips into the package and pulls out a small lens. "Thank you." She looks up at Stefano, and there's that heat again. "I can't wait to try it out!" I thank God when they announce that it is time to board. Jack looks relieved too. Maybe now he sees what I see.

"Good-bye, Stefano." I give him a hug, and Iva Lou and Jack Mac say their farewells. The three of us turn away, though I nudge Iva Lou to keep watching. She leans down to pick up one of her carry-ons and whispers, "Kiss on the cheek. That's all."

*

Iva Lou eats everything the flight attendants offer on the trip home, including the mixed nuts (hers and mine). "I was too excited on the way over," she says, apologizing.

"No, no, eat."

"It-lee triggered my appetite. For food. For shoes. For jewelry. And Lyle Makin better watch it. My sex drive increased in the land of love."

"I'm sure he'll be thrilled about that. And, of course, the crocodile loafers you bought him."

Jack Mac stands and stretches in the aisle. He is sitting with Etta, who is reading a novel in Italian. Jack motions for me to meet him in the back of the plane, and when I do, he says, "Okay, she's suffered enough."

"Jack, I am not torturing her."

"You've hardly talked to her since the incident."

"I have a problem with teenage drinking, okay?"

"Ave, it wasn't a typical thing. She's on vacation in a foreign country, with *your* girlfriend, her cousin, and a young man I respect. It got out of hand, she told you how. She drank bellinis and—"

"I'm not interested in the 'how' of all of this. I only know that she got drunk. If we act like it's okay, you're going to find her on High Knob with the Alsup brothers drinking Night Train."

Jack laughs.

"I don't think it's funny."

"You know what? I am sick and tired of being the referee in my own family. You put me in the middle, and I don't want to be there. You work it out with your daughter however you want to. I'm out of it." Jack turns to walk up the aisle.

"I'll talk to her," I say.

"Good. I told Iva Lou I'd help her with her customs form, anyway."

We go back up the aisle and Jack sits with Iva Lou, while I take his seat next to Etta.

"Etta?"

"Yeah?" She answers without taking her eyes off the book.

"I'd like to talk to you."

"I really don't want to talk right now."

I look over at Jack, who is chatting with Iva Lou. He completely set me up. Etta is furious at *me*, probably more angry than I am at *her*.

"I don't want to end our vacation not speaking to each other."

"Too late for that."

"Wait a second. You're the fifteen-year-old who came home drunk."

"How many times a day are you going to remind me how old I am or that I drank too much at that stupid disco?"

"Till it sinks in that you're not twenty-one."

"I'm well aware that I'm your prisoner till I go to college."

"I resent that."

"I resent that you treat me like I'm a kid."

"You *are* a kid. You're my kid. And I don't want a daughter who drinks when she's underage."

"You're forever judging people." Etta turns and looks out the window.

"If you mean you, yes, I am judging you. That's my job. I don't like to be your warden. But you scared me. You did something that makes me think you don't understand the consequences of your behavior."

"You're old-fashioned. You don't get it."

She's got me there. I am old-fashioned (emphasis on the "old"). Most of the kids her age have mothers in their early thirties. I have two decades on them, so I am coming at things from a different perspective. And I know I'm alienating my daughter. She's not really *bad*. She's no Pavis Mullins, who spent more time in the county jail than he did in his mother's house. Why do I treat her this way? Why do I treat her like Fred Mulligan treated me? The thought of this makes me cry.

"Ma, please."

"Oh, Etta."

"What?"

"You have to try and understand: part of my nature is that I try too hard. I'm afraid for you. And I express myself in ways that hurt you, and I don't mean to do that. You're plenty mature. Usually you do just great with everything. But it seems like whenever we have a good run for a while, something like this happens and ruins it."

"Was your mother like this?"

"My father."

"Grandpa?"

"Fred."

I haven't told her much about Fred Mulligan. I felt I resolved almost all of that, but I can see by my actions that I haven't, really. On some level, the man I first knew as my father was a consistent parent. He controlled me, and I behaved. I hadn't realized that I have subconsciously taken that path with my own daughter because I know it works.

"You have a great future ahead of you. I don't want you to

compromise that with some dumb choice, like drinking, that you'd look back on and regret. That's all."

"I've told you I'm sorry. I meant it, Mom."

"I believe you."

"You're mad at me all the time."

"I don't like being mad at you."

Etta goes back to her book. I should feel that our situation is better. She has promised not to drink again, but I can't promise I will ever be the mother she might wish I were. Jack looks over at me. Iva Lou had plenty to declare, but they've run out of things to do. I motion that he can come back to his seat. He looks at me as if to ask, *How did it go?* I give him a peppy thumbs-up. But I feel far from a thumbs-up. I wonder how I'm going to get through the next three years. And then there's four years of college, worrying about Etta from afar. This motherhood thing just doesn't get any easier.

The timing of the United Methodist Church's "First Call for Fall" Covered Dish Supper is coming on a good night. Our vacation photos are back from Kingsport and everybody in town wants to see them, so I figure I'll just haul a bagful over to the church basement and form an assembly line.

Fleeta has whipped up five pounds of Swedish meatballs in a jumbo baking pan, which will be our contribution (that and a case of Coca-Cola, which is standard to-bring fare at a potluck when you come in a party of three or more).

"Hi, Mom." Etta and Tara come into the Pharmacy. Etta shows me a pack of gum from the display case and tears into it, handing Tara a piece. "Hi, Mrs. MacChesney."

"You girls look great. What's going on?"

"I got a perm." Tara twirls to show me her curly hair. "Ethel Bartee said you're only supposed to git one perm every six to eight months, but mine fell out, so she bent her rule and give me another one."

"Thank God. We can't have our lead flag girl with a flat head of hair."

"That's what I told her," Tara says soberly.

"Is Dad going to the church supper?" Etta asks.

"He's meeting us there."

"Can Trevor come with us?" Tara asks softly.

"Cute Trevor or Medium-Cute Trevor?"

"Ma," Etta says in a tone that means I've said something wrong. As a mother, I make it a general rule to remember only the things that embarrass my daughter and then, of course, to say that exact embarrassing thing in front of her friends.

"Oh, he's the cute one," Tara informs me.

"Then he can come. Aunt Fleeta made plenty of food, so we haven't hit our head-count limit yet."

The Methodist Sewing Circle has decorated the church basement with fall leaves made of construction paper and glitter. The main table has been set with a white tablecloth trimmed in twisted orange crepe paper.

"From Fleeta," I tell Betty Cline as I hand her the enormous tray.

"Good. We're short on meat," Betty says as she takes it. Then she lowers her voice. "If you're a deviled-egg fan, you better make haste to the Apper-tiff Table. I already caught Lottie Witt stuffing a few in her purse. They's almost gone."

"I'll get on it," I tell her.

It's so much fun to see everyone after the long summer. Nellie Goodloe has her first tan, compliments of a trip with her grandkids to Myrtle Beach. Kate Benton, the band director, has a beau in tow, a transplant out of Norton named Glenn who sells mining equipment. Iva Lou is entertaining the Dogwood Garden Club with stories of the natural wonders she observed in Italy (not many plants, mostly men).

"Father Rodriguez! Did the Methodists invite you?" I ask.

"Catholics have to eat too. How was your trip?"

"Great. I brought lots of rosaries back for you to bless, if you don't mind."

"I'm happy to do it," Father Rodriguez tells me.

I smell a cigarette, so I turn to look. In the corner, Spec is having a smoke by one of the basement windows, ashing out into the drainage area. "Spec!"

"I wondered how long it would take you to say hello."

"The place is packed."

"I know." Spec smiles. "Sorry I had to send Otto and Worley to pick you up at the airport, but we had our all-county Rescue Squad picnic at the Natural Bridge, and I couldn't get out of it."

"No problem."

"What did you bring me from It-lee?"

"Gina Lollobrigida wouldn't fit in the suitcase."

"Damn." Spec laughs so hard, it turns into a cough. I pat him on the back.

"So I brought you a tie and handkerchief set. Silk."

Spec whistles long and low. "You didn't have to do that."

I feel a tugging at my pant leg; it's little India Bakagese. She looks up at me with her huge brown eyes. I lean over and scoop her up.

"God, she's gorgeous, she's gotten so big," I tell Pearl.

"I know. She's already two and a half. Welcome home."

Fleeta, still wearing her Mutual Pharmacy smock, interrupts us. "Y'all took off without the serving utensils," she says, waving three large slotted serving spoons.

"Sorry."

"Use your heads, people. Vacation time is over. We all need to git back in the groove. Looky there. They let the Tuckett sisters out of Heritage Hall Nursing Home for the night. I'll be damned."

The Tuckett twins, wearing matching housedresses in a loud iris print, occupy side-by-side wheelchairs at the head of one of the picnic tables. Nellie Goodloe sits on the bench conversing with them.

"See how they tell 'em apart? The slippers. Edna's in the white scuffs, and Ledna's in the blue." Fleeta waves us off with the spoons and goes to the serving table.

"Ave, can I stop by later?" Pearl asks.

"Sure. You guys did a great job while I was gone. You really kept up with the prescriptions."

"Had to. We have to compete with twenty-four-hour chains. Can't let any grass grow under our feet." Pearl looks off into the distance.

"Are you okay?" I ask her.

"Why?"

"You seem upset about something. What is it?"

"Well, I do have news."

"I hope it's good news."

"It is. But it's also big. It would mean big changes."

"How so?"

"I was gonna wait till later to talk about this. But you know me, I can't keep anything from you."

I smile. It's true, Pearl has confided in me ever since she was a girl. In many ways, our relationship reminds me of the one I had with my mother.

"Taye got offered a job at the Boston Medical Center."

"Boston, Massachusetts?"

She nods. "He wants to take it. But it means that we would move with him. India and me, that is."

"Of course. You have to be with your husband." My mind races. This town without Pearl? This pharmacy? How would we do it? She is the passion behind the growth, she is the visionary. How would I manage without her? "But I'm worried about the business," Pearl says plainly. "I told you about selling the Lee County branch, well, it's a lot harder to do than I thought. There aren't any buyers for our kind of operation, and if I have to move soon, I can't really do a statewide search for partners."

"So you want to sell the business? All three pharmacies?"

"The problem is, I can't sell them even if I wanted to. I've been to the banks, and they said that Big Stone Gap is essentially a bedroom community now. Most of the young people commute to Kingsport to work. We haven't had any new industry move in, except for the wildcat coal operations, and you know how folks feel about them."

"I do."

"I wouldn't do anything without asking you."

"Pearl, you're the president. You're in charge. I'm just your partner on the Big Stone Mutual."

"I know. But there isn't anyone else I trust to oversee the three operations. I can sign this pharmacy over to you, but that's a full-time headache. The three branches are really interdependent. I've set it up so that costs are spread over all three. They work together, in a way."

"How can I help?"

"Lew Eisenberg seems to think I should put the company in trust and have you as the guardian. That way, the places could function until we find a buyer. I can't be in two places at once. When we move, I have to devote myself to something new in Boston."

"I understand."

"I've been agonizing about this." Pearl's eyes fill with tears. "I've been struggling to figure out what to do."

"Honey, when I gave you this place sixteen years ago, I did it without strings. There still are no strings. We'll find a way to keep the places open until we find a buyer, and if we don't find one, we'll figure out how to proceed."

"Hello, gorgeous." My husband interrupts us, giving me a kiss. "You two look serious. What's wrong?"

"Nothing," we say in unison.

I give Jack a look that tells him I will explain later. Reverend Manning calls us to stand as he blesses the food. I take Pearl's hand and hold it firmly. I don't want her to worry. We've been in this position before, and we made it through, and we'll make it work again.

Jack helps me fold down the quilt on our bed. I open the windows a bit to let the fresh air in, all the while filling Jack in on Pearl's plans.

"Pearl in Boston?" he wonders aloud.

"It's a great opportunity for them."

"Big change."

"She can handle it."

"Do you ever want to move?" Jack looks out the window.

"Are you serious?" I go to him and put my arms around him.

"Don't you ever want to try someplace new?"

"And do what, open a restaurant?" Why do I always say the first thing off the top of my head? Jack winces and sits in the easy chair.

"I'm sorry," I tell him sincerely.

"I'm getting tired of construction."

"I know." Before our vacation, I noticed that Jack had grown weary of the late-night phone calls, the haggling over bids, and the long hours. Rick, Mousey, and Jack have kept their operation small (the only way to make money), but it has taken a toll on them, since they do the primary labor. I tell him gently, "Honey, I want you to be happy. But we have Etta going to college, and with the Pharmacy in flux financially, I think we should stay the course for a while, if you can stand it. We need your income."

He nods and knows this is true. "But don't you ever just want to shake things up?"

I look at Jack and want to say sure, I love to shake things up. But truthfully, I don't. I like to have a plan that goes off without a hitch. I like knowing that Etta's schedule is consistent, that we do the little things that add up to a strong family life, things like eating dinner together every night. I know I'm set in my ways, but I don't know how else to do it. "Do *you* want to shake things up?"

"I do."

"How would you do that?"

"Move."

"Where?" Why am I asking? Why would I care? I used to dream of picking up and moving. Why does the idea of it scare me now?

"I don't know. Charlottesville. Kingsport."

I make a face.

"Tuscany." Jack smiles.

"Tuscany!"

"Giuseppe said he could use a man like me in his operation."

"Giuseppe? The Olive Oil King? Really?"

"Yeah."

"What did you say?"

"I said I'd think about it." Jack looks at me. "Life is going by so fast. I want to take some chances. I hope you do too."

We lie down in bed. I'm so surprised, I can't think of anything to say. Maybe I discourage Jack from dreaming big because I'm always worried about practical things, but I've never pegged him to be an adventurer. He always seemed happy here, living in the house where he was born, in the mountains he grew up around, with me, a girl he loved all his life and finally married. What more is there? Evidently, a lot.

The phone rings.

"It's probably for Etta," I say as I reach for it.

"It's always for Etta," Jack replies.

"Hello?"

The caller speaks so softly, I can barely hear her. She asks for me.

"This is Ave Maria."

"This is Leola Broadwater." Leola is Spec's wife. I

wondered why she didn't come to the Covered Dish Supper.

"Leola, are you all right?"

"No. It's Spec. He's had another heart attack. Worse than the one he had in Florida."

"Florida?" I can't believe Spec lied to me. I sit down as my heart begins to pound. "Where is he?"

"He's in the ICU up at Saint Agnes. He's asked for you. I think you ought might hurry," she says, and then she starts to sob.

"He was fine at the supper tonight!" I tell her, trying to be upbeat. "He looked great."

"Oh, Ave," Leola cries.

"I'm on my way."

Jack wants to drive me, but I tell him I don't want him to wake Etta or to leave her alone. The truth is, I need to be alone. It's strange, but I have to sort out things like this for myself. Jack understands this about me and doesn't give me an argument. I promise him that I will call once I'm at the hospital.

As I walk to my Jeep, I look down and realize I have two different loafers on. I wipe the dew off the windshield with my sleeve, feeling an odd sense of familiarity that keeps me from crying. This night reminds me of the times I joined Spec on emergency calls at all hours with the Rescue Squad. I never thought I'd be making an emergency run on his behalf.

The night receptionist at the hospital knows me. By day, she works as a clerk at the Norton Mutual's. She waves me in, and I take the short hallway to the ICU. Leola stands beside Spec's bed, and surrounding him are his five children. His son Clay cannot stop crying. I grab Dr. Stemple as she exits the ICU and introduce myself.

"He was asking for you," she says, looking back at Spec through the small viewing window.

"How is he?"

"You know he has a bad heart. He had a bypass a few years ago, but it's not the arteries that are failing him now, it's the actual heart muscle."

"Is he going to make it?" She does not answer me, and I already know the answer. "Was he at home?"

"No, he was at work. He had some mechanic working on the fire truck or something and was staying to oversee the job, and then he collapsed. The mechanic drove him here."

"Is he conscious?"

"Yes ma'am."

A nurse summons Dr. Stemple, and she hurries off. For a moment, I stand and look at Spec and his family. I refuse to let this man go. It's too soon.

I push back through the doors and go to Leola. I put my hands gently on her shoulders. She does not turn to look at me. She just places her hand on mine and continues to watch Spec, who is on oxygen and, as the doctor said, wide awake.

"Was it the Swedish meatballs, Spec?"

He smiles as I take his hand.

"Doc said you were gonna be fine."

Spec rolls his eyes. I should know better than to bluff a trained emergency technician.

"Let's give Pap some privacy," Clay tells the rest of the family.

Spec lifts the oxygen mask off of his face. "Git Ma some coffee," he tells the kids. Leola kisses him on the cheek, then moves to the doors, sheltered by her children.

"I'll be right back, you old mud turtle," Leola promises from the door.

"Mud turtle. Now, there's a sexy picture for you," I say.

Spec tries not to laugh. Then he pushes the oxygen mask from his nose and mouth onto his forehead. "This is just for show. They want it to look like they can save me."

"They *can*."

"No, this is the end of the road fer me."

"You may not go. That's an order." It's not much of an order as my eyes fill with tears.

"Don't cry on me."

"Sorry." I wipe the tears away with my sleeve.

"We had us some fun, didn't we?" Spec lays his head back on the pillow and smiles.

"God, yes. Liz Taylor choking on a chicken bone. Naomi and her buck. That Sturgill boy when he shoved a dime and three nickels up his nose."

"Made change for a quarter." Spec sighs.

I reach for water on the nightstand and try to help Spec with the straw, but he takes it from me and sips at it himself.

"It's a funny thing. I'm lying here on my way to God knows where, and all I can think about is John Wayne. All my life I modeled myself after the Duke."

Spec was forever quoting John Wayne's lines from the movies, and encouraged Jim Roy Honeycutt, the owner of the Trail Theatre, to have at least one Duke Film Festival a year.

"Yep," he goes on, "when I was a youngin, it was *Stagecoach.* And then when I got to be a man, it was *The Searchers.*"

"And now?"

"*True Grit,* I guess."

"You know I love you, Spec."

"I know." He exhales slowly. "I was thinkin' of your Joe and how I was his godfather."

I remember the day we baptized Joe. He looked like a tiny doll in big Spec's arms. Spec held him so gently, Joe didn't even wake up when the priest splashed water on him.

"My mamaw would've shot me if she knew I was in the Cath-lick church."

"You did it for me."

Spec nods. " 'Bout broke my heart when that boy died."

"I know."

"It wasn't right. Now, me? I'm old. I seen a lot. I lived. But I never did understand why the Lord took him."

"I never will either. I keep looking for the answer."

"You ought to stop," Spec says plainly.

"I know."

"I want to ask you to do something for me."

"Sure."

"Don't be so hard on Etta. She's country. You know, like us. She's got her own mind. You'll see in time that that's a good thing. Now, my youngins, they ain't gonna do too well with me gone. I set it up all wrong."

"How?"

"I didn't cut 'em loose. I hung on to 'em. Now, they's followers, all except for Clay, so it's partly their nature. But it's mostly how I raised 'em."

"You were a wonderful father." I want to say more to my friend, to tell him what he has meant to me, but I don't want to cry (Spec hates weeping and wailing).

Spec looks off in the middle distance and cocks one

eyebrow. "I done tried my best. God knows I ain't perfect." I'm sure Spec is referring to his long friendship with Twyla Johnson, and I wait for him to say something about her, but he does not. Instead, he reaches back and tries to adjust the pillow. I help him. "Now I'm gonna sleep." Spec closes his eyes. I slip the oxygen mask back on his face and check the levels on the machine. His mighty chest heaves in deep breaths. The nurse comes over to check on him.

"You should get the family," she says to me quietly.

I go into the waiting area, where Spec's children are gathered around their mother. They look up at me. I cannot speak, but they see why I came for them and rush into the ICU to gather about their father. The boys help their mother onto the bed, where she lies next to her husband with her arms around him. It is only minutes until Spec takes his last breath. The heart monitor hums a low whistle that tells us he has died. Spec Broadwater, the Mighty Oak, is gone.

Spec's funeral is not to be a simple Baptist affair with a service and a burial at Glencoe Cemetery. It is going to be a full-out, all-county memorial festival. Rescue Squads from Wise, Lee, Dickenson, and Scott have gathered (in uniform) to parade down Wood Avenue to the church, led by the town fire truck and brought up in the rear by the National Guard. Iva Lou insisted that the Bookmobile be in the parade as well, even though Spec said he never finished a hardback book in his life. Some folks are calling it a volunteer-military funeral, but for me, it is an appropriate send-off for a man who devoted much of his life, including his spare time, to serving others. Leola told me that Spec would be buried in his Rescue Squad windbreaker, a dress shirt and pants, and the tie we brought him from Italy. That made me very happy.

Nellie Goodloe organized the luncheon following the funeral. Fleeta has stayed up for two nights baking three coconut cakes, three chocolate sheet cakes, and pies from pecan to shoofly (Spec's favorite). Pearl opened the Mutual's kitchen for the prep. Jack made five trays of his lasagna, I bought out every head of lettuce at the Piggly Wiggly, and Hope Meade made so many rolls, she had to borrow our pickup to transport them.

"Do you think there's enough food, Nellie?"

"I sure hope so. Ole Spec had a bigger turnout than Eisenhower."

Etta is fanning the napkins on the buffet when she calls to me to look out the window.

"What is it?" I ask her.

"Bless their hearts," Nellie says aloud.

Emerging from their cars (there must be a dozen of them) are women opening their trunks and pulling out cooked hams in baking pans, roasted turkey, large pans of casseroles, even a case of champagne (they must be Episcopalians, not Baptists).

"Tennessee license plates, Ma," Etta comments.

We open the doors to let the ladies in. A tall spindly woman, around sixty, leads the group.

"We're from Johnson City. And we heard about Mr. Broadwater, and we wanted to do something, so we hope you have some use for this food."

"Thank you kindly." Nellie accepts a large platter.

"I better go get a couple more folding tables," Jack says,

motioning to Otto and Worley, who are setting up the seating area.

"You're from Tennessee?" I ask the tall woman.

"Yes ma'am."

"How do you know Spec?"

"We had a fire at our rec center about eight years ago. And he came and helped put it out. Then, later, when we were rebuilding, he showed up to help with the construction. We don't know a finer person, and when we heard he passed, we just had to do *something*." The other ladies nod in agreement.

"He'd be very grateful to you."

"Well, we're very grateful to him."

I don't hear much of what is said at Spec's funeral. My mind is off in the past, when I was single and young and rode shotgun with Spec all over Wise County, working with him on the Rescue Squad. I learned so much from him. I learned to not panic, to keep my emotions in check, to not jump to the worst-case scenario in a crisis. He was always level and clear in times of tragedy. And he never went to a funeral, not even my son's, didn't believe in them. He had some kin way back who were Cherokee, and they had a philosophy about death. You don't dwell on it, you bury your dead, and you walk away from that grave never to return. Now, that's a hard concept for someone raised Catholic, like me, who every Sunday visits her mother's grave with fresh flowers. And it's hard for the Protestants, who hold somber picnics at the cemetery on Memorial Day. But to Spec, the Indian way made sense. "Life is about the living," he'd say.

*

Jack, Etta, and I are exhausted as we make the turn up to our house. By the time the last of the Rescue Squad workers left and we put the Baptist Church Fellowship Hall back the way we found it, it was late afternoon.

I'm proud of my daughter. She helped her dad set up, and served and stayed for cleanup. Her friend Tara tagged along and served punch. Etta loved Spec; he's one of the first people she remembers from her childhood. He spent many early mornings here having coffee and telling us the local gossip while she was having cereal in her pajamas.

"Ma, whose car is that?" Etta points to a chartreuse four-door with a black cloth roof parked in front of our house.

"I have no idea."

As we pull in, I get out of the truck and go to the mysterious car.

"May I help you?" I look into the car. There is a woman alone, probably in her early sixties, as the slight lines on her forehead indicate. Her car has the scent of polished leather and Youth Dew perfume. She wears a pale, shiny lipstick but is not smiling.

"You don't know me."

"I can't say that I do, ma'am."

"I'm Twyla Johnson."

I hope I didn't gasp when I heard the name, but the truth is, I've always wanted to meet her. Really, I know very little about Twyla Johnson. She works at the Farmers and Miners Bank in Pennington Gap and she had a relationship with Spec. After his bypass, I thought Spec would leave his wife to be with her, but he never did. And since then, the only mention of her has been Fleeta's joking references.

"Please, come in," I tell her.

I introduce her to Jack and Etta. Jack has heard tell of her but gives no indication when he repeats her name aloud and shakes her hand. Etta has no idea who she is.

"Would you like a cup of coffee?" I ask Twyla as I turn on the lights.

"I would love it," she says graciously. Shoo the Cat makes a beeline for Twyla and sniffs her patent-leather high heels. She wears a trim navy blue suit with a crisp white blouse. She has twisted a floral scarf around her neck and anchored it with a gold brooch in the shape of a bird. Her handbag matches her shoes, and there is not a smudge on its shiny surface.

"Mama, I'm gonna go to bed. I'm beat," Etta says.

"Go ahead, hon. You were a big help today."

I show Twyla to the kitchen as Jack goes outside to unload his truck. "What a beautiful old house," she says.

"My husband's family homestead."

"All hand-done stone- and woodwork."

"You could never match this craftsmanship today." Do I think Twyla Johnson is here to talk about construction?

As I make the coffee, Twyla makes herself at home at our kitchen table, neatly placing her purse in the chair and unwrapping the scarf from her neck.

"You know about me, don't you?"

"Yes ma'am, I do."

"Spec often spoke of you. I know it must seem odd that I know lots about you but you never met me."

"It is a little strange," I tell her, placing a dish of cookies before her.

"I loved Spec very much."

"You must be so sad."

"I am," she says, her eyes filling with tears. I give her the Kleenex box from the phone table. "There was no place for me today. I wanted to be there. I even got there early and went into the church, but when I saw people driving up and getting out of their cars to come inside, I went back to my car. I didn't want to cause any trouble."

"Did you see the parade?"

"I did. I had no idea that he was so well known."

"Everybody knew Spec Broadwater. Do you mind if I ask you something?"

She takes a tissue and wipes her eyes. "Go right ahead."

"Why so many years with Spec when you couldn't marry him? You seem like the marrying kind."

"Well, there was only Spec for me. And he was already taken."

Under normal circumstances, I would never ask personal questions of someone I just met. But Twyla needs to talk about Spec, I can see that. She loved him too, and she has no one to turn to in her grief. "How did you meet him? Did the bank catch fire?"

Twyla laughs. "No, no, nothing that grand. He had an account at our bank, an old account that was left to him by his parents. And every once in a while, he'd make a deposit and we'd chitchat. He'd comment about my hair or my clothes, but all of it seemed to have a double meaning."

"Spec was a flirt."

"But he meant his flirting, it wasn't silly. He was a real man. A man's man. He made me feel safe, maybe because he was so tall and sturdy. I remember the second time I met him, this was twenty-three years ago. I was operating the drive-through window at the bank, and we were very busy. I said good morning into the microphone and didn't look up, and pressed the button for the automatic drawer. Well, was I stunned when the drawer flipped open and inside, instead of a deposit envelope, the thing was stuffed with field daisies. I mean stuffed!" She laughs. "So I looked up, and there in the car was Spec. I asked him what I was supposed to do with the flowers, and he said, 'Put 'em in water.' I went to lunch with him that day, and it was the start of our friendship."

"Were you married?"

"I never was."

"It must have been hard for you on holidays." Could I possibly say anything more lame?

"It was. And really, except for our lunches, we couldn't see too much of each other because of his work. He called me a lot, though."

I think of Iva Lou, who told me one of the sure signs that a married man is having an affair is that he frequents phone booths.

"Did you get to see him at the hospital?"

She shakes her head sadly. "I didn't get there. I got a phone call telling me that he was in bad shape."

"Who called you?"

"Fleeta Mullins."

"Fleeta? Do you know her?"

"I never met her. Do you know her?"

"She works with me. She has for years."

"She was very curt. But she said that Spec would want me to know."

I don't know what to say. Fleeta called Twyla? How could that be? Fleeta is so principled about fooling around.

"I'm not proud of being the other woman."

"I can tell that you're a very good person. Spec was a deep person, even though he never said much. I'm sure he wasn't happy about the situation either."

"He had his family. I knew they came first."

I want to ask Twyla why she settled for third place, after Spec's family and his work. How could lunch once a week with the man you love be enough? But this woman is in pain, and I put aside my own judgments (and, for Godsakes, my own experience in these matters) and ask her a simple question instead. "Would you do it all over again?"

Twyla thinks for a moment as she stirs her coffee. "No, I don't think I would."

"Really?"

"You give up everything when you give up the privilege of saying good-bye."

I make an excuse that my coffee needs a warm-up, but my eyes are stinging with tears. "When Spec survived his bypass, he came down to see me afterwards," Twyla continues. "We felt so lucky that he had dodged death. And I had it in my mind that I was going to break it off that day, but when I saw him, I couldn't do it. So here we are." Twyla reaches for her purse and pulls out a small square of tissue paper. "He said when he died, he wanted you to have this. When he came back from Florida, he went to the doctor, who told him that he had more scar tissue than heart left. Spec took this as a sign that he may not have a lot of time, so he began to settle things."

"He never said anything to me."

"Spec was too proud to admit any weakness. That's the one thing he saved for me. He could talk to me when he was afraid." She gives me the tiny package, and I hold it for a few moments, not wanting to open it; knowing that if I do, Spec really is gone.

"It belonged to his mother," Twyla tells me.

I carefully unfold the paper and pull out a fine gold chain with a fairy stone dangling from it. A fairy stone is a small brown wooden cross, delicate, squat, and square. Every girl in our mountains gets one at some point in her life as a gift, from either her parents, a friend, or a beau. There is a story behind how these fairy stones came to be. We are told that there is a valley in the neighboring Cumberland Gap where there is a grove of dogwood trees, and on Good Friday hundreds of years ago, the birds in the trees wept, and when their tears hit the ground, they changed into fairy stones. And until the end of time, the birds will cry every Good Friday until their sorrow is released on Judgment Day. This is an old Scottish myth brought here by the immigrants, but it has never died.

"I never had a fairy stone."

"Now you do," Twyla says softly and smiles.

I shake Twyla's hands as she goes. She promises to be careful driving home, and we make murky plans for lunch sometime down the road. I know as I watch her back down the road that I will never see her again. We met when we had to, and our business is done. She took a big risk in coming here. I'm sure

Spec shared my troubles with her and that she knows how I feel about fooling around. But I guess that now I understand, specifically because of Twyla, how these things happen. It's not like she planned this; how could she know that it was where the road would lead? As I turn out the lights and lock the doors, I feel unsure and full of questions. I am at a point where I need answers, and there is only one man who can provide them.

Jack is lying on the bed watching TV when I come up. He quickly turns it off. "What was that all about?"

"That's the famous Twyla Johnson."

"I figured that when she introduced herself."

"She gave me this fairy stone that belonged to Spec's mother." I lean in and show Jack Mac the necklace around my neck.

"She is an attractive lady."

"Spec liked beautiful women. It's so sad, though. There was no place for her today." As I undress, I think of her perfect suit and shoes and bag, and how there was a time when a woman never left her house without shoes that matched her bag, an appropriate hat, and gloves. Twyla Johnson is one of those women who live in a bygone era and refuse to give up the artifice. Maybe that stubborn nature kept her in a relationship with Spec. "She loved him very much, she told me."

"Complicated, isn't it," Jack says.

"Well, we went through it." I sit on the bed and look at Jack, who turns the color of the red throw pillow propped behind his head.

"We did," he admits.

"Yes, we did."

"Uh-oh," he says flatly. This makes me laugh.

"I always told you that I didn't want to know the nature of your relationship with Karen Bell."

"It's so far in the past."

"It seems like a lifetime ago."

"It does. And it is. We're happy now, and that's what matters."

"I learned something tonight that left me peaceful about all this stuff."

"What's that?"

"Spec and Twyla were friends. Outside of the romance part, which I'm sure was there, there was a friendship. A kinship. Spec wasn't a big communicator, and I'm glad that there was someone he could unload on who would listen. She was a sounding board, someone he could talk to. Isn't that the most important thing?"

Jack doesn't answer me. "Let's go to bed, honey," he finally says, softly.

"Jack."

"What?"

"There's something I didn't tell you about when it happened. I thought it was best not to say anything at the time. I saw Karen Bell at Holston Valley when Iva Lou had her surgery."

"She wasn't important to me, Ave," Jack says quietly.

"Yeah, but she listened to you when you needed somebody to talk to. I wasn't there for you. She was. That's the truth."

Jack considers this for a moment and then nods in agreement.

"That was really how you became friends, right?" I ask him.

"I don't even remember."

"Did you make love to her?"

I'm expecting Jack to bite my head off or roll over and dismiss my question, but he doesn't. He looks off for a moment and then looks directly into my eyes. "I've never lied to you, Ave Maria."

"But we have skirted issues sometimes. I need to *know* now, honey."

I'm not nervous in the pit of my stomach asking this, maybe because I feel secure in my husband's love for me now. Maybe I want closure. Or maybe I want to understand Spec. I do know I won't rest until Jack tells me what really happened.

"I didn't make love to her," Jack says simply.

I know that he is telling me the truth. I would like to tell him that it doesn't matter anymore, because I know now what we have in this marriage. Sex is sex, but deep emotional commitment makes a soul mate.

Jack continues, "She helped me through a rough patch. That was the extent of it. Now, I'm not going to lie to you. She fell in love with me, and I was very tempted, and I wasn't sure you wanted me. So I thought about that, and I decided that if you left me, I would have to go on. And I went into a sort of survival mode where I figured out scenarios that could happen. I think like that, analytically. But you came home when she began to really press me to leave you."

"Oh my God." The nerve of that woman, I'm thinking. I

should've slapped her at the hospital instead of giving her a big ole hidee-hello.

"That summer you were gone, Spec came to see me."

"Why?"

"To scare the hell out of me. One night I came home, and he was sitting on the porch steps. He must have been waiting there for a couple of hours. Well, he got up and put out his cigarette and motioned for me to come closer. When I got about a foot in front of him, he reached for me with those giant hands of his and he took me by the collar, yanked me to about an inch from his nose, and he said, 'You hurt Ave Maria and I will kill you.'"

"No!"

"He meant it too. He told me that he didn't want me to mess up your life."

I lean back on the pillows and think about this for a moment. Spec Broadwater was more than my friend. He looked out for me like a good father, offering protection and asking nothing in return.

I get up off the bed and go to the bathroom.

"Wait a second."

"Yeah?" I turn to him.

"What about you and Pete Rutledge?"

"Why do you ask?"

"Something went on there, didn't it?"

"What do you mean?"

"Etta told me that you and he were close that same summer."

"Etta said that?"

Jack nods. "Were you?"

I don't know which is worse, that my husband is asking the question or that my daughter noticed something and felt it was important enough to tell her father.

"He's a friend." I try to sound casual.

"He is now."

"And that's all he was back then."

"Etta wouldn't make up a story. What happened between you two?"

"You know, I don't really know."

"Now who's skirting the issue?"

"I didn't make love to him, if that's what you're asking."

"I figured that."

"How?"

"I'm married to you." Jack smiles, and in his smile I see relief.

"What does that mean?"

"You never create a new mess without cleaning up an old one first."

"Oh." I go into the bathroom and brush my teeth.

Jack joins me in the doorway. "When we were young, the thing I wanted the most was to get to here."

"Here in Cracker's Neck?"

"No. Here. To this stage of our lives." He continues, "I want to get old with you. Real old. And then, when the time comes, I want to die in your arms."

I put down my toothbrush and pull my husband close. I realize that I have exactly what I have been looking for all of my life. When you honor someone, he owns you. Jack MacChesney owns me, and maybe that's the only part of love that lasts.

*

The lunch crowd at the Mutual Pharmacy is proof that life goes on after someone dies. Spec's seat at the counter is left empty (at least for now). Otto is on the stool next to Spec's. Fleeta pats his hand as she refills his mug with coffee. This is the first sign of public affection I've seen Fleeta give Otto; I guess it's true that grief binds folks together. Fleeta takes a break to join Iva Lou and me in a booth for a cup of coffee.

"I heard you had a visitor." Fleeta cocks her head toward me.

"Who?" Iva Lou wants to know.

"Twyla Johnson." Fleeta drags out "Johnson" like she's singing it.

"You're kidding." Iva Lou's eyes widen.

"Where'd you hear that, Fleeta?" I ask her.

"I ain't tellin'." Fleeta chomps on a straw. "I guess we can expect her to start sneakin' up to the cemetery of the night-time and puttin' a lone rose on his grave. That's how they do it, you know. The other woman. She wants the wife to know that she ain't the only one."

"That's an awful lot of effort to make a point." Iva Lou cuts her brownie with her fork.

"Well, don't you think an extramarital affair is a lot of work?" Fleeta sniffs.

"Too much for me. Why do you think I gave it up and got married?"

Fleeta turns to me. "So. What did she say?"

"She said that she and Spec were just friends."

"Oh, come on." Fleeta laughs. Then she studies me for a moment and asks, "Really?"

"Swear to God. She said Leola was the great love of Spec's life and that she could never hurt another woman or take their daddy away from his children."

As Fleeta considers this, her stress-lined forehead smoothes out like polished marble for the first time in years. "Twyla Johnson is a goddamn saint," Fleeta says reverently.

"I think so."

"You know, Spec could piss me off worse than a blood relative. But I liked the man. I knew he was a good egg. I didn't want to think he was like all the other men, you know, that hit fifty and run around the county with their tongues hangin' out, looking for action." Fleeta gets up and goes behind the counter.

Iva Lou looks at me. "That was a crock of bullshit and you know it," she says quietly.

"And it's the story you repeat every time you stamp a book and someone inquires about the nature of Spec and Twyla's relationship. Okay?"

"You got a deal."

April is a month of great celebration in the MacChesney home. Jack is in the kitchen making homemade spaghetti. He's putting together a special supper for our seventeenth wedding anniversary.

"Happy anniversary!" Theodore sings.

"Thank you very much. Where are you?"

"At the office. I got your message about Spec. Jesus, that was fast."

"I know. How's Max?"

"Still cookin'."

"When am I going to see you again?" I ask Theodore sadly.

"Anytime. What's the matter with you?"

"It's just so depressing around here. Etta just got her driver's license. Pearl is moving to Boston with her husband. And I really miss Spec." I could go on, but I stop.

"Lots of changes in Cracker's Neck Holler."

"Too many," I tell him.

"You need to look at what you have, not what's missing. You have a good man who loves you, and if that's all you get, you've already won the lottery," Theodore promises me. He fills me in on his life, and I do feel better. When Theodore talks about Max, I hear such happiness in his voice. Max brings out things in Theodore that I have never seen before, all of them positive. Love hasn't changed Theodore but has made him more open and willing to take chances.

Jack has already written in our anniversary book. I still haven't had a chance. Usually I'm the one pushing *him* to write in it. This tradition of writing to each other every year has served us well; we look in it and see each other's thoughts as our marriage has grown, and there is always something that we have written in the past that helps us in the here and now. This year his passage is simple but slightly arty. At the top of the page he glued a picture that Sergio took of us kissing on the banks of Lake Como. Next to that he affixed a small wild rose he plucked from the bushes outside our room at the Villa d'Este. Then he wrote:

Dear Wife:

When I was young I thought seventeen years was a long time. And now I know it is just the beginning.

With all my love, J.

He has left the book next to my place at the table to remind me to write in it.

I'm using the good china tonight, and feeling in a generous mood. I invited Etta to bring her new boyfriend to dinner. He's a senior at Appalachia High School, an honor student who plays basketball. He has an old-fashioned name: Robbie Ramsey (his parents were not inspired by the Old West, as were so many other parents of his generation, judging by all the Austins, Dakotas, and Cassidys in Etta's class).

I hear the motor of Tara's cranky 1988 Dodge Dart coming up the road. Etta jumps out, and Tara toots lightly on the horn as she backs down the mountain.

"I'm home!" Etta calls out.

"Come on back," I holler.

"Where's Robbie?" I ask when I see Etta is alone.

"I decided not to invite him."

"Why not?"

"I just like it when it's the three of us sometimes." Etta shrugs and goes to wash up. When she returns to the table, Jack serves his excellent meal. At the end of it, our daughter presents us with a gift, a first edition of *The Trail of the Lonesome Pine*, the novel by John Fox, Jr., that our Outdoor Drama is based on. "I thought you guys would like it. Since you used to direct and Dad used to play in the band."

"We love it." I look at Jack, and he beams.

"I'm going to clean up. You guys go and relax," Etta says, standing to clear the dishes.

Jack looks at me, raises both eyebrows, and says nothing. I thank Etta and follow him out of the kitchen. We grab our jackets and go for a walk in the woods. We always promise each other we are going to take long walks, but we usually get too tired after supper and scrap the plan. When we were in Italy, we often did *La Passeggiatta* after dinner, and we were amazed at how it relaxed us for a good night's sleep.

"We have a good kid," Jack says after a while.

"We sure do."

"She knows you've had a rough winter with Spec gone."

"She misses him too."

"I know. But she understands what you're feeling."

"Is that the same kid who got plowed on bellinis last summer?"

"The very same."

Jack takes my hand and leads me down the old path behind our house, the one that carries a creek in the summer and becomes a dry gulch in the winter. The old trees planted years ago by my mother-in-law hover around the property, their top branches leafless and reaching like old fingers up into the sky.

When you live in the mountains, there are signs every day that life is changing. The terrain shifts when the mountains settle, and sometimes streams disappear never to return. One year you might find sweet raspberries growing by a field, and the very next summer they're gone. Take nothing for granted, because if you do, it will surely go. If an old tree gets leveled by lightning, it reminds you that you're vulnerable too. And even though these woods are loaded with trees, when one falls, you miss it.

"Next year I'm going to take Etta up to Saint Mary's to check it out. What do you think?" I ask.

"She keeps talking about UVA."

"I just want her to see my college. She doesn't have to go there, just consider it."

"You won't get bent out of shape if she decides not to go where you went?"

"I won't."

Jack pulls me close and kisses me. It's one of those good, long anniversary kisses (it goes on for a full forty seconds, not that I'm counting). As he holds me, I'm thinking that it doesn't feel like seventeen years at all, it feels like seventeen days. Jack reaches into his pocket and gives me a small package.

"What's this?"

"A present, you dummy."

I tear away the pink wrapping and ribbon (this is from Gilley's Jewelers; the gold monogram gives it away) to find a small black velvet box. It's dark out, so Jack pulls out a lighter and flicks it so I can see the contents of the box.

"They're gorgeous!" And they are. They are gold hoop earrings with a dangling diamond charm. "So Italian!" I throw my arms around my husband and kiss him again. "Thank you."

"Ready to go back?" he says, putting his arm around my waist.

"Your present is in the truck."

"What is it?"

"A table saw. I'm sorry. You asked for it." And it's true. I asked him what he wanted, and that was his choice.

"You always give me what I want, honey."

As if there weren't enough changes around here, the most seismic of all is happening now. Pearl must decide the fate of the Mutual Pharmacy. Lew Eisenberg is on his way over to meet Pearl and me in the Soda Fountain. Pearl and Taye are moving to Boston, and we have to settle our business. Pearl doesn't say much as she takes the last bite of her BLT. Fleeta wants in on the meeting, as she feels that she has the most seniority (and she does; she has spent more years in this Pharmacy than I have).

"Hello, girls." Lew ambles in and squeezes into the booth, taking one of Fleeta's cigarettes. Fleeta does not actually smoke them anymore. Her quitting technique is quite original and has worked for her where the patch, hypnosis, and the classic "cold turkey" have failed. She simply dangles the cigarette from her lips without lighting it.

Lew begins, "So, here's the deal. We're creating a trust for the business, in which Ave Maria is the trustee. And this will ensure the operation of all three pharmacies until an appropriate buyer makes an offer or you decide to close the places down. Right now business is profitable in Big Stone Gap and Norton; the Pennington Gap branch is barely breaking even. You have six employees there, and the manager is recommending that the place stay open twenty-four hours a day to compete with the chain. That's something for you to consider."

"Ave Maria, I know this is more work for you. But the managers of the other stores have agreed to come here every Friday with their weekly reports. This shouldn't be too much of a drag," Pearl promises.

"Whoa. Doesn't anybody want to know what I think?" Fleeta takes the unlit cigarette, now rimmed in "Mad for Melon" orange lipstick, and taps it on the table.

"Sure," Lew says, looking at Pearl, sorry that Fleeta was included in the meeting.

"My Janine just graduated from Mountain Empire in business management. She ain't a kid. She's thirty-six. Top of her class. And she's lookin' for a job. She's lookin' into managing something or another. Why can't she be the overseer of all these stores and report to you"—Fleeta points to Lew—"and to you"—she points to me—"and file some damn thing in the computer every now and agin so you"— she points to Pearl—"can keep up with what the hell is goin' on around here."

Pearl looks at me. I look at Lew.

"I like that idea," I say aloud. "Janine is a great girl."

"I think it could work," Pearl adds.

"Y'all are forever jacking your jaws about giving people jobs 'round here; now, here's your opportunity." Fleeta leans back in her seat.

"When can I meet her?" Lew wants to know.

"She's out in the car right now. I'll fetch her." Fleeta puts the unlit cigarette back between her lips and starts to slip out of the booth, then stops. "One more thing."

"What do you need?" Lew asks her.

"I put my sweat and blood in this here Soda Fountain. All the cookin' is mine and all the bakin'. I think it ought to be called 'Fleeta's.' "

The three of us look at one another.

"I think that's a good idea," Pearl tells her.

"Well, it's about damn time." Fleeta goes to fetch Janine.

Pearl laughs, and then Lew and I join her. Who'd have

thought Fleeta Mullins would have a viable business plan and the ego of a mogul?

Pearl lives with her husband and daughter on Poplar Hill, in an old house they renovated, down the road from her mother, Leah, and her stepdad, Worley Olinger, who still live in the house I gave to Pearl when I married Jack. Otto lives with them now, and Pearl likes that India has her grandma, grandpa, and honorary great-grandfather under the same roof. All that will change now, and that's very hard for her. I don't think Pearl ever imagined leaving Big Stone Gap. She made the big change in her life when she moved from the housing project in Insko into my old house in town. She commuted to college at the University of Virginia at Wise, and then took on the huge job of running the Mutual Pharmacy and expanding to other towns.

"I know this is best for my family," Pearl says as she packs dinner plates in bubble wrap.

"You'll have an adjustment period. But think of the fun you'll have in Boston. So much history there! You can take India up to Concord to see Walden Pond, and the house where Ralph Waldo Emerson lived, and the Alcott homestead. It'll be great."

"I wasn't thinking about side trips."

"What were you thinking about?"

"Not having you to talk to."

"I'm a phone call away."

"I know. But it won't be the same."

"Honey, you're goal-oriented. You like to set a plan and follow it through. Think how fulfilled you'll be when you invent new challenges. A long time ago I went to a fortune-teller, and she told me that when you have a dream come true, you must then redream. You must not stay in the past. Because all of life changes anyway, and if you try to hang on to happiness or success or even the people in your life, you will be unhappy. You have to set new goals. Look where you started. And look where you are. Aren't you amazed?"

Pearl thinks about this. "Not really. When you start out with nothing, anything you achieve is a surprise."

"Look at the move to Boston in the same way. You're starting over again, except this time you have nothing to prove, you're already a success."

Pearl smiles gratefully. When I give her advice, I'm never heavy-handed or preachy, I speak from my heart and she understands. Maybe it's easier to mother a girl who is not your own, to give advice freely when you don't feel personally responsible for her every choice. If only I could be this way with Etta.

Pearl tells me that she and India will fly to Boston in the morning and join Taye, who has begun his residency at the hospital. Their furniture and other belongings will follow in the moving van by the weekend. As Pearl lists what is left to do, there is a knock at the door. "They're early," Pearl says as she goes to answer it. I stop stacking dishes, and when I look up, I'm instantly glad I'm not holding anything breakable when I see who stopped to visit.

"Dad?" Pearl says in a whisper.

"Yep, it's me."

I haven't seen Albert Grimes since the Trail Theatre burned. After he was taken to the hospital and discharged, he seemed to want contact with Pearl, so she invited him to her wedding. I'd hoped that Pearl's wedding was a new start for them, but evidently it was not. Pearl hasn't spoken of him in years, and I sensed it was a painful topic for her, so I never asked. Albert looks much better than he did back then (I think he has new teeth). He has a close-cropped haircut, and he's wearing a neatly pressed khaki uniform. The tag on the shirt says GUARD.

"How are you, Pearl?" he asks.

"We're moving."

"I heard."

"You're working?" she says kindly.

"Yeah. Up to the Wise County prison. And I married me a nice girl out of Pound. She was an Isover. I don't know if you know you any Isovers, but they're good people."

"I think I've heard the name. Congratulations." Pearl looks away and says softly, "You have a granddaughter. Her name is India. If you'd like to see her, she's over at Mama's."

"I'll do that directly."

"We're leaving in the morning."

"I know all about."

"How'd you hear about it?"

"Funny thing. One of the guards is moving, and you're sharing the truck with him. So I asked about when the truck was comin' down here and figgered I'd catch you."

"I'm glad you came."

I realize that Pearl and Albert have been standing in the doorway the whole time, and say, "Should I throw on some tea or coffee or something?" They look at me. "Albert, I'm Ave Maria."

"I remember you," he says nicely.

"You look great," I tell him sincerely.

"Well, a good woman will do that to ye." Albert and Pearl stand in silence for another moment until Albert fumbles into his pocket. "Pearl, I want to thank ye fer looking out fer me fer so long when I had a hard time. This here is a check. I kept track of what you give me, and I want to pay you back."

"That's not necessary, Dad." Pearl's voice falters.

"No, no, you take it. My wife and I agreed you ought to have it. It's yorn. You got a girl to raise, and you may need this. Please." Albert gives Pearl the envelope, and she takes it. "I know it was hard fer ye, to take care of me. I know that I must've been a disappointment to ye in some ways, but I hope this lets you know that I believe in paying back and puttin' back. I'm just happy that I got me a job and can pay off my debt to ye."

Pearl wipes her eyes with the dishcloth she's holding, then reaches up and embraces her father for a very long time.

"I always knew you were a good man, Daddy."

"I was hopin' you did."

I'm mostly in the kitchen, but I can see that Albert Grimes has tears in his eyes too. I hear Spec's voice inside my head: "People do the best they can." And here's proof that they really do.

CHAPTER TEN

"*M*a you know I want UVA. It's where I want to go."

It is the fall of Etta's senior year, and she already has a plan in place. We spent the past year visiting every college in Virginia from William & Mary to Hollins, collecting applications, postcards, and sweatshirts, so that Etta would keep an open mind. But she's been set on UVA since she completed her internship at Thompson & Litton. I think she even has her dorm picked out.

When Etta was born, like every mother, I made a lot of plans for her. I made lists of my favorite books to share with her, most of which she has read (she's in the middle of *Pride and Prejudice*, next up *The House of Mirth*). I wanted her to see the world and have a fine education. I still hope she'll consider my alma mater, Saint Mary's College up in South Bend, Indiana.

"I know you're set on Charlottesville. But can't we just take a ride up to South Bend so you can see the place?"

"Okay. But don't get your hopes up," she tells me.

Jack begs off from the trip I've planned for Etta's fall break (smart man). I think the flat farm fields and never-ending countryside of Indiana, and its midnight-blue night sky with stars so low they dangle like crystals on a chandelier, might woo her to change her mind. It's a football weekend at Notre Dame, which adds to the excitement. Maybe when she sees the girls in their wool pea coats and Fighting Irish baseball caps, she will reconsider.

As we drive onto the campus, Etta is impressed by the lane, anchored on either side by hundred-year-old oak trees, so high they meet over the center of the road, forming an orange canopy over our heads. The buildings, so beautifully set beside a lake with an island at its center (the ducks are out, how picturesque), create a scene that far exceeds the beauty of the photographs in the brochure. Etta laughs when she sees an old Packard, painted white with silver fins and stuffed with nuns in black and white habits, whiz by. "They look like a tin of Aunt Fleeta's iced brownies," she observes.

Etta's never seen a nun in a habit. Catholics are rare in Southwest Virginia. The only nuns she knows are at Saint Agnes Hospital in Norton, and their habits are more like the traditional nurses uniform, not the long flowing robes of the order of Saint Joseph. Our priests down home are worker priests, missionaries really, so they rarely wear their collars. Etta is amazed by the first Catholic place she's ever been. The statues of saints tucked in alcoves, the angel statuaries in the gardens, and the heavy cross in Le Mans hallway are all new to her. I'm not sure she relates to it all.

Etta has a meeting with the admissions committee, who, I

can see by the looks on their faces, would love to have her. Etta tells them that she is grateful for their time, but she remains noncommittal, saying that she wants to check out the art department in Moreau Hall. A B.F.A. would be the closest match to the architecture studies Etta has in mind, and she wants to see what the facilities are like. As we tour, I remember taking photography classes, and when we enter the Little Theatre, I remember the plays I saw when I went here.

"Isn't this gorgeous?" I ask Etta as we walk across the empty stage of the Little Theatre.

"It's really nice." Etta looks at me with that *Don't press it* expression, so I don't. Why am I selling this so hard? Don't I know that if she picks where she goes, she will make it work? Doesn't the University of Virginia have the best architecture school in the state? What's the matter with me—haven't I learned to pick my battles?

The ride back home goes quickly, and soon we find ourselves in the blue hills of Kentucky near the border of Virginia. Etta has been quiet most of the way back (she slept a lot), and I notice that by the time we stop for food, her mood has visibly lifted.

"You're in a better mood," I say, handing her the ketchup for her hamburger.

"We're almost home."

"And that makes you happy." I don't pose this as a question.

"Yeah." Etta has a swirl of sarcasm in her voice.

"You didn't like Saint Mary's, did you?"

"It was nice."

"It's traditional and old and grand and well respected. I wouldn't call it nice."

"Ma. I don't want to go to Saint Mary's."

"Why?"

"Because it's not for me. I knew you were gonna do this. I knew you wouldn't make it a fun trip, you'd make it about getting what you want."

"I've already gone to college. I don't want anything except the best education for you."

"No, you want me to do what you did."

"You'd love those girls once you got there."

"No, *you'd* love those girls once I got there. I didn't see one person like me."

"What are you talking about? You're smart and you have a great personality. You'd fit right in."

"I don't want to fit in there."

"You really want UVA."

"You make it sound like a mail-correspondence college. It's the state university of Virginia, founded by Thomas Jefferson. It's not some dump."

"No, I know it's a great school."

"Then why don't you want me to go there?"

"I don't *not* want you to go there."

"You've never once said, 'Great choice, Etta.' Most of the kids in my class don't even go to college. Why can't I decide what's right for me? If you don't get your way, you act like the world's gonna end. You're so spoiled."

"Spoiled? Me?" The last thing I consider myself to be is spoiled.

"You're an only child, and you've gotten your way forever."

"You're an only child," I retort.

"No. I had a brother." Etta takes a sip of her Coke. I can see that if we weren't in a truck stop in Kentucky, she'd get up and leave. But she is trapped, and so am I. "You forget that I lost someone too."

"I'm sorry." I try not to cry, wiping my eyes with the napkin.

"And don't do that either. Apologize all the time. You can't say whatever you want to me and push your agenda with heaps of guilt and then apologize for it like you didn't mean it. You do mean it. It's your way or nothing."

"That's not true."

"It is true. You think you know best for everybody! You think you're above people. You even think your family is better than Dad's."

"I do not. I loved Mrs. Mac very much."

"As a friend. She died before she was family to you."

"What does that mean?"

"You could deliver her medicine and hang out with her, but that's not being family. You never get attached to people, Ma. Don't you notice that?"

"I have dear friends in Big Stone Gap. Aunt Iva Lou! Aunt Fleeta! What about Spec?"

"Ma, I'm a mountain girl. I'm a MacChesney. Look at me. I have brown hair and green eyes and freckles. I'm built like Dad. I like mechanical things and astronomy. I couldn't sew a button on my coat or work in a pharmacy. I'd be claustrophobic. I like soup beans and corn bread and divinity candy. I like mountain boys who talk like me. I like my girlfriends who live in the hollers and have babies when they're young enough to chase them around. I love the country, the back roads, the Powell River when it floods, and the fact that you don't need much money to survive in Big Stone Gap. I'm one of them, and I will be until the day I die. And whether I live there after college or not, I'm gonna carry all that inside me all my life. That's who I am."

I can't say a word. I hear her, and I know she believes what she says. I guess I was hoping that it wasn't true. I wanted more for her. I wanted her to love the world outside these mountains as much as the world within them.

"I guess when you were born, I thought I'd have a daughter just like me. And that was wrong. You are who you are, and you have a right to be that person."

"Thank you." Etta sounds relieved.

"I didn't want you to be like me because I thought I was better than everybody else. I wanted you to be like me because I was very much like my mother, and I found great comfort in my relationship with her. I'm letting go of hoping that you and I could be like my mother and me. It just wasn't our fate, I guess."

"Is this really what you're sad about, Ma?" Etta looks at me. "Is it really about me? Or is it about Joe?"

"I don't understand."

"All my life I just wanted you to be happy like you were before Joe died. You used to laugh more, and it seemed like you weren't scared of anything. I know I was little, but I remember that everything changed. I don't know what it's like to be a mother, I can't even guess, but it doesn't do you any good, or me, to be scared for me all the time. You can't protect me by putting me in a school in Indiana any more than you can lock me in an attic. If something were to happen to me, it would be because it was supposed to happen, and there is nothing you could do to stop it."

"Don't say that."

"It's true. It wasn't your fault, Mom. You didn't do anything wrong, and Joe died anyway."

She's right. I look at my daughter, and I don't see a little girl anymore, and I don't see a teenager. I see a whole person who thinks deeply about things and searches for answers. I set out on this journey of motherhood with a plan in place. I knew exactly how I was going to handle every challenge and what my rules were. What I did not consider was what kind of a child I would get. And I have to say that, even though I was hoping for something different, I was very lucky to have Etta for my daughter. She is far more intuitive than I ever was, and certainly more honest about her feelings.

"I'm happy you want to go to UVA, really I am."

"Are you sure?"

"Totally sure."

Etta smiles. "Thank you, Ma."

And those are the most important words my daughter can say to me. Mothers who try hard (I lead the pack) need to know that once in a great while, they do something right.

Jack and I sailed through the milestones of Etta's senior year of high school, including the spring musical (Etta was set designer for *Carousel*), the prom (she went solo with a group of girlfriends), and graduation (Jack cried, I didn't). Papa has sent Etta a round-trip ticket to Italy for her graduation present. We took her to the airport yesterday; it's her last fling before she starts college.

Theodore has been awarded an honorary degree by the University of Tennessee. I convince him and Max to drive down a couple of days early to stop in Big Stone Gap on their way to Knoxville. Theodore wants to show Max "Where the Big Orange Reigns Supreme" and, of course, Big Stone Gap.

There are many people who want to see Theodore, so I've parked him at Mutual's during lunch to have one central location for folks to stop by and say hello.

"I don't know what you were talking about. The food here is interesting," Max chides Theodore.

"I lived here eleven years, and I couldn't get past the first bite of soup beans and corn bread."

"That's your problem. I think they're delicious." Max goes back into the kitchen for seconds.

"So much for my cosmopolitan boyfriend," Theodore tells me. "Do you think the folks wonder who Max is?"

"Are you asking me if they think you're a couple?"

"Yeah."

"I think that everyone here is so old now that if they might have cared at some point, they don't anymore. Gay, straight, or tuckered out entirely, I think they just want everybody to be happy."

Theodore throws his head back and laughs. "I think you're right!"

One of the things I missed the most after Theodore left was spelunking into the caves of these old hills. I couldn't find anyone else who had the passion for it. I took Jack once, and he said he'd rather be in a coal mine. Another time, I took Etta, and she was busy measuring the walls for potential collapse instead of examining the lichen and stone formations. So I'm thrilled when Theodore agrees to go to

Cudjo's Caverns with me while Jack gets a lesson from Max on how to make profiteroles.

Everything is as we remembered it: the low ceiling entrance, the unwieldy footbridge, and the underground stream. "Isn't it weird nothing has changed?" I ask Theodore.

"This isn't like Disney World. They don't upgrade. It's whatever nature does. It took hundreds of years to get this way, and it will take hundreds more to change it."

"If I tell you something, will you laugh?"

"Never."

"I'm getting early empty-nest trauma. Every time I think of Etta leaving for good, I can't breathe. What's wrong with me?"

"You're like everybody else. You want to hang on to what you know. It's going to be strange not to have your schedule arranged around Etta. Work won't matter in the same way because you won't be doing it for your family, you'll be working for you. So you have to rejigger the whole picture. And it's scary to start all over again at our age. Who really does? No one. And you know why? Because it's too hard."

"Thanks. Now I feel worse."

Theodore laughs. "It's true. Sorry."

"That does not explain my physical ailments, like palpitations."

"Are you going through the Change?" Theodore asks bluntly.

"What?"

"You know, the Change. When your eggs take a vote and decide to close down the factory."

"I know *what* it is, I can't believe you asked me about it."

"Why? It's completely natural. And it also makes very sane women lose it over nothing in particular, and you've certainly been doing that lately."

"For your information, I *am* going through the Change. Well, really, it's the Changeover. I'm at the end of the ordeal. And the process made me realize why these mountain girls are brilliant. There's a reason to have your children at twenty. When you have them in your late thirties, they leave you just as your cycles do. It isn't pretty, and it sure ain't easy."

"Contrary to your standard self-recrimination, you are doing just fine with everything."

"Thank you for the support."

"Max and I are planning a trip to Lake Tahoe at the end of the summer. You want to come?"

"Jack and I always wanted to go there."

"You could drop Etta and join us after. I promise I won't let you ruin my vacation with your pity party. You'll have to leave your Etta wailing back in Virginia. Think you could do it?"

"Yes, I do." And I mean it. I don't want to spend a moment of sadness around Etta's great achievement. She's going to the University of Virginia to be an architect—what mother wouldn't be thrilled about that?

Throughout July, we get regular postcards from Etta, detailing her travels up the Mediterranean with Chiara, Giacomina, and Papa. Meanwhile, I'm here making lists for whatever she might need for her freshman year at UVA. Iva Lou and I drive over to Fort Henry Mall and pick up all sorts of dormitory necessities: new towels, bedsheets, and a leather book bag (I hope she likes it). Iva Lou helps me unload the packages when she takes me back to Cracker's Neck, and Jack meets us on the front steps. His face is ashen. I drop the bags on the porch. "Did something happen to Etta?"

"No, no. She's fine."

"Why do you look like that?"

"She called while you were gone and said she'd call us back in fifteen minutes. She wants to tell us something."

"But she's flying home tomorrow. Is something wrong with the ticket?"

"She didn't say."

"Why didn't you press her?"

"She wouldn't be pressed, Ave."

"It's probably nothing. She probably bought y'all matching ID bracelets on the Ponte Vecchio and wants to know how you want 'em engraved. For Godsakes, don't jump to conclusions." Iva Lou looks as though she might shake me.

The longest fifteen minutes of my life commence. Oddly enough, they give me ample time to play out several horrible scenarios in my mind. I don't have a best guess, but the feeling in the pit of my stomach is one of dread.

At last the phone rings. Jack motions for me to pick it up in the living room, while he sprints up the stairs to talk on our bedroom phone. Iva Lou pours herself a Coke in the kitchen.

"What's wrong?" I say without a hello.

"Ma."

I breathe deeply.

"I'm getting married."

I can't say anything, I drop the phone. Iva Lou runs into the living room, takes one look at me, and motions for me to sit down. She picks up the phone and hands it to me. Then she sits down next to me, sharing the receiver, and we listen together.

"Etta, what do you mean you're getting married?" Jack asks this question like he heard it wrong.

"I'm getting married."

"After college?" I ask weakly.

"No, next month."

"Next month!" In the back of my throat, I feel the cheeseburger that Iva Lou and I had at Pal's.

"Aren't you going to ask me who?"

"Who?" Jack, Iva Lou, and I say in unison.

"Aunt Iva Lou?"

"Sorry. I picked up the phone to see if Lyle wanted me to stop at Stringer's for a takeout."

"Stefano Grassi has asked me to marry him, and I said yes."

"What about school?"

"I'm going to go to the University of Bergamo. They have a great architecture school."

Jack raises his voice and sputters into the phone, "What about UVA? Are you abandoning all your plans just like that? Where is this coming from?" Every bit of his protest is lost on Etta, who sighs into the phone.

I blurt out exactly what I'm thinking. "Have you lost your mind? You're eighteen years old. Marriage? What in God's name are you thinking?"

"Mom. I'm an adult, and I can do what I want."

"The fact that you're eighteen, dumping out of college, and getting married tells me that you are far from an adult!"

"Please. Talk to Grandpop." Etta hands the phone to my father.

"Ciao," he says quietly.

"What is going on over there, Papa?"

"They're in love," he says simply.

"Jesus. Where was Chiara?"

"She's not a very good chaperone."

"No kidding. Neither are you!"

"I'm sorry, but you can't stop this sort of thing. I know she is young, but she knows her own heart. Stefano is a good man. You know him. This is what they want. It's like a boulder coming off the mountain. You have to let it be and get out of the way."

"Papa, I'm going to be sick."

"Ave Maria, listen to me. You cannot stand in the way of her happiness. You will lose her."

"Too late for that."

I hang up the phone. Let Jack deal with them, with her. I can't. I can't believe this is happening.

"What a shocker." Iva Lou gets up off of the couch. I begin to cry. Iva Lou doesn't know what to do, so she paces, then says, "Look, it could be worse. She could be miserable or hurt or something horrible. She's in love, and she sounds happy. Why is this so terrible?"

"She's a kid."

"Not according to the government."

"What do they know?" I wail. Jack joins us in the living room. He comes and puts his arms around me. "That kid is trying to kill me," I tell him.

"No, she's not."

"She deliberately pulls this stuff. She's ruined my life."

"Come on, Ave."

"We sat up here and did homework with her every night, sent her to Mountain Empire for college prep classes, supported her when she did her internship. . . . For what? It's all gone."

"She says she's going to go to college over there."

"Dream on! When? How? Who's going to support her? You know what happens to teenage girls who marry? They have babies and they get trapped and it's over. Over!"

"That's a little prejudiced," Iva Lou says politely.

"It's the truth!"

"This is a shock. And when the shock of it wears off, we will figure out how to proceed."

"Jack, wake up. The horse has left the barn. She's getting married. Did you hear her? She didn't ask for our blessing. She doesn't care. She does what she wants when she wants, and doesn't listen. She's never listened!"

"She's got a mind of her own."

"And look where her mind got her!"

"We know Stefano—"

"Him? I'd like to kill him."

"You don't mean that."

"Yes, I do. With my bare hands, I would like to kill him. How dare he subvert her college plans? What kind of a man discourages a woman from getting an education? I'll tell you what kind. The kind who wants a slave to cook and clean and wait on him."

"You know better than that. He's an educated man himself."

"Oh, please."

"He is. He's a good man. This could be worse. She could

have called home saying she was going to marry a stranger."

"What am I going to do?" I walk to the window and consider running all the way to Lee County, until my heart gives out and I fall over dead.

"You're gonna have a drink." Iva Lou looks to Jack. "Where's the hooch?"

The problem with drinking when you're upset is that it doesn't take quickly. I have several shots before I feel the first one. I'm not proud that I turned to Jack Daniel's in my crisis, but I realize there is a first time for everything. Iva Lou went home after a couple of hours of hearing me rant. She took all she could and then slipped out. Jack is in the kitchen making us something to eat. I muster all my strength and go into the kitchen. Iva Lou has stacked all of Etta's college supplies on the bench under the windows. The sight of them makes me cry.

"Come on, you need to eat." Jack puts the food out on the table.

"I'm not going over there."

"We have to go."

"I'm not going. I am not going to support this."

"Ave, it's too soon to say that."

"Plenty of people disown their children and go on to lead happy lives."

"Name one."

"I don't actually know anybody personally, but I am sure they're out there."

Jack sits down and takes my hand. "Ave?"

"Jack, how could she do this to us?"

"I don't like this any more than you do. But I don't think she's doing this to hurt us. She's following her feelings. She's in love."

"Ugh."

"I want you to remember when we fell in love."

"We were thirty-five years old!"

"Okay. Bad example. How about my mother? She was sixteen when she fell in love, and seventeen when she got married."

"That was in colonial times."

"Folks have always married young in these mountains. Now, I'm not saying this in defense of what she's doing, I'm just making the point that this is not a new concept to her."

"We didn't raise her to do something like this."

"You have to get past this feeling that she did it to spite you."

"Okay, let's say they are in love. A girl at eighteen can't know what love is. She's dated two boys, both of whom she dumped because they were too dull. She's throwing her life away without exploring any of the possibilities. He's probably the first man she's had sex with, and she got hooked." I can't believe I said that, but I believe it's true. She got caught up in the moment, and in that moment, she gave away the rest of her life.

"I don't think that's what's happening here."

I look at Jack and see that he is as wounded as I am; but he's better than I am, he is giving her the benefit of the doubt, trusting that he did a good job as a parent and that this will all work out. I wish I had his perspective.

"You're a cockeyed optimist," I tell Jack.

"Aren't you happy that she's marrying an Italian?"

"I don't want her to marry anybody right now!"

"Your father is there. Giacomina. Nonna. She has a loving family around her. It's not like she ran off to Albania with a convict."

"Jack, any way you look at this, it's wrong. She's out of her mind! She flip-flops! When I took her to Indiana, she went on and on about being a mountain girl, and being a MacChesney, and how she loved these mountains, and now she turns around and decides to live in Italy with her childhood crush. I don't get it."

"If all that is true, it must mean she really loves him. She was excited about UVA, thrilled about it. She wouldn't throw that away on a whim."

"I don't know her at all, Jack. I can't figure this out." I can barely get the words out. I'm drunk. I sound like an old booze hound somebody found on the floor of Ray's Café on a Sunday morning after an all-night binge.

"We have to accept this."

"Why is it so easy for you?"

"Because I know it's her life and she has to live it."

I shove all the college supplies off the bench and lie down on it, curling up in a ball so small you could play field hockey with me. I'm so sad and disappointed. It's like I built a beautiful castle and turned away for a moment, and a fire has broken out and burned it to the ground. Now I understand why people drink: there are days when the news is just too hard to take.

The flight to Italy is so turbulent that Jack and I have a moment where we truly believe that we won't make it to

Etta's wedding. Our initial plan, to stop this thing, entirely backfired on us. When we threatened to come over to bring her home, Etta pushed the date up. Jack and I went to Father Rodriguez to talk things through, and he helped me understand that I have to find a way to accept this because my daughter needs me and surely will more in the days to come. I haven't accepted this marriage yet, but I have decided to act like I do, and then hopefully one day I will have a change of heart and embrace my daughter's decision. Of course, this is my rational mind talking, not my heart.

Theodore will be meeting us at Malpensa Airport in Milan. When I called him to tell him about Etta, he quickly dropped the Lake Tahoe trip and rearranged his plans. Jack and I invited Max too, but he felt he'd be in the way, so he's going to see his family instead. We've rented a car and will drive directly to Schilpario, where the wedding is to take place a week after our arrival. Five weeks have passed since the fateful night of Etta's phone call, and we have spoken since, but the conversations are strained and overly polite. I received a five-page letter from Stefano Grassi, who outlined in nearly mathematical terms why this union would stick. I read it through once and haven't had the strength to read it again.

Jack thinks I'm doing better with the whole thing, but I find it hard to talk to him about it, because he is overly optimistic. I can't find a single soul who understands why I'm devastated. Even Fleeta said, "It's not like she's fifteen. She's eighteen. She's legal." The only person who is on my side is Theodore. Thank God he will be there for this wedding. I really need him now.

Jack falls asleep after the meal, which gives me a chance to think. Once again I feel cheated out of happiness. By getting married so young, Etta has deprived us of that natural order of maturity: graduation from high school, then college, then a life on her own in some new and exciting place, after which she finds a good man to settle down with, and then, at a mature age, children, if she so desires. I had so many plans for Etta's wedding day. I cut out pictures from magazines of bridal cakes and Italian *regali*—gifts left on the wedding table for the guests. I thought about what kind of gown and veil she would look good in, deciding that bright white was bad; an eggshell beige would go better with her skin tone. I would make her day a happy one, filled with sweet surprises and beauty. I would welcome her husband's family with open arms, and be a hostess with largesse and good manners. Instead, I've had nothing to do with the planning of my daughter's wedding. She has not asked for my input, telling us only where and when the service will be, and the address of the reception.

Malpensa Airport is packed with people. I doubt Theodore will be able to find us, and the way things have been going, I wouldn't be surprised. Jack corrals the luggage through automatic doors. I hear Theodore calling my name and see him in the crowd.

"I have the car. Let's go." Theodore kisses me, shakes Jack's hand, and takes a couple of bags. We pack everything into the trunk of the black Volvo and pile in.

"We're going to make this a happy trip, aren't we?" Theodore says, eyeing me in the rearview mirror.

"I'm doing my best."

"She really is," Jack tells Theodore.

"This could be worse," Theodore says.

"Yeah?"

"She could be marrying that Boggs boy who broke into the Mutual's and stole the Valium that time."

"True, Theodore," I say halfheartedly.

All the magic that makes the Italian Alps my dreamscape is lost on me as we ascend the regal cliffs. I might as well be on my way to the guillotine. I feel as though everything is ending, even though I know that my daughter is at the beginning of a new life. Despite everyone's protests, I still have an aching feeling that this marriage is doomed.

Papa and Giacomina meet us in the driveway. His embrace reassures me, and Giacomina's warmth makes us feel as welcome as always.

"Where's Etta?" I ask.

"She's at the church. She'll be home any minute."

"You should be pleased that she's getting married in church," Theodore says to me under his breath.

"Don't push it," I whisper back.

Giacomina shows us to our rooms and, when she gets the chance, pulls me into her and Papa's bedroom. "How are you?" she asks me tenderly.

"I'm here."

"I know this is hard for you."

"I wish I was an actress, so I could invent a character to be throughout all of this. I'm going to try really hard to be nice. To be happy. How's Etta?"

"She's in love," Giacomina says simply. Papa calls her from

downstairs, and she excuses herself and goes.

Love. What a tiny word that is used to describe everything and can mean nothing. These Italians. They're all for it. Love is the point of life itself, love is the great healer, love is the energy behind all things that are beautiful, whether it's a silver cup of berries or lovers on a bicycle built for two. Dreamers. They're all dreamers.

"Mom?" Etta stands in the doorway and looks at me.

"I'm sorry, honey. I'm so angry at you," I tell her quietly. I look at her and, of course, my heart melts. This is my daughter, and I want her to be happy more than I want it for myself. But I cannot hide my disappointment or my fear.

"I know." She sits on a chair and motions for me to join her. "How was your trip?"

"Not great," I tell her.

"You think I'm too young."

"Oh, Etta, it's more than that. You don't trust my judgment. You don't listen and benefit from my experience. Yes, you're young, but you're also impulsive. If you're really in love, and it will last, why are you rushing into this? Can't you come home and get your degree and then marry Stefano? Why are you doing this?" The questions I have longed to ask her come tumbling out, and not eloquently.

"Because it's right for me."

"How? You were accepted to college and you were excited about going. Aren't you sad about giving up your future?"

"I'm not giving anything up, Ma. I'm adding to my life. I'll have my studies and my husband at the same time."

"When did this happen?"

"Ma, I've known I would marry Stefano since I was eight years old."

My memory takes me back to the house on Via Davide, where Etta slept in the trundle next to my bed and told me that someday she would marry Stefano Grassi. At the time I thought it was cute, that she believed she was wise and could project into the future. I sure as hell didn't think she was serious. As I play through all the key events of her life, like I have done so often over the last few weeks, I realize that there was never a time when Etta lied to herself. She looks at me, waiting for me to say something. I can't. I hold my arms out for my daughter, and she rushes to me. I begin to cry.

"I'm sorry this is so hard for me," I tell her.

"It's okay."

"No, you deserve to be happy."

"So do you, Mom."

"Don't worry about me. I'm okay." Who am I kidding? I will never be the same. I'm letting her go and she may come back to me, but she won't ever be mine again. But that's my problem, not hers.

"I have so much to show you." She takes my hand.

"Is there anything I can do?"

"Tons!"

Etta takes me to her room on the first floor, which looks like a bridal showcase. She has made favors for the tables, small gold silk purses filled with pastel almonds, tied with a peacock feather.

"They're beautiful. How many people are coming?" I ask.

"Just family and a few friends. Maybe thirty of us in all."

"Do you have your dress?"

Etta nods excitedly and unzips a garment bag. "In Italy, the gown is white, but it's accented with color." Etta pulls a pristine, high-waisted, scoop-necked beige silk gown from the bag. It is embroidered with tiny pink and blue rosebuds on the hem, and down the back are satin streamers that match the roses.

"It's exquisite," I tell her.

"Do you think so?"

"I love it. It's exactly what I would have picked for you."

Etta hugs me so hard, I feel I might snap in two. "Oh, Ma, I'm so happy."

"Tell me about it. How, when, the whole thing." I sit down on her bed, and she sits down next to me.

"When I got here, Chiara and I went to Sestri Levante to hang out at the beach. When we got there, we heard that Stefano Grassi was working on a project there, and did I want to see him? He had come by Zia Meoli's house and asked me out to dinner. So we went."

"Did it happen just like that?"

"No, it took a while. But Mom, I think Stefano said when he wrote to you, he's loved me since our last visit. I know I was young, but he was seeing a girl seriously and gave her up because he felt like a phony with her and was hoping someday that he and I would be together."

"I remember that part in his letter."

"Mom, when I was little and you told me the story of your mom and Grandpa, it was so romantic, how they fell in love and would sneak around to see each other, right here in Schilpario like Romeo and Juliet."

I could kick myself for planting these romantic notions in

284 ☆ ADRIANA TRIGIANI

her head, even though they are true. This is all my fault! But I say nothing and motion for her to continue her story.

"Anyway, we began a proper courtship with Grandpa sort of chaperoning, and then Giacomina, and we just spent a lot of time together, and it was almost time for me to leave, and Mom, I couldn't get on the plane. Stefano wanted me to go home and go to college and come back when I had my degree. But I couldn't imagine leaving him. I tried. I knew that I had obligations back home, but nothing else mattered, only Stefano. I want to be with him for the rest of my life. And I don't want to wait. There's no point in waiting."

"But you told me you were a mountain girl."

"Ma, look out the window. There are mountains here too. They just have a different name. These folks are just like the people of Big Stone Gap. They have their own music and their own cooking and their own ways. They don't like outsiders to come in and change their way of life. They like that they're remote and that visitors get lost trying to find them. The lady who runs the patisserie is just like Aunt Fleeta, crabby but she'd do anything for you. There's another woman who works in the dress shop, she's just like Aunt Iva Lou, a free spirit. They even have a Spec Broadwater here, he's the forest ranger who checks for floods. It's not really different. I feel at home here."

"And I'm glad you do. Because it will be your home for the rest of your life. Stefano is Italian and not likely to leave his country."

"I'm fine with that."

"I accept that you're in love and swept away, and all the good stuff. But take it from an old bag: I'm not worried about your happiness this year or next, I know you'll be flitting around on the wings of bliss for a long spell. It's your future that concerns me. I'm worried about when you're thirty, or forty-one, when you wake up and realize that you've given up your youth to a grand romance. This is a time in your life that you can never retrieve. And I'm not trying to change your mind. Look, there's the dress and the shoes and the *regali*. You're all set. But I wanted to explain why I couldn't jump up and down when you called. I was worried sick for you."

"Mama, you're always going to worry about me."

"I know. I've done my best, and I tried to instill in you the values that my mother instilled in me. There wasn't anything complicated or fancy about what my mother taught me. It was to honor myself and be true to what I believed. And when I reacted the way I did, I realized that I was imposing my beliefs upon you. This is your life, not mine."

Etta embraces me, and for the first time since the day she was born, I feel that she needs me. "I want to promise you something," I tell my daughter. "By next Saturday, your wedding day, I will be where I need to be for you."

"I know you will, Ma."

Theodore and I take a long hike up the mountain, and we try in vain to find the peacocks. Either they moved or I took a wrong turn at the pine tree near the stream. Even so, the views are spectacular, and we reminisce about our days spelunking in Lee County.

"You're almost yourself again, Ave."

"You think?"

"I knew when you saw her, you'd come around."

"Yeah, you're right."

"The phone isn't your thing. Long letters bore you. Besides, you had to stew before you let Etta go. It's your way."

I put my arms around Theodore, so grateful for his friendship. Who drops their own vacation plans to suffer through a teenage wedding? Who else stays upbeat and sunny for me when I give in to my dire predictions? There is one constant in my meltdowns, and one person who consistently pulls me from the abyss: the one and only Theodore Tipton.

"So, what do you think of Schilpario?" I ask.

"I want to know where they're hiding Heidi."

"It *is* just like *Heidi*, isn't it?"

"Any minute I think your father is going to send me to the attic with a bowl of hot milk and melted cheese. Remember that?"

"That's all that poor kid ate, goat's milk, cheese, and every once in a while a slab of crusty bread." I can't believe I remember the story so well.

"The town is amazing. I love the architecture, and the people are so interesting."

"Thank you for coming all this way."

"First of all, I had no choice. You were suicidal. Second, who gives a flying fig about Lake Tahoe? I can rent *Guys and Dolls* if I get a yen for gambling Reno-style. No, this is big. This is your kid's wedding, and I belong here. I'm her godfather, for Godsakes. Who else could give a kick-ass toast this high above sea level?"

"No one."

"Damn right."

"Giacomina said she's making risotto tonight."

"I want those Italian babes slaving over the stove every moment I'm here. I want local dishes out the yin-yang. Before we head down, can you show me the field of cockerbells?"

"Bluebells. No. It's in the other direction. Way way way over there."

"I get it now." Theodore laughs.

"What?"

"How you got entangled with Pete Rutledge up here. It's like the rest of the world doesn't exist."

Theodore and I get back just in time to wash up for dinner. It's amazing to me, how I can bounce back when I'm on my home turf. Everything about these Alps soothes me: the air, the fragrant nettle, and the water, so clear and icy that it cleanses the deepest part of me. Jack meets us in the hallway on our way to the dining room.

"Stefano's here."

"I thought he was coming tomorrow."

"He wanted to see us tonight."

"Have you talked to him?"

"For two hours."

"Good. He's warmed up," I tell my husband.

"Back off, Kitten with a Whip. This is your future son-in-law. Leave some flesh on him for the ceremony," Theodore reminds me.

"Oh, I will."

This house has never been so quiet. I think even the stones in the wall are frightened that I may tear this place down board by board when confronted with the man who stole my daughter from the University of Virginia, Cracker's Neck Holler, and the American Academy of Future Architects.

The dining room is set for dinner. Stefano stands near the windows alone. He looks out as though he is watching something, but it is suppertime, and Via Scalina is empty.

"Stefano."

"Hello, Mrs. MacChesney." He extends his hand.

I embrace him instead. "Thank you for your letter. You covered every detail. So I'm going to make it short and sweet. I wish you all the happiness in the world."

"Etta told me you reconciled."

"We did. Thank God."

"I'm sorry if we caused you any pain."

"Oh, you did. But I'm getting over it."

"I will take good care of Etta."

"I know you will. And I know she'll take good care of you. But I want you to promise me something."

"Of course."

"I want her to finish college. It's very important that she have her education."

"I agree, and so does she."

"Don't let that fall by the wayside, or I will have to get on a plane, come over here, and make your life a living hell."

"Yes ma'am."

Theodore has thrown himself into the local culture and has arranged to go down to Bergamo with Stefano, Etta, and Jack. Papa insists that I rest before the wedding, and I agree I need it. I would like to look good in the photographs, and when you're over fifty, that requires an additional four hours of sleep per night. I remind myself that all the great Italian beauties are luminous in their fifties. There is a reason I keep a picture of Sophia Loren in my wallet. She is over ten years older than me but still the most gorgeous dish on the continental menu. My Etta trauma has put me in the smallest size I've worn since I was a teenager, and what Mother Nature streaked through my hair has turned a natural chestnut brown at the behest of Lady Clairol. I'm going to look good on Saturday, maybe the best I've ever looked. I'm wearing a pewter-gray party dress with a full skirt (my mother's, of course), and if I'm feeling daring, I'll wear a gardenia in my upsweep.

I love the mirrors in my father's house, because they are old and mottled and give off a golden aura that blurs lines and wrinkles. At my age I thank God and the Italian gene pool for my strong nose and jaw, because, as my mother promised, they hold everything up and take off ten years when you really need it.

"Ave, you have company!" Nonna shouts from the kitchen. No one has seen her for days. She's baking the wedding cake, and evidently, it takes more concentration than cracking World War II spy codes. I skip down the stairs, finally feeling myself again. I bounce into the kitchen and stop short.

"Pete?"

"Ave."

"Oh my God. What are you doing here?"

"Etta invited me to her wedding." Pete Rutledge smiles.

"She did?"

"She didn't tell you?"

"No."

"Well, it's all right with you, isn't it?"

"Yes, absolutely. It's wonderful that you came," I tell him. "It all happened so fast. She was going to go to college this fall and came over here for a final vacation, and fell in love, and here we all are, and here you are, and oh my God. Where's Gina?"

"We're getting divorced."

"No!"

"It didn't work out."

Now, Nonna is listening to all of this, even though she doesn't speak English. She looks at me, expecting a translation. Instead, I tell her that I am going to go for a walk with Pete. She shrugs and goes back to forming cherubs out of marzipan.

Pete and I walk almost instinctively up to the road beside the chapel of the angels. I try to swerve us up toward the rec center so I can show him the new ice rink, but he takes my arm and leads me to the old stone path that goes up the mountain.

"Where are we going?" I ask him.

"I don't know. Let's not plan it."

"Jack is in Bergamo. He'll be back tonight." I say this peppily, though what I'm really saying is, You may be divorced, but I am still very married, so please obey the rules.

"Great. I'd like to see him."

"So, what happened with Gina?"

"You can't get married to get married. You have to want it badly. I really think that's what makes it work."

"Who wasn't it working for?"

"Both of us. I travel a lot, and it seemed that whenever I left and returned, we started all over again, instead of picking up on what we had built. It was strange. I thought I loved her, I hoped she loved me, but we both found out that marriage is another matter entirely. It has to work separately from love, almost. Don't you agree?"

"I do, I guess."

"You don't sound so sure."

"The older I get, the more I believe in luck."

Pete and I catch up on his work as we climb the path. He keeps one foot in the marble business and one in academia at NYU. He finally took an apartment in New York City near Washington Square Park (and, therefore, Theodore). He comes to Italy a lot, mostly because he loves it, but often on business.

"Where are we going?" I ask, but I can tell where we're going from the direction we're taking. He's climbing up toward the field of bluebells.

"You know."

"This is a bad idea." I stop on the path.

"What?" he says innocently.

"The altitude is bad up there. Makes me do things I shouldn't do." Then I breathe deeply. "Things I don't want to do," I correct myself.

"Are you sure?"

"Yes. I love my husband. He's really the man for me. Of course, it's taken me almost twenty years to figure it out. No matter what happens, no matter what I do, he stays true. He was there when I went through menopause and had hot flashes so bad I almost drove my Jeep into Powell Valley Lake to cool off. When my friend Spec died, it was like losing my father, and Jack was there to comfort me. When the call came that our eighteen-year-old daughter was getting married, he held me together when I was falling apart. Maybe I have limited experience in these matters, but I don't think it gets any better than Jack MacChesney."

"I understand," Pete says quietly.

"So, the truth is, I'll never go back up there. Not with you, not alone. Not with anybody. I want to remember what it was, how it was, with you. We can have that, but that's all we can have. Okay?"

"Okay."

As we walk down the path back to town, I am thinking one thing, and one thing only: wait until my daughter gets home.

I help Giacomina clear the dinner dishes. The crew returned from Bergamo, happily surprised to find Pete Rutledge at the dinner table, but then thrilled as the wine flowed and stories of Etta's first trip to Italy when she was little and Pete's trip to Big Stone Gap were told in Technicolor detail amid much laughter.

Theodore comes up behind me at the sink. "We need to talk," he whispers.

"I'm almost done."

"Now." Theodore takes my arm and pulls me out the kitchen door. "Are you trying to sandbag me? Why didn't you tell me you invited Pete? You shouldn't scare me in this high an altitude."

"I didn't invite him. Etta did."

"Why would he come, even if she invited him? What does he want?"

"Me," I joke. "I thought I'd tell Jack that it's over between us at Etta's wedding and then I'd ride off on a donkey down the Alps with Pete."

"The way he looks at you, he wouldn't mind it."

"That's all in the past."

"Yeah, well, this is the Land That Time Forgot, so you better be careful."

Etta turns in early so she'll be rested for her wedding day. I give her a few moments to get ready for bed before I go in to say good night. She is sitting up in bed reading.

"Am I interrupting?"

"Not at all."

"What are you reading?"

"Shakespeare's *As You Like It* in Italian."

"Why did you pick that one?"

"Stefano gave it to me. It's about these characters who are displaced and find their way by falling in love."

"Sounds interesting."

"You know, all of Shakespeare's plays end in either a funeral or a wedding?"

"I remember that."

"It's almost as if the two most important days in your life are when you're married and when you're buried." Etta smiles.

"We never did have our big talk about sex, did we?" I ask my daughter.

"Sure we did. In bits and pieces, here and there, over the years. I got the facts, Ma. Don't worry."

"You know, there never is a perfect moment to have that

discussion. Believe me, I've been working on *that* one for seven years."

"You did great, Ma."

"I didn't come in here for you to tell me how great I am. I came in here to tell you how wonderful *you* are. It's been a great privilege to be your mother. I was thinking that I always made a big deal out of everything you did wrong, instead of honoring all the things you did right. And now I know what a waste of time it is to focus on the things that really don't matter. It took two children to teach me that. I'm just glad I got the lesson before you checked me into Heritage Hall Nursing Home to live out my days."

Etta throws back her head and laughs. "I won't put you in a home."

"Never promise your mother *that.* I may very well end up there making fudge with the Tuckett sisters."

"You're young, Ma."

"Thank you. I never thought I'd think that was a compliment, but by God, I'll take it."

"Ma, I love Stefano so much."

"I know you do."

"We know we're young, but we feel ready."

"Then it will work, honey. It works when you make it work."

"Would you marry Dad again?"

"Absolutely. We're very different, but somehow we admire our differences instead of letting them annoy us. And the real truth is, he's a great man. They don't make them any finer than your father, so why would I choose anyone else?"

Etta looks at me for a moment as though she wants to ask

me something; and I've known this girl since the day she was born, so I know what she wants to know.

"Why did you invite Pete?" I ask her.

"He's such a part of Italy to me. That summer we were here. I remember the trip to his marble quarry and when he took us to Florence on the train."

"You remember all that?"

"Oh yeah. He made you happy again, Ma. After Joe died, you hardly ever laughed. And when we came over that summer, you started to smile again. And one night, you even danced. That's when I knew you *could* be happy."

"Pete was, he is, a good friend." I look at Etta. "And that's all he was. A friend."

"I figured that, Ma."

"It's true," I tell her. "It was nice of you to ask him to come. Dad likes him too."

"I know! See, even that was meant to happen. Dad made a good friend because you did."

"Is that what the stars tell you?" I ask her.

"I don't need stars to tell me that." Etta looks at me seriously. "Do you have advice for me, Ma?"

"You really want my advice?"

"Sure."

"Well, I would just be patient with Stefano. He grew up very differently from you. He didn't have a mother and father, and that created a void in him that no one can fill. I know this because I went through it. When my mother died, leaving behind a letter that told me that Mario Barbari was my father, not Fred Mulligan, it took me a long time to understand what had happened and what it meant. And Stefano will spend much of his life trying to understand why things happened to him the way they did. And if you're smart, and you are, and if you're like your father, and you are, you'll know how to handle it."

"How did Dad handle it?"

"He let me be sad about it. And he listened. And he never tried to make up for what I didn't have, he just loved me for who I am, knowing that my sadness was part of me."

"I'll remember that."

"Ma, do I have everything?" Etta asks me.

"You did a more thorough job packing than Aunt Iva Lou did when she came to Italy when you were fifteen."

"That good?" Etta smiles.

"That good," I tell her. "You're going to have the best honeymoon. Rimini is perfect."

"Thank you for everything, Ma. For coming over and for your support."

"I have something for you." I give Etta a package wrapped in white paper with a pink satin ribbon.

Etta tears into it. "An empty book?" she says, flipping through the leather-bound journal.

"Your dad and I—"

"It's my own anniversary book! Isn't it, Ma? I always loved that you and Dad wrote to each other every year."

I try not to cry, but I realize now that she noticed every-thing, including the good stuff. All these years we watched Etta closely, and the whole time she was watching us. Maybe she is ready to write her own story. "I got the one with the extra pages, since you're getting married so young," I joke. "Dad and I went with a slimmer volume, since we got married later in life." Etta and I laugh.

"And one more thing. I don't want you to be scared about having children. We lost Joe, but it was out of our hands. I still don't understand why, but even if I knew why, I wouldn't trade one day of the time we had with him."

"Me either," Etta says quietly.

"If you can, don't make any decisions based upon fear. Try to choose the big things out of love, and I don't think you'll ever go wrong."

Etta and I hold each other for a very long time. Parenthood, the least permanent job in the world, just ended for each of us, and a new story begins tonight. This next chapter ought to be a doozy.

Etta and Stefano's wedding day, September 3, 1998, is the most beautiful day I have ever seen. The cobblestones on Via Scalina, on the way to La Capella di Santa Chiara, glisten. The sky is aquamarine blue without a cloud, and the air is cool enough to wrap yards of silver taffeta over my shoulders like a countess. My husband looks so handsome in his Italian-cut navy blue pin-striped suit with the red handkerchief. We didn't say a word as we got ready this morning. He just kissed me every chance he got.

Zia Meoli and Zio Pietro are sitting in the front row of the chapel. Before the procession begins, I go up the stairs to the tiny choir loft and say a prayer by the stained-glass window of the Blessed Mother that my great-grandfather designed and installed so many years ago. I pray to my mother and to Ave Maria Albricci, who took care of my mother when she was alone with only me inside of her to keep her company. Jack comes up the stairs to tell me it's time for the service to begin.

Don Andrea, the priest who married Jack and me, stands at the altar. The alpine air must be good for him; he seems as robust as the day he married us. Etta has asked her father and me to walk her down the aisle. We are preceded by Federica's daughter, Giuliana, who wears a pink tulle dress and carries a small bouquet of edelweiss and is followed by Chiara, in a simple pale green silk sheath with a small wreath of boxwood.

Giacomina is the matron of honor, and Papa is the best man. Stefano, in a black Edwardian suit with a pale blue tie, never takes his gaze off our daughter as we walk down the aisle. When we reach the altar, I kiss my girl and step away. My husband kisses her and holds her for a very long time. Only I could know what these two mean to each other, because I have seen from the moment she was born that she felt understood and heard by her father, treasured by him. They have always been the best of friends, and it gives me great comfort that she has the very thing I was missing all of my life.

I expect to cry through the ceremony, but I don't. I listen carefully to the instructions that the priest gives my daughter and my son-in-law. He tells them that love is central to a marriage, but forgiveness is the one element that makes a marriage last. Jack takes my hand when he hears this, because he and I know from experience that it is the truth.

"Isn't she beautiful?" my husband whispers to me. I nod. And truly, in all of my life, I have never seen a woman so lovely. Etta's long brown hair is twisted into a low chignon and set in place with tiny clusters of edelweiss. She is tall and slim, almost her husband's height, and as they stand beside each other, I see that she is every bit his equal. Her eyes are the same deep green as her grandma MacChesney's, the Scottish freckles peek through the pressed powder, and her rosebud mouth is set with determination.

Theodore must know what I am thinking. He reaches over the back of the pew and takes my hand. I don't let go. I turn around and smile at him. A couple of rows behind Theodore is Pete Rutledge, who smiles at me. Here, under one roof, are the most important men in my life, who have loved, accepted, and changed me. What sort of fate has brought us all together? What strange karma? Why does it feel that we have all been here before, in this chapel that smells of frankincense and white lilies? What connects us all is in some cases a blood tie, but more often than that, it's some centrifugal force that throws us together for reasons we can never understand. Did my mother have to leave these mountains to go to the hills of Southwest Virginia so I might find Jack MacChesney? And why, after all of that, does my daughter return to the very place where her grandmother was born to find her true love? I almost laugh, but I catch myself. We Vilminore women, we always take the long way home.

I saved up all my tears for the flight home. Jack tries to nap but wakes up intermittently just to see if I've dried up yet—I haven't. Etta and Stefano left for Rimini on their honeymoon, and for a few seconds, I thought I would jump in the car and join them. Jack held me back, or maybe he was resisting the urge himself. He and I have spent so much of our time and most of our conversation on Etta for the past eighteen years. So it seems strange that we hardly spoke about her this week. We didn't stay up and talk through the night before the wedding, we didn't analyze it at breakfast that morning, and we didn't say a word on the way to the church. Of course, this is my husband's way; when something really matters to him, he can't talk about it.

I take a walk up and down the aisles to stretch my legs. When I return, Jack is awake. I slide down into the seat next to him and lie across his chest. He encircles me with his arms, and I rest my hands on his.

"Why are we going home?" he asks me.

"Because we live there," I tell him.

"Our daughter's in Italy. What are we going to do back home?"

Jack is right. Pearl is in Boston, and with Janine in place managing the pharmacies, they don't need me. Spec is gone, and when he died, my anchor died with him. I love the old stone house in Cracker's Neck Holler, but it was made for a family, a family to eat in that kitchen by the fire, to rest in those rooms with the big windows, and to run in the field that faces Stone Mountain. The woods will get lonely with two middle-aged mountaineers passing through once in a while when the mood hits them. The woods should be filled with kids, hanging from trees, fishing in the stream, and eating the wild strawberries from the thicket by the Lonesome Pine tree.

"What do you want to do?" I ask him.

"Are you wide open to any possibility?"

"What does that mean?"

"Can you think with your heart, not your head?"

"I could."

"What are we going to do with the second half of our lives? I say half because I'm being generous." Jack laughs.

"I haven't thought about it."

"I have a little."

"Since when?"

"Since Etta told us she was getting married."

"We can't follow her to Italy," I tell him. The last thing a good mother does is horn in on her newlywed daughter.

"I don't want to follow her, I just want to be closer."

"Do you think the Olive Oil King still wants you?"

"Maybe."

As Jack holds me, I turn my head to look out the window, but there is nothing to see. It's as though a black velvet drape has been drawn on our window, in the dead of night. I know the Atlantic Ocean is under us and somewhere, buried behind these clouds, is the moon. In my husband's arms, these are the only two things I am sure of.

"We have to redream," I say.

"What do you mean?"

"Well, you have to be honest, to start with. You have to admit that one story has ended and another one needs to begin."

"We know one story has ended, Ave. What do you want that you haven't had?"

"That's a hard question for a goal-oriented girl. I always tried hard for what I wanted, and when I got it, I figured I was lucky."

"Do you think I'm part of your future?" Jack asks without an ounce of self-pity. "If you could, would you choose me all over again?"

"Maybe a thousand times."

"Good. Because I choose you every morning."

Jack settles in his seat to go back to sleep. I pull his arms close to me as he sleeps, and I decide to be completely open to his dreams and encourage him to follow his heart. If we wind up in a Tuscan olive grove, that is fine with me.

"Are you on your honeymoon?" a woman with white hair asks me as she passes.

"Yes," I tell her.

"It's always sweeter the second time around."

"First time wasn't so bad either," I say.

"Don't tell *him* that," she whispers, pointing to Jack Mac, and proceeds down the aisle.

I lean back on my husband and do what I always do, which is inhale deeply and exhale until my breathing is in rhythm with his. Of all the decisions I have made in my life, marrying Jack MacChesney was certainly the best.

As we fly through the night sky, it's good to know I did something right. Love may not be enough, but when it's right, it's plenty.